PRAISE FOR
MILLY TAIDEN AND HER NOVELS

"Taiden introduces readers to the Alpha League Federal
Agency (A.L.F.A.), a secret group of shapeshifters who
work for the government. The chemistry between Parish
and Melinda is off-the-charts hot, but there is also a great
story that goes along with it. Readers will enjoy the introduction to a new type of paranormal romance with characters who have fascinating backstories. A job well done by
Taiden!"   —RT Book Reviews

"Would I recommend this author? Yes! Milly Taiden does
not disappoint with this funny, sexy storytelling! This author
should be on all must-read lists!"

—Twin Sisters Rockin' Book Review

"I can always rely on Milly Taiden to write a fun, quick,
sweet and sexy romance."   —Angel's Guilty Pleasures

A.L.F.A.
INSTINCTS

MILLY TAIDEN

JOVE
New York

A JOVE BOOK
Published by Berkley
An imprint of Penguin Random House LLC
375 Hudson Street, New York, New York 10014

Copyright © 2018 by Milly Taiden
Penguin Random House supports copyright. Copyright fuels creativity, encourages diverse
voices, promotes free speech, and creates a vibrant culture. Thank you for buying
an authorized edition of this book and for complying with copyright laws by not
reproducing, scanning, or distributing any part of it in any form without permission.
You are supporting writers and allowing Penguin Random House to continue to
publish books for every reader.

A JOVE BOOK and BERKLEY are registered trademarks and the B colophon
is a trademark of Penguin Random House LLC.

ISBN: 9780399585845

InterMix eBook editions / January & April 2018
Jove mass-market edition / May 2018

Printed in the United States of America
1   3   5   7   9   10   8   6   4   2

Cover design by Annette DeFex
Book design by Laura K. Corless

For my kids, Aiden, Alan, and Angie.
Thank you for being so loving and pushing me to do better.
I love you!

And for my sister, Julie, and my mom, Angela.
Your support means the world to me.
I love you, too!

DANGEROUS MATING

PROLOGUE

─✂─

"He's been captured by the enemy." ALFA Director Josh Tumbel stood at his third-floor-office window overlooking Washington DC, hands jammed in his pants pockets. "There's no other explanation for him going dark." And that worried him considerably. He'd never lost an agent, and in ALFA's history, only one agent had been killed in the line of duty. He didn't want one on his watch.

"When was the last time we heard from him?" Agent Sheldon Loper asked. He sat in front of the director's desk. With two of the four agents on assignment and a third missing, this man was the only one he had available. Maybe time to train more. The world wasn't getting any nicer.

"It's been a week," Tumbel replied.

"For Bryon, that's definitely not normal. He'd never deviate from procedure." Agent Loper shifted in his chair. Loper was right about that. Bryon Day did everything to the letter. The man could probably recite chapters and subsections of the ALFA handbook from memory. But no one held that against him. His redeeming factor was he was also great at video games.

"That's what I'm thinking," Tumbel said as he made his

way back to his desk. "We need to send a team in to get intel or bring back a body." His stomach churned at the thought.

"What have you got in mind?" Loper asked.

The director leaned back in his leather chair. "You and a female go in as tourists, see what you can find."

Sheldon grunted. "I don't even know what country he's in. He's been gone a while."

Tumbel opened a file on his desk. "He's been in Cloustien for about a year."

"Never heard of it."

"Not surprised," Tumbel said. "I don't see how it's classified as a country. It's smaller than New Hampshire." He ran fingers through his hair. "It's somewhere around Liechtenstein."

"Germany, then," Loper said and nodded. "Where are we getting the female? We don't currently have any in training."

"I'm going to call the FBI to borrow one of theirs. She won't have to do much. As long as she can walk, she'll work."

CHAPTER 1

Kari Tomlin threw open the entrance door to the FBI building, stubbed her toe on the metal floor-transition piece, then stumbled into a lady holding a cup of coffee in the security checkpoint line.

"I'm so sorry," Kari said to the woman's scowling face when she looked to see who had run into her. The woman said nothing, just turned. Under her breath, Kari retorted, "Well, good morning to you, too." God, she hated being awake this early. Her brain didn't function until after seven A.M. And that's with two cups of coffee in her system.

She glanced at her watch. When her boss had called forty minutes ago, he'd sounded as if aliens were attacking the planet. The "director" wanted to see her right away. Top secret information had come and they needed her.

She'd met the director once, if you called shaking his hand as he handed over her FBI certification a meeting. She'd never forget that day, not because she became an official FBI agent but because she tripped over a taped-down microphone wire on the stage and took out the podium. It was the fault of the stupid high-heel shoes she'd worn. She was more of a flip-flop kind of gal.

After getting through security, she hurried to the elevators. One started to close and she dashed between the doors and stood facing the others. There wasn't enough room for her to turn around. She hadn't realized how crowded it was. She barely fit, and her bag didn't. The briefcase crunched, then the elevator doors popped open, the security feature kicking in.

"Oh, crap," Kari said. She pulled her case toward her and turned around, which required her to move back in the cab, jostling everyone behind her. She cringed at the moans.

The last to get off at the top floor, she rushed down the hall to the director's door. She took a deep breath and smoothed out her suit jacket, then knocked. She heard "Enter" and opened the door.

Director Lancaster, the head of her division, grabbed his cup of coffee off the desk and leaned back in his chair. On her side of the desk sat two older military men in highly decorated military uniforms. She didn't know the ranks of the armed forces, but she saw both men had two stars on their collars. "And here she is now, gentlemen." Lancaster looked at her. "Come in, Miss Tomlin." She plastered on a fake smile and reminded herself to breathe.

"Good morning, sir," she managed to get out.

"Good morning, Miss Tomlin." He gestured to the two men. "These are Generals Smithton and White." She nodded and mumbled a good morning as they did the same. "Miss Tomlin, thank you for coming in early. We've received intel from the field we need decoded urgently. The CIA has had it for several hours and are making slow progress.

"I've been telling these guys for a while now," Lancaster gestured at the men sitting in front of his desk, "that you are a miracle worker when it comes to this kind of thing." The director winked at her. "And now we get to put our money where our mouth is, if you get what I mean."

She had no idea what he meant, but she'd play along. "I'll try, sir." He handed her a sheet with *Classified* stamped on it. That was normal for her. Most of her work was fresh off the press with a get-it-done-yesterday deadline. "Do we know the originating country?" she asked as she scanned the lines of gibberish.

"Russia, we think," General White said.

"What about intended recipient?"

The director answered, "Mexico, we're guessing."

Russia sending coded messages to Mexico—not what she'd expected.

"Do you need to go back to your desk?" the director asked.

"No," she said. "I have my laptop with me." She pulled her bag around, the one crunched by the elevator. Inwardly, she groaned. Please, don't be broken. "I just need a place to set up."

"Go on next door to the deputy director's office. He doesn't get here till noon most of the time."

"Thank you, sir." She hurried out before she passed out. She'd forgotten to breathe, dammit. Standing in the hallway, she leaned back on the closed door and took a quiet breath. Why was she so nervous? She'd met high-ranking people without flipping out. Too badly. But those people weren't depending on her to decipher something important enough to start a world war if she got it wrong.

Sitting behind the desk next door, she pulled out her laptop and set the paper in front of her. She stared at the strange symbols and their layout. Russian and Spanish. In her head, the patterns and similarities formed. She Googled Russian language and took a minute to look it over. It'd been a while since she'd dealt with that part of the world. Ever since she'd started, the agency had been dealing with the Middle East.

Skimming through the Russian alphabet, diphthongs, and sentence structure, facts and figures soaked into her head. She puzzled out the basic possibilities. Her mind filled in letter combinations and translated them into Spanish and Russian for decryption. She counted characters, looking for a hidden pattern. Then she saw the trick to solving the puzzle. Every letter that corresponded with a prime number was a dummy character. Removing the fake characters allowed for meaningful arrangements of other pieces.

She went through and crossed out the third, fifth, seventh, eleventh, up to the last letter. Her mind sorted and resorted. She noticed something about the structure. The words were not arranged in sentences. They seldom were. Those were too easy. After a quick mix in her brain, it was done.

Reading the message, she thought Russia was trying to get their asses in trouble. If they thought they could get Mexico to fight a war against the U.S., they had another think coming. She closed down her laptop, stuffed it into her bag, and left the office.

She knocked on the director's door. Getting the go-ahead, she entered, trying to be more confident. She should be.

"I have the decoded message for you, sir."

The two generals gawked, then their eyes narrowed quickly. They didn't believe she'd done it. She got that reaction all the time. Nothing new. Ever since the childhood accident that nearly killed her, she'd been a wiz at math and puzzling solutions. She wished she had the same ability with her social and love lives, which were both in the toilet.

The director grabbed his cup of coffee and sat back in his chair. She came up to his desk and handed him the paper. When she scooted to the side, her elbow hit the picture frame on the corner of his desk. She quickly knelt to pick it up, apologizing profusely. She put her hand on the desk to help get her back to her feet and her hand knocked over a bronze flag statue, which in turn set a rubber band ball rolling across his desk.

She leaned over the desk to grab the ball and her fingers brushed over pens in a black mesh cup, sending them sprawling. Still apologizing, she scooped the pens back into their holder. The rubber band ball had rolled to the floor, so she wasn't worried about that. Then she straightened up and her elbow bumped the same picture frame to the floor.

She sighed and the two generals gawked at her again.

This time for a different reason. So much for coming across as a professional agent. That was the story of her life. Whenever she was on a roll, doing great at something, she'd ultimately end up with egg on her face.

The director leaned forward and put his coffee on the desk. "As I said, gentlemen, she's the best there is for decoding."

She looked at the military men. "Would you like me to explain the patterns or would you rather I just talk to your guys?"

"Just talk to our guys," was all they managed to say. Typical. Most people didn't understand the algorithms anyway. She took the business card one of the generals proffered and walked out of the room.

The card had the symbol of the CIA stamped on it. Looked important, unlike hers. Wait, scratch that—she didn't even have business cards. She figured someone had forgotten to order any or just deemed her unworthy of the distinction of having her name on something.

But despite all that, she was the first to know things no one else did or would ever know. The airplane crash over the Ukraine—it wasn't caused by local dissidents as the news had reported. Nope. The world knew North Korea was working on nuclear capabilities, but had no idea about the biological chemicals the country was stocking by the ton.

And some things, she was sure the world was never meant to know. One was what really happened in the infamous Area 51 and the other about a nonhuman species blending in and living among us. What would the world be like, she wondered, if the public knew of this species? It'd probably go to hell in a handbasket quickly.

The funny thing was no one would believe her if she did tell them all she knew. That was one thing that kept her from having the meaningful relationships she craved with girlfriends and boyfriends. Her social IQ was about as low as it could go. Growing up as a freak to her peers had started it. Now knowing little of the world beyond work, she had nothing to talk with others about.

She tried to get into the TV shows she overheard other women talking about. Oprah, Dr. Phil, Dr. Oz. But a lot of the things discussed were flat-out wrong. Especially about foods. One would think organic meant coming from your grandmother's home garden. Not the case. So much so that she ate fruits and vegetables from cans. Preservatives were better than things used in the organic world.

Once, she dared to tell a few ladies she wanted to befriend in her apartment building about the hidden aspects of the food industry. They looked at her as if she was from a different planet. Who would they trust more? Dr. Oz with all his commercial backing or a person they hardly knew who wouldn't tell them where she worked or what her job was.

Well, piss on them. She didn't need friends who didn't get her. She could make it on her own. As long as batteries for her Rabbit were in stock.

CHAPTER 2

Kari schlepped her bag down to her office bullpen. She needed coffee in the worst way. She wondered when she'd gotten so hooked on the stuff. It didn't help that all the adrenaline streaming through her body since the phone call from her boss was now draining. She was crashing hard. Maybe she could go back to sleep at her desk until her clock-in time. Not that she really punched a card. But this was the FBI building. Those who needed to know knew everything about everybody, including the minute you walked in or out a door.

Even dragging butt, and she had substantial butt to drag, she was glad to be here. She was able to decode messages important to *national security*. How many others could really say their job was as important as hers?

Looking around the room, she had no idea so many people came into work this early. They were the ones who had children to pick up from soccer practice or band rehearsal. Had a loving spouse to go home to, and whatever else that was wonderful in their lives. She wouldn't know. Never been there. No T-shirt.

She turned down the aisle toward the kitchen and was

startled by a man standing in the center of the corridor. "Hey, Marty. I wasn't expecting to see you there. What are doing standing in the middle of the hall?"

He grinned. His eyes were as round as plates. "Oh, just lucky, I guess, to not run into you at the corner. You've done a great job of teaching me how to be careful." He was fidgety, seemed a bit afraid of being close to her. "Well, need to get back to work." He scooted over, his back against the wall and sidestepped until he was a distance away, then hurried on.

She sighed. Yeah, she'd done the proverbial *run into a coworker carrying coffee while coming around the corner* act. But she hadn't done that for a long time. Not yet this year, and they were halfway through.

In the kitchen, someone had placed a dozen donuts on the table. Oh my god. She was so thankful. In her rush out the door this morning, breakfast hadn't happened. Not when the director wanted to see you right away. Maybe she should find an apartment closer to the office. But stuff was so expensive in this part of DC.

Coffee in hand, she sat at the four-person table and plucked a glazed donut from the box. And it was still warm. Oh my god, again. If they did this every morning, she was changing her work hours. The dough melted on her tongue, the glazing sliding onto her taste buds. Pure heaven, and the reason she had a lot of butt to drag around. Oh, well. She'd rather live shorter and be happy than live longer and be miserable.

From the hallway, she heard high-heeled shoes *clack* on the terrazzo floor. Annie, a lady who worked across the room from her, walked in. Upon seeing Kari sitting at the table, she froze in her tracks.

"Good morning, Annie," she said.

"Hey, Kari." The smile on her coworker's face was faker than shit. Even she could see that. "You're here early." Annie poured coffee into a mug designed as a cat face.

"Yeah, had a rush job come in. Didn't take long, so here I am eating donuts," she said. Surprising her, Annie took a cream-filled pastry from the box instead of running out of the room.

"But they're freaking good. Still warm," Annie said. *Ahh*, Kari thought, the draw of sugar was strong enough to create even the most awkward of meetings. The silence between them was thicker than the lemon goo squirted into the donut Annie held.

Kari noticed the diamond ring on Annie's hand. "How's it going with Keith?" she asked. She hoped that was the man's name.

"Good, good," Annie said. "Any men on your horizon?" Kari saw the slight cringe Annie made after asking the question. Yeah, the woman didn't care, just being polite and asking the wrong question to someone she didn't want to talk to. But Kari had a funny comeback for this. First time for everything.

Kari snorted. "The closest I've been to a man was when I wiped spilled tea off the TV when a commercial advertising the *Thunder from Down Under* tour came on. Then I had to wipe my drool from the screen."

Annie laughed. "Aren't they absolutely gorgeous? At least you can look at them. Keith turns the channel as soon as he hears the music for the commercial start, whether I'm in the living room or not." They both laughed over men and their jealousies. But in reality, she'd love to have someone who would be jealous. Shit, she'd be glad just to have someone. She sighed.

Her coworker's eyes turned sad, sympathetic. But she didn't come any closer. "Hey, now," Annie said. "Just because you haven't found somebody yet doesn't mean you won't."

"Yeah, I know." Though she didn't believe it. "But I'm in my thirties now and ready to do something with my life." She'd been here since college, day in, day out. The worst part was Kari had never even been in love.

Annie whispered back, "It will happen. You just have to find him, then kick his ass for not finding you sooner." She glanced at the clock. "I need to get back to my desk. Lots to do today." She hurried out of the kitchen. That was the longest conversation Kari had ever had with someone from her office.

Kari hefted her bag over her shoulder. Talking to no one in the room, she said, "Yeah, might as well get started. Maybe I'll leave early and check out the new spa that opened across the block. The pictures online made the place look incredible."

At the main aisle, she trudged to her desk in the back by the wall. She laid her bag on the desk and noted the message button flashing on her phone. Wow, no one used the phone anymore. All her correspondence was via email or some other electronic means. She couldn't remember the last time she actually used her office phone. They were too easy to tap into.

She listened to the message and about died. The director wanted to see her again when "she had a moment." Like she'd ever tell the director *Sorry, no moments available right now*. He probably wanted to ask questions about the message from this morning.

Kari loved her job. She loved solving puzzles and riddles and figuring out mathematical problems. But she felt tired now . . . tired of her mundane life. Maybe she needed some time off. Visit her family in Florida. Go to the beach, get eaten by a shark. She shivered. She had a hard time getting in the ocean knowing how many critters existed that could kill or hurt her.

She might even try one of those online dating services. She was leery of those. There were stories about women being robbed and also not knowing if the picture you saw online was who you'd see in person. But it seemed like a good way to "meet" a bunch of guys at the same time.

The elevator to the director's floor opened. She needed to pull herself together. It was time for work and not personal catastrophes like her love life. And she had to remember not to touch anything on the director's desk.

CHAPTER 3

For the third time today, Kari knocked on the FBI director's door. Hearing the obligatory "Enter," she stepped inside the office. The director grabbed his coffee cup and sat back in his chair.

"Please, have a seat. Thank you for coming up so quickly, Miss Tomlin." Again, not like she was going to tell him to bugger off.

"Absolutely, sir," she said. "What can I do for you?"

"Miss Tomlin," he began, "you've been with us for some time, now. Is that correct?"

Oh shit. Was he firing her? Was the message decoded incorrectly? No, it had to be right. Had she done something wrong? "Yes, sir. Since college, sir."

"And in all that time, you've never taken a full week of vacation," he continued. "Do you not enjoy taking time off, Miss Tomlin?" She heard the humor in his voice and relaxed a bit. She smiled.

"No, sir. I mean, yes, sir. I just don't have anywhere really to go."

"I see." He cleared his throat and set his cup on the desk. Funny how he always grabbed his cup and scooted away from his desk whenever she came in. "I just got off the phone with Director Tumbel." She had no idea who that was, but wouldn't ask, either. "His group needs a female to help on a project. I thought you would be a good choice for that."

Oh, come on. Couldn't they find a male who could type and file? Why did it always have to be a woman to do that work? Mainly because men couldn't get that shit right. She met the director's eyes and realized he was waiting for her to say something. Shit. What was the question?

"Yes, sir." Damn, she hoped she didn't make an idiot of herself.

"Is that a yes, I'd like to go, or yes, I wasn't listening and don't know what to say."

Kari busted out in a laugh. The way he said it was hilarious. He damn well knew which *yes* it was, but chose not to embarrass her. He was a good guy. Not many of those around. If she ever came across one who was single, she'd grab hold and never let go. Good luck finding one available, though.

"Yes, sir. I'll help them do whatever they need. Is it a lot of typing or more organizational?"

His brows drew down. What did she say now?

"The job is a field assignment in a foreign country," he said.

Kari heard the words because she was paying attention, but must've heard him wrong. "I'm sorry, sir. What did you say?" She scooted forward in her seat.

"Miss Tomlin," he leaned over his desk, "we need a female to go undercover for a short assignment."

She slid to her feet, jumping up. The director snatched his coffee cup. "Yes! I'd so love to go into the field." Her fist hit that damn copper flag statue again. She reached to put it back in place, and the director threw his hand up, stopping her.

"Let me get that. Please have a seat." He set the figurine upright, and she sat, almost buzzing with excitement. "Director Tumbel will brief you when you arrive, but I need to ask you a question."

Oh shit. She hoped it wasn't a true or false. She hated those questions, she always chose the wrong one.

"Miss Tomlin, you have decoded many classified items for us," he paused.

"Yes, sir." Where was he going with this?

His hands clasped together on the desk. "Do you know about the shifters in our community?

She sat quietly, thinking. What was the right answer here? If she said no, would that keep her from going? If she said yes, would someone hunt her down and kill her for knowing something she shouldn't?

"I have decoded a couple messages that had information about . . . others. Of course, I've never talked about it with anyone. So I just thought 'that's cool' and didn't worry about it." *Please be the right answer, please be the right answer. Please—*

"Wonderful, Miss Tomlin." He smiled. "Then I don't have to go into all that. I figured you had, so I knew you were the person for this assignment."

"Yes, sir. Thank you, sir." She was ready to come out of her skin. "What is the organization?"

"It's ALFA, Alpha League Federal Agency," he simply replied.

That meant absolutely nothing to her. Never heard of them. "Great." She sprang to her feet. "I won't let you down, sir." With that she hurried out the door. In the hallway, she held her first victory dance in a long time. Her arms pumped, booty shook. Yes, she was going into the field. Oh, wait. She knocked on the door again.

"Yes, Miss Tomlin."

She felt her face melting from embarrassment. "Um, sir. Where do I go for the briefing and when?"

The director came to her and handed her a sticky note with an address scribbled on it. "There is no name on the building, but the number is easy to see. Josh Tumbel, the director, would like you to go over as soon as you can for briefing."

After packing her laptop and talking with her boss, she made it to the ALFA building in record time. She had enough excitement built up inside to fuel a jet plane across the ocean. She knocked on the door that had a plaque that read *Director Josh Tumbel*. She wondered if his first name was Joshua. She couldn't imagine "Josh" being a shifter.

She wondered what his animal looked like. Would he have big teeth if he was a wolf? How about lots of hair all over his body? If he was an elephant, he'd have a six-foot dong, according to the Animal Channel. She couldn't imagine—six feet long.

The door flew open, startling her. A gorgeous man smiled at her. Damn, was he married? Hubba, hubba.

"You must be Kari." They shook hands.

"Yes," was all she could manage. Josh looked like a human, no hint of an animal at all.

"Come in," he said. He gestured to another gorgeous man sitting in front of a desk. Good god. Did they need a receptionist? Shit, she'd type and file the whole damn day if she got to stare at them.

"This is Sheldon Loper. You'll be working with him on this assignment."

She stepped up to the man sitting and shook his hand, exchanging greetings. Her foot caught on one of the chair legs, tripping her enough to lose her balance. Figures, she thought as she tried to catch herself. Story of her life. But hands were there to steady her before she had a chance to react. These shifters were damn fast. Carefully, she sat in the second chair in front of the desk.

"So," Josh started, sitting behind his desk, "first off, I want to thank you, Miss Tomlin, for volunteering."

"Please call me Kari," she said. "Unless we have code names." She perked up instantly at that thought. How cool would that be?

"No, for this mission, you can use your real names," Josh said. He glanced at Sheldon in the chair next to hers, then back at her. "Is this by chance your first undercover assignment?"

Her heart about stopped. How could they tell? Did she look like a kid in a candy store? Well, she sure as hell was! "My first field assignment," she replied.

Josh nodded. "That's fine. This op isn't too . . . demanding. Your role is to be a girlfriend to Sheldon and you're on a trip to visit the city."

"What city would that be, sir? she asked.

"Cloustien."

Her jaw dropped. "No way." She looked at both men to make sure they weren't joking. "This is so awesome."

Josh said, "I guess you've heard of the place?"

"Well, yeah? Who hasn't?" she said.

Josh looked at Sheldon. "Indeed." Sheldon shrugged. Josh held out a packet to her. "Here is information about the organization you're touring with. They arrived in Cloustien yesterday, but are allowing you two to join them. Their organizer has no idea you are undercover. She thinks you are regular people coming at the last second."

She took the envelope from him. "What is the mission? What are we really doing?" she asked.

Josh slid a file folder onto his desk. "One of our agents, Bryon Day, has gone missing and Sheldon will be searching for his whereabouts." He handed the folder to her. She opened to the headshot inside. Her breath caught in her throat, her eyes fixed on his, and her panties became very wet. Could you fall in love with a photograph? This man was the most stunning thing she'd ever seen.

She scanned his stats on the sheet under the picture. The only one she really cared about was marital status. On that line was the letter *S*. She could cry at this moment; he was available. As long as he didn't have a girlfriend. And let's be real, how could a man like him not have an equally gorgeous female draping off his arm. Maybe female*s*, plural.

Both men breathed deeply and turned away from her.

Was the director hiding a smile with his hand? She hadn't done anything, so the joke couldn't be on her.

"Kari," Josh asked, "you were told about our kind, right?"

She nodded. "Yes, my director told me you guys are shifters."

"Do you know much about shifters?" Sheldon asked.

She knew one thing, and knew it well. "When a shifter finds its mate, they are instantly in love and stay in love until the day they die. They never cheat on each other. Don't even look at the opposite sex anymore. Their souls are half of each other, bonded together the instant they become one."

That's the kind of love she wanted. The type she could devote herself to and know he would always appreciate everything about her, and she, him. She let out a little sigh then looked at the guys. They stared at her with . . . fear or humor? She couldn't tell.

"Uh, yes," Josh finally said. "That's one thing. But we also have extraordinary senses of smell and hearing. We can see in the dark and smell fear or lies or whatever scent the body excretes."

Her face paled. "Any scent?" Oh god. Her panties were still wet. Oh, well, nothing she could do about it now. She was not letting a little embarrassment keep her from going on this assignment. She straightened in her chair and cleared her throat. "So, when do we leave?"

"Your itinerary and tickets are in your packet. Plane leaves in a few hours. You need to pack for cool evenings and warm days," Josh told her.

"How many days?" she asked.

The two men looked at each other. Sheldon shrugged. "I would think I'd know something in a few days. Pack for five days. Just in case."

Josh nodded. "Sounds good."

She hopped up from her chair. "I gotta go, guys, if the plane leaves in few hours." She glanced at her watch.

"Oh, don't worry too much about that," Josh added. "We

get special security clearance and seating. You don't have to wait in any lines."

Sheldon then asked if he could drive her to her home, if she was taking the bus. He would also pick her up to go to the airport together. That was so thoughtful of him. He seemed like a really nice guy. Single? He didn't wear a ring. She shook her head to clear her lusty thoughts.

This was it! She would be on her way to Europe with a gorgeous male, looking for the man whose picture she had fallen in love with, in a town known for people disappearing under the earth and never coming back.

CHAPTER 4

B ryon Day scrunched against the back wall of his cell, cringing every time the whip stung his back. He preferred that to the fire torture or cattle prod they used. His eyes glanced at the group on the other side of the thick cage bars—several guards and the Big Dick himself.

"I will ask one last time, Mr. Day," Prince Goddard said, "why are you in my country?"

He had to remain strong, fight the wolf that wanted to tear into their throats and rip out their guts for the rats to feast on. Section Four, Chapter Two of the ALFA procedure handbook stated agents were not to give away their cover or their animal. If captured, allow yourself to be taken and find a place away from humans to escape, if possible. If not, wait for backup to find you. That's what the book said and that's what he had to do.

He just hoped backup was on its way. Each day he went without food or water, his mental and physical capacities worsened. His wolf would win control at some point. Then he'd be fucked. No telling what these bastards would do to him.

The whip split open the skin on his back. He ground his teeth. He could do this. He would.

Prince Goddard stopped the whipping and stepped closer to the cell imprisoning him. "Mr. Day, answer my question correctly, then I will set you free." That got his attention. Of course, his wolf helped him smell the lie. He wouldn't answer shit.

"One of the townspeople said they saw you go from a human to a wolf. Is that true? Are you a werewolf?" The way the prince said those words sounded asinine. Bryon broke into laughter, scratchy from lack of water.

"Are you listening to yourself?" Bryon whispered. "You think werewolves are real? Is Dracula hanging around, too?" He pressed his laugh louder, enraging the prince. He thought he saw the prince's eyes glow red for a second. The bastard ordered the whip again. This time, Bryon caught the thin rope and yanked it toward him. The guard holding the whip slammed headfirst into the bars then fell away unconscious. Took care of that.

Now if they would give him the opportunity to take care of the rest of them, he'd get the hell out of there. He already had a plan. He'd heard some of the other prisoners talking about underground tunnels under the entire city. Supposedly, there was an entrance somewhere here in the dungeon. It was fabled as a death trap maze in which once lost, there was no finding your way back. Being a shifter with a decent nose, he wasn't worried about that. It was getting past the extra-thick iron bars they kept him behind.

It was as if this cell were created with shifters and their strength in mind. He wondered if this part of the world openly believed in shifters. If someone was bold enough to say something to the prince without fear of rejection, then that did not bode well for his kind. Any surprise advantage he might have would be expected.

The prince stepped up to the bars again. "Don't worry, Mr. Day. I know what you are and you will give me a new outlook on life very soon. Arrangements are being made as we speak. We've caught one of your kind before and are prepared to kill you if you try to escape. In your weakened state, you're no stronger than my guards, so rid yourself of any thoughts of overtaking my men.

"You'll be part of the entertainment tonight. I will put you on display and they will all see you and know I speak the truth. You people aren't priceless. Not at all. But no one will have you until after I get my piece. Then later, I shall take every bit of you. I can almost feel it now."

The man's arousal floated on the musty air. If Bryon had had anything in his stomach to vomit, he would have. He understood what the sadistic prince was saying and he'd be damned if he was just going to let anything happen to him. He would let his wolf out at that point to kill all it wanted.

The prince backed away and nodded at one of his men. The man slowly approached the bars and slid a narrow bucket into the cell. When Bryon's wolf picked up the smell of water, it forced him to grab it. He chugged mouthfuls in desperation to hydrate his body.

The prince smiled. "Drink up, Mr. Day. I will see you soon. And I do mean all of you."

Bryon watched as the men picked up their guy lying on the ground and headed toward the door. They placed their torture equipment on a shelf before leaving. How he would love to take the cattle prod and shove it up the bastard prince's ass.

He shuddered and put the empty bowl on the ground. His preference did not swing that way. He knew plenty of LGBT folks, some even shifters, but he liked the ladies. No one in particular yet, unfortunately. He was still holding out on the hope of finding his true mate. But now in his midthirties, his dreams of finding that perfect one were dying.

In this last year, he felt that he clung to that hope tighter than he ever had before. Maybe because he saw it would not happen. Or he knew it was his only chance of finding real love. Could be the wolf griping at him constantly to have pups. It was ready to have a family whether or not Bryon was.

Which he was for, for the most part. He wanted happiness and to share his life as much as any other person. But did he settle with someone who made him feel loved and would make a great mother even though he didn't love her in return? Would he grow to resent her or her him because he couldn't give his entire soul in return?

No, he couldn't do that. That wouldn't be fair to anyone, including his pups. His parents were mates, one of the few in those days. They were perfect for each other and their kids. He saw the love they shared in the way they looked at each other, the way Dad held Mom's hand everywhere they went, and the physical desire—he stopped right there. The thought of his parents getting it on wasn't something he wanted to picture in his mind.

He ran his grime-covered hands through his hair. If he got out of this alive, maybe he'd take a break. He'd been going nonstop for years. Maybe go to one of those resorts they show on TV where every female has long hair and is wearing a bikini. That wasn't his type of girl, though. His type would more likely be found in a library cooking a cow. What the hell? Where did that come from?

He eyed the water bowl, then brought it to his nose. Fuck. There was a light smell to the water. They just played him well. He'd been so dehydrated, he didn't stop to think they would drug him. But they had no reason to.

Goddard mentioned entertainment. What did that mean? He'd be taken from the cell certainly. That would be where he'd escape. It was damn hard to hold a shifter and an ALFA was near impossible. Unless he were drugged. His body would burn through the chemicals faster than a human, so that would be his element of surprise.

This was great news, in a way. He'd been undercover in this town for a while tracking clues to an international human trafficking ring. There was a ring organizer somewhere in this region he was trying to get in with. He thought he was probably in Liechtenstein just a few miles away, so he had a small apartment in Cloustien where there was less threat of discovery and less concern over communicating to headquarters.

So much for that thought. The leads he had were going nowhere. He was in contact with a ring member, but the guy was low on the totem pole. The contact thought something big was going down soon and he was right.

Before he was captured, Bryon observed dignitaries and other affluent people showing up in this area. The few restaurants in town were much busier than they had been. But he couldn't find a location big enough to hold the number of people this ring usually dealt in. Unless it was in the palace itself. His current plan didn't include breaking into the palace. Now he was here, but on the wrong floor. They really should clean better down here. Ice cream would help.

He shook his head. He was losing to the drug. Shit. The effects were pulling on his mind. How much had they given him? They said they'd had a shifter before, so they knew what they were doing. His eyelids were too heavy. Even his wolf was out of it. Maybe he could rest for just a second until his body—

CHAPTER 5

Kari had the window seat and Sheldon took the aisle side of the propeller flight. After changing planes in London, they were loaded in and quickly on their way to the center of Europe. She loved staring out, watching the clouds float like pieces of cotton. Such dazzling white in the sun. Occasionally, she'd gotten glimpses of the ocean below, though now it was land only.

She pulled out the packet Director Tumbel had handed to her at the office. Inside was information on different aspects of the mission. First thing was their tour schedule.

"Sheldon," she asked, "what's the plan with the touring agency?"

He looked up from his puzzle book. "We're simply visitors with the group and will do everything they do. Except I won't be there all the time. You will be my cover and alibi if needed. Basically, you just walk around. Easy."

She looked at the agency's brochure in her lap—ITA, International Touring Agency. This assignment was a bit of a letdown. She'd hoped to do exciting thing like hold a stakeout, spy on the enemy, transfer secret messages to HQ.

Just like in spy movies. *Kingsman* and *Bridge of Lies* were her favorites.

"What wrong?" Sheldon asked. "You're upset."

She whipped her head toward him. "How do you know that?"

He pointed to his nose. "Remember, we can smell emotions."

"Smell emotions?" she questioned. Uh-huh. Not falling for that.

"You're right. Not really emotions," he clarified. "Emotions cause the brain to secrete certain hormones that flow through the body. That's what we smell coming through the skin."

"That I'll believe," she said. Sounded logical.

"So," Sheldon continued, "why are you upset?"

God, she felt stupid now, letting her romanticized image of spies affect her. "It's nothing. Growing up, I always loved romantic spy movies. It's one reason I wanted to work with the FBI. And I guess I just keep imagining this to be a movie. But I know it's not. So it's okay. I get it."

Sheldon moved in his seat. "You're right, this isn't a movie, but we are going into a foreign place with possible hostile factions. It is still dangerous. No matter how light I make of it. Your life could be in danger."

She took in a small gasp of air. Then saw his grin. He was trying to make her feel better. She appreciated that. But it was okay that she wasn't being a real agent. Hell, she sat around in offices all day playing with words and numbers. How was she remotely qualified for something that required experience? That's why her director thought of her for this assignment. He knew she would be safe. *Just accept it and try to enjoy the trip.*

"At the office," Sheldon said, "you mentioned you've been to Cloustien."

"Oh, not to it. Just saw a bit about it on the Travel Channel. The country is tiny, and their claim to fame is their underground tunnels. These tunnels were supposedly dug two thousand years ago. Researchers think the Germanic tribes in the area built them to hide and move around without the Romans killing them.

"Then in the 1930s, it's rumored the Nazis used the tunnels to store artworks and treasure they stole from conquered lands, then set up booby traps to keeps others out until they returned after they ruled Europe."

"But they lost," Sheldon said. "What happened to all the stolen stuff?"

"That's the cool part. Nobody knows," Kari said. "Some have tried searching for it, but were never seen again. Most think it's just a story made up like so many other lost treasure stories. No one takes it seriously."

"That's interesting. Maybe we can see some of the tunnels while we're there."

"Well, the government pretty much blocked all the entrances to keep people for going in and dying from getting lost. There is probably a museum with pictures and stuff, but not the real tunnels themselves."

"We'll check out all the museums before we leave." Like usual, the silence turned awkward and she couldn't think of a word to say. She never trusted herself to say the right thing, so she'd just keep her mouth shut.

He turned back to his puzzle book. She watched him write a number in a Sudoku board.

"You might want to try a different number there," she said. Shit, she couldn't believe she'd said that. Dammit, now he'd think badly of her, nosing in and acting all smart. She just told herself to keep her mouth shut. No trust in herself.

His brows scrunched. "Is it wrong?"

She had to continue with what she'd started. No telling what he'd think if she didn't reply. Stick with the facts. Nothing else. She said, "Yes, you can't put a three there because it has to go in the bottom square."

Sheldon flipped his pencil and erased the number. "It goes down here?" He scratched it in. "So, what goes up here?"

"Four," she said.

He pointed to another square and she gave the number for that box, then he did the same with another. He looked at her then his puzzle. "Do you have the numbers for this whole thing?"

Great, here came the "freak" part. How had this happened already? She hadn't even had time to screw up anything. She shrugged. "Yeah, I figured it out a while back when you started the first one," she said, scanning the back of the brochure, pretending like it was nothing. Hopefully, he'd drop it there.

He flipped the page to the five star grids, sixteen by sixteen. "How about this one?"

No, no, no. She stared at the page. She let her mind relax and do its thing. Numbers flashed in and out of each space, spinning through possibilities. The squares started to fill in, a few more in the middle row . . . done. "It's not hard, really. You can do it." She rattled off the first row and he checked the answers.

"That's amazing," Sheldon said.

"That's my job," she replied. The silence between them felt uncomfortable once again. She tried to think of something to say. "You have any children?" Everyone loved talking about their children.

He sighed. That didn't bode well. Maybe she shouldn't have asked. Kept her damn mouth shut. "No," he began. "I'm still holding out, hoping to meet my mate. I hoped with all the traveling we ALFA agents do, I would come across the one meant for me.

"What you said about mates in Tumbel's office is more true than you know. I want a family before I get too old to enjoy them. But I have several years before it gets that far. I'll just keep a *nose* out." He winked at her. "What about you?"

She shrugged. "I guess I always thought I'd find someone who would sweep me off my feet and live happily with our kids and white picket fence. But, you know . . ." She shrugged again. Maybe she had things in common with this hot shifter. She could handle being coupled with him. She'd eventually fall in love with him, right? "Do you like going to the movies? I love watching all kinds. I can spend all weekend sitting on the sofa laughing, crying, and screaming at the TV."

"I prefer RPGs when home. I have enough of the real world during the day. At night, I'll gladly be anywhere else."

"RPGs?"

"Oh, sorry. Role-playing games. Video games. *Assassin*, *Warcraft*, *Final Fantasy*, that kind of thing."

"Cool," she said. She had never heard of any of these. "Do you cook when home? I have several of my mom's recipes. Some she got from her mother. Creating natural food dishes is my second love. As you can see." She gestured to herself.

He gave her a questioning look. "You look great. Don't ever think you don't. Any man would be lucky to have you. Especially if you cook. I usually order pickup or delivery. Pizza, Chinese, fusion, whatever I feel like."

"You sound like you work a lot. Do you ever take a vacation? This is my first time out of the office for several days. I'm thinking a cabin retreat would be fun, though. Reconnecting with nature, hot cocoa in front of a blazing fireplace."

"We do work a lot," he said. "It's what the job calls for. But I have taken time off. I've gone to the beach with lots of women. My wolf loved it. All the sand to run around in and heavenly bodies to enjoy."

Okay, obviously, they didn't have a chance in hell of having a relationship. The only thing they had in common seemed to be this job. "Do you know the agent who's missing?" She wanted to know everything about this man. But didn't want ask until they had a conversation going.

"Yeah, Day is a great guy. He's dedicated, really smart, nice. He keeps to himself a lot. He's always working."

"Does he have family?" she asked.

"I've never heard him talk about anyone, but that doesn't mean they don't exist," Sheldon replied.

"Any pictures on his desk?"

Sheldon thought about the question. "I don't think he even has a desk anymore. He does a lot of undercover stuff and is seldom in."

She nodded. Day wasn't sounding like good boyfriend or husband material. If he didn't want a desk to tie him down, would he even consider a wife? Maybe he'd like an assistant to travel with. That was something. Who knew. She started thinking of him as a big, sexy cowboy type. Yeah. A cowboy or a rancher. She shut her eyes and let her mind drift off while still visualizing all kinds of crazy things with a man she didn't even know.

"You seem so natural around animals, Kari. Like you were meant to be part of their world in some way."

She looked up at Bryon from where she stood petting the horse's velvet nose. He was so tall and broad and she licked her lips at the glimpse of muscled chest peeking through the open buttons on his flannel shirt. She dared let her eyes dip to his crotch and her mouth watered. Holy moly!

He stepped behind her and moved the hair from her neck and his breath fanned against her skin. She shivered from the tickling sensation, but also from how close his hard body was to hers.

Oh god, if he kissed her now, she'd let him have her right then and there in the barn. She closed her eyes and as if he could read her mind he slipped his hands over her bare arms and walked her backwards.

"Where are we going?"

His lips slid into a smile against her skin. "Wherever you want."

She sighed and leaned into him. "This feels like a dream."

Bryon turned her in his arms and lifted her onto a high hay bail. "That's because it is, Kari. I am whatever you want me to be. I'll do whatever you want me to do. Just let me have you."

She gasped as his hand tugged her blouse loose from her skirt, his fingers slipping over her breasts to pull the cotton fabric over her head. It fluttered to the ground as his hand plundered her cool flesh. Heat streaked across her body, his rough hands teasing her nipples as his mouth took hers.

She cupped his firm buttocks and pulled his hips close, spreading her legs to feel the full bulge behind his zipper and the rough denim against her thin panties.

"You smell delicious, Kari. I just want to bury myself in your scent and taste every inch of you."

His lips feather over her jaw to the tender flesh beneath and further down to the full mounds inside her lacy bra. He tongued the delicate fabric, sucking the hard peaks through the material, his teeth grazing the sensitive flesh until she gasped.

"Are you wet and throbbing, Kari?"

She croaked out a yes, fisting his hair.

"What do you want?" He looked up from her breasts and his eyes were green and hungry and his untamed desire left her breath locked in her throat.

She reached for his zipper, but he locked her wrists, shaking his head. "I do. You feel."

He shoved her skirt to her hips and then pulled her to the edge of the hay bale, spreading her knees. He dipped his mouth to her slick slit and flicked her moist folds apart, delving and teasing with his tongue. He swirled her clit, nipping and sucking until Kari's fingers dug into the hay as she arched for more.

Her head dropped back and she cried out, fisting his hair as she ground her pussy farther into his mouth. With a sly smile he lifted his face, dragging his lips over her inner thighs, nibbling her flesh.

"I want to fill you, Kari. Stretch you and ride you boneless until your legs shake and your body screams with pleasure. You're mine, love. To keep, to fuck, to love, to have—"

He freed his cock and with a deft thrust drove his member deep, lifting her ass from the hay bale. He scooped her up and pushed her back against the high stack, his hips grinding and owning every thrust, every pound balls deep.

Kari cried out as her body spasmed, her inner walls

clutching his thick cock as her fingers clutched his back. Tiny barbs scored her walls with every thrust, pushing her past the limits until waves of pleasure eclipsed all thought.

With a feral snarl Bryon's fingers grasped the soft flesh of her ass, his body tense as every muscle tightened with the need to release.

"Tell me!" he snarled.

"Come! I want you NOW!"

Bryon roared, keeping his cock rock hard and deep. He pulled back once more and with a final plunge, let hot jets pulse from his engorged head.

Kari clung to him, weak but sated.

"You know you're dreaming, right?" he whispered against her ear.

"I don't care."

He chuckled against her damp skin. "Good, because I'm ready for round two."

"Giddy up, cowboy cat."

The pilot over the intercom woke her with a start. Her heart pounded and her entire body throbbed. Man, she hadn't had a dream that . . . real, in ever. She needed to get laid.

CHAPTER 6

⟶

Their plane from London taxied to a small building, but instead of pulling up to the terminal to walk through a connecting tunnel to the inside, they stopped away from the building.

"Damn, I almost forgot." He pulled a square, velvet-covered jewelry box from his pocket. Her heart picked up speed. What was he doing? He flipped open the top to reveal a shiny silver bangle bracelet. "This is for you. I want you to wear it all the time. Never take it off because some-one will steal it. It's brand-new and fine to get wet."

She was taken aback by such an extravagant gift. "I can't wear that. It's beautiful, but—" but she wasn't dating him and had no plans to. Was she reading him wrong? She wasn't getting any "love" vibes from him. He was a shifter. Maybe they were unlike human men. No, human men didn't show love very well, usually.

Sheldon took her hand in his and slipped the bangle over her wrist. "I insist you wear it."

Oh god. It must've cost him a fortune. The people in front of them were pulling down their carry-ons. She'd find a way later to thank him and give it back. Hopefully, he could still return it.

They stood and he handed her the bag from the overhead bin. His smile was awfully cute. From the plane's entrance, she stepped onto a set of stairs butted against the door. Kari grabbed the rail with a death grip. This was something she would fall all the way to the bottom on.

"By the way," he said, "the bracelet is a GPS tracking device." Her cheeks warmed from the completely wrong romantic ideas she'd had about him. His sly smile made her entire body flame from embarrassment. "You didn't think I gave that to you because I was sweet on you, did you?"

She didn't know how she could be more discombobulated, but she was. "Of course not." She tilted her head down to study her hands. Oh god, how could she look him in the face again and not die from mortification?

"This is different," Kari said, looking around the area. A few bigger planes were sitting, but what surprised her was the number of small jets like Gulfstreams scattered about. Almost looked like a sales lot.

"Especially for a private airstrip," Sheldon added. "Maybe there's a big convention in town."

She laughed. "You definitely don't know much about Cloustien. There isn't a place that holds more than fifty people. And that'd be the local tavern. It's an old town, back when they built things small and compact."

An airline employee unloaded the cargo bay at the bottom of the plane. Her suitcase was easy to spot. When she'd shopped for a new case, she'd wanted something that would be easy to find among a mass of black. As soon as she laid her eyes on it, she knew it was the one.

Everyone seemed to stare at the luggage, waiting to see who the owner of such a case would be. She sighed, used to the stares. It was the largest canary yellow piece of luggage she could find. With the handle extended, the bag was almost three-quarters her height. She thought about practical issues, not the color. Again, she couldn't trust herself to do anything right.

She wrapped her fingers around the handle and pulled. The bag rocked, but remained standing, dragging her backward with it. She lost her balance, but straightened before making a big scene. This time, she used both hands and stepped back, tipping the suitcase onto two wheels. She'd have to get a bag with four wheels so she wouldn't have to tip anything. Maybe something a bit smaller, and maybe not Tweety Bird yellow.

She looked around for Sheldon, her boyfriend for the next several days. When they got inside the terminal, she'd have to make a pit stop. She really needed to pee. That last soda had gotten her. But he stood among cars parked at the back of the building, holding the rear door to a car open. She'd just have to wait until they got to the hotel to use the restroom.

Snuggled into the backseat of the small car, she watched as they left the private airport behind. The driver was bald headed and looked jolly. He smiled back at her and said, "You Americans?"

Sheldon answered before she could. "We are. We're with a tourist group that came in yesterday. We're a bit late."

"Tourists," the man said. "We love tourists. Not many come here because we're so interesting." His smile got bigger. "I give you small tour. Yes, I show you."

She looked as Sheldon. He didn't look thrilled. That made her laugh.

The driver started the expedition right away. "Cloustien is very old country. Oldest bone found here is six hundred *thousand* years old."

"What?" she asked.

"Yes, ma'am. Is true." They drove over a bridge that looked six hundred thousand years old. She glanced out her window and could see the river through the warped and cracked wooden planks. "This river is very old, too. There are places where water goes underground and disappears. Then come out somewhere else."

He pointed out the window. "You see there?" She leaned forward to look out Sheldon's side. On a hill in the distance sat a castle. It was so cool. "Our prince's family used to live there. But now it's haunted by the old, old King Alheim. My grandmother said the old king had found a way into hell. That he go there to get riches and power beyond the human world.

"The king's rule began to spread far. My oma talked of war and great battles where many enemy died, but few of the king's men were ever harmed. Oma said it was the devil within the king that worked sorcery to win."

"But Cloustien is so small," Kari said. "What happened to his rule?"

"You know what happen when make deal with the devil. No good come from it. After time, his payment was due. Old king died. Then his much younger brother returned from Rome. Oma said they never knew of the brother, but he was kind and good for the people. They liked him."

"And the land," she said.

He shrugged. "In time, all things change. But at night, if you watch the castle, sometimes you see old King Alheim's ghost walking the halls and lighting rooms. They say he's angry because of how he lost everything. Stay away from castle. Those who go in sometime never seen again."

Kari asked, "Your royalty doesn't live there anymore?"

"Not for long time. No electricity or water. The prince lives in town in his modern palace. Beautiful home. He talks with people of our village. Others kings, no bother with common people. We didn't see them much."

"Prince?" she replied.

"Yes, Prince Goddard is good man. He take care of our town. Especially when money needed. He is very generous."

"Does the prince hold any power in the government?" she asked.

"Some. But he mainly let us decide for ourselves. He is always busy with important people. Our prince very important and educated in world goings-on."

Sheldon perked up. "Really, what kind of important people?"

The man shrugged. "Big military men, men with own planes, royalty. That kinda thing. In fact, earlier this week, I drive around several of them. Good people, give lots of money to driver." He turned toward her and winked.

Sheldon handed the driver a picture of Bryon Day. Shit, just glancing at his gorgeous face got her hot and bothered. "Have you seen this man?" He stared at the photo a long time, and not the road. She felt around for the seat belt. Twisting around, she squished her bladder, reminding her she needed to go. The driver handed back the photo.

"No. Never seen him. Does he live here? American, like you?"

Sheldon didn't reply. She looked at him and he gave her a small shake of his head. The car jolted in a U-turn and stopped in front of a building. "We are here." The man jumped out of the car and headed toward the trunk and luggage. She let herself out and looked around. This village was like nothing she'd ever seen.

This place was old. You could almost feel the time that had passed. The streets were made of worn-down cobblestones. The buildings were smallish and sat pushed against one another. No alleys. The door to the building in front of her opened and several people walked out. One woman carried a clipboard and wore a white visor. She looked at Kari and stopped.

"Are you Kari?"

That surprised her. She glanced at Sheldon behind the car getting the bags. "Uh, yes?"

The woman laughed and waved her hand in the air. "You're so funny, dear." She looked at her clipboard. "Kari and Sheldon. From Virginia."

Sheldon came up behind the tour guide. "Yes, that's us. Sorry we're late."

"You're just in time," she said. "We have a short tour right now, then going to dinner at a local restaurant." She stuck her head in the door and hollered. A boy came running out and tried to take the suitcases from Sheldon. He growled at the kid.

"It's okay, Sheldon," the woman said with an extra-white smile. "They're going to check you both in so you can come with us now. Your suitcases will be waiting for you in your room when we get back." The boy grabbed the bags again and rolled them inside.

"Okay, everybody, let's go." The guide had her hands in the air. "And we're walking, walking."

Kari looked at Sheldon. He shrugged and gestured for her to go in front of him to follow the group. They walked down the street looking like tourists. This might be fine, she thought. Then her bladder spoke again. Oh shit. How long would it take to get to the restaurant? They turned another corner and the area changed entirely. Instead of little old town, it was modern with concrete buildings and nice sidewalks.

She stopped and squeezed her thighs together. If she peed her pants, she'd just kill herself instead of letting Sheldon smell her.

"What's wrong?" he asked.

"Nothing," she said. The urge went away and she caught up with the group. They all stopped to look at something. She didn't get to see it because she was doing the potty dance.

Across the street, a van was backed up to a large door to a building and people were carrying in silver warming trays and chafing dishes. Maybe she could sneak in, use the restroom, and get out with no one being the wiser.

She whispered her plan to Sheldon.

"What? You just can't sneak in there," he said. "It looks like a museum or something fancy."

"If not in there where the public is welcome, it will be on your shoes. Choose."

He stood silently for a second. "Do you need help getting over there?"

CHAPTER 7

———✂———

I t was coming! Nature had called, and it had called loudly. Screamed. She gritted her teeth and bent over. Squeeze those Kegel muscles. Fuck. After this, her Kegels would be able to lift weights. The sensation passed.

"No. I got it." She stepped off the sidewalk toward the building. At the van, she glanced in the driver's-side window and saw an apron and clipboard. Looking around and seeing no one watching her, she opened the door and grabbed both items. She tied the apron around her waist and put on a pained expression. People seldom talked to others who looked mad. If she came in like she was supposed to be there, then maybe no one would notice.

The fancy bracelet Sheldon gave her caught on the apron's material. She slid it off and shoved it in her back pocket. It didn't seem like women here wore anything expensive. In her back pocket, no one would steal it. She wasn't going far. There'd be no need to be tracked.

When she walked around the back of the van, she was startled to see armed guards standing on each side of the door. She didn't miss a beat, though. She pulled a pen from the top of the board, frowned and pushed down her brows and looked at the ground as she walked through the door. The guards didn't move. She wasn't sure they were even awake.

Out of sight of the door, she hurried down a hall, checking each door. There were three doors down each side. Most looked like conference rooms with tables in the center. One room was filled with gold items. They shined like a thousand mirrors. It took her breath away. She slipped the apron off and set it on the floor inside the door. A couple catering employees passed her. They didn't even look at her. She came to the end of the hall and found no bathroom.

The space opened into a huge lobby-like area with amazing artwork and paintings on the wall. This had to be a museum like Sheldon had said. Everything was too incredible, too ancient-looking to be anything else. There had to be a restroom in a public place. She tried a door close to the corner. The sight that greeted her almost made her cry.

She rushed in and never in her life had she gotten her pants down as fast as she did now. As she sat, she sighed. So much better. The room was very small. Must be for the staff who worked in that area. After washing her hands, she stepped out and closed the door behind her.

On the wall next to her was a beautiful framed painting. She couldn't read the artist's name, but it looked old, the paint faded. That would make sense. Museums weren't for new things. That would be called a *store*.

Across the way, a group of men came around the corner. The one in front of the group was dressed in flashy clothing and looked important, but the others were wearing the same uniforms as the two guards at the back door. And they were dragging another guy who looked unconscious. The guy in the shiny clothes abruptly stopped and stared at her. Oh shit. He must be a manager.

He pointed a finger at her and yelled words she didn't understand. That wasn't what made her run. It was the guns leveled at her. She had no idea they shot people who didn't pay for a ticket to get in. She should've never assumed this place was like the U.S., the greatest country in the world.

If she headed to the back door she had come in through,

she'd never get out once those chasing her yelled to the guards outside the exit. She had to hide and find another way out.

She grabbed a doorknob and threw herself inside. She tripped on the carpet, rolled, then popped up to her feet and ran for the door on the other side. As she opened it, the door behind her opened with guards stepping in. This was bad. She couldn't do anything right.

Slamming the door, she ran to another door. She didn't see the guards, but heard the door open. This room had a twenty-person conference table in the middle. The room being somewhat narrow, and her not being narrow, she bumped into an antique buffet and went down. She rolled under the table, wondering if she could hide.

The door at the other end of the table opened. The swishing of clothes headed toward the door on the far side. The second door opened, then she heard someone yell a word she didn't know, but the sound of moving clothes stopped.

Chairs clunked as they were moved around, scooted away from the table. She held her breath and squeezed her eyes closed and lay as still as she could. After several seconds of silence, the voice said another word and everyone left the room.

Air rushed out of her lungs. She reached up from where she lay curled up on the floor, pushed away from the table, and promptly rolled to the floor. She had extra padding, so nothing hurt, too much, when landing. After getting to her feet, she peeked into the room she just left and saw nobody. She rushed to another door, hoping to find the hallway to the lobby where she could walk out the front door. Bingo!

She stepped out at the same time one of the guards did two doors down. Shit! She dove forward into the room across the hall. The room was dark, no lights. Her hand slid along the wall which felt like books. She kept going, came to a corner. The door opened. She flattened herself against the wall.

Lights came on, but they were small spotlights shining

on the rows and rows of books lining the walls. She was awed by the amount of leather and paper this room held. At the end of the shelf, she squeezed back, hoping they wouldn't see her.

The small of her back rubbed against two small objects in the wall behind her. Wait, she wasn't against a wall, but a double door. She quietly opened it and backed in. Her eyes stayed on the men on the other side of the room, searching for her. Her shaky hands eased the door closed with barely a *snick*. She blew out the breath she held.

A throat behind her cleared. She jumped and twirled in the air, then flattened against the doors, her heart beating way too fast. Standing behind a desk was the sparkly important man who had pointed and sent the men after her.

Perhaps this was her last time not trusting herself to do anything right.

CHAPTER 8

Kari stood with her back against the double door staring at the man who would determine her fate. All this because she didn't buy a ticket to get in? Time to beg. "I'm so sorry." She unzipped her fanny pack. "Here, I'll pay the admission price. Even more for a donation. I just had to use the bathroom very badly." She stood in front of the desk, holding out money.

His brow raised, head tilted. "Are you American?"

Oh shit. If she said yes, would he kill her or throw her in jail? If she said no, could she fake an English accent? Her initial thought was to lie. But she knew her luck too well.

"Yes, I'm American."

The man broke into a big smile, his arms spread wide. "Well then, welcome to my home."

Her jaw dropped. Home? The only person in this town who could afford the kind of stuff on display would be the—oh, double shit. She was in so much trouble.

"I am Prince Goddard and this is my palace. What brings an American female to my doorstep?" The way he said "American female" sent a shudder through her. She smiled anyway.

"My boyfriend and I are touring." The words sounded robotic even to her. She was so dead. On her first mission and gone missing, never to be seen or heard from again.

"Are you sure you're not with the CIA?" he asked. Was he joking? A spot of red flashed in his eyes.

"No. We're with ITA."

The prince's face took on a questioning expression.

"International Touring Agency. That's the name of our group, I swear." So much for being a strong spy. She wasn't even being interrogated and she gave out information.

"That's wonderful, Miss . . ."

"Oh, I'm Kari Tomlin." She leaned forward and put her hand out to shake. He took her fingers in his soft ones and brought it to his mouth. Ever so lightly, he brushed his lips across her skin. Oh my god. She was in complete shock. Was this normal in this country for greeting females?

"We have so few American women come here. You are truly a treasure worth a fortune." His smile seemed predatory. He looked at her like she was an object, not a person.

Someone knocked on the door. The prince said a word and the door opened. It was a guard. When he saw her, his eyes widened. The man spoke and quickly left, closing the door.

"Miss Tomlin, you're just in time," the prince said.

She narrowed her eyes. "In time for what, may I ask?"

"For dinner." He smiled and opened his arms wide again. "You will be my guest this evening. We have a fantastic show I'm sure you'll like. Yes, I think you will like it very much." His eyes flashed red again. It unnerved her even though she wasn't sure what it was.

Her head shook side to side. "Oh, thank you. That is so kind of you, but I should be going. My boyfriend will be worried." Her phone buzzed in her waist pack. She stared at it, not sure if she should pick it up. The prince gestured for her to go ahead. She dug it out and pushed the icon for text messaging.

"Who is it?" the prince asked, standing over her shoulder, deliberately reading her message.

"It's my boyfriend wondering where I am." She stepped away. "I really should—"

"Miss Tomlin," he backed her against the desk and put a hand on the wooden top on each side of her, "you don't want problems with our police. Any crime against the royal family is punishable by death. And you are trespassing on my property."

Fuck. He was a bipolar psycho. Charming one second, threatening her life the next. That red glowed brighter and larger, then died back. She put on a smile to save her life. "On second thought, it would be nice to sample some of the best food your country offers. Let me text my boyfriend and he'll be here shortly."

"I haven't invited him, Miss Tomlin," Goddard said.

Oh, shit. This couldn't be good. But what could she do? She swallowed hard. "Of course, you haven't. How presumptuous of me."

He stepped back. "Wonderful. Now send your friend a message telling him you'll be fine. I will deliver you to your hotel safely."

She picked up the phone from the desk where she'd dropped it and brought up the on-screen keyboard. There had to be some way to let Sheldon know she'd be okay or he would barge in and get himself shot. Or worse yet, get them both put in jail and cause an international incident. Just what she needed on her first trip into the field.

She typed, "Guess who I just met. Prince Goddard! He's invited me for dinner and a show. Enjoy the tour. Don't wait up." Why, now that she needed to be clever with words, could she not think of one secret code or clue phrase? The spy business wasn't for her. She needed to stick with her movies and fantasies.

"Very good," he said after reading what she'd typed. "Send it and we'll go." She tapped the envelope icon, then the prince snatched the phone from her hands.

"Hey!" She tried to grab it back. "That's mine. Give it back."

Goddard tsked. "You Americans and your toys. Dinner

is not the place for such distractions. After we finish, I'll return your phone." She had no choice. And she was hungry.

"Lead the way," she said. He took her hand and opened the door for her. Every other step, another amazing piece of art dazzled her. His stash had to be worth billions. "Your collection of art is astounding. You must've spent a long time searching for everything here."

He smiled. "It is quite impressive, isn't it? Many items are from the castle and very old. But a majority I've found here and there in my life." He flipped a hand in the air like it was nothing. Just a watercolor he found at a starving artist sidewalk sale. Whatever.

After a maze of hallways, they came to a set of doors that looked solid gold. Wasteful, but beautiful. He pulled them open with grand flourish and strutted into the room. This was not what she expected for a dining room.

The lighting was low, very low. How would they be able to see their food? As they walked, she realized the room was bigger than she'd thought. Others were in the room already. They sat on giant pillows leaning against the walls. In front of each person was a tray of fruit. And she noted they were all men who held an air of importance. Some had a scantily clad female draped over them. One had her hand down the pants of a guy in a military type uniform.

Her eyes snapped forward. She suddenly wasn't hungry. What had she gotten herself into?

CHAPTER 9

Kari's mind swirled with ways to get out of the "dining" room and palace as quickly as possible. She felt like she was walking into a bizarre porn movie.

The prince led her to the back wall where more pillows were stacked and trays sat waiting with what looked like fruit. Goddard assisted her with the pillows.

"Are you comfortable, Miss Tomlin?" he asked. He had returned to his charming self. As long as she did what he wanted, he seemed happy.

"I am, thank you," she replied. As soon as he sat, soft Arabian music played and more women came out of a side door, carrying pitchers. The prince's wineglass was filled first and hers next. The liquid was dark. He leaned toward her.

"This is wine from the finest vineyards in France. It is superb. I hope you like it." When the ladies filling glasses left, he raised his glass. Everyone followed suit. "Welcome, all, to tonight's feast and show. I see some of you have started your entertainment early." He smiled at his guests. Maybe she had misunderstood what was going on. The prince nodded toward the couple where the lady had her head bobbing in his lap. Then again, maybe she had understood this too well.

And Goddard called her phone a distraction? He needed to get his shit straight.

He continued. "We have a special guest tonight." He looked at her. "An American female visiting my lovely country." The word "American" turned their heads. Her heart suddenly tripled its rate. "A beautiful woman like you is a treat in itself. For tonight, you are my stunning princess." His head bowed toward her. If he was trying to win her over, it was working. He turned back to the group and spoke foreign words. Everyone took a drink and so did she.

The wine was surprisingly very good. She wasn't a drinker. Had never acquired the taste for it. Guess she'd never had the good stuff. Side doors opened and women poured out, carrying steaming food on platters.

Those eating sat against the walls in a semicircle. Well, since the walls had corners, it was more like a semi-square. That left the middle open for the ladies to serve or even dance, it was so big.

The prince was kind and gracious, explaining what each item they ate and drank was. He paid no attention to the nearly naked women or the other men with ladies attached to their body parts. When they were halfway finished eating, he gave a nod to someone on the other side of the room and the lights dimmed even more.

From the ceiling in the middle of their semi-square a blue spotlight shined down. Now that she was looking up, she noticed a rack of stage lights and spots. This must be for the entertainment. The sensuous and slick Arabian music got louder and beautiful women dressed in draping material and shiny jewelry appeared under the light. As the floor filled with gyrating bodies, more lights shined down.

The men were entranced. They watched without eating. One man discreetly raised a finger, the prince nodded and the woman selected was directed to the man. That couple left the room. A disgusting little man with food on his face and shirt pointed a greasy finger at some poor female.

Without complaint, she went to him. He remained seated, but pushed her head to his lap. Kari turned away.

The females didn't seem to object. In fact, they looked quite happy to be there. Except one young lady in the back. Kari only caught sight of her occasionally. The lady didn't know the choreography well and kept looking at the door. The woman was too far away for Kari to see her face, so she couldn't tell what was wrong, if anything. Could be that she was new and didn't know the dance and felt out of place. Sorta like she felt at the moment, staring at sexy women.

The prince didn't look at the ladies either, but watched the men as they chose females. After a few minutes, the prince clapped his hands and the remaining women left. That's when the familiarity of the show hit her. This was the prince's harem, and this whole dinner was a ruse for men to get partners for the night. But a few men hadn't chosen. Neither had the prince. A chill raced down her back. Did being his princess include her sleeping with him?

Panic seized her and she readied herself to bolt. That was not happening. He leaned over and whispered, "This is the part you and I will appreciate most." He clapped his hands and the single spotlight appeared center stage again.

Doors opened in the dark, then a guy in painted-on leather pants and no shirt strolled into the light. His chest was slick, shiny with oil. His dark eyes drilled through her, sending shivers down her back. He came to a stop, feet shoulder-width apart. In his hand, he held a black strip of leather.

He skirted the circle of light showing those who watched his tight body and impressive hard-on. When he turned his back to her, she saw his ass cheeks were bare. Lines buried in his skin crisscrossed his entire backside. When he stood in front of her and the prince, the man swung his arm out, releasing the whip he held. It snapped in the air, startling her with a loud crack.

Other men came into the light. Some were dragged in with cuffs on wrists and ankles.

She asked, "Why are some restrained and not others?"

The prince didn't take his eyes off the men. "It shows the level of play they enjoy." She translated that to mean whips and chains were welcomed.

They filled the middle similarly to the females. And every one of them was to-die-for hot. The prince licked his lips. The panic in her quickly vanished once she realized she was not the prince's dessert. The men were on the menu.

She let out a silent breath and watched the event before her. The other men were dressed in nothing but a small loincloth that in some cases did little to hide their willingness to participate. Oh my god. One was almost up to his bellybutton. How can they grow that long? He'd shove her uterus into her stomach.

Instead of dancing, the men stood on a turntable. The next man came into sight. She had never seen a chest so chiseled or abs so square. It was to the point that he looked . . . strange.

The table continued turning and men were taken out of the room.

"Where are they taking the guys?" she asked.

"Once chosen, they are taken to the guest's room for preparation and quality time."

She snorted. "Quality time," her ass.

The man coming into view was swaying slightly on his knees instead of standing. His head dipped forward, hands chained behind his back. Water dripped off the ends of his hair hanging in his face. He looked ready to fall over any second. Tingles spread throughout her body. That was strange. She'd never had that feeling before when seeing a man. She couldn't even see all of him because he was slumped over. She leaned toward Goddard.

"What's wrong with him?" she whispered. His head snapped up, and he locked eyes with her. Her breath stopped. This man was the most gorgeous thing she'd ever seen. There was something familiar about him. Beside her, the prince chuckled.

"I knew you'd like him. I've chosen this one for us

tonight." The prince's eyes were consumed with red. He pointed and a couple of guards grabbed the kneeling man and dragged him closer. He fought his captors. They stabbed him with a cattle prod. His jaw clenched; she jumped at seeing his pain.

"Stop that," she yelled then slapped a hand over her mouth. She hadn't meant to say it, but was glad she had. No human should be treated that way whether they wanted the "punishment" or not. She had problems with BDSM that passed a certain pain threshold. How could people truly enjoy agony? She just didn't understand.

The man was shoved to his knees in front of her forgotten tray of food. Air heaved in and out of his bedraggled body. The guard reached down, wrapped a fist in the man's hair and yanked his head back.

Kari gasped.

CHAPTER 10

⤚⤙

Bryon knew he was no longer in the dank cell, but some-where quiet and fragrant. He felt his body jerked around, but couldn't control any part of himself. His eyes wouldn't even open. The toxins in the water he drank were still too concentrated in his system. More needed to burn off before he could move of his own will.

His clothes were ripped off. Cold water and a scrub brush bit at his skin. He smelled floral and citrus scents. Soft hands rubbed warm oils over his chest, abs, legs, and under his balls.

He forced his eyes open to find himself on a concrete floor, a woman kneeling over him. She glanced at his open eyes but quickly looked away and continued rubbing oil on him. He tried to speak but wasn't coordinated enough. He relaxed and closed his eyes. The hands on his beaten, ach-ing muscles felt too good to ignore.

Next thing he knew, rough hands jerked him up. His legs barely held him standing and the men dragged him more than helped him walk. A cold stick was jabbed into his side and a paralyzing shock constricted his muscles. His lungs froze and abs contracted, curling him into a partial ball.

When his body loosened, his strength was gone. They certainly knew how to handle a shifter. From the moment he drank the water, he'd been completely in their hands. Question was what were they going to do with him?

They entered a dark room with exotic music, and he was tossed to his knees. The smell of food made his stomach cramp. How many days had he gone without anything to eat? His wolf came to the forefront, ready to seize control. His arms tugged against the chains wrapping his wrists together behind him. ALFA policy and procedures strictly forbade shifting with humans around. But he wasn't strong enough to hold back his other half.

Then another scent captured his attention. The most incredible scent he'd ever experienced. His wolf immediately knew what the smell meant. Bryon couldn't think. *Mate!* Bryon didn't understand. Mate? Here? In Cloustien?

His world was slowly spinning, although he wasn't moving his body. There were several others in the room with him. He smelled them all and they were disgusting. Sex permeated the air. Seductive music played. He searched for that divine smell. Where did it come from? Then his ears picked up a voice. A soft voice that filled his heart with longing. *What's wrong with him?*

The scent he longed for returned to him in full breaths. She was here, close to him. He could feel her presence, but he couldn't move. He was so tired. Once again, rough hands grabbed his arms and dragged him forward. The cattle prod was again shoved into his side. He clenched his teeth together to fight the pain. Then it was gone.

He fell forward and hit his chin on the floor. But that pain was little compared to the wrench of his head being shoved back. Then there she was, right in front of him. Her eyes showed concern and compassion for him. Then widened to complete surprise. Did she know him? He'd never seen her before, and he'd been in the town for almost a year. He thought he would have seen her by now.

She was so beautiful, so perfect. Except she was sitting beside *him*. He had to get her away from that bastard before he hurt her. Suddenly, he was lifted from the ground and moved away from her. He struggled to get free, to get back to her. Then she was gone from his sight. Everything inside him died. He had to find her.

He was shuffled into another room and tossed onto something soft and welcoming. Cool, slick material rubbed against him. Unceremoniously, his loincloth was jerked off and he was kneeling again, but this time, his hands were chained straight up over his head. His knees sank into the same soft material he lay on.

Then the room was quiet. With one breath, he knew he was in the prince's personal room. The stench filled his nose. He was finally able to lift his head and look around. He was chained to the ceiling in the middle of a huge bed overflowing with pillows. What the fuck was going on? What kind of weird shit was this asshole into?

Bryon shook his head trying to clear the fuzz, but it hung on. The door opened and her smell hit him. He breathed deeply. She was here. As well as that son of a bitch. Would that bastard ever go away?

The bed jostled. The prince was pulling the beautiful woman onto the bed. Seemed she was rather short or the bed high. Maybe both. The wolf in him growled. Nobody should touch their mate.

The prince looked at him and smiled. "Well, what is this? Sounds like we do have an animal inside, Mr. Day." The wolf came closer to the surface. It wanted to be closer to their girl.

She looked at him then back at the prince. "His name is Day?"

"Yes," the prince said. "Bryon Day, if my intelligence is correct. Isn't he just scrumptious?" The prince reached over and ran his hand along Bryon's crotch. There had been so little activity there for so long, he wasn't sure there would be any response. Hopefully not to the prince's touch, but hers . . .

"Here, my little *schatzi*." The prince brought her hand up and placed it on Bryon's chest. Her eyes locked with his.

Controlled panic seeped from her pours, along with a hint of desire. Her hot touch crashed through him, zapping his nerve endings, sending his wolf into an ecstatic high. Something else was starting to go high also. The prince smiled. "Yes, that's what we want." Goddard moved back so the woman could kneel in front of him, only inches away.

He felt her heat, smelled her want growing. God, this was going to kill him. She pulled back, shaking her head.

"This isn't right, Goddard. Can't you see he's in pain? Let him go. He can lie on the bed."

He tugged on the chains, but his arm strength had yet to return. Yes, he'd lie on the bed with her. The prince forced her hand back onto his chest, pushing her close again. The touch was burned into his skin. His head dipped, his nose close to her hair. Sunshine and lemons. His most favorite smells as a child and now. Fresh, clean, uplifting. Warm.

She leaned against him, putting her mouth to his ear. "Play along," she whispered then clamped her teeth on his earlobe. He growled from the slight pain. When she leaned back, her eyes begged him for something. What did that mean? She was playing, toying with him?

Chills slicked over his torso when her fingertips brushed his flesh. Her breath was hot against him. Fuck, he wanted her and there was no hiding his desire. He nuzzled his nose along her hair. A low rumble vibrated his body. She looked up at him with large eyes. She felt it, too.

Her wet panties told him how much she liked it. He arched toward her, pressing his painfully hard cock against her stomach. He wanted her taste, whether from her mouth or her pussy. Didn't matter. She'd taste so good both ways. Her hands slid up around his neck and she looked up at him.

CHAPTER 11

Kari knelt with her hands on the man of her dreams. This was way better than her little fantasy on the plane. Except in her fantasy, she wasn't scared out of her wits nor did she have a creepy prince watching her make out with a man chained to the ceiling. She had to find a way to get him free.

Her entire plan to escape had been blown to bits as soon as she'd seen his face in the dining room. When he looked into her eyes, she knew immediately it was him. The agent they were here to find. How and why he was here, she'd work on finding out later. She had to focus on getting him—them—out alive.

Her new plan required her to pretend she wanted to have sex with the agent. Which wasn't *really* pretending. She would like that, but it was too soon. When she made love to someone it was because she was making love, not having sex.

The prince had led her out of the dining room and down more hallways to another set of double doors. A guard was posted to the side; he didn't budge an inch.

The plan was on track so far. The prince had taken her

to where the agent was. Then when she was alone with the agent, she'd sneak them out a window to safety and she'd be the hero and they'd get married and have lots of kids. Easy peasy.

Until she realized the prince wasn't leaving the room. And he wanted to *participate*.

She nearly freaked out. Holy shit. She'd barely had sex with one man at a time, much less two. And the prince wanted a piece of the agent. Now, she wasn't being judgmental. To each his own. Some of her friends were gay and they were the best, most caring people she'd ever met. But for her to be on one side of the tied-up agent and the prince on the back side was just too much. It would wig her out.

Then when Goddard put her hands on the completely naked agent on the bed, all thought flew from her mind. This hunk of man was hers to do with as she wished. His skin was hot to the touch. Electricity zapped low in her stomach.

Whoa, whoa, whoa. She leaned away from him. He was too intoxicating for her starved soul and heart. All reasoning and logic flew out the window when she was this close to this man. She was here to rescue him, not seduce him in some bondage fantasy.

She argued with the prince about unchaining him. Tried to get the agent released. Together, they could overpower the prince and escape. Goddard probably realized that also. Thus his telling her no. The prince forced her hands back onto the hot flesh.

His head tilted down and his cheek rubbed against her hair. He breathed her in. Despite the agent's advances, she had to stay focused. How could she get the prince in a position where she could tie him up or knock him out or something?

It was obvious what Goddard had in mind for the three of them. Maybe if she played along until he was distracted, then she could attack. What about Agent Day, though? He had no idea who she was. She could be in the harem as far as he knew. Would he hurt her given the chance? Probably, if he could escape.

With the prince behind her, lying on pillows against the headboard, she leaned against Agent Day and whispered, "Play along." Then bit his ear to complete the ruse for the prince. She pulled away and begged Day to understand what she was saying: She was here to help, so stop making it so difficult to pay attention.

She brushed her fingers over his chest. A deep grumble vibrated in his chest. What the hell? Was that his animal side peeking through?

Her undies were instantly soaked. Goddammit, Day. Did the man not know how to read eye sign language? Her eyes tried to tell him to stop making this hard. Joke was on her. His hardness pressed against her stomach.

She looked up at him. God, she wanted to kiss him so badly.

Then the bed bounced and the prince snuggled up behind her agent. She snapped her hands away and leaned back. What should she do? She wouldn't let anyone be taken advantage of against their will, male or female.

"Kari," the prince said, "would you open the drawer on the table beside the bed and pull out the white tube."

White tube. Yeah, she could do that if her lust-consumed brain would get in gear. She leaned over the side of the bed and pulled the drawer open. Never in her life had she seen a bed so tall. Her legs didn't lift that high. The prince had had to help her onto the top mattress. Good thing they weren't in the mood at that moment. It was the most un-sexy thing she'd ever done.

In the drawer, there were two white tubes. Figured. She stretched for the nearest one. Her fingertips barely reached the plastic. Just a little closer. In between her fingers, she held it up. "Is this it?" She looked over her shoulder and startled. Unprepared for the scene, her hand slipped off the slick comforter's edge, banged her head on the open drawer, and she fell to the floor. Shit.

"It's the other tube," the prince said, leaning over the side, looking at her.

"Got it." She pulled the other one out and tossed it to him.

"Come up the back way." The prince nodded toward something behind him at the back of the bed. She stepped around and saw a two-tread step. Why didn't he show her that to begin with? Then she realized what was in the white tube when the prince squeezed stuff in his hand. The agent rattled his chains but could do little else.

She would not let this happen. She looked around for a weapon or something. Everything in the room looked so expensive; she didn't want to break anything. But this was an emergency. The only thing that looked viable was a pair of tall pewter candlesticks. She grabbed one, snuck up the steps and swung it with all she had at his head.

The candlestick was so heavy that the prince's head wasn't enough to stop the momentum her swing created. Her arms continued around, twisting her body and knocking her off the steps with a loud crash. A sound came from the door. The guard called from the other side. He didn't speak English, but she could guess what he said.

"Sorry," she hollered. "Everything is good in here. Just got carried away." She made a couple grunting noises. "You know how it is."

Agent Day looked down on her with a *what the fuck* expression. She shrugged and whispered, "What was I supposed to say? We're killing your asshole prince?" She leaned over Goddard to look at his bloody head. "Oh shit. Did I kill him?"

Agent Day tried to clear his throat. "Look, lady." He broke into raspy coughs. "The guards put the key to these cuffs are on the dresser where that candlestick was. If you let me go, I'll pay you."

For some reason, that rubbed her the wrong way. "I'm worried about killing someone," she said, "and you're talking about money?"

"He's alive. His heartbeat is strong," he replied.

"Oh, good." She'd never thought about having to kill someone. Yeah, she really liked her desk job now. She wondered what to do with the prince's body. She had to hide it.

"Lady—" Agent Day started.

"My name is Kari. I'm with the U.S. government. I'm here to help."

Day snorted. "If that isn't an overused oxymoron."

"I read that on a T-shirt somewhere." She looked for the key on the dresser. Sliding it between her fingers, she climbed the steps at the back of the bed and stepped onto the mattress. Putting her weight on one foot, she sank deeper than expected and fell forward into Day's back. Her hands wrapped around his chest from behind. His pecs hardened with her contact. She couldn't keep her fingers from squeezing.

He sucked in a harsh breath and she stiffened against him. "Sorry," she breathed onto his back. Pushing away from him, she held on to his arm and inched her way around to the front side where the slot for the key on the manacles was.

Looking at her, he snorted. "You can barely take care of yourself. How can you help me?"

His weight kneeling on the bed made a deep hole. When she got in front of him, she sank into the indention, pressing her body against his. Damn, he smelled so good. His hair was freshly washed, still damp. The oils on his body smelled citrusy. His eyes snapped to hers. The fire in them ignited her want again. How was she so horny over a stranger—a gorgeous stranger, but a stranger.

Wait. Did he just call her incompetent? Her sex-hazed mind came out of the gutter a moment to realize he'd just made fun of her. "For your information, Agent Day, do you have any idea how much talent it takes to look so clumsy? How many people have you seen fall off a bed? Or have to be pulled onto a bed by her one arm. It's not easy making the enemy think you're not a threat. And," she held up the key, "who has the key and who's in handcuffs?" There, suck on that, Mr. Hotshot Agent.

Handsome or not, the man was a jerk. She should've known. Now she knew why he wasn't married. His eyes narrowed at her. She hadn't told one lie, so there wasn't a lying smell floating out her ass. Ha.

Kari reached up and her body leaned against him more. She felt pressure against her shirt and glanced down. His eyes were at her chest level. Embarrassment tinged with anger edged with desire washed through her. She brought her hands down. "Stop looking there," she reprimanded.

He huffed. "Like I have a choice."

She frowned and leaned back. "Yes, you do. Turn your head," which he did. She reached up again, leaning forward. His nose sank into the side of her boob. That wasn't happening. Her hands came down. "Okay, Day—"

"Lady, I'm not trying anything. Would you please unlock the cuffs?"

Hands on her hips, she said, "First off, my name is Kari, not lady. Secondly, I'm trying to unlock you, but you keep feeling me up."

"What?" he barked. "I am not feeling you up. Your breasts are in my face and I can't move." His words may have been harsh, but his eyes melted her panties. He was right, but that didn't make it better.

"Shut your eyes, then." He rolled his eyes then closed his lids.

"Fine. Hurry up and unlock me before Prince Charming wakes," he said.

She almost laughed as she stretched. "Your Prince Charming, maybe. I don't have the opening he wanted." She thought about that. "Well, I do, but I have two built-in hills he didn't want."

Agent Day groaned and his wrist came free. Then the other. She stepped back.

"There, Mr. Day. You're free. Now let's get out of here," she said. The prince groaned and moved his head. Oh shit, they were goners now.

CHAPTER 12

———

Damn, that woman was gorgeous but irritating as hell. Shit. She smelled so fucking good. He was tempted to take her to the comforter and tear all her clothes off. They were on a bed. Fuck, he started getting hard. Couldn't have that.

The prince moaned. Shit. He looked around for something to tie him up with. Kari hurried around the bed. She opened the drawer on the side table farther out and shoved around things inside.

"Here," she said and tossed him handcuffs. He rolled the prince over and restrained his hands behind him. "You can use this, too." Something landed on the bed beside him. A gag with a red ball attached to elastic lay at his knee. His brow raised. What else was in that drawer?

She pulled out rope and a sleeping mask. "You can tie his feet, then we can put him under the covers with the mask so if anyone looks in on him they can't tell if he's awake or not."

That was a good plan. Maybe this little lady wasn't so bad. He followed her instructions and the prince was soon under the covers with pillows around to hide him a bit without looking like they were hiding him.

"Perfect," she said. "Now what?"

"Now we get the guard in here so we can kill him and get the hell out of Dodge."

She cringed. "Do we have to kill him?" she whined. "Can't we just go out the window or something." Oh, no. She was one of those—a save-the-world kind of agent. Give-the-benefit-of-the doubt agent. Get-herself-killed-because-of-that agent.

He lifted his arms. "Sure. You point out the window and we'll go through." She looked around then dropped her chin to her chest. He smelled her embarrassment.

"Sorry," she said. "The room is so dark, I didn't realize there weren't any windows. I don't have shifter eyes that can see in the dark, like others in this room." She looked around again. "Besides, I was distracted."

Her arousal wafted lightly on the air. He grabbed her arm and turned her around. She wouldn't look at him. He lifted her head with a finger along her jaw. "It's okay, beautiful. I was quite distracted, also."

Her eyes got big then returned to normal and she smiled. That's what he wanted. She was breathtaking. He shook his head. Now wasn't the time for hitting on his mate. He had to get her out of danger.

"Here's the plan," he said as he searched the drawers for clothes to put on. "You scream for the guard. I'll stand behind the door and when he comes in, I'll knock him down—" she tried to interrupt, but he knew what she wanted, "But not kill him." She nodded and smiled again. He would do anything to keep her happy.

After dressing in what he knew as parachute pants from the eighties and the shirt with fewest sequins he could find in the closet, he slid behind the door and she stood next to the bed. He nodded to her.

"Oh, no! Prince, Prince, wake up. Wake up! Guard, something is wrong with the prince." He thought she'd do well for a Shakespeare play, but not modern-day acting.

The door opened and the guard rushed in nonetheless. He took the man down as he was trained, with nonlethal force, then grabbed her hand and hurried to peek out the door. No one was in the hallway. Since he had come to this room from the dining room, he didn't know where a door to the outside was.

He looked back at her. "Do you know where an exit is?"

"The only one I know is where the caterers bring in the food," she said.

"Where's that from here?"

"I don't know."

"But you just said you knew," he commented in a huff.

"You asked if I knew where it is, not if I could get to it," she replied in a mimicked huff. He wiped a hand over his face. This was going to be rough. Smells of humans were thick everywhere. He couldn't discern if one hallway was any better than the other. A side door opened and a guard stepped out. One he recognized from the dungeon. Fuck.

He stopped and she bumped into the back of him. "Ow, warn me next—" He grasped her hand as he whipped around and ran down the hall. The guard yelled behind them. She was much too slow as a human. That wasn't going to fly. He stopped, she ran into him, and he used her momentum to toss her over his shoulder.

He expected a surprised noise from her, but not the high-pitched squeal he got. He picked up his own scent. It was either from the dungeon or the dining room. Sifting through the scents, he noticed mold and mustiness. It had to be from the dungeon. He followed that smell like a string through a maze.

The guard was still behind them. It would be hard to lose him. He had only one option since the guard would pull a gun. Stopping in the middle of the hall, he put his mate on her feet and raised his hands. The guard came closer, gun aimed at him. With shifter speed, he rushed the guard and knocked him out. Picking up the gun, he stuffed it in his waistband and ran for his mate.

"You didn't kill him, did you?" she asked.

"It's his lucky day," he said. "Now come on." With her hand in his, he led.

"Where are we going?" she asked.

"To the dungeon."

She pulled back on his arm. "What? The dungeon? Are you crazy?" He yanked her back into motion. From other parts of the palace, he heard scuffling. The guards were on to them.

"I know what I'm doing. They know about us missing." She didn't fight when he pushed forward. He was close to the dungeon door. He remembered seeing the familiar painting on the wall. He turned at the corner and saw a couple of men down the way. The guards hollered, telling them to stop or they'd shoot.

He snatched a vase off a side table and launched it at them. Being a shifter, the throw was direct and very fast. It smashed into one of the guys' heads, knocking the guard down. He picked up a small, decorative box on the same table and threw it, then grabbed his mate and continued on.

The remaining guard was ready for the attack and ducked under the missile. On the go, Day chucked another vase behind them, hoping to slow them down. Didn't really work, but whatever. They were at the door.

It was heavy, thick metal and he had to lean his weight into it to open it. A bullet dinged off the door close to his head. He bent forward, shoving his mate through the doorway. From the shelf beside the entrance, he snagged two flashlights and a cigarette lighter. That's all he had time for. The door opened.

Training instincts kicked in and took out the guard. They were safe for the moment but he felt the floor vibrate from others running.

"I really hope you know what you're doing," Kari said. He handed her a flashlight and directed her down the center aisle. *So do I*, he thought.

"Trust me," he said.

This would lead them to either safety or their deaths.

CHAPTER 13

Kari hustled down the aisle in the dungeon. It was like she'd stepped back in time to medieval London. They had to have purposely made the cells so formidable since the palace was modern. The prince was quite the drama queen.

There were a few men among the cells, and they looked like skeletons. When she got out of this, she would make sure they were rescued from this hellhole.

Bryon pushed ahead of her and stopped at the rough-hewn rock wall.

"Now what?" she asked. "Where's the door?"

He stood looking around. "Not sure."

Panic zipped through her. Along with anger. "What?" He had to be joking. "You bring us down here not knowing how to get out? Are you crazy?" Her arms slapped down at her thighs. "We're gonna die. That's all there is to it."

He sniffed along the wall. "Hush. Don't be so over-dramatic. That's not becoming of an agent."

She straightened up immediately. He was right. She wasn't being professional at all. For pretending to be a girl-friend who was supposed to only walk around a lot, she

sure was busy. And now she was going to die. All because
she had to pee. Funny how life sucked.

"Got it." Agent Day pushed against the rock and she saw
a portion slide back. He gritted his teeth and the muscles
popped out on his arms. His shirt sparkled in the low light
from the dungeon. She would've giggled if not in this situation. The dungeon door opened and men's voices echoed.

"Hurry." She pushed against the section of wall like she
was really helping. She had to do something. Shit. They
were going to die! Day suddenly seized her hand and pulled
her through a narrow opening. She sucked her belly into
her chest. Her boobs were already big enough, she didn't
need this.

She breathed out as a flashlight lit the dark tunnel.
Where were they? It looked like the escape tunnel El Chapo
used in his getaway. Then it hit her. They were in the infamous tunnels that no one ever escaped. They existed. At
least, one did.

Agent Day guided her through turn after turn, sometimes pausing before taking another direction. The tunnel
was high enough for her co-agent to stand, and he was a lot
taller than she was. The walls were far enough apart to almost walk side by side. The floor was somewhat smooth for
being cut from rock. Probably from years of people traveling to and from this area.

Running into another dead end, they backed out. Now
that she thought about it, the palace had to be purposely
built where it was to have such access to an entrance. She
wondered if the Nazis had a previous structure there and
used the tunnels to hide things. Holy shit. There could be
treasure somewhere down here.

They slid down another narrow passageway and stopped.

"What?" she asked. "Why did we stop?"

"I think we're safe for a bit. We hit so many dead ends
and made so many turns that the guards couldn't have possibly followed us. You can rest while I search ahead for a
way out."

Once again, she did not believe his words. "You brought

us into the fabled tunnels which have had all their exits
bulldozed and blocked, and you don't know the way out?"

He looked at her. "*All* the exits bulldozed?" he asked.

"Oh my freaking god." She didn't care if she was being
unprofessional. They were definitely going to die. What
was she going to do? She absolutely didn't feel safe, like
he'd thought. Acting in anger, she stomped down the trail
and took the first turn she came to.

Everything was so dark. She could only see a narrow
swath of the area that her flashlight landed on. This really
creeped her out. If she had had claustrophobia, this would
not have been the place for her.

The tunnel narrowed to a one-person passage. Her toe
hit a rock in the middle of the path and she tripped forward,
losing her balance. Her shirt was grabbed from behind and
a breeze hit her face. What the hell? She straightened and
turned around. Fixing her shirt, she scowled at the man.
That was quite rude. "Agent Day," she said, "there is no
need to be manhandling me. I can take care of myself."

His brow raised. "Call me Bryon. I'll call you Kari." He
looked over her shoulder to whatever was behind her. "You
can take care of yourself?" He shined his light past her and
nodded for her to turn around.

She spun around and inches from her face was a metal
spearhead. She screamed and jumped back. Bryon shined
his light over the area. Not only was there one spearhead,
but two dozen heads attached to wood boards that shot out
from both sides of the wall. And to make matters worse, a
partial skeleton hung from several of the spikes. Oh, fuck.
She'd have been a shish kebab if he hadn't snagged her
shirt.

She looked at him. "How did you know?"

"I smelled a dead body and figured since it wasn't on the
ground, there could be a trap. As soon as you stepped on
the trigger, I knew that was right," he replied.

Her face scrunched. "What trigger?" Then she remembered. The rock she'd tripped on in the first place. "Never
mind."

Bryon stood close to the spears and sniffed. "This trap has caught more than one person. It must reset itself somehow," he said.

"How could it do that?"

He shrugged. "Could use gravity to eventually pull down a rock attached to a pulley to yank a rope to pull it back. Something like that."

"You mean we have to wait for this to open before we continue through?" she asked. Patience wasn't a virtue right now. The guards could still be behind them. Bryon put a hand on each piece of wood and pushed out. Nothing happened for a second, then slowly, the boards moved. When his arms were fully stretched, the spears were spread enough for her to pass through. Which she did. He slid his hands across to the other side then jumped out when close to the far side.

Kari swiped her light along the path in front of them and wondered what other traps lay ahead.

CHAPTER 14

B ryon pushed ahead of his mate. His pulse and mind had yet to slow to normal. He'd almost lost her. After years of waiting and praying, losing her before he even got to kiss her. That wouldn't happen. He wouldn't let it happen.

She was his mate, and he wanted to know everything about her. He smelled her anger, but wasn't fazed. He'd win her over. What do women like to talk about?

"Kari, tell me something about yourself."

"Myself?" she asked.

"Yeah. Something about your childhood or anything interesting," he replied.

"There's nothing interesting about me. I'm rather boring," she said.

He laughed. He loved her modesty. "I doubt that. I bet you're extremely fascinating."

She snorted again. "You really don't know me."

That was the purpose of this conversation. He wanted to know what made her laugh, what made her cry, what made her love someone, what made her want to *make* love to someone.

"Well," she started, "I almost died once."

Panic shot through him. He didn't want to know that.

"When I was twelve, one of my friends was toting me on the front of her bicycle. She hit a pothole and I flew over the handlebars." A million horrific images flew through his mind. He looked back at her to make sure she was fine. He chastised himself: of course she was fine. But still . . .

"I don't remember anything after that. Mom told me a while later. Supposedly, I hit the asphalt face-first. My front two teeth were knocked out." Her voice changed as if she were poking at her teeth as she talked about them.

He wondered about other things in her mouth. What did she taste like? How would her tongue feel gliding over his? How soft would her lips be? Shit. He adjusted his pants as he walked. Good thing he was in front of her. He turned when they came to another side opening.

She continued. "The skin on my chin and forehead was scraped off. And I'd managed to break my arm."

"That doesn't sound that bad," he said. He could live with such minor injuries on her. Of course, he'd have taken care of her until she was perfect again. Then he wouldn't have let her out of bed.

"The bad thing was the concussion," she continued. His wolf flipped out. Their mate had gotten brain damage when he hadn't been there to protect her, hadn't been there to save her. Bryon reminded his animal they didn't know her then. They were only fifteen or sixteen themselves.

"I was in the hospital for several days, in and out of consciousness. Mom said the tests the doctors took showed extensive damage to the left side of my brain. They said I could be partially paralyzed or challenged in some way."

"Were you?"

They came to a sudden stop at a pile of rocks that blocked the tunnel. With a sigh, he turned her around to head back. Kari hadn't said anything to his question. Her delayed replied couldn't be good. What did he say?

"You make it sound like you can't tell if I'm brain damaged or not. Is that what you think?" Her pitch rose with the last few words. He cringed.

"No. Of course, not," he said with as much authority he could muster. "You're extremely smart and beautiful and I'm keeping my mouth shut."

She giggled. His heart lightened. Another hallway opened to the side. He sniffed the entrance, then went in to see where it led.

"Actually," she continued, "I was damaged, but not in a bad way, really."

He glanced back at her. Again, to make sure she was fine. What was wrong with him? Why was he worried she was injured? It was in the past. "What way?"

"Before the accident, I didn't care much for math or numbers. Afterwards, answers to math problems appeared in my head. I didn't have to think about the numbers. They just showed up. And were always right. My sophomore year in school, I discovered I knew how to play the piano even though I'd never taken lessons. After someone showed me how to read music one time, I could play Beethoven."

"That would be pretty cool," he said. "I always wanted to play an instrument in school. My one attempt with a trombone was disastrous. My siblings complained I sounded like a dying whale." She laughed. The beautiful sound echoed in the tunnel. He wanted to listen to it all day. "Did the doctors give a reason why all that was happening to you?"

"They said that maybe since the left lobe was injured, the right lobe tried to compensate for the deficiency. Since the right side of the brain is the creative side, my brain re-wired itself to do the left side's job more creatively. Or something like that. So I'm able to visualize on the concept level better than most."

Damn, dead-end wall. With a groan from both, they turned around to the previous path. "Anything else?" he asked.

"When I breezed through geometry, my teacher suggested I get a puzzle book with different kinds of visual riddles to see if I could do anything else easily. That's when I found out I was really good at cryptograms. That led me to being a decoder in the FBI."

FBI? He stopped. He'd been so caught up in getting his mate to safety, he hadn't even thought about why she was here or who had sent her or anything. Damn, he was such a sorry mate. His wolf said he'd better get it together or it'd kick his ass.

"What?" She stopped behind him.

"*You* work for the FBI?" He had no idea his mate was so awesome. There were women in the department, but not many compared to men. He knew she wasn't with ALFA since no women were training for a position.

When she stomped past him again, he realized he'd said something wrong. Now what? "Kari. What's wrong." She kept walking without saying a word. He sighed. "Whatever I said, I'm sorry. I didn't mean anything negative. Just the opposite." She must've heard them as a put down.

It wasn't that he couldn't believe she worked for the FBI. Women had every right and were highly qualified to work in that male-dominated world. He just never imagined his mate would be from something so prestigious.

He always thought of his wife as a hearty beauty who would rustle up the pups when time came to eat and hose them down before bedtime. Not necessarily someone he could carry an intellectual conversation with. But that's what he had gotten. How did he get so lucky?

"Yes, that's exactly it. I meant just the opposite of how it must have sounded," he pleaded.

She slowed, said "Whatever," then picked up her speed. No, she didn't walk away from him. He wasn't letting her. In a flash, he had his arm around her waist, lifting her off her feet.

"You're going to listen to me whether you want to or not," he growled. He breathed deeply and took in her sudden wetness; the growl intensified on its own. She was hot for him. Fuck him, goddammit. He wanted to take her here on the floor.

Then he noted the rock was damp. The humidity had risen quite a bit.

Ahead was a branch off the tunnel they were in. He

carried her there. It turned out to be a small cavern or hole in the wall, but had a high ceiling with stalactites and straws. He sat her on a large rock so he wouldn't be tempted to flatten her to the ground.

A strange vibration ran through his body. From the stone below his feet? It was like a train in the distance rumbling the ground as it approached. His wolf picked up on the scent of fresh water. He looked around for a pool, but the room was too small to have much of anything.

"You can't just go walking off on your own," he said. "You would be filled with holes right now if I hadn't smelled a corpse back there."

She crossed her arms over her chest. "Fine. You lead. I'll follow." She saw something on the wall behind him, but he wasn't taking his eyes from her. "I'm sure that's how you like it anyway. I know how you shifters are."

How shifters are? What did she mean by that? He was about to retort when she got up and walked past him. He noticed what she'd seen behind him and his curiosity was piqued. He followed her up a steep ramp that put them several feet higher than the floor.

Stretched side to side before them was a stone shelf extending from the wall. At one end of the shelf stood a double-pan balance or dual-weight scale. It looked like a letter T with the top bar resting on a narrow rock. On the left side of the bar's middle pivot point sat a bowl that appeared made from bone; on the far right side lay a rock about the size of a bowling ball.

He lifted the bowl and tilted it to see inside. The bar both items sat on see-sawed so the rock side slammed down. He quickly put the bowl back onto the bar, but the ball side didn't rise to balance the bar again.

She slapped at his hand. "Didn't your mother teach you not to touch strange things? You have no idea where that's been."

A loud crash shook the room. He spun around to see the ceiling above the door had crashed down, blocking the entrance. They were trapped inside.

The vibration he felt grew more intense. Water poured through the hole in the rock ceiling. He gawked at what was happening. Quickly, the floor at the bottom of the ramp was covered.

"Oh my god. Don't you ever touch anything again. We're going to drown if we don't get out," she yelled.

CHAPTER 15

Kari stood at the top of the ramp that would lead to their watery deaths if they didn't find a way out of the room quickly. She watched Bryon pull a small boulder from the rock pile in front of the blocked door and toss it aside. That would work . . . about an hour after the room filled.

She turned back to the scale. It had started when he'd touched it. Maybe that was how to stop it also.

Next to the bowl side of the scale sat two other bone bowls: one slightly smaller than the bowl on the weight and one just over half the weight bowl's size. A large of pile of pea gravel sat at the other end. The solution looked rather obvious to her. She had to fill the big container on the weight so the sides balanced again.

She scooped handfuls of rock into the small bowl and dumped it into the big bowl. Two scoops filled it a little over halfway. When pouring in the third batch, the half of the bar that held the bowl twisted, letting the bowl slide off and spill. What the hell? She repeated the same process, and again, when she poured out half of her third deposit, the bar twisted and dumped.

The water was at her knees. Bryon was still throwing

boulders into the middle of the space from the door. The ten-foot-square room was quickly filling.

Alright. The small bowl didn't work, so she filled the middle-sized bowl and dumped it in. The weight bowl was almost full, but not completely. She put several scoops of pebbles in the middle bowl and poured it in. Again, while filling it, the bar turned and emptied the contents. Damn. What was the issue?

Bryon hollered behind her, "Having fun playing with the rocks?"

"Yeah, I am." Jerk. "Seeing how this is the way out, I'm having a fucking blast." With that statement, he waded to her.

"What have you got?"

"I have to fill this bowl on the scale so it balances with the rock," she said.

"That looks easy enough," he smirked.

She stepped back and motioned for him to try. "Go for it, genius." He went about the procedure that she did and came to the same conclusion.

"It doesn't work. Maybe it's broken."

She rolled her eyes. "Yeah, that's it. Then we're dead. This has to have a solution that will stop the water flowing. We just have to figure out what it is."

Bryon kept filling and refilling the bowls while she treaded water. She could solve this problem. The answer was on the edge of her brain. Maybe she could use math to work numbers.

The water had filled the room enough that she couldn't touch the ground without going under. Since the ceiling was so high, they had several minutes before they would drown. Her mind spun into a panic making her start to hyperventilate. Bryon pulled her to him.

"Hey now. Everything is going to be fine." He pressed her against his chest and rubbed the hair away from her face.

She snorted. "I'm not stupid, Bryon. We're going to die very painfully, very soon." He just sighed and held her.

"Because I had to pee, this is the last day of my life," she said.

He pulled back from her. "What?" he asked. Going back to try different bowl combinations, she recalled her misadventure of trying to find a bathroom. They laughed about it. She could now that it didn't matter.

Once the shelf with the weight was under water, she stopped trying since the rocks floated in the water and took forever to settle into the big bowl. Their heads were nearing the rock ceiling.

Bryon wiped hair from her face and met her gaze. He was inches from her. The heat from his gaze melted her insides. She wanted him badly, but he was so . . . much. Clearly an alpha male, she wasn't used to someone so big and sexy giving her his full attention. It was overwhelming and dizzying. Her body heated and her hormones danced like she was a teenager in her first date.

"May I kiss you?"

Instead of a reply, she wrapped her hands around his neck and pulled herself closer, her lips meeting his. The sensation was electrifying. The intense pull from him made her press herself as close to him as possible. She couldn't get enough of his touch. This was new and intoxicating.

Suddenly, the answer to the three bowls was in her mind. "I got it," she gasped, pulling away from their kiss. "Stay here." She gulped down a big breath, dove under the water, and pushed off the ceiling. She picked up bowls, filling and dumping. The process took much longer than originally as the pebbles floated in the water, but did eventually settle.

She had reached the point where she'd either found the solution or would have to go back to the top for a breath. There was so little air left when she came down, she doubted any remained now. The water had squeezed its way into every crack and crevice. She stayed and finished for Bryon. Maybe there was a chance he would go on if he hadn't drowned already.

She was amazed how quickly he'd wormed his way into

her heart. She hadn't even felt it. Anger seemed to be the dominant trait in her when he was around.

As she poured pebbles into the final bowl, the air in her lungs depleted. She watched to make sure the big bowl lowered and balanced with the round rock on the other side. She hoped that did something to save Bryon. She fought to get into the position she needed to swim up. There was no way she could get all the way back to the top in time to breathe. Her body couldn't move that fast.

Her short arms stroking through the water, barely moving her along, she closed her tearing eyes. Her lungs burned so badly, she could no longer fight the need, even though she knew it would be a long, painful way to go. Kari smashed her lips together refusing to give in to what her body demanded she do. Her body convulsed, needing to suck in what wasn't there.

She could stand it no more. Her mouth opened and she pushed the built-up carbon dioxide from her lungs.

CHAPTER 16

If he was going to die, this was the way to go. Kari's lips were soft and warm. She tasted like she smelled, of sunshine and lemons. Refreshing, invigorating. He felt like he had enough energy to run for hours. But he had nowhere to go. Just being beside him, she turned his life around.

The past several months, he had been slipping more and more into a funk that wouldn't let him go. If not for his mission to take down a group of people who sold and abused others, he had no reason to get out of bed. He realized how much his family gave him purpose. He was born to protect and that's what he'd die doing.

Suddenly, Kari pulled away. Her words didn't register in his lust-hazed mind until after she was gone. She got what? Then he remembered the rocks and balance they were working with. Did she really think that contraption was the key out of this mess?

His head bumped against the ceiling. He hoped she was right. If not, it wouldn't matter in a few minutes. If they died, it was his fault. He'd led her into this cave because he thought his shifter senses could get them out, could save them no matter the situation. Maybe he'd grown too dependent on his animal's abilities, choosing to use them instead of his brain. Taking risks he shouldn't, thinking he could get away before the danger became too great.

Maybe he could've, but his human mate was fragile. Bad injuries usually killed them. The delicate body didn't repair itself fast enough. He would always have to remember that. He could rely on his instincts, but he needed to get back to the basics of work: using his brain.

He'd gotten cocky, figuring no one would be able to stop him with his abilities. How did he get caught in the first place? He was depending on his wolf's sense of smell, but the bad guys used hunters' scent block to keep him from smelling them. He'd walked right into their trap. Not thinking twice.

His head tipped back to keep his nose above water. If this was it, he wanted his last sight to be of his mate. He'd hold her through the last moments of their short time together. He sucked in a couple of breaths to build oxygen in his bloodstream to last him longer underwater. His lungs filled with the last bit of air available. Then a section of rock let loose from the ceiling inches above and in front of him. He jerked his head back to keep his nose from getting bonked.

Access into an upper cavern just opened. He popped his head up through the opening. It was another small room, and it was water free. He gulped down another breath and went for his mate. He prayed she still had air.

He pushed off the ceiling, diving straight for the side where the bowls and rocks were. Her eyes were closed, mouth open. Bubbles trickled out of her mouth. He wrapped his hands around her head and pressed his mouth completely over hers. His tongue slid forward past her lips and her eyes popped open as he breathed oxygen-rich air into her body.

Another breath shared and she nodded she could make it. He took her hand, pushed off the rock and glided them to the hole in the ceiling. They burst through, both gasping in the musty room.

She clung to the edge of the opening. "Where did this hole come from?"

"The ceiling section fell into the water." He wondered . . . "Did you balance the bowl?" he asked. He examined the edges of the hole and discovered two slots with wooden dowels in them. If he was a betting guy, he'd say the stone chunk that fell also had dual holes. By solving the problem with the bowls, the dowels slid back, releasing the escape route.

"It balanced a few seconds before you showed up. The final rocks had just settled and I—" she choked back a sob, "I was about to—" Her eyes squeezed shut and it was more than water dripping from her hair that ran down her cheeks. He wrapped an arm around her waist and muscled them out of the water, onto the rock floor above. He set her in his lap and scooted back to the wall. Then drew himself around her shaking body.

He held her tightly and gently rocked, whispering reaffirming words until her racking body had quieted to small shudders and hiccups. Hopefully, his body heat was enough to keep her from shivering and going into shock. He knew from experience she would suffer post-traumatic stress. How could you come within a breadth of dying and not be affected?

Fortunately for him, his wolf was able to keep him from dreaming. After so many years of barely escaping death and seeing all the atrocities men do to other men, his dreams became only nightmares waking him in the dead of night in a cold sweat. He didn't sleep much anymore. Even his animal was having a rough time consoling his psyche. But now that he had his mate, she could help him through the difficult times. He once again looked forward to living.

He rubbed his hands up and down her arms, building friction to keep her warm and aware he was there. She wasn't alone. She never would be again. He had to figure a way to break the mate news to her. It'd be really nice if they got out of here without her hating him. First things first. He was going to hold her, right now, as long as she would let him.

After several minutes, she let out a deep breath and settled against him. His wolf was content, as was he, with her there. When he'd embarked on the undercover assignment a year ago, his wolf was pissed at him. How would they ever find a mate if he was hiding his ass in a room, spying on men? Maybe that had been the reason he'd taken the job.

If he didn't search for her, there was always the hope she was out there, waiting for him. If he searched and never found her, then knowing he'd never have true love would crushed him. Was that fucked up logic or what?

She asked, "Where do you think the water came from? That trap was well planned."

He thought about her question. "The taxi driver said the river disappeared underground somewhere. Maybe we were close enough that when the rocks fell to block the door, it opened a small channel that flowed through the hole. How did you solve it? What were we doing wrong?"

She sighed and leaned more into him. "I didn't understand what was going on until I applied math concepts. There were three different-sized bowls. Say the smallest held three pounds of rocks, the middle held four, and the big bowl on the scale needed five pounds. I had to come up with five pounds exactly; any more or less triggered a dump, and I had to fill the big bowl in two trips or it tipped again."

That was confusing, he thought. "How do you get exactly five out of three and four?"

"I filled the four pound and dumped it into the big bowl. Then I filled the four again, but dumped it into the three bowl, leaving me with exactly one pound in the four bowl. I dumped that into the big bowl to make five exactly."

"Holy shit, woman. That was brilliant. I would've never thought of that."

She moved in his lap. He smelled a sweet shyness from her. She said, "You really think so?"

"Hell, yes, I know so. If you weren't there, I would be floating belly-up right now," he said.

"More like if I weren't here, neither would you. It's my fault we're in this mess."

He looked at her even though he knew she couldn't see him in the darkness. "How do you get that idea?"

"I don't know," she said. "I just feel responsible for everything."

He leaned her head to his lips and kissed her. "Don't think that for one moment, beautiful. If not for you, I would be in a much worse place." She breathed out and settled into him more.

"Do you think the guards are after us still?" she asked.

"Nah," he replied, "I'm sure they've given us up for dead."

"Have you?"

"You forget, I'm an ALFA, baby. No way I'll ever give up on this, on you, on us."

CHAPTER 17

On you, on us.

She heard his words clearly, but understanding wasn't so clear. Did he mean he wasn't giving up because his boss would expect more of him being an ALFA or because he cared? It would be nice if this gorgeous man cared for her, but she wasn't holding her breath. Shit, she'd almost died holding it minutes ago. It would hurt if she fell for him and he saw her as only part of his job.

But his kiss when she was sure they were going to die . . . she wondered if she had crossed over into heaven. Her body had never felt so alive. Like her nerve endings were being overloaded with sensory details she couldn't take in. Heat suffused her from head to toes. If not for the cool water, she'd be sweating though her clothes. Then she'd have to take off those clothes and get all naked with this man holding her . . .

She'd better stop that line of thought before he smelled her and broke her heart by telling her she didn't have a chance with him. That was what scared her the most: rejection. Her self-confidence was never high. Only when she was solving problems, putting her brain to work, did she not doubt herself.

She let out a sigh. "It's pitch-dark for me. I can't see a thing. I'm guessing you can see?" she asked. Stupid question, probably. But she wanted to know more about this species. What made them tick? How were they different? How the hell did they shove an animal body inside themselves?

"I can see, but not very well. Our eyes need some light to magnify," he said. "It's much the same as night-vision googles. There has to be some light to magnify to get it all to work." He inhaled deeply. "I smell wood and a strange . . . oil maybe." He moved to get up. "Stay here for a moment."

"No problem," she replied. "Like I'm going to walk around in the dark. I can't walk in the light without tripping, much less this." She heard him scuffling and then a click. Several feet away, a blaze erupted from the darkness. She covered her eyes from the sudden brightness. "What is that?"

"I'm guessing it's an old-fashioned torch. The material covering the sticks has been doused in fuel or oil. Whatever it is, it's flammable."

"That's convenient," she said. Then she thought about all she'd read about the tunnels. The Nazi theory was sounding more viable every minute. If the Nazis knew they had to flood the cavern to get up here, then they knew flashlights wouldn't work after the batteries got wet. So they made sure to have a supply of torches available. "Is there more than one?" she asked.

"Yeah. How did you know?" he said.

"Lucky guess. Let's get going." She was getting tired and who knew how long they'd be in here. The little she had eaten at dinner was about through her system. She'd do cartwheels for a protein bar right now.

Bryon handed her an unlit torch, then took her hand in his. "There's only one way," he said.

She smiled. "You lead and I follow." He frowned at her words, but led her out of the cavern. That had been status quo most of her life, especially with the FBI. Men would always lead and the women would follow. But sometimes that was perfectly fine. The bad guy usually took out the first person to enter the room. It was the second person who took out the bad guy.

"That's not what I meant earlier when I said you shouldn't go walking off," he said.

She knew his comments weren't a simple chauvinistic remark, but was pissed at him at the time she said that to him and the words flowed from her mouth. "Yeah, it's all right. I really didn't mean what I said. I was just upset that you thought I wasn't good enough to work at the FBI."

He added, "I didn't mean that either. I was saying that I always figured my ma—" he coughed and cleared his throat, "my rescuer would be from ALFA. I didn't know we even had a relationship with the FBI. I'd thought someone from the CIA would be the first choice."

"I agree. It should've been the CIA since they are international and FBI are domestic. But I deciphered a code the CIA was working on. Maybe this is a multilayer joint mission. I don't know. Maybe the generals in the director's office told him to assign me."

The tunnel they were in seemed different from those before the water trap. These felt older, more worn, more lived in. The walls' sides were smoother as if millions of shoulders and hands had quietly sanded them down over hundreds of years. Same for the floor. It was a bit dusty as feet scraped away pointy edges, leaving crumbled rock and granules in their wake.

She wondered how old this tunnel was. Rome was in power long before the common era began. This could easily be over two thousand years old. A sense of admiration and respect filled her. Many people gave their lives in building these underground routes to save more lives in the future. Like hers, right now.

That made her think about what she was leaving behind that would benefit the world when she was gone. Had she done anything worthy with her life? She thought about her job. She had decoded several things that related to war and threats. Perhaps in some way, she had helped calm a volatile situation with feuding countries or stopped a coalition that would have taken over a people.

That was all a *maybe*. What certain things had she done? Not much. Took the bus to work instead of driving. But honestly, that was because parking spots in the FBI area were few and expensive. The only thing she could leave behind were children that believed in saving the world and being kind to your neighbor.

Did she want a family? She wasn't afraid of raising children, even as a single mother, though she preferred both parents to help balance children's mental and sociological development.

"Bryon, do you ever think about having children?" Her words startled her. She really didn't mean to ask him. "I'm sorry for being so personal. No need to answer. That was a dumb thing to ask."

He stopped, turned to her, and smiled. Instant panty melt. "No, that's a fair question. Actually, I'm thinking about starting a family more and more. I'm in my mid-thirties, now. I've put in more than my fair share of time at ALFA. It's time that I put effort into my mate and making a home where we can share love and raise children."

Good god, if that wasn't the most romantically perfect thing to say . . . she'd love to share love with him.

"So you'd quit your job," she asked, "just like that?"

"Those who work ALFA for years get a pension, but it's not enough for a great living. I'd probably find a side job I enjoyed. Or maybe my wife will work full time and I'd take care of the pups. I'd be an official 'house dad.'"

He sounded so enthused by the idea, she laughed. He would make a great house dad. Those kids would be lucky to have him as a father.

"What about you, Kari? Are you a career woman or do you want a family?"

"I've always worked, as did my mom. So I wouldn't know any other type of lifestyle. But I do want children and a family. I've never *not* wanted one, just haven't thought about it much till now."

"If you could live anywhere in the world, where would it be?" he asked.

She knew that answer right away. "Somewhere with forests and mountains would be great. I like being in the woods and in touch with nature. Whenever I get too much city trash in my system, I head toward a park and camp out under a tree for several hours, reading, people watching, smelling the grass, whatever."

He laughed. "Smelling the grass. I like that."

"One of my favorite smells is freshly cut grass. I roll down my window in residential areas when folks are mowing. It's so calming." She read somewhere that cut grass had the same natural chemicals as men's semen. Oh god. She must be getting horny again. How could she not, following the scrumptious ass in front of her. He reached back for her hand and pulled her closer.

He whispered, "I meant it when I said I didn't want you following. I'd rather have you in front of me."

She giggled, thinking about watching his ass. "What? To see my ass wiggle?" She slapped a hand over her mouth. Her face felt on fire. "Sorry," she said, hand still over mouth.

He laughed . . . hard. With a huge smile she couldn't erase, she hit his arm. "All right, get over it." She fanned her face with her hand. When she turned to hide her face, she saw black marks on the wall. "Hey, bring the torch over here."

Bryon stepped closer. "Is that writing? What are those pictures of?"

Kari examined the script. "It looks like hieroglyphics mixed with something else."

Bryon grunted. "By chance, read Egyptian?" He was joking.

"I actually do," she said. "I was fascinated with this stuff after the accident and picked up on it quickly."

A warm body snuggled behind her. "I knew you were

amazing." He kissed the top of her head. A happy feeling flowed through her. Maybe he really did care for her more than just a job hazard. Maybe she could fall for this man in a heartbeat.

She refocused on the wall. "See this umbrella with two poles," he nodded, "that represents the Underworld or the Land of the Dead."

"So this is probably some warning to scare us off?" he asked.

She kept studying the drawings. "Maybe. This bird thing is *Ba*, which we call soul or personality. It leaves the body when it dies. This line with a split bottom is called a *was*; it's a symbol of power, more like a scepter carried by royalty. Then the square without a top is *ka*."

"*Ka*?" Bryon asked. "As in someone's spirit?"

"That's it. You're pretty smart yourself," she said.

"No, I just know *ka* from somewhere," he corrected.

"Then this last symbol is *ra*, which is the sun god representing resurrection." She stood back and let the images mix in her mind. "It's talking about the royals, so in our case, the prince. Then we have two symbols that mention the soul or personality; souls can resurrect or they can go to places like the underworld." The idea that came to her was so crazy, she didn't want to voice it, so she waited for another answer.

"What do you think?" he asked. "Sounds like our prince died, went to hell, and came back."

Startled, she looked at him. "You really got that?" He nodded. "Well, this may not sound so crazy, then. What I'm getting is the one who rules the land, his personality is taken away like when the body dies, but a *ka* from the underworld resurrects the body."

Bryon looked at her. "You mean the prince is possessed by a demon *ka*."

Yeah, that sounded ridiculous to her, too. She leaned toward the last symbol of *ra* which was the image of a single eyeball. When the fire light was just right, she thought she saw red paint in the eyeball circle. Her mind recalled the red flashes in the prince's eyes she'd seen on several occasions. Had to be just coincidence. Maybe a hereditary issue dealing with the retina.

"That's exactly what this means, but it couldn't be the current prince," Kari said. "It must be myths from ancestors because this was put here possibly two thousand years ago." She stepped back. "Demonic possession doesn't exist. Science proved diseases were the cause of weird things in humans. Not demons."

CHAPTER 18

B ryon mulled over these new ideas in his noggin as they
continued through the tunnels. He took her hand wanting to feel her close. They came to another fork in the road.

"Which way?" he asked.

"Whichever way has fewer spiderwebs," she answered.
That would be straight ahead.

"You scared of spiders?" he asked.

"Eh," she replied, "I wouldn't say scared. But I definitely
don't want to give them something to stand on and bite. But
less spiderwebs could mean the path had more travelers to
keep spiders away. But given how old all this is, it's probably a moot point."

He nodded. Why hadn't he come to that conclusion? It
seemed a lot of her thoughts were common sense that
wasn't common until someone else said it. Then you're like,
duh. Their pups would be freakin' geniuses.

"You know," Kari said, "I don't know anything about
you. Not even what kind of shifter you are. How did you get
into ALFA?"

He could easily talk about that. "I'm a wolf shifter. My

pack is rather big compared to most. We live within a community, or a town, I guess, that is all shifters."

"All shifters," she asked. "How many?"

"Our population is several thousand. Other shifter places across the U.S. vary depending on who's there."

"Wow, I had no idea."

"Yeah, we keep a low profile. Believe it or not, the government actually helps with that," he said.

"How so?"

"ALFA is short for Alpha League Federal Agency. Basically, a long time ago, shifters were 'discovered' by the military. Our kind is much stronger than normal humans and can do things humans can't. So when the military decided they wanted to harness that strength for themselves, they decided to approach us with a deal."

"Oh god," she replied, "I can just imagine what 'deal' the government had for you. We all know what they did to the Native Americans."

"Yes," he said, "we did, and we made sure that kind of thing wouldn't happen to us. So the deal was that some of our young shifters, after graduating, would join ALFA to do special jobs humans weren't able to do. It's sort of a shifter military, except we usually don't go into battle situations where live munition is fired. Unless on a special project."

"Why not?"

"I'm not sure. Something about accidentally shifting and exposing our secret, maybe?" He shrugged.

She asked, "So you joined after graduating high school?"

"Yes and no. After high school, if you sign up for a four-year stint, they will put you through college first. My parents at the time took jobs the community needed instead of jobs that paid a lot of money.

"Dad was a first responder, what they called back then a volunteer fireman. He was usually one of the first to arrive at accident scenes or where medical emergencies existed. He was a trained EMT, certified as a crisis and hostage negotiator, top-rated marksmen, and a bunch of other stuff."

"Wow, he sounds amazing. That must be where you get your drive for AFLA work."

"I think it is. When I was older, he took me with him on several calls and I helped out where I could. Talk about a rude awakening to the real world. I saw firsthand what drinking and driving could do. Saw what happened to people in motorcycle accidents who weren't wearing protective clothing or helmets. I even saw a baby born in the backseat of a car. *That* was traumatic."

Kari laughed. "Made you glad men didn't give birth, huh?"

"Damn straight, it did."

"What about your mom?" she asked.

"My mom was a social service agent who watched over underprivileged and abused pups. She was proud to say that during her time there, pup abuse dropped tenfold and more abusers than ever were punished. She brought home a lot of pups, too.

"I had 'adopted' siblings coming out the nose for years. But there was always enough love to go around, even if the food was a little short sometimes."

"You know," she said, "that's one thing about America I wish would change. All the professional sports stars are paid millions and millions of dollars, yet teachers, police, and firemen can barely support their families."

"Yup. People are willing to pay for what they want, not what they need. They want the fancy slam dunks and homeruns and touchdowns, but they need others to teach them how to read and write, to save their lives in dangerous situations, and to protect them from others who would do them harm over a pair of stupid athletic shoes with some sports star's name on them."

"I completely agree. Priorities are messed up. It's sad," she said. "Are your parents still around?"

"Yeah, they still live in town and still bring in pups and cubs. No one is safe from the Day's home." They laughed.

"They had no problems with you joining ALFA right out of school?"

"Nah, not at all. They were quite proud of me. Taking after them in honorable jobs without a lot of money. After college, I went into training. Talk about getting my ass kicked. Fucking A." He realized his harsh language in front of his mate. "Sorry 'bout that. I'm used to being around men all the time anymore."

"Not a problem. I'm okay with some. It comes out of my mouth occasionally. A sign of the times." She smiled at him. Fuck, she was so beautiful. He wanted to stand where he was and just stare at her. That would probably creep her out, though.

She pulled him forward. "With all this cave-and-tunnel stuff, I feel like I'm in an Indiana Jones movie," she said.

"That is the best movie on the planet," he said.

She shoved him to the side with her hip. "No way. *Bridge of Spies* is so much better."

He rebounded toward her and wrapped an arm around her shoulder, pulling her to his side. "Would you believe I got to shake Steven Spielberg's hand once," he whispered.

Kari stopped in front of him and gasped. "Seriously? Oh my god." She looked at their linked fingers. "Is this the hand you touched him with?" She put it on her cheek. "I got to feel the hand that shook the movie god's hand." She let out a long breath.

His heart jumped. Her face was so soft, so perfect. Her eyes rolled up to meet his. Her smiled faded, but her pupils widened, and her smell became irresistible, loaded with pheromones. Fuck, she wanted him as much as he wanted her. Could he have her? Just one more taste.

She licked her lips. That did it. His animal roared inside. She was soft and sweet but there was a definite aggression in her that he fucking loved. She was everything he wanted and more. The way her tongue swept over his drove him crazy and made him groan into the kiss. If he survived more of these kisses, he deserved an award. As it stood, his body was wound tighter than a rubber band ready to snap.

They had come to another intersection. "All right, pretty lady. You pick the direction: straight ahead or right turn?"

Holding on to his hand and the second torch in her other hand, she studied both ways. "One looks the same as the other. Flip a coin?" she said.

He frowned. "I don't have a coin, but I'll flip you."

Her eyes got big. "What?" She stepped in front of him, trying to hide her smile, and eased forward. "I don't think that's a good idea. I don't flip well."

He took a step toward her. As long as he could get his hands on her body, he didn't care what she did. He could push her against the wall, rip her clothes off, and claim her here and now. There definitely wasn't anyone around to catch them. His wolf loved the idea. Its tongue fell out the side of its mouth with the thought.

He must've looked predatory because she squeaked out a laugh and took off running down a path. Oh, that wasn't a great plan. He chased her. His wolf got all up in his business, wanting to play, too.

Quickly, he gained on her. "Kari, running ahead is dangerous. You could get hurt."

She looked back over her shoulder, then abruptly stopped. "You're right."

He was going too fast to stop without hitting her. She cringed, seeing him coming, and he dove to the side of her, landing on solid ground. After a roll, the ground dropped out from under him. The torch he held showed him the location of his landing, twenty feet down.

CHAPTER 19

—◁—

"Bryon?" she called out. There was no response. Oh, fuck. "Bryon!" She got on hands and knees, feeling out for his body. Did he knock himself unconscious? He was a shifter. The move he made wouldn't even faze someone like him.

"Kari, don't move," echoed from someplace lower than her current place. She froze. She didn't need to be told twice.

"Bryon, what happened? Where are you?" she asked.

"I fell into a pit a short distance in front of you."

"Are you okay? Are you hurt?" Probably a silly question for a shifter, but that's what humans always ask: Even if the injured looks nearly dead, they say, "Are you okay?"

"Nothing a shift won't fix," she heard. She climbed to her feet and backed toward the wall. She wasn't stepping on any trigger this time. But a pit didn't really have a trigger. It was just a pit.

When she leaned against the wall, she felt a rock behind her butt move back with her weight. She popped forward. Did she just push on something?

A rumbling sound came from deep in the cave and a slight tremor shook the stone under her feet. The shake became stronger and the sound of rock dragging over rock pierced the air. What was happening? She thought she heard a "Well, fuck me," but wasn't sure.

"Bryon? What's happening," she asked.

"Don't move, baby. The walls on each side of the pit are closing in."

Oh, shit. She must've done that. Dammit. Next time she seriously wouldn't move an inch. A few feet in front of her a light suddenly appeared. The torch Bryon had been carrying landed on the edge of the pit. She could see somewhat better, but the torch wasn't blazing like it had been. She wondered how it got there.

Then she saw something pop into the air above the edge. It was dark and fell out of sight quickly. She scooted closer and realized what she saw was Bryon's wolf jumping up, trying to get out. Then she saw the side walls closing in. They were giant squared-off boulders that ground over the ground and would end up smashing anything between them.

The wolf jumped again, but wasn't close enough to get a paw on land. She couldn't imagine how he even got that close. It was straight down twenty feet. He had to get a running start. The next jump started too close to the wall, and he slammed into the side halfway up. The rocks were feet from closing.

"Come on, Bryon. You can do this," she yelled. The wolf looked up. She couldn't see its eyes, but he could see her and she would send him confidence and courage. Power of positive thinking. He got a running start, but didn't even reach the top. He was getting tired. The walls were closing. He had one more shot.

Kari leaned her head over the side. "One more time, baby. Give it all you got to get back here. You're not leaving me alone." He backed, prepping for the sprint. The walls were so close, it really scared her. It would be her fault if he died. It seemed to always be her fault something bad happened. Maybe she was cursed.

Bryon sprinted for the wall. He sprang into the air. Kari could tell from the angle she stood, he wasn't close enough to get both paws and upper body onto the ledge. She panicked at losing him. Shit, she'd just met him.

CHAPTER 20

How did she get into this predicament? It seemed like days since she'd potty danced with Sheldon. Now she'd fallen for an Adonis and because of her, he was about to die. Being squished between two boulders would probably be a quick death. Her heart broke thinking she would never see him again. He had one last chance to get out.

His head rose above the surface and her instincts kicked in. Her hands shot out and latched on to his ears, then she threw herself backward with all the strength she had. She landed on her back hard, knocking her breath out. The floor vibrated with a *thud* when the rocks slammed together.

She desperately wanted to see if Bryon was alive. Had she held on to him or had he slipped through her fingers? After she could breathe again, she'd check. But it turned out she didn't need to. A slobbery lick up the side of her face told her he was fine.

Bones snapped and clothes rustled. He must've been shifting to human. Warm hands grabbed her upper arms then she was surrounded by his manly scent. He didn't speak. Didn't need to. His hold on her said volumes. Tears came to her eyes.

"I'm so sorry," she cried. "I didn't mean to push any-thing. I was trying to get away from it."

He didn't loosen his squeeze on her, but he did talk. "What did you push?"

"I leaned against the wall to make sure I didn't step on anything and my butt pressed against something. I'm sorry. I think it started the walls moving." She readied for him to yell at her, to cringe at his angry words that she'd almost killed him.

He sighed. "Sounds like I should spank that butt, then."

She gasped. That was not what she was expecting. And the way his voice oozed sensuality, she creamed her panties on the spot. He breathed deeply and she cursed herself. A growl started deep in his chest and his arms tightened. He was about to suffocate her.

"Damn, woman, I can't resist you much longer. We'll start with a spanking, then."

Another *thud* came from inside the walls, interrupting his poetry to her pussy. The two stones that had come to-gether were now sliding apart, returning to their places in the walls. She hurried to stand, now that the moment was gone.

"I guess we should backtrack to our last turn, huh?" she said.

His brows drew down. "That was quite a distance. Why would we go back?" She turned to look across the distance the pit presented. Her foot landed on something and her leg rolled out from under her. She was going down. "I gotcha." Familiar hands settled around her waist. He pressed her back against his chest. "Maybe I should carry you the rest of the way," he joked.

She rolled her eyes. "Yeah, yeah. I've heard it before." She bent over and picked up the second torch she'd dropped earlier. "Do we need this one?" She looked at the dim em-bers of the first one on the ground.

"We should wait until we're on the other side," he said.

"Other side?" she replied. "You might be able to jump

that distance, but this butt isn't even thinking about it." She pointed to her ass. The look he gave her could start its own fire. No torch needed. She snapped her fingers in front of his face. "Hello? What are we doing?"

"I'm shifting into my wolf, then you're getting on my back and we jump together."

She busted into laughter. "That's the funniest thing I've ever heard," she said. Good to know he had a sense of humor. Even if he was frowning at the moment. She slapped the torch against his chest as she passed him headed back the way they'd come. "*Hasta luego*, my friend." He snagged her wrist and pulled her back to him.

"I don't think so, love. You can do this. We have to hurry before the other torch goes out completely."

She groaned and took the bundle of sticks from him. "Fine." He began to take his sequined shirt off. Her brow raised. "What are you doing?"

He smirked. "I have to undress to shift," he said smoothly.

"But," she stuttered, "you didn't change for the jump a minute ago."

He gave a single shoulder shrug. "Didn't have time. And it constricted me. With you on my back, I'm not taking any chances." His eyes held hers as he unfastened and dropped his pants. She didn't dare move—body or sight line. His smirk grew. "Grab my clothes before we go over. Do you mind?" He glanced down at his shirt on the floor; she just glanced down. Holy sausage on a stick.

He looked up and she jerked her head back, cheeks warming. "I didn't see anything." He didn't say a word. His shift began and she watched, mesmerized. He went to his knees, head elongating and teeth sliding out of his jaw. The waning light hid most of the change, but she watched the structural shift. It was one of the most extraordinary things she'd ever seen. Everything about him wowed her.

Before her stood a beautiful, fluffy wolf. Damn, he was the size of a small horse. How the hell was she getting on his back? She picked up his clothes and the second torch. Okay, her hands were full; she could ride him without holding on. Whatever.

She slipped his shirt over hers. It smelled of Bryon and the prince. Next, she tied the torch to the outside of her thigh using his pants. Hands on her hips, she turned to the wolf.

"Unless you have a ladder, you need to get lower," she said. He snuck a lick up the side of her face and lay on his belly. She would swear he was laughing at her. She swung a leg over his back and he stood. Immediately, she slid off to the side. She lay there, staring at the tunnel's ceiling. "This isn't going to work." His reply was another wet tongue up the face. And another, and another. "All right! I'm getting up." Under her breath, she grumbled, "Just you wait and see what I do with that tongue of yours, buddy."

She took off the shiny shirt she had put on a minute ago and twisted it into a rope. She climbed onto Bryon's furry back and tied the shirt sleeves under his stomach, strapping her to the animal. When she pulled the fabric on his stomach tight, he looked back at her.

"What?" she said. "Suck it up, buttercup. This is your idea, not mine." The body under her legs tensed, muscles hardened. Her fingers dug into fur, legs clenched at his sides.

Her spine stretched as he sprang forward, and rounded when he pushed off his hind feet. Wind rushed in her face. Her eyes were closed, but she didn't remember closing them. In less than a second, they were floating over the fifteen-foot-wide chasm.

CHAPTER 21

Bryon and his wolf loved the feel of her straddling his back. He could imagine her riding him a different way. He shook his head to get his concentration on getting her to the other side to safety. This wouldn't be an easy leap for him. Fifteen feet was a long way with limited takeoff space.

When she finally stopped wiggling around, he sprinted for the pit. The light was almost gone, limiting his depth perception. This wasn't a good time for that to happen. At the end of the path, he pushed off rear legs, thighs releasing their stored strength. Just past midway, he felt her slide to the side.

Fortunately, the shirt she'd tied around her kept her from dropping into the hole, but now she hung below him. If he didn't land exactly right, she would slam head first into the rock.

He was losing altitude and the other side was within sight. He made the distance easily, but now had to stick the landing. Kari's grip tightened and her head tucked up to his chest. Smart girl. He came down on stiff front legs, hind legs coming forward to balance momentum.

He stopped as quickly as he could, then fell onto his side

to not squish her, waiting to see if she was okay. Kari lay on her side, facing him. She opened one eye and looked around. He breathed and his tongue fell out the side of his mouth. Thank the gods.

His mate laid her head on his side, her fingers digging into his fur, and laughed. Laughed? Bryon wanted to take her into his arms, but his wolf wanted to keep her. He had to be fine with that. His human side did get most of the time.

Kari untied the shirt holding her to his wolf. Her hands rubbed down his fur, sending a thrill through him. She reached up and slid a hand along the side of his face. That felt so good.

"I feel silly talking to an animal, but you're not really a critter, are you?" she said. He yapped. He heard her heart racing. He wasn't sure, but she might have a slight tremble in her hands. His mate was strong. She was scared shitless, yet didn't complain. Pride filled him. He kissed her hand. Maybe a bit slobbery.

"You know, you're really pretty in your fur." He cringed a bit at the feminine word, but he knew what she was saying and was happy she liked his other half. "Well, since you're a guy, it would be better to say you look *manly* in your fur." Her stomach growled. "Hmm. Guess you don't have any food on you, do you?" she asked.

His wolf hopped to his feet. They had to feed their mate. He had to show her they could take care of her.

"Hey, what are you doing?" she asked "Hold on. Let me light the torch."

His wolf heard material rustle and knew she'd be fine. He sucked in a breath. Was that . . . He inhaled through his nose. It was food. He yapped twice and headed off in search of the source of the scent. After passing a couple turns they'd have to check out, he hit pay dirt. A roomful of dried fruits, berries, and other preserved things stood unattended.

He raced back to his mate. She stood holding the fire sticks. She must've found the cigarette lighter in his pants pocket. Time for the human to retake control. The wolf backed down and let the other form come forward.

His mate yipped and turned as his two-legged body reformed. Her arm was straight out from her side, his pants and shirt hanging from her fingers. He snuggled up to her back and tilted his head down. He blew his warm breath on her shoulder.

"Thank you for taking care of my clothes."

Her body stiffened, but she didn't step away. "You're welcome. Where did you go a minute ago?"

He slipped on his pants and the damn sequined top. "I've made reservations for two at the best restaurant in town." Her brow raised. "What? You don't believe me?" He bowed and swept his arm through the air. "This way, my dear."

"Restaurant or not, I need to rest. My feet are blistered, my knees ache, and I'm about to pass out from hunger."

"Hold on to the torch," he said.

"Why?"

He swept her into his arms. She squeaked. "What are you doing? Put me down."

"You said your feet hurt, so I'm helping you along," he said. He was so close to her lips. He remembered their last kiss and wanted more of her taste. More of her scent. More of everything.

"That's very kind of you," she said. Her breath was wispy, her eyes darted to his lips. "But I can walk."

"We're here, madam. Your table is ready," he said. He set her on her feet and took the torch from her. He looked around to see a few more torches in holders on the walls. He lit a couple more, giving the small room a soft, warm glow.

"I can't believe this," Kari said. "Why is all this stuff here?" There were figs, nuts, dried fruits, jerky meats, and anything else that could be preserved. Along the wall lay thick rugs and blankets. Several muslin-type robes hung from hooks.

Why *was* this stuff here? It was obvious these food items

were put here recently. An exit had to be nearby. Then again, not necessarily. This place was a hideout for someone. They probably didn't have it near an exit for fear of being found. They had passed a couple side paths in coming to this room. Maybe one of those led to an open exit.

He wondered if this place could have any relation to human trafficking. Could the bad guys be hiding people down here until the time to go came? Or it could be that those who got away were kept here until they could escape further? It would explain why he hadn't found any clues to where the ring was, who was part of it, and who had been taken.

While Kari gathered food, he pulled out several rugs to make a suitable place to lie down. It was late at night, or rather, early morning in Cloustien. Washington DC time was about bedtime. No wonder her human body was exhausted. But it was also aroused.

He debated telling her that she was his mate. Would this be a good time or not? His wolf wanted to tell her then bite her—within the next five minutes, please. That wasn't happening unless they wanted to scare her off. Even though she was his mate, she had no idea what that meant to shifters. Mating meant for life. No changing your mind. No divorcing. It really was "till death do us part."

But what if she rejected him? How could he be so close to her without having her? Holding a wooden bowl, Kari sat next to him on a rug, leaning against the wall.

Time to find out.

CHAPTER 22

She couldn't believe this food was here in the middle of nowhere. And she was starving. The food and drink from the prince's dinner were completely gone from her stomach.

A bowl of dried fruits in hand, she sat next to Bryon on rugs he'd moved around. With a sigh, she toed off her shoes and wiggled her toes. "I won't be able to walk for a week without Band-Aids."

"Guess I'll have to carry you around for that time," Bryon said. So gorgeous, so perfect.

"Uh, probably not," she replied. "But we can work something out." Whoa. What did she mean by that? Great. She was delirious now. Delirious with love? Good god, that was lame.

"Kari," he said, "how much do you know about shifters?"

She halfway shrugged. "I've learned a few things besides what you've told me. You guys have super senses and your mates are forever."

"You know about mates?" he asked, surprise in his voice.

"Not that much. Just that once you find your mate, your

heart is theirs forever." She hadn't mentioned this to Director Lancaster, but she had known shifters existed before she'd decoded any messages. When she was eight years old, her mom worked two jobs for a while. During that time, the older neighbors, Tabi and her husband, Joe, would watch over her at night until her mother came home. Kari considered Tabi to be her grandmother since her real grandmothers were with the angels in heaven.

Even at her young age, she saw the intense love between Tabi and Joe. The couple was really old and had been together since they were in school. They always held hands when they sat on the swing on the front porch. Joe kissed Tabi every time he walked in or out of a room she was in. And they always ate dinner together at the table.

Kari had known the couple were shifters when one of the young grandkids accidentally shifted when she was there. It had become their little secret. When Kari once asked how they could be together so long without getting bored of each other, Tabi told her, *When you find your true mate, your heart is theirs forever.* Then Kari asked if that was for shifters only, or if she could find her own mate.

Tabi told her if she had a true mate waiting for her, then she would be cherished and loved by her mate unconditionally. But humans didn't usually have shifter mates back then. Well, they did, but shifter law forbade the races to mix at the time.

One day, Joe was in an accident and died. Kari hadn't grasped the concept of death except that the person went to heaven to be with angels, like her grandmothers. The next day, Tabi said she couldn't take care of Kari any longer. She had to go where Joe, her mate, was because she loved him too much to be away from him.

Kari never saw Tabi after that, but as Kari grew older, she'd come to understand the meaning of all Tabi had shared with her. She'd never met another shifter, that she knew of, anyway.

She decided that was why she accepted Bryon so readily. She'd romanticized shifters into great lovers and heroes.

And she had secretly prayed that one day she would meet her mate and have what the old couple had.

"You're absolutely right about that. Mates are born to be together," he responded. "Many times, our mates are human, too."

"Really," she said. Man, oh, man. What she would do to be the mate to the delectable man sitting next to her. She'd win the Powerball if that were true. Hot sex with shifter alpha 24/7. She'd never leave her bed. Hell, she'd never let him leave. She stuffed more fruit into her mouth to keep from drooling.

He rubbed the back of his hand on her arm. He was warm in the chilly air. Chills ran down to her fingers. She loved when he touched her. Loved when he stood so close. Loved his smell, loved his body. All right, she needed to cut it out. He'd catch her horny scent soon.

"What would you think if you were my mate?"

Her heart stumbled over itself, fell flat, then pumped overtime. "Was that a 'Let's pretend I'm your mate' or 'You want me to be your mate, for real'?" She wasn't hungry anymore. Her stomach was too busy being nervous.

Bryon slid closer on the thick rug, his eyes never leaving hers. "The question wasn't rhetorical nor was it a hypothetical."

"Why me?"

He glided his knuckles over her arm, grazing her breast, and she closed her eyes at the promise in the not-so-innocent gesture.

"No one's ever gotten to me like you do, Kari."

"But?"

He shook his head. "No buts. I would go through captivity all over again, especially if it means meeting you."

Kari's eyes searched his. Bryon the badass agent wanted her. Not for a night. Not for the hottest sex she would ever have, but for himself. For her to be his mate in front of god and the entire world. She chewed on her lips and he smirked.

"What?"

"Nibble, nibble. You know you only do that when you're arguing with yourself."

Heat bloomed in her cheeks. "How'd you figure that?"

He leaned in so his lips were no more than a breath from hers. "Because I've gotten to know you, Kari. Not just your scent branded on my brain, but you. Inside and out. Whether you want to admit it or not, you are mine. MINE. My mate. Now and for always. But I can't do anything about that alone. I need you."

That was it. Every question, every misgiving that reached up and grabbed her was silenced. Bryon took her mouth as if he knew it, too, muzzling any remaining doubt in a hungry kiss.

He fisted her hair, his tongue plundering the sweet cavern of her mouth. "I want you, Kari. Forever. Let me have you."

His words were a whisper in his kiss and they rang in her head. They were the same words he'd said to her in her dream and she gasped. Taking the sharp intake as an invitation for more, he unbuttoned her shirt, pushing the front wide, exposing her breasts.

"If I had known we'd be doing this I would have worn sexier underwear," she joked.

He rolled his thumb and forefinger over her nipple and pinched the puckered flesh. "You're sexy enough no matter what you wear, but I'd prefer you in nothing at all."

Kari's mouth slid into a sexy smile and she shrugged out of her shirt. "Your wish is my command." She had to laugh at the *1,001 Arabian Nights* feel of the moment. An evil prince somewhere above them. A cavern full of dried fruits and nuts and every kind of stored delicacy and a carpet that was about to become magical beneath them.

"Watch that, Kari. My wishes can be pretty primal, especially when it comes to you and the thought of your pretty pink pussy."

His raw language made her panties wet. "I'm a tough cookie, Bryon. Bring it, baby."

His eyes darkened to a feral green and he slid onto his knees, reaching to slip his shirt over his head. "Now you."

Knee to knee, they each stripped off a piece of clothing one by one. Kari's blood raced with anticipation, especially with Bryon's thick member so prominent and clearly ready for action.

He pulled her close, wrapping his arms around her waist. "Do you know how lush and full you are? I could eat you up."

She smirked. "Now there's an idea." Disentangling herself she stretched out on the rug, pulling her knees up and letting them fall apart. "Juicy is best, don't you think?" Her fingers stroked her pussy, and she let her index finger slide through her slickness, lifting her finger to her mouth. "I think so."

Bryon growled low in his throat and crawled toward her open legs, burying his face between them. He lapped and laved at her slit, circling her nub until the sensitive bud swelled beneath the rough barbs on the tip of his tongue.

She fisted his hair as she had in her dream, urging his mouth deeper, harder. Her body tensed and a climax crested, but Bryon held her at the edge, pulling his mouth away.

She cried out, protesting but he shook his head. "My wish, remember?" His smirk made her clit jerk and she slid her hand down to give herself relief, but he held her wrist. "I want to watch you come, Kari, but by my hand, not yours."

He raised her wrist high and held it over her head and she lifted her other hand clasping her fingers together. He kissed her mouth, her chin, her neck, working his way to her breasts. He sucked and flicked her nipples, teasing each with his tongue and teeth until Kari locked her legs around his waist.

"Bryon! Please!"

He reared back and drove his cock deep, his hips grinding against hers with thrust after thrust. Again he brought her to the edge and held her there.

"Are you ready, Kari?"

"Argh! I've been ready, you son of a bitch! Make me come!"

He chuckled. "You're so sexy, Kari. Hot and flushed and frustrated, and ready to eat my head or my cock, whichever you could sink your teeth into first, but I need you even more ready . . . ready for the bite of your life."

His words pulled her back from the precipice and she looked at him. Their bodies were joined and in that moment so were their hearts, their souls. This was it. He was asking her again.

"Make me come, Bryon. I'm ready . . . for everything. For it all." Her eyes locked on his. "For you."

In one fluid motion he flipped her onto all fours and plunged his cock deep. He rode her hard, driving over and over, his sex swelling inside her as the ridge on his head scored her walls. She cried out as she came, rockets exploding behind her eyes.

Bryon threw his head back and the roar that ripped from his throat shook the room. Hot jets pulsed from his cock and as his body released he bit down on her nape, his mark penetrating her flesh as his sex penetrated her core.

The two fell forward, letting the spasms ebb. Sweaty and sated, he wrapped his arm around Kari's waist and held her close against him. He licked the bloody mark, his saliva sealing the wound and making it permanent.

"You're mine, Kari. Now and always."

She snuggled in closer, letting the heat from his body sooth her tender bits. "Just the way I dreamed it would be."

CHAPTER 23

⤙—⤚

Bryon curled around his little mate on the rugs. The tunnels were silent—no cars, no sirens, no wind. Just him and his dream woman. She felt so good in his arms. It had seemed like forever that he'd had to wait to hold her. But now she was his. He was hers. And he had to get her out of here and to his den.

Reluctantly, he pulled away from their shared warmth under the blanket. He gathered two bowls of food and sniffed at the bags of red wine. Didn't make him gag, so it was probably safe to drink.

Behind him, the blanket rustled and a beautiful yawn brought music to his ears. "Good morning, my love," he said, setting the food next to the rug they had slept on, among other things.

Kari picked up the bowl. "Thank you. That's so thoughtful. I'm not used to having stuff done for me."

"Well, now," he said, sitting next to her, "you need to get used to it because I'm always going to be there to do stuff for you."

Her head tilted toward him. She asked, "Aren't you going to be working at ALFA?"

Yeah, he hadn't fully thought all that through yet. Two of his other co-agents had found their mates recently. Each had taken time off to be with his mate. Sort of a honeymoon getaway. That left one guy, Sheldon, in the office with Director Tumbel.

"Our procedures say if we find our mates while in service, we are allowed to leave with full benefits after a replacement is found and trained."

"But what about this case you've been undercover for for the past months? Don't you want to find these trafficking rings?" she asked. He smiled at her. She was perfect for him. She knew exactly what he felt and wanted and they'd known each other for a very short time.

"Yes, I'd like to put a stop to this evil and gut those in charge," he replied.

Her eyes widened then returned to normal. "Wow, remind me never to piss you off." He laughed.

"No worries, love." He kissed her forehead. "When you're ready, we need to get going. It's morning here. And I'm thinking an exit is nearby."

"Because of this room being relatively clean and stocked?" she asked.

"Yup. My thoughts exactly," he said. Bryon helped her to her feet and pulled her body to his. He inhaled her fresh scent. He could stand all day, just breathing her in. That wouldn't get them out of the cave, though.

Taking a couple of torches with them, they stepped from the room into the aisle. "We passed at least two side tracks on the way to this room. Either could be the exit," he said. Kari looked behind them where the tunnel continued on. The path made a sharp curve.

"Hey, Bryon," she said, "look at this." Torch held high, she made her way toward the turn. There on the wall was a big arrow pointing the other direction.

"Careful, Kari. Could be a trap," he reminded her. She stopped midstride. When he took the lead, sniffing for booby traps, he felt relieved she listened and didn't argue about her independence. At the bend in the trail, they leaned forward to peek around the edge. Seemed to be a continuation of their way. But it was a dead end into another wall.

"Look," Kari said. She scuttled to drawings on the wall. They resembled the hieroglyphs they had seen earlier, but the swastika was a big clue this was not Egyptian in nature.

"Any idea?" he asked.

She stared at the symbols. "I'm sure you've guessed it's not original to the tunnel's creation. And maybe the answer will reveal a door or some way to continue."

"Yup. But that's about all I got from it."

"You speak the language of this area?" she asked.

"Pretty much fluent," he replied.

"I just know basic root words based on Latin. But this may not be all that complicated. May not even need specific language." She rubbed a finger across the broken cross and the tip came back with a smudge. "They didn't even use paint. It looks like charcoal," she said.

"Thoughts on who 'they' are?"

"I'd say the rumor about Nazis stashing treasures in these tunnels is true. And I doubt the SS took the time to come up with a ball-busting puzzle."

He bent closer to the images on the rough rock and pointed to the last picture. "That looks like it could be the earth. Europe here and that resembles Africa." His finger traced the crude outlines. "Maybe."

"Yes, that's good. The swastika could mean the Nazi regime or Germany. But what the hell is this?" She pointed to stick figures, some with hats, some behind vertical lines. Those lines reminded him of the cell he was in before joining the prince for dinner.

"Could that be Nazis wearing the hats putting others in jail cells?" he asked.

Her eyes lit up. "That's it. It says the Nazis will punish the world. In other words, they will rule the planet." She bounced to her toes and kissed him. When she started to pull away, he grabbed and brought her back to him. He loved her taste. Wanted all he could get.

She laughed and pushed back. "All right, lover boy. More when we get out of here."

He raised his brows. "Promise?"

"How about an entire week? Honeymoon style." Heat infused her eyes. Her arousal scented the air. Good god, he couldn't wait. He was ready to plow through rock walls right now. "But first, we get out of here." She turned back to the puzzle. Below the row of drawings were two holes with a rope dangling from each. Above each hole was a word. "I bet those say yes and no, right?" she asked.

"Sharp as a tack, I'll tell you," he joked. She grinned and moved her hand to the "no" rope. He grabbed her arm. "Wait. Even though Germany lost the war, they didn't know that when they stashed the stuff. So to them, the answer would've been yes, don't you think?"

She stood back and chewed on her lip. First time he'd ever felt jealous of a body part.

"You're right." Kari grabbed the "yes" rope and pulled.

From deep inside the walls, a low rumble vibrated. Similar to the water room, but different. To his sensitive ears, the sound was coming closer.

"Bryon, do you feel that?" Her voice wavered. The ground shook, dust fell from the ceiling. They had to run, but he didn't know to where. It sounded from all around. His instincts screamed to get away. But which way?

CHAPTER 24

———

Kari stared at the ceiling and walls around them. An earthquake shook everything. She looked for an opening in the rock, somewhere they could go. The dead-end wall was still a dead end. Hopefully not literally.

She whipped her head around to see the wall and ceiling from the turn in the path to where they stood disappear under tons of boulders and dirt. Bryon tackled her, keeping her away from the deadly pileup.

"What?" she yelled. "I can't believe they would've answered no to that." She pushed him off her and sprang to her feet. There was simply no way Nazi soldiers would've thought they'd lose the war. Maybe she'd interpreted it wrong. She grabbed the "no" rope and pulled. She wanted to see what would happen. Nothing? Was it a trick?

"Kari, don't." Bryon was airborne in a heartbeat, yanking her arm toward him as the ceiling above her gave way to more boulders. She screamed and ducked her head, landing on a soft body. Dust coated her throat and she coughed, her hand waving away the particles from her face.

"Those bastards cheated," she said. "Both options were

bad. Good thing they lost the damn war." She stood in the small space between the second dump of rocks and the dead-end wall and dusted her pants off. "Now what?"

The powder floating in the air swirled where there should be no breeze or movement. "Bryon?" she said.

He stood behind her and faced the wall. "I see it. Hold on a second." He picked up the one torch that had survived the landslide and blew on the dying embers to reignite the flames. He held it in front of the wall and watched the smoke waft to the side. He handed the torch to her and put his hands on the wall. Bracing his feet against the floor, he shoved against one side.

The wall/door pivoted so quickly, the far side of the door whipped around and smacked him in the ass, throwing him into a new part of the tunnels. She almost peed her pants laughing so hard.

"I see now," she started, "why both ropes were sabotaged. They didn't have to solve it to make the door move. You just had to push it. Lightly."

Bryon picked himself up off the floor and wiped his hands on his pants. "From your position, I can see this being funny. But not really from mine." She laughed more and walked through the cleared doorway. She reached for his hand and continued forward.

"I hope this ends soon," she said. "I'm so tired of this stupid tunnel. I want sunshine and fresh air."

"Me, too, love. I'd really like a bed to take you in." His brows slipped up and down. She laughed.

"Is that all you think about? Sex?" she teased.

He lifted her against the wall and she wrapped her legs around his waist. "Until you pass out screaming my name, it is. You got a problem with that?"

"Not at all," she said and kissed him.

Needing air, they parted, each panting. "We can do it right here on the floor," she said.

"I don't want to bruise your back or knees. It'll have to wait until I can lick you from head to toe and eat your creamy center before making you come."

Damn. She shivered from the image of that in her mind. Her legs unlocked from around him. "Let's get going, then. Time's a wastin'." When he set her feet on the ground, she slapped his ass. "On your toes, soldier. Get me the hell outta here."

"Yes, ma'am." He laughed, grabbing her hand. Despite the levity in their conversation, she knew he was careful of traps and surprises waiting for them. They turned a corner and were met with another dead-end wall. But this end sported designs different from any they'd seen. The rock was even different from the sidewalls. The ground was covered with dirt and sand. It looked much . . . newer.

Bryon held up the torch to the newest obstacle. From top to bottom, side to side, twelve circles lined up. "Well, damn," she said, "yet another death-defying escape required. I'm so over this shit."

Bryon's brows drew down and his head tilted. "You hear that?"

She closed her eyes and focused on listening. "No. What is it?"

"Voices. I hear voices on the other side of the wall," he said.

She lifted her arms into the air. "Hallelujah. It's about freaking time."

"We just need to solve this last riddle," he said as he stepped back to see it all. "What do you think?"

She stared at the circles, which all had straight lines zigzagging through them. As she gazed, her brain reproduced the images and mixed and matched them in her mind. When overlaying and turning the figures, a pattern slowly emerged.

It seemed to be a sequence in which each circle design built on the previous one by adding one more line. Various lines were here and there, but all circles had one path in common. The twelfth circle had three lines no others had sprouting from the previous circle's line: one hooked left, one right, and the last pointed straight ahead. Obviously, they had to pick one of those. But which one? What was this diagram supposed to be?

"You know," Bryon said, "if you rotate these, they all have matching lines." He pointed to top left. "These three lines are identical to these three," he pointed to the circle below it, "but this bottom one has one more length to it."

Wow, she was impressed with him for recognizing that so quickly. Brawn and brains. She'd keep him. "You are correct, my dearest." She pointed to a circle on the far right with a lot of lines. "This is the last one with these three lines being new to the circle." She traced those lines for him. He nodded, brows down in concentration.

She thought the last three circles' lines were like the path they'd taken since the food room: straight, left turn, straight, right turn, this dead-end wall. "Hold the phone," she said. She knelt and drew a circle in dirt. She closed her eyes and visualized the path they'd taken since leaving the dungeon. Her finger mapped the lines in her mind into the sand, taking out the dead ends and blocked exits.

When finished, she stood back. Her diagram and the one on the wall matched, more or less. She never claimed to be an artist.

Bryon pointed to the last circle. "According to your drawing, this right turn is the correct choice." He grinned. "Damn, woman. You are creepy smart."

"Are you calling me creepy?" she asked, brows up to her hairline.

He put his arms around her and kissed her hair. "Yes, but you're my creepy. Creepy is sexy." His grin turned into a full-on smile with a twinkle in his eye.

She punched his chest. "Yeah, yeah. Come on, I want out of here."

"All right," he said, "we have the last line, but now what?"

"I don't know," she replied. "The only thing I can see is to trace the correct path in the last circle, maybe?" Bryon stretched to the top left.

"This is the one." Since she couldn't begin to touch the diagram even standing on her toes, he gallantly took on that responsibility. He looked at the drawing on the floor. "Start here?" She nodded and guided him the rest of the way. When they came to the last line, he looked at her. She shrugged.

"Go for it," she said.

CHAPTER 25

His little mate was a freakin' genius. He loved her so much already. If anything happened to her, he'd never forgive himself. If voices weren't on the other side of this wall, he might've taken a second to rethink this.

He moved his finger to the right and at the end of the line, his finger slipped into a hole he hadn't noticed. Above their heads, rocks shifted. He lifted the torch higher and saw the trap in the ceiling.

One end of a piece of rope stretching back several feet was wrapped around an oblong boulder. If the boulder were loosed, it would swing down like a pendulum and smash anyone standing in its path. That would currently be Kari. And the pendulum was in motion.

He dropped the torch and grabbed his mate around the waist and plastered them both to the sidewall. The breeze of the falling rock ruffled his hair. Kari's eyes were as big as the boulder as it swung down.

The rock hit the diagrammed wall, ricocheted back a few feet and knocked against the stone again. He held the woman of his dreams to the side until the plumb came to a complete stop. After peeling themselves from the wall, he saw the purpose of the battering. A narrow hole was punched through the wall and the voices flowed louder, but were still at a distance. It sounded like a large crowd. What the hell?

"Let me go through first," he said. "I'll see what's going on and come back. I want to make sure it's safe. Okay?" He kissed her head then wiggled through the hole.

"Okay," he heard her say as his feet slipped to this side of the wall. He wasn't giving her a chance to say no or argue. With the trap sprung and nobody behind them, she was safe there. He wasn't so sure about the people ahead of them.

The trail was well worn and no longer a tunnel, but a path along the top of a cliff that overlooked a massive stone chasm. He squatted behind large rocks and peeked around the side at the goings-on below. There had to be hundreds of people milling about. With further scrutiny, he realized the people were gathered around platforms with females standing together.

Narrowing his supersonic hearing to the closest group, he tried to find out what was happening. One man spoke German, calling out numbers. Others in the crowd, all men, raised a finger occasionally.

Then one of the men reached up toward a girl onstage. He grabbed a . . . leash around the girl's throat? Oh my fucking god. This was the trafficking event he had been searching for when he was captured by the prince's forces. That bastard son of a bitch. He wanted to rip off the prince's testicles. He had to force his wolf back. They wanted to run down and save all the helpless ones. But that would be suicide.

He pulled back from the cliff's edge and slinked his way back to his mate. He wasn't sure how they were going to get past all that. Maybe they could wait it out.

Kari paced side to side in front of the hole in the wall. Was the man ever coming back? What if he got hurt by another trap? Something he didn't see? Her stomach churned. He could be dying and she wasn't doing a thing about it.

She stopped and looked through the hole. It was at the height of her chest so she didn't have to bend too much. Listening intently, she did hear the voices Bryon was talking about. She put her arms through the wall, followed by her head, then rose onto her toes. From there, she couldn't get any further. Wait.

If she put her foot against the hanging rock that smashed into the wall, she could maybe push the rest of the way through. She was still too short to get her chest in. She needed to jump, but with her arms on the other side of the wall, that would be impossible.

Kari pulled out and stood, straightening her shirt. Okay. With her hands on the hole's edge, she could lift herself to get her upper body into the gap. Then she could push off the oblong rock to get the rest of the way.

Hands on the edge, she jumped up and leaned forward. Halfway through, she realized her hands faced the wrong way. Her wrists were folding backward. She didn't know how, but amid her panicked wiggling and twisting, she had gotten her hands turned. But now they were pinned under her, mashed between her stomach and the rock. When she tried to pull her arm out, skin tore from the back of her hand pressed against the jagged stone edge. Shit.

If she rocked to the side, she could maybe pull out her hand with minimum damage done. Contorting her body to one side, she yanked and gritted when her flesh gave way to rock, but her hand was no longer under her.

With her head on the other side of the wall, she could barely see anything. Not that there was much to look at. The same damn rock she'd seen the past million freaking hours. Light bounced off the ceiling from somewhere ahead. Trying to pull her free arm to the other side, she quickly found the hole wasn't big enough to bend her arm to get through. She groaned.

On the side of the wall opposite her head, she kicked her legs, pointing her toes, but the floor wasn't within reach. Shit. She lifted her leg, searching for the rock to push off.

Her shoe brushed the pendulum, setting it into a slight motion. Shit.

Her mind spun through the options. If she kept her leg straight, locking it at the knee, the rock would swing back and hit her foot, either pushing her forward or shoving her thigh bone into her ribs. Almost good, but not quite. If her leg remained flexible, bending at the knee just a bit, then that would push her while not breaking her. Her knee quickly bent a bit and the force of the swing pushed her forward.

She bit her tongue holding back the holler from the pain of her hand scratching along the rock under her stomach. She twisted to free the arm before the rock bumped into her foot a second time. If she could get a few more inches, she might be able to get her elbow out far enough to free her arm. The rock's return pushed her farther, but not enough. Shit.

She wiggled her arm free and let it dangle. Thank god. She pushed against the wall to get her other arm out. She rested a second. Her body was not meant for going through holes in walls.

With a deep breath and heave with her arms, she pushed until she came to a sudden stop. Shit. She hadn't stopped to think if the gap was wide enough for her hefty hips. Well, it wasn't. Shit.

"What the hell are you doing?" She looked to see Bryon coming up the path.

"What does it look like?" she whispered loudly.

He stared at her. "I'm not sure, sweetheart." She heard the laugh in his voice. She'd kick his ass when she got out of this.

"Shut up and help me." She lifted her arms. He leaned over to hook his hands under her arms. When he pulled, nothing moved.

"Darling," he started, "can you suck it in a bit?"

She huffed. "No. You can't suck in hips. If I could, I would've a long time ago." He released his hold, letting her upper body hang. Then he put his hands around her waist.

"What are you doing?" she asked as he pulled. "Ow," she whined.

"Be quiet. I'm doing what I have to here," he said. With his hands on the small of her back, he twisted, shook, and yanked her body. After a few aching moments, her legs slid through. Apparently, he wasn't ready for her to pop loose. He quickly wrapped his arms around her waist, flinging her legs into the air.

"What the hell?" Upside down, her hair hung in her face and shirt slid toward her breasts. She snagged her top from falling farther. "Put me down right this second." Blood rushed to her head. He flipped her over, putting her on her feet. "That was a damn nightmare," she said.

"Okay, now we have to go back through it," he said.

CHAPTER 26

Peeping around the side of a boulder, Kari gazed over the crowd of people on the cave floor below them. There was no way she was going through that damn hole in the wall again. She'd walk naked among the people before she squeezed her oval body through a round space. Of course, her mate was fine with that. She had to punch his arm for being so male.

On the side of the pit below, she watched as women came from behind a curtained-off area. Most were practically dragged by a leash around their necks. An older lady stepped from behind the curtain and opened one of fifty plastic containers stacked just beyond the barrier. Colorful material was packed inside and she pulled out a red fabric. She wrapped it around one of the females' waist.

"This is how they sell people?" she asked. "There are kids down there." She stood to march down the path and give them a piece of her mind and escort every one of the females and children out the door.

He grabbed her arm and pulled her to sit. "Where are you going?"

"Someone has to rescue all those people. And you're just

sitting there. We have to do something." She didn't want to sound whiney, but this was atrocious. Males selling women because they were stronger and could beat the female into submission. Pure hate and anger bubbled in her chest. Something had to be done.

"We will rescue them now that we know this is going on. But we have to get out first and call for backup. The two of us can't fight all the bad guys down there." She hated that he had a point.

"All right," she said. "How do you propose we get out? And don't say through the hole in the wall."

"Of course not. The plan is to walk through like everyone else. I will hold on to your arm and we walk out."

That seemed reasonable. They would blend in perfectly. Hand in hand, he led her along the steep path descending the side of the chasm. Nobody noticed them.

She whispered out the side of her mouth. "Where's the exit? I didn't see it."

Bryon nodded ahead. "On the other side of the cavern."

"Of course," she mumbled. Suddenly, he pulled on her arm and walked a different direction. "I assume you know what you're doing."

"Prince Goddard is that way talking to several men. He doesn't look happy."

She looked over her shoulder, but couldn't see over the crowd. "What is he saying? Can you tell?" she asked.

"He's giving them a description of us. He must know about the tunnel leading here." He scooted them to the side of the plastic containers she saw the older woman at a while ago. Using his shifter speed, he restacked the boxes by taking containers in the back and placing them up front to build a wall to hide them. Another great idea. Her man was good at this spy stuff.

"Grab a couple more containers and let's see what's in them," she said. They popped the lid on a few and saw female clothing, scarves, wraps, robes, shoes, and loose pieces of makeup. She now understood the purpose of the curtained zone. It was a staging area where the older women dressed up those being sold.

She felt like puking then burning down everything in this insidious place. "I have a plan to get us out of here," she said, pulling stuff out of containers. Bryon stood by quietly. He must've known her thoughts or expected the worst. Which would be correct.

"Here," she handed him two fist-size rocks, "hold these to your chest." She wrapped a long length of material around him several times, firmly holding the stones against his skin.

"What are these for?" he asked.

"Insta-boobs." She handed him a white muslin robe. "Put this on." She continued to drape scarves and material over his head. She worried he was too tall, but not much she could do about that. "Damn, your feet are hairy, boy. No way they'll pass for women's feet."

There weren't shoes big enough for his clompers so she tied scarves around his knees to hang down and hide the grizzly things.

"Almost done," she said. She pulled up the black tulle material covering his face. "Open your mouth wide."

He frowned. "Why?"

She sighed. "Do you trust me?"

"Yes, sorta. Depends what you do with that lipstick in your hand." Damn, he saw her pick it up.

"You have to look like a female. This lipstick will do that. Now open your mouth." He did as she requested. "Now do this." She pressed her lips together, showing him how to set the makeup.

"Ew. This stuff feels disgusting." He lifted a hand to wipe at the color, and she smacked it down.

"Don't smear it. You can take it off as soon as we get out of here." She tossed the lipstick into a bin and pulled out a robe and scarves for herself. In another container, they found fake gold jewelry and leashes. She draped herself in gold, making her look quite wealthy. She pulled Sheldon's bracelet from her pants pocket and slid it on with everything else.

Bryon grabbed her arm and held it up, exposing her last fancy addition. "Have you had this the entire time?"

"Not on, but in my pocket." She didn't want to tell him about her earlier erroneous thoughts about Sheldon liking her and giving her such an expensive gift.

"Good," he said. "Keep it on."

She shrugged. "Not a problem." She wrapped her hair in a dark turban then draped her face with black tulle. "How do I look?" She twirled for him.

"Like a fancy brothel owner." His grimace said he didn't like the look. Good. She didn't want to look pretty. He picked up a leash and tied it around his neck. "You know, this will look silly with you holding me on a leash. I'm a foot taller than you. How about I just shift and go out that way."

Kari rolled her eyes. "Yeah, like a huge-ass wolf walking through the crowd won't draw attention?"

"I see your point." He handed her the other side of the leash. "Let's go, master." She huffed, then peeked around the wall of containers they had built. Everyone around them was focused on the stage fifty feet away with three scared, nearly naked teens. She told herself to wait for backup like Bryon said. Nothing could be done now that would help.

She headed for the exit, falling in line behind others going the same direction, some with multiple girls in tow. Ripping that man's balls from his body would make her feel really good at that moment.

Ahead, one of the women lashed out, fighting her captor. From nowhere, guards surrounded them. One shot her with a dart gun and she calmed, then passed out and fell to the floor. Her owner picked up a leg and dragged her behind him.

Suddenly, a man was in Kari's face, rattling words she didn't understand. "I'm from America." She lifted her chin. "What do you want?"

The man's eyes got big and he looked her up and down. "You lay one goddamn hand on me, mister, and your balls will decorate the rearview mirror in my car."

"No, you misunderstand. You are short for American. I used to tall men," he managed to get out in English.

"What do you want. I'm done here and leaving." She changed her voice to be annoyed and impatient. She should try out for the community play. This acting stuff wasn't too hard.

"I pay half million dollars for your slave," he said. Her jaw dropped open. The man didn't notice because he was making twinkle eyes at her Bryon. His foot hit hers, snapping her thoughts.

"No. She is not for sale. I just purchased her."

The guy reached up and squeezed Bryon's rock boobs. "Firm, just like I like them. One million American dollars. I must have her. I've never seen anyone more beautiful."

She turned and looked at her mate. "Mister, you got yourself a deal," she said.

"Wait here for me to return," he said, hurrying away.

Bryon bent down to her ear. "What the hell are you doing? You can't sell me."

"Suck it up, buttercup," she whispered back, trying to move her lips as little as possible, "I just made myself one million bucks." She smiled at him. "Just go with him. If we're not together, they'll be less likely to suspect something. I'll be behind you." He huffed and straightened.

The man fought his way through the crowd, carrying a briefcase. He held it out to her. She took it and nearly dropped it from being heavier than expected. She handed the leash to him.

"There you go. She's all yours. Have fun." She smiled and stepped away. The man led Bryon toward the exit. She watched as the new owner's hand slipped behind Bryon and rested on his butt cheek. She barely held the laugh in when Bryon batted it away. She quickly melted into the group heading out.

CHAPTER 27

B ryon couldn't believe his mate had sold him for a million dollars. He would've held out for at least two million. And when the man put grubby paws on his ass, it jumped to three mil.

As they approached the guards at the exit, he kept his eyes to the ground. It would be a miracle if this worked. His temporary owner thought nothing of the security and continued without even looking at the guns the men held. Then Bryon felt the hand on his arm.

His new owner went ballistic cussing at the guard in at least three languages. That drew the attention of others with guns. He wanted to tell the guy to chill the fuck out, but he couldn't do anything without being made.

Bryon looked back to find his mate, making sure she was okay. He noted the crowd gathering to see what was going on. Kari was among the mass. Just as he turned back, a large hand grabbed her arm and jerked her out of his sight.

His wolf jumped forward wanting to kill everyone between them and her. Fuck his disguise, he would give his life to save her. He should've known not to let her walk around with a briefcase holding money. Why did he go along with this insane idea?

Kari's angry voice came from the middle of a gathering. He shoved his way through to find an olive-skinned man cowering on the ground while his mate beat him with the case. Bryon grasped the briefcase on its swing down and dragged his mate from the crowd.

Right behind him was his owner pulling on him. And on his owner's arm was a guard yanking him. What a lovely train they made. Kari smacked the case into his owner's chest.

"I reneg," she said. "You keep the money. He belongs to me." A warmth filled him. His mate wanted him. He took her hand and headed toward the exit, but of course, it wasn't that easy. Mr. Moneybags latched on to the back of Bryon's robe, jerking it halfway off. Bryon punched the guy in the face, knocking him into others. The briefcase hit the ground and spilled open, dollar bills scattering.

The orderly mass quickly became chaos with people pushing and shoving to get their hands on the money. Bryon fought his way through, his mate with him—her disguise mostly ripped away in the bustle. When they reached the point to break free, the prince stepped through the exit.

Bryon locked eyes with the bastard. The red glowed to life then died back. Goddard was possessed by a demon, just like the hieroglyphics said. He didn't want to think about the implications. He just wanted his mate out of here.

The prince yelled and guards surrounded them. Kari was torn from his side. His wolf had enough of her being taken from him. His shift was fast. In a heartbeat, his teeth sank into the thick arm holding his woman. Blood splattered on his muzzle.

High-pitched screams erupted along with more chaos as people scrambled to get away from a monster killer. He nosed Kari to get her up and going. His wolf growled as men with guns narrowed their escape route. A sting hit his hind quarters and he yipped. A dart like the one that hit the lady who passed out earlier stuck up from his rump. Fuck.

His mate's voice faded in his mind. He was going down.

"Bryon!" Kari yelled. She saw the dart come from the pistol one of the guards held. She was thankful it wasn't a bullet. Struggling to get to Bryon, she ripped her arms from grasping hands. "Bryon!" She stumbled to her knees by his side. His chest rose and fell. He was alive.

Fancy shoes stopped beside the wolf's head. She looked up into red eyes.

"I'm impressed you two made it this far. After the water chamber, I could no longer track you." His eyes scanned the wolf's body. "I've been waiting for another of these for so long."

"Another what?" she asked.

His eyes never left the animal. "Shifter. I knew he was." He snapped his fingers. "Take them both to the castle—now. I will be there shortly." He twirled around and hands lifted her off the ground. She struggled as a natural reaction, though it did no good.

Two of the men tried to lift the wolf's dead weight. In the end, four guards carried/dragged Bryon.

The other side of the exit wasn't outside but inside a large warehouse with several cargo vans and limos with blacked-out windows. Men in expensive suits, some with, some without women on leashes, got in and out of the cars.

A white van with a business logo on the side was packed with bodies. One of the women caught her eye. She had dark draping hair and big fear-filled eyes. The two back doors of the van slammed shut and a man walked around to the driver's side. A long garage door in front of the van slid up letting bright sun into the space. The first sun she'd seen in a while.

The buildings she could see outside the door weren't familiar. Gone were the quaint houses and brick roads. Instead more metal warehouses and industrial structures. They were far from where they'd started yesterday.

The van drove out and away. Sadness and anger overwhelmed Kari. She had no idea what those women would endure, but their lives wouldn't be happy. They wouldn't fall in love, have a caring relationship with a man who respected them. If she got out of this, she would rededicate her life to stopping this inhumane crime.

One of the two men holding her arms jiggled her, bringing her attention back to her own situation. They stopped at the side of a van. Her escort opened the double doors and shoved her in followed by the guys with her mate.

Kari scooted around in the back to cradle her love's furry head in her lap. Her hand rubbed down the side of his snout and neck, again and again. She wondered how long he would be out. After the handful of men had settled inside the van, they exited through another lifted door and drove into the sunlight.

She had to cover her eyes from the sudden brightness, but was quickly able to see a bit of the world around them. They drove out of the industrial park and onto asphalt roads barely wide enough for two vehicles.

The steep hills were covered in green, either trees or fields. They passed the occasional townsfolk walking bicycles along the side of the road. One was walking a cow. She had watched the movie *The Sound of Music* several times as a kid. Much of the landscape reminded her of that movie. The huge sweeping hills of grass and countryside begged for picnickers and dogs chasing balls.

In the far distance, she saw the old castle the taxi driver had pointed out what seemed like weeks ago. From this angle, the structure looked huge. Several stories high with turrets and ramparts and pointed towers. In its day, she imagined the place was spectacular. But as with almost everything, its time had come and gone, giving way to the new and improved.

The men spoke the local language she didn't understand. The way they glanced back at her and the wolf didn't bring her comfort. Sometimes their faces reflected fear, other times anger. What did it mean that they were going to the old castle? If the prince wanted to hold them, the dungeon cells under the palace would be fine without the added problem of transportation.

What if the castle had old torture devices like the rack and all those other things she always saw in movies about time? Was the prince going to torture them to get information on who they were? Then she remembered how the prince reacted to realizing Bryon was a shifter. The man had said he'd waited a long time for another shifter. That meant he had a plan for them. Whatever it was couldn't be good. She needed to come up with an escape plan that included getting past five guards and moving a wolf that was probably twice her weight. No problem.

CHAPTER 28

❧

Sitting in the back of the van, Kari lost sight of the castle on the hill. She didn't want to move with Bryon's wolf's head in her lap. The driver turned onto a bumpy road and they climbed a hill. The path narrowed as they drove past trees that became a forest the higher they went.

After a short amount of time, they passed through a gate in a stone wall. If she was correct, they were at the back of the castle. The part not seen from the town. The van stopped and the men got out. The two side doors opened and men grabbed the wolf by his fur.

"Hey!" she hollered, even though she doubted they understood her. "Be nice." She held his head in her hands and scooted him closer to the door so they wouldn't have to yank and pull on him. She followed her mate's procession with the last guard behind her.

They came to a rounded door that would've looked perfect in a castle if it wasn't made of shiny metal. The guard punched in a passcode on the electronic entry device and the door popped open. Quite modern, especially when there supposedly wasn't any electricity in the castle.

Inside, the air was musty and old, but the corners were relatively free of cobwebs. So either it was so old that all the spiders had died or there was enough activity to keep them from making a home. She wasn't sure which was better.

The men led them down a set of stairs where a switch on the wall turned on a single light bulb. The wire was attached to the stone and ran up through a hole in the rock floor. The whole place was probably wired in the same fashion.

At the bottom of the steps, the room opened into a large space that looked multifunctional. Cells with thick bars lined one side. Chairs and foldable tables were stacked against a wall. The other side held a fire box and what looked like a stone altar. All the horror and witch movies she'd ever seen flashed through her mind. All the scenes where the sacrificial victims had their throats slashed or heads cut off or a knife driven through their hearts. A shudder passed through her. She and the wolf had to get out of there fast.

She looked around for possible escape routes. No windows or other doors except the one they had come through at the top of the stairs. The men dropped the wolf inside a cell and pushed her in before closing and locking the door. The guys whispered as they left. She found that interesting. Were they trying not to draw the attention of the old ghost king? She wanted to laugh at that, but the surrounding environment made the story feel more real.

Kari sat on the floor next to the unconscious wolf's head and petted him. "Well, wolf, any ideas how to get out of here?" she waited for a reply not coming. "Yeah, me neither." She sighed.

"I have to say, this has been an exciting trip. When I came on this project, your boss told me I would just have to walk around and pretend to be a girlfriend." She laughed. "I failed at that spectacularly. I haven't seen Sheldon in forever.

"But in a way, that's fine. Because with you, I don't have to pretend to be in love. You're exactly what my Tabi talked about when she spoke of Joe and his love. Shifter love." She looked down at him, stroking her fingers through his soft fur. For years, she'd dreamed about a shifter being her white knight, or black wolf, in this case. He would love no matter her looks or how smart she was. He would love her for who she was.

And she would love him with all her heart in return. They would have three kids, two boys and little girl. The boys would always watch over their sister and keep her safe from bullies and those who would be mean to her. She'd wanted a cat and dog, until she realized that if her husband was a shifter, he would probably scare the crap out of the cat. But the dog would be okay. But why have a dog when her shifter husband could play fetch with the kids? And he'd walk himself. Huge bonus.

When she'd reached her late twenties, that dream slowly went away. Replaced by bills, a mortgage and car payments, and reality. She watched as her friends, one by one, married and grew their families with children and animals—regular ones. The thought of shifters no longer entered her head. She'd forgotten for the most part that they existed. Everyone looked and acted human.

She sighed and leaned forward, resting her elbows on her legs. Her wish of finding the man of her dreams had come true, but now it seemed they would never have their happily ever after. She felt certain they would kill Bryon. Biting tears flooded her eyes. Her heart sank and a pain inside her ached like she'd never felt before. That was what losing someone you loved felt like.

She felt helpless, overwhelmed by the circumstances. How could she fight men trained to kill? Thinking back, she was trained how to defend herself against those types of people and how to go on the offensive. But she'd had a desk job her entire working life and she used her brain, not brawn. Perhaps it was time to kick her own ass into gear.

She'd been relying on Bryon to get her out of the tunnels. Now that they were, it was up to her to get them out of this. She would do whatever it took to protect him. She could do this.

The door from the upstairs opened, and the stair treads creaked and moaned under someone's weight. She got to her feet, ready to go head-to-head with whomever. Of course, it would be the red-eyed prince prick himself. What did he want? She was almost too afraid to ask.

CHAPTER 29

Kari stared at the bastard with his red eyes glowing on the other side of the cell.

"What do you want?" she asked. "Going to try to sell us off to the highest bidder? I swear to god, when we get out of here, I will make sure every single person in that warehouse is found and either set free or put in prison. Starting with you." She shoved a finger through the bars and poked his chest.

The prince frowned and stepped back. He rubbed the spot where she'd touched him. "Do not worry yourself with such trivialities. Soon, your reality will be what I want it to be."

"What are your plans for us?" If he would give her a hint, maybe she could figure a way out.

"I will take possession of the shifter's body and live once again. I've waited for such a long time."

"You've already taken possession of him and me," she said. He laughed and walked up the stairs. A few minutes later the guards brought food and water then went back upstairs. Did they really think she was dumb enough to eat their poisoned food? That trick was in every story ever told. Instead, she shoved it in the corner.

Behind her, a cracking sound startled her. She turned to see her Bryon back in human form, lying on the ground. And naked. If not for their dire situation, she'd have kept this view for a while. But she turned and wiggled her robe off for him to cover himself. After shimmying it from her shoulders, she turned to see Bryon set down the cup of water.

"No." She would've slapped the cup from his hand, but he'd already drunk it all.

"What?" His voice was scratchy. "Where are we?" His head shook and he wiped at his eyes. "Everything is blurry. Do you have more water?" Whatever they drugged him with dehydrated his body.

"There may have been poison in that drink," she said.

He looked at the cup then around them. "Well, shit. There probably was if the prince had anything to do with it. It will knock me out in a few minutes." He sat up and ran fingers through his hair. "Where are we?"

"At the old castle on the hill," she said. She held out her robe. "Put this on to cover some of you. Probably not all of you, though." Her eyes strayed down his chiseled chest and abs. When his thighs separated, her look snapped back to his face. He caught her checking him out. Again. She raised her chin as her cheeks flushed hot. "You're my mate," she said. "I can . . . can . . . ?" she waved her arm in the air over his body, "look all I want." She dropped the robe on him.

He laughed and pulled her down to his lap. "Yes, you can, my love. And I like that you do. But the fear I smell tells me we have other matters to attend to first." He kissed her neck. She sighed. She felt so much stronger when with him. He gave her the belief they could get through everything. They practically had already. "Now tell me what's happening. Why are we at the castle? I heard this place was haunted by one of the old ancestors."

"I heard that, too, but I don't believe in ghosts, so that's the least of my worries." She scooted around on his lap. "Have you seen anything weird about the prince?"

"Weird like what? He's flamboyant as hell, but that doesn't bother me."

"Remember the drawings on the wall talking about the royals being possessed by demons?"

"Yeah."

"I think it is true. Several times I've seen red in his eyes. And that is not a human trait."

He rubbed his chin. "I have to agree based on what I've seen."

"But I don't know how that applies to us," she replied.

"Have you talked to him any? Did he say anything?" he asked.

She thought back to what the prince had said recently. Dammit to hell. Now the bastard's comment made sense. "He said he's going to take possession of your body. That he's been waiting a long time to find another one of you. *You* being shifters."

Bryon nodded. "He said something similar to that before—waiting for another me. But doesn't he know shifters can't be possessed? The wolf will kick out the demon before it gets a chance to move in."

"Thank god. That's a relief. I don't think he knows that. Should we tell him?"

"Let's wait until telling him benefits us in some way. We might be able to use it somehow," he said. His eyes drooped and head fell back against the bars.

Panic ran through her. She slapped his cheeks. "Bryon, wake up. You can't pass out. We have to get out of here." His head snapped forward.

"I'm awake. But won't be soon."

"How long were you out before?" she asked.

"I don't know. It wasn't too long. Maybe a couple hours. But that was a full dose for me. This was meant for you, right?"

She whipped around to look at him. "You're right. You were out when they dragged you in here. Why would they bring it for you? That means you got a partial dose."

"That would explain why I'm still conscious," he replied.

"But barely." She took a deep breath. She had to think to come up with a plan. Goddard would try to take over her mate's body, but wouldn't be able to. What would Goddard do when he discovered he couldn't? He'd kill them both on the spot. Shit. Think, Kari, think.

This wasn't a puzzle easily solved by analytics or moving things around in her head. She'd always wondered if that accident hadn't happened when she was twelve would she be "normal," just like the average Joe who watched *Wheel of Fortune* because *Jeopardy!* made him feel dumb?

He rested against the stone wall. They were running out of time. His shaky hand lifted to her face. Fingers brushed against her cheek. "I loved you the first time I set eyes on you in the prince's dining room. That second, I knew you were mine."

He spoke like he was dying. Maybe they were on their way to meet death. Tears rolled from her eyes. "I loved you the second I saw your picture in the director's office. The guys could smell it on me. I was so embarrassed." He chuckled. She leaned forward and kissed him. Much too quickly, his body went limp.

The door to upstairs opened, again. More than one person was on their way down. This was where it began.

CHAPTER 30

———✂———

With nearly closed eyes, Kari sat on the cell floor and stared through slatted eyes at the surreal image of those coming down the stairs. Since she was supposed to be unconscious from the drink, she positioned herself next to Bryon leaning against the wall. From this vantage, she clearly saw the steps.

Prince Goddard led the procession down, wearing a deep red cape-like robe. The collar and sleeves were wrapped in fur with long flowing fibers that almost floated in the air when he walked.

Behind him came those she recognized as the guards, but they were wearing black robes with hoods over their heads. They carried down armfuls of fluffy rugs. What were those for? Were they going to lie around and tell ghost stories?

The prince continued toward their cell while the men laid out the mats. He spoke the native language, but she could guess what he was basically saying. A black-robed person took a key from a pocket and opened the cell. The guard pointed at Bryon and asked a question. Probably wondering why Bryon was in human form and not animal. Shit.

The prince paused for a moment, but told the guy to bring Bryon out. Her poor Bryon, once again, was dragged across the floor. Fortunately, this was smooth stone and not jagged rock. His body was laid on one of the rugs. Worry made her feel like puking. What should she do?

The prince spoke to the group, raising his arms to the sides and dropping his head back. He looked to be preforming a miracle. In a way, he was. Demon possession was only in fiction. The light bulb in the room faded for a brief second. When Kari returned her eyes to Goddard, she gasped out loud. Oops. All heads turned toward her.

She couldn't take her eyes off the prince as he made his way toward the cage. "Well, I see you didn't drink the water," he said. He smiled when he saw her expression of horror. "You like what you see, young lady?"

Her brain was trying to make sense of the image before her. Goddard was in human form, but looked like a zombie fresh from a grave. His skin was loose and discolored, teeth and nails looked like they'd been soaked in black coffee for years. His face was sunken and hollowed as to appear skeletal.

"What happened to you?" she asked.

"Time happened, my dear. Flesh only lasts so long. Ever since finding out about a superhuman race, a species with immense physical power and beauty, I've waited and hunted for a creature I could have."

"So you're not really the prince, are you?" She was starting to catch onto the logic here.

The creature laughed. She blinked and suddenly, the prince was standing in front of her. "You are correct, child. Goddard and several of his 'ancestors' have been purely contrived by me. I would be Goddard's great-great-grandfather, King Alheim."

What would allow him to change his image like that? There was only one reason she could come up with. Black magic.

"You've used glamour to disguise yourself as members

of the royal family. But the logistics of that would be completely insane," she said. "You'd have to—"

"Kill lots of people and limit exposure. Yes, of course." He waved his hand like it was nothing. "When you get to my age, life means little except for what it can do for you." He turned back to the black-robed men gathered around her mate's body lying on the rug. "And as soon as I have this new body, I will be invincible for generations to come. Hopefully."

Two thoughts came to her mind. This creature roaming these halls would explain the rumors of the castle being haunted by the older king. And the reason he was part of the traffic ring was to find a body he wanted. Who better to scout for a shifter than someone who made a living finding and capturing people?

His last word registered in her mind. "What do you mean *hopefully*?" Halfway to the rugs, he stopped and glanced over his shoulder.

"The last shifter possession I tried didn't turn out so well. The poor creature suffered horrible pain before dying. I waited too long for him to bleed out, among other things. That won't happen again."

Oh shit. This was not happening. Panic seized her. She had to find a way to stall whatever the hell this monster had planned until the poison burned off and Bryon woke. The only thing that came to mind was their last option. Bryon said not to use it unless dire. Now looked pretty dire to her.

"Do you know why you failed, dumbass?" she said, making her voice as smooth and haughty as she could. The sick shaking she felt inside wouldn't be good to show right now.

Goddard swung around, his robe flying out behind him. He stomped his way back to her cage. His arm shot between the bars, aimed for her throat. She lunged backward to hit the wall.

"What do you speak of, child. How would you know my failings?"

Kari rolled her eyes and huffed. "Everyone knows you can't possess a shifter. The animal half will beat the shit out of the demon before he even gets in."

The demon's eyes flashed red, locked onto hers, then narrowed. "And how do you have this information?" he asked.

She swallowed hard. Please god, let this work. "You don't know who I really am, do you?" She cocked her hip and crossed her arms over her chest. "You happen to be talking to the only human on this planet who knows all there is about the shifter species."

Goddard stepped back and looked her over. "So fortunate for me. How have you, a female human, come to such knowledge?"

She pulled her shirt collar to the side revealing her mating bite marks. "Remember that boyfriend of mine? He happens to be my mate. My *shifter* mate. I've studied their traditions and ways and understand their history."

His eyes grew wide. "Your boyfriend is a shifter? Another one in my town?" He stepped up to the bars. "You will tell me where he is."

She frowned. How long could she keep this going? *Wake up, Bryon!* "Like I'm going to tell you that and let you find him." She crossed her arms over her chest and rolled her eyes.

"Then I have no further use for you." He walked away. "Guards, have someone kill her."

CHAPTER 31

—✄—

Fuck! That's not what she wanted. She clutched the bars in her dungeon cell and scrambled for something to say that would make Goddard want to keep her alive. She'd already told several lies. Why not a few more. If the poison didn't wear off Bryon soon, they would both be dead shortly.

"There is a way to possess their body if you really want it." The prince stopped and turned to her.

"You said there is no way because of the creature inside."

She swallowed again. A glass of non-poisoned water would be great. "That's right. You have to draw out the animal essence before you can take over."

He hiked his fists onto his hips. "Why have I never heard of that before?"

"Duh, how many shifters have you dealt with before now? That would be the huge, grand number of one."

Goddard pinched the bridge of his nose and paced. "Female, you have been a thorn up my ass for too long."

"Usually it's a thorn *in* your ass. But up it sounds just as painful if not more so." She sneered at him.

He spoke to his men and pointed to her. The guy with

the key came forward and unlocked the door. He grabbed her arm and jerked her front and center.

"Now, tell me how you draw out the essence of the animal." He stared down at her, only inches away. Fear almost pounced on her heart—rephrasing: being scared shitless almost stopped her heart.

"It's a ritual that requires proper setup and procedure to work."

He remained quiet for a second. Would he buy this? She was selling some really deep shit here. Time to get her waders on.

"What do we need?" he asked.

She scoured her mind for something, anything, to help. Ritual scenes from movies she'd seen popped into her mind. "Candles. We need lots of candles."

He looked at his men standing around. "You heard her. Bring me every candle in the castle." The men disappeared quicker than she thought possible, leaving her alone with him. "You know, female. If this doesn't work, you will die slowly and painfully."

Words did not make their way to her mouth. That *being scared shitless* thing was back in full force. Not that it had ever left.

She cleared her dry throat. "It will work. I know what I'm doing."

"It better. For your sake." She'd heard that exact line in a movie more than once. She felt like looking around for hidden cameras, waiting for that guy from *Candid Camera* to walk in and tell her this was all a setup. Damn. She was becoming delirious. She needed to focus on a plan, not break down. FBI agents didn't do hysterics. Quickly, men returned with candles. By the looks, the wicks and wax may have been original to the castle. She wondered if they'd even burn.

"Set the candles in a circle around the ceremony site and light them. We're creating a circle of protection. It's important to keep evil from entering." She glanced at Goddard. "I mean, keep evil from leaving."

"Next," the prince said.

Yeah, next. What else did they use in rituals? "Chanting. We need chanting next." The prince's brows raised. "Have you heard of Lady Gaga?" she asked.

"Who?"

"Never mind." She turned to the men. "Here's the chant: Rah rah ah-ah-ah. Ro mah ro-mah-mah." She repeated the lyrics several times and they picked up on it quickly. It was the perfect chant if done with a slow tempo and deep, male voices. She knelt next to Bryon's head and pushed up his eyelids. She jerked back, startled at the very eerie look of only the whites showing.

The prince frowned. "What's wrong?"

"Nothing. It's just when eyes are like that, with only the whites showing, it looks like the person is"—the irony didn't escape her—"possessed."

The prince laughed. "Not yet, dear child. Not yet. Now make haste. I grow weary and skeptical of this. If this is a charade, your pain will be immense and long-lasting."

She was very sure it would be. The thought kept her brain processing, thinking of ways to stall to give the poison time to get through the wolf's system. "We have to call to the powers that be and beseech their guidance and prayers for success."

Goddard wrapped a hand around her throat. "There are no deities on this planet with power. You lie."

"No," she squeaked. "This isn't godlike power. It's . . . it's . . ." Oh god, this was it. She was going to die at the hands of a demon older than dirt unless she thought of something good. Her mind reeled through every book she'd read and movie she'd known, searching for something that would remotely make sense as an answer. The solution came to her. "It's the force."

His grip loosened enough for her to breathe. "What is the force?"

She prayed he'd never seen *Star Wars*. Best movie of all time. No arguments. "It's an energy field created of all living things. It surrounds us, penetrates us, binds the galaxy together." She cringed a bit with the last part. "Galaxy" sounded a little over the top.

Goddard stared at her, probably wondering if this was all bullshit. She had to push him. Get him off balance and take control of the situation. "Do you want to possess the body or not? It's not going to work unless you do it the right way. You failed once already. I won't." Oscar-worthy performance. Did she smell shit in someone's pants? Oh, wait. That could be her.

He released her. She stepped back and sucked in air. Skepticism shined on his face, bringing back his zombie eyes and scowl. He said, "This will kill your friend. I'm having a hard time believing you'd simply comply with my wishes. Why are you helping me?"

That was a damn good question. One she couldn't answer truthfully and expect to live. Hopefully, God would forgive her for the lies she was about to tell. If they didn't work, she would probably be meeting the Almighty and could explain then. Kari gave him her saddest, most vulnerable expression.

"Look," she started, "I just want to get back to my boyfriend so we can go home. I'm tired and hungry and dirty. My feet hurt. I didn't want any of this to happen. I'm scared and willing to do whatever I have to in order to stay alive." So far everything was true. She looked at the wolf lying on the rug and continued.

"If that means telling you how to possess this shifter, fine. It's no skin off my back. Once you have his body, then you can let me go. I'm no threat to you. If I tell any police that a demon-possessed werewolf is the royal ruler, they'd throw me in the looney bin and forget I ever existed." And that was the damn truth, too. Except she had a few business acquaintances in high places who would believe her story. She was thankful for that.

The king laughed at her. She hadn't meant anything to be funny, but apparently something was. "Continue on, girl. We'll see the outcome before we decide anything," he said. She hoped they didn't get that far. This *making up stuff as you went along* was difficult. She now understood how hard it would be to write a book. She gained more respects for storytellers.

"Okay," she said, "it's time for your part." She turned to the prince to see the ancient skeletal-looking man and jumped. That horrid face was enough to make anyone ill. The skin on his face continued to sag with gravity, pulling away from the bone. The little substance in her stomach churned. She needed to keep it together. How much longer could the damn toxin last?

Kari took a deep breath and slowly let it out. Maybe it was time to trust herself in that she could do other things not related to numbers and puzzles. She'd always felt like a failure when it came to things outside the realm of her job. Perhaps if she put faith in her heart and didn't overthink it, she could find she could be a success. Now more than ever, she needed creativity.

She opened herself to everything around her—*the force*, she thought as she laughed to herself. But she felt something she'd never experienced.

Her fingertips buzzed like energy from the air vibrated around them. Through her shoes, her feet tingled as if soaking in the life of stone she stood on. She closed her eyes and her ears heard the sounds of bugs and insects milling in the rotten wood, scurrying around. She heard heartbeats, all those around her. She focused, listening to blood rushing through the bodies nearby.

Calmness filled her as she felt the unconditional love from the man before her. In the tunnels, she'd been so caught up with everything going on that she blocked out all emotions and feelings to let her brain work in a sterile environment. But now it was different. Her mate, her forever love, was sending her what he could to help her. With him, she could do this. Could do anything.

She let everything flow, just hanging on for the ride as her soul and mind went to work. She said, "The whole point of this is to entice the wolf spirit to come out of the body. If it's more pleasant out here than in there, then it will

willingly depart the body. Get it?" God, she hoped he did.
He didn't say anything. She asked him, "Do you know the
Latin language?"

"No. It was obsolete long before I was here," he replied.

"Good." Kari knelt by Bryon's head again. "I need to
start the process. Get the spirit's attention, if you know
what I mean." Shit. The man's scowl scared the piss out of
her. It went along with the shit already there. She breathed
in deeply again to get back in touch with that life, the energy she felt around her.

She put a hand on Bryon's forehead and the other over
his heart. She rattled off Latin phrases words she knew
from books and movies. "*Carpe diem, anno domini, deus
ex machina, e pluribus unum, Se agapo.*" That last one was
Greek for *I love you*, but he didn't know that. Hopefully.

Dropping her chin to her chest, she tried to talk without
moving her lips. She knew the wolf inside the body would
hear her no matter how softly she spoke. "Okay, wolf. Snap
him out of it. If not, it won't be pretty. Listen for my cue—"

A hand squeezed her shoulder and pushed her back.
"What are you saying?" Goddard demanded to know.

CHAPTER 32

⚓

Kari looked up at the man towering over her as she sprawled on the floor. The pain in her shoulder inflicted by a bony hand digging into her joint flared with each heart thump.

She needed to answer his question quickly. "You wouldn't let me invoke the force, so I had to say an extra prayer." With a huff, she picked herself up and dusted off her hands. Fortunately, that gave her brain a few moments to think. The old wives' tale of how cats killed babies came to mind. How or why, she had no clue. She was just rolling with it. "He's ready now. Kneel down and lean over his face. You're going to steal his breath and his wolf along with it."

"Steal his breath?" Goddard said. "What nonsense is—"

Kari put her hands up. "I'm telling you what I know. It's your choice—"

"Yes. I recall that from earlier." He leaned over Bryon's face. "How do I steal breath?"

"Whenever he exhales, you inhale, sucking his air to you. This will draw the wolf spirit to the surface to protect its human form." By God's grace, the demon bought it. If something sounds logical . . .

"Keep going." Kari knelt on the other side of Bryon. "His body should begin to shift into his wolf as it comes forward to save his other half. It's the last stage of the wolf's ability to hang on." Please let Bryon or his wolf be conscious. Please. When nothing happened, she cleared her throat. "I said the wolf will shift as—"

When the sound of a bone cracking ripped through the air, she nearly passed out from relief. The poison had worn off. About fucking time. "Keep breathing, Goddard. Open the animal's mouth and stay with it. The wolf is fighting you. You have to take it. Now!" She shoved the wolf's back. Nothing happened. "That's the cue. Now!"

As the prince looked up at her, the wolf lifted its head from the floor and sank teeth into the old man's scrawny neck. Snapping it instantly.

A black mist escaped the prince's mouth and dissipated in the air.

It happened so quickly that the guards were still chanting the Lady Gaga song lyrics she had taught them minutes ago. When realization hit, black robes went flying into the air, whipped off by the guards in record time. Guards who still had guns.

Kari lunged in front of the wolf, hoping to keep it from getting shot. "Wait! Stop!" Among the confusion of men running toward their deceased prince, men running away, and robes catching fire on the candles, the armed guards stood over her as she blocked most of the wolf with her body. One big guy shouted to others and pointed to the fires breaking out around the room.

"Woman . . ." The man in charge looked at her with steely anger. Then his eyes slid down her body. Her clothes were torn, revealing more of her than she would ever allow. Chills ran through her and the wolf growled against her back. "Step away from the beast and we will let you live." The grin on his face told any idiot that he was lying through his teeth.

In the confined space, the room quickly filled with smoke. Throat already dry, Kari coughed with the first wisps of contaminated air. She seriously doubted this lower hold was equipped with a fire extinguisher. She pulled the front of her shirt over her nose. It helped some. Not enough. The riflemen steadied their guns aimed at her and her mate again. She shook her head and coughed.

The guard who spoke to her lowered his brows and snarled. "So be it." He lifted his gun and she squeezed her eyes shut. Behind her, the wolf had dropped the king's body and leapt toward the men lined in front of her.

Two shots fired. She waited for the burning sting she was sure a bullet wound made. The room instantly became silent except for the popping and snapping of the fires and two thuds that sounded like bodies hitting the floor. She peeked through a slatted-open eyelid and saw two dark forms in the smoky air lying face down on the ground. The others were turned, gazing at the stairs.

On the steps, men in camouflage with guns poured in. They yelled in the native tongue and guards put hands up and fell to their knees. This had to be the rescue party, right? When Sheldon appeared on the steps, tears sprang to her eyes. Partly from relief, partly from acrid smoke.

They were saved.

He caught sight of her and wolfy Bryon and headed their way. She wrapped her arms around him in gratitude then coughed against his chest. She mumbled a sorry. A growl began behind her. She laughed through tears and bent down to hug her mate. "We're alive. You saved us, my love." She placed a kiss on his ear. He started his shift and she sat back realizing that he was naked and turned her eyes to Sheldon. This was so embarrassing.

In human form, Bryon man-hugged Sheldon. Bryon hollered over the ruckus, "Let's get out of here." But it was too late for her. With each hack, she sucked in more smoke. Her throat swelled from the burning irritation, cutting off her air. Her heart sped wildly. Her hands scratched at her throat. Forcing her lungs to expand, she sucked in hot air, making it worse.

In the next instant, she was lifted and carried upstairs

and out the back door where several military vehicles were parked and more men milled around the area. She fought for a breath of fresh air now that she was in the sunlight at last. She'd never take the sun for granted again.

Her coughs went so deeply, her gagging reflexes kicked in. She squirmed out of Bryon's arms, fell to her knees, and puked the little food in her stomach. Her throat loosened and air slid into her lungs, but her chest still felt like it burned on the inside. A tin cup of water was handed to her and she swished it around her mouth and spit out, drinking the remainder until she suddenly coughed it up.

Bryon picked her up and carried her to a car. He sat with her in the backseat as Sheldon drove. After a few more gagging fits, her lungs and throat started to feel better. She collapsed against her mate, exhausted for the sudden exertion and drain of adrenaline.

"Where are we going?" she asked.

"Sheldon is taking us to the airport. By plane, we can be at the U.S. military base in Liechtenstein in thirty minutes. They have equipment and medicine to take care of our dehydration and make sure your lungs are clear. I don't like the sound coming from your chest."

"I'm feeling much better. We don't need to go to the base. That's way too much hassle."

Bryon's face scowled. He was angry. "Don't think for one minute I don't know how to take care of my mate, missy. You're going to a military hospital I can trust not to try to kill you while you sleep."

She laid her head back on the seat and sighed, which started another short bout of hacking. "Fine." But she really was feeling better. All she wanted was toxin-free water to drink or a glass of refreshing lemonade would be awesome.

She noted he wasn't naked. "Where did you get the clothes?"

"Sheldon has your suitcases in the trunk. These are his."

She nodded and coughed. "Did you tell him about the warehouse?"

"Some," Bryon said. "Enough to get his men on the move."

Kari sprang forward on the seat. Saving the women being tortured by the traffic ring was more important than her dang cough. "Sheldon, how many men do you have here?" she asked.

"Half of the base I'm sending you both to," he replied. Another cough crept forward. She motioned for Bryon to tell Sheldon whatever else that needed to be relayed. If Sheldon's men would surround the facility, they could take care of the criminals and free the women. Sheldon pulled his phone from his pocket and made a call. She hoped it was to get more men there. There could never be enough men. She almost laughed at that. But it was no longer true for her. One man would be more than enough for her.

Her heart ached for those who'd already left the warehouse before she could help them. She remembered one of the girls shoved into the van as she was escorted to theirs in the warehouse. The woman with beautiful dark flowing hair and big eyes. There was something about her that drew Kari's attention. She could see any man wanting a female like that.

Meanwhile Bryon debriefed Sheldon on what had happened the past twenty or so hours. Was that it? It felt like days. But she did have one question that couldn't wait. "Sheldon, how did you find us in the castle?"

"Your tracker beacon suddenly popped up on the radar. We just followed it," he said.

She looked at her wrist. Some of the costume jewelry she donned with her earlier disguise remained. "Then why didn't you find us earlier?"

"We were underground," Bryon said. "Unfortunately, the bracelet's GPS doesn't work in places like that. As soon as we came out, they received the signal."

Not that it mattered, but she would've liked to have known that from the get-go. She slapped a hand on her forehead. God, she wanted to go home. Wanted to be in a deep

Jacuzzi with bubbling water floating around her. And Bryon on the other side of the tub in all his naked glory. Hmm. The things she wanted to do to that man.

"Hey," Sheldon said from the driver's seat, "keep that smell to yourself. We'll have none of those thoughts in a car with a guy who is still mate-less." He smiled at her with sad eyes in the rearview mirror. Her heart broke for him. She remembered how much he wanted a mate and family. He would make a great dad and husband to the right woman. She prayed he would find her soon.

She glanced at her mate. The past day had been incredible. She'd gone from being lonely to the happiest person in the world with a wonderful man. And his eyes shined with exactly what she was feeling: wanton desire.

The car slowed. "Saved by the airport," Sheldon mumbled. "Thank god we're here. I was going to step out if things got any smellier back there."

Bryon laughed. "Just you wait till you find yours. You'll see."

CHAPTER 33

—✦—

Bryon was glad when they pulled into the private airfield's driveway and parked around back in the passenger drop-off area. His mate needed medical attention and he'd make sure she got it.

As they got out of the car, a plane sat on the tarmac not too far away with its engines running. An attendant was in the process of closing the plane's door. With his mate he'd be on their own plane hopefully very soon. He was as tired as she was.

They went inside the small office building and heard a very angry person yelling at the man standing behind the counter. When the door closed behind their group of three, the screaming man turned to look at them. He snatched papers on the counter and marched out.

Sheldon shook hands with the man on the other side of the front desk. They seemed to know each other. That would make sense seeing that half of the closest military base had just flown in under Sheldon's authority. Bryon looked around for his mate not by his side.

She stared out the window, watching the attendant roll away the mobile stair unit that was attached to the leaving plane's door. In the driveway outside, a white van with a business logo drove past. Seeing she was safe, he turned back to the conversation between Sheldon and the company's employee.

Suddenly, Kari spun around and pointed to the van waiting to pull onto the street. "Where are the people who were in that van?" she hollered. He and the other two men looked where she pointed.

The employee said, "The man who was yelling when you come in. We have problem with plane and delay a couple hours. He's pissed we not give money back."

"What about the people who were in the van?" she stammered. "Where are they?"

He nodded at the plane rolling away from the loading tarmac. "They all in plane. Mostly ladies. Two males."

His mate ran toward him but she looked at Sheldon with panic and fear in her eyes. "Give me the car key."

He fumbled around, shocked by her sudden demand. "What? Why?" Sheldon pulled the key from his pocket and she snatched it from his hand.

"I'll explain later."

He called after her as she ran for the door. "Be careful. It's a rental."

Bryon watched the door close then turned to Sheldon. "Is she getting the suitcases out?" He ran for the door. "She doesn't need to do that. I will."

Rushing through the entrance, the men were outside to see the rental car speeding away . . . after the plane. Bryon slid his hands into his pockets. "Did I mention she might be crazy?"

A couple of employees came running out of the plane's storage building and the office, staring at the car now cutting across the first landing strip. They were as speechless as he was. Bryon slapped his partner on the chest and headed for the employees. He yelled out if anyone had keys to the company truck sitting in the parking lot. One of the men hurried over, pulling a fob from his pocket, and pointed at a vehicle. They jumped in the truck and took off after his mate.

The man asked what was going on. He and Sheldon shrugged, though he had his suspicions. They watched as she rolled through the median between landing strips. A small ditch ran down the middle of the grassy area. Did she see it? The front end of the rental car dipped and slammed up the other side. The front bumper came off and spun to the side. That would be a *No, she didn't see it*. Sheldon groaned.

The plane slowed on the back taxiway, making the turn onto the runway for takeoff.

The employee driving the truck wore a headset with voices screaming through the ear speakers. Bryon plucked them from the man's head and slid them on his. The microphone extended around from the side to lock in place at his mouth.

"Listen up, boys. This is Agent Bryon Day with the United States government." That shut up everyone on the line. "We have a situation we need your assistance with. There is an escaped crazy woman driving the car that just stopped in the middle of the back airstrip. She is armed and very dangerous. I suggest you do whatever she says."

Sheldon slapped his arm and whispered, "What are you doing?" Bryon waved him off.

"We have the situation under control. Do not approach her. Stay far away from her. I repeat, stay far away from her. Do you copy, tower?" Bryon finished.

"Copy, Agent Day. We will inform the pilots as soon as they contact us that they are ready." That was strange, they should've done that when leaving the tarmac.

"You mean the pilots haven't confirmed already?" Bryon asked.

"That is correct, Agent. I'm sure they will respond any second now." The controller's voice didn't sound too positive. More worried. He realized why when he glanced at the runway and plane. Kari had stopped the car sideways in the middle of the strip the jet stopped at. Why did she not want the plane taking off?

The plane rolled forward. Oh, fuck. The pilots couldn't be serious. They'd damage more than just the landing gear if they tried to run her over. His mate had her heart set on something. He knew Kari was strong of heart and will. She wasn't moving an inch until the wrong she perceived was righted.

His bet was that plane was loaded with females who had been purchased at the sale in the back of the warehouse. How she knew that, he'd ask later.

The plane continued forward. He was relieved she was safely inside the car at least. The jet would have to go through the car to get to her. The car door opened. What the hell was she doing now? Hopefully getting away.

To his unbelieving eyes, she got out of the car then stepped on the back bumper and hoisted herself onto the trunk. Said bumper now sagged on one side. Sheldon moaned again. From the back part of the car, she climbed onto the roof and put her hands on her hips. She stuck out her one arm, turning the palm toward the plane. Dear god, if she thought that would stop them taking off . . . Sheldon groaned again.

The plane wasn't slowing; she wasn't budging. This would not turn out good for one of the parties. He urged the truck's driver faster. As soon as they were in reach her, he'd yank her gorgeous ass off the roof and spank her. Naughty visions flashed in his head. Oh, the fun they would have when they got home. Wanting to focus on his mate surviving, Bryon closed down the images.

Still not moving fast enough, Bryon moved his leg to the side and stepped on the driver's foot on the gas pedal. The vehicle jerked forward. Their driver's eyes grew huge and his hands wrapped tightly around the steering wheel while he yelled at Bryon. Some of those words Bryon had never heard before.

They had to reach Kari before the plane did. Just in case the pilots were stupid enough to plow into her. The thought of losing her sent his wolf into a panic. It jumped forward wanting to break free and run to her. Bryon reminded it the truck would be there by the time they shifted and got out. It didn't like that answer, but would abide by it for now.

The jet kept coming. What the fuck were they thinking? Their vehicle nosed into the ditch and popped up on the other side. Almost there. No one was backing down. Goddammit, Kari. She was getting it from him for scaring the shit out of him. What "it" was he'd decide later.

They raced the jet toward the car parked on the strip. He prayed one of them would bail. Now would be better than later. The jet's speed had reached the point where it couldn't slow in time. Shit! How would he save her?

The company truck hit the concrete the same time the jet slammed on its breaks. Loud peals of screeching filled the air as smoke from the jet's and truck's tires floated close to the ground from their skids. Long black marks marred the pale strip.

The plane stopped within a foot of Kari's outstretched hand. He'd be damned; she pulled it off. She had freaking superpowers. She was in so much trouble.

He jumped out of the truck with Sheldon. Through the headset, he heard the tower trying to reach the pilots, but they were not responding still. Running toward his mate, he glanced at the cockpit. A man stood between the pilots, pistol in his hand. That would be the reason the pilots weren't responding to the tower's requests. The gunman looked familiar. Bryon thought he might've seen him in the cave earlier.

The three in the cockpit seemed to be arguing, the guy with the gun waving it around. One of the pilots gesturing out the windshield at Kari on the car's hood. He must have been the reason the plane hadn't stopped, not his mate's superpowers. Thank god for small miracles.

They reached the car together and Bryon reached for Kari. Sheldon held his arms out to his side, eyes scanning the damaged vehicle his mate stood on. "The car is a wreck. The boss won't be happy."

"What?" Kari said. "It's a rental. You got the insurance, right? Never mind. I need your gun."

"What? No way—" Sheldon stepped back from her reaching hand.

"Sheldon," she yelled over the jet's slowing engines, "there are twenty women and children on this plane who will be sold into slavery and sex crimes if this jet leaves this airport. I'm not allowing that to happen. Now give me your gun."

Without further argument, Sheldon lifted his gun to her hand. She turned toward the pilots, weapon aimed at them. She fired four shots, breaching the windshields, making the plane too dangerous to fly. It wasn't taking off any time soon. When the pilots peeped over the dashboard, she pointed to the loading area and building. They had no options. They had to go back. The guy with the weapon was gone.

Pride soared through Bryon at what his mate had done. She had put her own life in danger to save complete strangers from a horrible existence. Her heart was as big as any he'd ever seen. And she belonged to him.

CHAPTER 34

Kari stood on the roof of the rented vehicle staring down the plane stopped in front of her. Any normal person would've passed out from fear. Shit. She should've been rolling on the ground—her knees being too weak to hold her up.

But she wasn't.

Her body was fueled with energy. She felt incredibly strong, righteousness giving her courage, but also stealing her common sense to not stand in front of a jet rolling down a runway.

Really, though, the jet would stop. No way could it take off after smashing into a car. The front landing gear would be torn to shit. The pilots knew this and, she had no doubt, they would back off. This game of chicken was over before it began.

The hijacker didn't know she had been called the Chick-enator by the kids on her block while growing up.

One of the older boys used to bully the younger kids on her street. On a cold day before she turned twelve, she stood with her bike at the end of the block. Billy the Bully was picking on her next-door neighbor kid. She yelled at him to leave the kid alone. Billy's head snapped around to see who had called him out.

"Well, if it isn't Scary Kari, scaring everyone with her fat, ugly face." Billy sneered then laughed. She'd had as much as she could take of the bastard. She got on her bike and pedaled toward him. She was going to show him she wasn't scared of him anymore.

Billy picked up his bike lying in the neighbor's yard and pedaled directly in her path. "You wanna play chicken, Scary Kari? Let's rumble." Their eyes met and locked. Neither giving an inch. She figured the worst that could happen was they crashed into each other and got bumps and bruises. She could live with that to make Billy leave them alone.

Kari hunkered down over the handlebars, her new aerodynamic helmet strapped on tightly. Seconds before they crashed, she saw the fear in his eyes. Someone was standing up to him, not cowering in a corner. She'd let him have it.

A moment too late, Billy turned his front wheel to the side and she crashed head-on into him. Her helmet slammed against his forehead, effectively knocking him out cold. Her bike bucked, throwing the rest of her body over the bikes and rider in front of her. She landed on her butt on the other side of the collision.

Her neighbor kid ran to her, mouth gaping, eyes as wide as basketballs. "Oh my god, Kari. You killed Billy."

The boy bled from the nose and his cheek had a scratch. She saw his shirt move up and down; that was a relief. "No," she said. "I just knocked him out."

The kid stared between her and the bully lying on a bent bicycle as if watching a tennis match. "Wow. That was awesome. You weren't scared of him. You're the Chickenator. You ate him up and spit him out. I gotta tell everyone." Well, she was afraid, but she contained that fear and did what she had to do to protect those she cared for.

And she'd do the same here, except it was her versus a jet.

As it turned out, Billy had a broken arm and wasn't

allowed to ride his banged-up bike anymore. So unless he walked, he wouldn't be coming down their street much. And Billy wasn't much for walking or anything else that required a bit of exertion.

Her biggest hurt came when she tripped over the curb and skinned her knees. She was used to that, so no biggie.

Now she stood on top of a car instead of bicycle telling the bully where to go—back to the garages. Once she put four bullets into the windshield, the pilots were happy to accommodate her signal to go back. This plane was not taking off.

As the plane started moving in the right direction, she was yanked off the hood of the car, the gun taken from her hand. "What the hell do you think you're doing?" Bryon hollered.

Sheldon joined in his love in shouting at her. "Shooting at a plane is a federal offense, you know."

"Good thing we're in Cloustien, then," she replied as Bryon held her in his arms. Sheldon harrumphed and got into the rental. As he slid into the front seat, his knees slammed into the steering column.

"Careful, I moved the seat up. I got short legs," she said.

Sheldon looked to grumble under his breath, but she heard every word. A thought hit her. "Bryon, when you bit me, you said it was to claim me as yours forever." He nodded and kissed her head.

"Yes, and now I'm going to kill you for that stunt," he said.

She rolled her eyes. "Yeah, yeah, but listen. Did your bite do more than just claim me?" she asked.

His brows rose high. "You're gonna blame me for you suddenly going crazy and facing down a plane?"

She huffed. "No. Let's get back to the tarmac and arrest these guys." Riding back to the main building, she thought about the sudden and dramatic change in her thoughts, trust in herself, and physical prowess. Not only had Bryon made her his mate, but he had also enabled to her to be a better person inside and out. She wondered if she'd be able to shift. She'd have to ask when they were alone.

The plane came to a stop in the same place it was when she and the guys had arrived. The man driving the company truck they were in parked next to the metal building housing the jets. Bryon put his hand over an ear with the headphone, pressing the speaker closer to his head.

"Damn. Not good," he said.

"What?" The plane had powered down and they were rolling the portable stairs to the door. What could possibly go wrong? They had them.

"I was afraid of this," he said. "The man on board is threatening to kill the women if they don't get another jet for takeoff."

"What?" She wanted to kick herself. Why hadn't she thought of that before? Duh. Must be the lack of water, food, the vomiting, battling a demon, solving puzzles to save their lives, and turning into a superhuman that made her a little tired.

She dropped her head into her hands and groaned. This wasn't how it played out in the movie she had made in her head. It was supposed to be an HEA—happily ever after—ending. The bad guys would be arrested, the hostages set free, and the heroine got the guy.

Sheldon knocked on the passenger-side window of the truck, scaring the bejesus out of her. By the frown on his face, he'd heard the news, too. Bryon opened the door.

"You heard," her mate asked.

"Yeah, one of the managers told me he was to prep the other plane. They are giving in to the traffickers' demands."

"No!" she cried. "They can't do that. Don't they see these women are in danger already?"

"I doubt they know anything about the crime ring," Sheldon answered. "By the casualness of the employee who told us they were on the plane, it seems like it might be a normal thing to have a lot of women fly out together."

Her heart squeezed. So many more women and children were out there, praying to be found and released. Or simply wanting to die to end their misery. Bryon put an arm around her and scooted her closer to him.

"Hey, now. You've done all you can to help these people. I haven't heard from the military commander yet, but they should have the warehouse surrounded and be arresting the men involved. You've saved hundreds there alone."

She glanced up from her hands. "*We* saved them. I never would've gotten through that damn wall if you hadn't yanked me out. By the way, with all the walking and lack of food, I think I've dropped ten pounds."

"That's okay. We'll get those back on you in no time and I can pound, suck, and lick, every inch of you."

That sounded great to her. They needed to get home ASAP.

"Okay, guys." Sheldon still stood outside the truck. "It's getting a little too mushy for me. We still have a problem to take care of before you two go off and mate like rabbits." Sheldon sighed. "We don't need twenty dead women on our hands."

While she talked naughty with her new lover, her brain churned in the background. Now she trusted herself to come up with solutions that didn't have numbers involved. She let herself relax and let both sides of her brain mesh and do their thing. If she could've done this in the water trap and the rocks, maybe they would've gotten out of it much sooner.

"No, we don't need any dead people," she said. "Sheldon, what color is your wolf?"

"I'm solid black. Why?"

"I have a plan."

CHAPTER 35

B ryon knew his mate was a fucking genius, and maybe a bit crazy, but this was a great plan. As long as he and Sheldon didn't mess it up. So many things could go wrong. The private airport crew worked feverishly to ready another plane for the traffickers and their booty. All he and Sheldon had to do was lie around and look pretty.

Well, as pretty as a wolf can be with vibrant colored scarves tied in bows around his neck, feet, and tail. He was so glad no one else would ever see him like this. His wolf was not happy at the moment.

He lay in the plane's aisle between the cockpit and main compartment, waiting for the action to start. Sheldon was hidden in the back of the plane in a dark kitchenette area next to the toilet.

He heard someone coming up the stairs to the plane's front entrance. Male, by the smell. With a gun. Fuck. One of the traffickers. The guy who stepped in was dressed in an expensive suit. He must've bathed in exotic cologne. It was strong enough to make a wolf gag. The guy looked down at him.

"There's a fucking dog in here. Fucking hell?" Americans? These fuckers were from the same country he was. His wolf wanted to jump up and tear out the bastard's throat. Bryon had to remind it that the opportunity for that was coming later.

The pilot turned. "He belongs to me. He's trained. You won't even know he's here." Bryon gave the man his best puppy-dog eyes and wagged his bow-covered tail. Humans were suckers for it.

"Yeah, fine. He doesn't look dangerous. Kinda cute, if not for the damn bows and shit."

A voice outside the plane piped up. "What the fuck is going on up there, Heady? Is the plane secure or not?"

He hollered out the door. "Give me a second to check the back."

This was the do-or-die moment. If this guy, Heady, saw Sheldon hiding in the back, they were done for. They'd left the lavatory door open with the light on to distract the bad guy from the dark kitchen area. Bryon held his breath. Please let this work. Please let this work. Please—

The man glanced in the lav, slammed the door shut, and his eyes skimmed the area above Sheldon's body, not looking down over the countertops. Thank the gods for little miracles. The guy then turned and headed up the aisle. He yelled out the door, "All's clear. Get them up here." Feet clomped closer to him.

For the plan to work, one of the men needed to stand in the back of the plane, preferably with his back facing the lav so Sheldon could jump out and take him down. But the man stood up front shoving the women and kids down the aisle.

"All the way to the back," he said. Person after person he pushed, treating them as if animals. Smacking some of them on the head and face.

A small voice came from the back. "Mr. Heady, the bathroom door won't open."

"Sit down, kid. You can hold it," he growled.

"Please, Mr. Heady. I don't want to make a mess in the plane." The man grumbled about damn kids and smelling piss and shit all the way back to the States.

"For Christ's sake, kid. Hold on." He cut into the line of females taking their seats, pushing them aside. This could be it. He would be at the back of the plane for Sheldon's wolf to take down. But the man held his gun. If it went off when Sheldon tackled him, someone could get hurt. The kid moved back into the dark area for Heady to get to the door. Oh shit. Now Sheldon was blocked in. He wouldn't dare hurt the kid. He'd wait for another time. And the last of the passengers were coming up the stairs.

The narrow lavatory door in the back opened. Heady turned toward the front and the girl stepped inside and closed the door. A black flash zipped down the aisle and the man was on the ground, Sheldon's wolf teeth firmly clenched around the guy's neck. With a quick twist of his muzzle, the man's neck snapped and he stopped fighting. Not that he got started, it all went so quickly.

Some of the women squealed and fell into the closest seats to partially hide, but no one screamed. A woman with flowing dark hair and big eyes stepped into the aisle, hushing everyone. Bryon could tell right away that this woman was of strong heart and soul. She wasn't a victim.

Sheldon gripped dead Heady's pant leg and tried to drag him back. Needless to say, teeth were not the best choice for that task, continuously sliding off. The woman in the aisle lifted the other leg and muscled her way to the dark posterior of the plane. The first phase of the plan was completed. His part was next.

The second guy of the twosome was backing up the steps, holding a female in front of him as a shield. Fucking coward, no better than chicken shit on the bottom of a shoe. But that did put a crimp in his plan of attack. The girl the bastard held on to could get seriously hurt. The man stepped back onto the carpeted flooring. He pushed the girl away and leaned forward to grab the door.

Bryon launched himself at the human and latched on.

They slammed into the door, knocking it open, and they tumbled down the steep stairs. He would probably regret this in the morning when he tried to get out of bed. He was getting too old for this kind of shit. Young ones were supposed to do the physical crap.

His wolf and the bad guy landed on the ground with a *thud*. In a flash, he was on his four feet, jaws stretched tightly around the trafficker's scrawny neck. Military men from Sheldon's group came out from behind parked cars and the office door, guns at the ready. A male and female ran up the steps into the plane. Good. In no time, the man was cuffed and dragged off. He hoped they locked up this guy for the rest of his life.

His nose caught a whiff of his only love. She was close. "Bryon." She wrapped her arms around his furry neck. "I about freaked out when the guy held the girl going up the stairs. I was sure you wouldn't be able to jump him." She pulled back and ruffled the spot between his ears. That felt so fucking good. "I have your clothes over here." He followed the gorgeous woman, watching her glorious wiggle with each step. He couldn't wait to be pounding into her. He had to push those thoughts to the back of his mind. Morphing with a hard-on wasn't appreciated by others.

"Where is Sheldon? Why hasn't he come off the plane yet?" Kari asked. That was a good question. Where was he? He shifted and quickly donned pants then his shirt. He wanted to check on his co-agent. Make sure he was okay.

Sheldon appeared at the top of the stairs. He held the beautiful lady that had helped him drag the dead body down the aisle. Sheldon and the woman slowly descended. Surprisingly, he didn't trip; he didn't take his eyes from her for one second. What the hell?

Bryon took his mate's hand and hurried toward the two. Sheldon stopped and gently lowered the woman to her feet. He wrapped an arm around her dainty shoulders. "Bryon, Kari, meet Elna. She's my mate."

EPILOGUE

━━━✂━━━

Kari set down her mug of cocoa on the silver tray on the side of the Jacuzzi she and Bryon sat in. Sweet-smelling bubbles foamed around them. Their view from the tub was atop a mountain, overlooking a majestic valley covered in glistening white.

She leaned back, placing her hand over her belly. She might not be showing yet, considering she was already on the plus side and her belly had had a curve even before she'd become pregnant. But soon, there would be no mistaking her for anything other than a woman with a baby in her womb. Their little one was growing inside her and she couldn't wait to meet him. From what Bryon said it was a boy and he was walking around like a proud father. It was so stinking cute.

Outside their rental cabin, the storm blew another foot of snow against the front door. She was fine with that. That meant no one would be disturbing them for at least a day. This was day three of their ten-day getaway. Her first real vacation and her boss joked for her not to make a habit of it. She would miss that place a little. But she liked the new contract she had worked out with the FBI.

When she was needed to decode, she would come in or they would come to her. If the situation arose, she and her ex-ALFA mate would go undercover to get the intel. But they aimed to keep those types of operations as limited as possible. She had better things to do with her new mate.

Bryon looked at his phone. It was time for their scheduled call with Director Tumbel from ALFA. Usually, she'd frown at mixing work and pleasure, but since it was planned beforehand, she was fine with it.

At the sound of Indiana Jones's main theme song, he swiped across the screen. "Director Tumbel, how are you this evening?" Bryon asked.

"Probably not as good as you are," Tumbel replied.

Bryon took her hand. "You got that right, sir."

"So let's make this quick, you two." They heard papers shuffle on the director's side. "According to workers in Cloustien, Prince Goddard specifically said where he wanted his palace and the warehouse placed. They found fifty-year-old subterranean maps in the palace. Along with an incomplete map of the underground tunnel system."

"Hi, Director, it's Kari. What did they find out about the art in the palace?"

"You're going to love this," he said. "Most of the items were treasures that had been missing or stolen from the time of the Second World War."

Kari smiled. "I knew that had to be the case. Everything there was just too over-the-top to be in one place, and a personal home at that."

"And the cave entrance where the trafficking ring set up was the room the Nazis kept the stash," the director added. "The story from some oma who 'knows' the history said one of the ancestor kings was digging area mines for precious stones and they came upon the cavern by accident."

"If that's the case," Kari started, "then that was Alheim who found it. He probably put the building there, eventually becoming the warehouse, to cover it and sneak out the treasure little by little."

"Then after that," Bryon said, "it made the perfect spot

to smuggle traffickers in and out. All under everyone's noses."

Tumbel said, "There is a group of international artwork people working on returning pieces to the rightful owners. Those alive, anyway. I bet most of the stuff will be going to museums around Europe."

"Director," Kari said, "did anyone find out about the room with the dried fruits and food?"

"That was actually the first mystery we solved. The townsfolk gladly provided the answer," Tumbel replied. "They knew about the trafficking for a while, but wouldn't do anything against their royalty. So when they could, they rescued women and hid them in the tunnels until it was safe for them to leave. Seems everyone knew about it except the prince."

"What's happening prosecution-wise for those traffickers caught in the warehouse cavern?" Bryon asked.

"Liechtenstein, the country, is taking over the extradition process. I believe someone told me the monarch of Liechtenstein was a distant cousin or some relation to the 'missing' Prince Goddard. I'm sure we'll hear about many of the trials in the news. You two did a great thing for the world."

"Nah," Kari said, "just doing our jobs."

Tumbel found that extraordinarily funny by the laugh coming through the phone's speaker. It was sort of funny since what she did wasn't close to her "girlfriend" job description.

"Have you heard from Sheldon or Elna recently?" Tumbel asked them.

"Not a word," Bryon said. "I'm sure they are enjoying their private island beach as much as we are our cabin escape."

Tumbel sighed. "I'm sure they are, too. Can't wait for my turn to find my mate."

"Gotta get out of the office sometime, Tumbel. Unless your mate is a pizza delivery person, you aren't going to meet her there."

"Yeah, I hear you. I have to wait for you two clowns to get back before anything can happen. We have a whole new group that needs to be trained. Oh, one more thing since I've got you. ALFA will be getting a plaque in the new National Intelligence Building for so many years of service blah, blah, blah."

"Really?" Bryon questioned. "But we're a secret organization."

"The group isn't really that much of a secret around here. All the bigwigs know we exist. The secret is about the agents who work here. On paper, we look like a normal intelligence-gathering agency. The point is you and Kari need to be at the dedication ceremony. Be ready to dress up."

"Whatever you say, boss man," Bryon said. He was ready to get the call over with so he could get back to loving his mate.

"Well, gotta go," Director Tumbel said. "Stuff to do before heading home. See you when you're back. And, Kari, you guys give some thought to you training and joining us. I'd hate to lose Bryon because I didn't try to sweet-talk his mate."

"Yeah, yeah, we got it. See ya later, boss." Bryon tapped the end call button on the phone.

"Speaking of things to do," he said, his eyes filling with desire, "I have a little mate that needs some doing."

Kari laughed. "So you're going to *do* me?"

"Damn straight, I am." He stood and stepped out of the tub. "How else am I going to get started practicing for baby number two?"

She shook her head, giggling. "Maybe we should let the first one be born?"

"No way! We have to be ready. And I'm going to love seeing how many ways I can get you to moan and scream. Just you sit back, relax, and enjoy the show." He lifted her from the bubbly water.

"I hope it's better than the first show you gave. That one was hot, but you were a little out of it being drugged and all." He took a towel from the warming rack and wrapped it around her body, then took a second one and dabbed at her hair.

"Oh, don't you worry. I've seen a TV commercial for a group of Aussie guys who know a thing or two about entertaining women. I'm taking lessons. My first show is tonight in the other room. I got front-row seats for you."

"I love the sound of that."

FEARLESS
MATING

CHAPTER 1

Josh Tumbel, director for the Alpha League of Federal Agents, had finally found his mate. She sat in front of his desk, talking about something. Her luscious lips were moving and her bedroom eyes were fixed on him. And god, how he wished he had her in his bedroom. Naked and begging him to take her. It didn't seem likely at the moment, though. Not with the frown on her face.

She introduced herself as Sergeant, or was it Lieutenant? Maybe Major? Candace Obermier. He'd call her Candy. He wondered how many licks it would take to get to her creamy center.

Her beautiful eyes narrowed and her scrumptious mouth puckered. Ah, fuck. She'd stopped talking. Hopefully, she hadn't said anything important.

Her brow raised. "Director Tumbel, did you hear a word I said."

"Of course," he lied. "Every word."

"And you have no comment?" she asked with a sniff.

Fuck. He'd never expected to make an ass of himself in front of his mate. That had been a long-standing fear of his. He'd find the one, then chase her off with his caveman mentality. His mama had taught him well. He knew all the mistakes shifter men made and how to avoid them. But would he? Obviously not.

"I'm sorry, Major—" he started.

"Sergeant Major," she corrected, her gorgeous lips pressing into a tight line.

Well, shit. He just called her a rank four levels lower. She was not happy with him. The military took their rank and file so seriously.

"Sergeant Major, I apologize. I was a bit preoccupied . . ." *fantasizing about licking you all over*, "and missed your last remark."

"I said," she repeated with a soft growl, "I am shutting down your department."

That certainly got his attention. How could she possibly shut them down? They were specifically commissioned by the National Intelligence Board to do dangerous assignments that would kill any normal human. Was it possible she didn't know they were "special"? Looks were deceiving. Should he tell her? No. That was above his pay grade.

Calmly, patiently, he knitted his fingers together and laid his hands on his desk. "Sergeant Major Obermier," he breathed out, "my group has been in operation for many, many years. Longer than most other organizations in DC—"

"I am aware of that, Director Tumbel—"

"Please, call me Josh." He flashed her his white smile with perfect teeth. He'd spent his entire teenage years wearing braces and stupid retainers, so the damn things had better be nothing less than flawless.

By her frown, he could tell that apparently, looking impeccable didn't mean shit to her. Which was good in its own way. He didn't want a mate stuck on superficial, material qualities. But then again, how was he to woo her if she didn't like things easily bought? If he'd have to rely on his own self and personality, he was screwed.

"Director Tumbel," she continued, her voice containing a bite of impatience, "let me explain something to you. This new president and his administration are all about cleaning up the quagmire DC has become. That means cutting some serious budget. Not just a couple million by changing office supply companies but hundreds of millions. It is my job to figure out where the slack is and tighten it up."

Slack? His group was thought of as slack? Had she any clue who they were? "Sergeant Major Obermier, do you know what we do here in ALFA?" he asked.

She opened a file on her lap. "I do." She paused then continued. "You destroyed a one-of-a-kind viral specimen that now is extinct to the world."

He opened his mouth to explain, but she raised a finger, cutting him off.

"You nearly incited a mafia war in one of the largest tourist destinations in the world that could have killed hundreds if not thousands of innocent civilians," she said. He could explain that one, too, if her scathing look didn't say *keep your mouth shut*. "And last, but not least, one of your agents was captured after almost a year undercover," she finished. He couldn't say much to that, except the investigation did end up closing down the biggest human trafficking ring in Europe.

"Oh, wait," she added, "one more thing. You called in an unqualified agent to assist in an international cover-up."

What the fuck? That was going too far. "I don't know what you're talking about." Then again, maybe he did.

Her brows raised again. "A field-inexperienced FBI agent was sent overseas for an undercover operation. How many wrongs is that, Tumbel? First off, everyone knows only CIA deals with international issues. Secondly, sending an untrained female—"

Getting more than a little pissed with his mate, he interjected, "Agent Tomlin was a highly skilled agent—"

"In doing crossword puzzles." Obermier's voice rose, followed by her body. She leaned over his desk. "She was a decoder, for god's sake. She plays with words all day."

He rose from his desk, bending over to meet her across the desktop. "And she's damn good at it. We would be at war with Russia, right now, if not for her." He smelled her sweet breath just inches from him. She must have had a piece of candy in her mouth. Fuck, he couldn't wait to have a piece of Candy in his mouth. His pants were shrinking in the crotch area. Trust the animal in him to see the bickering between them as foreplay.

He could launch over the desk this instant and take her on the floor if she'd only give him a sign. Fucking hell, there it was. The ambrosial scent of her arousal. His knees weakened. Thank goodness he was leaning on the desk or he would've collapsed to the floor. He inhaled deeply, taking in all he could.

His rebel-roused emotions settled along with the angry thumping of his heart. She wanted him as much as he wanted her. He had started to wonder if his wolf was wrong about her being their mate. No doubts now.

She glanced at the watch on her delicate arm. How had he never realized that wrists could be so sexy? "I'm sorry to have bothered you so late at night, Director Tumbel," she said.

"I'm going to the ALFA dedication in thirty minutes." *This is ironic*, he thought. "A dedication ceremony honoring my group and all they've contributed to America's safety in the past years. Isn't that strange?" he asked. "Dedicating a plaque to an organization you want to shut down."

One side of her lips curled up. "The ceremony was commissioned by the previous president, not the current one." She straightened up and crossed her arms. "Will all your men be in attendance tonight?" she asked.

"Yes." Finally, he'd have everyone together again. Each of the guys had recently found his mate and had been on paid leave. Now they were all about to take permanent vacations if this woman had her way.

"Good," Obermier collected her briefcase. "Tell them tonight at the reception not to come in Monday morning. We'll have their personal effects in a box outside the door by noon." She hurried to the office door. "Goodnight, Director Tumbel."

And she was gone from his life, just like that. How the hell had he lost control of the situation so quickly?

CHAPTER 2

Candy parked her car on the third floor of the garage to the National Intelligence Building where she worked. Shit, she had needed to get out of Tumbel's office fast. Never in her life had her body reacted to a man the way it had to his. And he was fully dressed and not even clean shaven. But those eyes. That face. Lord have mercy.

He was fucking gorgeous. Drop-dead-with-a-side-of-beard-and-bedroom-eyes-that-made-her-knees-weak gorgeous. Her body shuddered. She needed to get a hold of herself. He was just a dumb male. Stupid, pain-in-the-ass, piece of shit like all of them. Bitter much? She snorted to herself. She definitely had a reason to feel that way with all she'd been through in her life.

Looking up as she exited the garage, she saw the helicopter sitting on the rooftop pad of the National Intelligence Building. That meant the NIA director was already there for the ceremony even though it didn't start for an hour. Maybe he was working late, too. That would be a first. Damn, she needed to shake off this negativity. She wasn't usually like this.

It was this damn assignment she'd been given. She was responsible for researching and digging into the workings of each department to find their mistakes, cover ups, and secrets. Then anyone deemed less than perfect, she had to inform they were out of a job. Even if the organization was well run like this ALFA group she just visited. A few issues could shut them down.

In the alleyway between the parking garage and building, she saw the catering truck for the ceremony being inspected by two of her four men in outside security. Even though this event was quite low on the terrorist-attack priority list, she insisted everything be checked before strangers were let in.

This habit was a throwback to her time in the field. She'd spent years in Afghanistan and other sandy countries fighting to keep this country's freedom so those who wanted to complain, protest, and burn the flag could have their opportunity. Land of the free and home of the brave. Got that damn right.

She never regretted her choice of joining the military at eighteen. Running away and enlisting probably saved her life. Candy just wished her mother had had a choice. In a handful of years, she would be able to retire with full benefits after twenty years of putting up with sexual harassment, bullying, and men's shit in general. She felt like she was going on sixty instead of thirty-eight.

She shook her head, wanting this slow building anger and resentment to go away. This was how it was lately. She was losing the last shreds of patience necessary to deal with her line of work. Who pissed in her Cheerios this morning? Speaking of food, that was one good thing about the event tonight. There would be munchies and drinks. No alcoholic beverages, her order, but punch and tea were acceptable. She was not babysitting a bunch of drunks on the job this evening. Her job was to make sure security was staffed and ready to go.

This was her building. She knew it inside and out. Every door, every hall, every hidden passage. Built in the 1950s along with many other structures in DC after World War II, the building design was simple and a pain in the ass to update with technology. Made mostly of concrete, each floor had to be drilled through to run new wires and pipes. Replacing the old sprinkler system a few years ago nearly brought down the lobby ceiling. That was fun. They had to reinforce the wide expanse with I beams and supports.

But despite that, the building was solid as a rock. The windows were fitted with electromagnetic shields so inside communications couldn't be intercepted outside, and the halls were somewhat of a zigzag maze to cut off any radio transmissions within. She'd miss this place when they moved into their new offices currently under construction.

She was proud of her contribution to the new NIA building. Because of her efforts in security, the new facility would have its own power plant, phone/Wi-Fi system, and police force to handle situations with classified information. She laughed when she found out the place wouldn't have an address, but did have its own zip code. How silly was that? It wasn't like they were hiding where they were. Shit, Google had the building on their maps. When it came to the government, who knew what all they would do.

After entering the front doors, she used her badge to bypass the metal detectors, also a retrofit, but before her time. As she walked toward the back of the lobby, Candy had to weave around tables and chairs set up for the show. New plants had been brought in to attempt to warm the harsh concrete walls. Nice try, but they'd need a jungle for that to happen.

She passed the elevators on both sides of the aisle, then the stairwell that led from the roof to the tunnels connecting all of DC underground. Hurrying down a narrow, mostly hidden hallway at the far end of the building, Candy made her way to the security door and punched in the code to access the inside.

As the door opened, her men came to attention and saluted. She returned the salute. "At ease." Her eyes skimmed over the multitude of small monitor screens, each showing a different shot of the interior and exterior. "Did I miss anything good while I was out?"

Her group of guys were great to work with. They had a camaraderie rarely found in military circles. That was only because she allowed that to happen. Candy could chew someone a new asshole, if needed, but she would give her life to protect her men.

"No, Sergeant Major. Just folks decorating and the regulars coming and going. The caterers pulled up not too long ago," said Dotson, seated in front of the monitors.

"I saw our guys checking out the truck. Good job on making sure that happened, Dotson," she said.

"Thank you, ma'am."

She ran a tight, clean ship, even though the "ship" was practically the size of a broom closet. Another "make do with." When upgrading the security system, the old office had become too small to house everything required. So it was moved to the side of the elevators and stairs where a janitor's closet had been expanded to include the small office space behind it. The room had an exterior door and secret stairwell to the tunnels that the other didn't, so that was a perk.

"Nice and boring," she said. "Just how I like it." She lightly slapped her hand against Dotson's shoulder. "Carry on, Dotson. I'll be in my office until this damn thing starts. Call if something doesn't go as planned."

He smiled, stood, and saluted. "Yes, ma'am."

She saluted and walked out the thick metal door. With a sigh, she pushed on the door to the stairwell and climbed to the next floor. She could take the elevator, but what was the point? By the time she waited for it, she'd already be on the second floor and down the hall to the last office, hers.

She plopped into the chair behind her desk and pivoted to look out the back window. They were blessed with a park behind the building so she could watch owners walking their pets, and parents with their kids, playing. A cute little family happened to be on the grass. A small pain tinged her heart. She told herself, again, that she wasn't family or mom material. Her temper was well known. She was best on her own. Alone. It didn't matter that others had told her once she had a baby she'd fall in love. Not like she had anyone to have babies with anyway. Besides, her busy lifestyle allowed for her only to be single. Busy? Whatever.

The family in the park looked so happy, talking and laughing. And they had a wiener dog. How adorable. Now she was a puddle. She'd always wanted a dog, but her father had killed the stray she'd brought home as a child, and after that, she didn't have the heart.

Watching a dog being kicked and beaten to death had destroyed something inside her. She couldn't stand by and see that again. Even now that she lived alone, she couldn't think of getting a dog and watching the animal age and have to be put to sleep.

Candy popped to her feet, automatically pushing away memories of her past. She'd become good at doing that. And a little action on the front lines of the battlefield helped take her mind off home.

At the side window that looked over the alley separating the garage and building, she saw the caterers loading rolling carts with goodies. At least she wouldn't have to cook tonight. If you called spaghetti with hot dogs and a salad cooking.

She found her chair again, sat back and stared at the white sofa and gas fireplace opposite the side window. A crocheted blanket in the design of Old Glory draped over the sofa. With red and blue throw pillows, it looked like someone had barfed up patriotism all over the floor. The whole ensemble had been here when she'd taken the office, and she'd liked it, so she'd kept it.

And a fireplace in an office. Really? One time last winter, she turned it on to see if it worked. Lo and behold, it did. It was kind of nice to have a fire going when the wind chill was twenty below zero outside. She'd never had a fireplace at any place she'd lived. Surprising how homey it felt.

Candy slapped a hand on her desk and laughed at herself. Several minutes ago, she was feeling like the biggest bitch the world had ever seen and now she was mushy over burning wood. "Crazy" did come to mind, but that was silly. She was a soldier, and soldiers didn't have issues like that, no matter how bad the past had been.

CHAPTER 3

Josh chose to walk to the dedication ceremony instead of driving and having to find a place to park. He could've paid to keep his car in the garage, but he and his wolf loved being outside as much as they could. Which wasn't a lot in a sea of concrete.

Some days, cabin fever got so bad, he'd take the metro to the mall where all the statues and war tributes were and walked the path around the edges of the grass a few times. He'd already memorized the words on the Lincoln monument and watched the complete exterior remodel of the national obelisk. That was no short-term job.

But now, he had something to think about. Something that wholly engulfed his mind and soul. Candy Obermier, goddess. Hard to get, but a definite goddess. In his eyes, anyway.

He knew that once he got a chance to get to know her, he'd see more than the ice princess she tried to project. Didn't matter she was trying to shut down his organization. A quick discussion with the right people, namely the NIA director, and the issue would be moot. Hopefully. Then he could focus on taking his sweet to bed and get started counting the licks to her candy center.

The image of licking his way up her thighs and watching her squirm and moan made him tug on his collar. He hadn't been laid in too long. But first he had to get her to see him as more than some dick whose team was too expensive to keep on board. It would take all his patience to keep his beast leashed when she was around. After all, he wouldn't be getting into bed with anyone but his sweet Candy.

Shit, he slowed to shake his leg to reposition his hard-on. Good thing black pants were his normal attire. Otherwise, walking around with a hard-on would probably get him some strange looks. He hadn't had that problem for a long time. No woman had ever really appealed to him or his wolf. Sure, he'd had urges and dated a few times, but none of those women had made any impact on his animal. His manly needs were what got him to go out and meet women. From the moment he laid eyes on Candy, he knew there would be no other woman he'd want to see naked or watch squirm as he thrust balls deep into her sweet, sticky center.

That had him visualizing some really dirty shit. Him. Candy. Every position known to man and some he'd make up as he went along. When she finally gave him the chance, he'd get her screaming in seconds. Fuck! His body shuddered. He looked around to see if anybody saw. For being after-hours, too many fucking people were out and about. Though that was the norm here. Guys were always running the sidewalks, shirts off, trying to impress women.

Yeah, he looked like they did, but didn't care to attract attention to himself. He favored lying low and being ready for the attack. Surprises were a wonderful thing—when it was him doing the surprising. Come to think of it, Candy was making him think of doing some covert work to figure her out.

Damn. He should get something to surprise Candy with. Would she like flowers? Hell no. She seemed the type to chew 'em up and spit 'em out. The thought did something to the animal in him. It made him think of what an amazing alpha she would have been as a shifter. But she was human. His little sweet tart was all human.

Maybe chocolate. He thought for a second. Most women loved chocolate or cake or something. What about strawberries and champagne? Too personal. Besides, that was something that spoke sex and as much as he wanted to get her naked, he didn't want her to freak out. He'd save the surprise for their first time together. He had to think about something else before people wondered if he'd taken a damn blue pill and been left by his female without getting his rocks off.

So, Candy wanted to close his office. Director Pommer would be at the dedication tonight, so they could speak briefly and clear it up. Pommer was one of a few in intelligence who knew about shifters. Certainly, he could influence the president if need be. Maybe not this current president; he was a bucking bronco, fearless of others.

He needed to come up with a way to prove to her that his department was important despite some of the mess-ups they had. The destruction of the virus Candy had mentioned had been for the sake of mankind's continued existence on the planet. And the mafia incident, that ended with the city and "the family" working together to make a better place. And yeah, Agent Day was captured, and they brought in an FBI operative instead of a CIA person. But the special intelligence the FBI agent had provided had saved their lives and helped take down a human trafficking ring.

So whether Candy saw it or not, his team was fucking amazing and no humans out there could have done what they had. Try putting a human in place of his guys. They would be dead in a heartbeat. But he had to remind himself that she didn't know they were shifters with abilities beyond humans'. Fuck! Should he just tell her? She was his mate. He'd have to tell her eventually. Would she freak out? He would be breaking his oath to secrecy. He'd play it by ear.

He looked at the cars parked in the garage next to the NIA building. Fancy cars decorated the bottom floor.

Reserved spots for those in power who were seldom there to use them. Always so much going on, never enough time to go to the office.

A nice-looking family with a dachshund walked toward him on the sidewalk. They appeared so vibrant and cheerful. That was what he wanted with his mate. Candy would make him happy just by standing next to him. Or lying under him. No, not going there. Too fucking late for that.

The dog on the leash sniffed, looked him in the eye, and slowed. A near-silent growl came from the adorable mongrel. The child holding the leash picked up the dog. She was gentle and loving, not reprimanding or yelling at the dog. Well-trained dog and child. He wanted that, too, a pack of well-disciplined pups. And a big pack. He was confident Candy would have no problem with the discipline part. That thought brought a smile to his lips. Then he took it somewhere else. Thinking about her disciplining him with handcuffs and leather— Dammit, man.

Opening the door to the NIA lobby, Josh stepped in and gave the guard his badge to check his name on the list. A short man in a black jacket, holding a glass of punch watched as he cleared the metal detector. He hoped people walked around with platters of finger food. He wouldn't have to order takeout for dinner later, then.

Not seeing any food or serving dishes by the short guy, Josh stood at the edge of the small crowd, looking for his men. He glanced at his watch: half past the hour. The dedication would be starting soon, but he had time to schmooze and talk with the director about their "issue."

Hearing a familiar laugh, Josh headed for the table with spreads of meat and cheese on tiny crackers and even smaller shrimp in creamy dip. His favorite appetizer was the small meatballs drowned in spicy barbeque sauce. Candy reminded him of that spicy sauce. He could eat a whole meal of those and her. His stomach growled and his dick throbbed. Good thing the twenty or so people here were talking loudly and nobody was paying his lower body any attention.

Josh slapped one of his men on the back. "I knew I'd find you all where the food was." He met the eyes of each mate. "Ladies, you all look amazing. It's great to finally see you all in the same room. Thank you for making sure these men got here on time."

"Old habits, man," Parish replied. Parish was the agent involved in the destruction of the virus Candy had mentioned.

"What are you talking about?" Frank asked. Frank and his mate Amerella had taken down the mafia while in hiding.

Bryon snorted. "Forgot already, Frankie boy? The 'can't pass up free food' bachelorhood motto."

And last was Bryon. He and Kari had brought down a human trafficking ring. How could Candy even think his team could be cut? There was no other group like them.

The women laughed.

"You probably won't go to half of the free-food events now that someone's cooking for you." Kari winked at Melinda.

"Not on your life," Amerella said, gripping Frank's arm. "Frank will be going to every one and bringing back enough free food for me, too!" She glanced up to look at Frank. "I need to show you how to stuff shrimp in your clothes so nobody notices."

Josh saw Frank's eyes widen. Josh guessed that since Frank and Amerella were newly mated, Frank wasn't sure how to take his wife. She was a mobster, after all. Amie slapped his chest. "I'm joking, François. Breathe."

Frank was looking a bit purple.

This was what Josh wanted, too. The playful banter of mates who loved each other unconditionally. The teasing, laughing, touching. Everything he desired so badly. But Candy didn't seem like the touchy-feely type. She looked more like the stab-you-in-your-sleep type. He sighed, tossing down another meat-on-cracker.

"Hey," Bryon said, "I know that sigh. I've heard it enough times to have nightmares about it. What's up, boss?"

What's not up, he thought. "Sheldon isn't here yet. Let's wait for him and his mate to arrive." *His mate.* Now he had his own mate. Someone born only for him. But she would be a tough nut to crack. Was he up to the task? Fortunately, he wasn't up at the moment.

That could change if he thought about Candy, though. And what sucked about that was his men would smell his mating desires. Then all hell would break loose trying to get the information out of him. He was good at giving interrogations, but not good at taking them.

"Just tired. Ready for some candy." He smiled to himself. He was an idiot but that line made him relax without having Candy by his side.

"Candy?" Melinda said, scanning the food table. "I have gum if you want that."

Josh bowed his head. "Thank you, but no. I was just spouting off. Candy sounds good to me is all." She raised a brow and looked at Parish. Josh could hear her unspoken question: Is he off his rocker? It made him chuckle. He loved these guys. No matter how bad things were, together, they created an unstoppable team. They would give their lives for one another.

"Director Tumbel." Josh turned to see the NIA director, Ike Pommer, lift a cheese cracker from a platter.

"Director Pommer, good to see you again." Josh gestured to his men. "You remember Parish Hamel, Frank Dubois, and Bryon Day." The director shook each man's hand and gave a nod to the ladies. "Of course. Your team has been doing a great job. Too bad we have to keep you all a secret from the public. But tonight's for you. Your time to shine in front of some of the bigwigs here. And just so you know, this plaque will be going in the new NIA building."

"Thank you, sir." Now was his chance. "Sir, there's something I'd—"

The director lifted a hand and looked over Josh's shoulder. "Ah, here she is. Josh, there's someone I'd like you to introduce you to. Director Tumbel, meet Sergeant Major Candace Obermier."

CHAPTER 4

Well, if this wasn't awkward, she didn't know what was. She grabbed Josh's hand for a strong shake. She was no wilting flower and that meant her handshake was strong, too. Not knowing whether to acknowledge they were already acquainted, she looked into Josh's eyes. Let him take the lead on this one. A good commander knew when to take charge and when to back down.

Now that she was this close to him, she could see his beautiful eyes. They were a stunning color she'd never seen. Hazel but with a yellow-gold outline around the iris. Breathtaking, really.

Something about him drew her in. She didn't normally have that type of reaction to a man. Any man. Her body's temperature rose rapidly. Sweat beads formed across her forehead and above her upper lip. What the fuck was wrong with her. He was just a cute guy like any other cute guy. But he wasn't.

Still holding her gaze, his eyes flashed gold. Well, she thought they did, but that was impossible. What the hell? She wasn't the type of person to see things that weren't there. People's eyes didn't change color like that. Then a memory tickled the back of her mind. A recollection of seeing eyes that turned gold, and stayed . . .

"Nice to meet you, Sergeant Major," Josh said. She'd follow his lead of keeping their previous engagement between themselves.

"Nice to meet you, also, Director Tumbel." She saw a tiny smirk start on his lips and he held his grip on her hand longer than necessary. Ass. Gorgeous ass. But an ass, nonetheless. No, she wouldn't think about him that way any longer. The last thing she wanted was to walk around thinking of him and his smile. Those eyes. The slight beard growth that made her want to rub her face on his jaw to get the full effect of it. Nope. She wasn't going to think about him being hot.

Her go-to persona kicked in. Anytime she felt emotions coming on, she'd slide into this alter ego that let her be the strong woman she'd had to be to survive childhood and the military.

By the happy faces of the men gathered around Tumbel, she doubted he'd told them about shutting down the department. Glancing at the men, she noted they wore shocked expressions. One of the guys breathed deeply and smiled.

"I get it," the man said. "I bet you would like a piece of candy." The others covered their smiles with their hands. Nothing she hadn't heard before. He breathed deeply again.

Tumbel scowled at him. If he wanted a piece of her, then that's what she'd give him. She cocked her head to the side. "Director Tumbel, may I have a moment with you and your team?" His face paled and his smirk disappeared. Ha, take that, jerk. "In my office," she added.

"Don't keep them too long, Candace." Director Pommer smiled. "We have a show to put on."

"No, sir. I'll make sure they are back in time. This'll be short and sweet," she replied.

Tumbel's eyes flashed. She knew he was flustered, to say the least.

"Just your team, Tumbel," she said. "I apologize, ladies, but this is confidential." That ruffled some feathers, but everyone seemed calm and the men stepped away. Candy moved toward the elevator not looking back to see if they followed. Inside the elevator, she pushed the second-floor button, holding the door open for the men.

Tumbel was arguing with the guy who'd made the smart-ass comment about her name. From what she heard, Tumbel was telling him to shut up. Her hearing was exceptional for an ex-pilot who'd been around for a while.

The short ride to the second floor was silent. As well as the walk down the hall to her corner office. Once inside, Tumbel grabbed her elbow and pulled her to the side next to the fireplace. She snatched her elbow free, narrowing her eyes at him. "I suggest you never touch me again," Candy said.

Tumbel growled, and for a second, she blinked at his features. Fuck, he was close to losing his control. Then he took a deep breath and sighed, running his fingers through his hair. "Look, Candy—"

"It's Sergeant Major to you, Director," she sneered, standing defiantly in front of him.

"Fine," he rumbled low and deep, curling his hands into fists at his sides, "Sergeant Major, I haven't told my men about our discussion. And this whole mess is bogus. If we could just talk with Pommer, he will explain our special circumstance."

"Pommer has no say in this decision. I report directly to the president," Candy retorted now slapping her hands on her hips.

"That's not what I mean." Tumbel looked as frustrated as hell. She smiled. "Relax, Tumbel. I'll do this gently."

A voice came over her shoulder. "Can we watch you do it gently?"

"Day," Tumbel snarled so roughly, her jaw almost dropped open. She couldn't believe that sound came from him. It was so animalistic. "Go over there." He pointed to the other side of the room.

"Sergeant Major," he continued in that low, churned-gravel tone that was starting to make her skin hot. She'd never been turned on by a man calling her "sergeant major" until now. "Let's hold off until after the ceremony. Can we at least do that?"

He was so cute when he was trying to sound composed, but she saw the lust in his eyes. She raised her hand, wanting to brush his bangs from his eyes. When she realized she was moving closer, she crossed her arms over her chest hoping to hide her silly intention. What happened to her go-to personality?

Being a hard-nosed bitch around this guy was nearly impossible for her. What was up with him? She cleared her throat and tugged on her green uniform top. She could do this. She'd been in a lot worse circumstances and come through rather unscathed. It would be the same here.

"I think we should do this beforehand, Tumbel." She sounded like such a bitch in her own ears. A horny bitch wanting to jump every bone in this man's body. God. She was disgusted with herself.

A noise like firecrackers popping in the distance reached the room. Her mind told her instantly that it wasn't explosives, but gunshots.

CHAPTER 5

⚞⚟

Candy stood in her office with Tumbel's three men. Her mean, angry side was ready to show them who was boss: She was. But the gunshots halted her. The men stiffened, looked at one another, and bolted for the door. Were they seriously going to run into enemy fire without having a plan?

"Stop!" To her surprise, the men obeyed. "Leaving this room without having a clue about what is going on will get you killed. You all know that as trained paramilitary. Now get your asses back in here." Of course, the guys deferred to their boss, waiting for his say.

"Fuck, she's right," he said. "You can't rescue your mates if you're dead as soon as you walk through the door."

While he argued with his team, she dialed the security room. It picked up on the first ring. "Dotson, shut down all elevators and lock exterior doors, except the main entrance."

"Already done, Sergeant," Dotson responded.

"Good. What do we have?" she asked while she brought up the security camera footage on her laptop. "Tumbel, come here. This is no prank."

Dotson responded, "Looks like four armed men entered through the catering staging area. They shot into the air. Nobody is hurt, as far as I can tell."

"What about our perimeter guys?" she asked. Suddenly, she was very scared for her men. A good plan of attack usually involved taking down the outer defense first, then infiltration.

"They seem fine," he said. "No, their uniforms. They are different. Wait." Candy locked onto the in-house wireless cable signal. She saw the same images Dotson did in security. The masked men in the lobby were collecting cell phones.

Suddenly, a tall man put the tip of his automatic rifle to a man's head. Candy didn't breathe. Please, no deaths. The bad guy reached into the man's coat and pulled out a hand gun. A shot lightly echoed from a distance and the man crumbled to the ground. Those around the fallen man scuttled away. The masked guy looked around, saying something. Dammit. She didn't have audio on this remote site.

She snatched up the phone. "Dotson, what is he saying?"

"He said if anyone else has a gun, they need to put it on the ground or he'll shoot them when he finds it on them."

"This is a federal building," Candy said. "It's illegal to carry firearms into this facility. No one else should have one, according to the guest list."

"What about the guy who did have a gun, then? Why did security let him through?" Dotson asked.

"He was an agent with another department, cleared to carry a concealed weapon," she said. She knew the agent by sight, but never talked with him. Then a thought hit her. "How could he know who's carrying, anyway?"

"Shit," Tumbel said. "When I came in the front doors, I saw one of the caterers—who I thought was a caterer—standing close by, watching. He would've seen everyone who came through the metal detector."

Candy turned to him. "Can you pick him out?"

"Not in these images. They are too fuzzy and far away," he said.

"Ma'am," Dotson cut in, "another thing, he has a thick accent. Somewhat hard to understand." A clue. Their bad guys were from another country where English wasn't the main language.

"Do you know what language it could be, Dotson?" she asked.

"No, ma'am. I don't," he replied.

"That's fine." She didn't expect him to know but thought she'd ask anyway.

"Ma'am, look at the lower right exterior camera." Wide views of the outside of the building showed men standing guard. Dotson zoomed in the camera's focus on the bushes alongside the building. There was something there, but she couldn't tell what.

Then she recognized the face of one of the guards. He lay in the shrubs, his body sprawled out like he had been thrown carelessly. She felt positive the three other guards were in similar conditions. Candy swallowed the shot of pain coursing through her. In war, there were casualties. And now she had a clear goal: Take down the bastards who'd killed her guys. No jail sentences, but fast execution.

"I see it, Dotson," she whispered on the phone.

"Yes, ma'am," he replied, his voice wavering.

"Hey," Josh leaned against her, "what's wrong? What's going on?"

Candy held a finger up telling him to wait a minute. With Josh closer to her, she had to hold herself together. There was no time to get emotional. Now she had to think and strategize on what to do. "Dotson, stay put. Do not open the door unless it is me and then only if I'm alone. You got it?"

"Yes, ma'am." She hung up and closed her eyes. A deep breath helped her put everything into perspective and prioritize.

Tumbel's team gathered around her, looking at the computer screen. "We have four gunmen inside. Outer defenses have been taken over by the enemy—"

"You mean . . ." Tumbel said, resting his hand on her shoulder.

With a jerk, she leaned away from him until his hand moved off. "I told you not to touch me," she tried to say the words calmly but knew they came out like an ice-cold demand. It didn't matter. Best for him to learn now. People didn't touch her. Ever. "And yes, all four guards have been compromised."

One of the guys behind her said to call 911. Tumbel snorted. "We are the 911, Hamel."

Yes, that was true. She was the one in charge of the situation and she had to find a quick, peaceful resolution.

One of the men leaned over her, tapping the screen. "There, our mates are there."

Candy looked at the camera shot. So not good. One of the bad guys had his gun pointed at a woman in Tumbel's group downstairs. She was going to be the first casualty.

CHAPTER 6

⚔

Candy stared at the image of the "mates" on the screen. The one at gunpoint was calm and poised. "Which one is she?" Candy asked.

"That's Amerella," the one named Dubois said. "My mate."

What the hell was up with this "mate" thing? Made them sound like a bunch of animals.

"She's been at gunpoint so many times, this is nothing for her. Living in a mobster family unfortunately prepares you for this kinda thing." Despite his words, Candy felt the tension roll off him like water. Mobster? One of their fucked-up missions was with the mafia. She hadn't read the particulars of the reports that had been messed up, but now she wondered if Amerella was connected to that.

Amerella said something and turned her back to the gunman, looking bored at the whole thing. The woman was brave. A sense of pride for all womankind spread through Candy. Women were stronger nowadays. They didn't back down from fights when they stood up for what they believed. They did whatever it took to keep their loved ones happy and safe. Exactly what she had been fighting for the past twenty years of her life. Equality.

She watched as Amerella loaded a plate with finger foods and handed it to the man. Then she returned to the floor with the other two girls by the table. The guy stared at her for a moment then walked away. The tension in the room dropped.

Hamel flicked the lights off. She should've thought about that. Giving away their presence on the floor above the action wasn't good. If they sent someone up to check out the office, she'd have to kill him. Since no one had come yet, she hoped those outside hadn't paid much attention to a light being on.

The laptop gave off enough light for her to see. The others walking around her office were on their own. How they hadn't tripped over furniture yet surprised her. They didn't have any night-vision goggles, did they? Dubois then hurried to the side window.

"I see the guard's body on this side. Dead." He went to the other window. "Damn. Same thing." He gave a heavy sigh.

"How can you see that at this distance?" she asked. "It's dark outside." The men shuffled, but said nothing. Movement on the laptop screen drew her attention. The guests were lying facedown on the floor with their arms extended past their heads. Well, shit. Candy scooped up her phone and pressed the speed dial for the White House security.

"Hey, Candy—"

"We have a hostage situation at the NIB," she spit out. "This is not a drill. Repeat, *not* a drill."

"What? Fuck," the man on the other side of the line said. "Call me when you have intel." The phone beeped that the call had ended.

"Who was that?" Josh asked.

"White House security," she said. "Protocol is to immediately inform the Secret Service about any threatening activities. They'll then call in reinforcements to protect the president and his wife." He probably knew protocol, but she said it more for her own benefit than his. She pressed another speed dial number.

"Dresden here."

"This is Sergeant Major Candace Obermier. We have a hostage situation with four inside and four outside at the NIB."

"Shit. Candy, what the hell is going on over there?" Dresden said.

"Dres, this is bad," she replied. "The NIA is having a dedication ceremony tonight."

"Yes. I was invited as head of national security," he said.

"Before the ceremony began, four armed men took over the lobby, holding everyone hostage. My four outside men are down, replaced by their men, I'm guessing. Pommer and several other high-ranking officers are here. This could get ugly if our top guys are retired permanently. We need help now."

"Dammit, Candy. You know it will take a couple hours to put together an operation with men, munitions, and planning."

"Yes, sir. Until you arrive, the Alpha League of Federal Agents are with me in my office one floor above the scene," she said.

"You're with the ALFAs?" he asked.

"Yes, sir."

"Hell, Candy. You don't need me, then. Let those boys take care of it. They're more than qualified."

"Sir, I'm sure they are, but—"

"I'll have a group of my guys go over there to assess and do what they can. But without knowing Director Tumbel's plans, we would only be getting in the way. I'll have them there in an hour." Her phone went silent. She tossed the phone on the desk and ran her fingers through her hair, pulling back the strands that had fallen from her bun.

Time to make a plan, then, she thought.

Josh stood back and said, "It's time to make a plan."

She looked up at him. The side of his lips tilted up and

he winked at her. Fucking god, her heart sputtered. Disgusted with her weakness, she got up and moved away from him. He was too alluring, too enthralling, and the man hadn't even done anything but wink! She was in so much trouble.

Hamel paced. "We need more intel on the situation before we can assess anything. Then we need to figure out the best way to get our mates out."

"Whoa, there, buddy," she said. "We're getting everyone out, not just your wives or mates or whatever the hell you call them. Leave no man behind." Due to the darkness in the office, she couldn't see his reaction. Probably a good thing. "Okay, we have to get closer to the terrorists and listen in. See what we can find out."

"Shimmy down the elevator shaft?" Day asked.

"Good thought," she replied, "but the with the doors closed and the concrete encasing each shaft, it'll be impossible to see or hear anything."

"Is there a way to get over or under them?" Tumbel asked.

The answer slapped her upside the head. "Yes, there is." She felt her way around her desk toward her chair, scooped up her phone and pocketed it. "The lobby ceiling has been reinforced with steel beams and there's enough space to walk." She put her hands out, blindly, feeling her way. "Where's the damn door?"

Light slipped into the room from the door opening. Tumbel breathed deeply, then motioned to her. What the hell was up with these people's heavy breathing? She was starting to think none of them were playing with a full deck of cards.

"The hall is clear," Josh said, stepping back. "Lead the way, Sergeant Major."

Candy stopped at the light's cusp and said, "I can do this on my own, Tumbel. Your team isn't needed for this."

"That's fine," he said. "My guys will stay and watch the monitors. But I'm going with you." She put a hand on her hip and stared at him. Was he really going to make an issue out of this? she wondered.

He pointed to the hallway floor where he stood. "If your cute fanny isn't out here in five seconds, I'm grabbing your hand to drag you out." That got her moving. No way did she need him touching her again. But she had to admit his touch was pleasant. Nothing like her father's or that of some men she'd had to deal with on the base.

Focusing on what she was doing, she scoured the hall, looking for an air return duct. She knew one accessed the space above the lobby ceiling to suck out the hot air that built up in the summer months. On the other side of the elevators, she hit pay dirt. A large opening covered by a metal grating was cut into the wall several inches from the ground. She leaned over and grabbed her shoe.

"You need to take your shoes and socks off if you're going down with me."

"We're going down that?" He pointed to the grate.

"Yeah," she said, "you scared?"

His face hardened and she almost laughed at his change in expression. "No. I'm just not sure I'll fit."

Candy shrugged. "If not, you stay up here, then."

Again, his face morphed, but this time his brows came down and his lips pursed. "I'm not letting you go alone. You have no idea what you might run into." She did, but there was no telling him that.

After opening the metal grid and removing the air filter, she wiggled her way in, feet first. Since getting a desk job a year ago, she'd put on weight. More than she ever had, even though she ran daily and worked out regularly. It was just the feminine body she had. Her mother was the same way.

The jerk laughed at her the entire time she stuffed herself into the vent shaft. She'd see if he even had the guts to go through with this. She'd kick his ass if he chickened out.

CHAPTER 7

Josh could not believe he was going to crawl down an air duct. What the fuck was he thinking. *Fuck* was exactly what he was thinking. Damn animal and its one-track mind. Good thing he had the wolf to blame. Otherwise, he'd have to kick his own ass for being so chauvinistic. He needed to pull his shit together. He growled at his mating needs. He was a professional. The last fucking thing he needed was to mess up what they were doing because his animal had taken control of the situation.

Taking his shoes off, he chuckled as he watched his lovely mate stick her ass end in the air and crawl backward into the shaft. "You need to use the friction from your skin to keep from sliding down."

Ain't she a little genius, he thought. Friction on skin—sounded sexy as hell to him. "You do this often?" he asked. She snorted at him and disappeared down the hole.

"Okay, Tumbel," he said to himself, "you volunteered for this craziness." He scooted closer to the vent and repeated Candy's movements. He scraped his knee putting his leg inside the hole. "Oww, shit, that hurt."

"Shhh," Candy called up. "You voice carries in here."

He looked down. "Sorry," he whispered. What the hell was he thinking when he said that he could do this? There was barely enough room for him to get a grip on the walls. But just like his mate had said, he used the friction between skin and metal to inch his way down. This would be a total disaster if he fell.

So don't fall, idiot, his wolf told him. Great time for you to show up, Josh thought back. He diverted his attention to his mate below him. "So what's the plan after this?" he whispered.

She glanced up at him and said, "We get above the bad guys and use my phone to record what they say and maybe try to get some closer visuals, too. See faces."

That sounded easy enough. Once he reached the bottom of the shaft, he removed his feet from the metal sides and landed lightly on the balls of his feet. From there, he bent down to get out of the tunnel. The view before him was surreal.

He wasn't sure what to make of it. The dim space seemed to be a mix of old and new that weaved together creating a chaos of pipes and beams. At his side, Candy stretched her stride to cross to the first I beam. Instantly, he and his wolf didn't like this idea. If she lost her balance, she'd crash through the ceiling tiles and plunge twenty feet to the tile floor below.

"Don't move," he whispered-hollered to her. He stepped forward to join her and leaned down to her ear. "I'll go first, then help you over." He saw storm clouds gather behind her eyes. Oh, shit. "Look, it's not a gender thing. I happen to have excellent balance and flexibility."

A grin lit her face. "What? You can do cartwheels and flips?" she asked. He was sure if he tried, he could.

"That's not the point here," he continued.

"Yeah," she agreed "I get it. Then get your ass to the next beam." Josh stepped over crisscrossing pipes and wires bundled between the I bars. He held his hand out to her. She stiffened and stared at it. Dammit, he thought, what was the deal with others touching her? He'd have to find out and get her over it quickly. He intended to touch her *all* over when this was done.

"It's just like a handshake," he said. "You can do that. I've seen it. Just put your hand against mine." He'd do the rest.

Hesitantly, her arm moved forward as she prepared for the leap. Midair, her hand slipped into his and he pulled her directly in front of him, using both hands to make sure she was steady. When she started to freak out and shuffle away, he snapped his arms back, hands in the air.

She scowled at him and pointed to the next location. The terrorists staged themselves at the reception area midway in the room. They had several more jumps to make before they got close to the desk.

His mate was doing a fantastic job of beam hopping, for a human. She had strength for the distance and balance when it came to standing. She probably could've done it without him. But he wasn't about to tell her that.

The next crossing was a bit more difficult. A PVC tube lay on top of existing pipes, making it stick up in the air. He had to make sure his feet were high enough to clear it. He pointed at it when he made it over. She drew her brows down and swished her hand in the air like she would've hit him if he were closer and mouthed, *I see it.* She grumbled under her breath about men thinking women couldn't do anything. That made him smile.

She'd better get used to it. That's how it was going to be for the rest of their lives together. He would never let harm or danger come close to her. He would always be there to make sure she was safe, though he had a feeling she was good at getting herself into trouble.

Her eyes followed the length of the elevated pipe, running from the front to the back of the space. If she wanted to avoid the pipe, she was out of luck. He waved her over, mouthing, *Come on.*

She huffed at him then swung her arms back for the leap. When she was in midair, he could tell immediately she wouldn't make it. And she knew as well. Her leg

snapped down and pushed off the pipe giving her the
needed oomph. The pipe bent under her weight, but she was
off so quickly, no damage was done.

He reached out for her with both hands. Sorry, she'd
have to get over it. This landing was not going to be pretty.
Seeing what he planned to do, she twisted away in the air,
but that wouldn't stop him. He grabbed her arm and guided
her body against his for a base to hold on to. Her feet tangled with his and his balance was thrown off. He was going
down.

He wrapped an arm around her waist, holding her tightly
to him while his other arm went under him to grip the
beam. His hand broke most of the fall, but he curled his
back and rolled along his spine on the beam instead of
landing flat on his ass. Candy was able to stretch her arms
to the sides and hang on to pipes to keep them still.

The look of shock and horror on her face made him want
to burst out laughing, after he realized they were okay and
safe again. He was sure the fall wasn't what had scared her,
but the fact that she was lying on top of him, her entire
body aligned with his. The arm he wrapped around her
waist remained.

Her mouth moved with no words coming out. He put a
finger over her luscious lips and shushed her. "Calm down,
love. You're okay. I'm not going to hurt you."

She stopped her wiggling, though he did like it. Her
mask—the other person she became when she needed to
protect herself—appeared. He'd seen her make this change
a couple of times now. He wasn't sure why she felt the need
to hide herself, but even her smell changed slightly. It was
less Candy and more machinelike. No emotions, no
feelings.

He wasn't sure she even realized she slipped into another persona, she did it so smoothly. Her brows came
down and eyes narrowed at him. Her chin rose in indignation.

"I know you're not going to hurt me," she whispered.
"It's this." She moved her arm in the air along their bodies

to indicate the compromising situation. God, he wanted to kiss her so bad. To lay soft baby kisses down her slender neck to the spot he would very soon bite. He wanted those damn clothes off. To see her flushed and naked and slick with need. Fuck fuck fuck his body hated him. Now was not the time to get a hard-on.

CHAPTER 8

Candy stared into the eyes of the hottest man she'd ever seen who was lying underneath her on an I beam over the heads of a terrorist hostage crisis. Could this day get any worse? His body was hard below her soft spots. And she meant hard *everywhere*. A fire shot through her that she hadn't felt since she was a teen with raging hormones. No. This was not the time or the place. And most importantly, he was not the person. She'd just fired him and his team. What the hell was wrong with her?

Did she like this? It scared her. She didn't feel helpless or overpowered—she didn't want to feel anything. She had people to save and a job to do.

"You know," Tumbel said, "to get up, you're gonna have to slide over me." She schooled her face to a neutral expression. Then she thought about what he said. The image of his body rubbing hers as she slid over him made her warm all over. He was right. She either dragged her v-jay over his nose, or her mouth had to go over his . . . johnson. Her face felt ready to burst into flames. This would be a great time to spontaneously combust.

He smiled at her as she tried to hide her true self from

him. "Well," she started, "I'm damn sure not sliding up so your face . . . your face . . . You know what I'm saying." Damn, she was flustered. Why was she so embarrassed? When men had sexually harassed her before, she'd gotten fighting mad and made them back off. In camp, she'd been named the Virgin Bitch because no man had ever gotten a piece of her. She was even fine letting them think she batted for the other team.

Except, he wasn't harassing her. He was stating facts. And he was the first man she'd found sexually attractive in as long as she could barely remember. The images going through her mind were so inappropriate she was glad he couldn't know what she was thinking.

"Slide down, then," he quipped quietly.

"I will," she whispered. Her body squirmed and slid over his. Her breasts against his chest, her hot core gliding over his johnson. Fuck, he felt so good. When her head reached his crotch, she put a hand on the beam to lift her upper body. She wasn't giving him any ideas. She may have let him touch her, but it was an emergency.

She got to her feet as did he. Time to focus on the job at hand, getting intel. After leap-frogging a few more I beams, they were in the center of the space. She couldn't hear much, just the mumbling of the men below. Tumbel kneeled and put his ear onto the ceiling tile.

"They're directly below us," he said. That was good. She pulled her phone from her pocket. "They're speaking a foreign language," he added. Just like Dotson had said.

"Can we get my phone in for a visual?" she asked.

Tumbel sat back on his heels and pointed behind her. "Scoot back. If we get behind them, we can lift one of these tiles and they won't see it." He was smarter than she gave him credit for. Maybe he did know what he was doing when it came to agent work, even though the department's record showed otherwise.

Moving back several tiles, she settled and looked to him for an okay. He gave her a single nod. While he pried up the mineral-fiber square, she pulled up her camera on her phone.

His look waited for hers. She nodded and he lifted the tile. Her fingers slid the phone through the narrow gap.

"Don't drop it," Tumbel whispered.

"No shit," she replied. She kept her head down so he wouldn't see the smile on her face. What a dweeb. Like she planned on letting her phone fall.

With the fiber material raised, she now heard the men talking. She didn't know what language, either. It wasn't a Romance language, didn't sound Asian. So that left northern Europe and at least five languages. Not a lot of help.

After several moments, she pulled her phone out of the slot and stopped the video recording. She looked around, wondering if there was anything else they could do while they were here. She climbed to her feet and slipped the phone into her pocket. Then she noticed her hand was in Tumbel's.

The instinctive reaction was to jerk away, run so he couldn't hurt her. His grip tightened slightly, keeping her there. He lifted her hand to his lips and kissed the back of her fingers. Her heart raced. No one had ever done that before. She saw it in movies and rom-coms, but never in real life. Her life. She stood staring at him, at a loss for what to say or do. Her stomach flipped and fear grew wings in her chest.

A tangle of emotions she didn't know how to deal with bubbled up inside her. Away. She had to get away from him. She had to pull herself together and push down the feelings she'd suppressed almost her entire life.

Screw the fact of him going first. She leapt to the closest I beam and her momentum kept her going until she reached the wall. With little effort, she was up and out of the air return shaft. She never looked back to see where Tumbel was. Didn't care. He knew where her office was.

Reaching the door to her sanctuary, she stepped inside the dark room and froze. What was going on? She never turned the lights off.

"Sergeant Major?" a familiar male voice came from the darkness.

It took a moment for reality to catch up with her. Pulling her cell from her pocket, she chastised herself for being so pathetically out of it. Shit like that would get someone killed on the battlefield. The light from her phone got her to her desk.

Staring at the laptop's screen, not much had changed since they'd left the office. Wait. In one of the monitor's squares, she noticed someone was standing, no—sitting— in front of the entrance doors, back turned so he faced outside. She brought up the video footage on her phone and zoomed in on the screen, making the person in question larger.

With a gasp, she recognized the back side of Director Pommer. He was sitting in a chair, hands tied behind the seat's back and staring ahead at the darkness outside. Smart, she thought. Any attempts to get inside, shoot through the glass, or throw in a gas bomb were effectively blocked. Okay, fine. That didn't change much on her part.

Candy tapped the green *Play* triangle on the screen. The others in the room crowded around her. The voices were low, so she turned up the volume as much as possible.

Agent Day said, "They are speaking Russian."

She looked at him. "You're sure?" How could he know when no one else did?

"I spent a year in that part of northern Europe, scouring for clues. I know Russian and five other languages," he said with a bit of snobbishness. That was a bit impressive. She'd give him that.

"What are they saying?" she asked. They were quiet for a moment before he spoke.

"Their discussion is weird. They are talking about a movie one of them saw last week," Day informed.

"A movie?" She found that hard to believe.

"Yeah," Day affirmed. "One just asked if the others were going to a wedding. Strange."

She never gave thought to what hostage captors talked about, but she doubted it was so casual. It was like this was nothing out of the ordinary in their day. Why were they here and what did they want? Why weren't they making any demands? She paused the footage.

Accessing the classified files in the National Intelligence database, she searched for Russian-born men. "Guys," she addressed the group, "what you see here goes nowhere. All of it is highly classified." After a general mumble of agreement from them, she continued her search.

There were so many, a lot of them from the Cold War. Most of those spies were probably dead by now, she thought, if even still in the business. She came across a set of brothers she knew all too well. A couple of years prior, the bastards had abducted a French family on vacation as hostages for money. In a joint top secret mission with France, she flew the transport that was to whisk the family away once freed by the American and French forces. In and out. Easy peasy.

Well, the brothers weren't giving up their cash cow that easily. In a desperate attempt to salvage their cowardly act, they attacked her chopper when she landed nearby, damaging it beyond repair. She and the family had to hitch a ride on the assault team's getaway, aborting the mission before the brothers were apprehended.

Not long after that, she was promoted then asked to work in DC.

Wondering what the brothers were up to, she Googled their names on the Internet to see if any news had been posted about them: Yulian and Mikhail Steganovich.

"Holy fuck," she spit out and clicked on the link to YouTube. The brothers had posted a clip a while back for the world to see. Of course, they spoke Russian and she had no idea what they were saying, but she had a clue. They wore paramilitary uniforms and were in front of a graffiti-covered wall. It was nighttime and small fires glowed in the background.

Day grunted. "They're idiots."

"What are they saying?" she asked.

"Nothing of big importance," he responded. "They're talking about some French family and how they—the brothers—released the family out of kindness in their hearts—"

"That's a load of horse hockey," she said, crossing her arms in front of her. "Lying sacks of shit."

Day pointed to one of the brothers in the video—Yulian. "He's one of the guys talking on the video you recorded."

The voices all sounded the same for the most part to her. "What about the brother?" she asked.

Day shook his head. "Don't hear him. He's not one of them."

"You're sure?" she asked, trying to make sense of the insane situation they were in. "They do everything together. One of the others has to be the brother."

Day shook his head again. "I'm sure. Play the video on the phone." She tapped the green arrow button and listened to the hollow echoes coming from the small speaker. Day and the guys all nodded. Consensus was it was Yulian.

"How can you tell it's not Mikhail?" she asked. "They sound identical on the video."

All three guys shook their heads. Hamel said, "There is a slight pitch variation between the two. The one on the left is higher than the brother on the right." The rest of the team agreed.

"You must have damn good hearing because they sound the same to me," she said. Exceptional ability to see in the dark, extremely sensitive hearing, ability to think on their feet and remain calm under tense pressure. They seemed to be decent agents. She wondered why none of them had military careers or even served.

That was what clued her in to the group being a bunch of screwups. They had no formal military training. How could they possibly perform as well as the SEALs and Rangers if they had no experience in the armed forces? It was unheard of. Maybe there was more to these guys than what was in their files. She still wasn't convinced they were worth keeping.

She paused the image of the lobby filled with guests and the four men wearing all black with knit hats covering their faces. "Can you tell which one Yulian is?" From the high camera angles, she couldn't assess how tall the terrorists were. "Yulian and Mikhail are short for males."

"That should be easy to figure out," Dubois said as he came around the desk to her side. "They're carrying ASh-12.7s which are about forty inches long—"

She sucked in a breath and leaned closer to the laptop. "Are you sure that's what they've got? How can you tell in this stupidly small image on the screen?"

Tumbel, who had followed her in, pointed to an image where one of the men leaned against the elevators keeping watch over the back area of the lobby, his gun hung from a strap over his shoulder. "Look at the bullpup design," he said. "All the action is behind the trigger."

Good god, he was right. A sick sensation took over her stomach. Things were a lot worse than she realized.

"And the short nose." She turned to Tumbel. "Did you know the old KGB asked their designers to specifically make this gun for urban terrorists?" she asked.

Tumbel's face showed surprise at her question. He probably never expected a female to know anything about weaponry. He replied, "But have you noticed the design similarities to our cartridges that used to hold .50 Beowulfs?"

"What?" she shot back. Excitement about talking guns almost made her giddy. "Like the Russians need to copy us? Besides, they have longer cases and heavier bullet loads."

He smirked. "Our lighter weight makes it more practical for close urban situations."

"Really," she said, "have you given thought to stopping power—"

"Hey, guys," Dubois interrupted. "Let's focus, here. We're working on height, not combat assault rifles normal people know nothing about."

Candy sat back in her chair and rolled her eyes, but noticed the grin on Tumbel's handsome face. She quickly moved her eyes to the laptop. Enjoying his company wasn't on her to-do list.

Dubois tapped the screen on one of the men downstairs. "I'd say this guy is the shortest at about five-and-a-half feet. This guy is over six foot."

Looks like they had their man. But why just one brother? Where was the other?

CHAPTER 9

⤳

Victory rushed through Josh's body. The fact that he and Candy had something in common thrilled him to death. This was only the beginning of their coming together. They needed to get this shindig over with so he could take her home. His girl liked guns. Goddamn, that was something he never expected. Candy seemed so uptight. But he bet she would be soft and sweet when he got to know her.

Finding out who their terrorists were was good, but did nothing for him. He wanted them gone. "We need a plan," he said.

"Agreed," Candy said. "We should take down the outer perimeter first, then we can focus on inside. But we need to watch for the brother. He could be outside, ready to pick off anyone trying to get in." She sighed. "What can we do until backup gets here?"

The guys looked at her. "Backup?" they said in unison. Josh and his men didn't even know what backup was. On their assignments, it was them and no one else, for several reasons.

By her incredulous look, he needed to clarify. "Sergeant

Major, we are used to doing things on our own. Backup does not exist in our world."

His mate sat back in her chair and crossed her arms over her chest. "Then tell me how you plan to get rid of the men outside."

He hadn't intended on letting her in on their secret just yet. But what else could he do? He doubted very seriously if she would stand in the hall for a few minutes while they stripped and shifted. His guys looked at him. "Uh," he started, "yeah, about that . . ." Damn, how did he get her out of the room for a few minutes? "Do you need to go to the restroom or anything?" he asked. God, if that wasn't the lamest.

Her brow rose. "No. Do you?"

"No, that's not my point."

Both eyebrows rose. "Then what is your point?" she asked.

Dammit. What could he say that would not be suspicious? "Would you mind standing in the hallway for minute?" Her eyes narrowed and mouth puckered. He guessed that was out of the question.

Hamel spoke up. "She's your mate, right?" he asked.

Well, damn. He hoped the men wouldn't have realized that, but the nose never lies. He ran his fingers through his hair.

Candy stared at Hamel, then flicked her eyes to him. "What the hell is up with you guys and the word '*mate*'?" she asked.

Josh sighed. "It's what we use where we come from."

"You all come from the United States," Candy said. "Your files say so."

"Yeah, that's not what I mean," Josh mumbled.

"Having a hard time with your words, eh, Director?" she poked at him. He had a hard time lying to her. That was the problem. "I thought so. I think my plan will be better."

Her plan? She had a plan? Where the fuck had he been when that happened?

Her eyes narrowed in on him again, a twinkle of desire lit in her eyes. "You had better not be thinking that a woman cannot come up with a plan," she growled. "I will so kick your ass into next week, soldier."

Fuck. If that wasn't the hottest thing he'd ever heard from a woman. He wondered how many men underestimated her. Probably all of them.

"No, Sergeant Major." He tried to stop the oncoming grin. "That thought had never occurred to me."

"Good," she said, clearing her throat and stepping back. "Keep it that way. I need to get down to the security office and take charge in there. There's no audio on my laptop, plus there's access to the outside and the tunnels below to maneuver."

"*I?*" Josh questioned. She wasn't going anywhere without him.

She huffed at him, pushing the few strands of her hair that came loose behind her ear. "Yes. Me, myself, and I. All of you can't fit in there, much less sneak down the stairs and past the bad guys," she said.

That would be the perfect way to get her out of the room for them to shift. But he wasn't letting her go alone. He stared at the camera views and where all were positioned. "I'll agree with that. And with the guard standing at the elevators, you're not sneaking around him, either. As soon as you open the stairwell door, he'll see you."

"I'm aware of that," she conceded. It shocked him that she gave in so easily.

Day, standing at the window, tapped on the glass. "We need a diversion and I think we just got it." Standing over his mate's shoulder, Josh watched the laptop screen as an exterior camera showed a news van pulling up to the sidewalk in front of the building.

"How the hell did the media get wind of this?" Candy said. "The DC police aren't even here yet."

Sitting on the sofa, Hamel hit Dubois in the arm. "Didn't one of your ex-girlfriends work for a news station?"

Dubois frowned. "Yeah, but don't mention that to my

mate. A jealous mafia wife isn't the best thing to have. You can go to bed a rooster and wake up as a hen."

Josh ignored the dumbass remark. "What station did she work for?" he asked.

"I think it was WADC. Something with DC in it," Dubois replied.

"How about WWDC?" Josh said.

"Yeah, that's it." Dubois got up from the sofa and joined him. He leaned closer to the laptop when the passenger door of the van opened. "Huh, that's her. Claire Carter." A shapely woman wearing a jacket and pencil skirt stepped out from the vehicle, microphone in hand. The driver came around to her side and opened the van's sliding door, setting out equipment.

"Still got her phone number?" Josh asked his agent.

Dubois pulled out his phone. "Maybe." A moment passed while Dubois flipped through his contacts. "Yeah, I have it, as long as she hasn't changed it since we went out. What do you want me to tell her?"

Good question. He asked his mate, "Candy, what do you think is the best way to use them?"

She sucked in the side of her cheek and one eye squinted. She was so adorable when in deep concentration. "We need all the guards' attention away from the back of the lobby so I can go from the stairwell around the corner to the hall leading to security."

He knew she meant "we" and not "I"; he'd let her know that shortly. He stood at a window and looked for a locking mechanism. He asked, "Do these windows open?"

"Originally, they did. Now you have to remove the electromagnetic screens from the inside to get out," she replied. "You're not thinking about jumping, are you? It's twenty feet to the ground. You'll break a leg. And they'll see you hobble away." Her voice had a slightly amused tone.

He shrugged, playing off her statement. "Just curious." He turned to Dubois. "Frank, call the girl and tell her we need her help. Get her on the line for me." On the laptop, he saw the woman reach into the van and pull out something, then put it to her ear. Her voice came over Frank's phone. Frank spoke a moment and handed the phone to him.

"Hi, Ms. Carter. I'm Josh Tumbel, Frank's boss."

"I remember your name. How are you doing?" she asked.

"Well, I could be better. We need your help."

"I'm on assignment at the moment," she said. "Can I call you back?"

"Actually, Ms. Carter, your assignment deals with our problem. How did you get information to come to this building?"

"My producer got an anonymous call at the office. Someone said a news crew should get to the NIB immediately. So, here I am. Are you inside? What's going on?"

"Ms. Carter, I need you to stay calm and be professional," he said.

After a pause, she replied, "Okay . . ."

"Inside, approximately twenty people are being held hostage by Russian gunmen." On the monitor, the lady's body stiffened, but she didn't react further. "If you got an anonymous call, I suspect they wanted you here to make a statement or demand. Whatever you do, don't go live. This would only cause panic that isn't necessary. Do you understand?"

"Yes, sir. I get it. What do you want us to do?" she asked. He was impressed with her ability to stay calm and think. "We need a distraction of some kind to get the men's attention away from the back. Something that would draw them toward the front."

She waved a hand in the air. "That's all? That's easy. When do you want it?"

"Give us two minutes. Is that long enough for you?"

"Oh, yeah. I'm ready whenever. It's not like this will be hard or anything," she said. That had him a bit worried. But he didn't have time to question her.

"Great, thanks." He hung up and handed the phone back to Dubois. "You all heard—"

Candy glared at him. "Of course not. You were on the phone. How could—"

"We'll talk later," he said to Candy, then to his men, "After my mate and I are gone, do your thing and wait for my signal outside. Pick a guard. First will be the one at the back on the west side." He held the door open and looked at Candy. "Let's go."

She was taken aback. "Go where?"

Goddammit. Now was not the time for her to get uptight about a man taking charge. Sometimes it was just that way. "Candy—"

"Sergeant Major—" she started.

"Whatever," he growled. "We have only seconds left before we miss this window of opportunity to get to security. Are we going to stand here and argue over semantics or get your sweet ass down there?"

Her widened eyes and dropped jaw were comical. She was cute when surprised, too. Hell, who was he kidding? She was cute no matter what.

He raised a brow. "Don't make me stop this car."

The corner of her lips twitched and she stalked forward. "Fine." She breezed by him into the hallway, leaving her alluring scent in her path. He gave a nod to his guys and closed the door.

CHAPTER 10

⤙

She was pissed enough to spin bullets. Once again, a man presuming the little lady couldn't take care of herself. As long as they didn't get in her way, all was fine. It was when men interfered that shit hit the fan.

He did ask her opinion on how to use the TV reporter, but he'd also used her first name. She let it slide. Wasn't sure why. She doubted he even realized he'd said it. He was a very personable guy. He seemed kind, like he'd never hit anyone, but you never knew a person until the worst happened. Then the man behind the curtain revealed himself.

And how dare he call her ass sweet. He was being sexist and she shouldn't put up with that crap. But it was flattering he noticed—anyone else, no—but he was okay.

She shook her head. What the hell was wrong with her? Never was she fine with men being overbearing and controlling. What was it about this one man that was turning her world upside down? Maybe if she worked with him instead of against him so much, they could compromise and get through this alive. But he needed to do the same, dammit. This wasn't a one-way street.

When they reached the bottom of the stairs, Tumbel put

his arm out to stop her from approaching the door. Like she was going to walk out without checking first. When he put his hand on knob, she jerked him back.

"What the hell are you doing?" she whispered-yelled, slapping him on the side. "Stick your head out there and it'll get shot off."

He rested fists on his hips. "I may be able to see in the dark, but my X-ray vision is in the shop."

She huffed. "I don't expect you to see through doors, dumbass." God, he was impossible. She pulled her phone out and stuck it in his face. "Technology." She opened the camera app. "Help me push the door open enough to stick my phone out. Like we did on the ceiling."

Slowly, quietly, he pushed the door barely open. She pushed her phone out then glanced at the screen. The guy standing at the elevators earlier was no longer there. The reception desk was vacant also. "It's clear. Let's go." Pushing the door farther open, she slid out, keeping her back to the wall the few steps to the corner leading to the security hall.

Safely around the corner, she let out a breath. It'd been a while since she'd seen any real action and it appeared she was getting soft. Later, she'd buckle down and chew on some nails. After a few seconds without Josh coming around the corner, she backtracked and peeked into the lobby. Josh stood staring at the front like the rest of the guys who were glued to the entrance glass.

Outside on the sidewalk, a tall, slender woman with long hair had taken her suit jacket off and was stretching, doing a fabulous job of showing off her boobs. Big ones at that, of course. She unbuttoned the top of her blouse and fanned herself as if hot. Candy knew for a fact the nighttime temp was around seventy degrees.

The woman then slowly bent toward the glass, her top gaping, to pick up something. That was enough. Candy grabbed Josh's ear and dragged him around the corner. She said, "Keep it in your pants, big boy. That's our distraction, which seems to be doing a perfect job."

He batted her hand away and followed. "Sorry, I was just making sure the men were watching," he retorted.

"Don't worry. Their eyeballs were as glued to the door as yours were." The thought almost made her laugh. Men were so easy sometimes. A little sex and a little beer and they were in heaven. Except when they were mean drunks. Her father had been one of those.

She waved at the camera, realizing she'd forgotten to call Dotson to let him know they were coming down. She gave a thumbs-up and pointed to the guy behind her. Her instructions were to not open the door unless she was alone. And Dotson wouldn't; he was an excellent soldier. If she didn't give the right signal, he would have his gun at the ready and fire immediately.

Candy punched in the passcode and the magnetic lock disengaged. When she opened the door, Dotson was already standing, saluting. She pulled Tumbel inside and quietly closed the door. Returning the salute, she introduced Tumbel to Dotson then went to the board with all the video screens.

The woman outside, Claire—she remembered the name, continued her routine. The woman was bent over, running her fingers over from her ankle over her calf muscle. And interestingly enough, two of the Russians were arguing close to the front. She heard the voices, but it didn't matter as she didn't know the damn language. She needed Day. But that wasn't happening. He was in her office waiting on some signal from Tumbel. She had no idea what that exchange of words between Tumbel and his men meant. He didn't tell them to go anywhere, so . . .

Tumbel leaned toward her, but didn't touch her. She was sorta hoping he might. Dammit, no she wasn't. No one touched her. Maybe she could allow— No!

"Hey," Tumbel whispered.

"What!" she said louder than she intended. Not that they could be heard outside this room. It was soundproofed as well as blocked to all radio emissions, in or out. He frowned at her anyway. She had pulled herself together to fall apart after five seconds of being close to him. Maybe she needed a week's vacation—with the men from Chippendales.

God, great time for her to think about that silliness. Here was Tumbel making her all kinds of distracted and her body doing insane things just from being near him. She should really reconsider her usual stance on men. Tumbel was proving to be a nice guy so far. Hard-headed and gorgeous, but nice. Not one of those jerks that was full of himself.

"Sorry," she said. He motioned her to the side. She accommodated his wish and followed.

"I, uh, I need to do something and it would be best if you and your boy, here, did not see it," he said.

"What?" she asked. Candy couldn't fathom what was going through his head. "What are you going to do? Steal the computer? And where do you think he and I could go?" What could he possibly do in there that she couldn't see?

She held her hands up for Tumbel to just be quiet for a moment, then turned to Dotson. "I need you to go through the tunnels and cross under Peters Avenue to the metro exit then double back to the TV van out front."

"Yes, ma'am," Dotson replied. "Any reason I shouldn't use the tunnel exit here on the corner?"

She picked up his firearm and handed it to him to holster. "They may have men in the tunnel disguised as normal civilians. We don't know. You being in military garb makes you a target. The farther you get from here, the less likely you are to come across anyone."

"What are my orders after getting to the TV crew?"

She needed a second to reason out the best tactical strategy. "We need a man on the outside to communicate with Dresden's men and the police when they show up."

Josh interjected, "I thought we didn't want police."

"We don't," she said, "but I doubt there's any way around it. Maybe they can serve as an added distraction while we figure out a solution." She turned back to her guard. "Tell Dresden and the police we are working on the inside and to stand by. Be ready for anything. But don't initiate." She pushed him toward the wall.

"Yes, ma'am." He pulled up the hidden panel in the floor that led to the narrow stairwell going to a thick metal door to the tunnel. From there, she hoped he had a clear path away from any ambush.

Now she had to figure out what to do with Tumbel. What did he need to do that she couldn't see?

CHAPTER 11

Well, shit. Josh didn't know how he was going to shift with his mate in the room. Was now the time to tell her? He had to do something. His guys should be shifted, out the window, and hiding in the night, waiting for his signal. He scanned the camera angles to see where the four guards outside currently were.

He almost laughed. All four were toward the front, watching Frank's ex-girlfriend do her thing. He was surprised at how undisciplined the men were. But the men inside were the same, having everyday conversations over pizza and beer. Something wasn't right. But he'd worry about that later after the hostages and his men's mates were free.

Josh turned to his mate. "Stay here for now. I'll take care of the guards outside. Then I'll come back and we'll figure out where to go from there."

"You're going to take on four men armed with ASh guns?" She stood with her fists on her hips. "Are you high? All there is to hide behind are shrubs and some trees that edge the park. And you don't even have a gun."

Candy whipped around in the small room and edged her

way to a corner locker. With keys from her pocket, she opened a metal cabinet door to reveal an arsenal of weapons. Enough to stage a small army if need be. His mouth fell open. They were beautiful.

She saw his expression and smiled. "Beauts, aren't they? Never had the opportunity to break them out. What do you need? Let's get the party started."

His mouth snapped shut. It was really going to freak her out when he told her he didn't need anything. On the video monitors, the guards were moving around. The show out front must've finished. Shit. "Hold that thought. I'll be right back. Don't come outside." He slipped out the heavy metal exit door into the cool air.

Leaning against the door so his little mate wouldn't be able to open it, he immediately began stripping and let out a little whistle to his men letting them know the time was close. Calling his wolf forward, he went to all fours then slinked into the trees and bushes separating the National Intelligence Building from the green area behind it.

The four guards had retaken their original positions at the corners of the building. Josh had to time everything correctly for a surprise attack. Sliding with stealth in the darkness, he smelled for his three men. They were spaced around the building, hiding behind the bushes.

Bryon hunched in his wolf form, waiting behind the shrubbery at the back of the building. Of the current shifters in ALFA, Bryon was easiest to spot at night. His multi-brown coat was best for desert camouflage. He looked more like a domestic dog than any of the others. Damn monster domestic dog.

Josh whimpered and that told Bryon what the plan was. The agent continued the whimper and crawled through the shrubs, sticking his head and paw out the other side, lying on his stomach. Once he got the attention of the guard, Bryon played the injured puppy, drawing the guy toward them. When the man knelt and reached out to pet Bryon, his wolf sprang forward and snapped his jaws around the human's neck, then dragged him to the rear of the shrubbery.

It had been a long time since Josh and his men had been able to work as a team. Most assignments required only one, sometimes two, of his men. With them all together, they were unstoppable. Adrenaline pumped through his veins, giving his wolf more strength and his human more clarity of mind for quicker strategizing. They were a force to be reckoned with.

Next was the other man at the back. He'd been on the side of the building when Bryon lured the first one into the bushes. This second guy didn't even know his comrade was missing. But it didn't take long for him to notice once so he came around the corner.

Bryon shifted into human form then started groaning as if badly hurt. Josh hid in the shadows of the shrubs several feet from Bryon and the dead enemy body. When the guard whispered, Bryon answered in Russian, drawing the guard to them quickly. Bryon scurried to the shadows, out of the immediate sight of the man coming through the bushes to find his deceased buddy.

When the Russian guard knelt to feel for a pulse, Josh sprang forward and took him down in similar fashion. Two down, two to go.

Candy stared at the exterior camera monitors and sat speechless. When Tumbel ran out, she tried to go after the idiot, but he must've held the door closed so she couldn't open it. Fine with her. If the stupid man wanted to commit suicide, so be it. Her emotions went all over the place and her mind argued with her about letting him die. He was cute and she was growing attached to his company, but she wasn't in love with him.

He was the first man who hadn't tried to talk down to her. And he had been professional even when she'd been a total bitch to him. Something she was now trying to rectify, even though it was damn hard. But she still didn't want to see him dead. She'd never know what more time with him would be like. Ugh. She had to stop getting emotional with him. Tumbel wasn't her boyfriend. Maybe working on serious lust issues . . .

Then one of the guards in the rear of the building moved toward the bushes. She figured Josh had to be hiding there, but she couldn't imagine what the agent could do. When he fired his weapon, that would draw attention from the others, making it one against three. He couldn't be that dumb, could he?

She watched as the guard squatted, then a scuffle that she couldn't really see, and he suddenly slid through the foliage and disappeared from camera view. Not a single shot fired. She jumped to her feet. Wouldn't she have heard the gunshot outside, considering they weren't that far from her position? He must've had a silencer.

On a monitor below the exterior views, something was happening at the front of the lobby and on the sidewalk just outside the door. Front monitors showed the man with the news truck had the TV camera set up on a tripod and a bright light shined on the news reporter as she talked into a microphone. Fuck! Dubois had told her not to go live. Were they?

She snatched up the TV remote and switched on the twenty-four-inch box to the station matching the call letters on the van outside. Some kind of cop show was playing. One with police or firemen depicting the "real" lives of those who put their lives in danger for others. Except for some of the hot men, she had no interest in seeing Hollywood's version of what she did for a living.

At least the camera crew hadn't gone live. Candy glanced at the front monitor angle. The woman outside was handing off the microphone to one of the captors inside the building. The short one, Yulian, stood behind the NIA director still tied to a chair blocking the door from any frontal attack. Guess the Russian was too chickenshit to stand in the clear. Not that anyone was set up to take him down yet. It had been less than an hour since this had all started.

Candy reached out to turn up the volume of the lobby mics, but her eye caught the image in an exterior view of something she was completely at a loss for how to handle. Where the fuck had the panther come from?

CHAPTER 12

Josh and his two agents had come around to the side bushes to see the TV camera aimed at the lobby. The microphone cable snaked on the sidewalk in through the door, so he figured one of the bad guys was making a demand or pontificating his views for his fifteen minutes of fame around the world.

He noted the satellite equipment on the truck wasn't up and running, so they weren't on live television. Apparently, their Russian guest didn't know how a satellite broadcast should look. Josh had seen plenty of those in his days working high-profile security cases.

The last enemy guard stood at the building's corner, watching over the crew and scanning the area for trouble. The man had frisked the camera guy when the two newscasters had approached the doors, then he'd edged back into the shadows. During that interlude, Josh and his men had taken care of the third guard. Frank had stayed behind to drag the body to a hidden location.

The problem with this guy was that he was too close to the front of the building for any of them to sneak up on. Too much open grassy space didn't provide any of cover needed to get close. So the plan morphed into a let's-play-it-by-the-panther's-ear.

Parish was a black jaguar that people constantly mis-identified as a panther. As humor between the coworkers, they called him a panther and bought him pink prank items for his birthday. But when it came to stealth and surprise attack, no one was better than Parish, the jag.

Josh, along with Bryon, made their way to the rear of the building, staying out of sight behind bushes. The jaguar had slinked its way to the bushes along the middle of the building wall where the enemy had dumped the NIA security guard's body before taking over. The only evidence Josh could see was the hint of green eyes when Parish looked directly at him. Even Josh's animal's night vision couldn't pick out the jag from the shadows.

With Parish set, the agents threw rocks at the wall to draw the guard's attention to the back. When the guard didn't see his other man, hopefully he'd go to investigate. And that was the case. The enemy hurried back, passed the bushes, then put his back against the wall, sliding toward the corner.

At that moment, the metal door to the security room opened and Candy came out, draped in guns. Josh drooled. The only way she could be any sexier was to be naked with the guns strapped to her. He didn't start to freak until she headed in the same direction as the gunman ready to turn the corner.

Where the fuck was Parish? Why hadn't he taken down the guy yet? He watched as both his mate and the bad guy rushed to an intersection. Josh was ready to spring over the bushes and tackle the man in a frontal assault, probably getting shot in the process. But he'd do that to save his mate. She was now his reason for living.

The man inched closer to the corner as well as Candy. Josh's human form tensed. He wanted to shift, but didn't have time for that. Bryon put a hand on his arm, then hollered out words that sounded guttural. The man stopped and faced the bushes where he and his agent hid, his face full of confusion.

Candy came around the side, almost slamming into the guy. Guns swung into motion. Josh jumped to his feet and froze while Parish's cat body slammed into the guy's backside, taking them down to tumble to the edge of the bushes. Parish ended up under the guard, sharp teeth deeply sunk into the man's neck.

Josh had thought he would shit his pants, if he'd had any on. Then he would kick Parish's ass for waiting so goddamn long.

"Josh," Candy yelled, "don't move. There's a wild jaguar on the . . ." she paused and looked more closely at the heap that was the dead man next to the bushes. Parish, in jaguar form, moved from under the body, and she snapped the gun into position faster than Josh thought possible. Bryon jumped up, distracting Candy for a second, Josh following suit.

"Don't shoot," Josh and Bryon said at the same time.

She looked at the agent next to him and frowned. "Day? What are you doing out here? You're supposed to be in my office. How did you get out?" She then eyed both of them. She noted the bushes came to just below his waist.

Her brows rose and then lowered in confusion. "Do I want to know why the two of you are hiding behind the bushes, buck naked?"

Josh felt his face ready to melt off from hot embarrassment. "No, it's not how it looks." He started to push through the prickly bushes, but quickly discovered that wasn't a good idea for his man parts. "Just hold on a second." He jogged toward a narrow path cutting through bushes between the park and the NIA building.

Candy kept her shotgun aimed at Parish on the ground, but her eyes followed him. How was he going to explain this to her? He couldn't possibly make up a scenario that would begin to make sense. He dashed for his clothes on the ground outside the security door where he'd dropped them before shifting.

When he bent over to pick up his pants, Frank came around the far corner and smacked Josh's butt sticking up in the air. "Great job, guys. Need to do that more often. Whoa." He saw Candy and stopped. "Boss, did you know your mate's standing out here with a gun pointed at Parish?"

"Yes," Josh huffed, "I am quite aware of that." He slipped his pants on, foregoing the boxers. "Turn around." A growl came from him. "My mate sees no one else naked."

Frank spun on his heel. "No problem. I'll just go back to where no guns were pointed at my nuts."

Josh glanced at his mate. Her face was as red as his had to be. She aimlessly pointed the gun in his direction. She probably didn't even know she'd moved when seeing Frank. She glanced at Bryon, back to him, then dropped her eyes to the cat hiding under the dead person best he could.

Her voice was strong but unsure when she said, "That's not Hamel's body."

Josh hurried toward her, pants done up, but no belt. "No, you're right. That's not what Frank meant." He stretched for the gun in her hands and she jerked it out of his reach.

"This is mine," she said and stiffened her stance. "Will somebody explain why we're not worried about the man-eating animal, and why you're all naked, and how the hell you guys got outside, anyway?"

Josh put an arm around her shoulder and directed her back toward the security door. "We'll discuss this inside."

She looked up at the building toward her second-floor office. "What the fuck?" She stopped and turned back to Bryon. "You jumped out the—"

The jaguar had climbed out from under the guard and was following them. Candy twisted around and pulled the trigger. If not for Josh's shifter speed, Parish would've been toast. The bushes to the side of the cat's body had a new entrance to the park. Smelling feline blood, Josh snatched the gun from her hold.

At the same time, Parish shifted, feeling around his ribs. "Son of a bitch, man. Your mate freaking shot me." He rubbed his hand over his chest and abs.

"You were barely touched," Joshed huffed. "The pellets mostly went over your back."

"Yeah, mostly," Parish complained. "I was still bleeding to death."

Josh looked down at Candy's face and sighed. She was white as a sheet. "Shit." He turned them toward the security office, away from Parish's full monty. "You guys hang out somewhere close, but stay out of sight."

"Wait," Candy said, "are you all "—she flipped her hand in the air—"animals or whatever?"

Josh continued walking with his arm around her shoulders. "We'll talk inside, love." Well, he hoped they would talk and she didn't just decide to shoot them all.

CHAPTER 13

Seeing the guys without clothes carried Candy into the past, about ten years ago. Casualties were heavy on the front line that day and medevacs were in high demand. Night had fallen and the temperature in the desert was dropping rapidly. After three full transport runs for injured soldiers, Candy's helicopter was grounded for fuel. Which was fine since the mission was about over. A few more helos were on their way in, but that was it.

As she stood outside the depot, she watched doctors and nurses frantically trying to save the lives of brave men willing to die for their country. She heard that several chopper pilots had been injured during their pickups. In the midst of all the goings-on, a shout came out for a SF pilot. SF pilots were a group of specialized flyers who picked up certain combat units.

As far as she could tell from her few conversations with those pilots, they did nothing different from what she did with her medevac chopper. Except the pickup locations were in more dangerous combat zones.

Someone hollered that no SF pilots were available. They were either en route back to camp or down in the battlefield. The coordinates for the pickup were not too far from her last field landing location. When a second call came in, she knew it was dire. The men needed help now. With nobody moving toward any choppers, she decided to take the call. If the situation was that bad, the unit would not mind a non-SF pilot dropping in.

With all the medevac helos down for service, she headed for one of the bigger non-emergency 'copters and powered up. Even though the helicopter was not equipped with full medical supplies, she would be able to fly the guys out. After giving the call letters of the helo and her ID, she confirmed grid coordinates and lifted off.

According to protocol, she should've waited for authorization to go, but sometimes when speed was the key, they cheated a bit and left early. There was never a time when departure was not approved. None she ever knew of. And of all times, now was a time to cheat. The first medevac request had come in over fifteen minutes prior. A transport should've been on site already. Every second she waited, another soldier could be killed.

Well on the way, she was surprised when a deep harsh voice came over her headset. "Lieutenant Obermier, this is Sergeant Sanders. Do you copy?"

She almost laughed. She didn't deal with this sergeant much since he worked with the SF teams, but she still laughed when the men called him Colonel Sanders when chicken was on the menu.

"Copy, Sergeant Sanders."

"Lieutenant, you are not authorized for a SF pickup. Copy."

Oh shit. It was too late to turn back. She couldn't turn back. There were no others available to save the men. "Copy, sir. Over." She heard garbled noise and an electronic squeal through her headset. Then the normal dispatch person came on.

"You cheated, didn't you, Obermier," Dispatch said. "You're already in the air." Candy breathed a small sigh of relief. This guy in dispatch was a friend. He usually worked the combat runs when medevacs went out.

"Kellems," she whispered, though not sure why, "no one was going to help these guys. I can't just leave them to die when I can fly just as well as any SF."

"Candy," Kellems said, "you are disobeying a direct order." He was silent a moment. "How close are you?"

"Almost halfway. ETA ten minutes," she replied. "Is Sanders there?"

"No, he left after he talked to you. I don't think he knew you were airborne."

"I think that's obvious, Kellems," she said. "Do you want these men to die because I don't have *SF* at the end of my name?"

"No, Candy, but that's not my job. I can't make that decision."

"Okay, here's the deal, Kellems," she said. "I didn't take off. I heard what Sanders told me and I abandoned the mission. I'm now in my bunk getting ready for dinner. That's all you know. Radio silence begins now." She flipped the mic button, cutting off any sound on her side.

"Dammit, Candy." Anger came from his voice, but she wasn't worried about him. She saw the familiar landmark of her last pickup and passed it to reach the coordinates given earlier. Finding a flat area behind a rock outcropping, she set it down. Sand whipped into the air, creating her own dust storm. She had no idea where the men were. Hopefully, they saw her.

Through the hazy view came a group of men. One giant of a male carried an injured soldier over his shoulders. Following him, two others continued shooting their guns as they backed through the kicked-up grit. Those two were bloody, but on their feet. As soon as they were in, she started lift off.

The men shouted for her to wait. There was another coming. One of the soldiers yelled out a name she knew, telling this guy to hurry his ass up. If it was the same person she knew, she hoped he was okay. She liked him. He was funny and sweet. Big, though, over six feet tall and muscles out the wazoo. In fact, all these men on her craft were exceptionally big.

On the front of the helo, bullets from enemy fire ricocheted off the metal moving up to the windshield. Time was up. Despite the men's objections, she lifted off the ground. One sacrificed for the good of the many. Barely off the ground, her head turned and she saw a wolf materializing out of the sand-filled air. With a leap, the animal covered fifteen feet of ground and slid through the open side door.

Candy banked away from ground zero, intensifying the mess of debris in the air, hopefully making the enemy's shot off-target. Her heart pounded and adrenaline rushed through her system. That was the norm for combat evacs. But she'd never had her helo hit before.

Two things stood out on that mission, besides the Alpha Charlie ass-chewing she got after landing: On the way back, a guy said she didn't smell like one of their pilots. She thought he must've said "spell" as some jargon of theirs meaning she didn't have SF at the end of her name indicating special certification. And after they landed, no four-legged creature got off the chopper, but the guy whose name they called climbed down from of the back, buck naked. She knew he didn't get onboard in that condition. That wasn't something she would likely miss.

She never got the chance to talk to any of the guys as they were shipped out almost immediately while she carried out the punishment of being Latrine Queen for a week. They went easy on her since she did save the lives of five men, or four men and a dog/wolf.

Now, in the security room of the NIA building, she looked into the gorgeous eyes of the hot man close enough to kiss and said, "Are you a wolf?"

CHAPTER 14

Josh didn't know what to say to his mate's question. There was so much to tell her and they had another crisis to handle at the same time. He guided her inside. As if she were in a long-lost memory, she followed him quietly then sat in one of the desk seats. What clued him into her being in a quasi trance? The fact he had his arm around her without her threatening to kick his balls into his throat and that she then let him hold her hand.

He plopped into his own chair and rolled to her so their knees touched. He placed his elbows on his thighs then sat back and rubbed a hand over his face. "Sergeant Maj—"

His mate held up her hand. "I've seen you *naked*. No more military titles. I don't want to think of military men in the buff."

About fucking time! He didn't want her calling him anything weird when he finally got her naked. This was a big step forward.

"Okay, Candy," he said. "Yes, I'm a wolf. And so are my guys, except Frank is a cougar, and Parish is a black jaguar, as you saw." He watched her eyes carefully, ready to take her down if she went for the gun cabinet. She just nodded, chewing on the inside of her cheek.

"That makes a lot of sense, now," she said, running shaky fingers through her hair. "I knew a wolf got on, but a very nude man climbed out."

A growl rumbled in his chest. What man and why was he undressed?

She blinked wide eyes at him. "Is that you? Are you growling?"

He told his wolf to chill. He had no idea what or when she was talking about. Now was time to pay attention to their mate, not jump to conclusions.

"So," she said, "that's what makes your organization so special." Still nodding, she continued. "And that's why you're all so big, stature-wise."

"Not all of us, but those working with the government usually are because of what we do," he said.

"And that's, what, exactly?" she asked.

"Well, in ALFA, we do what's needed, from personal security to tracking down international bad guys."

"Oh," she blinked at him. "Like watching over a mafia female or discovering a human trafficking ring in Europe."

"Yeah, like those," he said, running his fingers through his hair. She had called him out on those recent jobs. Though the missions weren't totally screwed up, they had their moments. His mate seemed too quiet. "You have any questions?"

She shook her head. "No, not right now. Not really. I'm sure I will eventually. A lot of them."

Okay. She was going through a bit of shock. That was normal and understandable. "I'm sure this comes as a huge surprise," he said.

"Well, sort of," she responded, her voice still lacking that bite he was used to. "Not as incredible as what happened in New Mexico, but yeah."

"What happened in New Mexico?" he asked.

Her hand covered her mouth. "Oops. Nothing. You're really messing with my head."

He sat forward in his chair. "You talking about Area 51? That New Mexico?" he questioned.

She spun her chair to face the wall of monitors and pushed buttons on the board. "I wonder what we missed while outside?"

"Hey," he said. "That's not fair."

She grinned at him. "Sorry, dude. If I tell you—"

Josh flopped back in his chair. "Then you'll have to kill me." He winked at her, hoping to make everything normal again.

"You got it." Her smile lit him up inside. Candy continued to mess with buttons and knobs, as camera footage ran backward.

He wasn't sure what had happened, but he felt as if they'd crossed a long and scary slatted-wood bridge dangling a hundred feet above snapping crocodiles. He was light and happy. She looked relaxed and focused. She smelled content with a tinge of arousal. Was that for him? It had better be, or he'd be kicking someone's ass.

"Here it is," she said, pushing buttons.

"What are you looking for?" he asked.

She said, "Before I came outside, Yulian was talking to the newswoman. I think he may have said something important."

"We saw the camera guy turn the light on and the mic cord stretched inside, but that was it," Josh said. "Any idea what Yul said?" He glanced up at a small TV mounted on the wall. A five second commercial promo identified the station as the same as the letters on the van outside. A regular nighttime show played—no live footage, so this crisis was still under some control.

"No clue what he said, but we're about to find out." She twisted a knob. "Hopefully, it'll answer some questions we have. Like what the hell is going on? And where is his brother?"

He noted her usage of "we." That was a good sign, right? The security camera footage played on a larger monitor sitting on the desk in front of them. He watched as the reporter hesitantly stepped toward the glass door to hand off the microphone, then hurry back toward the camera.

The guy argued with one of his men in Russian, then stood behind the NIA director tied to a chair. "'Ello, Americans and people of Washington, DC—"

Candy looked at Josh and asked, "Is that the same voice as the YouTube we heard upstairs?"

He nodded. "Yeah, the one you said was Yulian, so that much we have right."

The video continued: ". . . your government do dis to my family. I am here to tell you my story. My American father marry my Russian mother then you kill him years later—"

"What the hell?" Josh asked. "Is he giving us his life story?"

"Sounds like it," Candy replied as she typed into a laptop sitting to the side. "God, does he think this is Lifetime or something? I can't believe he's telling the truth. There has to be a good explanation if he is."

He grunted. "He's trying to justify why he's doing this. What has that got to do with him taking hostages?" Josh couldn't believe this joker. There was no reason ever to threaten innocent lives, to bully others into doing what you wanted.

"Great," Candy said, scanning through the laptop's screen contents. "He and his brother have a grudge against the U.S. government."

"Why?" he asked. "What happened to them?" The CIA logo rested in the corner of the website Candy clicked and typed into.

"According to their intelligence file, the boys' father was an American who married their Russian mother. They lived in Russia as their father worked as an ambassador-like person of some kind." She paused and scrolled farther down on the screen. "In the early 2000s, he was recalled to the States."

"Why?" Josh said moving closer.

"Espionage charges," Candy continued.

"Did he have a trial?" Josh asked. Candy skimmed longer.

"Shit. The father was killed on a street in DC, coming to the NIB," she said.

"By whom?" he placed a hand over her shoulder, and she sat up but didn't say anything to him touch.

"Case unsolved," she replied. "But notes say they think another Russian spy already here took him out before he could testify. Not much after that," she said. "Bunch of gibberish." She clicked the back button a couple of times.

"So you're telling me this guy and his brother are seeking revenge on the U.S. government fifteen years after their father's murder? And we didn't even do it." Josh found that cowardly. Yeah, it was a shitty hand dealt to them, but what they were doing now was more wrong.

"Here's something more," Candy said, her voice excited. "Looks like we kept eyes on the mom and boys for a while in Russia. Says here the mom died from illness a couple years later, leaving the boys on their own. The two dropped out of school and melted into the Russian underground. End of file."

"How old were they," he asked, taking a few steps back and trying to calm his animal.

"Yulian was fifteen. Mikhail was seventeen," she said. "God, poor kids. No wonder they are the way they are as adults. To survive on their own in that environment . . ."

Her expression and smell turned sad. Even though these guys were terrorists, his mate was caring enough to feel sorry about their situation as children. She may show a hard-lined bitch face to the world, but underneath she was a gooey chocolate chip cookie. One he'd spread open to let the hot chips drip like honey as his tongue caught the ambrosia. He licked his lips and pivoted his chair away from her, hiding his filled dick.

"Oh, this isn't good," she said. She wasn't talking about cock, was she?

CHAPTER 15

———✂———

In the security room of the NIB, Josh snapped from his sex-filled daydream before it even started. His mate was a couple of feet from him and he couldn't touch her without her freaking out on him. Apparently, something had happened to her in the past to make her afraid of touch. He needed to find out what and get her past it.

Candy slid down the counter in front of the monitors to the side, closer to the computer.

"What isn't good?" he asked.

"Director Pommer worked with the two boys' dad, but Pommer wasn't director back then, but in charge of the State Department." She paused, eyes whipping side to side across the form she had pulled up on the computer. "Shit. Pommer was the one who authorized the boys' father for interrogation."

"Well, that explains why here and why tonight," Josh surmised. "This dedication was the perfect opportunity to get back at the people who the boys think ruined their lives."

"I agree." Candy sat back and rubbed her eyes. "Shit. So not good." She returned to the camera footage of Yulian's speech and fast-forwarded through it. Josh guessed she wasn't concerned what story the terrorist told. She knew the truth and that's all she needed. "Let's see if he offers any type of demands at the end of his boohoo," she said.

They watched and listened. The accent was thick. The man went on about Russia and the true motherland. Blah, blah, blah.

Candy jerked forward to stop the video. "Did you see that?"

Josh about fell out of his chair from her sudden movement. His little woman was as fast as a snake strike. "What?" he asked. Of course, he didn't see it. He was staring at her. The screen showed rewinding material.

She leaned forward and placed her finger on the monitor. "Look what he does." She clicked the mouse and the picture played at normal speed. Josh watched as Yulian's arm and head moved with no interruption of his story. "Did you see it?" She turned to him. "He looked at his watch."

Yes, that was what the slight movement was. "That's interesting," he said.

"Exactly what I thought." Candy sat back, finger tapping her chin and pressing her lips into a pucker. "What is he waiting for? Obviously, there is an agenda in the works."

"What do you think it is?" he asked. "You seem to know more about them than anyone else right now."

"All I know is they are unpredictable," she came back. "They are smart and in with technology. They don't do anything old school. And I don't like this." She pointed to the screen again. "Look at the other guys. Their guns are hanging at their sides. This is all a joke to them."

As Josh studied the image, Yulian knocked the microphone on the director's head and threw it at the door. "Ve are about to have fun soon, Pommer. Let's get de party started." His mate sucked in a breath and snapped her eyes to the camera. Something was going through her head and he suddenly felt very worried.

Candy popped up from her chair and headed for the gun locker. Her smell wasn't right. It was desperate, irrational.

Josh was on her tail. "What are you planning, Candy?" he asked.

"I'm going to pick them off one by one before they kill someone." She pulled out a sniper rifle and whipped around to face him.

"Whoa there." He blocked her way. "I don't think that's a good idea. There are too many of them and you have no good vantage point to set up." He grabbed the rifle barrel and jerked the weapon over his head, dragging her toward him, right to his bare chest.

He hadn't taken the minute to put his shirt back on since coming in from outside. In fact, most of his clothes still lay on the ground on the other side of the door. Going commando in his pants gave him a free, wild sense.

Her hands landed on his chest. The little fingers were hot. His skin sizzled, though he knew it was the electricity between them. Their chemistry would be off the charts.

She was pissed, shooting daggers from her eyes. He backed her against the closed locker. Quickly her mood changed to sweet arousal.

"Candy." Her name slipped from his lips after a deep breath of her. His eyes still locked on hers, he leaned his head down to take her lips. He didn't waste any time. Hunger for her made him desperate. Rough. Ferocious. Her open lips gave him an easy entry into her sweet depths. His tongue plundered, tasted, dominated, and took. He'd wanted her and now he was getting her. He was beyond thinking. It was time to feel. She pulled him closer. Time stopped. Everything got foggy as his sole focus became the moans he heard and the scent of her arousal.

The kiss turned wilder, desperate and consuming. He should stop. He should stop right now. Her whimpers grew, and he envisioned ripping off her clothes. Fuck, but she felt so damn good.

When he pulled back, her breath feathered over his cheek. "J-Josh . . ." The scent of fear slapped his face.

"Candy, it's okay. I would never hurt you." He moved slightly so he no longer touched her, but barely. Her face reddened and she reached out for the rifle in his hand. The diversion hadn't worked. Fuck. He'd been too rough. Let his control slip too much and he'd scared her.

"Hey," he said gently, "did you hear me? I would never hurt you."

She pushed away from him, her eyes not meeting his. "I know that." She sat on the task chair at the monitors and stared at one of the screens.

"Candy," he said. She cringed a bit. His heart died a little. He wanted to ask about her past, but he couldn't bring himself to do it. If it was bad, he didn't want her remembering things that would make her angry or sad.

Sirens suddenly reached his ears. In the exterior views, black-and-whites with red lights flashing on top screeched to a stop up and down the street. Police officers swarmed the area, some even coming onto the back of the property.

"Oh, shit," she said, face in her hands. "There goes the neighborhood."

CHAPTER 16

Saved by the red flashing lights, Candy thought. A moment ago, when Josh had her cornered and his incredibly ripped body had been within inches of her, she had about come undone. She'd been secretly drooling over him since she'd first laid eyes on him in his office hours ago. But being that close to him, smelling his manly scent, she about gave in to the building desire.

Shit, when he'd been naked outside, she couldn't take her eyes from him. He was freaking perfect. Muscles defined like the marble of a Greek god statue. And if a normal male's johnson was supposed to be small when in the cold, dammit to hell, he'd be huge when excited. Her stomach churned, making her feel sick. But she squashed that weakness immediately.

She was surprised by her reaction—or lack thereof—to him telling her he and his team were shifters. That explained her one SF mission. Actually, the idea of changing into an animal wasn't foreign to her. When she was little and her parents yelled at each other, she used to pretend she was a fairy princess in a distant kingdom where families loved each other, never hurt each other. Not much of a difference between fairy and wolf, except one was real. One was deadly and scarier than shit. Okay, maybe there was big disparity.

And then when his lips touched hers. Oh, fuck—that was exactly what she'd wanted to do to him. She wanted to feel Josh touch her in ways no man ever had. Perhaps it was the genuine concern she saw in his eyes or just how cute he was whenever he grinned, but she'd never wanted to have sex this badly. She wasn't a virgin, by any means, but she wasn't that experienced, either. When in camp with no solid walls and people always moving around, there was little opportunity for sexual encounters.

Sex wasn't that big of a deal to her, anyway. Her early trysts had been short-lived and quick. A lot of the time, she never reached orgasm. But that was what she got for hooking up with young guys who had little idea exactly where her clit was, much less what it took to bring a woman to climax.

She felt sure Josh wouldn't have that problem. Not at all. Then imagining his hands on her body, that old fear came screaming forward. Goddammit, she thought she could handle these stupid feelings. This gorgeous man weakened her emotionally and physically. If she stayed with him, he would break her down until she was a blubbering mess like she had been when she'd enlisted.

Life had taught her how to not let her feelings and emotions get involved where logic was needed, but with Josh, the line was getting fuzzy. Josh made her feel things. Things she wasn't sure she could explain. Things she shouldn't even be considering. Too long had she lived in a dark corner, and he tempted her to go out into the sun.

Her body responded to him in ways it never had to any other man. She'd never cared much about having sex or how good it could be. Good was never really in the cards. But here she was, really thinking and questioning, hoping and, hell, even daydreaming of what he might do. Of all the ways he could bring pleasure to her and take her over the edge.

The military philosophy was to cut each soldier to the bone in basic training, making them nothing, lower than dog shit. Then build them into the amazing soldiers who protected the liberties this country enjoyed.

Didn't take her long to get to the building stage since she was already at rock bottom. But once in, she never looked back. The men and women around her were her new family, one she would fight for, die for. Now, for the first time, she was considering what life would be like if she married and had children.

No! She couldn't think that. She couldn't let that ever happen. Children were not an option. How did that even slip into her mind? She'd been determined her whole life about that and suddenly she was having visions of kids and by god, they had Tumbel's eyes and adorable grin. Her heart raced. She was sweating. What was happening to her?

A diversion. She needed to change her thoughts. She didn't want to go down that lane of memories. Too much hard work had gone into getting past her childhood. Moving on.

She sighed, watching the police swamp the street. She looked around for Dotson in his uniform, saw him heading toward one of the lead cars. He should be able to keep the force in line, doing what they should outwardly, and not planning anything covertly. Later, she'd have to ask how the police had gotten word of the situation. Someone had finally gotten to them.

Her eyes glanced at the image of Yulian and his men to see their reaction. The man snapped his phone closed and looked at his watch again, then walked to the front of the lobby.

"Hey," she said to Josh, not looking at him pacing behind her, "we have movement." He stood behind her chair—right behind. Heat poured off his hot skin. She shuddered at re-membering how silky and hard his chest was. Oh god, she felt wetness slip from her core. He breathed deeply and she knew he smelled her. Oh god, oh god, oh god. Could she be more embarrassed?

A voice came over the speakers from the mics out front.

Yulian stood with the news reporter's microphone again, talking to the camera. "As a consequence to hurting my family, I demand $100 million to be deposited in de next hour or everyone in here dies." Yulian threw the mic on the floor by the door.

Behind her, Josh said, "What? That's it? What the hell?"

Candy was breathless. She knew a lot of the people in that room. And all of them killed? What did Josh mean by "That's it"? She could only gape at him. "What?" she said.

"He demands money," Josh said, "but doesn't give a bank account to put it into? No demands of unmarked bills?"

He had a point. Yulian had set this up to fail. No matter what. He said "deposit" and not "cash," which was what she'd guess was the preferred way. The terrorist was arguing with one of his guys again. Dammit, she needed Day to translate. He was outside, naked, or in animal form, or whatever.

"I don't care how fucked up the scenario is, we have to do something," she said. "If all the bigwigs here are killed, our intelligence community will be in chaos for months. If our enemies found out about that, all hell would break loose." She stood and pulled her phone from her pocket. "I need to call the president."

"You have the president's personal number?" Josh sounded astonished.

She laughed and replied, "This president is different from any other in history. He knows who he trusts and he likes to work directly with the source, not the 'in-between' people. He wants the facts firsthand."

She dialed, hoping the president was available. It was close to eight o'clock already. She waited for his atypical answer: "Talk."

"Mr. President, it's Sergeant Obermier."

"That's what my caller ID says."

Shit, she knew that. The president was a strict no-nonsense kind of guy. His sense of humor lacked, but his negotiating skills and law smarts were top of the line. "Yes, sir. Sorry, sir. We have a situation in the NIA building needing your attention."

"Go on," he said.

"As you know, we are under a hostage situation with the Steganovich brothers from Russia."

"Yes, I've been briefed on that. What's changed?" he asked.

"The leader has made a demand for $100 million for deposit but left no account numbers or anything. Has information of that type come to you?"

"No, nothing yet but we do not negotiate with terrorists." The president sounded calm and cool. She had been until this last statement.

"Sir, do you know who all is here? Our intelligence department will be decimated. We'll be vulnerable." She couldn't believe this. The people downstairs were among the top intelligence in the community. Pommer, the NIA director; Lancaster, FBI director; Homeland Security, and others were all here to congratulate their highly regarded and most rigidly kept secret, the ALFA team.

"I've just been handed the attendee list. Stand by one minute." The line turned silent. Candy couldn't sit any longer. Her legs were too anxious, as was her mind. When she paced to the door, she opened it a crack and whispered-yelled for Agent Day.

Josh and all his sexy skin came up behind her. When she turned, he was there, in her face. And she loved it. She took in his smell: woodsy and all male. A growl vibrated from his chest, surprising her. Her eyes snapped up to his. Their golden glow lit a flame in her lower stomach. Another memory wanted to surface. She refused it. Her breath left her. She had to force wind into her lungs. A whine behind her got her moving. Josh pushed the door open for the wolf to enter.

She smirked as she was about to talk directly to the animal. "We need your translation skills. They're talking a lot." She tilted her head toward the monitor board. Her eyes glanced at Yulian answering his phone. She turned up the volume knob then went back to pacing. After another minute of phone silence, Candy looked at her phone's screen to make sure the signal was still intact. It was. What was taking so long? It couldn't be good. She leaned her forehead against the cool metal of the gun locker.

Finally, noise traveled down the line. Sounded like several voices. "Candy, someone'll call you back. I've got a damn dog sniffing my feet." Then the president was gone. She looked at her phone and sighed. Her peripheral sight caught the movement of the hidden floor trapdoor leading to the tunnels, that Dotson had left through earlier.

She turned to see a stranger's face pop up from the stairwell, ASh gun in hand, pointed at her. A shot echoed in the small room.

CHAPTER 17

A s his mate wore a path into the terrazzo floor, Josh let
in Byron and grabbed his boxers and shirt on the
ground next to the building. Josh was high on pheromones.
His mate wanted him, even though she tried to keep her
distance. He smelled her want and saw the heat in her eyes
when she looked up at him. Now if he could cut through the
fear she had, they could move on to mating.

His agent shifted after Candy explained what she needed
Day to do, and he slapped the clothes in his hands to Day's
chest. His woman would see only him naked. Day rolled
his eyes, but slid on the clothes while staring at the monitor
showing the live events in the lobby.

Josh kept his eye on his mate. She was intensely concerned with a bit of trepidation flowing through her. The
general rule with terrorists was not to negotiate or fall to
their demands. If they caved to one, then every damn bad
guy in the world would copy the first to get whatever he or
she wanted. That simply couldn't be allowed.

If this had happened any other time, any other place,
he'd be getting a phone call and assigning one or two of his
men to a mission to go in and bring out the hostages alive.

ALFA had done so many jobs with SF teams and Navy SEALs in the past that he wondered why his organization was kept separate from the military.

He guessed their time had come, though. Since they weren't part of the armed forces, his group became expendable when it came to cutting costs and tightening the belt. But that wasn't his mate's fault. She was just following orders like any good soldier. She was good at her job and kept a cool head under pressure. He could see why she had been promoted to this leadership position. His mate would make a great mom.

When Candy got close to the locker, he meandered closer to make sure she didn't decide to pull a Rambo again and go all gung-ho to shoot up the place. He had no doubts she could walk into the lobby and take out a couple of the men before they got her.

With that thought, a pierce to his heart stopped him. The idea of losing her was more than unsettling, it was deadly. If he lost her during this, the world would lose two destined lovers today.

"Josh," his agent said to him, "who is Mikhail? Wasn't that the other brother?"

"Yeah. Why?" Josh asked.

"'Cause the short guy on the phone asked Mikhail, who I'm assuming he's talking to, if he was 'done at the house.'"

That was interesting. So Mikhail was around, doing something. He'd have to tell Candy when she got off the phone. Maybe she knew what they were talking about.

A strange smell reached his nose. It grew stronger the closer he came to Candy. The smell was familiar, but he couldn't place it. Then he heard a tap under the floor, and another coming from the secret exit to the tunnels. Had Dotson returned, climbing steps? No, this person smelled different. Smelled like alcohol, vodka to be exact. A lot of vodka.

Josh's shift started before he realized it. His animal put the answer together and took control. The trapdoor in the floor raised and the nose of a gun slid up in front of a face covered in a knit cap like the terrorist's out front. How this guy found his way in he'd figure out later. Maybe he'd seen Dotson leave.

Josh lunged forward, diving for the man's throat at the same time the terrorist's eyes locked on Candy and his gun took aim. Unfortunately, to get to the terrorist, he had to get past the gun first.

Josh felt the sting, then the burn of the bullet as it entered his body. This wasn't his first time getting shot, but it was the closest to point-blank he'd ever been. With his jaws open, he crashed into the guy, snapping down on the tender flesh and muscle that tore away as the man fell from the ladder leading to the secret door.

With no control over his body, Josh rolled across the floor and slammed into the wall. A ball of fire rolled through him from tail to ears. The scent of blood, his own, clogged his wolf's nose. His mate was suddenly there, kneeling beside him. She'd taken off her uniform jacket to reveal a white T-shirt tucked into her pants.

A pressure pushed against his side, right where the fire ate at his fur and skin. He watched his beautiful mate's lips move, but heard nothing but a continuous buzz in his ears. That was strange. He'd never experienced that sound before, but he'd never been standing next to an assault rifle exploding in a small, metal-lined room.

He felt tired, so tired, like he'd run all day in the woods chasing rabbits and other critters without a break. But that wasn't right. He'd been with his mate. He'd met her, finally. After all these years. He wondered if he'd ever get to touch her again. Maybe after he rested for a moment, just a quick minute—

CHAPTER 18

"Josh, don't you fucking leave me, do you understand that, soldier?" Candy nearly screamed at the wolf lying in blood on the floor in front of her. She pressed her uniform coat to his wound, trying to stanch the red flow. She'd flown enough medevacs in her life to know how to treat battlefield wounds. Funny how she thought that part of her life was over.

She never would've anticipated not only meeting, but also falling for a male from another species living side by side with humans. No, she wasn't falling for him. Dammit, yes she was, ever since she'd walked into his office. How had he gotten through her defenses when no man ever had in her life? And he thought he was going to take a bullet for her and die. Fat fucking chance.

Agent Day knelt beside her and laid his hands on his boss's pelt. "He needs to shift to heal. Like Frank did. When he does, the body will eject the foreign material and regenerate muscle and lost blood."

Her mouth dropped open. "Are you kidding me? You're instantly self-healing?" They were the perfect soldier that science had been trying to create for years.

Day frowned. "Yeah, sort of. But it's hard to grow a new head once the original is removed and you have to be conscious to shift. Which Tumbel isn't."

She looked down at the creature. He looked like he was sleeping, taking a long-deserved nap, and not dying. His fur was gorgeous. She wanted to slide her fingers through it, but her hands were busy trying to keep his blood inside his body.

"So how do you get him to shift?" she asked.

Day's worried eyes met hers. "You don't. Pray that either his wolf or the man inside is with it enough to make a shift." Day glanced away. "There is possibly another way, but if it works, he'll kick my ass into next month."

"Who the fuck cares? Let him kick it into next year. As long as he's alive to do it," Candy retorted.

He grumbled to himself and ran a hand over his face. "Okay. Long story short. You are very special to him and he will do whatever it takes to make you happy." He pinched the bridge of his nose. "I'm so dead when he wakes. But if you *demand* that he shift, he will."

If that wasn't the strangest thing she'd ever heard. Why would she be special to him? How could she make his subconscious mind do what she wanted?

"Oh, shit." Day jumped to his feet and returned to the monitors.

"What?" she asked. "What's going on?" She twisted around to see the screens while keeping pressure on the wolf's injury. Yulian was talking to the NIA director's wife. Poor thing looked scared to death. Didn't help that the little prick held a gun to her. "What is he telling her?"

"He's instructing her to relay a message about using a helicopter," Day said.

"For what?" she wondered out loud. She and Day watched as the wife stuck her head out the front door and spoke to the female reporter. Yulian stood behind the director, resting a hand on the seated man's shoulder. The newswoman nodded and ran toward the police.

When the director's wife returned to her husband's side, Yulian raised his gun and shot her.

Shocked, Candy watched the woman crumble to the floor. Screams erupted in the lobby, echoing in the security room. Agent Day turned down the volume.

Why? Why did the terrorist bastard have to kill an innocent woman? Then a sick thought crossed her brain. Perhaps this was the boys' way of getting back at Pommer for taking their father. Murder the man's wife.

Anger and hate swept through her. Burning bloodlust settled in her heart. She wanted to rip the fucker's balls off and feed them to him. He deserved no mercy in her book.

Director Pommer sprang from his chair, hands tied behind his back, and one of the men hit him over the head with the butt of a gun. He fell to a knee next to his prone wife. Two of the gunmen lifted Pommer to his feet.

"Ve're almost even, Director," Yulian said. "Only one last thing and my part is done. And I'll be rich. Now, ve take your helicopter and escape back to our beloved country."

"It only holds four people," she heard the director say. Yulian looked at his four other team members, turned to the man he'd argued with a couple of times, and shot him in the head.

"Now ve have four. Let us go."

"The son of a bitch shot his own man," Day said, his incredulous voice wispy.

That was it, Candy thought. "Day, they are headed to the director's helo on the roof. You've got to get up there and stop them." The agent was out of his chair in a blink. "Wait," she said. "Turn off the roof lights." She nodded to a panel on the wall with labeled switches. He also switched off the heliport lights. "No, leave those on. They'll light the chopper, luring them so you can take them down."

Day gave her a weird look. As if the thought of what she said would've never crossed his mind. He flipped the switch back on. "Can we get to the roof without the elevator?" he asked.

Shit. With the elevators shut down, the stairwell was the only way to the roof. And they had to go into the lobby to get to the steps. The monitor above the desk showed the group of three gunmen and the director walking toward the elevators. Then it hit her.

"The garage. The upper level has a bridge connecting to this roof so the director can go directly to his car from the helo without having to come inside the building. That's the only way. Go. All of you." As Day opened the exterior door, she added, "Agent, grind his nads off with your teeth for me. The director's wife didn't deserve that."

He gave her a sad nod and was gone.

Candy turned her attention back to the wolf in front of her. Her hands were covered in red stain, her coat completely soaked through. How could so much blood be lost and it still be alive? Her heart hurt, which seemed ridiculous for her. But it did. She raised a silent prayer to the One listening. If Josh lived, she'd do anything. Anything.

Banking on Agent Day's words about Josh obeying her orders, she sat straighter and put on her commanding persona. "All right, Tumbel. You've lain around long enough. Get your ass in gear and shift." She waited as nothing happened. Maybe she shouldn't come off as such a bitty, but more personal. Day did say Tumbel would do whatever to make her happy. She leaned down to his ear.

"Josh, if you shift right now, I'll be the happiest person in the world. If you don't, I'll be so pissed off at you that I'll never talk to you again."

The first crack of bone made her heart smile.

CHAPTER 19

⤖

Josh felt his body shift even though he had not initiated it. He remembered there was a reason to shift, but his mind refused to land on a thought and adhere to it. His wolf howled in his head to pull his shit together and wake up. They had a mate by herself in a dangerous situation, which she could handle, but they didn't want her getting the idea in her head that she didn't need them. They would always protect her, always be there for her.

His eyes popped open and he stared into the most beautiful hazel irises he'd ever seen. Worry filled them, then they smiled. His mate was inches from him and thinking about kissing him. He saw the hesitation, but when her pink tongue slid out. Screw it. He lifted the small distance and gently pressed his lips to hers.

Their lips met again in another scorching kiss. A kiss that deepened the strange connection they seemed to have. At least in her eyes. He seemed to think it was all normal. From the moment she saw him, she'd felt the pull to him. She knew there was something strong between them. It scared her, but it excited and pushed her to trust him at the same time. Her mind and heart told her she was delusional if she thought she could deny this. Them.

She pulled away with a smile and blush that made her too adorable. His mate was shy. That endeared her so much more to him. When she looked over her shoulder, he realized they were still in the security room of the NIA building. Shit. He'd been shot. The memories rushed in.

He rubbed his hands over his chest feeling for holes. His hands came away sticky.

"You got blood everywhere. Don't move," Candy said. At the water dispenser, she wet several paper towels and brought a dripping handful to him. The second the cold water hit his bare chest, he was wide awake. Goose bumps crawled over his body. "Hold still, you big baby. If you want cold, I'll drop you in the Potomac." He looked at her to see if she was serious. Her eyes were severe, then they rolled. "Yes, I would do that, but only if you made me mad." She winked at him. His heart fluttered. He was in love.

Sitting up, he noticed he still had on his pants. They were shredded, and the button and zipper were busted, but they covered him for the most part. He'd have to find something else to wear if he went into public.

He looked at the wall of video images she kept glancing at. "What's going on? What did I miss?" he asked.

Handing him another wad of wet paper towels, she wiped her hands and threw the waste into the trashcan.

"The little bastard shot Pommer's wife for no reason other than to be a fucking prick," she started. "Then he grabbed Pommer and they were headed for the elevators last I looked to get to the helicopter on the roof. They'd have to take the stairs since we shut down the shafts. I haven't seen them come out the top yet."

"Dammit," he said, trying to stand. His legs felt like gummy worms. "They're getting away. I need to get my men up there."

She grabbed him around the waist and lifted. He couldn't believe how strong she was. No wimpiness for his mate. "Your men are up there, and hopefully, set up to do whatever. I have faith they can make plans without you. Think on their feet." She pulled out a chair and sat him in it.

"My team can do more than just think in the middle of a crisis," he said, injecting pride into his voice.

"I'm starting to see that," Candy mumbled. She pushed a button, changing the large monitor on the desk to the view of the rooftop. The wide-angle shot covered the entire roof with one video unit. The helipad shined like the sun in contrast to the darkness around it. He couldn't see much more than a few air conditioner units and other shadows.

A rectangular swath of light cut through the darkness where the door from the stairwell opened. One of the men slid out, gun at the ready. He quickly circled the space behind the door checking for an ambush. Josh held his breath, praying his men didn't make a liar out of him. The gunman waved those in the stairwell out and their shadows passed through the rectangular light on the roof's ground. Four in all.

The group hurried through the darkness between the door and helicopter. Yulian, even though short, kept a gun to the NIA director's back. When they reached the 'copter's illuminated area, only three of the men stepped into the light. Josh sat forward in his chair. Candy sucked in a breath.

The first guy looked over his shoulder as if hearing something. The director stopped behind him, stalling the group. The two Russians exchanged words and Yulian pointed toward the dark area. Maybe telling the guy to look for their comrade. If Josh knew his men, and he did, they had taken down their first victim without so much as a murmur or scuffle of shoes.

Yulian poked Pommer with the gun and they headed toward the helicopter. When the director opened the rear plane door, he jerked as if a loud noise had startled them. Yulian spun around and fired several shots into the darkness.

"Don't by chance have mics on the roof, huh?" he asked.

"Nope," she replied. "Never needed them."

The remaining Russian pushed the director inside and slammed the door shut. Facing the darkness, holding his ASh in front of him and firing blindly into the dark, Yulian reached behind him and pulled open the pilot's door. As he turned to get in, a black mass with shiny white teeth launched from the seat.

Josh shouted, "Sheldon. Where the hell did he come from?"

The black wolf pinned Yulian to the concrete by the neck. Josh and Candy jumped from their chairs, cheering. A wave of dizziness rocked his world and he fell to the side. Candy was there, her arms around him, setting him back into the seat. "You stay here," she said. "You lost a lot of blood and it'll take a while for your body to regenerate it."

Josh opened his mouth to argue, and she pointed a finger at him and gave him the stink eye. "Don't give me any smack, boy. I've eaten men like you for breakfast." She planted a kiss on his lips and was out the door into the hallway leading to the lobby.

Wow, he couldn't wait for tomorrow morning's breakfast.

CHAPTER 20

———

Candy opened her office door with her naked entourage and their mates filing out of the elevator. The room was freezing. What the hell? She flipped the light on and the curtains fluttered at the open window on the far side of the room. This confirmed the ALFA guys had jumped from the window earlier. That seemed like a day ago, but it'd only been hours.

As she crossed to the window, the others followed her in, Josh between two of his guys helping him along.

"It's cold in here," one of the women said. "Does this fireplace work?"

"It's gas," Candy said.

"Put him down here on the rug, Parish," the woman continued. "The fire will keep him warm." Another lady grabbed the flag blanket from the sofa and draped it over Josh, sticking a toss pillow under his head. A streak of jealous anger raced through Candy. These women had their own men to fret over. Josh was hers. She swallowed hard. Where had that thought come from? Never had "jealous" been used to described her. Or overly caring for that matter.

She could thank her father for that. "Thank" wasn't the word either.

Director Pommer walked in. He looked broken after three hours of intense strain and the murder of his wife in front of him. "Director Tumbel," Josh started to sit up, but the NIA leader put up a hand. "No, don't get up. Please, rest. I came in here to thank all of you for an excellent job saving everyone you could tonight."

"I'm sorry about your wife, sir," Candy said.

"Thank you, Sergeant Obermier. She was a wonderful woman." The man paused, dropping his chin to his chest. Candy thought about what he must be feeling. For the past decade, she'd been surrounded by death. They'd walked together, hand in hand, on the battlefield, scooping up those still breathing and flying them to MASH units, and eventually, CSH facilities, to be patched up and either sent home or back into the field.

But of all those gone, she had not mourned one of them. She was sad for every soldier who no longer walked the earth, but she was never overcome with grief. She'd not let anyone into her heart to cause her pain if they were suddenly not there. In combat, tomorrow was not promised. She didn't know any other way.

The director cleared his throat and continued. "As I was saying, thank you, men and Sergeant, for your working in taking out the terrorists while keeping your profile low. We really need you out of the media, especially since y'all are . . ." the director's eyes glanced around then looked at his hands "naked."

"Thank you, Director. We appreciate your trust in us," a weak Josh said from his prone position in front of the fireplace.

"Of course, Tumbel. Of all our teams, you guys are the most amazing, for obvious reasons." He turned to her. "Sergeant Major, excellent job. I knew you were the one for this position when I submitted your name for the vacancy. Your record is spotless."

"Sir, thank you for the acknowledgement, sir."

"Now, don't worry about anything downstairs," the director added. "I want you out of the spotlight as well as you, men." He looked around. "Feel free to . . . get dressed and leave through a back door anytime you're ready." The tension in the room grew. Words unspoken hung heavy.

Sheldon, bare-bottomed, came through the door, holding a couple of trays loaded with finger food from downstairs. "Let's get the party started." When he saw the director of the NIA standing, staring at him and the food, he said, "Someone's got to eat it all."

Candy smiled at this newcomer's boldness.

Pommer slapped the naked guy on the back. "And you, Sheldon, are the perfect wolf for that. Congrats on your engagement, by the way." The director walked into the hallway. "And put some pants on, boy."

"Yes, sir. Right away, sir." Sheldon's smile was contagious. He pushed the door closed with his foot and put the trays on the desk. "Hey, guys, my wonderful mate and I are here. What did we miss?"

Everybody groaned and the guys gathered their clothes and redressed. Sheldon's new mate, Elna, handed black and white garments to him. A pair of boxers covered in cartoon wolves sat on top.

On the floor, Josh said, "Yeah, you guys go on home. You did a great job tonight."

"What about you?" Sheldon asked. "You can't even stand up yet." Hamel leaned closer to Sheldon and whispered in his ear. Mr. Wolfy Boxers looked at Candy and smiled.

"Got it. Nice job, boss man. I met my mate on a plane in a little-known country." He pulled a pretty, dark-haired lady with stunning eyes to him and kissed her. On the lips. And was still kissing her.

Josh sighed. "Loper, you're making it hard for the rest of us in here to not tell you to get a room."

Sheldon pulled away and smiled. "I bet I'm making you all *hard*—"

"That's not what I said," Josh huffed. The comment made Candy blush.

She never even had the sex talk with her parents. Her mom died before a young Candy was old enough for the discussion and her father she hid from every night.

One of the ladies carried the food trays and set them next to Josh then pulled a paper cup of water from the dispenser in the corner. Damn, she should've thought about that. Why hadn't she?

The woman placed the cup on the tray since he lay on a thick fuzzy rug. "There. You need to eat and drink a lot to get your strength back. Your body can't heal without extra substance to fix it all."

That was good to know, she thought. Wait a minute. Why would she care about knowing information on a shifter? The strong emotions she felt when the wolf was shot and close to death came to mind. Terror of him dying. Fear of never seeing him again. And other emotions she didn't understand. Feelings she'd never felt before. All centered in her heart and stomach.

Hamel looked at her as he tucked his shirt it. "Sergeant, why were we called up here in the first place. Did you want to tell us something?" Her eyes flashed to Josh. She hated eating crow, but it was called for, and she would do the right thing.

"It can wait. We'll see you all on Monday."

"Sheldon," Josh called out, "how the hell did you know to be in the helicopter on the roof?"

"Elna and I were a little late. When we saw the news van parked out front, we veered to the side so we wouldn't be caught on TV. That's when I smelled the blood of the killed security guards. After I got Elna in a safe place, I called 911. Figured you could use a little distraction out front."

"That doesn't tell me how you knew about the helicopter," Josh said, uncharacteristic impatience plaguing him after his injuries.

"Hold the phone, boss man," Sheldon responded. "I'm getting there." He picked up a piece of sausage and tossed it to Josh. "Here, eat this. You're grouchy and I don't have a Snickers bar." Josh scowled at him, but caught the meat and ate it.

"Now, if I may continue," Sheldon said with a British accent, trying to be funny. "When the cops showed up, we hung out with them. The news reporter lady relayed a message from the hostage takers. They were going to take off in the helicopter with the director in tow. If anyone followed or attempted anything, they would kill him like they killed his wife." Sheldon shrugged. "I took the garage up to roof."

Josh nodded and fell back on the rug. "For once, I can say I'm glad you were late. Now, everyone, get out." He winked at Candy. "See y'all Monday."

All the couples said their good-byes and began leaving the room.

"Wait, guys. What about him?" She pointed to Josh. They weren't leaving her alone with him, were they? No, no, no. Not good.

Sheldon nodded. "Oh, yeah." She followed the agent to his boss on the floor. He knelt and put a hand on his shoulder. "Boss, just remember that women are not equal to men."

Instant anger rose in her. She'd dealt with this problem her entire life. She would so kick his ass—

"No," Sheldon continued, "they are far better us. Smarter than us. And always right." He patted Josh's shoulder. "You get that and you two will be happily mated forever." He stood and walked out, then before the door closed, his arm slipped in and flipped off the light switch.

CHAPTER 21

⚮

Candy stared at the closed door to her dark office. Her heart raced and stomach felt like it could empty itself through her throat.

This was pathetic. She'd been on the front line for a medevac. Bullets flying everywhere, grenades and RPGs exploding feet from her helo. Sand and dust clogging her sinuses, choking her lungs. And she was more scared at this moment than then.

"Director Tumbel—"

"Candy, relax. We're adults; we're allowed to be in the same room, alone," Josh told her.

Irritation set her off. "Please, I know that. You're hardly dangerous." She gestured toward his prone body.

"Then sit next to me," he offered, patting the rug close to him.

Oh shit, she thought. Maybe she should turn the lights back on. The glow from the fire softly lit the room, making it all romantic-like. But also giving her shadows to hide in. Lights stayed off. She turned and headed to her desk chair.

"I need to do some work," she replied, hoping this would

give her the distance from him to not succumb to his sexy everything.

"Then bring the laptop over here," Josh said.

"I'd prefer not to. You need to rest to get better and leave." Hint, hint.

He lay back, his hands settling behind his head, elbows in the air. "That's fine. I understand your fear of shifters. Most people are scared when they first meet us."

A chill ran up her back. She was not scared of anything. Including dying. And a sexier-than-hell man lying naked under a blanket in her office. Fuck! Speaking of coitus, she hadn't done that in over a year. Okay, maybe it was years. Too many other things, like keeping her evac passengers alive, occupied her mind.

When a physical need arose, she'd work herself to exhaustion until the desire went away. After a few years, the basic human needs stopped coming, as well as all other emotions and passions and things that made humans human.

She leaned her face onto her hands, elbows resting on the desk. What the hell was wrong with her? A list of wrongs she'd be writing for days. Forget that. What was wrong with being with a man? It wasn't like she was a slut if she did the wild thing with him. Because that would be exactly were it'd go if she got close to him. She felt like a virgin on prom night.

"For your information, Director, I'm not afraid of you or your agents," she said.

"Prove it," he dared her. "I bet you can't sit next to me for five minutes."

"You want to bet, huh?" she retorted. "What do I get if I win and if I lose?"

She saw him around the side of the monitor, smiling. "The same thing, baby. Me." She leaned back in her chair and laughed. Full-on, belly-busting laugh. He was so damn cute when he said that. Like a two-year-old being so proud that he pooped for the first time on the potty.

She sighed, a giggle popping up—remnant of the laughter. "Fuck me," she said under her breath. She closed the laptop, but kept it in hand, and stood. "All right, Director. You win. I'll join you." She glanced at the finger-food tray next to him. "But only because I'm hungry, not because I'm attracted to you."

"Who said anything about attraction? Not me. I just asked you to sit." His smile was huge. Well, fuck her. She'd totally given herself away. This was going to be really bad. She'd be getting herself into a whole lot of shit. Some of it she wouldn't know how to handle, but she was a big girl wearing her big-girl panties. Besides, didn't everyone have a one-night stand with a gorgeous stranger in their lives? This would be hers.

And well, dammit, he'd made her feel special. That's one thing in the army you didn't want: to stand out, to be special in any way. Those who made impressions were the ones picked on the most. And she'd almost forgotten: He loved small arms as much as she did. Maybe they could talk guns for a while. Great idea! Now she felt better about this.

She plopped down on the fluffy rug next to him and pilfered a cracker with a sausage slice and cheese. "Did you know the ASh first came out in 2011?" she said.

"Do you know beautiful you are?" Josh asked totally ignoring her question. That shocked her. She was as plain Jane as they came. Well, she'd ignore his comment because a, she didn't know how to respond, and b, she had no clue how to respond.

She continued, not missing a beat. "Shortly after that—"

Josh partially sat up and leaned toward her. His warm lips were over hers before she realized what was going on. All kinds of shit blew up inside her. More stuff she didn't know how to respond to. The thought occurred to her that she'd forgotten how to kiss. When his tongue glided along the seam of her mouth, she opened more than her lips to him.

His lips were on hers. An instant fire burst in her veins and rushed through her body, pooling at her groin. She'd never felt anything like this. So hot. So raw. So desperate. Her hands crawled up his torso, tracing muscles, memorizing every delicious inch of him. She whimpered in the back of her throat and took and gave. Her heart thudded hard with every harsh breath shared between them. He kissed her neck, then her jaw. Her clothes came off in a rush of broken kisses and desperate pleas.

She moaned, her pussy aching for his attention. "Josh, please."

"Soon, baby. Very soon," he murmured, his tongue going around a circle over her curved belly and dipping into her belly button.

Her breaths reeled. Lord have fucking mercy. This guy was amazing. He continued his journey south, and she prayed she could survive this because she so wanted to know how it would feel to actually have an orgasm. Then he was there. His hot breath on her inner thighs. His cool tongue gliding over her heated flesh and working its way closer and closer to her pussy. She held her breath as his tongue dipped into her entrance, and she was lost to the bliss he was imparting on her pussy. He licked around her pussy lips and proceeded to fuck her with his tongue. She panted and ground her hips down, closer to his face.

"Please . . ."

She whimpered when he did a slow trail around her clit with his tongue.

"Tell me you want this, Candy," he growled against her pussy, sending electric pulses up her spine.

"God, yes. I want this. I want you. Please, Josh."

"Fuck, Candy. You're sweeter than honey. I could eat you for hours." He flicked his tongue twice over her clit. Her brain cells melted at that point. He rubbed his fingers up and down her pussy, wetting them with her dripping heat. Feeling his callused fingers over her sensitive flesh turned into a new point of pleasure. She groaned and tightened her hold on the blanket. Her hips rocked into his face involuntarily.

He sucked on her clit while his fingers curled and thrust

in and out of her. It took very little for her to go over the edge. Her heart pounded in her ears, each beat a fierce, wild gallop. Tension unraveled inside her, pushing her headfirst into an all-consuming orgasm. She screamed when a wave of pleasure rushed through her.

Panting like she couldn't get enough air in her lungs, she blinked the haze of happiness away.

When he pulled back, she could barely move. Her entire body tingled, breathing in quick gulps. She guessed he didn't want to talk about guns. He breathed deeply, moaned and lay back on the rug. "Candy, what you do to me is driving me crazy. You smell so good, yet you won't let me do more. Why? What are you afraid of?"

There was that word again implying she was flawed, less than perfect, that she'd bow down to someone instead of ruling the roost. Her father knew exactly what he was doing when he reigned in the house.

She frowned. "I think I'll just let you touch me a lot. All of me, actually. As I said before, I'm not afraid of anything." Way to ruin the fucking mood. Literally.

"That's not what your body is telling me. It's says you're frightened of something and need sex really, really, badly."

Oh my fucking god. She wanted the fire in the fireplace to jump on her and burn her to ashes. No need. Her body was about to spontaneously combust from embarrassment, anger, and shame. She rolled away from him and started to get up to gather her clothes and leave. She didn't give a shit if he was here all night by himself.

"No, wait, Candy. I apologize," Josh said. His hand was on her forearm. She stared at it. Since physical contact was rare and far between in her life, when someone did touch her, it made an impact on her. The fingers wrapped around her wrist were strong, rough from manual labor. His palm was hot like he'd held it to the coals.

She met his gaze, his eyes glowing around the blue irises. The radiance brought up a long-forgotten memory.

One that had tugged at her brain earlier. A time when she was young, before her mother— "Holy shit," she let out. "My mother's eyes sometimes glowed like yours."

His look narrowed and he was quiet for a moment before asking, "Were those instances highly emotional for her?" Josh asked.

She didn't want to think about those times. They were the worst. She looked away from him. "Yes."

He rested his hand on her bent knee, sending goose bumps to her foot. "You have shifter genes in your family tree. That explains a lot," he said, lying back.

Her head snapped around. "What does it explain? Tell me."

CHAPTER 22

Josh lay on the furry rug in Candy's office, thinking about her traits. "For starters," he began, "that's why you're so damn strong. You've excelled more than ninety-nine percent of the men, and it makes even more sense why we're true ma—" Shit. He'd almost said "mates." No way was she ready for that info. Damn, this relationship would've ended before it got started. "Sorry, I misspoke. I meant to say, it hints at why *you're* in the military." He stressed the pronoun, hoping she'd forget about the word "true."

"What's that got to do with anything?" she asked.

How did he explain shifters to a newbie to their world? "Shifters are survivors. They can fight their way out of just about anything. Nothing scares them." He pointedly looked at her. "Sound familiar?"

Candy rolled her eyes. "Yeah, whatever, what else does it say about me?"

"A lot of shifters are adrenaline junkies. Sometimes they do things just for the rush."

She thought about the medevacs from the battlefield and front line. Did she crave the rush? Hell, even the time she picked up the SF boys. "What does SF stand for?" she asked.

"Shifter forces."

"Seriously? That's it?" By the dramatic way those groups were talked about and treated, she figured it was big Latin or Greek words standing for "almost a god to everyone else."

She became lost in thoughts. Thoughts that caused her emotional pain. His wolf jumped forward wanting to console their mate, make everything all right, make her happy. "Where are you, Candy?" he whispered. "What do you see?"

She shook her head, coming back to the present. "Nothing. Just childhood stuff." He noted her shiny eyes that went along with her smell. She didn't want to talk about her past, so it had to have been difficult. What had she survived? "Tell me about yourself," Josh said, taking a different route.

"Dear god, this sounds like an interview for a corporate job," she said. They laughed lightly. "I don't know. I'm pretty boring. Enlisted when I was eighteen. Made sergeant quicker than most females who earn that rank." She shrugged.

"What is your job?" he asked, wondering about her shifter blood.

"Until this job, I flew medical evacuations during combat."

"Shit," he said. "Talk about adrenaline rush. You were all over that."

She smiled. "Yes, I was. I loved it. Miss it sometimes."

He asked, "Do you have a lot of family?"

"No. I have a younger brother and sister. My mother died when I was twelve. I don't know if my father is alive or not. Don't care, either." There was that agony he kept smelling. It had to do with her past.

Putting a bit of calming control in his voice, he said, "Why don't you care if he's dead?" He needed to be very careful not to scare her away, but he needed to know what had happened if he was to help her. If she truly didn't want to answer, he wouldn't force her.

It drove him crazy when a woman said nothing was wrong when it was obviously the opposite. If he didn't know what he did wrong, how could he change it? Women thought men should be able to read their minds and just *know*. But Sheldon was so right. Women were way more complex than men, too much shit always floating in their heads. Men were BSS: beer, sex, sports, not necessarily in that order.

Her body stiffened a bit from the command he gave. "I'd rather not talk about it right now."

He scooped her hand into his and kissed each finger, as he had earlier, to comfort her. She stared at him with wide eyes. "What?" he asked.

"It . . . you . . . I never had anyone do that before," she whispered, looking at their joined hands. "You've done it twice."

His heart broke for his mate. She'd been deprived of love for a long time. He didn't need to know her past to realize that. Once she knew everything, he would give her so much love that she wouldn't be able to stand it. That made him smile to himself. But there was a huge obstacle in the way of getting there: her. Something was blocking her emotions, her ability to care and love. He had to figure out what it was if they were to have any hope of mating.

"Candy, you have to know I'm attracted to you as much as you admitted you're attracted to me." He held on to her hand tightly in case she tried to bolt. "Are you going to be strong and face those feelings or cut and retreat?" He hoped using her language would help the communication between them.

A touch of anger floated in the air. "I am not a coward," she ground out between clenched teeth.

"I know you're not. That's why we're talking through this. Would you like to know how I see you, in truth?" he asked. She locked eyes with him, that fright returning.

"I want to ask you a question first," she pleaded. He

nodded. "What is a mate? I've been called that several times tonight."

Damn, she'd caught those references. He groaned and squeezed his eyes closed. This wasn't the time. She wasn't ready. But he wasn't starting the relationship by telling lies.

"The answer is complicated, but I'll give you the easy answer now. Is that all right?" God, he hoped that was all right. She nodded and he breathed again. "A mate is a companion, someone who sticks by you through good and bad."

"Oh, like a best friend," she theorized.

"Yes, like a best friend." And whole lot more, which included sex, which was why his body was saying to take her now. Again, she wasn't ready.

"So I'm to be your best friend? I've never had one of those. Your guys called me your mate. How can they know that? What if I don't like you?" she asked.

He cringed inside at the words. It was possible that mates wouldn't like each other, but he'd never heard of it. Even with a human mate.

"We're here right now to work on that. I want to get to know you, inside and out." She didn't miss his innuendo. Her arousal rose thick in the air. His wolf was about to have a cow. It wanted her NOW. *Chill out*, he told it.

Her chin dropped to her chest. "I don't think it's a good idea for you to know about me," she whispered.

"Why not?" he replied.

"Because . . ." she paused and sighed. "Because my growing up wasn't pretty. I hated my life." Tears were building in her eyes, but she straightened her back and held them in. She was strong; she wanted the world to see she wasn't a pushover or weakling.

Josh scooted closer to her so he could touch more of her. She hadn't objected, yet, so he took that as a positive sign. "Candy, you are one of the toughest people I've ever met."

She rolled her eyes to meet his. "Really? You think that?"

"Absolutely. How many female sergeant majors are there?" he asked.

"Well, I'm the first, actually," she replied. Holy shit, his mate was a powerhouse of a woman.

"That says enough, right there," he commented. "I see a beautiful woman who will kick ass when required. No one sees you as weak or vulnerable."

"I hope not," she said. "I've spent twenty years proving my worth to this military."

"Yes," he responded. "So opening up to someone, like your best friend, won't make you look feeble. We're here to strengthen each other. Make each other better, more loving people."

"I can't do that," she said.

"What do you mean?"

"Jeez Louise, how do I say this and not sound . . . stupid?" Her hand wiped her face.

"To me, you will *never* come across as stupid. Don't ever think that." Her personal self-image needed help while her professional image was buttoned down. No wonder she slipped into that tough-as-nails persona when she felt threatened. If he could just get her to relax and trust him, he would get past whatever blocked her.

Candy sighed. "I've never been in love. I don't even know what love feels like."

He asked, "You love your family, right?"

"No, but I did once. That was so long ago, I don't remember anything about it. My father did a great job of shutting down any happiness in the family."

"Was he mean?" he asked.

She tilted back and looked at the ceiling. "'Mean' doesn't begin to describe it. I think 'sadistic drunk' would be a better description. An angry, hate-filled bastard whose misery wanted all the company it could get."

"Did he hurt you?" His anger at a man who'd put his hands on her grew. He hadn't been there in her childhood to protect her. But he'd do his best now.

"Every day. But I got used to it. Even took the prick's attention away from my siblings when they got in his crosshairs." That was why she didn't like to be touched. In her mind, touch equated to pain. When her father touched her, she knew what was coming. This was killing him. She needed to be happy again. He'd get her there with time.

Josh swallowed hard thinking how to phrase this question. "Did he ever . . . did he . . ." Not a good start.

"Did he ever touch me inappropriately?" Yeah, that's what he'd tried to say. "No. The bastard was too drunk to do anything but hit with his fist. Couldn't make it up the stairs to our rooms where we hid when he fought with mom in the beginning."

"In the beginning? Did they stop fighting after a while?" he asked.

A boatload of emotional agony and grief came over her. She scowled and sat straighter, sliding into the other person she used as an escape. Her having an alter ego, a mask to hide behind, made all the sense in the world now. When things at home went to hell, she pretended to be someone— somewhere—else who was happy and had a better life. Coping strategies. Psych 101.

"In a way, they stopped fighting. I killed my mother."

CHAPTER 23

A s Candy sat on the floor of her office with a man who
enticed her too much, emotions she didn't want to deal
with bubbled inside her, ready to explode like a volcano. It
had taken her a long time to suppress the tumultuous disaster her life was, to push it down so far inside, it would
never see the light of day. Apparently, that wasn't enough.

Here she was pouring her heart out to a man she didn't
know, but was highly attracted to. There was something
about him that made her want to trust him. Believe in him.
Talking to him was so easy, too easy. Like they had been
best friends for years. Mates.

Thinking back to when her mother died made her want
to curl into a ball and cry until the pain was gone. But that
wouldn't happen. She hadn't cried since she was twelve.
The ache would forever be there, ready to eat her alive
when helpless against it. Solution: don't be vulnerable. She
sat up straighter and yanked down her white T-shirt.

"You didn't really kill your mother. Did you?" The way
he asked sounded funny in her ears. Like he didn't believe
she would do that. Then again, maybe he would. She
laughed, releasing some pent-up emotion.

"No, I didn't," she confirmed. "The drunk prick did. But I was the cause of it." She took herself back to that awful day. She would finally tell someone the horrible truth of the moment that had changed her young life.

"I had come home from school angry because my favorite teacher was going on maternity leave and would be gone for a few months. Her substitute was a grouchy old man who liked to call you out in front of the class to 'teach you a lesson.'

"When I came through the kitchen door, Mom was cooking dinner. Spaghetti with hot dogs cut up in it. My favorite, but it didn't cheer me up. I stomped over the linoleum toward the other room. I told my mom I was mad at Mrs. Carpenter and wasn't going back to school, ever. She smiled and asked me how I had arrived at that conclusion. I had reached the stairs in the living room at the point and hollered back to her, 'She's leaving because she's pregnant.'

"My father popped up from his recliner, nearly empty bottle of Jack clutched in his hand. I knew right away I shouldn't have yelled. He looked around confused, like he'd never been in the house before. 'Who's pregnant?' he stammered, holding on to the back of the stained recliner for support. His expression turned to the mean hate I knew meant trouble.

"He staggered toward the kitchen. 'The bitch ain't ever leaving me.' I ran after him when he burst through the swinging door into the kitchen. I pulled on his arm, telling him it was a mistake. My teacher was pregnant and leaving, not Mom. He didn't hear me. He had an excuse to rant and rave and he was going to take it.

"Mom was holding dinner plates in her hand when Dad tromped in. Before she could react, he bashed his glass whiskey bottle into her head. She crashed to the floor and the plates fell from her hands. It was so loud with my father screaming at my mother that he didn't want any more twat waffles to feed, Mom screeching back, and the dishes smashing into pieces. I wanted to cover my ears, block it all out.

"Then my dad did the unthinkable: He kicked Mom in the stomach, over and over, saying he would beat her until she miscarried, and if she ever thought about leaving him, he'd kill her." A sob choked her throat. The image of her mother on the floor, bloody and beaten, tore at her. It was her fault. A single tear slid down her cheek.

Suddenly, a warm blanket was wrapped around her, holding her tightly against a hot body. Josh had scooted behind her and enveloped her with his silent strength. With his comforting touch, she felt stronger, able to get through this nightmare he'd asked her to relive. Only for him. She wouldn't do it for anyone else.

"I hit and pulled on Dad's arm, screaming at him to stop. It was all a mistake. My mistake. He laid his hand on the top of my head and shoved me against the wall, hard enough to crack the wallpapered surface."

She snuggled back into his warmth. She'd never felt anything so good, so relaxing. She let out a breath and let him gently rock her.

Josh asked her, "What happened after that? Did the police arrest him?"

She laughed, but it sounded angry and hate-filled even to her ears. "You'd think that would be the case. That's when I learned something about my father I'd never forget. Just how much of a motherfucking piece of shit he was." Her hands fisted and she brought them down hard on her thighs. The momentary pain felt good. For the tiniest sliver of a second, it took her mind off the agony inside her. She did it again. Another small repose.

Josh grabbed her fists from behind where he'd snuggled up to her. He whispered soothing sounds, gently swaying side to side. With an incredible sense of peace in her heart overcoming the pain, she relaxed into him. This man's touch, his closeness, his protective cocoon around her was like nothing she'd ever experienced. She didn't know this . . . this . . . bliss existed.

Josh asked, "Is there more you want to tell me?" She nodded. She wanted to tell him everything. She wanted him to make all the ache go away, all the burden of knowing her mother was killed because of her carelessness.

She took in a deep breath. "After he pushed me into the wall, the next thing I remembered was waking in my bed to sirens and red lights flashing through my bedroom windows.

"In the twin bed beside mine, my younger sister and brother slept, holding on to each other for dear life, it seemed. I had always protected them when our parents fought, but I wasn't there for them this time. I was a part of the battle, a casualty.

"I sneaked downstairs to see what was happening. It was nighttime. Hours had passed. Police cars were parked in the driveway and along the street, their emergency lights giving the dark room a surreal feel. I went to the kitchen to see Mom, to make sure the police had her safe. What an idiot child I was back then.

"I walked in and saw a white blanket over a lump on the floor. At the bottom of the blanket, my mom's feet stuck out. They, too, were bloody.

"Someone called my name, probably my bastard father. I looked up and saw him sitting at the breakfast table, crying. I—I was so shocked that I couldn't move. I just stared at him, not recognizing the man. My father was dressed in a suit with his tie loosened around his neck. His hair was combed back and his black shoes shined. He looked like any respectable father coming home from work.

"One of the officers knelt in front of me. His eyes were friendly, unlike my father's. He asked me if I'd seen the intruder who had come into the house, hurt my mother, and took off with her purse.

"At first, I didn't understand what he was saying. That wasn't what happened. My eyes caught my dad's, glaring hatred at me. I knew at that moment he would get away with my mother's murder. Blaming it on someone who came in the unlocked door to steal money—during the daytime, when people were out and about."

She came back to the present to find herself in the hold

of a man she truly desired to be with. Inhaling deeply, she took his scent into her, calming her, bringing her comfort.

Josh said, "That's what we call scenting."

"What?" she replied. "Breathing in your smell?"

"That's part of it. For a shifter, our ability to smell the slightest molecule of a scent keeps us alive in dangerous territory."

She nodded. "I can see that." They sat quietly, the rocking motion lulling her into contentment. The pain in her heart subsided, almost to the point she could bear it. Where did it go? She didn't understand.

"You know," Josh said, "they say when you tell someone about something you've kept inside a long time, you're sharing your heart, and you and that person will always be connected through that sharing. You've given me half your pain so you are not burdened alone anymore. I will carry it for you as our connection grows stronger. As your mate, I will do everything in my power to make you happy."

She twisted around in his hold to see his face. The fire lit one side, keeping the other in darkness. But she only needed half to see he meant what he said. Even though she'd never seen it after her mother died, she knew the look in his eyes was love, directed at her.

She snaked her hand behind his neck and pulled him to her. She wanted this kiss more than anything. That damn cliché about wanting him more than her next breath was true. A laugh almost burst through with that thought, but the touch of his lips on hers sent every logical piece of her scurrying away.

CHAPTER 24

"Mmmm . . . I could kiss you all night." Josh whispered against her lips, the glow from the flickering fire making his eyes even sexier.

His lips feathered over Candy's chin and across her jaw to the tender skin beneath. His body was a hard-muscled line against her naked flesh and she shivered, feeling the dampness spread between her legs. How they got to this point still stunned her, almost as much as the memory of his tongue on her private parts. Her lower body jerked just thinking of how he'd made her come, her legs going liquid as he plundered her pussy with his hand and his mouth.

The feeling was nothing like she'd expected. She'd been happy without sex most of her life. Now she wanted to know how it would be with Josh. He was different and she knew it.

Josh's lips continued down, kissing the hollow of her throat, skimming over her breasts to take one nipple into his mouth. She gasped at the tender yet rough feel as he drew the stiff bud deep.

Skating his hand over her hip, he cupped her pussy once more, stroking her slit. "You're so wet, baby." His tongue played along her breast. As he slid one knee between hers, he climbed between her legs. "Spread yourself for me."

Candy's whole body stiffened and she shoved him from her, scrambling back.

He blinked, his face clearly stunned. "Candy, what just happened?"

She shook her head, bringing her knees to her chest. "It's not you, Josh. It's me. I can't. I just can't—"

"Look at me, babe."

She shook her head.

"Yes . . . Candy, baby, please. Look at me."

Wiping a hand across her wet eyes, she lifted her gaze to his. He reached out one hand and held it toward her. "Whatever this is, we can talk about it. I'm not going to force you to do anything you're not comfortable with. Is it something I did? Did I hurt you?"

Her eyes widened and she took his hand. "No, Josh. None of the above. You're the only man who has ever made me feel like you care."

"I do care. If I didn't hurt you, what's wrong?"

"I hate feeling powerless and out of control." She shrugged. "Sex does that to a woman. Men tend to over-power and do what they want. It's part of the reason why I'm not as experienced as you'd think when it comes to sex."

"You were made to submit with sex?" he asked, concerned.

She nodded again. "Something like that, yes. Not to mention the times I tried were less than satisfying. You combine that with my aversion to feeling not in control and it makes for a recipe of 'why bother.'"

"Less than satisfying, huh. Sounds to me like the guys you were with wouldn't know what to do with the equipment if they read the manual."

She cracked a smile. "To say the least. They made it all about them and I was nothing more than a means to an end. They got off and I didn't."

His eyes took her in and he nodded. "I have an idea."

She cocked her head, wary. "I don't know, Josh. It's been

a really long time since I've found myself in a situation like this, and with my history I really don't want to freak again."

He reached for his clothing pile on the floor. Candy's throat tightened. "You're leaving?"

Josh turned with his necktie in hand. "Nope. I don't scare that easily." He walked toward her. The silk tie wrapped around his palm.

"Um, Josh—what are you doing?"

Sliding in beside her, she scooted away the moment his body touched hers.

"Don't be afraid, Candy. I think I know how to help you relax and enjoy sex the way it should be." He stuck two pillows on the floor behind him and then held his tie out to her.

"Josh," she said unsure.

He nodded. "Trust me. Take it."

She slipped the silk length from his hand and he held his wrists together. "Tie me up, love. No touchy, no feely. It's all you."

With a smirk, she bound his wrists. "Too tight?" she asked.

He shook his head, slipping his hands behind his neck. "Nope. Perfect. Now I want you to take that pretty scarf of yours from behind the office door and blindfold me with it. That way you won't have to watch me watching you." He winked. "What better way to be taken than bound in silk that smells like you?"

She moved to the door and slid the shimmering scarf from the hook, tying it around Josh's eyes. With the crooked smile still on his face, he nodded once. "I'm all yours, baby. Exposed and completely in your hands."

Candy inhaled, kneeing beside him. "Yes, but—"

He shook his head again. "No buts. Not unless that's the part of my body you want to tease and tempt. You call the shots. Just don't leave me hanging too long." He chuckled. "Though with my cock as hard as it is right now, I'm not going to *hang* for a while. Not without help from you."

Unsure, she climbed over his legs, and sat on his thighs. Leaning over, she spread her palms over his chest. The feel of his skin and the rasp of soft chest hair sent tingles to her lower belly. Feeling emboldened, she raised and moved up his body, the length of his erect cock grazing between her legs.

He moaned gently as her slick part brushed his shaft and head, but she took his mouth instead. Sinking her hands into his hair, she concentrated on his lips and tongue. "Kiss me like you want to own my mouth, Josh. Like you want nothing more than the feel of my tongue on yours."

He obeyed, devouring her lips as she tightened her grip on his hair. His cock jerked against her thigh, his head swelling as he strained for contact.

As he had done before, she broke their kiss and nibbled her way over his throat to his chest, circling his nipples with the tip of her tongue.

Josh grinned. "Now I know why you like that so much."

"How about this?" She grazed the narrow bud with her teeth and he hissed. "You like it a little rough, Josh?"

"I aim to serve, beautiful."

Raking her nails along the hard planes of his chest, she licked and stroked his torso past the sexy V-shaped muscles leading toward his cock. She scooted down his thighs and wrapped her hand around his thick shaft. His member jerked in her palm and she froze, all her bravado gone.

"Relax, Candy. Just loosen your grip and run your hand over my hardness."

She nodded.

"Okay." She slid her hand up and down, her movements tentative.

Josh groaned, licking his lips. "Harder, baby. Run your palm over my head." She did what he asked and he sucked a breath through his teeth. "That's it. Now faster, get a rhythm. Mmmm."

The low rumble in his throat made her pick up her pace even more and his thigh muscles clenched beneath her thighs, his ass tight. A grin tugged at her lips at his reaction and she dipped her head, her tongue flicking the satin of his swollen head.

"Oh, babe, yes . . . use your mouth. I want your tongue and your lips wrapped around my dick. Take me deep."

She inhaled and opened her mouth, slipping his engorged head over her tongue. Josh bucked his hips pushing his member to the back of her throat.

"Keep your hand on my base, work my shaft as your mouth works my head. That's it." He said the words in a tight mutter and then let his breath out in a *woosh*. "Circle your palm over my head as you pull your mouth up and off and then plunge in deep again."

Candy took his full length into her mouth and a growl left Josh's throat, the sound raw and full of need.

"Faster, baby, tongue my balls and work my length. *Ahhh,* yessssss," he hissed.

Candy ran the flat of her tongue up the corded base of his cock and then sucked his head between her lips. Letting her teeth graze his sensitive flesh in and out.

"I'm really liking this," she stopped to say with a grin before taking him deep again.

"What's that?" he groaned with each suck.

She stopped again, licking his cock from root to tip. "Your grunts and your sexy animalistic noises. They make me want to suck you harder, until you come in my mouth. Do you want that, Josh?" she asked, giving his head a quick lick, taking the pearl of cum from the top. "Want me to make you come?"

Josh's entire body went rigid and his cock flexed, hard and unyielding in her hand. "Let me fuck your mouth, baby. I want you to swallow everything I give you."

"Tsk, tsk. That might be what you want, but that doesn't mean I'm going to let you."

"Candy! Fuck!" he snarled, a massive shiver shaking him.

She laughed low. "What do you say, Josh? What's the magic word?"

"Jesus! For fuck's sake! PLEASE!"

She took his cock deep once more, but then pulled back when he tried to buck his hips. He growled in frustration, but she lifted her ass off his thighs and hovered over his straining member. Gripping his rigidness, she rubbed his head along the slick folds of her slit.

"Candy, God . . . I'm not going to survive this. Come on, baby. Either fuck me or suck me. Pick one!" He strained trying to push his head higher.

With a smirk she lowered herself onto his tense dick and with a growl he reared up, his ass and thighs grinding his cock deep. Candy pushed his chest and shoulders down and lifted her ass, taking him as she rolled her hips. She kept the grind slow and forceful. Gritting her teeth, she let the tension build, moving her body so his cock hit her spot with every in and out.

Her thighs clasped either side of his hips and her body went taut as her orgasm crashed, her walls squeezing his cock tightly inside. She cried out as waves took her, her body spasming until her legs went weak even with his dick still rock-hard within.

Josh's ass coiled beneath her and she leaned to take the scarf from his eyes. "You saw me come. Now I want to see your face as you climax."

His gaze was dark and full of need and he held himself taut and unmoving inside her. She lifted her ass and rode him, her eyes never leaving his as she milked his cock, faster and deeper. His back arched and he bucked, raising her high until with gritted teeth, his cock head bulged as hot spurts filled her core.

CHAPTER 25

C andy luxuriated in the haze between sleep and consciousness, snuggled against a hard, hot body that pleased her to no end. She wanted to fall into dreams, as long as they weren't some screwed-up, brimstone-and-hail visions. Her father and mother's death always comprised those types of dreams for her.

Now, after telling Josh the story, the whole incident seemed less traumatic. She saw and felt things differently. Yes, the gamut of emotions were still there, but muted. She was able to separate herself from the memories and put them away gently, not shove them into a box that wanted to explode any second a crack presented itself.

Josh had shown her she had the power to let go and forgive her father, not the other way around. If she released the pain, it would go now. And that's what she wanted. She'd never forget her past, but it would no longer affect who she was. It would no longer make her hateful and angry. Her father's power over her was gone. Her mother's death caused her sadness, but it wouldn't dictate her feeling for others.

Candy scooted closer into the arms of her "mate." He

spooned her on the office rug. The fire popped and crackled.

Mate.

She thought back through the night and recalled the other men calling their wives mates. Wait a minute. Was a mate a companion like "married spouse" and not just "best friend"? Josh had said it was the simple definition. Ha, more like the understated definition of the century.

She knew wolves in the wild mated for life. Did the same go for the human version? It'd probably be similar since instincts drive those innate things.

"What you thinking about, love?" Josh asked.

She rolled her body onto her stomach and reached for a cracker with meat on the food tray beside her closed laptop. "Just wondering when you want to get married and how many kids I want."

When his mouth dropped open, she laughed, blowing cracker crumbs from her lips. His hands were instantly on her, tickling her sides. The laughing heightened as she wiggled and begged him to stop.

Grabbing his hands, she pulled them out to the side, making his body fall closer to hers. She stared into his eyes, seeing love reflected. The love that gave her the strength to face her demons and conquer them.

All these ideas about her and Josh mating and having children worried her. What if he wasn't the right one? What if he was? Her body and heart screamed yes, but her head said to clamp on the brakes.

She could accept this gorgeous man with her would be her husband, but she didn't know the first thing about love. Even though she was getting an idea of what it felt like in her soul, she didn't know what to do when in love or how to act for that matter.

PDA—pubic displays of affection—was strictly prohibited in the military. She'd never had problems with that. Never had affection to show anyone. But now she knew she had to express herself or there would be problems. Was there a book or video she could watch that gave her the answers she needed?

There had to be websites that would tell her exactly what to do. She'd learn like she had her schooling and practice with the same fervor she did her military training. Then their lives together could get started.

At that moment, something in her changed. It was infinitesimal, but it shook her world. She had no reason, now, to keep running. Since the day she'd walked out of the house with her siblings in tow, she'd been running from her memories and emotions. She couldn't handle them on her own.

With Josh in her life, it was all different. She had someone to lean on, someone who would keep her strong during those times when she felt the world would overtake her. She was no longer alone.

Her biggest fear flew forward. The smile faded from her face. A worried looked came from him.

"Promise me something," she said.

"Anything," he replied.

"If you ever see me turning into my father with you or the kids, intervene. Kick my ass, if you have to. Just don't let me treat them badly."

He kissed her forehead. "My love, the fact that you are asking this of me means you won't ever let that happen. But if it does, I will spank your scrumptious ass."

She lifted her hips off the ground. "You mean this ass?"

Josh disappeared under the blanket covering them. "Yes, this." Playfully, he bit her butt cheek. She squealed and laughed. A sense of happiness she'd never felt slid over her. Was this love? She felt light and free. She could face anything the world threw at her with her mate beside her. This was how she wanted to be the rest of her life, which wasn't likely. Life would hand her shit on fine china, but once she got through it, the end was priceless.

But something else niggled at the back of her mind.

As if enough hadn't happened in the last four hours. She'd gone from saving the intelligence department to saving herself with her mate by her side all the way. The last hour alone blew her mind. How her brain even functioned was a miracle.

She was perched half on her guy, arm over his chest, thigh across his lower abs. It was the most comfortable position she'd ever been in.

"What's wrong, love?" Josh asked.

She let out a sigh. "I don't know. Something's bugging me and I don't know what it is."

He partially rolled to face her. "Is it about us? Are we moving at light speed for you?"

"Absolutely." She laughed at his slightly panicked look. "But that's doesn't bother me. It's something else."

"Oh, good." He lay back and closed his eyes. She pinched his nipple and twisted it slightly. His eyes popped open, gold rings flaring.

"Don't be an ass," she said. "Help me figure this out."

"Figure it out? So this doesn't mean you want more sex?" He whimpered like a hurt puppy. She laughed again. When was the last time she'd expressed such happiness twice in the same minute? This man was a godsend.

"Wanting sex and figuring this out are not mutually exclusive. One doesn't dictate the other," she replied.

He drew a brow down. "Sooo, does that mean yes or no to sex right now?"

She giggled. Giggled! Her. Sergeant Major Obermier, giggling. Hell was definitely freezing over and the pigs were flying south for the winter. "It means no, horny toad."

"Hey," he said. "Get your shifters straight. I'm a horny wolf, not frog."

She gasped. "There are frog shifters? Really?"

"Uh, maybe," he said with all seriousness. "I haven't met any, but they would've been frogs so I wouldn't have talked to them in the first place."

She didn't want to think about herself talking to every creature she came in contact with asking if they were a shifter or not. Rather quickly, she'd find herself in her own padded room playing with small plastic G.I. Joes.

"Okay, I'll let that go for now," she said, not sure how to approach such a statement. This conversation was getting weird. "We're way off topic here. I'm forgetting something and I don't know what."

"Oh, yes," her mate replied. "And it's not sex."

Exasperated, she sighed. "No, it's not sex. We've confirmed that."

"Damn," Josh said. "I was hoping you'd forgotten that you said no already." His smile warmed her heart. It would take a little time to get used to his serious-faced, playful banter. "Playful" wasn't a word in the military handbook.

"You're such a dork," she responded as she scooted away and rolled onto her stomach. He laughed, smacking her on the ass. She could get used to that. No, no, no, stay focused. After pulling her laptop in front of her, she logged onto the Internet to see the latest news. "Shit. Look."

She angled the monitor for him to take a peek. The bold headline read *Hostages in the NIB?*

"What's NIB?" he asked. "I've heard you say it before."

"That's what we call this building, National Intelligence Building of the National Intelligence Agency. I think they are naming it after some senator when we move out of it soon." She scanned the article, looking for anything scandalous. Clicking a link, she was taken to a page with various photos of the night and a few statements. Director Pommer was quoted giving the standard spiel when pressed by the media too soon.

Nothing about her or shifter involvement. And thank god there were no photos of the four dead men on the roof. She googled Yulian's name again to see what else she could find. The fact that Mikhail wasn't a part of this bothered her. They were a pair, it seemed. Maybe they got in a fight and no longer talked.

"You think we're missing something?" Josh asked.

She sighed. "I just can't believe that the brother Mikhail had no part of this. Of the two of them, he's the smarter one. Yulian was always the more brute-force type."

"Mikhail was part of something," Josh replied.

She looked at him. "What do you mean?" she asked.

"When you were on the phone with the president, Day listened to Yulian's phone call. It had something to do with Mikhail finishing up at a home," Josh informed her.

"What home?" she asked.

He shrugged. "Didn't say. Does he have relatives or know someone here in DC?"

She didn't know. He could've, but that didn't seem right. Why hold a group hostage just to wait until his brother did something at someone's house?

Josh snuggled up to her side. "What you said about Yulian not being the brains was definitely true. The men with him weren't highly trained. We took out the four guards with little effort, and the guys inside seemed to be joking around a bit much. I'd have been pissed if they were my men."

"I'm with you there. Very unprofessional, which wasn't how the last run-in I had with them seemed. Their part was well planned and executed. It took us a while to locate their hideout. Here, it appeared they were just waiting for something. Yulian looked at his watch a lot. And if their plan all along had been to take the helicopter, he'd known only two other men could leave with him and a hostage."

"He was going to leave his guards behind, wasn't he?" Josh said. "What a bastard to sacrifice his own men. He should be shot and hanged by his balls."

She felt something coming to her. The answer to all this. They were close. "How long after the conversation Day listened to till the time they left?" she asked.

"They started moving out right afterward," he replied.

She sat up. "That's it. Yulian's part in this was to be a distraction. Like the newswoman and Sheldon calling the police to distract the hostage takers."

"Distraction for what?" he asked. "A robbery of some kind?"

"The brothers aren't the stealing type. Not flashy enough for them," she said. "They ransom people for money, so I don't see them coming all the way over here to shoot out a

Tiffany's when they have the same thing much closer to home."

"What about abduction? That makes sense if they took someone from a home," Josh theorized.

"That works for me, but why the big distraction, then? Why not just go in, take the person, and leave?" she wondered. Damn, they were missing something big.

"If you need a distraction, then that means the target has to have eyes on it or is out in public," her mate said. "What house is out in public or easy to see?"

"Oh, fuck," Candy said, dropping her face into her hands. "The White House."

CHAPTER 26

From his place on the rug in front of the fireplace in his mate's office, he watched her throw the blanket off and run to her desk. Damn, what a sight to see. She was gorgeous. He knew she would be by the way she filled out her uniform. Tight across her chest and hips, her ass a scrumptious bubble he'd love to sink his teeth (dick) into.

She paced in front of her desk, phone pressed against her ear. "Come on, pick up the damn phone." He heard the personal message for the president answer. Irritated, she bashed her finger against the phone's screen a couple of times then lifted it again. Deep concern floated from her.

"Dresden," she nearly shouted, "are you with the president?"

Thanks to his superhuman hearing, he could hear both sides of the conversation. "He went to his private quarters on the second floor. Why?" he said.

"I believe the Steganovich brothers had a plot that included something at the White House," she said.

"The one brother is dead, correct?" he asked.

"Yulian, yes. We heard part of a conversation he had on

the phone about Mikhail being at a house. They are dumb enough to think they can pull off kidnapping the president."

"Shit," Josh heard Dresden say. "I left the president not more than ten minutes ago. He's in the shower now for approximately fifteen more minutes." Huh, Josh wasn't sure he would want everyone to know his schedule that intimately. Did the president have a toilet break scheduled, also?

"I'll be there in ten minutes. Let the gate know I'm coming." Candy dropped the phone on her desk and went to a closet. When she opened it, he about shot his wad where he sat. The small cubbyhole was a military enthusiast's dream. She dressed in a multi-gray camo design he'd never seen before, and without shifter eyes, he probably couldn't see her in the shadows. Her boots appeared lightweight and flexible, not heavy like combat footwear.

She picked up a small plastic bottle and squirted dark liquid onto her fingertips. "Seriously," he said, "you're painting your face? Is this that dangerous? I'm thinking I don't want you to go, love."

Candy rubbed the lotion onto her face. "First off, *love*, you have no say whether I go or not. And secondly, this isn't the old face paint."

His feathers were a bit ruffled with her stating he had no control over her safety. Shit, he'd better get used it. That was the kind of person she was. If there was trouble on the horizon, she was there before sunup.

"If it's not paint, what is it?" he asked as he watched her beautiful pink skin turn dirt brown and black.

"This is made of synthetic material that, among other things, will protect my face from the heat of a bomb blast."

That got him off his ass quickly. "Fuck, no. You are not going if bombs are involved." He was sure her brow rose even though he couldn't see it under the coloring. He rapidly realized that was not the thing to say to her. "Stop." He cupped his hands around her face. "Just listen to me for a minute."

How was he to tell her how much she meant to him and

he wouldn't let her die without coming off corny as hell? Fuck, he better make it fast; a hurricane was brewing in her eyes.

"Candy. I know we just met, but I'm here to protect you whether you like it or not. I cannot allow you to go into a dangerous situation unless I'm with you. Please, baby, you have to understand it's a shifter thing. You are so precious to me—"

She placed a finger over his lips, which he kissed. "I understand you wanting to keep me safe. It's how I feel about the men and women under my command." Her grin brightened her face. So beautiful even with dark smudges everywhere.

He brought his lips down to hers, giving and taking everything he possessed in his heart. He wouldn't let her go alone. No way around it. If her had to tie her up, then so be it. That actually sounded rather tasty.

She turned back to the closet. "I don't have clothes your size, so do your shift thing if you're coming with me."

He stood, taken aback.

"What?" she said. "You said you wouldn't let me go without you, so you better get on getting on." She glanced up and down his body. "With you naked, we'll never make it to the White House."

He scowled. "That's true. Too many cops around, right now," he agreed.

"No," she replied. "I was thinking more along the lines of me shoving you into a back alley and taking advantage of your naked situation."

Air coming into his lungs and words coming out choked him into a coughing fit. He couldn't believe Candy had made a sexy joke. She had been so shy an hour ago. What had he unleashed?

Taking a backpack from a hanger, she shoved in a couple of flashlights, a cigarette lighter, and a small first aid pack. From the small refrigerator by the water cooler, she scooped out a couple of bottled waters and dropped those in as well.

On the desk, she grabbed her phone and turned to him. "You still look human to me, wolf."

With a cheeky grin, he let his animal come forward and shifted. His mate watched with awe. She wasn't scared. In fact, she was slightly aroused if the air told the truth. Candy pivoted toward the door.

"Let's go. We have one more stop before we're on the move."

CHAPTER 27

Since the NIB was a couple of blocks from the White House, Candy decided running would be faster than getting the car from the garage. Plus, when she and her new wolf buddy exited the building after stopping in security to load up on fire power, the garage was closed off with guards watching the entrance. No doubt they had made their way up to the kill scene on the roof. It would take hours while they went through the entire route down to the lobby looking for whatever clues and evidence they looked for.

Josh knew those details better than she did. He was more detective while she was more blow 'em up.

At the security gate, a transport buggy and a handsome guard were waiting to take her, and her *dog*, to the north side of the White House. When she smiled at the driver, Josh growled. She almost laughed then scratched between his ears.

As they approached the White House, Candy fell into a sense of awe. The building was massive with the West Wing housing the Oval Office and the East Wing with its "secret" underground bomb shelter.

At the main entrance, one of the two glass doors opened

and Colonel Dresden hurried out. Candy stepped off the cart as soon as it stopped and came to a salute. Dresden returned her gesture.

"Candy? Is that you all dressed-up for the occasion?" the man said, trying to cover a smile with his hand. She was sure he referred to her synthetic paint and shadow camo. The wolf barked once. She knew *her mate* was agreeing with the colonel.

She leaned closer to the wolf. "Just wait till we get home."

"When did you get a wolf as a pet? I'm hoping it's a pet," he said. She and her animal climbed the steps as the cart drove away.

"Colonel, sir. This is Director Tumbel with ALFA." The wolf sat on its hind legs and lifted his right paw to the colonel. The man stared at the furry extension, then looked back to her.

"This is . . ." his hands swished up and down implying the animal, "his shifted form?"

"Yes, sir," Candy replied. The colonel frowned and glanced around.

"Let's do this inside so some media big shot doesn't get a picture of me shaking a wild animal's paw."

Candy stifled her smile and followed the retreating officer through the front door. The grand entrance was truly grand, from the massive marble columns to the shiny pink and white square floor pattern. The simple design elements were huge. The ceiling had to rise twenty feet, or close. A mirror at the side stretched from the floor to the crown molding. Standing here, she felt small, insignificant. But she had an important job to do.

Josh took a whiff of the air. She waited as he sniffed around the area. He slowed when he came to the large planted fern. If he even began to lift a leg, she'd freaking kill him. She relaxed when he returned to her side.

"Has the president been secured somewhere?" she asked.

"After your call, I sent up extra security to guard the

second floor and all entrances," he said. She wasn't happy the president was still in residence. But this was all conjecture on her part. She could be completely wrong. How humiliating. She understood why the colonel had done what he had since they had no solid proof of anything. His phone rang and he answered, quickly hanging up. "The president wants to see us now. He's out of his shower."

"Oh, shit," she said under her breath. The president was a bear of a man. Always serious, never smiling, with permanent lines indented into his forehead. He was a great leader, not much of a partygoer.

They climbed the red-carpeted stairs to the second floor. They passed the guards with concerned looks for the wolf who trotted beside her. Josh raised his nose into the air and stopped.

"What?" she asked. He trotted around the stair landing they had just come off. After a moment, he padded after the colonel. Must not have been anything. From what seemed like a mile away, a man came out of a room.

"Mr. President," the colonel called out.

"Hi, Colonel," the president said in his characteristic rumbly voice. "Let's meet in the family room—"

The floor shook just before a wave of drywall slammed into her back, quickly followed by a heat surge followed by an explosion. Next thing she knew, hands were on her upper arms lifting her to her feet from the floor. Josh stood in front of her, his hand on her face, terrified eyes blinking at her. His lips moved, but she didn't hear anything.

The smell of burning wood and a thick layer of dust floated in the air, making her cough.

"What happened?" she asked. Josh's voice slowly became a mumble. But she read his lips. Bomb.

She glanced over his arm to see the colonel getting to his knees. Her hand snagged Josh's and he helped her to the colonel's side. The man shook his head as if to clear it then pulled his radio from his pocket. They hurried down the hall to meet the president running toward them.

"Mr. President, we need to get to your closet." Dresden

turned the president around and stumbled after him. Candy and Josh caught up within a few steps. At the end of hall, they entered a no-nonsense bedroom, sparse with furniture, but still welcoming.

They navigated turns and doors and found themselves in the president's wardrobe room. She was amazed by all the cool gadgets and containers and a ton of identical, perfectly pressed white, long-sleeved shirts. On the section of wall where shoes perched on shelves, Dresden pressed his hands against the wood and the panel slid back and out of the way.

On the other side of the wall, the handrail for a spiral staircase came into view. A red light shined from above. Dresden started down.

"Wait. Stop!" Josh hollered. He elbowed his way to the front. "Let me go first. I know what I'm smelling for." Dresden leaned back and let Josh pass. The rest trailed behind, Candy as the caboose after the first lady, who had rushed to join them. Several steps down, the group came to a stop. "Candy," Josh called, "I need you up here."

She made her way, trying not to slip on the damp metal steps. "What did you find?"

Josh knelt on a tread, leaning over to the next step. "Look here." He pointed to a thin wire strung across the width of the stair.

"A trip wire?" Candy asked. "Where is it tied in?" They followed the line to the outside wall then underneath the stair they kneeled on. Attached to the bottom side of the stair was a backpack hanging open so they could see inside. "Oh, fuck," she whispered. Both straightened.

"What is it?" Dresden asked.

"Colonel, sir. There is a trip wire here connected to enough C-4 to bring down this side of the building," she said.

Josh said, "I smelled the taggart chemical, so I knew something was rigged."

"Should we step over it and continue down?" the colonel asked.

Josh shook his head. "I wouldn't chance it. There could

be more ambushes along the way. The person came from below up to this spot."

The president's voice echoed in the narrow area. "How do you know that, son?"

Josh stood, helping Candy up a step. "From what I can tell, most of the Russians at the NIB had a hint of alcohol to them. Like it was part of their clothes. I smell that here, but not higher up. Where does this go?"

"Everybody back up," Dresden commanded. "We'll take another route." Candy waited for an answer to Josh's question. But it never came. Guess they didn't want her or Josh to know.

The group gathered by the bedroom door as Dresden talked on his radio and paced the hallway. Candy noticed the first lady blush after looking her direction. Josh put a hand on her shoulder. The touch was nice. She'd have to get used to touching and being touched. Then she noted Josh was buck-ass naked. That was why the first lady had blushed. Candy stepped in front of her mate.

"Uh, Mr. President, do you have a T-shirt and a pair of sweatpants or shorts Director Tumbel can wear? Shifting requires they be undressed."

The leader's eyes narrowed on Josh, staring him down. With both hands on her shoulders, he stared right back. After a moment, the president smiled and reached out his hand.

"Nice to meet you, Director Tumbel. I've heard about the great work your organization does."

Josh reached around her and shook his hand. "Thank you, sir. I'm sure Candy agrees with you." Behind her, he bumped against her back. Yeah, yeah. She got the joke— her shutting down the group. Based on paperwork only, anyone would've made the same initial decision she did to close them down. Of course, that was all different now.

The president leaned toward his wife and kissed her cheek. "Dear, would you get the director something from my dresser. You know where my clothes are better than I do," he said softly.

Candy was about to pass out with shock. Her big, growly, bear of a scary man turned into a cub around his wife. Josh leaned down to her ear. "What's wrong?"

How the hell did Josh know? She'd have to figure out her emotions so she knew them before Josh smelled them. This relationship was getting more complicated with every superhuman trait Josh revealed.

"Is the goddam passage clear or not?" Dresden yelled from the hallway. He was still on his radio.

"Colonel," Candy said, sliding into the hallway, "anything I can help with?"

He pinched the bridge of his nose. "Seems we're having a hard time contacting our bomb-sniffing dog trainer."

"He was here earlier, right?" She recalled the president needing to call her back after the dog left. His words were akin to "damn dog sniffing my feet."

"Yeah, finally," the colonel said.

"What do you mean?" Candy asked.

"It took him forever to get here," Dresden ranted. "He knows he's part of protocol. Dipshit should've been in the truck already. By the time he got here, the bug sweeper had already gone through and nonessential rooms were cleared."

He didn't do a good job seeing as they'd found two bombs in a matter of minutes. She wondered. "Colonel, is the bomb guy alone when he does his sweep?"

"I have one of my guys help him out. But tonight, he was so damn late that all my men were stationed and I had to pull somebody. The dog got started before my guy got here. I didn't want to wait any longer," Dresden said.

His radio came back to life. "Are you sure? The dog's not here yet." His hands fisted. "I'll tell you what, how about I just try it myself. Get me a motherfucking dog!" He stomped down the hall and turned a corner.

Dressed in gray sweats and plain T-shirt, Josh came out of the bedroom and stood beside her. "Where's he going?"

"To the first floor. There's an elevator and stairs in the

cove on that side of the hall," the president said, his gruffness back.

Josh frowned and stepped forward. "He really should let me go fir—"

Another blast erupted. This one was closer. Much closer.

CHAPTER 28

Candy found herself on the floor again as she had been a few minutes ago, except this time, a heavy body covered hers. She opened her eyes to stare into hazel ones with a gold ring around the brown and green. So much concern filled the look and she knew it was for her. Someone cared if she lived or not.

"You okay?" Josh asked. A surge of emotion roared through her. From the terror of almost dying to the elation of . . . love? There was that damn *L* word again. Creeping up on her. A word she'd never used, and a feeling she'd never had. But that had all changed now, right? She'd had a taste of utmost happiness and it was highly addictive. She wanted more, but didn't have a clue what to do to get it.

Josh scooted off her and helped her sit up. On the other side of the hall, the president was doing the same with his wife. The first lady leaned her forehead onto her husband's and put her hand on his cheek.

Taking the cue, she leaned forward, but Josh wasn't close enough, so she grabbed him around the neck and dragged him toward her. Being a bit anxious and adrenaline-filled, she pulled too hard and his head bonked into hers.

"Sorry—" she said, rubbing over her eye.

"No, my fault," Josh threw in. "I wasn't ready."

She wouldn't let him take blame for something that was her doing. "No, it was my fault since I tugged on you."

Josh huffed. "Well, I should've been—"

"No, dammit," she growled. "I—"

The president cleared his throat. "Tell me when you two are done figuring out who's wrong so we can get the hell out of here."

"Sorry, Mr. President," they said in unison.

Everyone got to their feet. Farther down the hallway, a gaping hole extended past walls exposing bedrooms on both sides of the corridor. Through the hole, she saw the pink and white marble floor of the downstairs entrance. Firemen had hoses putting out small flames from the first bomb on the stairs. Shocked faces looked up at them from below the hole.

Candy hurried forward to see what had happened to Dresden. He had been in the middle of the explosion, may have accidentally triggered it. Josh leapt forward and grabbed her arm.

"Whoa, where you going?" Josh said.

She jerked from his hold. "I have to see if Dresden is hurt."

"Candy," he whispered. Tears instantly came to her eyes. She understood what he was saying without him voicing the words. Colonel Dresden had been a great friend for a long time. He went to battle for her when other men told her she couldn't. He always said she could. And she proved him right, time after time. She let Josh pull her back toward the end of the hall.

"Now what?" Josh asked, looking at the group. Candy didn't know this building like she knew the NIB. That was her building, this wasn't.

The president frowned. "That bomb took out two escape routes. Besides the closet, there isn't any other in the area."

Several feet of flooring around the hole fell, making the gap reach past the doorway to the president's bedroom.

They scrambled back toward the window at the end of the west-side hall.

Shit. This was not good. The only other room they could get to looked to be a small kitchen opposite the bedroom. Just inside the door was an elevator.

Behind her, Josh said, "I wouldn't chance it. Don't push any of the buttons." He stepped inside the door and sniffed, walked in farther, nose in the air. "I don't smell the vodka, so I don't think anyone has been in here, but they could have planted something below." He kept sniffing, passing the elevator, stopping at a case of shelves holding counter-top appliances and dishes.

"What are you doing?" she asked him. "We need to find a way out of here before the rest of the floor gives way."

"Just a minute," he said, "I'm smelling musty air and . . . fresh air?" He got down on his knees and sniffed along the floor. "It's coming from the floor." He got to his feet and grabbed dishes off the shelves. "Help me move this bookcase."

Taking a handful of items, Candy noticed it was a book-shelf, like someone had stuck it there from the library or something. Once the breakables were stacked on another counter, Josh and the president scooted the casing aside. Behind it was a door with a round glass window. Almost like a porthole.

"Everyone get back," Josh said. "Even though I don't smell anything, it doesn't mean it's safe. I'll open it."

Candy grabbed his elbow. "No, what if you get hurt? There's nowhere to take you for help. I—I don't . . ." She didn't want to lose him. She never wanted to lose any of her men and women, but this felt different. This hurt her heart.

Josh leaned down and kissed her. "Don't worry, babe. I got this."

"Babe"? He'd called her "babe." No one ever called her "babe." She kinda liked it from him. "Fine," she said. "You get hurt and I'm throwing your furry ass out the window, got it?"

"Yes, ma'am." He grinned, knowing he got his way.

He'd better not get used to it. Candy took the president and his wife to the far end of the kitchen by the south-facing window. He put his arm around his wife and pulled her against him, turning his back toward the room. If anything exploded, he would be hit before she was. Candy stepped between him and potential flying debris to prevent that.

Over his shoulder, the president glanced at Candy in her shadow fatigues and all. "Dressed for the occasion, I see."

She blushed. Having the president's attention was more than she'd ever asked for. "Yes, sir."

He continued, "I gather you and the director are in a personal relationship."

"Yes, sir," she said. "We met this morning."

"This morning?" he repeated.

She glanced at her watch. "Yes, sir. Almost twelve hours on the dot." She shook her head. "Been a hell of a day."

After a glance at her, Josh pulled the door open, then sprang toward the hall. All remained quiet. Josh came in and Candy hurried toward him. She pulled a flashlight from her backpack.

"What do you see?" she asked. Before he answered, she saw for herself. About the size of a broom closet, the space contained a spiral set of metal stairs, thick with cobwebs and dust. No one had been on these in a long, long time.

"Of course," the first lady said. "This is the stairway that connects all the kitchens from the ground floor to the second floor. I remember someone mentioning it. They haven't used the stairs anymore since the elevator was installed. It's been here since early 1900s."

"Well over a hundred years?" Candy blurted. "It can't be sturdy, can it?"

"Guess we'll find out," Josh said, taking the first step. A loud creak and pop echoed down the tunnel.

"Wonderful," Candy huffed. "Lead the way, wolf. I'll bring up the rear." She took the second flashlight from her pack and handed it to the first lady since she was second to descend.

Slowly they circled down and down, lower and lower.

On the next floor—the first—was an identical door with a round look-through porthole. It was blocked by something too. They continued down.

"Mr. President," Candy started, "do you have any idea, besides the obvious, why the Steganovich brothers would target you? We know why they chose Director Pommer for his supposed role in their father's death long ago."

A deep sigh came from the man in front of her. "I was afraid this would come back and bite my ass—"

"Dear," the first lady scolded.

"Sorry, love. Bite my butt," he continued. He stopped and turned back to Candy. He stood a step below her, yet he met her eyes. "You can never take the schoolteacher out of a woman." He winked and stepped down.

Candy stood in shock. The president of the United States had winked at *her*. He was really a nice guy. Who woulda thunk? She was amazed how this man combined immense power and responsibility with being personable. Her one male role model only had shown his ability to bully and hurt.

She hurried down the stairs to catch up. "You were saying, Mr. President, about the brothers."

"Oh, right. Those boys nearly started World War III."

CHAPTER 29

With white knuckles, Candy gripped the railing in the small shaft in the kitchens. "World War III, sir?"

"That entire incident was *FUBAR* from the beginning," he said. Candy grinned at his use of the military term: "fucked up beyond all recognition."

The president continued. "Russia was getting ready to arrest their father on charges of espionage, spying for the U.S. I had Pommer immediately pick him up—"

"Wait," Candy cut in, "*you* ordered Pommer?"

"Yes, that was my role in the fiasco. I was over Pommer at the time. We needed to get their father back to the U.S. to ensure his safety. Then, of all things, he was killed on the way to the intelligence building here in DC." The president shook his head. "What a mess."

"The file said a Russian spy may have been responsible for his death," Candy said. "Is that true?"

"We believed so since no one else knew what was going on. Of course, we had to cover it up from the media or Russia would've started a bunch of shit with NATO and us harboring spies and who knows what else."

"What about the boys and mom?" she asked.

"By the time things settled down enough to figure out what had happened, the family was no longer where they had lived in Russia. They were gone. We tried finding them, but we weren't able to get inside help at the time with the situation."

"So the boys think the U.S. government made their father come back and killed him or made him disappear forever," she theorized.

"That's what I'm taking from all this," the president said. He shrugged. "It's too bad, really. He was a nice guy and really loved his family. I wish we had been able to see what evidence Russia had to accuse him. He had to be innocent of any wrongdoing."

Candy thought about what he said. If she had been in charge of that operation, she'd be ranting and raving about Russia's interference with Americans living in their country. She'd throw their commie butts in prison and let them rot for wanting to hurt people in this country. Even now, she'd still be angry and hot over the deal. But the giant who could chew new assholes with one bite felt sorry about the situation.

Now she knew why the president was such a great leader. He cared for human life no matter who they were or what they did. He didn't judge. Innocent until proven guilty. That was what she'd spent the last twenty years fighting for.

She noted how calmly the president was recalling the event. He didn't bring in anger or physical violence. Like her father would've; like she would've. She never thought about a different way to react to negativity. Even in the military, she was taught to holler and yell to get attention. Maybe her way wasn't the best way.

Not paying attention, Candy almost smacked into the president's back. The group had come to a stop. "Are we there?" she asked. No one answered, but they all stepped into an old, musty basement-like room. After she exited, Josh got on his hands and knees, his face on the stair flooring.

"Where are we?" she asked.

The first lady's face lit up. "We are in the subbasement." She pointed to the door down the hall. "If I remember correctly, that's the laundry room. And down the big hall, it's mostly electrical and heating machines. I've only been down here once. Several passageways come through here also."

"Secret passageways?" Candy asked.

The first lady nodded. "Mostly."

Candy tapped her foot on the dingy white floor. She thought about what she'd learned in school history classes. This sounded dumb, but she'd ask anyway. "They had tile like this back in the 1800s?"

The woman laughed. Candy knew it was a stupid question, but she didn't expect it to be funny. "I don't mean to laugh at your question. But it is the exact same thing I asked when I toured the house." The lady smiled at her. "Great minds think alike." She reached out a hand. "I'm Monica. We haven't had the chance to meet properly."

Candy shook her hand. "Sergeant Major Candace Obermier, ma'am. Good to meet you." The woman's smile turned to a frown. What? Had she done something wrong?

"With my husband," the first lady said, "it's fine for you to be Sergeant, but with me, you're Candace."

After an initial shock at such friendliness, Candy relaxed. "Ma'am, please call me Candy."

"And you call me Monica, not ma'am." Both ladies smiled at each other. "And the answer to your tile question is no. The original house didn't have basements. In the late 1940s, Truman discovered the wooden beams supporting the house and floors were about to completely fail. Most everything was original from 1814 at that time."

"Oh," Candy said. "I thought the White House was built around 1776 when we took our independence."

"The original was 1790s," Monica said.

"Original?" Candy replied. "It's been rebuilt?"

"Twice, actually."

Damn, she was feeling stupid as shit now. Did she sleep through this in school? Monica smiled. "I'm a schoolteacher. Well, *was* until I became the first lady. I teach American history. Learning it once, like you, I wouldn't expect anything to stick past the test; there's so much. But me, I don't even need a textbook anymore."

That made Candy feel better. She was sure she'd known all this stuff at one time, like twenty years ago. "So how old is everything here?" Candy asked.

"The first build was 1790s. In 1814, the British burned down most of Washington DC, including the inside of this house."

"All of it?" Candy couldn't believe the White House had burned down.

"The walls stood since they were brick, but the inside was gutted."

"So nothing from before that time exists. All the documents and letters from the presidents were destroyed? All that history lost."

"Unfortunately, yes. Everything of James Madison and earlier is gone. When people say they have authentic things from that time period, you can almost bet it's fake. Unless it was brought in after the fire and put here."

"What happened the second time it was rebuilt?" she asked, now curious about the history on which her feet rested. Who had stood and walked where she had, hundreds of years ago?

"Rumor has it that President Truman was sitting in his tub, which happened to be on the second floor above the State Dining Room where the Daughters of the American Revolution were having dinner.

"Supposedly, the tub almost fell through the ceiling and onto their table. Truman was so embarrassed by the near catastrophe, he had the entire structure inspected. Turns out he was living in a death trap, practically."

"Wow," Candy commented. "The same frame since 1814? Grew strong trees back then," Candy said.

"Can you imagine?" Monica gushed. "*All* floors could've collapsed on whoever was here." She shook her head slowly, concern evident on her face. She cared, too. "Anyway, Truman had the place gutted and they dug the basements then. This tile is from the 1950s."

If Candy ever had a friend, she'd want her to be like Monica. Sure, Candy socialized with other females, but in the military, having a close friend wasn't the best idea. Like she'd said before: Tomorrow wasn't guaranteed for them.

That got Candy's imagination going. She replied, "I bet they added secret rooms and hidden passages."

Monica smiled. "Yes, they did. Several of them. And at the end of each term, the outgoing lady has to be sure the incoming lady commits them to memory."

"Couldn't you write them down and keep a list in a safe?" Candy asked. That seemed logical.

Monica laughed again. "I asked the same question. Then got a lecture like I hadn't had since grade school. No way are we to keep anything written, or hints, or clues."

Candy saw the purpose, but still . . . "Couldn't a passage be forgotten?"

"My thoughts exactly, but I see the purpose of it. Safety for my husband." Candy watched Monica turn to her husband, put an arm around the back of his waist, and slide under his arm. From there, she kissed his check and asked, "What are we waiting on?"

An explosion came from far away, but still the ground shook and dust fell from the ceiling. Candy had let her guard down too much. With no danger directly in front of them, there wasn't as much immediacy to get away. She was back and wouldn't be forgetful again of her responsibility.

A loud crack startled her, whipping her head around to look at Josh and his foot currently sticking through the floor. "What the hell are you doing?" Candy asked.

Josh pulled out his foot and leaned over the hole he'd made. "It only looks like the bottom is here. The steps continue lower."

"Lower?" Monica said. "There isn't a blueprint for anything lower than this floor. I've looked. This is it."

CHAPTER 30

Josh heard the story the president told Candy about the Steganovich boys. Tragic, really. And now they were running from one of the brothers' scheming.

On hands and knees again, Josh peered through the hole he'd made in the plywood at the base of the stairs. Well, not really the base since the stairs continued down. The heavy smell of dirt overwhelmed his senses. Old steel and wood floated to him. The mustiness of material that had sat in hot, humid weather too long; old cardboard and paper; and oil paint and . . . ? What the hell?

He tore up chunks of wood revealing another level.

"Wow," the first lady said, "this wasn't on any plans I saw of the house. Is it safe?"

Josh didn't smell the telltale sign of alcohol, nor did he smell any human presence. That was a first. Never before had he been in a place where humans hadn't been for years. Their scent lingered for a long time, so not smelling it— Wait. He took a deep breath. Yes, there it was again. Death, decay, but so minute.

He responded to the first lady. "I'm pretty sure there are no bombs, but I can't promise anything else." He'd ripped away enough flooring to continue down the spiral. "Give me a second to check it out."

Sliding down the rail, he curved around twice then dropped to the ground. Ground meaning dirt, not tile or concrete, but dry, dusty earth. Then he couldn't believe what his eyes were seeing. He was *below* the mansion. Literally. If there was an earthquake, or big enough bomb, the entire house could fall on him.

As he looked across the expanse, steel girders and I beams stuck up from the ground like skinny tree trunks supporting a ceiling. Except these were holding up the basement floor and five levels above that, not counting any roof.

Suddenly, he realized what he was looking at: the crawl space under the house. But you could stand and the space was huge. Old air shafts and pipes traveled the length of the floor above their heads, coming out one side and back up the other, as well as old wooden beams that didn't look very healthy.

"Josh?" His mate called down, worry in her voice.

"It's safe to come down. You won't believe this," he replied. He stepped up to the stair when he saw the first lady coming through the hole. He assisted her down and waited for the next person. When no one came, he tuned his ears into the upstairs area. Arguing? What the hell?

Josh hurried up the steps to see what was going on. He stuck his head above the floor level. His mate and the president were in a heated discussion.

"No, I insist, young lady. You go before me," the president said.

"No, Mr. President. You go next. I go last," Candy replied.

"Sergeant," the president said, "you should go first—"

"Mr. President—" Candy huffed.

Josh couldn't believe this. He clarified, "Mr. President, it is my mate's job to protect you with her life, which means you come down next."

Candy straightened her shoulders and smiled like she'd won a hard-fought victory. Note to self: mate is highly competitive and probably doesn't lose well. An ass-kicking or two may be in the future.

Josh stood farther down on the steps as the president made his way around the metal pole, not very happy. Candy followed directly behind him.

"You wait," Josh pointed a finger at his mate. When the stairs were clear, he rushed up and held on to Candy. She rolled her eyes at him.

"I am quite capable of going down stairs on my own," she retorted. "I handled the previous several floors just fine."

He scowled at her. "Let's make a deal for here on out."

"About what?" she asked.

"You let me coddle and overprotect you everywhere we go," he said.

"What?" Candy snorted. "That's not a deal. And I can take care of myself."

"Okay, let me rephrase," he said. "You *pretend* to let me coddle and overprotect you and we'll all be happy." His mate let out a soft laugh. Her eyes twinkled beautifully in the dim light from the upper floor.

"All right, I'll *pretend* you're saving me, a damsel in distress, everywhere we go."

He leaned in and kissed her fully on the lips. She tasted fantastic. He wanted more of her and took it until a clearing throat interrupted.

"We should be going," he said. "Even though I think we're safe, we're not out of the hole yet."

"Nope," she agreed, "we are definitely in a hole." He tagged her ass for the smart reply and helped her down the rest of the steps.

The bottom of the stairwell was completely dark to human eyes, but the flashlights took care of that. Ahead, the president and his wife were kneeling, looking at something. There were a lot of things clustered together. This was where the musty material, old paper, and oil paint smell came from.

Candy waved her light around. "What is all this . . . stuff?" Old flowery upholstered furniture lined the wall.

On their cushions was an eclectic mix of boxes, painted portraits, curtains, silverware.

"Oh my goodness, dear." The first lady held up the silverware she'd spied. "These are the missing pieces to Truman's silver set." Her hand lay on a massive heap of curtains. "I think these are the curtains Roosevelt had in the Oval Office that had been lost. This is incredible."

Not as impressed as the first lady, Josh meandered farther along the wall. Candy came up behind him and slipped an arm around the back of his waist. Her touch surprised him and when he lifted his arm to go around her, his elbow bumped her nose.

"Oh, babe. I'm so sorry. I didn't know you were there until too late."

She waved him off, tears from the nose pain gathered in her eye. "It's okay. I must've missed something."

"About what?" he asked.

She shook her head. "I watched the first lady do it and it looked easy. Guess not." She wiped away water from her eyes. Then she reached down and pulled on the tip of a piece of paper sticking out between the pages of an old book. The light beige paper was folded into quarters and the edges looked burned. When she unfolded it, a section along the creases crumbled in her hands. "Oh, shit." She quickly set it on the book, the only flat place nearby.

Slowly, Candy lifted the top half and lay it flush against the tome's leather cover. It was an old letter in fancy script. The first thing Josh read was the date at the top: 1813.

CHAPTER 31

Candy almost shit her camo pants. "Do you see this?" she whispered to Josh. "Oh my freaking god. Josh, this is history at its best. It's *pre*-1814."

In the header next to the date was written "White Palace." Candy handled the paper gently. "Ma'am, I mean, Monica, I think you might have the answer to my question."

"What do you have?" she asked as she made her way toward them.

Candy pointed to the top of the page. "Does this refer to this building? Palace?"

The first lady's brows drew down as she picked up the book the sheet sat on. After a few seconds of reading, she looked up at Josh and her. "Do you know what this is?" They shrugged and shook their heads. "Where did you find it?" Monica asked.

Candy gestured at the book in the lady's grasp. "The edge was sticking out of that book, and I pulled it. Some crumbled when I opened it. Sorry."

The president came up behind his wife. "What are you looking at?" Candy observed how the man stood close his wife. She leaned against him and he wrapped his arms around her waist. Being in Josh's arms was incredible. She could lean against him like Monica did her husband. She scooted over and back to get closer to him.

At the same second she leaned back, Monica fumbled with the old book she held. Josh reached around Candy to help stabilize the leather-bound relic, completely moving away from her target location. Her arms flailed in the air as her ass headed toward the dirt. She got her hands under her in time to stop her humiliating dirt dive.

Josh was with her in a second, helping her up. When on her feet, she slapped at his hands. "I'm fine. Don't touch me," she quietly ground through clenched teeth.

Her mate drew his brows in. "What?" he whispered.

"Nothing. I said I was fine. I tripped. That's all." Her mate glanced at the ground.

"On flat dirt?" he asked. She wanted to scream: Yes, on flat dirt, goddammit. But she remained calm as opposed to earlier where she would've gone off on his ass. She straightened and turned back to the presidential couple.

"If I'm right," the first lady said breathless, "these are notes made by James Madison when he was president. He lists items he wanted in the Treaty of Ghent."

The president leaned over his wife's shoulder. "Are you serious? This is amazing."

Candy knew Madison was known as the "Father of the Constitution" and the fourth president but wasn't sure about anything else.

"Ma'am," Josh started, "I didn't pay much attention in American History class. What it the Treaty of Ghent?" Candy dropped her head into her hand. Don't ask a teacher a question like that and expect a short answer. They knew too much to make it quick. As evidenced by the lecture they received.

Monica laughed, probably seeing their eyes glaze over. "No worries. The only reason I know this is my obsession with this house. When we started campaigning, I started researching. If I was moving in, I wanted to know everything I could about it. And the Treaty of Ghent marks the end of the American-British War of 1812."

"How does that relate to the house?" Josh asked. Candy elbowed him in the stomach. "What? That's a fair question," he said.

She rolled her eyes. "For someone who snoozed through school, maybe."

"It's okay, Candy. My husband did the same thing as a kid."

"I beg your pardon. I paid attention and passed the tests," Mr. President rumbled playfully.

"You squeaked by, dear, if I remember correctly," the first lady said.

The president looked at Josh. "Word of advice, don't marry someone you went to school with. You'll never live down the stupid stuff you did as a teen."

Josh looked down at her with sparkling eyes. *Marriage?* she thought. He didn't want that right away, did he? When she mentioned getting married and kids earlier, she was joking. And kids—no way in hell. Ever. Womb closed for remodeling, eternally.

The first lady pushed on her husband's arm. "I don't bring up half the things you did in school. You should be glad." She went up on her toes and pecked him on the lips. That, Candy could do. Josh was a lot taller, but on her tip-toes, she could reach his lips. PDA as obvious as that would have to wait. Besides, given how her moves were working on him, she'd probably end up kissing his armpit or some shit.

"Back to the question." The first lady drew her attention. "I didn't mention this, Candy, but in 1814 when the British set the house on fire, it completely destroyed everything inside *except* the painting of George Washington that Dolley Madison had cut from the frame and fled with. So this letter dated before that is a miracle."

"And apparently that book," Josh added. "What's the title?"

Carefully, Monica let the book lower while holding the front cover level. She smiled and nodded. "Of course. It's Dolley's family bible. She wouldn't leave without that. The president's notes she must've grabbed on her way out or used them as a bookmark maybe." The first lady carried the book and letter to a small side table, still talking about the find; the president followed.

"Cool," Josh said. "History is so much better in person."

Candy shook her head and rubbed her hand over her face.

"What?" he whispered in her ear. Should she explain to him that history means not being there in person? Nah. She'd let him be happy in his own little world where everyone knew him.

He kissed her on the head and took her hand. "Let's see what the rest of this looks like before we drag those two farther in," he said, motioning with his head to the president and first lady.

On the way, she noted a slightly worn path in the dirt. Not much, but they were not the only ones to have walked this. She wondered if this open space was meant for something secret. Not built out yet. Josh tapped her on the arm.

"Babe, shine your light on the ground in front of us," he said. Kneeling, he examined faded small spots.

"What is it? I don't see much there," she said. He pinched the dirt between his finger and thumb and brought it to his nose.

"Blood."

CHAPTER 32

"Old blood," Josh said. Finding something like this in as remote a place as this, put his senses on alert. Searching for more, he saw a pattern of drips farther under the house.

"How did you see that?" Candy asked. "It was nothing."

"That's what I'm trained for, babe. My job. And that's why you've changed your mind and are letting my department remain open."

She hit him on the arm with the flashlight. "Don't gloat or I will change my mind back." The smell of happiness surrounded her.

"Let's see where this blood trail goes." He took her hand and led the way. He had to admit, it was sort of creepy walking *under* a huge-ass building. But the beams and bars, though rusty, looked sound.

Then he caught that smell again. Death, decay. "Shine the light over the area," he asked his mate. Slowly she scanned right to left. And there it was. She saw it too and walked ahead of him.

"Is that what I think it is?" she asked. When they reached the disturbed earth, he had to say yes.

"I do believe that is a shallow grave with bones and clothes sticking out. Rather hasty job on the cover-up. The government's gotten better at that since this guy." Behind him, she heard a gasp. The president and first lady had come up behind them. "Mr. President, I believe we found the reason why this secret passage was closed up."

The big guy stood beside him. They looked like linebackers for the Dallas Cowboys in white T-shirts and sweatpants. "This is certainly a surprise," the man said. "Wonder who it was."

"We'll send a crew in to collect evidence and figure that out," Josh responded. "I wonder if that has anything to do with all the stuff over there." Meaning the artwork and furnishings.

The first lady shook her head and said, "Probably not. I think when remodeling, they needed a place to put those things until the basement storage room was completed. The tunnel connecting East and West Wings displaced several storerooms. They probably forgot it was down here."

"And whoever dumped this body was in too much of a hurry to care if it stayed down here," his mate said. "Is this a secret passage, or just the underside of the house that happens to be six feet off the ground?"

"All the secret passages I know of converge in the subbasement. I wasn't told about anything *under* the house," the first lady said.

"Me, neither," her husband replied. "I'm thinking that spiral staircase and all of this space was purposefully forgotten."

"Because of the dead body?" the first lady asked.

"Maybe," he replied. "We need to find out who that is before we can make any conclusions."

Josh nodded and turned in a circle, surveying the space. "Should we further examine the area or go back up to the basement? Think there's anything on the other side?" Both flashlights swept the distance. Scores of structural materials, wires, and pipe were all there was to see—until Candy moved her light to the far right corner. Something shined when the light hit it.

"There's something in the corner. It could be a door. Let's have a look-see, shall we?" Josh scooped up her hand again, leading around ground obstacles and overhead impediments.

"Director, Candace," the first lady said. The two stopped and looked where her flashlight was pointing along the wall. In the expanse of cement block was a black circle about a yard wide and a few feet off the ground.

Josh glanced at Candy. "Any ideas?"

"No," Candy said. "Let's check out the corner then we can backtrack if needed."

Josh hoped this corner had a door that led to somewhere safe and *out*. As soon as they did get out of this hellhole, he needed to make plans to mate and get married. They should get hitched right away. Maybe Vegas. Unless she was one of those girls who wanted a big shebang for a wedding. On second thought, hopefully they could hold off. He'd wait for her to bring it up.

Unless she waited too long. He wanted to start their family right away. Like, when they got home tonight, right away. Her having siblings, he guessed she'd want several pups, too. At least a half dozen. That reminded him, she never told him what happened to her siblings and her during the years after their mother died. He'd have a brother- and sister-in-law. Cool, a family of their own. He and his wolf had waited so fucking long for this. He was so excited, a thrill ran down his spine, giving him a shudder.

"You okay there, son?" Mr. President asked.

"Yes, sir. Fine, sir," he replied. "A bit cold. That's all." His mate stared at him with concern. If she could trip on flat ground when she didn't take a step, then he could be cold even though shifters ran hot.

He winked at her and quickened his step. Going from one side of the house to the other was a long distance. Candy shined the light in the corner again and the shiny metal turned out to be a door. Thank god. They could go home.

"Where are we in relation to the house?" Candy asked.

The first lady looked around. "I'd say we're at the far east side." She pointed to the door. "See the letters on the door." Josh easily read PEOC. "They stand for the Presidential Emergency Operations Center."

"Never heard of it," his mate said.

The president banged on the door with his fist several times. "It's a bunker shelter and comms center in case of national emergencies or disasters."

"Oh," Josh said. "I thought that was hidden in the mountains somewhere."

"There's a couple there, too," the president added. He banged again.

The first lady tapped a finger on her chin. "You know, we are still a long way from the East Wing. Will they hear us?"

The president sighed. "When I toured the PEOC, we started down a dark hall that led to one of the escape passages never used by any president, they said. I was in a hurry and decided to come back the next day to walk it. Never did, though."

Josh put his hands on his hips and said, "Seems strange. If I were in one of the safest places in the world like the PEOC, why would I leave?"

"Agreed. Leave a nuclear protected bunker?" Candy asked and looked over her shoulder. "Not sure I'd call the spiral steps an escape route since you're still stuck inside the house, even if in the subbasement."

Josh shrugged. "Semantics."

The president knocked on the door again. Josh felt their luck at finding a door was low. No one could hear them. They'd have to go back up to the house where more bombs could be waiting.

CHAPTER 33

Candy wandered off, following the cement block wall. If someone came to the PEOC door, then she'd hurry back. But that didn't seem likely. The first lady was right: They were too far away for anyone to hear them.

Josh hurried to catch up with her. She smiled at him. He had always been there for her, even when she didn't want his cute ass around. He was more dedicated than she thought he would be. Not many guys in her past were award worthy when it came to sticking around. But that was nearly impossible in her career situation. She could get used to him being nearby. She wasn't telling him that, though. Boy needed to work harder before that.

"We pretending again?" she asked.

"Always," he replied. "Where you going?"

"Looking for the black circle in the wall," she said. "I have a hunch about something." She was thinking that maybe this space was designed on purpose, despite the dead body. She needed proof before spitting out her crazy idea. And to her, her idea seemed over the top.

After a few steps she asked him, "Does your wolfy sense tell you which direction north is down here?"

His eyes closed and head tilted back. She thought he'd be able to do this since the pull of magnetic north tugged on every object on the planet. Including animals. Ducks used it to fly south. Sea life used it to navigate north thousands of miles to give birth. A wolf would know.

He put his hand on the wall next to which they were walking. "This is the north side of the house."

"Good." One of the criteria was correct. Now if all the others worked. When they came upon the circle, she saw it wasn't what she'd expected. A four-inch pipe came straight down the wall through the bottom of the house and curved into a pipe, three-feet in diameter, that extended forward from this point. She squatted and shined her flashlight down the tube. "See anything?" she asked.

"Nothing different than the hundred feet before it," he replied.

"Can you see the end?" That would be astonishing. There would be no way she'd shut down these amazing creatures. That would be doing the U.S. a disservice. And besides, she couldn't handle him with her 24/7. If she didn't get a break, she'd run around the block screaming. Him following, of course.

"I can see pretty far, but it ends in black, so I don't know if that's all I can see or if it's the end."

Only one way to find out. She slipped her upper body and a knee in and that's as far as she got. "Let go of my leg. Josh? What the hell?" She tried to shake him off but knew it was futile.

"Hell no, I'm not letting go," he growled. "I'll go if you tell me what you're thinking."

She conceded and backed out onto her feet. Monica and the president were coming to join them. So much for getting proof beforehand.

"What have you got there, Sergeant?" the president asked.

"Well, sir, the black circle we saw is actually a pipe extending a long way." She gave Josh a stink eye. "I was going to see where it went, but my associate didn't like that idea."

Josh stood with arms crossed over his chest, not fazed one bit about her tattling on him. The president looked between the two of them. She could only imagine what he was thinking.

The president cleared his throat. "Sergeant, your job is to protect me, right?"

"Yes, sir," Candy replied.

"Then since I am here, I suggest Director Tumbel be the one to go," he concluded. Not the answer she wanted, but one she respected. Diplomatic.

"Yes, sir." She turned to Josh. "Get going. If we're not here when you get back, someone from PEOC opened the door. I'll come back for you. Maybe." Yes, she would always come back for him.

Josh leaned down and gave her a big kiss. She was mortified and loving it. She pushed him away, breathless. "I'll always come back for you, too. Don't forget it." With that, he was gone.

Her face felt on fire. She steeled herself for the smack-down the president had a right to give after such a display. How many times had she gotten on others for just holding hands, also prohibited?

She contemplated pulling a pistol from the pocket of her camo pants and shooting once down the tunnel, knowing it would hit Josh in the ass. His wolf would heal him with their mojo or whatever it was they possessed.

"Sorry, sir. I . . ." She had nothing to say.

"Sergeant—" the big man barked.

Monica cut in. "I think that was an ambush, don't you, dear?" Her husband stared at her with a questioning look. "Yes, an ambush. She had no warning of such an attack and was unprepared to handle it according to regulation." She winked at Candy. "I think we should be very happy she survived."

The big man sighed, wrapped an arm around his wife and kissed her on the forehead. "All right, dear. I pick my battles and this one I'll give to you. It's not like we're in public, anyway."

Candy was speechless, but instantly knew why these two people had been together so long. She had witnessed the secret to a loving relationship that would never end. The couple made it look so easy. But Candy knew better. Her father did beat her mother to death.

A loud explosion startled them and the steel beams shifted and groaned above their heads. The front of the White House was collapsing.

CHAPTER 34

"In the tunnel. Now!" Candy hollered. The first lady was already moving in the direction of the mysterious tunnel under the White House and the president had enough smarts not to argue. Candy brought up the rear, her flashlight illuminating the way so the first lady could crawl faster without using the one she held. She heard Josh's voice echoing. She answered, "We're behind you. Keep going."

They hadn't left the second floor that long ago, but long enough for the bomb dog and the explosives crew to get there. Hopefully, that wasn't the team's attempt to disarm a device. Tears came to her eyes, which surprised her. She'd been a hard-as-nails, don't-give-an-inch-on-anything, badass leader. Never once, even as a child, had emotions overwhelmed her. She always found a way to hide from them.

Then she met Josh and twelve hours later, she was a mush. But a happy mush. These feelings Josh created in her were new and exhilarating. She saw the world in a different light. Everything wasn't bad, not everybody would hurt you, and some things weren't worth getting mad about.

Was she okay with this change in herself? Yes. Yes, she was. Sheldon was right. Women were not on the same level as men. Women were continuously evolving creatures, growing and broadening with every new experience. Women see the world and internalize it, taking the good in it and throwing away the rest. That was how she'd coped all these years in hell's home with her father and then on the battlefield.

When her face was suddenly close to the president's proportionally large backside, she pushed herself backward. Oh, god, how horrible would it have been if her head plowed into the ass of the man she was sworn to protect? At least then no one could accuse her of having her head up her own ass. A giggle forced itself from her throat. God! Now she was really losing it. Sergeants in the United States Army didn't giggle.

Then she heard Monica's voice up front. "You're not passing laughing gas back there, are you, dear?"

The president grumbled, "Teachers and their kiddie jokes."

That was too much for her. She covered her mouth with her hand and laughed out loud. She'd get in trouble, but it was worth it.

A gruff "Sergeant" echoed back to her and she took a deep breath.

"Here, sir. Sorry, sir."

The man grumbled more and she had to bite her lip. This couple was amazing. She needed to learn all she could from Monica. Maybe then she would be good enough for Josh. His voice was just ahead of her. He was helping the first lady from the tunnel. The president crawled out next and Josh was there for her.

She emerged in a small round room lined with more cement bricks identical to those under the house. Steel and wood beams supported a flat roof with a machine of some kind in the center with a pipe sticking up from it, through the ceiling. The others were looking around, gaping as well.

This was not what she was expecting. "Is this really the fountain in the north lawn?" she asked.

"Huh," the president said, "this must be what the POEC meant when they said the door led to a passage."

His statement made her feel better at least. Her crazy idea about the fountain being a way out wasn't so crazy. Now they just needed to find the "out" part of it.

"Everybody watch your eyes," Josh said. A red light in a green mesh cage filled the room. If that didn't scream military design, she didn't know what did.

"What's that?" Candy asked, pointing to the boxed machine sitting on a platform in the center of the space.

"I'm guessing that's the water pump for the spray heads in the fountain," the president said. With all the pipes snaking everywhere, that made sense.

Candy set her backpack on the ground and pulled out two bottles of water, giving one to the president and first lady. Monica passed hers to Josh and took her husband's when she finished. Josh smiled and came to her side, handing her his bottle.

"Amazing couple, aren't they?" he whispered, leaning against her. She made sure she didn't move while he leaned, unlike him. "They remind me a lot of my parents." A little sadness crossed her heart at the memory of her parents and how fucked-up her family was. Josh kissed her head and snuggled a little closer. "You're with me now, sweetheart. We'll make a future that will erase the pain of the past. Okay?" He took a step back and smiled.

Once again, he left her speechless. There was little doubt in her mind that he would make an incredible husband. He was perfect. And she was far—too far—from perfect. She was damaged goods in just about every sense. Josh deserved someone better than her. She couldn't make him happy; she'd never made anyone happy. She slipped the half-full water bottle into an empty side pants pocket.

"Okay, folks," Josh said on the other side of the room, looking at a panel on the wall. "We've got the choices of *off, on,* and *drain.* Unless someone sees another way of getting out of here?" Candy pressed on the cement blocks to see if a hidden wall opened. The ground was dirt, so it didn't look conducive to a door for secret stairs going down. Seemed Josh was right. The way out was through the fountain.

"If up is the only option," the president said, "we'll have to drain the pool or get flooded in here."

"Drain, it is," Josh commented. He pushed a button, and the motor in the pump changed its sound, and they heard water rushing down one of the pipes.

"Should you have turned it off before draining?" Candy asked.

Her mate looked at her. "I don't know. Is the pump sucking the water out?"

"I'm thinking it's gravity fed, so the pump is still trying to push water out when there's no water coming in," Candy thought.

"Turn it off, Director," the president said, "just to be sure. We can always turn it back on. Last thing we need is a motor blowing up in this small space."

The first lady laughed. "You would know," she said, poking her husband's arm. "You and Dad are lucky the barn didn't fall on both of you."

He wiped a hand down his face. "Monica, you know that was an accident."

"Yes," she said, "but I still love to tell it to everyone." She looked to Candy. "When we were dating, your president and my dad were elbows deep in grease in some old truck engine."

"It wasn't a truck." He said it like he couldn't believe she'd said "truck." "We were fixing up a Willys CJ-2A, sixty horsepower, 134-cid, with 'Go Devil' engine."

Josh looked up from the drain pipe. "No way. Where'd you find one of those?"

Monica dismissed the guys and turned back to Candy. "Anyway, the two men managed to blow it up and take down half the barn with it."

Normal. They had the normal kind of life Candy had always dreamed of. She looked at Josh standing next to the president, figuring out what to do next. Could she make a normal life with him? Would she give up everything she knew, including the military, to be with him?

Josh placed a hand on each side of the pump box and the

president put his on the other two sides. Together they lifted it, shoving the pipe going through the ceiling even farther up. A spine-tingling metal-on-metal grinding tore around the room as the center of the ceiling raised as the pipe wrenched through. The farther the men pushed the pipe up, the farther the ceiling went.

Candy covered her ears and clenched her teeth. "Stop! What are you doing?" she yelled. It took the men a few more stubborn seconds to quit. She stared up at the now vaulted roof of their room.

"Hmm," the president mumbled to his partner in crime, "don't think that worked like we thought."

Monica lowered her hands from her ears. "What did you *think* would happen?" she asked. As the men discussed the miscalculation of whatever the hell went through their brains, Candy shined her light along the newly arched ceiling, examining the damage.

Supposing the roof was the base of the fountain, the water feature probably looked more like a mini volcano with a pipe sticking out the middle. Closer to the outer rim, four black lines in the form of a square caught her eye. No other place on the ceiling had that. She scooted around the guys to examine her discovery.

Upon closer inspection, the lines resembled strips of rubber used to help stop leaks. Why would that be on the underside of a fountain? An old ladder made of metal piping leaned against the wall close by. She dragged it over, drawing the attention of her mate, always protecting her.

"Whatcha doing, babe?"

"Looking for sensible alternatives," she said.

"Like what?" he asked. "A hole in the ceiling?"

Climbing the ladder and pushing up the center of the square, she was startled when it easily rose. Then stopped after a few inches. "It's stuck," she grunted. "Probably an obstruction from the newly sloping bottom."

"Let me," Josh said and lifted her around the waist and set her on the ground like she was nothing. She was not used to being picked up and thought she was falling when he moved her. The man was lucky she didn't pee her pants when he yanked her down.

Josh climbed the stairs as she stood at the base and looked up. With strength and effort, he was able to bend the metal piece back enough to squeeze through. Then suddenly, his body flew up and out of sight.

CHAPTER 35

———

Josh smelled the soldiers and their gun oil gathered around the fountain. Thank god, they were finally out of this mess. He and Candy could go home and spend the rest of their lives together. A couple of the guys approached just as he bent the lid back far enough to stay put.

Before he could turn to greet them, he felt hands under his armpits and his body was hoisted away from trap door. He didn't think much of it until he was slammed down on his back. The butt of a rifle smashed against the side of his head. His wolf burst forward ready to tear into the bastards stupid enough to attack him.

His hands morphed into claws and he swung haphazardly, gouging chunks of flesh out of the unfortunate legs that got too close. A few kicks got through, but nothing his wolf couldn't fix. His main fight was keeping his animal at bay. It wanted to maim and rip apart.

"Stand down!" he heard his mate scream. Several of the men bristled, undoubtedly surprised by the command coming from a female under a water fountain. "I am Sergeant Major Candace Obermier. I order you to stand down." Those with guns backed off, but the men kept beating up on Josh. And he wasn't stopping his defense of himself, claws included, until they did.

A booming voice shouted, "She gave you a command, men. Disregard it further and I will have you arrested for insubordination." That worked. They all snapped to attention and he lay back on the ground.

Whispers of "the president" erupted in the group. Suddenly his little mate was there helping him to his feet. She pushed the men in her way and muscled him back to the president's side. In the distance, a man in uniform ran toward them across the lawn.

"Mr. President, sir," the man hollered as he neared. He stopped and saluted, waiting for the president to reciprocate. All formalities done, the soldier continued. "I'm Captain Hayden Bridges, sir. Second to Colonel Dresden. We have a car ready for you, sir." He turned to the house and waved. A black SUV jumped the curb and roared toward them.

"Oh," the first lady groaned, "not through the flower garden."

"It's all right, dear," the president said. "We'll invite a class of children to come help you replant. You can teach them how birds mate and flowers pollinate."

She popped him on the arm. "They are way too young to learn about birds and bees." Discreetly, she hit him even harder. "And I can't believe you made such a lame joke and I fell for it."

Josh smiled at his mate. That's what he wanted with her. Happiness and love strong enough to survive bad jokes. After the president and first lady were swept away to safety, the captain dismissed the soldiers gathered.

Candy was on her game. "Captain, status of Colonel Dresden."

"Injured, but alive, ma'am. He was thrown down the stairwell next to the elevator, the biggest part of the blast nicked him."

"Do you have a suspect for the bombs?"

"No, ma'am."

"His name is Mikhail Steganovich. Russian terrorist. We killed his brother at the NIB earlier tonight. Has the bomb dog gone through the house yet?"

"Uh, we've . . . There's a situation with the bomb dog and trainer," the captain said.

"What?"

"When we weren't able to contact him via phone, we sent someone to his residence." He paused.

"And?" she pushed.

"They found his body inside the home. Shot once in the head. The dog was outside the fence, waiting to be let in."

"Let in? I don't understand, Captain," she replied. Josh didn't get it either. How did the dog get out if the man was dead?

"We've speculated, ma'am, that someone killed the trainer and impersonated him, including uniform and credentials, and brought the dog the first time according to protocol. That was how the bomber gained access to plant his bombs. Afterward, he dumped the dog and it found its way home."

"Are you serious?" Candy shook her head. Josh smelled her anger building quickly. She'd done so well with her temper the past several hours. He knew she was trying. This fuckup, though, was irreprehensible.

She took a deep breath. "Captain, please help me understand how this unknown man could get through."

"Ma'am, he had on standard paint and looked like the rest of us. And how would someone else know when we'd get a call to the White House? He had the credentials."

"Stolen creds," she mumbled.

Josh looked around at the hundred scattered men. The captain was right. Every man looked identical with matching uniforms and black face paint. He understood the problem humans could have with identification. That wasn't a problem shifters had. They identified others by smell, which would be nearly impossible to copy.

"Captain," his mate said, "if someone wants something bad enough, it's hard to stop them. Our man, Mikhail Steganovich, had his brother set up a diversion at the NIB building."

"Of course," Josh chimed in. "Mikhail knew protocol would be for a group of men to go to the White House to secure the president, including the bomb dogs. He just had to blend in."

"Well, son of a bitch," she muttered. He heard the exhaustion in her voice. "Lock down the house, Captain. Keep everyone out of it in case there are more bombs. Tomorrow morning, we can debrief and have the ALFA group search for bombs. They are specially set up for that."

She looked at Josh. "Think your guys can handle that?"

He nodded. "Yup, that's what we're trained to do." They reached the driveway to the north entrance and stepped onto the concrete. Several men stood ready, assault rifles shouldered.

"Yes, ma'am. We'll meet you in the PEOC at 0700," the captain said.

"Make it 0800," she replied. "I've had a hell of a day."

"Yes, ma'am. Do you need a ride anywhere?"

"If you could have someone takes us back to the NIB, that would be great," she said, sagging against him. He loved her delicious weight on him.

The soldier standing nearby turned to them. "Captain, sir, I'll volunteer to drive them over."

"Thank you, soldier. Take one of the Humvees. Report back to me when you return."

The soldier started to one of the trucks then stopped to salute.

Candy turned back. "Captain Bridges."

"Yes, ma'am."

"If you see anything remotely suspicious, I don't care if it's a groundhog waving a Russian flag out its ass, follow up on it until the end. Mikhail Steganovich is extremely smart."

"Understand, ma'am."

"Oh, and have an explosives team to diffuse a C-4 in the secret escape in the president's bedroom."

"Ma'am, I don't know where that is—"

"I know," she said. "In the morning. Just don't let anyone in tonight." His mate turned to him. "Take me home before anything else happens."

"Yes, ma'am," he said. Gladly.

CHAPTER 36

In the back of the Humvee, Candy closed her eyes. She was exhausted. It'd been an eighteen-hour day now that it was midnight. Nothing would be better than passing out in her mate's arms. With that thought came all the worries about him not wanting her once her got to see how she really was.

Maybe she'd take all she could in their time together, then when he left, it wouldn't be a big deal. Well, she doubted that, but she'd deal by throwing herself into her work. Perhaps even ask for a transfer for another tour overseas. She could easily move into a commander sergeant major role with any battalion.

Josh grabbed her hand from the other backseat. "What's wrong?" he asked.

Oh, shit, she thought. The man could smell everything she felt. Damn, how would she ever get away with anything around him? She couldn't even have a surprise birthday party without him smelling it.

"What's wrong? I'm tired, for starters," she said. "The list is a lot longer, if you care to take notes."

He smiled. "Don't need to. Eidetic memory."

She dropped her head back and laughed. Oh my fucking god! The man *was* a god. There wasn't one thing wrong with him. Nothing. Pure perfection. It felt so good to laugh.

The truck turned the corner and the street was partially blocked by federal agency vehicles in front of the NIB.

"Damn, they are still here?" she said.

Their driver tensed. "Ma'am?"

"It's all right, soldier. There was an incident at the building earlier. These guys are still working it apparently."

"Do you think they've cleaned up the roof yet?" Josh asked.

"I would've thought they would have, but maybe not," she said. "Soldier, would you mind driving us to the roof of the parking garage?" She sat back. "It'll be much quicker than going inside to the elevator. Besides, my car is parked there."

"Good idea," her mate said.

"Yes, ma'am," the driver replied. She noted Josh's grip on her hand tightened for a second.

She stared at Josh, trying to figure out what he was responding to. Maybe he needed a morale boost? "This here director's men and I took down several uglies. Their bodies needed to be removed. That's it." He shook his head then glanced at the rearview mirror up front. She mouthed, *What?* to Josh. "We make a good team," she finished.

The director's helicopter came into sight. The driver stopped at the bridge connecting the garage to the NIB roof. She and Josh climbed out and the soldier drove away. Josh remained standing where he got out, staring back at the Humvee.

"What?" she asked.

He shook his head again and shrugged. "Nothing, I guess I must be overly tired too."

A guy wearing an FBI jacket stood on the roof, staring at the floor. He looked up when they crossed the metal bridge. He offered his hand to her first. Smart man. "Sergeant. I'm Agent Mike Ward, FBI."

"Good to meet you. I'm Obermier."

Ward turned to Josh and gave him a nod. "Good to see you, Director."

That surprised her, though she wasn't sure why. "You know each other, obviously."

Josh smiled. "Yeah, he's one of us."

Her brow raised. "*Us*, us?"

"Mike, this is my mate, Candy. Found her this morning."

The agent's face lit up with happiness and he gave Josh a manly hug/slap on the back. "That's fantastic, man. I'm so jealous." She hadn't realized how big of a deal it was—

A gunshot rang out and all three dropped to the ground. Josh and she were near the helipad while Mike was several feet away, closer to the door leading into the building. "What the fuck now?" Candy growled.

"Mike," Josh called out, "you all right?"

"I'm hit, but will survive," he said.

"Get behind one of the air ducts. Try to get inside the building. Stay low," Josh instructed.

"What about you?" Mike said, scooting away.

This man was injured and worried about her and Josh. "Don't worry about us, Ward. Just go," Candy said.

From the garage, the soldier who'd driven them here strode out with ammunition and automatic weapons. Rifle pointed at them, he stopped in front of the couple, still on the ground.

His face was twisted into a snarl. "I should fucking shoot you both, right now, and let the birds eat your fucking guts." He hitched back his leg and kicked toward her head. "You fucked up everything." Josh caught his foot, sending him to the ground. He kicked with his other foot, making Josh release his hold, then scooted away. Through it all, his rifle was steady enough to shoot.

He looked around. "Where did the other go?"

"You hit him," Candy said. "He's probably dead already." Partially behind, partially on top of her, Josh cursed quietly. She could tell he was pissed off about something. This wasn't his fault. He shouldn't get overly stressed about what he couldn't control. She snorted to herself—like *she* should be giving anger advice to him.

The gunman shuffled back to a large pipe exiting the roof and quickly looked around it. Josh moved to stand and helped her up. The man hurried back, gun raised. "You're not going anywhere," he said.

Josh's chest rumbled against her back. "I thought I recognized your voice. But you didn't say enough in the truck," Josh said. "What do you want, Mikhail?"

Candy whipped her head around and stared at the bastard pointing a gun at him. With the dark paint on his face, Josh didn't recognize the man from the YouTube video. But he wasn't looking for similarities, either. Plus the heavy vodka smell wasn't on his clothes like with the others. That was because the asshole was wearing the uniform of the dog trainer he'd killed earlier.

Loudly, she said, "Mikhail Steganovich, who would've thought you'd get by Captain Bridges's men who are at the White House right now? Men who are highly trained, standing around, ready for something to do. Yup, Colonel Bridges. At the White House. Right now."

Josh leaned down to her ear. "You okay?"

"I know what I'm doing," she said, trying to move her mouth as little as possible.

Mikhail stared at her like she was nutso. "Uh, yeah, it was easy, actually. Your fucking procedures make it so predictable." The Russian stepped closer to her, squinting his eyes. "I've seen you before, haven't I? You're that woman promoted to some position no other woman's ever had." He nodded and grinned. "We're keeping tabs on all you. We know who you are and how to get to you."

That sent a chill down Candy's back. She assumed the "we" he spoke of was Russia. That country and the U.S. had always had a tentative friendship. This could cause an international incident that wouldn't be pretty.

Down a ways, the door to the roof slammed. Hopefully, Mike had understood her earlier instructions and was on the way to the White House.

She looked at him. "You're on a clock, Steganovich. Just go back to the truck and drive away. Any direction you want. We won't see it." She read the uncertainty in his eyes. Josh should smell it, too. Then a nasty smile grew on the man's face.

"You killed my brother." His body shook, his face red from more than the cool wind. "I will enjoy watching you both being interrogated. I will avenge his death."

"Come on, Mikhail," she said, disgust pushing her buttons. "Your brother killed two people and held the NIA director hostage. What the fuck did you think would happen? It was his own damn fault that he died. He could've just walked away."

The Russian screamed and fired his automatic gun, narrowly missing them. Josh squashed her into the concrete. Her heart raced so hard, it hurt. Could a thirtysomething have a heart attack from the heart beating too fast?

The man stood, panting, staring behind them. "How fitting. Instead of my brother taking the helicopter, I will in his place with better hostages." He waved his gun at them. "Both of you get in the helicopter. We're going for a ride."

"We don't know how to fly," Josh lied. She wondered if he knew or not. Knowing his skill set, he probably knew how to do about everything there was.

"Then I'll kill you both and be on my way." He raised his gun level with Josh's head.

CHAPTER 37

⤙⤚

As Josh stared down the barrel of a rifle, he hoped this asshole believed they didn't have a chance of getting off the roof of the NIB. With Mike on his way to the White House, help was coming. If they could stall long enough, then Bridges could get here with his guys. That would take a while, but that was the only possibility he saw.

"I can fly," Candy said. "Put the gun down, Mikhail."

Josh dropped his chin to his chest. Why did she confess? No, no, no. That wasn't how this kind of game was played.

"Put the gun down, Mikhail," Candy repeated, climbing to her feet. Josh tried to edge in front of her, putting himself between her and the gun. His mate spun on him. "If we are going to try this mating thing, you have to be fucking alive to do it. If you—"

"Or you," he added.

"Yes, if one of us dies, then forget it."

Was that her way of saying she wanted to be with him? Elation and true fear struck him at the same time. He was so close to having her, and so close to having her taken away.

"Enough talking." Mikhail raised his aim overhead,

specifically at Josh. "The only reason I'm keeping you, Mr. Smart Ass, is because you're a director. I will get paid well for you. And I will enjoy beating you when you are tied and can't defend yourself. It will be for Yulian."

"Someone is paying you to kidnap people?" Candy asked. That was surprising. "What happened to you and your brother doing it all yourselves?"

"It's a lot easier than trying to get the money myself. Now get in the helicopter. I'd hate to give up the director's worth, but I will if either of you cause problems. Director, get in on the other side. Any moves and I'll put a bullet in Miss Army's head."

Shit. Hands in the air, he walked around the helicopter. He'd bide his time and wait for the opportunity to attack. There would be one. He just needed to be patient.

As he settled in the seat, Mikhail shoved his mate forward. That was enough for a death sentence in his book. Patient, he'd be patient. Candy opened the pilot's door and climbed in. He read the confidence in her eyes. He hoped she had a plan. He knew she was good. She wouldn't be where she was if she wasn't.

Mikhail hopped into the back and held a pistol to his mate's head in the pilot's seat. The rifle slid behind the back seats. No chance for him to reach that without getting up. No opportunity there.

Candy started up the helicopter and they all put on headsets. He prayed she didn't do anything to get herself killed. But Mikhail now knew how to get her to bend to his wishes. Threaten him, her mate. Dammit.

"Where are we going, Mikhail?" she asked.

"To the cargo docks, where the ships are," he said.

Josh caught her eye. That was a strange place to go. Was the man planning to take a cruise home? Candy lifted off, quickly turning them in the wrong direction. But Mikhail wouldn't know since he wasn't familiar with the city. He glanced at her, but kept his poker face. He hoped she knew what she was doing.

The local air traffic control man spoke through their

headsets. Mikhail poked his gun into Candy's head again. "Don't talk to them."

"I have to," she explained. "They need to know who we are and where we're going."

"No, they don't," the Russian said in perfect English. "We will be gone before they can get anyone to find us."

Air traffic came on again, asking for identification and destination. Candy maintained radio silence. After a couple of minutes, Josh saw the White House come into view. Oh, shit. Was she going to do what he thought?

His mate glanced at him and grinned. Oh, fuck. She was.

Candy kicked their air speed much faster than it should have been. At the same time, she dipped them to treetop level. Air traffic control screamed over the headset, warning of restricted airspace and threatening to shoot them down. Candy switched them off.

"What are you doing?" Mikhail yelled. "Get out of here. Go to the docks or I will shoot you."

"Mikhail," Candy said calmly, "if you shoot me, you will be a red smoldering splotch on the back lawn of the White House. Now be quiet while I buzz the place."

"You're buzzing the president's home?" Mikhail looked out the window. "Isn't that illegal?"

"Damn right, it's illegal," his mate laughed, "and you should be loving it. Your flyboys do this to our ships at sea all the time. It aggravates the hell out of them."

"That's why we do it," Mikhail proudly said as if he had some personal role in what the Russian military did. "Circle again," he directed with glee on his face.

He hoped she remembered about the snipers mounted on the roof. That would explain her gut-wrenching, vomit-producing flying.

"We need to keep going," Candy said, "before they mount an attack."

"Yes, yes. Go, then," the Russki said.

Candy turned them in the correct direction and high-tailed out of the city.

"Mikhail," Candy said, "you've pulled off an incredible

feat. Having the hostages to divert attention away from the White House was genius." Josh looked at Candy. Was she going over the edge? Lack of food and sleep making her loopy? "How did the men get inside the building to take hostages?"

"That was easy, Miss Army Girl. You Americans think you're so safe here in your little country. We made our own truck with fake floor where my men hid until they passed security."

"How did you get the caterer to use it?" Josh asked.

"We took his family." The Russian shrugged like it was an everyday thing, common sense.

"Army Girl, how did you get to the fountain?" Mikhail asked. "No one in Russia has that information. You do well to hide it."

"That fountain escape route?" his mate said nonchalantly. "Lots of people know about it. It's been there a long time. How many bombs did you plant in the president's home?" she asked.

The terrorist smiled. "You would like to know, wouldn't you?"

She scowled. His mate did a good job with a sneak interrogation, pumping the guy full of praise. Josh hadn't realized her ploy until a few minutes ago, either. The bastard played along for a bit, giving information that meant little, though.

The water and large cargo ships came into sight. "Where are we landing?" Candy asked.

"Not here," he said. "We're landing on a boat at sea."

CHAPTER 38

The son of a bitch had to be joking, Candy thought. No wonder he didn't complain about dive-bombing the White House. She was taking him out of the country immediately. Fuck!

"Here." She felt Mikhail's arm press against hers. He handed her a scrap of paper with numbers written on it. "Follow these coordinates exactly." Shit, shit, shit. She couldn't do this. There had to be something she could do.

"You know, Mikhail," she said, "even on the water the Coast Guards can arrest you."

He laughed. "I know the rules as well as you, Army Lady. If a boat is flying a foreign flag in international waters, you won't interfere to avoid a diplomatic mess with Russia."

Dammit, she knew Mikhail was smart enough to pull something like this off. Think.

"Yeah, you got me there, Mikhail," she said. "I had to try. How far out is the boat? We only have enough fuel to go so far." International waters started about twelve miles out, so it wasn't that far for the ship to be in neutral territory.

"We have fuel to get there. No worries." He seemed too calm for the situation. Was that good or bad? She thought about bringing up Yulian, his dead brother. But that might piss him off enough to shoot her or her mate after they landed.

Passing over the open water, she gradually slowed their speed and kept a high altitude. She'd stay in radar range as long as she could. Not that it would do much good where they were going.

She glanced at Josh from the corner of her eye. He stared out the side window. She wondered what he was thinking. Did he have a plan? Formulating one? Did he have some animal skill that could help them? Unless he shifted into a kraken, too, she doubted there was much he could do.

The side of her head pounded. A bottle of aspirin sounded good right now. When was the last time she and Josh had eaten? Other than the finger foods from the caterer's tray in her office, she'd had nothing since her late lunch.

"Mikhail," she asked, "do you have the radio frequency for the ship? I'll need to talk with them to land."

"They know we are coming. You don't need to talk to anyone."

She wanted to stand in her seat and scream at the fool, but instead took a deep breath. "Mikhail, it is the middle of the night. There isn't a damn thing to see except stars. If the ship is a little bit off the coordinates, they could be miles away and we'd never see them."

"Just stay on the route," was all he said.

At a loss for what to say or do, she'd just fly until something came along. At least Josh was with her. She wasn't alone to die. Not that she wanted him to die with her. But he was a calming comfort to her erratic personality.

Up ahead, she saw something on the water. Lights. Well, damn. *There is the ship*, she thought. They hadn't been in the air all that long. Too long to swim to shore, but easily within range to fly back.

Candy hovered high over the ship, looking for an open area. "Where do I land?" she asked.

"At the front of the boat," he said.

She snorted. "Where? There isn't a big enough space."

"Yes, there is," he replied.

"No, there's not," she came back. "I need at least thirty feet. The damn blades are that long."

"I've seen it done before," he ranted.

"On this ship, this space?" Candy asked.

"No, but—"

"Exactly," she yelled, "it can't be done."

Mikhail put *two* pistols to Josh's head. "Land. Now."

"Goddammit," Candy yelled. "I should crash this fucker into the ship's bridge to teach you a lesson, asshole." The weather devices on top of the bridge's roof gave her wind direction. At least she knew that. Wind on her nose, she gauged the ship's speed. Come in too fast, the rotors would slam into the metal shipping containers stacked against the front edge of the deck. Come in too slowly and they would miss the ship completely, crashing into the water.

She slowed the hover making sure the containers cleared the rotor diameter. Then descended farther. Immediately, the helicopter began to violently shake. Warning buzzers screeched. The 'copter rolled and pitched, threatening to crash.

"What's happening?" Mikhail hollered.

"Exactly what I told you, moron," she hollered back. The craft started to drop. "We're in a vortex. Pulling out, now." She increased lateral airspeed and banked to the side, pushing for altitude. White caps from waves appeared out the window. "Come on, baby," she coaxed as the water came closer with every second. "You can do this." The controls came back under her command, the alarms shut off, and she leveled out.

She was ready to throw up now. Check, please. Josh gripped the seat and door handle with white knuckles. "What's a vortex?" Josh asked.

She answered: "Remember back when the SEALs went in after Bin Laden and one of the helos crashed inside the compound?"

"Yeah," he said.

"The pilot probably got caught in what we call a vortex-ring state. It's when you try to land in your own down-wash."

"What's downwash?" Josh asked.

Now was not the time for flight instruction. "Downwash is the air the rotors are pushing down to keep the helo hovering. When the air hits the ground, it bounces back up, messing with all the dynamics and rotors, causing the craft to rock and roll."

"How did we not crash when the SEAL did?" Mikhail asked.

"I was able to increase speed and get out of it. The SEAL had high walls surrounding him. He had no options. He had to settle with power," she explained.

"He what?" the Russian asked.

"He had to land extremely hard. Enough to damage the helo, obviously, since they abandoned it."

"So," Mikhail said, "try again."

She fisted her hands. "Mikhail, did you not understand—"

"Yes, I've seen it done," he replied. "Try again."

Shit. He was going to get them killed. Now or later. She checked wind direction again and would try a different angle where the air didn't bounce off the metal containers as much. Maybe that would help.

Hovering over the ship, she tried again. This time the ride was less rough and they landed with a thud.

"Now get out. We're going to see your executioner." Mikhail laughed.

CHAPTER 39

Josh had never been prouder of his little mate than he was at that moment. She had nerves of steel and hands as steady as they came. Her knowledge and expertise had let them do the near impossible. Hopefully, that wasn't all for naught.

He climbed from the passenger's side and was met by three huge Russians. Damn, they grew them big in that country. They rivaled him in size and they were human. As he looked at one of them, the other bashed him in the head.

Pain zinged through his scalp and neck, taking him to his knees. He heard Candy screaming over the cheap shot, not far away. He pretended to stay down so they would think him less a threat. He needed to get his bearings and come up with an escape plan.

They dragged him through doorways and down stairs to a cell made with iron bars welded to the floor, walls, and ceilings. His hope was that his mate would be with him. One of the men spoke in a language he didn't understand. The cage door opened and he was thrown in. Candy was pushed in behind him. Thank god.

He had to laugh at her. She was chewing them a new

asshole and was pretty damn good at it. If they'd understood her, they might be afraid. When the men had left, she was at his side in a second.

"Dammit, Josh." She tore off a piece of her shirt and pulled the bottle half full of water from her pants pocket. She soaked the scrap of material. "Sit up. You need to drink." Her hand slipped behind his back to help. She held the bottle as he sucked in lukewarm liquid.

She dabbed at the sore spot on the back of his head. His wolf had sealed the cut, but the area was still a bloody mess. "Can't you go anywhere without getting into trouble?" she said. Exasperation and humor flitted through her voice. "Seems everywhere you've been the past eighteen hours some disaster has occurred." She lay his head in her lap.

He smiled. "If I'm correct, you happened to be in all those same places. You sure it's not you attracting trouble?" The top of his skull was incredibly close to her hot folds where his face had been hours ago. He couldn't help but breathe deeply, taking in what she offered.

"Me?" she replied, "I'm completely innocent." Her eyes were drooping.

He did laugh at that. "That's not how you were in your office earlier. You seemed quite the wanton sex goddess." Yes, just what he hoped. She was aroused by his statement and she flooded the air with her want. Her face flooded red, her eyes wide at his comment. Damn, she was so cute. And his. Her shoulders slumped. Not normal for her.

"You know," he started, "when we get back home, you'll have to move in with me."

Her brow rose but eyes remained closed. "Why can't you move in with me?" She had a point. His apartment was still a bachelor pad with mismatched furniture, and his dinnerware consisted of Hefty paper plates. He had real silverware, though. It was impossible to eat a steak with a plastic knife and fork.

"Okay, I'll move in with you," he agreed.

Her head was back, breathing slowing. They had been

going nonstop for a long time. Geared up on adrenaline and fear, they had been sharp and in the zone for hours. Now his mate was crashing hard as adrenaline drained. Humans couldn't sustain that heightened state of existence shifters could. Her mind would be shutting down, insisting on sleep.

He'd let her rest, but not sleep. He needed her to be ready to go on the spot. "Would you like a big wedding or something simple?" he whispered.

She sighed but remained quiet, which unnerved him. She wasn't having second thoughts, was she?

"Josh," she said, "you are as perfect as they come. I'm about as fucked-up as they come."

"And your point?" he said. "Opposites attract."

"Oh, Josh," she sighed again. "You'll get bored of me quickly and want to leave. I don't know the first thing about love or how to love someone the right away." A tear trickled down her cheek. She was too tired for this topic to frustrate her that much.

He raised his head from her lap and moved her around until she sat against him with his back to the wall. This was so much better. Having her in his arms after all this time. She felt so good. Perfect.

"You spent all night watching the president and first lady, didn't you?" he asked. She nodded, her head back on his shoulder. "You even tried to get close to me, but I messed up both times." She nodded again. "But you tried." He kissed the side of her head. "I think you want to be loved. To love. To know what it feels like. And now you have it from me." Her head bobbed.

"But when you find out who I really am, the hard-nosed sergeant bitch, you'll run screaming. I have temper issues like my father did."

"But how many times did you purposefully quell that anger? I saw you controlling it," he said. "You have techniques to call on when you get into those situations. You are so strong, Candy. You've lived through what would have killed others."

He rubbed his hands up and down her arms. "And see

this. Almost a day ago, you would've kicked my ass for touching you this way."

She barked out a laugh. "You are so right, there."

"So see?" He kissed her hair again, loving her smell. "We are meant to be. Your body accepts mine and mine more than accepts yours."

She smiled at the comment, eyes still closed, head back. "Maybe."

"No maybe about it, love. Your body is made for loving and we're going to have our own pup yard."

She sat up and turned to him. "Our own what? You don't mean pets, do you?"

"No," he shook his head, "that's what wolf shifters call their children. Pups." The smell of fear stung his nose. Gently, he brushed back hair from her face. "What do you think about having children?" Shit, he should've waited to bring up this subject. He was just so ready to move on to the next stage of his life. She wasn't resting anymore, either.

"Josh." Her eyes turned to the floor. "I'm . . . I don't think I want children." Her fright ramped up more than ever. She was calmer during the bombs.

He pulled her back into his arms to lean against him. With what she'd told him about her past, he knew why she held this fear. Question was, did she understand it?

"Why don't you want kids?" he asked.

She shrugged, but didn't say anything. Her pulse was slowing and her breathing was returning to resting mode.

"Raising pups is a community thing where I'm from. It's not just the mother alone with the kids from dawn till dusk. I will be there a lot of the time. In fact, I plan to be there most of the time. I want to be a big part of our pups' lives. You never have to worry about becoming too rough or . . . violent with them. It won't happen."

In a tiny whisper, he heard her say, "How do you know? How can you be so sure?"

"Because you know what it's like and won't let it occur," he responded. "You won't be saddled or overwhelmed with stress. When it's playtime, a lot of the neighborhood kids get together and play outside or go to the pool, or jump on the neighbor's trampoline and break their arms." Her body cringed against his. "But we heal super fast, so the arm will be fine after an ice cream cone and chocolate syrup."

"Or a DQ chocolate Blizzard with M&Ms," she said.

"No way. Reese's peanut butter chunks blow M&Ms out of the water," he came back.

"Huh," she retorted, "I'll show you blowing chunks, buddy. Get you and me back in my chopper."

He laughed. The return of her smart ass meant she was about rested enough to help get them out of here. Just one more thing he needed to know. He snuggled her tighter to him. "Tell me about your life after your mom passed."

She stiffened then relaxed into him. Her throat cleared. "I would've run away, except I couldn't leave my younger sister and brother behind. I knew if I told anyone about my father, we kids would've been taken by Child Protective Services and probably split up.

"I did my best to feed my siblings and hide them when needed. Kept Dad's attention on me when he needed to rage and vent." She sighed and paused.

"On my eighteenth birthday, I had my brother and sister pack the few things they had and we snuck out of the house when Dad finally passed out. I drove them to our aunt and uncle's a couple towns over and dropped them off. I gave my aunt a journal I'd kept since the day Mom died.

"In it I wrote down everything that happened, everything I felt, and chronicled my dying childhood dreams. That way she would fight to keep my siblings if Dad came around wanting to take them back."

He asked, "Did he?"

She shrugged. "I don't know. After I dropped them off, I went to the recruiter station and signed up for the army and left for basic training that day. I haven't talked to or seen any of my family since then." She sniffled. "Happy birthday to me. Freedom."

CHAPTER 40

———✂———

Candy felt energized, a little saddened at recalling the end of her childhood, but that gave her the impetus to get moving. She must've caught her second wind. Her brain kicked into *drive* from *neutral*. She stretched her legs and realized something. She slapped a hand on her forehead.

"Well, fuck me," she growled.

Josh moved behind her. "If you insist."

She batted at his hands and scooted away. "Josh. They never frisked me." She unzipped her side pant pocket and pulled out a hand gun. Then did the same on the other side for pistol number two. "I just remembered I had them."

Josh picked up a weapon, though he didn't usually carry one. Shifters preferred to use brute strength and stealth, but on a boat at sea, that wasn't always possible.

"Okay," she said, feeling back on her game. "Can you bend the bars?" she asked Josh.

"Let's see." He got to his feet and positioned his body just right then gritted his teeth and pulled the rods. For a second, nothing moved, but then slowly, the bars formed a bow-legged exit. Josh took her hand and they slipped out.

"Have your nose get us back topside," she said. To her,

the halls looked identical with gray paint and pipes running everywhere.

She opened a door, and salty air hit her nose and tongue. The wind was brisk and chilly with no sun to warm it. If she waited a few more hours, it would be time for it to rise. But, yeah, she wasn't in the mood.

Through the shadows, Josh led them along the stacked containers crowding the center of the ship. He stopped and peeked around a corner, then turned back to her.

"Doesn't seem to be anyone up here. They're all in the stern or below deck. We should be able to get in and take off. Can you do that quickly?" he asked with a smile.

Her eyes rolled. "I don't know. Never tried to be fast before."

He pecked her on the lips then they took off running. Josh got her in her seat and closed the door then hurried around to his side. Her fingers danced over buttons and switches in a routine she'd done thousands of times over the years.

At a tap on her window, she turned her head. Mikhail stood frowning, gun resting against the window. Son of bitch. Where had the fucker come from? They were so close. Then she realized Josh hadn't gotten in the bird yet. Her heart leapt into her throat. Where was he?

She heard a noise. Maybe a gunshot, but the spinning rotor blades made too much noise to be sure. Either way, Mikhail disappeared from her door. Where did he go? Where the hell was Josh?

One of the guys who escorted them to the cell came around the corner. She opened the pilot's door and shot at him, hitting him in the chest. Others followed behind him. Before the men saw her in the cockpit, she dropped to the deck and rolled under the craft to the few feet of deck left before going over the railing.

Her hair whipped around her face and stung her cheeks. Keeping low, she scrambled to the side looking for cover. A bullet ricocheted off the railing beside her head. She dove toward a crate but it was too far to do her any good.

Another shot bounced in front of her, showering splinters from the decking onto her.

She dropped her gun and raised her hands, though she doubted it would do any good. Killers like Mikhail killed with no remorse or second thoughts. The only thing to stay his hand would be money.

Another man charged her, gun aimed at her. Instead of shooting, he grabbed her by the hair and dragged her to her feet. He drew her backside against his chest, placing the gun under her chin. He asked in a heavy accent, "Where is your boyfriend?"

Anger and possessiveness rolled through her. Josh wasn't a boyfriend, he was her mate, which meant he loved her and would never hurt or leave her. "How the fuck do I know?" She threw her head back and smashed her skull into his nose. The feel of cartilage giving way was satisfying.

With a double-arm elbow thrust to the man's stomach, she doubled him over and pushed him back a few steps. Grabbing his hair, she drove a knee to his head, sending him sprawling, out cold. Thank god for the exhaustive self-defense training the army forced recruits through.

More bullets bounced off a beam at her side. She fell flat, snatched the prick's gun from him and fired blindly until the clip was empty. The shots at her stopped. But more rounds were blasting on the other side. Was Josh over there? Stupid question. Trouble followed him, right? Or was it her? Either way, they made great contenders for Mr. and Mrs. James Bond. She'd be happy with the Boring family instead.

All the things Josh had said in the cell were right. She was afraid of being like her father if she had children. She'd seen Monica and her husband interact and already knew she wanted to emulate them. And she'd already decided Josh was perfect. He kept saying he'd never leave, so what the hell?

A shot flew over her head and Josh came out of nowhere, tackling her to the deck. Blood had soaked the front of his white T-shirt, which was smeared with mud, cobwebs, and grass stains. His breathing was heavy, face alarmingly pale. He needed to shift before he died.

A voice came from behind her and she turned on her knees, keeping Josh protected at her back. Mikhail, bloody and beaten up, pointed his gun at her and slowly limped toward them. She had nowhere to go and no weapon to defend her and Josh.

She sat with her back to Mikhail and scooted Josh's head and shoulders onto her knees. "Josh, you need to shift now." He rolled his head side to side.

"Can't protect you then," he managed.

"You aren't now, either," she hollered over the helicopter's engine. "You die if you don't shift and what good are you to me, then?" He still refused. She looked over her shoulder at Mikhail. The man was determined to kill them point-blank. That would be fine for her, but Josh would survive if it was the last thing she'd do.

"Listen to me," she said. "You may not be in the military, but you're damn close enough. So that means you are under my command since I'm one of the highest there is. And I'm ordering you to shift this instant and hide." A hard object poked at her head. She saw Mikhail's feet at her side. This was it.

Josh reached toward Mikhail, still trying to protect her to his dying breath. Not if she had her way. She looked into Josh's eyes locked onto hers. Her last words: "I love you. Have since the moment I walked into your office. Now, *shift*."

She threw her body backward, slamming against Mikhail's legs. A gunshot rang in her ears.

CHAPTER 41

⚓

As Josh lay on the cargo ship's top deck, he cursed him-self for letting his mate get into such trouble. How many times could he have done something to change this outcome? Who knew?

Mikhail had made his way to them. Josh had to admit, the guy looked like shit, but refused to die. True psychos were hard to kill. Something about them refused to give up.

He heard his mate's beautiful voice, but didn't under-stand what she was saying. He was surprised his heart was still beating. Actually, no, he wasn't. He had just as much will to live to protect his mate as the psycho killer had. But he'd lost so much blood. If he shifted, he'd be too weak to do anything. Who was he kidding? He'd reached that point in his human form also.

He heard his Candy say "shift." No, he couldn't. No. She said it again. He felt his wolf wanting to obey her com-mand. Unable to disregard it. She was alpha. She com-manded his shift and he had to comply.

The first bone in his body cracked as loud as a gunshot. The shift swept through him like a cold fire, reshaping, rearranging. In the end, he lay on his side, panting, staring at the Russian and his own mate, entangled and lying motionless on the ground. A puddle of blood grew underneath them.

The helicopter quieted and the blades began to slow. Shadows moved silently all around him. Some slipped through doors, others out of sight.

A familiar smell passed him and a dark figure knelt beside Candy. A growl rumbled out his weak body. His wolf would attack if this person didn't move away from his mate this instant.

"Chill out, Tumbel," Mike Ward said as he pivoted in his squat position to face Josh's wolf. "Damn, I have to say those old man sweatpants are sexy as hell on your wolf." Mike patted the animal's shoulder. "Don't worry, Director, we got this covered. We'll have you back on land shortly." He started to stand then turned back to the wolf. "Bridges wants his men back ASAP. And no more buzzing the White House. He wasn't amused." Mike laughed.

Healed mostly, but too weak to shift back to human form, he closed his eyes and relaxed. They'd made it.

Josh woke, but didn't move. He was in a place he'd never been before. Surrounded by the smell of his mate, he felt safe. The only thing he heard was the gentle popping of a small fire and the breathing of his mate snuggled against him.

He opened an eye. Like earlier in Candy's office, he lay on the floor in front of a fireplace, his mate wrapped in his arms. After another breath, he realized he must be in her home. This was a nice surprise. But how had he gotten there?

The beautiful woman under the blanket with him moved, rolling toward him. Her eyes opened and they smiled. Stunning.

"Good morning, *mate*," she said.

"Same to you, love," he replied. "Are we at your place?"

"Yes. Mike said you'd be okay after sleeping for a while. Your wolf just needed time to recover since you let yourself get so . . . so far gone." She choked on the last words. "Don't you ever do that again," she ordered. "You had me so scared." A frightened sob entered her voice. He kissed her forehead.

"I'm sorry, love," he said. "I was so worried for you. I didn't know where you were or if Mikhail had you. I had to find you before anything else."

"Well, we're safe at my home. Mike's men carried your wolf in and put you here. I figured we'd take a shower and go to bed when you woke. In about three hours, we're meeting Bridges in the West Wing to debrief."

"Three hours, huh?" he said, smelling his mate's arousal as she slid her fingers along his bare chest. He must have shifted when he'd gained enough strength. "I do feel dirty. How about that shower now?"

"Are you okay?" Candy asked, watching Josh wince as he sat up.

He nodded. "Yeah. *Ow,* Christ. Fucking Mikhail. I guess I should be grateful it wasn't that bad."

She frowned. "Too close for comfort if you ask me."

"I guess it could have gone a lot differently, but I'd do it all again to make sure you were okay."

Candy moved to Josh's side and slid her arm under his, helping him up. "Josh, you hardheaded mutt. We've got three hours to get you tip-top and I think the first thing you need is a hot shower. It'll loosen you up."

He slid his free arm around her waist and pulled her against his chest. "I've got a surprise for you too and it ain't loose."

She grinned against his lips as he bent to claim hers. "Really. Could it be your hard ass, or maybe its countermeasure, here." She moved her hand around to grip the hard bar of his cock.

He took her mouth and kissed her, hungry and greedy. "All I've done is lie in this bed thinking about your sweet ass and how many ways I can tap it."

"Really. And how many is that."

"Care for a demonstration?" In one fluid move, he

grabbed her waist and tossed her over his shoulder, not waiting for an answer.

Injuries forgotten, he kicked in the door to the bathroom and let her slide down his muscled chest.

"You're still hurt," she argued, taking a step back.

He shook his head. "When it comes to your body, I will never be that hurt." He gestured to the bathroom. "You said I needed a shower, so turn on the tap and then strip."

"I guess I can help, if you need me." She stopped and opened a nightstand, pulling out a bottle of lube. "You mentioned ass," she said innocently.

Pushing her to the tiled shower, he took the bottle of lube out of her hand and placed it on the ledge. "This will come in handy very soon."

She laughed at the devil-may-care grin he gave her. "You're a pervert."

"Maybe, baby. But I have needs, too." He wrapped his hand around his thickening cock. "Right now, I need your mouth on my dick."

Candy turned on the spray, water sluicing down her body first. She turned to Josh. He stared at her with enough hunger in his gaze to make her pussy clench. He took two steps toward her. He swept them both into the warm cascade, letting the water continue to drench them. With his hands on her shoulders he pushed her to her knees. He pressed his cock to her lips and with a smirk she sucked him deeply. It amazed her how easy it was now, how the thought of his rock hard rod made her wet.

Gripping his shaft, she worked the hard length, running a curved palm over his head as her tongue curled under its ridged edge. Josh growled and tightened his grip on her hair, pushing his dick deeper. With a yank he pulled free of her mouth with an audible pop.

"Your body is soaked, babe. Now let's see if your pussy is, too." He cupped her chin, running his thumb along her mouth. "On all fours, love."

Candy sat back on her heels and looked up at him. "What are the magic words, bossy?"

He grinned, sinking down to the wet tile along with her. He slid his hands into her wet hair and took her mouth, hungry again. "The magic words are 'I want to fuck you so hard, you scream as you come.' Then I'm going to spread you wide and fuck that fine ass of yours."

The raw words had heat sliding down her thighs, the slickness mixing with the shower water trickling from her hair. She bit his bottom lip. "Well, since you put it that way." She turned, dropping to her hands and knees.

Josh reached down and spread her juice wide. His thumb circled her clit as his fingers curled into her wet slit. "So fucking wet."

She turned, shoving her wet hair from her face. "Lick me."

Eyes on fire, he dipped his face to her pussy and dragged his tongue to her ass, ringing her tight hole. He growled lifting his face from her, and with a sharp yank, pulled her hips up and back. "I'm going to stretch you front and back." He drove his cock into her pussy fast and hard and then pulled back, his fingers gripping her hips as he slammed his dick into her again, balls deep.

Candy cried out as he hit her G-spot, forcing an orgasm, quick and cruel. "Yes!"

Josh turned back to licking, driving her crazy with his magic tongue.

"More! God, Josh. If I had known sex with you was this fucking amazing, I'd have jumped you yesterday in your office," she moaned.

He growled.

"Oh, god. Oh, Josh. Oh, yes, yes, yes!" Her words were little choked noises as waves crashed through her making her legs shake.

His entire body pulsed with need and he fisted her hair again, riding her as each thrust crested her closer to another climax. Her body shuddered again and her walls squeezed his shaft, the sensation pushing him toward the precipice.

He pulled out with a snarl and spread her cheeks. Then he grabbed the bottle of lube on the ledge of the shower and dropped a generous amount between her cheeks and on his cock. He slid his hand over his cock, spreading the lube on his dick. Her sexy ass came next. He rubbed the lube over the rim of her ass and dipped one and then two fingers in and out of her.

She moaned, her body tensing at first but as he continued to slip in and out of her, she relaxed to his touch. He curled a hand around her hip to rub it against her clit as he added a third and then fourth finger driving into her ass. She was panting and begging for more when he removed his hand.

"I've fucked your mouth and your cunt, now I want your ass." Pressing his swollen head to her slick hole, he pushed, invading her body inch by slow, torturous inch.

She moaned, not wanting to wait and reared back so he slid deep in one full stroke. Holy fuck.

"Christ, baby. Hang on a second."

He pulled back slowly and drove back in a smoother slide.

Her body squeezed his cock in a vise grip. "Tight. So fucking tight." His words were half growl, half moan, and he pulled back slipping deeply into the snug sheath, his body rigid with the need to come.

"Goddamn! I'm going to come, Candy. I can't—" he choked.

"Do it, Josh. Fill me again," she moaned, gripping the shower ledge.

"Where? Over your ass or inside?"

"Stay right where you are. Don't you dare go anywhere. You finish right here."

He reached down and cupped her pussy, his thumb working her clit. Her body clenched and she cried out again and with a guttural snarl he let go, his body emptying deeply. Josh held her against him, his cock pulsing with the intensity of his orgasm. He held her pussy clutched in his hand, her aftershocks rocking her until they both sank to the warm tile, letting the shower water puddle around them.

"You okay?" he asked.

She shivered. "Me? I'm not the one who got hurt."

He chuckled against her moist throat, his still-hard cock jerking within her. "Oh, I'd say you got something just now. Good and deep."

Candy leaned back against his shoulder. "So, are you loose or do you still need a little more?"

He grinned biting her shoulder. "Greedy. That's what you are."

She wiggled her ass and he slid from her body. "You've got no one to blame but yourself if I'm greedy when it comes to you."

He turned her in his arms and skimmed a hand from her neck over her nipple. "Then I should be the one to pay the price." His tongue darted to flick the stiff bud.

She laughed, arching her back, pressing her breast farther into his mouth. "You're the one who said you live to serve."

"Give and take, baby."

EPILOGUE

❦

Candy slowly walked her lineup, inspecting each of her men and women at attention. She made sure her scowl was stern. No easy offs here. A giggle was heard somewhere back in the line. She growled and a few more giggles erupted. Clearing her throat, the laughter stopped.

So far, the group had been fairly clean, a few smudges here, some sticky stuff there. Then she came to the male she knew would be the downfall of mankind.

"Junior Private Dubois," she said, stopping in front of him.

"Yes, ma'am," he squeaked, standing with his shoulders back, chin up.

"Boy, you are a complete mess. Look at you. Mustard on your face, ketchup in your hair. Juice all over you." She shook her head. "Knowing who your father is, I would have expected as much."

The boy looked up at her smiled. "Does that mean I win?"

Candy stepped back and saluted. The young boy returned the salute. "Junior Private Dubois, lead the battle cry."

The kid took off running, yelling "Chargem!" and cannonballed into the decorated red, white, and blue community pool as the other neighborhood kids fell in behind him, screaming and laughing.

"Candy!" One of the moms waved her over to one of the food-packed picnic tables in the town's park. "Come sit down before a baby falls out of your womb." She rolled her eyes. Never had she sat so much in her life. Just because she had the whole pregnant thing going, didn't mean her feet had to be up all the time, but she had to admit with each passing month, she did find reclining nicer and nicer.

Melinda, Parish's mate, handed her another hot dog with relish. Since getting pregnant, she'd never craved meat as much as she had the past several months. She suspected that had something to do with her mate's part of the pregnancy.

"Who won?" Melinda asked.

"No," Kari cut in, pulling away from her mate Bryon. "Let me guess." She turned to Candy. "Does the winner take after his father?"

Amerella turned to Frank. "See, Mr. Dubois, I told you your son was a walking laundry detergent advertisement."

Frank feigned surprise. "*My* son?"

"Yes," Amie said, "*your* son when he's an animal. *My* son when he acts civilized."

Frank snuggled up to her and whispered into her ear. "You didn't mind the animal last night, all *un*civilized."

Candy settled onto Josh's lap and joined in the laughter. She'd gotten to know all the shifters and their mates after Josh had taken her to his hometown shortly after her retirement from the military. She suddenly had a large family and was overwhelmed with love and support she hadn't known possible.

All her life, being what it had been, she had never been a girly girl. But now, she had gained full confidence in being a woman and all she wanted it to entail. The women showed her how to apply blush to bring out her cheekbones, and she showed them how to paint their faces so they blended into the forest when playing paintball against their shifter counterparts.

They also had infamous sausage parties where Candy

learned important skills her mate very much appreciated and which had gotten her in her current physical state.

"So, Mrs. Tumbel," her mate nibbled on her neck, "how is your first July Fourth in civilian clothes feel?"

She wiggled farther into his arms. "Pretty good. Except I feel like a bloated whale."

"But you're one damn sexy bloated whale," he said, rubbing his hands over her extended belly. He pressed his filling cock into her backside. God, she loved the feel of him hard against her. A whistle came from the sidewalk. They turned to see Colonel Dresden in his dress uniform and cane. The fruit salad on his chest was impressive. Candy hadn't seen many as highly decorated as he was.

When he stepped onto the grass, she wiggled out of her mate's arms and stood at attention, salute extended. The crowd quieted and several men and women also came to attention. Even all the kids in the pool clung to the side with one hand and saluted like she'd taught them.

As the colonel came to stand in front of her table, he returned her salute. He said, "I'd forgotten how many in this town have served their country in one way or the other." He shook hands with her mate. "Director Tumbel, good to see you again. And all your team." His eyes gleamed at her. "Well, Sergeant Tumbel, seems you're well on your way to having your own platoon."

Candy nearly choked. "Maybe the smallest platoon that ever existed. Three the first time out the chute may be the only time out the chute."

Josh smiled. "Two girls and one boy. She's used to having lots of boys around. She'll want more." Her brows rose to her hair line. Josh cowed a bit. *He'd better*, she thought.

The colonel smiled. "Director, I have something in the back of my car I need you to get. Now might be a good time."

"Yes, sir." Her mate kissed her cheek. "I'll be right back." Candy watched him hurry away, wondering what Dresden had brought with him. The colonel helped her to sit on the bench and joined her after shaking hands with the rest of the ALFA team.

"Men," Dresden addressed the guys at their table, "again, the president sends his gratitude and thanks for your work that night of the dedication. He's had a special plaque commissioned for the event with your names that will be in the old building since that's where it all began."

"The department dedication plaque is in the new building, right?" Candy asked.

"It is. It looks lonely, and over the years more will join it," Dresden confirmed. He glanced at the guys. "How are the new recruits coming? I haven't been over to see them yet." He shifted on the bench and frowned, his hand on his cane. "Don't get around as much as I used to. Getting old."

Parish answered, "They are doing great, sir. We have a full class. First time in years. Several females also."

"Good," Candy said. "No more pilfering from different departments." She looked pointedly at Kari. "Even if the best one happens to be elsewhere." Candy winked at one of her new best friends. "You know, girl, these men would've made such a mess of that whole thing without you."

The men groaned. They knew Candy and her *woman gung-ho* attitude. And she loved to tease them all with it. Just as a reminder that the weaker sex usually wasn't.

Those sitting on the opposite side of the picnic table from her and Colonel Dresden looked behind her. Candy turned to see what had their attention. Walking with Josh were several adults and a few children.

She recognized the two older ones right away. They were her aunt and uncle on her mother's side. Then her eyes fixed on the younger woman with a little girl on her hip. The woman was the spitting image of her mother before she'd died. One of the men looked like her father in the wedding picture that once hung in her childhood home.

Tears sprang to her eyes. Shaking hands covered her mouth as she glanced at Dresden smiling beside her. He nodded, not saying a word. He didn't have to. She knew who these people were. Not able to sit any longer, she got to her feet and met them a short distance from the table.

She stared into the faces of two people she realized she'd

loved and missed for the past twenty years. She gathered her little brother and sister into her arms and cried.

Josh stepped away, back to the table, to let his mate have a private moment with her family. He sat next to Dresden. "I guess her father passed away?"

"Yes, not long after Candy took the kids to her aunt's. Police report says alcohol poisoning. Bastard drank himself to death."

Josh sighed. He wasn't sure if he wished the prick had done that sooner than he had, for Candy's sake. Didn't matter. The past was the past, and his woman was stronger for it.

"Oh," Dresden said, "before I go, I wanted to let you know what we found out about the body you discovered under the house."

"Oh, yeah," Josh said, "who was it? Anybody important?"

Dresden said, "Ever hear of a guy named Hoffa?"

Ready to find
your next great read?

Let us help.

Visit prh.com/nextread

Five-Star Praise for THE CEREAL MURDERS
and the Nationally Bestselling Mysteries
of Diane Mott Davidson

"[A] DELICIOUS COMBINATION of unique
personalities, FIRST-RATE RECIPES and
SUSTAINED SUSPENSE." —*Publishers Weekly*

"A WINNING COMBINATION of character, plot
and setting." —*Library Journal*

"A CROSS BETWEEN MARY HIGGINS CLARK
AND BETTY CROCKER." —*The Sun*, Baltimore

"Diane Mott Davidson's CULINARY MYSTERIES
CAN BE HAZARDOUS TO YOUR WAISTLINE."
—*People*

"THE JULIA CHILD OF MYSTERY WRITERS."
—*Colorado Springs Gazette Telegraph*

ALSO BY DIANE MOTT DAVIDSON

Catering to Nobody
Dying for Chocolate
The Last Suppers
Killer Pancake
The Main Corpse
The Grilling Season
Prime Cut
Tough Cookie
Sticks & Scones
Chopping Spree

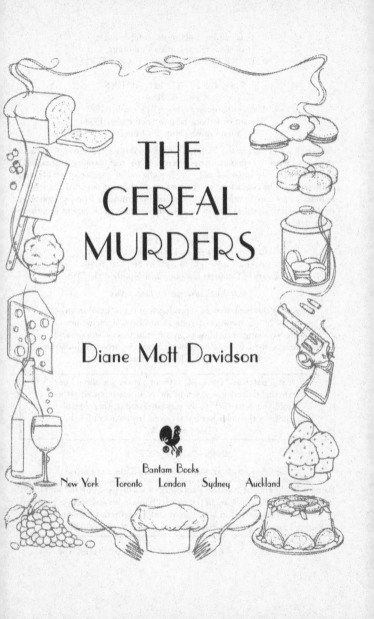

THE
CEREAL
MURDERS

Diane Mott Davidson

Bantam Books

New York   Toronto   London   Sydney   Auckland

THE CEREAL MURDERS
A Bantam Book

Bantam hardcover edition / December 1993
Bantam paperback edition / September 1994
Bantam reissue edition / June 2002

Although set in part in the Tattered Cover Bookstore in Denver, Colorado, this is a work of fiction. Any references to real people, events, and establishments are intended only to give the novel a sense of reality and authenticity. The characters, events, and establishments depicted are wholly fictional or are used fictitiously. Any apparent resemblance to any person alive or dead, to any actual events, or to any other actual establishment is entirely coincidental.

Interior illustrations by Jackie Aher.

ISBN 978-0-553-56773-1

Published simultaneously in the United States and Canada

Bantam Books are published by Bantam Books, a division of Random House, Inc. Its trademark, consisting of the words "Bantam Books" and the portrayal of a rooster, is Registered in U.S. Patent and Trademark Office and in other countries. Marca Registrada. Bantam Books, New York, New York.

PRINTED IN THE UNITED STATES OF AMERICA

For my outstanding teachers,
Emyl Jenkins, Pamela Malone, Gunda Freeman,
and the rest of the superb faculty
at Saint Anne's School in Charlottesville, Virginia.
With love and thanks

"I have never let my schooling interfere with my education."

—*Mark Twain*

Acknowledgments

The author wishes to thank the following people: Jim Davidson, Jeffrey Davidson, J. Z. Davidson, and Joseph Davidson, for their loving support and unflagging encouragement; Sandra Dijkstra, for being a superb and enthusiastic agent, and Katherine Goodwin Saideman, for being a steadfast and wise associate agent; Kate Miciak, for showing what a truly brilliant, insightful, and meticulous editor she is; Deidre Elliott, for her excellent and careful reading of the manuscript; Paul Krajovic, for his wide-ranging knowledge and his wonderful stories; Lee Karr and the group that assembled at her home, for their good-humored critique and patience; the Reverend Constance Delzell, for being an outstanding priest and incomparable friend; Joyce Meskis, Margaret Maupin, Jim Ashe, and Jennifer Hawk, for generously allowing the author to prowl through their domain; Mrs. Harold Javins of Charlottesville, Virginia, Cheryl Fair of Evergreen, Colorado, and Rosalie Larkin of Tulsa, Oklahoma, for testing the recipes; John William Schenk and Karen Johnson of J. William's Catering, Bergen Park, Colorado, for providing their usual culinary insights; and, as always, Investigator Richard Millsapps of the Jefferson County Sheriff's Department, for providing invaluable expertise and assistance.

THE
CEREAL
MURDERS

October College Advisory Dinner for Seniors and Parents

Headmaster's House

Elk Park Preparatory School

Elk Park, Colorado

SKEWERED SHRIMP

LEEK AND ONION TARTLETS

SALAD OF OAK LEAF LETTUCE AND RADICCHIO
WITH RASPBERRY VINAIGRETTE

ROAST BEEF AU JUS

YORKSHIRE PUDDING

PUREE OF ACORN SQUASH

STEAMED BROCCOLI

EARLY DECISION DUMPLINGS

IVY LEAGUE ICE CREAM PIE

1

"I'd kill to get into Stanford."

A you've-got-to-be-kidding laugh snorted across one of the dining tables at the headmaster's house. "Start playing football," whispered another voice. "Then they'll kill to get *you*."

At the moment of that sage advice, I was desperately balancing a platter of Early Decision Dumplings and Ivy League Ice Cream Pies, praying silently that the whole thing didn't land on the royal blue Aubusson carpet. My job catering the first college advisory dinner for Colorado's most famous prep school was almost over. It had been a long evening, and the only thing I would have killed to get into was a bathtub.

"Shut up, you guys!" came the voice of another student. "The only kid who's going to Stanford is Saint Andrews. They'd kill to get *him*."

Saint . . . ? Using the school's silver cutter, I

scooped out the last three slices of pie. Thick layers of peppermint ice cream cascaded into dark puddles of fudge sauce. I scooted up to the last group of elegantly dressed teenagers.

Ultra-athletic Greer Dawson, who wore a forest-green watered-silk suit, moved primly in her ladder-back chair to get a better view of the head table. Greer, the school's volleyball star, was an occasional helper with my business: *Goldilocks' Catering: Where Everything Is Just Right!* Apparently Greer thought listing *power serve* and *power lunch* on her Princeton application would make her appear diversified. But she was not serving tonight. To-night, Greer and the other seniors were concentrating on looking spiffy and acting unruffled as they heard about upcoming tests and college reps visiting the school. I needed to be careful with her slice of pie. Watered silk was one thing; ice-creamed, another. With my left hand I lowered plates to two boys before I balanced the tray on my hip and gingerly placed the last dessert in front of Greer.

"I'm in training, Goldy," she announced without looking at me, and pushed the plate away.

The headmaster stood, leaned into the microphone, and cleared his throat. A gargling noise echoed like thun-der. The bubbling chatter flattened. For a moment the only sound was the wind spitting pellets of snow against the rows of century-old wavy-glassed windows.

I zipped back out to the kitchen. Fatigue racked my bones. The dinner had been hellish. Not only that, but we were just starting the speeches. I looked at my watch: 8:30. Along with two helpers, I had been setting up and serving at the headmaster's house since four o'clock. Cocktails had begun at six. Holding crystal glasses of Chardonnay and skewers of plump shrimp, the parents had talked in brave tones about Tyler being a shoe-in at

Amherst (Granddad was an alum), and Kimberley going to Michigan (with those AP scores, what did you expect?). Most of the parents had ignored me, but one mother, anorexically thin Rhoda Marensky, had chosen to confide.

"You know, Goldy," she said, stooping from her height with a rustle of her fur-trimmed taffeta dress, "our Brad has his heart *set* on Columbia."

Greeted with my unimpressed look and decimated platter of shrimp, Rhoda's towering husband, Stan Marensky, elaborated: "Columbia's in New York."

I said, "No kidding! I thought it was in South America."

Refilling the appetizer platter a little later, I berated myself to act more charming. Five years ago, Stan Marensky's fast-paced, long-legged stalk along the sidelines, as well as his blood-curdling screams, had been the hallmark of the Aspen Meadow Junior Soccer League. Stan had intimidated referees, opponents, and his team, the Marensky Maulers, of which my son, Arch, had been a hapless member for one miserable spring.

I walked back out to the dining room with more skewers of shrimp. I avoided the Marenskys. After that painful soccer season, Arch had decided to drop team sports. I didn't blame him. Now twelve, my son had quickly replaced athletics with passions for fantasy-role-playing games, magic, and learning French. I'd tripped over more dungeon figures, trick handcuffs, and miniature Eiffel Towers than I cared to remember. These days, however, Arch had dual obsessions with astronomical maps and the fiction of C. S. Lewis. I figured as long as he grew up to write intergalactic travel novels, he'd be okay. With my career as the mother of an athlete over, I had heard only through the town grapevine that the shrill-voiced Stan Marensky had moved on to coaching junior basketball. Maybe he liked the way his threats reverberated off the gym walls.

I didn't see the Marenskys for the rest of the dinner. I didn't even think of Arch again until I was fixing the desserts and happened to glance out the kitchen windows. My heart sank. What had started that afternoon as an innocent-looking flurry had developed into the first full-blown snowstorm of the season. This promised icy roads and delays getting back to Aspen Meadow, where my son, at his insistence, was at home without a sitter. Arch had said it would make him happy if I didn't worry about him any more than he worried about me. So the only things I actually needed to be concerned about were finishing up with the preppies and their parents, then coaxing my snowtireless van around seven lethal miles of curved mountain road.

The last two rows of Early Decision Dumplings beckoned. These were actually *chômeurs*—rich biscuit dough-drops that had puffed in a hot butter and brown sugar syrup. I had added oats at the behest of the headmaster, who insisted even the desserts have something healthful about them or there would be criticism. The parents would use any excuse to complain, he told me regretfully. I ladled each dumpling along with a thick ribbon of steaming caramelized sauce into small bowls, then poured cold whipping cream over each. I handed the tray to Audrey Coopersmith, my paid helper this evening. Audrey was a recently divorced mother who had a daughter in the senior class. Gripping her platter of china bowls chattering against their saucers, she gave me a wan smile beneath her tightly curled Annette Funicello–style hairdo. Audrey wouldn't dream of complaining about the healthfulness of the *chômeurs;* she spent every spare breath complaining about her ex-husband.

"I just have so much anxiety, Goldy, I can't stand it.

This is such an important night for Heather. And of course Carl couldn't be *bothered* to come."

"Everything's going to be fine," I soothed, "except that whipping cream might curdle if it doesn't get served soon."

She made a whimpering noise, turned on her heel, and sidled out to the living room with her tray.

The *chômeurs* had steamed up the kitchen windows. I rubbed a pane of glass with my palm to check on the storm. Brown eyes like pennies, then my slightly freckled thirty-one-year-old face came into view, along with blond curly hair that had gone predictably haywire in the kitchen's humidity. Did I look like someone who didn't know Columbia was in New York? Well, those folks weren't the only ones with high SAT scores. I'd gone to prep school, I'd even spent a year at a Seven Sisters college. Not that it had done me any good, but that was another story.

Outside the headmaster's house, a stone mansion that had been erected by a Colorado silver baron in the 1880s, lamps dotting a walk illuminated waves of falling snow. The snowbound setting was idyllic, and gave no indication of Elk Park's tumultuous history. After the silver veins gave out, the property had been sold to a Swiss hotelier who had built the nearby Elk Park Hotel. A day's carriage ride from Denver, the hotel had been a posh retreat for wealthy Denverites until interstate highways and roadside motels rendered it obsolete. In the fifties the hotel had been remodeled into the Elk Park Preparatory School. The school had been through erratic financial times until recently, when Headmaster Alfred Perkins' elimination of the boarding department, all-out PR campaign, and successful courtship of wealthy benefactors had put "the Andover of the West" (as Perkins liked to call it) on secure footing. Of course, one of the benefits of being a fund-raising whiz had been the current headmaster's decade-long residency in the silver baron's mansion.

The wind swept sudden, white torrents between the pine trees near the house. During the college advisory dinner we'd gotten at least another four inches. Late October in the Colorado high country often brought these heavy snowfalls, much to the delight of early-season skiers. Early snow, like a winning season for the Broncos, also helped yours truly. Wealthy skiers and football fans needed large-scale catered events to fuel them on the slopes or in front of their wide-screen TVs.

The coffeepots on the counters gurgled and hissed. Headmaster Perkins had given me a dire warning about the old house: any sudden electrical drain would bring the wrath of blown fuses down on us all. For safety, I had brought six drip pots instead of two large ones, then had spent forty minutes before the cocktail hour snaking extension cords around the kitchen and down the halls to various outlets. The parents had found the old house—with its Oriental rugs, antique furnishings, and higgledy-piggledy remodeling—charming. Clearly they had never had to prepare a meal for eighty in its kitchen.

After the cord caper, my next problem was finding room for salad plates and platters of roast beef as they teetered, askew, on buckled linoleum counters. But the real challenge had come in making Yorkshire puddings in ovens with no thermostats and no windows through which to check the dishes' progress. When the puddings emerged moistly browned and puffed, I knew the true meaning of the word *miracle*.

From the dining room came the ponderous throat-clearing again. I nipped around the corner with the last row of dumplings as the headmaster began to speak.

"Now, as we prepare these youngsters to set forth into the fecund wilderness of university life, where survival depends on the ability to discover dandelions as well as gold . . ."

Spare me. Headmaster Perkins, who wore tweeds no matter what the weather, was smitten with the extended metaphor. I knew. I had already had to listen to a slew of them at parent orientation. Arch's sixth-grade year in public school had started badly and ended worse. But he had survived Elk Park Prep's summer school to become a new student in the school's seventh grade. To my great delight, a judge had ordered my wealthy ex-husband to pay the tuition. But as Audrey Coopersmith would soon discover and add to her list of complaints, like most single mothers, I was the one duty-bound to attend parent meetings. Already I had heard about "our trajectory toward the stars" and "harvesting our efforts" whenever things went well, or when they didn't, "This is a drought."

Now Headmaster Perkins intoned, "And in this wilderness, you will all feel as if you are navigating through asteroid fields," and held a pretend telescope up to his eye. I sighed. *Galileo meets Euell Gibbons.*

I finished serving the desserts, returned to the kitchen and with Egon Schlichtmaier, one of my faculty helpers, poured the first eight cups of regular coffee into black and gold china cups. German-born and bred, olive-skinned Egon possessed a boyishly handsome face and a muscular physique that threatened to burst out of his clothes. The school newsletter had stated that the newly hired Herr Schlichtmaier was also highly educated, having just finished his doctoral dissertation, "Form, Folly, and Furor in *Faust.*" How *that* was going to help him teach American history to high school seniors was beyond me, but never mind. I told the muscle-bound *Herr Doktor* that cream, sugar, and artificial sweetener were on the tables, and he whisked out with his tray held high like a barbell. Without missing a beat I poured eight cups of decaffeinated coffee into white and gold china cups. I hoisted my tray and marched back out to the dining room in time to hear the headmaster direct his audience to ". . . galaxies in a universe of opportunities."

I came up to the table where my other usual paid helper, Julian Teller, sat looking terribly uncomfortable. Julian, who was a senior at Elk Park Prep, was a vegetarian health-food enthusiast. He was also a distance swimmer, and sported the blond whipsawed haircut to match. Living with Arch and me the past four months, Julian earned his rent by cooking and serving for my business. Julian was, like Greer Dawson, exempt from service tonight because of the importance of the meeting. I had tried to sneak supportive smiles to him during the dinner. Each time, though, Julian had been involved in what looked like agonizing one-way conversations. Just as I was about to ask him if he wanted coffee, he extricated himself from the woman who had been chatting to him and half stood.

"Did you change your mind? Do you need help?"

I shook my head. It was nice to hear his concern, though. Faced with platters of roast beef, Julian hadn't had much to eat. I had offered to bring some *tofu bourguignon* that he had left in the refrigerator the night before, but he had refused.

Julian sat back down and shifted his compact body around in the double-breasted gray suit he had bought from Aspen Meadow's second-hand store. While helping me pack up for the dinner, he had recited the ranking of the thirty seniors in the class. Most small schools didn't rank, he assured me, but most schools were not Elk Park Prep. They all laughed about it, he said, but the seniors still had one another's academic statistics memorized. Julian was second in his class. But even as salutatorian, he would need bucks in addition to smarts to get a bachelor's degree, as the threadbare suit made plain enough.

"Thanks for offering," I whispered back. "The other pots are almost ready and—"

Loud *hrr-hrrm*s rattled from the throats of two irritated parents.

"Do you have regular coffee?" demanded Rhoda Marensky, shaking her head of uniformly chestnut hair dyed to conceal the gray. She still hadn't forgiven me for the Columbia comment.

I nodded and plunked a black and gold cup down by her spoon. I dislike giving caffeine to people who are already irritable.

Julian raised one eyebrow at me. I worried instinctively about how his close-clipped haircut would fare, or rather how quickly the scalp underneath would freeze, in the blizzard raging outside.

"Are you serving that coffee or are you just thinking about serving it?" The harsh whisper came from Caroline Dawson, Greer Dawson's mother. Fifty-five years old and pear-shaped, Caroline wore a burgundy watered-silk suit in the same style as her daughter's. While the style favored athletic Greer, it didn't look to advantage on Caroline. When she spoke sharply to me, her husband gave me a meek, sympathetic smile. *Don't worry, I have to live with her.* I placed a white cup at Caroline's side with the reluctant realization that all too soon I would be catering to this same group of people again. Maybe the decaf would mellow her out a little.

"Students moving from high school to college are like—" The headmaster paused. We waited. I stood holding the tray's last coffee cup suspended in mid-descent to the table. "—sea bass . . . swimming from the bay into the ocean. . . ."

Uh-oh, I thought as I put the cup down and raced

back to the kitchen to pour the rest of the coffees. Here we go with the fish jokes.

"In fact," boomed the headmaster with a self-deprecating chuckle into the microphone that came out as an electronic burp, "that's why they're called *schools,* right?"

Nobody laughed. I pressed my lips together. Get used to it. Two more college advisory dinners plus six years until Arch's graduation. A mountain of metaphors. A sea of similes. A boxful of earplugs.

When I came back out to the dining room, Julian was looking more uncomfortable than ever. Headmaster Perkins had moved into the distasteful topic of financial aid. Distasteful for the rich folks, because they knew if you made over seventy thou, you didn't have a prayer of getting help. The headmaster had squarely told me before the dinner that such talk was as much fun as scheduling an ACLU fund-raiser at the Republican convention. Tonight the only adult not wincing at the word *need* was the senior college advisor herself. Miss Suzanne Ferrell was a petite, enthusiastic teacher who was also advisor to the French Club and a new acquaintance of Arch's. I checked Julian's face. Lines of anxiety pinched at the sides of his eyes. At Elk Park Prep he was on a scholarship that had been set up on his behalf. But the free ride ended after this year, salutatorian or no.

"And of course," Perkins droned on, "the money doesn't rain down the way it does in the Amazon . . . er—"

Caught in mid-simile, he attempted a mental swerve.

"Er, not that it rains on the Amazon . . ."

Oh, for the right meteorological metaphor!

"I mean, not that it rains *money* in the Amaz—"

Greer Dawson snickered. At the same table, a senior in a beige linen suit began to giggle.

The headmaster made his horrible phlegmy noise. "Actually, *in* the Amazon—"

Miss Ferrell stood up. Lost in a forest of images, the headmaster shot the college advisor a beseeching look as she approached the microphone.

"Thank you, Alfred, that was inspiring. Seniors already know they will be meeting with me this week to discuss application essays and deadlines." Suzanne Ferrell looked down at the anxious young faces with a tiny smile. "We will also be setting up meetings to go over our lists."

There was a groan. The *list* was what colleges the school—in the person of Miss Ferrell—would say suited your child. Elk Park Prep called it *finding a fit between a student and a college.* But Julian said if you wanted to go somewhere that the school didn't feel you *fit,* you weren't going to get a recommendation, even if you donated the Harriet Beecher Stowe Underground Wing to the library.

"One more announcement, and it concerns our last speaker." She beamed at the audience. "Our valedictorian, Keith Andrews, has just been named a National Merit Scholar." Miss Ferrell began the clapping. The valedictorian, a skinny fellow, got to his feet. *Saint Andrews,* I thought. He did look somewhat saintly, but perhaps that aura would attach to anyone who was first in the class. Keith had a head that was too small for his body, and his bowl-cut, blond-brown hair, unlike the sprouted-looking things that most of his classmates wore, shone like a halo in the light from the brass wall sconces. Nor did Keith Andrews favor the fashionable clothes of most of his peers. He was wearing a loose, glimmery suit straight out of Lawrence Welk.

Keith extended a bony wrist as he approached the microphone. A number of the parents stiffened up. They had come to see *their* children shine, not some National Merit nerd, buttoned inside polyester.

"What is an educated person?" Keith began in a voice that was surprisingly deep for such a slight, angular fellow. I had a sudden flash: With his awkwardness, downcast eyes, and lack of athletic presence, Keith Andrews reminded me of Arch. Was this what my son would look like in six years?

There was another squeak of laughter from one of the seniors' tables. Standing beside Keith Andrews, Miss Ferrell gave the group a slit-eyed look. Whispers from the parents filled the close air.

"Our word *education* comes from the Latin *ducere,* to lead, and *e-,* out," Keith pronounced, undistracted. "The point of education is to be led out, not to get high test scores, although we could do better in that area," he said with a grin. More snickers erupted, as well as groans from the head table. Even I knew what this was about: a recent *Denver Post* article had compared Elk Park Prep SAT scores with scores from area public high schools. The prep school's scores were lower than their public counterparts', much to the distress of Headmaster Perkins.

Keith went on. "Is education attainable only at big-name schools? Or is our pursuit of those institutions just a function of ego?" Parents and students turned to one another with raised eyebrows. This was clearly dangerous territory. "As for me, becoming educated means I'm learning to focus on the process instead of the outcome . . ." And on he droned as I headed back to the kitchen with empty dessert plates so I could start organizing the dirty dishes to cart home. Predictably, the antiquated kitchen at the headmaster's house boasted no dishwasher.

When I returned with coffeepots for refills, Keith was winding up with ". . . always asking ourselves, is this integrity or hypocrisy? Is this a ticket for a job or an education for a lifetime? Let's hope for the latter. Thank you."

Flushed with either embarrassment or pleasure, Keith left the microphone amid a smattering of unenthusiastic applause. Faint praise, if you asked me, but maybe that was because he'd come off less as a valedictorian than a political candidate.

"Well, we'll be seeing you all later . . ." Miss Ferrell was saying. "And seniors, please don't forget to check the schedule for college reps visiting this week. . . ."

My helpers were scooping up coffee cups, saucers, dessert plates, and forks. With my second tray I walked back to the kitchen. In the outer rooms the noise of people bustling about searching for coats and boots rose to a small din.

Then, suddenly, there was total blackness.

"What the—" No way had I blown those fuses. I had just turned off all the coffeepots.

Screams and shuffling filled the sudden darkness. After I stumbled into a cabinet and nearly dropped my tray, my eyes adjusted to the shadows. Neither the oven nor any other appliance, including the refrigerator, had stayed on. I could barely see my tray, and could not see the floor at all. I was afraid to take a step in any direction.

A loud female voice cried, "Well, I guess that's the last time the headmaster invites us!" There was more shuffling, the scraping of chairs, and shrieks of laughter. Frigid air gusted from a door or window that had been opened.

"Wait, wait, we'll shed some light on this situation in a moment . . ." urged a man's voice that sounded like the headmaster's. There was a shuffle, a bump, and what sounded like an exceedingly creative curse, then a flashlight glimmered near me. The person holding it clomped across the linoleum and down the wooden stairs to the basement. Out in the dining and living rooms the talking, laughing voices rose in volume, as if cacophony could fight back the terror of unexpected darkness. After several moments the lights flickered. Then they came back on. There were more shouts of laughter, and exclamations of relief from the outer room.

I looked around for my helpers. Together, Egon Schlichtmaier, Audrey, and I quickly schlepped the rest of the dishes out to the kitchen and clattered stacks into cardboard boxes. I thanked them and told them both to go home; the roads would be terrible. I could load the cartons into the van myself. From the entryway with its huge carved wooden doors came the high-cheer sounds of people calling their final good-byes as they donned their minks and cashmere coats. After my helpers departed, Julian made a sudden appearance next to one of the buckled counters.

"Hey, let me help you with that," he said, heaving up a box holding roasting pans. "What a drag! All night I had to listen to the kid on one side of me talk about how his folks had spent a thousand bucks on a prep course for the SATs, and did I know an antonym for *complaisant*? Then on the other side was this girl who told me that all the women in her family had gone to Smith since the beginning of time. Finally I said, 'I swear, those women must be *old*.' But before she could get pissed off, the lights went out." Julian looked around at the boxes scattered everywhere in the old kitchen. "You want me to close those up?"

"I'd love it."

Julian folded in the flaps of the boxes containing coffee cups. When the crowd had dispersed, I trundled the first box of silverware out to the dimly lit entryway. There was no sign of the headmaster. Maybe Perkins was already off dreaming of a metaphorical Milky Way. With a groan I shoved open the massive front door. Sharp cold bit through my caterer's uniform, and I scolded myself for leaving my jacket in the van. At least the snow had stopped. I was determined to get home as quickly as possible. After all, I still had six boxes of dishes to wash.

Luminous scarves of cloud floated across the inky sky. The moon lifted from behind a shred of silver moisture, illuminating silhouettes of mountains to the west. The bright, frosty landscape rolled away from the headmaster's house like a rumpled fluorescent sheet. Puddles of shadow from the guests' footprints formed stepping-stones out to the van. At one point I skidded forward into a shelf of snow and the heavy box slid from my hands. It landed with a loud metallic *chink*. Cursing, I decided to take my first rest of the evening. I inhaled deep icy breaths, sighed out steam, and looked around. Snow clung to the branches of the stand of pine trees next to the house. The little grove looked like an ice castle inside a Fabergé egg. At the end of the grove, someone had overturned a sled and left it abandoned in the snow. Gritting my teeth, I tried to worm my hands underneath the box to get some leverage. I took a deep breath, heaved the box up with iced fingers, and headed for the van.

It was slow going. Lumps of snow fell into the sides of my shoes; pinpricks of ice melted into my ankles. Approaching the parking lot, I could see my van wore a trapezoidal hat of snow. It would probably take me fifteen minutes to warm up the engine. I lugged the carton to the van door, slid it open, and heaved it inside. The moon dipped behind a cloud. The sudden darkness sent a shiver down my back.

I opened the driver-side door, turned on the engine, then flipped on the headlights. They shone on the evergreens frosted with new snow. Next to the overturned sled, half-buried in a hollow, lay a coat. I groaned. One of the unwelcome punishments that comes from catering big dinners is that you end up being the guardian of a bewildering cache of lost-and-found objects.

By the pale glow of the van headlights I trudged through snow and by trees to where the sled was upended. Skidding down the slight incline, I leaned toward the edge of the coat. It was dusted with snow; perhaps it had been dragged or dropped. I brushed some of the icy powder off. Something was wrong. The coat did not respond to my attempt to pick it up. It was too heavy. My near-frozen hands moved rapidly to find edges of cloth.

I could hear my breath rasping in the cold. The night air was frigid. I turned the heavy, hard thing over just as moonlight blazed out again.

It was not a coat. It was the valedictorian, Keith Andrews. Blood from the back of his head darkened the snow. Instinctively, I felt for a pulse. There was none.

2

"Oh, no. Please."

I shook Keith's shoulders. The boy didn't move. I couldn't touch his head. His slick hair lay in a dark puddle of blood and snow. The moon lit his frozen grimace. The openmouthed expression was ghastly, contorted with the fear of death. My fingers caught on an icy cord that had been wrapped around his torso and attached to the sled.

I pulled away. My voice made high, unhuman sounds. The deep snow disintegrated like quicksand as I clambered backward. I raced to the headmaster's house, careened across the slate floor of the empty entryway, and dialed 911.

The operator impassively took my name and asked for the fire number, a standard localization procedure in the mountainous section of Furman County. Of course I didn't know it, so I screeched for somebody, anybody, in the house. Julian appeared from the kitchen. A bewildered-looking Headmaster Perkins came tripping down the stairs from the living quarters. Behind him was a lanky, acne-scarred teenager who looked vaguely familiar —the one who had made the Stanford comment. The headmaster's tweeds were disheveled, as if he had begun to get undressed but had abruptly changed his mind. He couldn't remember the fire number, turned to the tall boy, who crinkled his nose and mumbled off six digits. Perkins then trotted off quickly in the direction of the kitchen, where, apparently, he believed I had started a fire.

The voice on the other end of the phone patiently asked me to repeat what had happened, what was going on. He wanted to know who else was around. I told him, then asked the tall teenager his name.

"Oh," said the boy. He was muscular in addition to possessing great height, but his acne made him painfully repulsive. His voice faltered. "Oh, uh, don't you know me? I'm Macguire. Macguire . . . Perkins. Headmaster Perkins is my father. I live here with him. And I, you know, go to the school."

I told this to the operator, who demanded to know how I knew the boy in the snow was dead.

"Because there was blood, and he was cold, and he . . . didn't move. Should we try to bring him in from outside? He's lying in the snow—"

The operator said no, to send somebody out, to check for a pulse again. Not you, he said. You stay on the phone. Find out if anybody in the house knows CPR. I asked Julian and Macguire: Know CPR? They looked blank. Does the headmaster? Macguire loped off to the kitchen to ask, then returned momentarily, shaking his head. I told them please, go out and check on Keith Andrews, lying still and apparently dead in the small ditch in the pine grove.

Stunned, Julian backed away. The color drained from his face; bruiselike shadows appeared under his eyes. Macguire sucked in his cheeks and his ungainly shoulders went slack. For a moment I thought he was going to faint. Go, go quickly, I told them.

When they had reluctantly obeyed, the operator had me go through the whole thing again. Who was I? Why was I there? Did I have any idea how this could have happened? I knew he had to keep me on the phone as long as possible, that was his job. But it was agony. Julian and Macguire returned, Macguire slack-jawed with shock, Julian even paler. About Keith . . . Julian closed his eyes, then shook his head. I told the operator: No pulse. Keep everybody away from the body, he ordered. Teams from the fire department and the Furman County Sheriff's Department were on their way. They should be at the school in twenty minutes.

"I'll meet them. Oh, and please, would you," I added, my voice raw with shock and confusion, "call Investigator Tom Schulz and ask him to come?"

Tom Schulz was a close friend. He was also a homicide investigator at the Sheriff's Department, as Julian and I knew only too well. The operator promised he would try Schulz's page, then disconnected.

I began to tremble. I heard Macguire ask if I had a coat somewhere, could he get it for me? I squinted up at him, unable to formulate an answer to his question. Was I okay? Julian asked. I struggled to focus on his faraway voice, on his anguished eyes, his pallid face, and bleached, wet hair stuck up in conical spikes. Julian rubbed his hands on his rumpled white shirt and tried to straighten his plaid bow tie, which had gone askew. "Goldy, are you okay?" he repeated.

"I need to call Arch and tell him we're all right, that we'll be late."

The area between Julian's eyebrows pleated in alarm. "Want me to do it? I can use the phone in the kitchen."

"Sure. Please. I don't trust myself to talk to him just now. If he hears my voice, it'll worry him."

Julian darted toward the kitchen with Macguire Perkins striding uneasily after him, like a gargantuan shadow. I was shivering uncontrollably. Belatedly, I realized I should have told Macguire my jacket was in the van. Moving like an automaton toward the front hallway closet to look for a blanket, shawl, jacket, something, I could hear Julian's voice on one of the phone extensions. I pulled a huge raccoon coat off a protruding hanger. I had an absurdly incongruous thought: *Wear this thing on the streets of Denver and you'd get spray-painted by anti-fur activists.* As I was putting the heavy coat on, one of my coffeepots tumbled out of the dark recesses of the closet, spilling cold brown liquid and wet grounds on the stone floor. What was it doing in there? I couldn't think. I was shaking. *Get a grip.* I kicked at the hanging coats to make sure no other surprises lurked in the closet corners. Then I walked down the hall, looking into each of the large, irregularly shaped rooms with their heavy gold and green brocade draperies, dark wood furniture, and lush Oriental rugs, to see if there was anybody else around.

The voices of Julian, Macguire, and the headmaster warbled uncertainly out of the kitchen. Then the headmaster cried, "Keith Andrews? Dead? Are you sure? Oh, no!" I heard footsteps moving rapidly up the kitchen staircase. I stood staring into the living room, where the recent exodus of guests had left the tables and chairs helter-skelter.

"What are you doing in here? Jeez, Goldy." Julian leaned in toward my face. "You look even worse than you did five minutes ago."

There was a buzzing in my ears.

"Did you get through to Arch?" I wanted to know. Julian nodded.

"And?"

"He's fine. . . . There was a problem with the security system a little while ago."

"Excuse me?"

"Somebody threw a rock through one of the upstairs windows. It hit one of the sensor wires, I guess. The system went off. Once Arch found the rock, he interrupted the automatic dial."

I tried to breathe. There was stinging behind my eyes. I had to get home. I said, "Can you find something to put on? We need to go outside . . . to be there when they arrive."

He withdrew without a word. I went into the bathroom and stared at my face in the tiny mirror.

I was not a stranger to death. The previous spring I had seen a friend die in a car accident that had been no accident. I began to wash my hands vigorously. Nor was I a stranger to violence. I tested my thumb, the one my ex-husband, Dr. John Richard Korman, had broken in three places before we were divorced. Trying to bend it, I winced. The warm water stung my hands like needles.

In the mirror, my skin looked gray, my lips pale as dust. *A problem with the security system.* I shook droplets off my hands. My right shoulder ached suddenly. In the middle of an argument, John Richard had pushed me onto the open lower shelf of the dishwasher. A butcher knife had cut deeply into the area behind that shoulder, and I had paid for my protest over his extramarital flings with twenty stitches, weeks of pain, and a permanent scar.

Now death, violence, brought it all close again. I looked down at my trembling hands. They had touched the cold, stiff cord wrapped around Keith Andrews' body. The water ran and splashed over my fingers, but it could not wash out the slimy feel of the wire. I thought of Keith Andrews' angelic expression. Saint Andrews. I had stared into his lifeless face . . . how like Arch he had looked, thin and pale and vulnerable. . . . What had Keith said? *I'm learning to focus on the process rather than the outcome.* Not anymore.

There was a knock at the door: Julian. Was I okay? I said yes, then splashed water on my eyes, picked up an embroidered guest towel, and rubbed the flimsy thing against my hands and cheeks until they shone red.

When I came out, Macguire called down that he and his father would be outside in a minute. I wrapped the raccoon monstrosity around my body. Together Julian and I trudged back through the deep snow to wait in silence next to one of the outdoor carriage lanterns, a respectful ten feet away from the corpse of Keith Andrews.

Tom Schulz was the first to arrive from the Furman County Sheriff's Department. When his dark Chrysler chopped through the snowy parking lot, his headlights sent a wave of light bouncing through the cluster of pines next to the old house. There was another car directly behind his; the two vehicles stopped abruptly, spraying snow. The Chrysler's door creaked open and Tom Schulz heaved his large body out. Coatless, he slammed the door and crunched across the frozen yard. *Finally.*

Two men got out of the second car; one joined Schulz. The other man came over to Julian and me. He introduced himself as part of the investigative team.

"We need to know about footprints," he said. He looked down at my shoes. "Were you the only one to go out to the victim?"

I told him two other people had been out there. He shook his head grimly and asked which way we had gone through the snow. I showed him. He turned and pointed out a large arc around our path for the other men to take.

Schulz and the man I assumed was a paramedic approached the body. They bent over it, murmured back and forth, then Schulz walked raggedly back and reached for the cellular phone. His voice crackled through the cold air, although I couldn't make out any of the words. The other men stationed themselves near the corpse, sentrylike, ignoring us. Julian and I stood, mute and miserable, our arms clasping our bodies against the deep cold.

Schulz walked over. He stopped and pulled me in for a mountain-man hug. He murmured, "You all right?" When I nodded into his shoulder, he said, "You want to tell me what happened?"

I pulled back to look at him, the man who had invaded my life a year earlier and stubbornly would not leave. Golden lantern light illuminated the large, unpretentiously handsome face that was now somber and grim. His serious mouth, his narrowed eyes with their tentlike bushy brown eyebrows—these showed willed control in the midst of chaos. His faded jeans, white frayed-collar shirt, and sweater the color of cornflowers indicated he'd been relaxing at something before the call came in. Now Schulz pulled himself up, his stance of command. "What happened here, Goldy?" he repeated crisply. *I'm in charge here now.*

"I don't know," I said. "I saw the sled when I was loading the van, and then I saw the coat, so I went over . . ."

Schulz's sigh sent a cloud of steam between us. Behind us, three more police and fire vehicles drove up. He reached out and pulled the fur collar snugly around my throat.

"Let's go in. That's quite a getup. The two of you. I swear. Come on, big J.," Schulz said to Julian as he put one arm around him. Behind us, strobe flashes went off like lightning. "Be lucky if pneumonia doesn't take you both. Honestly." Another deputy silently joined us. Schulz and the other policeman walked with Julian up the narrow path that skirted the pines and led to the big stone house. I followed, clumsily trying to step in their footsteps.

The headmaster was tripping down the carpeted front stairs when we pushed through to the house's elegant entryway. The upturned collar of Alfred Perkins' black trench coat framed his horrified eyes behind round hornrimmed glasses. Above his high forehead, the cottony mass of white hair was wildly askew. His boot buckles *clickety-clacked* as he marched across the foyer toward us. When Schulz identified himself, the headmaster demanded: "Is there any way we can keep this out of the papers?"

Schulz raised both eyebrows and ignored the question. Instead, he said, "I need some information about next of kin so we can get back to the coroner. Can you help me out?" The headmaster gave the names of Keith's parents, who were apparently in Europe. The deputy wrote the names on a pad, then disappeared. Schulz started his characteristic swagger down the hallway, poking his head through each doorway. When he found a room he liked, he beckoned with a thumb to Perkins.

"Headmaster, sir," he said with a deference that fooled nobody, "would you wait in here until I have a chance to talk to you?" When the headmaster nodded numbly, Schulz added, "And don't talk to anyone, please, sir. Press or otherwise."

The headmaster clomped to his assigned spot. Schulz closed the heavy door behind him, then turned and asked who else was around. Julian called to Macguire, who trundled in and was assigned to another room. Perkins' son looked deeply stunned. In a kinder tone Schulz asked Julian to sit in the living room until he'd finished talking to me. "And try not to disturb anything," he added. "But get yourself a blanket to warm up."

Julian's face had a lost look that tugged at my heart. He obeyed Schulz in silence. But as we headed down to the kitchen, I heard him choke on exhaled breath.

I said, "Let me—"

"No, not yet. I'll take you back in just a couple of minutes. We need to talk before the investigative team is all over this place." Schulz paused, then gestured for me to sit on one of the old-fashioned wooden stools. I obeyed. After looking around the kitchen, he sat on another stool and pulled out a notebook. He tapped his mouth with a mechanical pencil. "Start with when you had me paged and work backward."

I did. Keith's body. Before that, the cleanup, the after-dinner talks, the dinner itself. The blackout.

Schulz raised one thick eyebrow. "You're sure it was a fuse?" I said I'd just assumed so. "Who fixed it, do you know?"

I shook my head. "Oh, and one of my coffeepots was in the front hall closet. I didn't put it there."

Schulz made a note. "You have a guest list?"

"The headmaster would. Thirty seniors, plus most of the parents. About eighty people altogether."

"You see anybody you know wasn't invited, seemed out of place, whatever?" I didn't know who had been invited and who hadn't. No one seemed out of place, I told him, but the senior-year anxiety had been palpable. "Anything else palpable?" he wanted to know.

I stared at him. He was all business. *Anything else you could touch?* He gave me just the slightest flicker of a smile. John Richard Korman always said I expected him to read my mind; Tom Schulz actually could. I wished for the two of us to be somewhere else, doing anything but this.

Reading my thoughts again, Schulz said, "We're almost done." Then he tilted his head back and drummed the fingers of one hand on his chin. "Okay," he went on, "anybody who was *not* here who should have been?"

I didn't know that either, and said so.

He looked me straight in the eye. "Tell me why somebody would kill this boy."

Blood jack-hammered in my ears. "I don't know. He seemed innocuous enough, really more like a nerd. . . ."

Silence fell around us in the old kitchen.

Schulz said, "Julian fit into this scenario at all? Or the headmaster's son? Or the headmaster?"

Miserably, I looked at the big old aluminum canisters in the kitchen, the wooden cabinets painted a buttery yellow, before replying. "I don't know much about what was going on in the senior class, or in the school as a whole, for that matter. Julian and Macguire went back out to check for a pulse when I was on the phone with the 911 operator. I don't know if Julian, Macguire, Keith, anybody, were friends."

"Know if they were enemies?"

"Well." I involuntarily thought of Julian's recitation of the class rank. He hadn't talked about any nastiness to the competition. I refused to speculate. "I don't know," I said firmly.

The deputy stalked into the kitchen. Snow clung to his boots and clothing. Ignoring me, he said to Schulz, "We got drag marks to the gatehouse, where whoever it was got the sled. They haven't finished with the photos, but it's going to be a couple hours. You got a kid having a hard time down the hall."

Schulz nodded just perceptibly and the deputy withdrew.

"Goldy," Schulz said, "I want to talk to Julian with you there. Then I'll deal with Macguire Perkins. Tell me if this headmaster is as much of a moron as he looks."

"More so."

"Great."

Julian was sitting in the front room. His eyes were closed, his head bent back against the sofa cushions. With his Adam's apple pointed at the ceiling, he had a look of extraordinary vulnerability. When we entered, he coughed and rubbed his eyes. His face was still gray; his spiky blond hair gave him an unearthly look. He had found a knit throw that he had pulled tightly around his compact body. Schulz motioned for me to go on over by him.

I moved quietly to a chair beside the couch, then reached out to pat Julian's arm. He turned and gave me a morose look.

"Tell me what happened," Schulz began without preamble.

Wearily, Julian recounted how the dinner had ended. Everyone had been putting on their coats and talking. He had stayed afterward to see if a girl he knew, who sort of interested him, he said with lowered eyes, would like a ride home. She had airily replied that she was going home with Keith.

"I said, 'Oh, moving up in the world, are we?' but she wasn't listening." Julian's nose wrinkled. "Ever since I told her I'd rather be a chef than a neurosurgeon, she's acted like I'm a leper."

Schulz asked mildly, "Keith was going to be a neuro-surgeon?"

"Oh, no," said Julian. "Did I say that? I must have been confused. . . ."

We waited while Julian coughed and shook his head quickly, like a dog shaking off water.

"Do you want to do this later, Julian?" asked Schulz. "Although it'd be helpful if you could reconstruct the events for me now."

"No, that's okay." Julian's voice was so low, I had to lean forward to hear it.

Schulz pulled out his notebook. "Let's go back. Before the girl. We have a dinner party for eighty people and a kid ends up dead. Goldy said the party was about college or something. How's that?"

Julian shrugged. "I think it's supposed to help people feel okay about going to college."

"In what way?"

"Oh, you know, like everybody's going through the same process. Have to figure out what you want, have to look around for the right place, have to get all your papers and stuff together. Pressure, pressure, pressure. Have to write your essays. Be tested." He groaned. "SATs are Saturday. We had 'em last year, but this is the big one. These are the scores the colleges look at. The teachers always say it doesn't matter, it doesn't matter, which makes you know that it matters. It *matters,* man." There was a savagery in his voice I had never heard before.

"Was Keith Andrews nervous about all this? First big step to becoming a neurosurgeon?"

Julian shook his head. "Nah." He paused. "At least he didn't seem to be. We called him Saint Andrews."

"Saint Andrews? Why?"

A hint of frown wrinkled Julian's cheek. "Well, Keith didn't really want to be a doctor. He wanted to grow up and be Bob Woodward. He wanted to be such a famous investigative reporter that whenever there was a scandal, they'd say, 'Better give Andrews a call.' Like he was the Red Adair of the world of journalism or something."

Schulz pursed his lips. "Know anybody he was investigating? Anybody he offended?"

Julian shrugged, avoiding Schulz's eyes. "I heard some stuff. But it was just gossip."

"Care to share that? It might help."

"Nah. It was just . . . stuff."

"Big J. We're talking about a death here."

Julian sighed bleakly. "I think he was having his share of problems. Like everybody."

"His share of problems with whom?"

"I don't know. Everybody, nobody."

Schulz made another note. "I need some specifics on that. You tell me, I won't tell anybody. Sometimes gossip can help a lot. You'd be surprised." He waited a beat, then clicked the pencil and tucked it in his pocket. "So the lights came back on, the girl said no to you. Then what?"

"I don't know, I guess I like, talked to some people—"

"Who?"

"Well, jeez, I don't remember—"

"Keith?"

Julian reflected, then said, "I don't remember seeing Keith around. You know, everyone was talking about the lights, and saying, see you Monday, and stuff like that. Then I came out to check if Goldy needed help."

"Time, Miss G.?"

I looked at my watch: eleven o'clock. Schulz cocked his thumb over his shoulder. When had Julian come out to the kitchen? I said, "I don't know. Nine-thirtyish."

"Did anyone go into the kitchen looking for Keith? This girl you mentioned, for example?"

We both said no.

"Okay, now, Julian," Schulz said impassively, "tell me who Keith's enemies were."

"God, I told you, I don't know! You know, he was kind of holier-than-thou. Smarter-than-thou too. You know. Like, we watched an Ingmar Bergman film in English class, and the film's over for like two seconds and Keith's talking about the internal structure. I mean, huh? The rest of us are going, okay, but what was it *about*?" He grimaced. "That kind of smart attitude can lose you some friends."

"Who, specifically?"

"I don't know, you know, people just get pissed off. They talk."

"What about the National Merit Scholarship?" I said before I remembered I wasn't supposed to talk.

"What about it?" Julian turned a puzzled face to me. "It's not like they're going to give it to somebody else now. . . . Keith was number one in our class, president of the French Club. He did after-school work for the *Mountain Journal*. People can hate you just for that."

Schulz said, "Why?"

"Because it makes them feel bad that they're not doing it too." Julian said this in a way that made it clear any fool would reach the same conclusion.

Schulz sighed, then rose. "Okay, go home, the two of you. I'll be talking to the rest of the guests over the weekend, then I might get back to you depending on—"

"Schulz!" boomed an excited voice from down the hall. "Hey!" It was the deputy.

We found him looking at the coffeepot that had fallen out of the front hall closet.

"Oh, that's my—" I began. I stopped.

"Your what?" demanded the deputy.

"Coffeepot," I answered inanely.

The deputy regarded me with deepening skepticism. "Y'had a couple of extension cords on it?"

"Yes, three, actually. You see, they have a problem with fuses—"

But the deputy was holding up the machine's naked plug. Belatedly, I realized where the extension cords had ended up.

3

Julian led the way out of the parking lot in his four-wheel-drive, a white Range Rover inherited from wealthy former employers. I could see him checking his rearview mirror for me. My van crawled and skidded down the prep school's precarious driveway. Overhead, cloud edges glinted like knives. The moon slipped out and silvered the snowy mountains. As I thought about the events of the past few hours, my stomach knotted.

At some point in the evening the tortuous road between Elk Park and Aspen Meadow had been plowed. Still, we skirted the banked curves with great care. My mind wandered back to that upturned sled in the snow.

To the look of horror on Keith Andrews' young face.

I shook my head and focused on the driving. Gripping the steering wheel hard, I accelerated up a slight incline. I hoped Arch was okay. The rock thrown through one of our windows was worrisome. Halloween was coming up, and pranksters had to be expected. I should have told Schulz about the rock, though. I'd forgotten.

Schulz was going to call us. He would tell us what had happened to Keith, wouldn't he? I had plodded through the headmaster's snowy yard, found the lifeless form, touched the icy extension cord. It was like a personal affront. I had to know what had happened. Like it or not, I was involved.

Resolutely, I veered off this thought pattern and reflected on Schulz. Somehow, his behavior this evening indicated a sea change in our relationship, from a growing intimacy back to the distance of business. I turned the steering wheel slowly while negotiating a switchback. For one breathtaking moment on this curve, all that was visible out the window was air.

Tom Schulz. We had been dating off and on, mostly off, for the past year. Recently, however, we had been more frequently and more seriously *on*. This summer had brought a rapprochement, a French word for *getting back together* that Arch now dropped into conversation the way he sprinkled sugar on his Rice Krispies.

Schulz and I had not really become a couple. But he and I, along with Julian and Arch, had become a unit: the four of us hiked, we fished, we cooked out, we took turns choosing movies. Schulz's light caseload lately had consisted mostly of investigating mail thefts and forgeries, giving him time to spend with us.

Insulated by the presence of the two boys, my post-divorce ambivalence toward relationships had begun to melt. I had found myself thinking of reasons to call Tom Schulz, inventing occasions to get together, looking forward to talking and laughing about all the daily details of life.

And then there had been the issue of the name

change. What had started out as a small problem had developed into a symbolic issue between Schulz and me. Over the summer I'd learned of the existence of a catering outfit in Denver with the unfortunate name *Three Bears Catering*. They had threatened me with a suit over trademark infringement. In one of our jovial moments, Tom had suddenly asked if I would like to change my last name to Schulz. With all that that implied, I had immediately demurred. But you know what they say about parties: It was awfully nice to be asked.

Only now we had a catastrophe out at Elk Park Prep. Involving me, involving Julian, involving homicide. Something told me the future of my relationship with Tom Schulz was once again a question mark.

The brake lights of the Range Rover sparked like rectangular rubies as Julian and I continued the steep descent into town. We rounded the flat black surface of Aspen Meadow Lake, where one patch of shining ripples reflected elusive moonlight. Part of me wanted Schulz to say, Come back to my place. But another, saner, inner voice said this desire came from knowing it was impossible. A homicide investigation was when Schulz was the busiest. Mortality and the need for relationship loomed large since I had looked into the dead face of young Keith Andrews.

My tires crunched down Aspen Meadow's Main Street. The only cars were those parked at wide angles along the curb by the Grizzly Saloon, where music and flashing lights announced it was still Saturday night. Witnessing partygoing after what I'd just seen at Elk Park Prep brought light-headedness. I rolled down the window; my eyes watered from the gush of freezing air.

Moments later, Julian and I pulled up across the street from my house. White shutters gleamed against the brown shingles. The front porch with its single-story white pillars and porch swing seemed to smile. The old place had become very dear to me in the five years since my divorce from Dr. John Richard Korman. Arriving home at night, I was always happy that the Jerk, as his other ex-wife and I called him, was gone for good, and that my brand-new security system could make sure he stayed that way.

I hopped out of the van and landed in three inches of new snow. It was less than we'd received in Elk Park, which stood another five hundred feet above Aspen Meadow's eight thousand above sea level. A sudden slash of wind made me draw my coat close. A curse rose in my throat. I had unwittingly gone off wearing the stupid raccoon thing. I put my hand in the pocket and felt tissues and something flat and hard. The thought of a trip back to the school to return the coat brought a shudder.

I pressed the security buttons and came in out of the cold with Julian close behind. Arch, who of course had not gone to bed after Julian's call, clomped down the stairs in untied hightop sneakers. He was wearing a gray sweatsuit and carrying a large flashlight—defense against power outages. His knotted, wood-colored hair stuck out at various angles. I was so happy to see him, I clasped him in a hug that was mostly raccoon coat. He pulled back and straightened the glasses on his small, freckled nose. Magnified brown eyes regarded Julian and me with intense interest.

"Are you guys late! What are you doing wearing that weird thing? What's going on? All you said was that there was a problem at the headmaster's house. Does that mean we don't have school on Monday?" This prospect seemed to please him.

"No, no," I said. Weariness washed over me. We were home, finally, and all I wanted was for everyone to go to bed. I said, "Someone was hurt after the dinner."

"Who?" Arch pulled his thin shoulders up to his ears and made a face. "Was there an accident?"

"Not quite. Keith Andrews, a senior, died." I did not say that it looked as if he'd been murdered. This was a mistake.

"Keith Andrews? The president of the French Club?" Arch looked at Julian, full of fear. "The guy you had that fight with? Man! You're kidding!"

Julian closed his eyes and shrugged. A fight had not come up in the questioning. I raised my eyebrows at Julian; his facial expression stayed flat.

I said, "I'm sorry, Arch. Tom Schulz and the police are over at the school now—"

"Tom *Schulz*!" cried Arch. "So they—"

"Arch, buddy," said Julian. "Chill. Nobody knows what happened. Really."

Arch's eyes traveled from Julian back to me. He said, "A lot of people at school didn't like Keith. I liked him, though. He didn't drive around in a Porsche or BMW, like he was so cool. You know, the way some of the older kids do. He was nice."

Arch's words hung in the air of my front hall. How easily he had put the boy's life in past tense. Finally I said, "Well, hon, I'd rather not talk about it now, if that's okay. So . . . you had a problem with a broken window?"

He reached into the front pocket of his sweatshirt and pulled the rock out. So much for fingerprints. But the rock was tennis-ball-size and jagged. It probably wouldn't have held a print anyway.

"I'll bet it was some kids from my old school. Trick or treat." Arch sighed.

"When did this happen?"

"Oh, late. Right before Julian called."

I took the rock from him. Did I have any clients who were angry? None that I could think of. In any event, I was too tired to think about it. "Church tomorrow," I said to Arch as I pocketed the stone and started toward the kitchen.

"But it's been snowing!"

"Arch, I can't take any more in one night."

"Hey, guy," said Julian, "if you come up with me now, I'll let you show me that model you made from the Narnia book."

"You mean the wardrobe with the fake back?"

"Whatever."

And before I could say anything, the two boys were racing up the wooden steps. Arch let out a howl trying to beat Julian to the room they now shared. I looked around the hall and thought about the boxes of dishes waiting in my van to be washed. It was past midnight. They would keep.

I shrugged off the coat and looked at the thing in the pocket. It was a Neiman-Marcus credit card. The name on it was K. Andrews.

I swept up the glass shards underneath Arch's broken window, taped a piece of cardboard over the hole, slumped into my room, and fell into bed. Fitful sleep came interspersed with nightmares. I awoke with a dull headache and the realization that the previous evening had not been a bad dream.

There was no way Schulz could have left Elk Park Prep before midnight. Rather than wake him at home, I put in a call about the credit card to his voice mail at the Sheriff's Department. Neiman-Marcus for an eighteen-year-old? But Arch had said Keith did not show off, at least materialistically. What had he said? *Like he was so cool.*

On my braided rug, Scout the cat turned his chin in the air and dramatically flopped over on his back. I obediently scratched the long white fur of his stomach, light brown hair of his back, dark brown hair of his face. While Julian had inherited his Range Rover from the rich folks the two of us had worked for, my inheritance had been the feline. I felt content with my part of the unexpected beneficence. Scout was always full of affection when it was eating time. Perfect cat for a caterer.

Speaking of which, I had work to do. For me, cats were safer than credit cards. I had never even been *inside* Denver's new Neiman-Marcus store, I reflected as I began to stretch through twenty minutes of yoga. In general, Dr. John Richard Korman's child-support payments were late, incorrect, or nonexistent. My calendar shrieked with assignments for this busiest season for caterers, the stretch between Halloween and Christmas. During November and December people were social, hungry, and flush. This was my most profitable time of year. No matter what was going on out at Elk Park Prep, I had to earn enough money for our household to scrape through the first six months of the new year. Upscale department stores were definitely no longer a part of my lifestyle.

In the kitchen, Scout twined through my legs and I fed him before consulting the calendar. Unfortunately, my first job of the day was not even income-producing, although it *was* a tax write-off. In a moment of weakness I had agreed to prepare the refreshments to follow that morning's ten o'clock service at the Episcopal church. This would be followed by a more profitable half-time meal of *choucroute garnie* for twelve Bronco fans at the Dawsons' house. Trick of caterers: Always use the French name for food. People will not pay large sums for a menu of sausage and sauerkraut.

No rest for the weary, especially the catering weary, I

thought as I hauled in yesterday's crates of pans and plates and loaded them into my heavy-duty dishwasher. When I was done, I washed my hands and began to plan. I had to call Audrey Coopersmith and remind her that for the half-time meal she needed to wear a Bronco-orange T-shirt.

Despite the fact that she had worked late with me the night before, I knew Audrey would be up early this Sunday morning. With the depression brought on by her divorce trauma, Audrey rarely slept past dawn. I knew, because I was one of the people she started phoning around six. In fact, in the past few months I had become something of a reluctant expert on the life of Audrey Coopersmith.

For the mother of a high school senior, Audrey was young: thirty-eight. Her house was full of books. Despite marrying and dropping out of college at twenty, she was self-educated and extraordinarily well read. Rather than take direct care of herself, she took in strays: extra kittens other people couldn't give away, guinea pigs, hamsters, and rabbits left over at the end of the school year, stray dogs abandoned by families moving away. She also exercised fanatically at both the athletic club and the local recreation center.

But the shelves of books, the cadre of pets, the soft body that refused to become fit, had been no help, she had sadly announced at a meeting of Amour Anonymous, our support group for women who felt they were addicted to relationships. After two years of denial, Audrey Coopersmith had finally begun divorce proceedings against her husband of eighteen years. With a deviousness that had fooled no one but Audrey, Carl Coopersmith had been supporting another woman in Denver for the past fifteen years. This other woman had children by a previous marriage, but Carl had been hanging around for so long that the other woman's kids called him Dad and the other woman's neighbors all thought "Dad" was the other woman's husband. Which, when it came to financial support, made for a very confusing situation for everyone but the lawyers. With delays, requests for documents, filing motions and countermotions, the legal beagles were having a field day.

Bottom line was, Carl "Dad" Coopersmith had cancelled Audrey's cash card, credit cards, and provided a copious supply of lies about his salary and other accounts. The court order on permanent support for Audrey and their daughter, Heather, was supposed to come down any moment. But as was typical, it had been delayed three times. Two months ago Audrey had asked me for part-time work. She couldn't earn too much, she told me, for that would undermine what she was asking from Carl. But she was having trouble making ends meet. She balanced the work she had from me with a part-time job at the Tattered Cover, Denver's largest bookstore, a place she claimed to love. But as you might expect, Audrey was always exhausted, always broke, always unhappy.

The one bright spot in her life was super-achieving Heather, an eighteen-year-old science whiz who ranked third in the senior class at Elk Park Prep. To my utter dismay, there were only two things Audrey wanted in life: for Heather to get into MIT, and for Carl to come to his senses, leave the other woman, her kids, and her neighbors, and return to their home in Aspen Meadow Country Club.

Now, *this* was a woman who was addicted to a relationship. Not to mention that she didn't have too firm a grasp on reality. Audrey desperately wanted to return to the status quo. In Amour Anonymous, we had all tried to enlighten her, to no avail. Sometimes people just have to go through things.

The phone had not even rung one full time when she answered. Once she realized I wasn't Carl, her voice went from lively to remote. Yes, she remembered that she was supposed to help me with the football party. But then she remembered that she was supposed to make a stir-fry for a small staff meeting after she filled in at the bookstore that afternoon.

I said, "Filled in?"

She gave a short laugh. "Best department."

"Really?" I said. "Cookbooks?"

"Self-improvement."

So I asked if she could help with the church refreshments instead, and I'd see if I could get someone else for the Dawsons' party in the afternoon. She agreed and added that she had to get off the phone because for some reason the police were at her door.

For some reason. I hung up. So Headmaster Perkins had already given the police Audrey's name. But that surely would not be the end of it. I looked out my kitchen window at lodgepole pine branches heavy with snow. A number of Elk Park Prep parents were Episcopalians. By the time of the service, the investigative team already would have visited some of them. The official interrogations, not to mention Keith's bizarre death, would be guaranteed topics of conversation during the church coffee hour.

Cook, I ordered myself, you'll feel better. I folded shiny slivers of orange zest into a pillowy spongecake batter to make Bronco-fan cupcakes for the Dawsons' brunch. When the cupcakes were in the oven, I drained and chopped fat purple plums for a Happy Endings Plum Cake, a prototype for Caroline Dawson, who had promised to taste it at church. If she and Hank liked the cake, they'd said I could sell them at their restaurant, the Aspen Meadow Café.

For the rest of the church refreshments, I sliced two dozen crisp Granny Smith apples into bird-shaped centerpieces that would be surrounded by concentric circles of Gouda and cheddar wedges. I didn't even want to think about the price of the cheeses in this little spread. I reminded myself that this was an advertising opportunity, even if it was church. To complete the cheese tray, I cut several loaves of fragrant homemade oatmeal bread into triangles and threw in a wheel of Jarlsberg for good measure. Advertising could get expensive.

Arch dressed with minimal complaining, since he didn't want to wake up Julian, who was snoring deeply. The wind bit through our clothing as we climbed into the van. The sky was luminescent, like the inside of a pearl. Streets slick with newly plowed snow made the going slow. By the time we arrived at the big stone church with its great diamond-shaped windows, the parking lot was already half filled with Cadillacs, Rivieras, and Chrysler New Yorkers, with the occasional Mercedes, Lexus, and Infiniti.

I scanned the parking lot for my ex-husband's Jeep with its GYN license plate, but he was not making one of his rare church appearances. The personalized tags indicated who had already arrived. The Dawsons' matching vans advertised the presence of parents and offspring. Greer Dawson was known to her volleyball teammates as G.D., the Hammer, hence the tag GD HMR. Her parents' more sedate tag read AMCAFE, for the Aspen Meadow Café. There was MR E, from a local mystery writer, and UR4GVN, from who else? The priest. I pulled in next to the gold Jaguar belonging to Marla Korman, my best friend, who also happened to be Dr. John Richard Korman's other ex-wife. Her license tag said simply, AVLBL.

When Arch and I pushed through the heavy doors with our platters, Marla shrieked a greeting and rushed across the foyer toward us. Large in body and spirit, Marla always dressed according to the season. This morning, an early appearance of winter demanded a silver suede suit sprinkled with an abundance of pewter buttons across a jacket and skirt. Sparkly silver barrettes, my gift for her fortieth birthday, held back her eternally frizzed brown hair. She folded me in a hug that was all bangle bracelets and soft leather.

"What in the *hell* happened out at that school last night?" she hissed in my ear.

"How did you find out about it?"

"What, are you kidding? My phone started ringing at six-thirty this morning!"

The organist sounded the opening notes of a Bach fugue. I whispered back, "It was awful, but I can't talk about it now. Help me in the kitchen afterward and I'll tell you what I know."

Marla told me she had visitors she had promised to sit with during the service, but that she could help later with the food. Then she whispered, "I heard this kid stole credit cards."

"He did *not*," said Arch in a very loud voice behind us. "He was *nice*." At this, heads in the pews swiveled to stare at us. The Bach was in full swing. Marla lifted her double chin in an imperial gesture. I pretended not to know either of them and hustled the first bird-apple centerpiece out to the church kitchen.

We mumbled along through the service until the passing of the peace, when you wish the priest God's peace and then turn to your neighbors and wish them the same. But in this parish the peace was a signal to pass along news, commentary on weather, parish illnesses and absences, and so on, until the priest halted the ruckus to make announcements. Unfortunately, the peace discussion this day was devoted to the events out at Elk Park Prep.

Happy Endings
Plum Cake

1 cup (2 sticks) unsalted butter
¾ cup granulated sugar
¾ cup firmly packed dark brown
  sugar
2 large eggs
1 teaspoon vanilla extract
2½ cups all-purpose flour (high
  altitude: add 2 tablespoons)
2 teaspoons baking powder (high
  altitude: subtract ½ teaspoon)
1 teaspoon baking soda
½ teaspoon salt
2 teaspoons ground cinnamon
1 16-ounce can purple plums packed
  in syrup, well drained, the syrup
  reserved and the plums chopped
confectioners' sugar

Preheat the oven to 400°. In a large
mixing bowl, beat the butter until

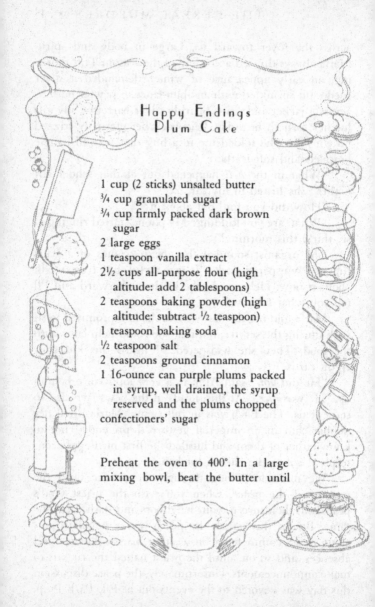

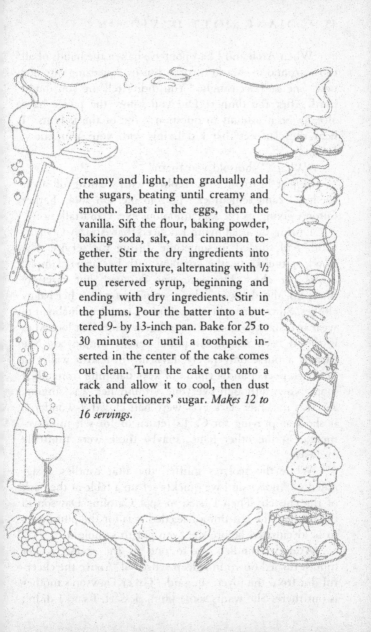

creamy and light, then gradually add the sugars, beating until creamy and smooth. Beat in the eggs, then the vanilla. Sift the flour, baking powder, baking soda, salt, and cinnamon together. Stir the dry ingredients into the butter mixture, alternating with ½ cup reserved syrup, beginning and ending with dry ingredients. Stir in the plums. Pour the batter into a buttered 9- by 13-inch pan. Bake for 25 to 30 minutes or until a toothpick inserted in the center of the cake comes out clean. Turn the cake out onto a rack and allow it to cool, then dust with confectioners' sugar. *Makes 12 to 16 servings.*

When Arch and I had politely shaken the hands of all those around us, Marla surprised us by squeezing into our pew. She said accusingly, "You didn't tell me you found him! After the dinner! Did you know the police have already been around to question some of the parents? I hear they suspect that kid living with you. You know, Julian."

"What? Who told you that?"

"I just heard it," she replied with a shrug of silver suede. "I can't remember who told me. Oh, look, Father Olson's giving us the sanctimonious eye. Can't talk now."

During the final hymn I noticed that Audrey Cooper-smith had slipped in sometime during the service. She stood, statuelike, in the last pew with her arms clamped across her chest. Her face was fatigued, but carefully made up, and she wore a long white apron over her baggy clothes. Since her separation, Audrey had been inclined to wear oversize chamois shirts and gray pants that looked as if they'd been issued for postal service employees. She carried a purse only rarely, favoring instead a wallet in her back pocket and a chunk of keys dangling from a belt loop. Now, although everyone around her was singing, she was not. Her dark eyes were half closed. I wondered if she was praying for Carl's return or for self-improve-ment. On the other hand, maybe these were mutually exclusive.

While the acolytes snuffed the altar candles, I sig-naled to Audrey and we quickly set up a table at the back of the church. Then I tried to spot Caroline Dawson in the bustle. The last thing I needed was for the plum cake to be decimated before she even got to sample it.

Audrey trundled up to one of the counters, her mouth turned down in a deep-set scowl. Above the cheer-ful din from the foyer, she said, "Greer Dawson's mother is out there. She wants some plum dessert. I said I didn't know anything about it. She said, 'Well, you just better go check, then.'" Audrey fluttered her free hand against her chest. "Why doesn't she ask Greer? She couldn't even manage to help us last night, why can't she pitch in this morning? Or is actual catering too difficult for the Hammer?"

"Audrey," I said in a placating tone, "Greer was listening to the program last night, just like Heather, just like Julian. Let me deal with Caroline Dawson."

Audrey grunted.

Of course, she had a point. Greer D., the Hammer, was interested in working for me only as a way to appear well-rounded to admissions folks. I didn't see why Greer couldn't round herself out working at the family café, but perhaps the Ivy League frowns on nepotism.

Anyway, Audrey was correct in saying Greer hardly ever managed to fit working for me into her busy schedule. But I couldn't afford to alienate her parents before I had wowed them with my baking. I handed an unsmiling Audrey a cheese tray. The enticing smell of cinnamon wafted up from the moist slices of plum cake. As I picked up the cake platter and headed for the Dawsons, I decided that the last thing I'd want to put on my college application was that working in food service had made me *well-rounded*.

"Ooo, ooo, ooo," crooned Marla when I breezed out into the foyer. She cast a greedy eye on the cake. "I still want to hear about last night. And let me tell you, Father Olson is in love with the spread. He already asked me if I thought you'd cater a high-powered clergy meeting."

"As long as he pays for it, I'm his."

"This is the *church,* honey." Marla pinched a piece of cake and popped it into her mouth. "He's not going to pay for anything." She chewed thoughtfully, eyes on something over my shoulder. "Here come Hank and Caroline Dawson," she said under her breath, "the king and queen of the short people. They'll eat anything in sight."

"Hey!" I protested. "*I'm* short! And I resent—"

"Behold your monarchs, then," Marla said with a lift of her chin. "They're right behind you."

The Dawson parents swept up to me. Hank's look was knowing.

He said, "Big game today. You nervous?"

I eyed him. Hank Dawson was a square-set man—square, leathery face with a sharply angled jaw, square shoulders, square Brooks Brothers gray suit. His short salt-and-pepper hair, receding hairline, and quickly appraising Delft-blue eyes all said: *No-nonsense Republican here.* When we could avoid the topic of how brilliant Greer was, Hank and I chatted knowingly after church about the upcoming Bronco games. We were hard-core fans who kept a separate orange outfit for Sunday afternoons, followed the plays, trades, and strategies with our own commentary, and had a standing prescription for stomach medication when the playoff season began. Talking shop with Hank after the Episcopal church service was like finding your kinsman who speaks Zulu in the middle of North Dakota.

"Nah," I replied. "The Vikings are sunk."

"You're right. The Vikings are sunk without Bud Grant."

"The Vikings have been sunk since Fran Tarkenton retired."

"Still," persisted Hank, "you have to worry about any team that can sustain a two-minute offense for a whole quarter."

"Hank. That was years ago."

"Yeah." He looked reassured. "That was Bud Grant's last year."

Then we said our refrain in unison, "And we have Elway."

"*Excuse me!*" shrilled Caroline Dawson. You see, they always get upset when you speak Zulu.

I suddenly wished I were trying to sell the Bronco-orange cupcakes to the café, instead of the plum cake. I turned an apologetic and only slightly saccharine smile to Caroline.

The queen of the short people touched the buttons of her scarlet Chanel-style suit, which was only a shade darker than the burgundy silk of the night before. Marla had once pointed out to me that this particular hue was favored by women in their late fifties. She had dubbed it menopause red. Standing, Caroline resembled a squat, heavy column abandoned by the Greeks. The two Dawsons reminded me of Arch's old square and round blocks that had to be hammered through the right holes.

"*Doesn't* that look lovely," Caroline murmured as she reached for a large slice. "I *do* hope it tastes as good as it looks." She gobbled it down and shoved another into her mouth. Hank picked the bars up and ate them two at a time. Mouth full, Caroline finally commented, "That was *quite* a dinner last night. Of course, Greer doesn't *really* need their college counseling. She has her pick of schools."

"Oh, ah, really? Well. I'm glad you enjoyed the dinner. Actually, it was very successful until the end."

They both looked astonished. Was it possible someone had not heard? Quickly, I explained about finding Keith Andrews. I prayed silently that the police did not arrive to ask their questions during the Bronco game today.

"My God," exclaimed Hank Dawson. I think he had just swallowed his eighth slice. He turned to his wife.

"Remember what Greer said after the state volleyball championships?"

Caroline took another bite. Then she smiled primly. "I think I was too excited to notice."

Eagerly, Hank turned back to me to explain. "Of course you know our daughter is responsible for the Elk Park Prep volleyball team being state champions."

"My heartfelt congratulations."

Hank narrowed one eye skeptically. "Anyway, after the final game, Greer did mention to us this rumor that Keith Andrews was having trouble with drugs. . . ."

I said, "Excuse me?" and momentarily lost my grip on the plum cake platter just as Caroline reached for the last slice, approximately her tenth. "Drugs? Keith Andrews didn't seem like the type."

Hank shrugged, world-wise. "The kind that seems the type rarely is. You know, Goldy, that's been true for the team too." We shook our heads together over the unspoken name of a former Bronco tight end. He had tested positive for cocaine three times in the last year, and had been banned from pro football. An All-Pro player too. At the time, Hank and I had agreed that the state flag should have been flown at half mast. "Take the headmaster's son, Macguire," Hank said after our moment of silence. "He looks innocent as can be, but I understand that kid's had quite a history with substance abuse."

"Substance abuse?" Marla sidled up to us with a tray. "What a nice shade of red, Caroline. It suits you."

"I can tell you where I got it if you'd like, Marla." Caroline and Hank reached simultaneously for cupcakes from Marla's tray.

"Oh," trilled Marla, "I don't think I need shopping advice—"

"Mrs. Dawson," I interjected briskly, "do you like this cake enough to sell it in your café?"

Caroline puckered her lips and closed her eyes. For an instant, she looked like one of those little Chinese demons who brings you nothing but rotten luck. "Not really," she murmured. "Sorry, Goldy. We do appreciate what you're doing for Greer, though. We'll see you in a couple of hours." And off she and her square husband plodded, licking the last cupcake crumbs off their fingers as they departed.

"Was that a rejection?" I asked Marla.

"No, no, my dear, the royal short people have cleaned the trays. Now they need to talk to some other Episcopalians who've come back from the Holy Land." I did not remember the overdressed couple the Dawsons were now chatting with as being particularly religious. Marla said, "You know, Goldy. *England.*" Under her breath, she added, "My question is, if she didn't like it, why'd she have so many pieces?"

I certainly did not know. I checked on the serving table, where Audrey had deftly kept the platters refilled. Across the room, Arch caught my eye. He was standing with the tall, skinny Marenskys, who were avoiding either me or the food or both. Stan and Rhoda Marensky were the kind of people caterers dislike most: They pick at their food, don't finish it, and then complain about how expensive it is. At that moment Stan was interrogating Arch, who shot me an imploring look that meant: *Can we go?* I held up my hand: *Five minutes.* Then I motioned him over. The Marenskys turned their backs.

"Has the headmaster's son been in trouble?" I demanded softly when Arch was by my side.

Arch pushed his glasses up on his nose. A bit of cheese hung on the corner of his mouth. I pinched a paper napkin and wiped it off.

"Do you *mind?*" Arch leaned away from my ministrations.

"Tell me about Macguire, the headmaster's son. And his trouble."

Arch shrugged noncommittally. "Well, he's kind of a goof-off. I mean, with a dad like that, can you blame him if he's weird? I don't think he's allowed to drive anymore. Listen, Mom, people aren't saying very nice things about Keith today. Like he deserved to die or something."

"Who's saying that, the Marenskys?"

"Oh, I guess. Them and other people." Another shrug. Arch, like Julian, wouldn't tattle if his life depended on it. "I'm telling you, Keith was a great guy. Even though he was a senior, he would talk to you. Most seniors just ignore you." Arch reached for another cupcake.

"I know, I know," I said, and felt a mother's pang over the way kids treated small-built, nonathletic Arch.

Marla sashayed up grandly. She had a piece of torte in one hand and a cup of coffee in the other. She gestured grandly with her coffee cup. "Van Gogh must have had to listen to people argue about the Ivy League. That's why he came home and cut off his ear."

I shook my head.

"Just go have a listen-in on the conversation between the Dawsons and Audrey Coopersmith. Caroline was going on about grade point average being less important than extracurricular activities. Audrey replied that besides volleyball, the only outside interest Greer Dawson has ever shown was in clothes. So Caroline said, now that you mention it, maybe dear daughter Greer could give Audrey's daughter, Heather, a few pointers in that department. For that matter—Caroline threw in, as long as she was on a roll—it looked as if Audrey *herself* could use a little advice in the fashion department."

I groaned. "Poor Audrey. As if she didn't have enough to deal with."

"Don't worry," said Marla. "I told Father Olson we needed a referee for a coffee hour argument. He said, Oh, theology or ethics? And I said, academics. He nodded. Said he learned all about it in seminary."

"Really?"

But before Marla could elaborate, the head of the Altar Guild came up and asked me to start clearing the serving table, as there was going to be a meeting in the parish hall after church. Arch sidled off.

To my relief, the cheese was almost gone, the plum cake was crumbs, and the bird centerpieces had been reduced to a few slices of apple-feather.

"Oh, Goldy!" Father Olson's face glowed with pleasure. "This was marvelous! And it gave rise to such a lively coffee hour! I wonder, could you be persuaded to do a luncheon-ministry for the Board of Theological Examiners? I'm sorry to say that we can't really afford to—"

"No thanks!" I called back gaily, scooping up the last of the Gouda. "I'm all booked for the next three months." This was not entirely true. But clients have to be willing to pay for their bread. I had a child to support.

". . . just don't understand why you think your daughter is the only one qualified . . ." Hank Dawson was gesticulating with a wedge of Gouda. As he chided Audrey Coopersmith, his tone was judgmental. "We have looked into this extensively—"

Caroline Dawson was nodding as she stuffed the last of a cupcake into her mouth. The lapels of her red suit quivered in indignation. She swallowed and continued her husband's thought. "Why, just the other day I was speaking with the director of admissions at—"

"And you think that makes you an expert?" Audrey fired back. Her face flushed with ferocity. "You don't know the first thing about the value of an education." She paused, and I felt myself chilled by the intensity of the dark-eyed glare she directed at the bewildered Caroline Dawson. Audrey's words erupted like a spray of bullets. "You think Ben Jonson is a Canadian runner. You, you" —she paused, grasping for another insult—"you think *Heidegger* is a box you carry to detect *radiation*!"

So saying, Audrey whacked her tray down on the table and stomped out the wooden door of the church. Her chain of keys made a loud chinking sound when the edge of the door caught them. She didn't stop to tell me good-bye. She didn't even take off her apron.

4

Father Olson tugged on his beard. "I do wish she hadn't made fun of Heidegger. . . ."

"Oh," I said sympathetically. "She's going through a bad time."

Father Olson moved off to smooth the Dawsons' ruffled feathers. Personally, I didn't know whether Audrey needed understanding, self-improvement, or a brand-new outlook on life. But she sure needed something. Pain seeped out of her like water from a leaking dam. I resolved to say a few carefully chosen words of support the next time we worked together. Carefully chosen, because Arch always said that what I thought of as support was giving somebody the Heimlich maneuver when all they'd done was hiccup.

Hank Dawson nodded at Father Olson and maneuvered his way back to me. "*Isn't* Ben Jonson a Canadian runner?" His brow furrowed.

"Yes, of course. Named after a sixteenth-century playwright, perhaps."

"Who does that woman think she is?"

"Well, she was upset . . ."

Hank Dawson poured himself another cup of coffee and blew on it. He looked down his broad nose at me. "Audrey Coopersmith has distressed my wife." This from the fellow who the night before had given me that classic henpecked look: *Don't worry, I have to live with her.* Maybe the more distress Audrey created for Caroline Dawson, the more there was for Mr. Caroline Dawson.

"Well, Hank . . ."

"Listen. Audrey's just jealous because of how gifted our Greer is. Heather is good in math and science, period. Greer, mind you, has been making up stories since she was eight. She excels in languages and is an athlete, to boot. She's well-rounded, and that's what they're all looking for, you know that. Heather and Greer in a contest? That's not a game, it's a rout."

"Of course," I said soothingly. "But you know we all feel so protective of our children. Especially after what happened last night."

Hank swirled the coffee around and regarded me with his stern ice-blue eyes. "Oh, tell me! Nine thousand bucks a year, and then you tell me you find a dead body after a dinner at the headmaster's house! Jesus H. Christ!"

"Father Olson is within earshot," I murmured.

Hank lifted a jaw that was so sharp it would have cut an Italian salami. He spat out his words. "Of all times for that school to get caught up in a scandal, this is the *worst.* These kids have their senior years, college applications, all that coming up. And what business does Audrey Coopersmith"—the blue eyes blazed as his voice rose—"who has never done a thing with her life, have judging our daughter? Greer placed fifth in the state in the National French

Contest. She's written poems . . . she went to a writers' conference and studied with the writer-in-residence at *Harvard*."

"Greer's wonderful, wonderful," I lied. "Everybody thinks so."

The king of the short people grunted, turned on his heel, and walked off.

The strange part about Audrey's outburst was that within ten minutes Caroline Dawson had a change of heart—not toward Audrey, but toward me. Or, more accurately, toward my plum cake. Wanted to show she wasn't all snob, I guess. Before the stragglers had left the church coffee hour, when I was cleaning up the last bird-built-of-apple slices, she bustled over and announced she'd changed her mind. What could she possibly have been thinking? Of course they'd love to have me sell plum cakes at the café. They were *absolutely* delicious, and would go over *wonderfully* with their clientele. Should we start with six a week?

Oh, definitely, I'd replied meekly.

The cake go-ahead wrapped me in a small cloud of good feeling, so I rashly informed Father Olson I'd do his clergy meeting if the church could pay for my labor and supplies. His right hand combed his beard in Moses-like fashion. He murmured that he'd check with the diocesan office. The clergy meeting was this coming Friday, and as the church bulletin announced, they were going to discuss faith and penance. So could I think of something appropriate? I gave him a blank look. What, bread and water? Then I assured him a penitential meal was no problem. I even had a recipe for something called Sorry Cake.

When Arch and I got home, Julian sat in the kitchen sipping his version of café au lait, a cup of hot milk flavored with a tablespoon of espresso. He said he'd called for a window-repair person to come out tomorrow, and he wasn't in the mood to do his homework, so could he help with the *choucroute* for the Bronco lunch? He also said I'd had six calls: two hang-ups and four with messages. The messages were from the headmaster, Tom Schulz, Audrey Coopersmith, and my ex-husband, who sure sounded pissed off about something.

Nothing new there. But two hang-ups?

"Did these anonymous callers say anything at all?"

Julian tilted back in one of the kitchen chairs. "Nope. I just said, 'Hello? Hello? This is Goldilocks' Catering, who're you?' And all I could hear was breathing and then *click*."

The air around me turned suddenly chill. Could it be the same prankster who had smashed our window last night? What if Arch had taken those calls? Was someone casing my house? Best to tell Schulz about this. But I had someone else to call first.

I reached for the phone; my ex-husband picked up after four rings. The Jerk's uninflected voice, the one he used to try to show he was above feeling, said only that he'd been trying to get me all morning. I asked if he'd been around our house last night, maybe with a rock? He said, "What do you think I am, crazy?"

Well, I wasn't going to answer that one. I asked what he wanted. Only this: Because of the early snow, he wanted to go skiing this coming weekend, his time to take Arch. He wanted to pick him up at Elk Park Prep early on Halloween, this Friday, to beat the rush. Just wanted to let me know.

I chewed the inside of my cheek. Since our weekend visitation arrangement did not include Friday, John Richard had to check with me about Arch's leaving school early. Of course, this checking actually meant announcing his plans and then waiting to see if I would get upset. Who, me? But I was concerned Arch might have other plans for Halloween. If Arch agreed, John Richard would no doubt take him to his condo in Keystone. His dad had had the locks changed, Arch had reported to me, to make sure I never used the place on the sly. Why should I be upset? Fine, I told John Richard, just let me check with Arch. I didn't even say what went through my mind, that some people had to *work* on Halloween. Or at least, like the Board of Theological Examiners, be penitent. But John Richard fit into neither of those categories, so I hung up.

I phoned Headmaster Perkins next, but got his son. Macguire acknowledged that he knew me by saying, "Oh yeah, hi. That was pretty heavy last night. You okay?" When I replied in the affirmative, he said, "Dad said to tell you he'd like to see you. Tomorrow. Just come into the office anytime, and, uh, bring some coat." He thought for a minute. "Tell him you just dropped in, you know, like a . . . meteorite."

I told him to expect a hit about ten the next morning, and hung up. Before I could dial Schulz, the phone rang.

"Goldilocks' Catering," I chirped, "where everything is just right!"

Breathing.

"Hey!" I yelled. "Who is this?"

A dial tone, then nothing. I pressed Schulz's number.

"How's my favorite caterer?" he said with a chuckle when I had greeted him.

"You mean your *only* caterer."

"Oops. She's in a bad mood. Must have been chatting with her ex-husband."

"That, and someone heaved a rock through one of our windows last night. Plus I just had an anonymous call, third one of the morning."

He snorted. "The ex up to his old tricks?"

"He says no. The security alarm went off when the

rock came through, and Arch handled it. The calls worry me."

"You going to let the phone company know?"

"Yes, yes, of course. But what scares me is that these things happened right after the Keith Andrews thing. Maybe there's a connection. I wish I'd never found him. I wish I'd never gotten involved. But I did and I am, in case you don't recall."

"I do, I do, Miss G. Take it easy, that's why I called you. There was a message on my voice mail from you, remember? You didn't want to wake me up, but you'd found something."

I told him about the credit card in the pocket of the raccoon coat. He asked for the number. I fished around for the card, then repeated the numerals. He said, "Don't return the card with the coat. Can you bring it over tomorrow? Stay for dinner?"

"Love to." I felt guilty for speaking sharply to him. Softening, I said, "Why don't you come here? I'll probably have a ton of leftover bratwurst. Then if we get an anonymous call, you can bawl the person out yourself."

"How about this . . . give the sausage to the boys and come out to my place around six. I need to talk to you alone."

His tone made me smile. "Sounds interesting."

"It would be if it were about us," Schulz replied reluctantly. "But this is about Julian."

Great. I said I'd be there and hung up. Packing up the *choucroute,* I remembered Audrey Coopersmith. Doggone it. Support, support, I told myself, and punched the numbers for the bookstore, where I asked for the self-improvement department. Part of psychology, I was told. Hmm.

"Oh, God, Goldy," Audrey said breathily when we were connected. "I'm so glad you called. I'm a wreck.

First the police and then those damn Dawsons at the church, plus I got this terrible letter yesterday from Carl's lawyer—"

"Please," I interrupted, but nicely, "you know I've got this Bronco thing at the Dawsons—"

"Oh, well, I've got a huge problem. We're having a seminar, Getting Control of Your Life, tonight and I promised to do a little stir-fry for the staff after the store closes at five and before we reopen at seven, and what with the police asking all those questions, I forgot all about the stir-fry, and they have plates and stuff here, but I don't have any food and I was just wondering if you'd . . ."

Fill in the blank. I stretched the phone cord, opened the door to my walk-in refrigerator, and perused the contents. "How many people?"

"Eight."

"Any vegetarians?"

"None, I already checked. And we've taken up a collection, five dollars per person. I'll give you all the money and buy you any cookbook you want, plus do the serving and cleanup myself. . . ." Relief and glee filled her voice, and I hadn't even said yes.

"Okay, but it'll be simple," I warned.

"Simple is what they *want,* it's part of getting control of your life."

I made an unintelligible sound and said I'd be down after the Bronco game. After some thought I got out two pounds of steak, then swished together a wonderfully pungent marinade of pressed garlic, sherry, and soy sauce. Once the beef had defrosted slightly under cold running water, I cut it into thin slices, sloshed them around in the marinade, and finished packing up the *choucroute* and trimmings. I couldn't shake the feeling, however, that it was going to be a long half-time luncheon.

. . . .

At the Dawsons' enormous wood-and-glass home, there was much discussion of the artificial turf inside Minneapolis' domed stadium. My appearance caused only a momentary pause in the downing of margaritas and whiskey sours and the assessment of Viking strategy. Caroline Dawson, still wearing her red suit, waddled in front of Arch, Julian, and me out to the kitchen.

It was the cleanest, most impeccably kept culinary space I had ever inhabited. When I complimented her on how immaculate everything was, she gave me a startled look.

"Isn't *your* kitchen clean?" Without waiting for an answer, she peeked underneath the plastic wrap of one of my trays. I thought it was to check how clean it was until her chubby fingers emerged with a crust of potato-caraway bread. She popped the bread into her mouth, chewed, and said, "Hank and I, being in food service, feel it's imperative to have a dust- and dirt-free environment. You know we asked you to cater this meal because, well, we're busy with the guests, and you *do* have a good reputation—"

Then she scuttled out, but not without filching another slice of bread. Julian, Arch, and I began to prepare the meal in earnest. But if I thought we would be uninterrupted, I was wrong.

Rhoda Marensky, as thin and leggy as an unwatered rhododendron, sauntered out first. It was well known in town that statuesque Rhoda, now fifty, had been a model for Marensky Furs before Stan Marensky married her. For the Bronco get-together, she wore a chartreuse knit sweater and skirt trimmed with fur in dots and dashes, as if the minks had been begging for help in Morse code. She stood in an exaggerated slouch to appraise Julian.

"Well, my boy," she said with undisguised wickedness, "you must have finished your SAT review early, if you can take time out to cater. What confidence!"

Julian stopped spooning out sauerkraut, pressed his lips together, and gulped. Arch looked from Julian to me.

"Unlike some people," I replied evenly, "Julian doesn't need to review."

Rhoda snorted loudly and writhed in Julian's direction, a female Uriah Heep. She put her hand on the sauerkraut spoon handle so that he was forced to look at her. "Salutatorian! And our Brad tells me you've never even been in a gifted program. Where was it you're from, somewhere in Utah?"

"Tell *me,*" I wondered aloud, "what kind of name is *Marensky* anyway? Where is *it* from, Eastern Europe?" Bitchy, I know, but sometimes you have to fight fire with a blowtorch. Besides, skinny people seldom appreciate caterers.

"The Marenskys were a branch of the Russian royal family," Rhoda retorted.

"Wow! Cool!" interjected my impressionable son.

I glanced at the butcher knife on the counter. "Which branch would that be, the hemophiliac one? Or is that technically a vein?"

That did it. Rhoda slithered out. A moment later her husband strode into the kitchen. Stan Marensky almost tripped over Arch, who scooted out of his path and grimaced. I tried not to groan. Stan's long, deeply lined face, oversize mouth, and lanky frame always reminded me of a racehorse. He was as slender as his wife, but much more nervous. Must have been all that Russian blood that wouldn't clot.

"What did you say to my wife about blood?" he demanded.

"Blood? Nothing. She must have been thinking of the football game."

And out went Stan. Arch giggled. Julian stared at me incredulously.

"Man, Goldy, chill! You've always told me you have to be so nice, especially to rich people, so you can get more bookings . . . and here you are just *dumping* on the Marenskys—"

Caroline Dawson interrupted his rebuke by waddling back into the room. The queen of the short people put her hands on her wide hips; her crimson body shook with rage. "*What* is taking so long? If I had known you three were going to be out here having a gab fest, I would have had Greer help you, or, or . . . I would have brought in help from the café—"

"Not to worry!" I interrupted her merrily and hoisted a tray with platters of steaming sausages. "We're holding our own. Let's go see how our team's doing," I ordered the boys.

Julian mutely lifted his tray with the sauerkraut and potato-caraway bread. Arch carefully took hold of the first serving dish of warmed applesauce. We served the food graciously and received a smattering of compliments. The Marenskys regarded us haughtily as they picked at their food, but ventured no more critical comments.

On the big-screen television, brilliant close-up shots made the football playing surface look like tiny blades. Happily, Denver won by two touchdowns, one on a quarterback sneak and the other on a faked field goal attempt. I predicted both plays in addition to serving the food.

Hank Dawson, flushed and effusive, reminded me I was booked again for next week's game. He brandished a wad of bills that amounted to our pay plus a twenty-five percent tip. I was profusely thankful and divided the gratuity with Arch and Julian. Unfortunately, I knew that next week the Broncos were playing the Redskins in Washington.

Maybe I could split the tip over two weeks.

We arrived home just before five. Early darkness pressed down from the sky, a reminder, like the recent snow and cold, of winter's rapid approach. Julian stared out the kitchen window and said maybe he should stay home and do SAT review instead of doing stir-fry at the Tattered Cover. Inwardly, I cursed Rhoda Marensky. Arch said he wanted to come along when I told him we'd be cooking on the fourth floor, usually closed to the public.

"Cool! Do they, like, have their safe up there, and surveillance equipment, and stuff like that?"

"None of the above," I assured him as I packed up the ingredients. "Probably just a lot of desks and boxes of books. And a little kitchen."

"Maybe I should take my wardrobe with the fake back for the C. S. Lewis display. Oh, Julian, *please* come with me so you can help me carry it. I know they have a secret closet there, did you? Do you think they'll use my display? I mean, if Julian helps me set it up?" He looked with great hope first at Julian, then me. I was afraid, as mothers always are, that the voice of expedience—"They probably have all the displays they need"—would be interpreted as rejection. I said reflectively, "Why don't we ask them when we get there?"

He seemed satisfied. Julian decided his homework and the SAT review could wait. He helped Arch load the plywood wardrobe into the van while I packed up the stir-fry ingredients. On the way to Denver, I decided to broach the topic of Arch's weekend. Despite his basically nonathletic nature, he had learned to ski at an early age and enjoyed the sport quite a bit. For Halloween, I asked, did he want to ski early with his father, go out for trick-or-treat, what?

"I don't have any friends from Elk Park Prep to go trick-or-treating with," he replied matter-of-factly. "Besides, if Dad wants to ski—wait! I could go around in his condo building!"

"And dress up as . . . ?" Julian asked.

"Galileo, what else?"

I grinned as we pulled into the bookstore's parking garage. Audrey was waiting for us in her silver van by the third-floor store entrance. She hopped out and swiped her security card through the machine next to the door. Arch, a security nut, had her repeat the process, which he studied with furrowed brow as Julian and I unloaded my van. While helping us haul in the electric wok and bags of ingredients, Audrey said the store was empty for the two-and-a-half-hour break between closing and reopening for the seminar. The other seven staff members present were doing some last-minute preparation . . . dinner was planned for six-forty, and she'd already started cooking some rice she'd found in a cupboard . . . was that okay?

"Is now a good time to ask her about the wardrobe?" Arch whispered to me in the elevator to the fourth floor.

We had fifteen minutes before cooking had to begin. I nodded; Arch made his request.

"A wardrobe with a false back!" Audrey cried. "You're so creative! Just like Heather . . . why, I remember when she was nine, she loved C. S. Lewis too. How old are you?" Arch reddened and said he was twelve. Audrey shrugged and plowed ahead. "When Heather was nine, she wanted a planetary voyager for Christmas, and, of course, she is *so* gifted in science, why, one summer she built a time-travel machine with little electric gizmos right in our backyard. . . ."

Arch rolled his eyes at me; Julian cleared his throat and looked away. I think Audrey caught the look, because she stopped abruptly and gnawed her lip. "Well, Arch, I'm sorry, but we probably can't," she said plaintively. "I mean, I can't authorize you putting up a false-back display, somebody might get hurt. . . ."

Arch looked disappointed, but then piped up, "Can I see the secret closet, then? I know you have one, a kid at school told me."

"Uh, I suppose," Audrey said, hesitating, "but it isn't exactly *The Lion, the Witch, and the Wardrobe*. Are you sure?"

Arch replied with an enthusiastic affirmative. Arch, Julian, Audrey, and I unloaded the supplies and rode down to the first floor. In Business Books, Audrey carefully pulled out an entire floor-to-ceiling shelf. In back was a small closet. Arch insisted on being closed into it.

His muffled voice said, "Yeah, it's cool all right! Now let me out."

This we did. Satisfied, he returned to the fourth floor with us and minutes later was stringing snow peas to go in the stir-fry under Julian's direction.

As I heated oil in the electric wok, Arch said, "Did you do stuff like that during the summer when you were nine, Mom? Make a time-travel machine?"

Julian snorted.

I replied, "The only thing I did during the summer when I was nine was swim in the ocean and eat something called fireballs."

Arch pushed his glasses up on his nose and nodded, considering. Finally he said, "Okay. I guess I'm not too dumb."

I gave him an exasperated look, which he returned. The oil was beginning to pop, so I eased in the marinated beef. The luscious smell of garlic-sautéed beef wafted up from the wok.

"Thank you, thank you," gushed Audrey. "I don't know what I would have done without you, I've just been *so* stressed lately—"

"No problem." I tossed the sizzling beef against the sides of the wok until the red faded to pink. When the beef slices were just tender, I eased them onto a platter and heated more oil for the broccoli, carrots, baby corn, and snow peas, an inviting palette of emerald, orange, and pale yellow. When the vegetables were hot and crisp, I poured on the oyster-sauce mixture, then added the beef and a sprinkling of chopped scallions. I served the whole hot steaming mass with the rice to Arch, Audrey, and her staff, who exclaimed over the fresh veggies' crunchiness, the tenderness and rich garlic flavor of the steak.

"I love to feed people," I replied with a smile, and then wielded chopsticks into the goodies myself.

On the way home, Julian ate a cheese sandwich he'd brought, pronounced himself exhausted, and lay down in the back seat. He was snoring within seconds. Arch rambled in a conspiratorial tone about the upcoming weekend, skiing, the amount of loot he'd collect trick-or-treating at his father's condo, being able to see more constellations in Keystone because it was farther from the lights of Denver. He wanted to know, if I hadn't read C. S. Lewis when I was his age, had I at least liked to look at stars? Did I wait until it was dark to see Polaris, and could you see a lot of stars, living near the Jersey shore? Like in the summertime, maybe? I told him the only thing I looked forward to on summer evenings when I was his age was getting a popsicle from the Good Humor man.

"Oh, Mom! Fireballs and popsicles! All you ever think about is food!"

I took this as a compliment, and laughed. I wanted to ask him how school was going, how he thought Julian was doing, how life was going in general, but experience had taught me he would interpret it as prying. Besides, he spared me the trouble as we chugged up the last portion of Interstate 70 that led to our exit.

"Speaking of food, I'm glad we had meat tonight," my son whispered. "Sometimes I think eating that brown rice and tofu stuff is what makes Julian so unhappy."

Monday morning brought slate-gray clouds creeping up from the southernmost part of the eastern horizon. Below the cloud layer, a slice of sunrise sparkled pink as fiberglass. I stretched through my yoga routine, then turned on the radio in time to hear that the blanket of clouds threatened the Front Range with—dreaded words—a chance of snow. The reason Coloradans do not use the eastern word *autumn* is that October offers either late summer or early winter, with precious little in between.

I dressed and made espresso. Arch and Julian shuffled sleepily out of their room and joined me. I flipped thick, egg-rich slices of hot French toast for them and poured amber lakes of maple syrup all around. This perked them both up. After the boys left for school, I worked on my accounts, sent out some bills and paid some, ordered supplies for the upcoming week, and then took off for Elk Park Prep with the raccoon coat rolled into a furry ball on the front seat of my van.

The winding driveway to the prep school had been paved and straightened out somewhat at the end of the summer. But the approach to the magnificent old hotel was still breathtaking. Several of the driveway's curves even afforded glimpses of snow-capped peaks. Saturday

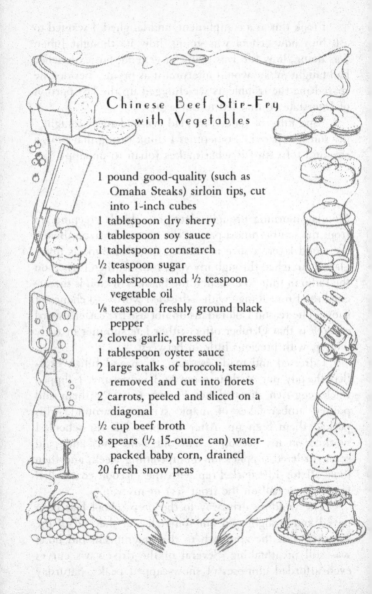

Chinese Beef Stir-Fry with Vegetables

1 pound good-quality (such as Omaha Steaks) sirloin tips, cut into 1-inch cubes

1 tablespoon dry sherry

1 tablespoon soy sauce

1 tablespoon cornstarch

½ teaspoon sugar

2 tablespoons and ½ teaspoon vegetable oil

⅛ teaspoon freshly ground black pepper

2 cloves garlic, pressed

1 tablespoon oyster sauce

2 large stalks of broccoli, stems removed and cut into florets

2 carrots, peeled and sliced on a diagonal

½ cup beef broth

8 spears (½ 15-ounce can) water-packed baby corn, drained

20 fresh snow peas

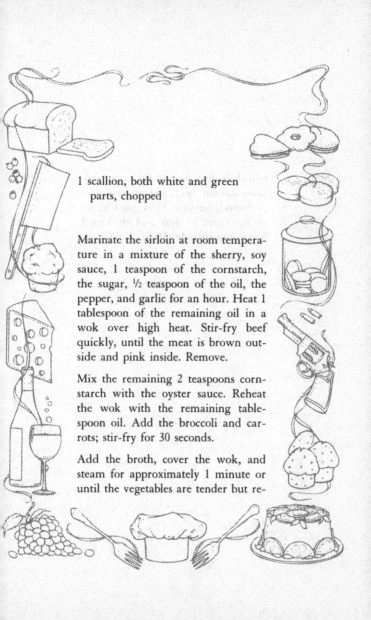

1 scallion, both white and green
   parts, chopped

Marinate the sirloin at room temperature in a mixture of the sherry, soy
sauce, 1 teaspoon of the cornstarch,
the sugar, ½ teaspoon of the oil, the
pepper, and garlic for an hour. Heat 1
tablespoon of the remaining oil in a
wok over high heat. Stir-fry beef
quickly, until the meat is brown outside and pink inside. Remove.

Mix the remaining 2 teaspoons cornstarch with the oyster sauce. Reheat
the wok with the remaining tablespoon oil. Add the broccoli and carrots; stir-fry for 30 seconds.

Add the broth, cover the wok, and
steam for approximately 1 minute or
until the vegetables are tender but re-

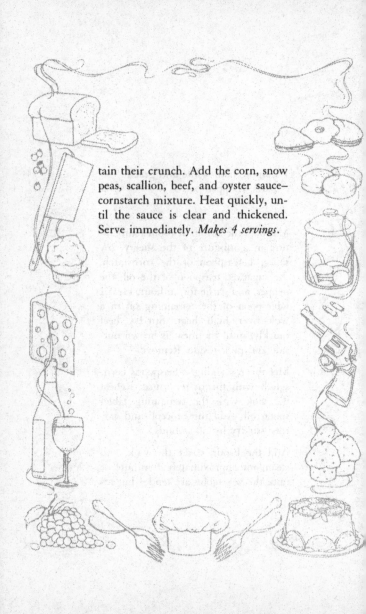

tain their crunch. Add the corn, snow
peas, scallion, beef, and oyster sauce–
cornstarch mixture. Heat quickly, until the sauce is clear and thickened.
Serve immediately. *Makes 4 servings.*

night's snowfall, now mostly melted, had reduced the roadside hillocks of planted wildflowers to rust-colored stalks topped with wrinkled flowers in faded hues of blue and purple.

As I rounded the last curve and rolled over speed bump number three, I noticed that the school had finished tearing down the chain-link fence around the pool construction site. In its place was a decorous stone wall surrounded by hemlock bushes. Looked like the administration didn't want kids thinking about swimming with winter coming on. Over the summer Arch had nearly drowned in that damn pool. I didn't want to think about swimming, either.

I parked, grabbed the fur coat, and leaped out onto the iced driveway. Over by the headmaster's house I could see two policemen methodically sweeping the ground with metal detectors. I turned away.

Someone had taped photocopied pictures of Keith Andrews onto the front doors of the school. Black crepe paper hung around each. The angelic, uncannily Arch-like face stared out from both flat photos. I closed my eyes and pushed through the doors.

In the carpeted lobby, chessboards left in mid-game were perched on tables with their chairs left at hurriedly pulled-out angles. Piles of books and papers spilled off benches. Through this clutter threaded Egon Schlicht-maier, my muscular faculty assistant from the college dinner. Today he was conspicuously spiffy in a very un-Faustian sheepskin jacket. Next to him clomped the much less sartorial Macguire Perkins in a faded denim coat. Macguire's acne-covered face had a dour expression; Egon Schlichtmaier's baby face was grim. They had just come in from outside, and they were in a hurry.

"You heff made us late," Egon was scolding.

"So?" retorted Macguire.

"Ah, there you are," trilled Headmaster Perkins at me. He approached in the tweed-of-the-day, a somber herringbone. "With Mrs. Marensky's coat. *Won't* she be happy."

Yes, won't she. Mr. Perkins escorted me into his office, a high-ceilinged affair that had been painted mauve to match one of the hues in the hand-cut Chinese rug that covered most of the marble floor. A buzz of his intercom distracted him. I sat carefully on one of the burgundy leather sofas profuse with brass buttons. It let out a sigh.

"You and me both," I said under my breath.

"Well!" said the headmaster with a suddenness that startled me. "Saturday night was indeed tragic." From behind his hornrimmed glasses, Perkins' eyes locked mine; we had the abrupt intimacy of strangers thrown together by disaster. There was the mutual, if unwanted, need to come to terms with what had happened. His usually forced joviality had disappeared; his anxiety was barely masked. "Awful, just awful," he murmured. He jumped up restlessly and paced back and forth in front of the windows. Sunlight shone off his thick mass of prematurely white hair. "It was like a . . . a . . ." But for once the complicated similes wouldn't come. "As you can imagine," he floundered, "our phones have not stopped ringing. Parents calling to find out what happened. The press . . ." He gestured with his hands and lifted his pale eyebrows expressively. "We had an emergency faculty meeting this morning. I had to tell them you were the one who found the body."

I groaned. "Does this mean people are going to be calling me to find out what happened?"

Headmaster Perkins brushed a finger over one of the brass wall sconces before moving toward his Queen Anne–style desk chair, where he ceremoniously sat. "Not if you can tell me exactly what you saw, Mrs. Korman. That way, I can deal with those who want all the details."

Hmm. In a small town, people *always* wanted *all* the details, because everyone wanted to be the first one with the complete story. How many stitches did George need when he fell while rock-climbing? Did Edward lose his house when he filed for bankruptcy? Did they take out Tanya's lymph nodes? And on it went. So the request did not surprise me. On the other hand, this wasn't the first time I'd had some involvement with a homicide investigation. I had learned from Schulz to talk as little as possible in these situations. Remembered details were for the police, not the gossip network.

"Sorry," I said with a slight smile, "you know as much as I do. But let me ask you a question. Who would have had the keys to your house to get in before I did that night?"

"Oh." Perkins didn't bother to conceal his distaste. "We leave it open. This is an environment of *trust.*"

Well, you could have fooled me. The receptionist buzzed once more. While Mr. Perkins was again deep in similes, I glanced around his office. The mauve walls held wood-framed degrees and pictures. The Hill School. B.A. from Columbia. M.A., Yale. There was a large crackled-surface oil painting of a fox hunt, with riders in full Pink regalia hurtling over a fence. Another painting was of Big Ben. As if the life of Merrie Olde Englande were available in the Colorado high country. But these hung decorations sent a subliminal message to prospective students and, more important, to their parents. *Want these accoutrements and all they imply? Go to this school.*

The headmaster finished up on the phone and laced his fingers behind his silvery-white hair. "I have a few more things to talk to you about, Mrs. Korman. We need to move the next college advisory meeting off the school grounds. Too much anxiety would be aroused if we held it at my residence again, I fear. Can you stay flexible?"

"As a rubber band," I said with a straight face.

"And you do remember that the SATs are this coming Saturday morning? You're making a healthful treat, something whole grain?"

I nodded. How could I forget? I would be bringing the Elk Park Prep seniors, as well as the visiting seniors from the local public high school, a buffet of breakfast-type treats, to be served before the test. Better than skiing at Keystone any day, I thought sourly.

"It's the morning after Halloween," the headmaster reflected, "although I don't suppose that will make a difference. But it may spook them," he added with a grin.

Getting back to his old self. I waited. Perkins pulled off his glasses and polished them carefully.

I said, "Well, if that's all—"

"It isn't."

I squirmed on the sofa. He put on his glasses, narrowed his eyes, and puckered his lips in thought.

Perkins said: "Your son Arch is having some problems."

Ringing assaulted my ears. Keeping my voice even, I said, "What kind of problems?"

"Academic as well as social, I'm told." To his credit, a shade of gentleness crept into Perkins' tone. "Arch is failing social studies. Missing most of the assigned work, is my understanding. He seems quite unhappy . . . not swimming with the currents of scholastic life. Reading books outside of the curriculum and wanting to report on them."

"Failing a course? Social studies?" The mother is always the last to know.

"We wanted you to be aware of this before midterm grades come out next week. Parent conferences are scheduled in two weeks. When you come, you can ask Arch's instructors yourself."

"Can I talk to his teachers now? Do they know why this is happening?"

He shrugged. His gesture clearly said, *This is not my responsibility.* "The instructors can see you if it's convenient. Remember, grades are only an indication of what young Arch is learning. Like the weather forecasts, this may mean a storm, but it may only be dark clouds . . . a wee disturbance in the stratosphere." This last was accompanied by a *wee,* patronizing smile.

"The instructors can see me if it's convenient?" I repeated. In public school, if you wanted to see a teacher, you got a conference, period. "Grades are like the weather forecasts?" Fury laced my voice. "You know what this school is like? Like . . . like . . . bottled water! You pay more for it than the free stuff out of the tap, but there's a lot less regulation! And the product is awfully unpredictable!"

Perkins drew back. How dare I invade his field of metaphorical expertise? I stood up and bowed slightly, my way of excusing myself without speaking. There was only one comfort in the whole infuriating experience: For the meteorological analysis of Arch's academic progress it was John Richard, and not I, who was forking over nine grand a year.

5

When I left the headmaster's office, I noticed that ultra-thin, ultra-chic couple, Stan and Rhoda Marensky, hovering around the receptionist. This day, Rhoda's fashionably short red hair stood in contrast to a blond-streaked fur jacket, the kind that looked as if the animals had their hair frosted. She stopped reading a framed article on the wall and turned a blank, prim face to me. Either she was angry to learn who had carried off her raccoon coat or she was still stewing about my hemophilia comment.

Stan, less like a clotheshorse than a horse who happened to be wearing clothes (in this case a rumpled green suit), paced nervously. His lined face quivered; his blood-shot eyes flicked nervously about the room. He looked at me, then away. Clearly, I wasn't worth greeting.

"I brought back your coat," I announced loudly, not one to endure snubs lightly.

"Hnh," snorted Rhoda. She tilted her head back so

she could look down her long nose at me, literally. "I *suspected* somebody had taken it. Compound grand theft with murder, why not?"

I could feel rage bubbling up for the second time in ten minutes. Now I really couldn't wait to tell Schulz whose coat had someone else's credit card tucked in its pocket. A *dead* somebody else, no less. We'd see about insinuations. To the Marenskys, I only smiled politely. I had learned the hard way not to respond directly to hostility. Instead, I purred, "How's the fur store doing?"

Neither answered. The receptionist even stopped tapping on her computer keys for a moment to see if she had missed something. Was it possible that Marensky Furs, a family business that had been a Denver landmark for over thirty years, wasn't doing so well? The newspapers are always full of doom-and-gloom analyses for the Colorado economy. But Marla, who was a regular Marensky customer, would have told me if the trade in silver fox had taken a hit. Perhaps I should have asked how Neiman-Marcus was doing.

The bell clanged, signaling the end of the second academic period. I wanted to catch Arch between classes but was determined that if anyone was going to back down, it was going to be the Marenskys. Stan stopped pacing and shoved his hands deep into his pockets. He rocked back on the heels of his unpolished Italian loafers and regarded me. "Didn't I coach your son in soccer?"

"Yes, briefly."

"Little guy, right? Kind of timid? What's he doing now, anything?"

"Building props from C. S. Lewis novels."

Stan Marensky continued to look at me as if I baffled him, or in some way presented an enigma. A wave of noisy students swelled down the hall. Stan Marensky said,

"I understand Julian Teller lives with you now, doesn't he?"

What was this, interrogation time? If he couldn't even tell me the status of the fur trade, what was I doing recounting the doings of our household?

I said merely, "Mmm." We were saved from open warfare by the sudden appearance of Headmaster Perkins at his doorway. He looked expectantly at the Marenskys, who turned in unison and made for the headmaster's office. Odd. *Two* people didn't need to come in to pick up an old coat. Something else was going on. But as the door to the office closed with a soft click, I knew I wasn't going to be privy to any confidences.

The second bell rang. I asked the receptionist how to get to seventh-grade social studies and then walked pensively down one of the long halls. Pictures of the old hotel before it had become a school hung between the bulletin boards and rows of metal lockers. In the first photograph you could see the lobby in its former glory. Once this had been an expanse of pink Colorado marble with replicas of classical statuary placed tastefully here and there. Now it was covered with dark industrial-grade carpet. Other pictures showed the wide halls to the guest suites; still others, the suites themselves, lushly decorated with floral-patterned rugs, matching wallpaper, and egg-and-dart molding. The faded photos exuded an air of quiet luxury that was distinctly at odds with the bulletin boards stuffed with announcements, the battered lockers papered with pictures of rock stars, the throb of young voices pulsing from classrooms.

Through the rectangle of glass in the door to his classroom, Arch was visible in the back row of desks. At the front, a video ran on a pull-down screen. A shot of the Acropolis flickered on the screen, accompanied by some loud droning from the announcer, then a shot of the Colosseum. I could see the chalked words on the blackboard: *Early Cities: Athens, Rome.* Arch, turned away from the teacher, his legs splayed out in front of him, paid no heed. His glasses had ridden down on his nose as he hunched with a book held to the light from the projector. I didn't need to see the title: *The Voyage of the Dawn Treader,* his current favorite.

I fought a powerful instinct to slip in and lift the volume right out of his hands. He was flunking this class, for goodness' sake. But I held back. I even managed not to rap on the door window and embarrass him. But then a sudden touch on my shoulder made me shriek. So much for my Mother of the Year Award: I lost my balance; my forehead bonked the glass. All the heads in the classroom turned. Hastily, I drew back, but not before I saw Arch put his head in his hands in embarrassment.

"What is it?" I demanded brusquely of Audrey Coopersmith, dressed this day in a periwinkle gabardine shirt and baggy pants complemented with hightop sneakers.

She winced. The perfect curls shook slightly.

"Sorry," I said, and meant it. *Support,* I reminded myself. "What're you doing here?"

"Delivering books. I've just been to the headmaster's office, but the secretary said you were here." Her tone was tentative; maybe she feared I would growl at her again. "Listen, that was a great stir-fry that you did. Thanks again. Anyway, after the seminar, one of the staff people said the bookstore was having a, a . . . reading this Friday night. I thought I'd talk to Perkins about it this morning, but he's in a meeting. The secretary let me talk to him over her phone, though, since the notice was short—"

"Notice was short for what?" I had a vision of stir-fry

for a hundred people. The last thing I needed was another job in an already busy week.

"The headmaster wants to use the reading as a college advisory thing. You and I would do the treats. After the reading, of course."

"Don't tell me. Halloween? Clive Barker. Stephen King."

"Nooo," Audrey said. She shifted her weight back and forth on her hightops; the keys on her belt hook jingled. "It's for Marshall Smathers." To my look of confusion, she explained, "He wrote that best seller, *Climbing the Ivy League*. It gives tips for the admission process."

True horror. I asked, "Will the bookstore pay for the treats?"

"No, the school will. The seniors and juniors from Elk Park Prep are all supposed to go. It'll be over early because of the SATs the next morning. The headmaster's office is going to call around and tell the parents. Perkins said the school would pick up the tab if you put out a little sign that says refreshments compliments of Elk Park Preparatory School. I suggested that part to him," she said with a slight snort.

"Audrey, you're an advertising whiz."

She said bleakly, "I'm a whiz, all right."

I didn't know whether the irritation I felt was from Audrey's cynical tone or just my increasing impatience with her chronic unhappiness. "Okay, okay," I said. "Tell Perkins I'll do it and that I'll call him." At that moment, I would have preferred to be a pelt in a Marensky coat than face another metaphor.

She said she'd leave Perkins a message because she had another meeting to go to. Then she turned and traipsed off. I went in search of Miss Ferrell. She did not teach Arch, but she did advise the French Club, which he enjoyed immensely. Maybe she could give me some perspective on his problems.

After about ten minutes of pointless wandering through mazelike halls, I located Miss Ferrell's room. Actually, it wasn't that difficult: it was the only door with a poster of a giant croissant on it. Above, a hand-lettered sign was posted: SENIORS: DISCUSS APPLICATION ESSAY AND ROLE-PLAY COLLEGE INTERVIEWS TODAY—THIRD PERIOD. From inside the room came the sound of voices. I opened the door and slipped in, heeded only by five or six of the thirty seniors within. Audrey appeared to have just come in also; to my surprise, she was sitting in the back. The Marenskys, apparently finished with their powwow with the headmaster, plus the Dawsons and several other sets of parents, were seated over to the side. A couple raised eyebrows at my entrance. I shrugged. Just me, the caterer. I noticed that a number of the seniors were mourning their valedictorian with black armbands.

A short, round fellow whispered, "Did you bring any food?" When I shook my head, he reluctantly turned his attention back to the front of the room.

Miss Ferrell's toast-colored hair was swept up into a large topknot held on the crown of her head by a trailing red scarf that matched the red of her tent dress. The dress itself was one of those bifurcated triangles, half bright red, half raspberry pink. She looked like a pyramid of sherbet. I took the one empty chair at the back of the room. Julian gave me a high-five sign and I smiled. Guess I had shown up at the right time.

"Okay now," said Miss Ferrell, "it seems to me that too many of you are becoming obsessively worried about what colleges want—"

A hand shot up.

"Yes, Ted?"

"I heard that for the most selective schools, if you aren't in the top ten percent of your class, you are *dead*."

There was a collective sharp intake of breath at Ted's infelicitous choice of words. Miss Ferrell paled slightly and reached for a response.

"Well, the ranking may have some effect, but it also helps to have good grades showing your effort . . ."

"But what about a composite SAT score between 1550 and 1600?" prompted another student fiercely. "Don't you have to have that too?"

"I heard you had to play varsity soccer, basketball, and lacrosse," catcalled another, "and get the good sportsmanship award too."

There were whispers and shaken heads. Miss Ferrell gave her audience an unsmiling look that brought a hush.

"Look, people! I could tell you that the ideal applicant walks a minimum of six miles each way to school! That he's a volunteer vigilante on the subway! Is that going to make you feel better or worse about this process?"

"There's no subway in the mountains! Good or bad?"

Audrey Coopersmith decorously raised her hand. "I heard that the ideal applicant comes from a low-income single-parent family." Over the murmurs of protest, she raised her voice. "And I also heard that if the applicant's after-school job helps support the family financially, it shows character, and *that's* what top colleges are looking for."

Cries of "what?" and "huh!" brought another stern look from Miss Ferrell. Did Heather Coopersmith have an after-school job? I couldn't remember.

"That is one possible profile." Miss Ferrell drew her mouth into a rosebud of tiny wrinkles.

Hank Dawson raised his hand. "I heard that the top applicants had to do volunteer work. I don't think it's safe for Greer to hang around some soup kitchen with a bunch of welfare types."

"Nobody *has* to do anything," replied Miss Ferrell crisply. "We're looking for a fit between a student and a school. . . ."

Rhoda Marensky raised her hand. Her rings flashed. She'd draped her fur over her lap. "Is it appropriate for the applicant to discuss minority connections? I understand there is renewed interest in applicants with Slavic surnames."

Hank Dawson bellowed: "What a *crock*!"

Greer Dawson cried, "Daddy!" Caroline Dawson gave her husband and daughter a be-quiet look which made both droop obediently.

Macguire Perkins swiveled his long neck and smirked at his classmates. "I flunk. I quit. Guess I'll be at Elk Park forever. You can all come visit me here. There's no way any school's going to let me in."

"You've already demonstrated how not to get in," said Miss Ferrell quietly. There were snickers from the listeners, but I missed the joke. Miss Ferrell demanded of Macguire, "Did you write to Indiana? I asked you to have it ready by today, remember?"

"Yeah, yeah," he said under his breath.

"I would like you to share it with us, please."

"Oh, shit."

"Macguire, let's go."

Macguire grumbled and slapped through an untidy folder until he found some papers.

"Up here, please," commanded Miss Ferrell. "Now, everyone, quiet, please. As I've said numerous times, *honesty* and *creativity* are what we value in these essays. Parents"—she nodded meaningfully at the tense adults in the back of the room—"would do well to remember that."

Macguire groaned again. Then he unfolded his long

body from his desk and slouched to the front of the class, where he towered over the diminutive Miss Ferrell. The holes in his tight jeans showed muscled flesh. His oversize shirttails hung from beneath his sweatshirt. He gave a self-deprecating grin and blushed beneath his acne. It was painful.

Miss Ferrell warned, "If there is any disturbance during Macguire's presentation, the offender will be excused."

Macguire gave a beseeching look to the class. Then, reluctantly, he lifted several crumpled pages and started reading.

" 'I want to go to Indiana University because their basketball team needs me. I have always been a fan. I mean, you'd never catch me yelling at the TV during the NCAA finals, "Hoosier mother? Hoosier father?" ' "

Someone snickered. Macguire cleared his throat and continued.

" 'I'm using my essay to apologize for the way I acted when I came for my campus visit. And also to set the record straight.

" 'It started off because some of my basketball teammates from last year's senior class are at I.U., and they all pledged SAE. And also, I didn't get along with my campus host. I mean, in the real world we wouldn't have been friends, so why pretend? I'm just trying to explain how everything went so wrong, for which I am sincerely sorry.

" 'After my campus host and I parted company—I did *not* ditch him, as he claimed—I went over to SAE to see the guys. They were having a keg party and invited me to join in. I didn't want to be rude and I did sort of feel bad about the campus-host situation. So I thought, well, this time I would be polite.' "

The laughter grew louder. Macguire looked up. To Miss Ferrell, he said in a low voice, "I know you just said one page for the essay, but this is a long story. I had to add extra sheets."

"Just read," ordered Miss Ferrell. She gave the giggling mass of students a furious look. They fell silent.

" 'So anyway,' " Macguire resumed with a twitch of his lanky body, " 'there we were, and I was being polite and a good guest. Yes, I *know* I am underage, but as I said, I was trying to be *polite*. Now, after I was polite for all those hours, of course I couldn't find my way back to the dorm, because you've built all those buildings out of Indiana limestone, and to be perfectly honest, they all look alike. While I was lost I was real sorry I had dumped my campus host.

" 'I did finally find the dorm, and I am truly sorry for the guy on the first floor whose window I had to knock on so he could let me in. He was mad at me, but it wasn't *that* cold out, I mean I'd just been *lost* out there for over an hour, and *I* wasn't cold. So why should he have minded so much to come outside in his underwear? And why would you lock up the dorms on a Friday night, anyway? You must know people are going to stay out late partying.' "

I looked around. All the senior parents looked somewhat shellshocked. Macguire plunged on. " 'I don't want to be, like, too graphic, but my college counselor is always telling us to write an *honest* essay. So to be perfectly honest, after I passed out for a couple of hours I woke up and had to puke. It was an overwhelming urge brought on by all that time I was being a good guest over at SAE, and you should be glad that I didn't ruin all that nice Indiana limestone outside my window but instead hauled ass down to the bathroom.

" 'After I hurled I felt better. I wanted to go right back to sleep so I could be on time for my interview the next morning and tell you how I helped bring Elk Park

Prep to the state finals in basketball with my three-point shots, and not have to listen to you ask me a bunch of questions about Soviet foreign policy. Okay, I told you in my letter that I did a paper on it my junior year, but who cares now? I mean, the world has *changed*.

" 'Anyway, at three A.M. I was in the bathroom ready to go back to bed. Here's an honest question: *Why do you put the exit to go back outside right next to the bathroom door?* So there I was again, outside, and not smelling too good this time, knocking again on that guy's window to be let in, and this time he was *pissed*.

" 'You know really, now that I look back on it, he didn't have to get that ticked off. It was Friday night! He didn't have classes the next day! But as I told you . . .' "

Macguire looked hopefully at Miss Ferrell. "You see, I'm not one of those guys who use bad grammar and say, Like I told you. That ought to count for something."

"Macguire! Read!"

Macguire cleared his throat and found his place. " 'I am sorry,' " he read. " 'I'm sorry to the guy in the underwear, I'm sorry for drinking when I was a minor, I'm sorry that when you asked me about Soviet foreign policy I said, *Who gives a shit?* and I'm sorry to my campus host, can't remember his name. You can tell him that if he wants to come out to Colorado, I'll show him a good time. Promise.' "

The applause from the students was immediate and deafening. The parents sat in stunned silence. Macguire, flushed with pleasure, gave the class a broad smile. I began to clap too, until I saw Miss Ferrell's frown. My hands froze in mid-clap. She rapped on her desk until she had quiet. "Can I go back to my desk?" implored Macguire.

"You *may* not. I will talk to you later about that . . . essay. Meanwhile, I want you and Greer Dawson to sit down and role-play an interview. Greer will be the director of admissions at . . . hmm . . . Vassar. Macguire, you will be the applicant."

Macguire slumped unhappily into a chair while Greer Dawson walked primly to the front of the room. Today she was dressed like an L.L. Bean ad: impeccable white turtleneck, navy cardigan, Weejuns, and a tartan skirt. Being paired with Macguire Perkins obviously annoyed her. Miss Ferrell directed her to the desk at the front, then crossed her arms. Macguire gave Greer a goofy look. Greer closed her eyes and exhaled deeply. It seemed to me that Macguire would be better off auditioning with Barnum and Bailey than trying to go to I.U., but I was not in the college advisement business.

Thank God.

"Gee," said Macguire in a deep voice. He tilted his head and eyed Greer lovingly. "I'd really like to go to Vassar now that it's coed. I want to watch the Knicks play in New York and I can't get into Columbia." Laughter erupted from the gallery.

"Miss Ferrell!" protested Greer with a shake of her straight, perfectly cut blond hair. "He's not taking this seriously!"

"I am too!" said Macguire. "I really, really want to go to your school, Hammer, uh"—he opened his eyes wide at Greer and she *tsk*ed—"Miss Dawson."

Miss Ferrell gestured to Greer to continue.

Greer's sigh was worthy of any martyr. "I understand you are interested in basketball, Macguire, and foreign relations. We have a year-abroad program, as you know. Does that interest you?"

"Not that much," drawled Macguire, his mouth sloped downward. "I really hate Spanish, and German is too hard. What interests me is your coed dorms. I did my senior thesis on sexual liberation."

"Macguire, please!" cried Miss Ferrell over the

squeals of amusement. "I told you not to talk about sex, religion, or politics!"

"Oh, God, fuck, I'm sorry, Miss Ferrell . . . well, I don't care about politics anyway."

"Mac-guire!"

"Well, I don't want to go to Vassar anyway," he whined. "I can't get into Stanford or Duke. I just want to go to Indiana."

"Yes, and we've all seen just how likely that's going to be," snapped Miss Ferrell. "Let's get two more people up here. Julian Teller," she said, pointing, "and Heather Coopersmith. What school interview do you want to role-play, Julian?"

Julian shuffled between the desks. He flopped into the chair formerly occupied by Macguire, ran his hand nervously through his mowed hair, and said, "Cornell, for food science."

"All right," said Miss Ferrell. "Heather," she said to Audrey's daughter, a dark-haired girl with her mother's face, pink-tinted glasses, and thin, pale lips, "let him ask the questions."

"This is not fair." Greer Dawson was miffed. "I didn't really get a chance."

"That's true, she didn't," piped up her father.

"You will, you will," said Miss Ferrell dismissively. "This is a learning experience for everybody—"

"But the period's almost over!" Greer cried.

Miss Ferrell opened her eyes wide. The sherbet-colored dress trembled. "Sit *down,* Greer. All right, Julian, what are you going to ask Heather about Cornell?"

From the gallery came the cry, "Ask her about home ec! Can I learn to be a smart caterer here?"

Julian flushed a painful shade. My heart turned over.

Julian touched his tongue to his top lip. "I don't want to do this now."

The exasperated Miss Ferrell surrendered. "All right, go back to your desks, everybody." During the ensuing chair-scraping and body-squishing, she said, "People, do you think this is some kind of joke?" She put her hands on her sherbet-clad hips. "I'm trying to help you." She panned the classroom. She looked like a Parisian model who had been told to do *peeved.* And the class was taking her about that seriously.

To my great relief, the bell rang. Miss Ferrell called out, "Okay, drafts of personal essays before you leave, people!" I fled to a corner to avoid the press of jostling teenage bodies. By the time everybody had departed, Miss Ferrell was slapping papers around on her desk, looking thoroughly disgusted.

"Quel dommage," I said, approaching her. *What a pity.*

"Oh! I didn't see you here." She riffled papers on top of her roll book. "It's always like this until a few days before the deadlines. What can I help you with? Did you come to see me? There's no French Club today."

"No, I was here to see the headmaster. Forgive me, I just wanted to drop in because, actually, Arch loves French Club. But he's having trouble with his school-work—"

She looked up quickly. "Did you hear about this morning?" She drew back, her tiny body framed by a rumpled poster of the Eiffel Tower on one side and a framed picture of the Arc de Triomphe on the other. When I shook my head, she walked with a *tick-tock* of little heels over to the door and closed it. "You've talked to Alfred?"

"Yes," I said. "Mr. Perkins told me about Arch. About his academic and . . . social problems." Come to think of it, he'd only mentioned the schoolwork mess.

"Did he tell you about this morning?"

"No," I said carefully, "just that Arch was flunking a class." *Just.*

"This is worse than that."

"Worse?"

Miss Ferrell eyed me. She seemed to be trying to judge whether I could take whatever it was she had to say.

I asked, "What happened to Arch this morning?"

"We had an assembly. The student body needed to know about Keith." Her abrupt tone betrayed no feeling. "When it was over, I'm sorry to say Arch had a rather strenuous disagreement with someone."

I closed my eyes. For being basically a kind and mature kid, Arch seemed to be getting into quite a few disagreements lately. I wondered what "rather strenuous" meant. "Who was it, do you know? We've just had someone throw a rock through one of our windows, and maybe . . ."

"Later Arch came and told me he'd gotten into a fight with a seventh-grader, a boy who is frequently in trouble. The other boy apparently said Keith was a tattler. Puzzling . . . most seventh-graders don't even know seniors."

"Is that all?"

"No. When Arch arrived at his locker, he found a nasty surprise. I went to check and . . . there was something there. . . ."

"What?"

"You'd better let me show you. I put my own lock on the locker, so it should be undisturbed."

She peeked out into the hallway. The students had settled into the new class period, so we were able to make it down to the row of seventh-grade lockers without being seen.

Miss Ferrell minced along just in front of me. Her

bright red scarf fluttered behind her like a flag. She fiddled expertly with the clasp on Arch's locker. "I told him to leave it alone and the janitor would clean it out. But I don't know what to do about the paint."

What I saw first was the writing above Arch's locker. Block letters in bright pink pronounced: HE WHO WANTS TO BE A TATTLER, NEXT TIME WILL FACE A LIVE . . .

Miss Ferrell opened the locker door. Strung up and hanging on the hook was a dead rattlesnake.

6

It was all I could do to keep from screaming. "What happened when Arch saw this?"

When Miss Ferrell did not answer immediately, I whacked the locker next to Arch's. The snake's two-foot-long body swayed sickeningly. It had been strung up just under its head, and hung on the hook where Arch's jacket should have gone. I couldn't bear to look at the expanse of white snake-belly, at the ugly, crimped mouth, at those rattles at the end of the tail.

Miss Ferrell closed her eyes. "Since my classroom was nearby, he told me."

I felt dizzy. I leaned against the cold gray metal of the adjacent locker. More quietly, I said, "Was he okay? Did he get upset?"

She shook her head. I recognized generic teacherly sympathy. "Of course he was a bit shaken up. I told the headmaster."

"Yes, right." Tears burned at the back of my eyes. I was furious at the crack in my voice. Hold it in, hold it in, I warned myself. "What did Perkins do? Why didn't he tell me about it this morning? What happens now?"

Suzanne Ferrell drew her mouth into a slight moue. Her topknot with its bright scarf bobbed forward. "Alfred . . . Mr. Perkins said that it was probably just one of those seventh-grade pranks. That we should ignore it."

Beg to differ, I said silently as I whirled away from Miss Ferrell and headed back to the headmaster's sumptuous office.

"Is he still in?" I demanded of the receptionist.

"On the phone. If you'll just take a se—"

I stalked past her.

"Excuse me, *sir*!" I barked as heartily as any marine. "I need to talk to you."

Perkins was staring at the oil painting of Big Ben, droning into his receiver. "Yes, Nell, we'll see you then. Okay, yes, great for everybody. We'll be like . . . underground bookworms who have come up to feast on—"

At that moment he registered my presence. Just for a fraction of a second he raised the bushy white eyebrows at me, and I knew Nell had hung up. No worm feast for her. Perkins finished lamely, ". . . feast . . . on volumes. Ta-ta." He replaced the receiver carefully, then laced his short fingers and studied me. There was a shadow of weariness in his pale eyes.

"Yes? Here to check on Friday night's event at the Tattered Cover? Or about the muffins and whatnot before the SATs? Or is it something else?"

"When you told me how my son was doing academically, you oddly *neglected* to mention that someone had left a threat, along with a dead *rattlesnake,* in his locker. And you say he's having a little trouble socially? You're not only the master of metaphor, Perkins, you're the emperor of euphemism."

His expression didn't change. He unthreaded his hands and opened his palms, a mannered gesture of helplessness. "If we had any idea—"

"Have you tried to find out? Or are you sticking with the environment-of-trust idea?"

"Mrs. Korman, in seventh grade—"

"First of all, Mrs. Korman is not my name. Second, you've just had a murder here, at your school, as a matter of fact in your home. Third, somebody threw a rock through our window the night of that murder. You can't dismiss that snake as a *prank*! This school is not a safe place!"

"Ah." He adjusted his glasses and pursed his lips. Portrait of pensive. The wild white hair gleamed like a clown's. "Goldy, isn't it? I do believe we have a safe environment here. Whatever happened to unfortunate Keith was . . . out of the ordinary."

I swallowed.

Headmaster Perkins drummed his fingers on the antique mahogany desk. "The kids," he mused aloud, "engage in this . . . alternative behavior . . . all the time. I refer to the reptile, of course. If we become authoritarian, they'll rebel with . . . more antisocial behavior, or with drugs. Look around you." His delicate hands indicated his elegantly appointed office. "Do you see any graffiti here? No one is rebelling. And that's because we make this school an environment where our students don't need to rebel."

"Thank you, Mr. Freud. Threats are worse than graffiti, don't you think? Maybe the kids rebel in ways you don't know. A murder, Mr. Headmaster. Rattlesnakes. Now, let's get back to it being *your* job to at least try to find out who—"

The headmaster waved this away. "No, no, no. That simply is not possible, Mrs. K—Goldy. We do not have a regimen of conduct, and we do not go after offenders. We encourage *responsibility*. This . . . reptile incident should be viewed as a challenge for your son, a social challenge. It is young Arch's responsibility to learn to cope with hostility. What I am trying to say to you, what I have to say to so many parents, is that we simply cannot legislate morality." Perkins gave me his patronizing grin. "And Mr. Freud is not my name, sorry to say."

Oh, cute. A social challenge. Can't legislate morality. I stood. At the door, I stopped.

"Tell me this, Mr. Perkins. Why exactly do you spend so much time and effort raising money for this school? And worrying about its precious reputation?"

"Because money is the"—he pondered for a moment, then spread his hands again—"money is the . . . yeast that . . . leavens this institution's ability to provide the best possible education. Our reputation is like our halo—"

"Is that right? Well. You can have a huge doughball of responsibility, Mr. Headmaster, sir, but without morality it's going to fall flat. Halos are elusive. Or, put another way, even a reptile knows when he's in the dirt. Ta-ta."

At home I forced my mind off the school and set it onto the penitential luncheon four days away, the bookstore reception that same Friday evening, and the SAT spread for Saturday morning. Thank God I was going to Schulz's for dinner. But not until I set some menus, ordered food, and had a heart-to-heart with Arch.

For the clergy luncheon I decided on triangles of toasted sourdough spread with pesto, followed by Sole Florentine with fruit salad. The original recipe for Sorry

Cake called for a rich batter developed to offer penance, my cookbook told me. The offender, a thirteenth-century French baker, had confessed to overcharging for bread. The local priest had ordered that the baker give away sweet cakes to all the villagers on Shrove Tuesday. Let the punishment fit the crime, I always say.

For the bookstore affair, there were soft ripened cheeses—Gorgonzola and Brie and Camembert—to order for the Volvo set and Chocolate-Dipped Biscotti to make for the young crowd. Better than trick-or-treat any day.

Which reminded me. Since I had to be at the school for the SATs very early in the morning after the bookstore reading, I'd have the pleasure of baking fresh corn, blueberry, and oat bran muffins at four A.M. Saturday. That ought to make me real sharp for dealing with lots of hungry, nervous seniors.

Arch traipsed in and groaned deeply, not a good sign. Over the summer Arch had fallen under Julian's spell. In the clothes arena this had meant eschewing sweatsuits and working to coordinate school outfits, holding pants up to the light to see if the color matched a shirt, trying on leather bomber jackets and baggy pants in our local used-clothing store until he resembled Julian as closely as possible. But the three shirts that Arch had carefully layered in hues of blue and gray this morning now hung in uneven tails over his gray cotton pants. His face was unnaturally pale; his eyes behind the glasses, bloodshot.

I said, "I saw the snake."

He slung his heavy bookbag across the kitchen floor. The bookbag, another new accoutrement, had replaced his elementary-school backpack. Not that the new books seemed to be getting a lot of use. Arch dropped heavily into one of the kitchen chairs. He did not look at me, and he was fighting the tremble in his bottom lip.

"Arch, do you have any idea who—"

"Mom, don't!"

"But I've been so worried! And that painted message! Tattle about what? What do you know that you could possibly tattle about?"

"Mom! Quit babying me!"

This would get us nowhere. I asked, "Where's Julian?" Since Arch no longer took the bus home, Julian was in the habit of driving him.

"Left me off and went to the newspaper office." He pushed the glasses up on his nose and released another sigh, as in, *You are so nosy*. "The *Mountain Journal*. Okay? Can I go now? I don't want a snack."

I ignored this. "Arch, I also need to talk to you about your grades—"

"Seventh grade is hard for everybody! Just let *me* worry about my grades!"

"*Are* you worried about your grades? Are the other kids doing this poorly?" I changed my tone. Try soft, I ordered myself. "Do you think we need to go back into therapy together?"

"Great! This is just *great*!" My son's thin face was pale and furious. "I come home after a horrible day and you're just going to make it more horrible!"

"I am not!" I hollered. "I want to help you!"

"Sure!" he screamed before he banged out. "It really sounds like it!"

So much for adolescent psychiatry. I looked at my watch: 4:45. Too early for a drink. I slapped bratwurst on a platter, cooked spinach and previously frozen home-made noodles for the boys' evening meal, wrote them a note on how to heat it all up, and wondered vaguely about the suicide statistics for *parents* of teenagers. But self-preservation as a single mother meant not dwelling on such notions. If things got worse, I promised myself, we would

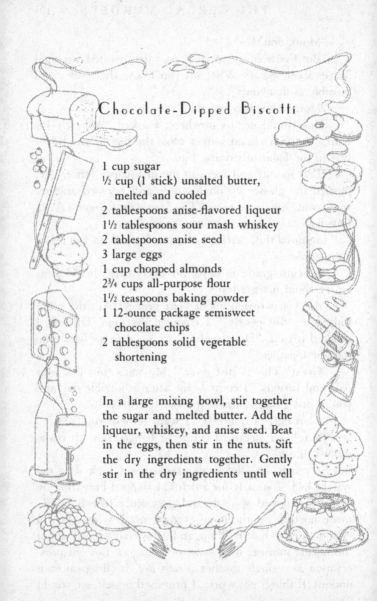

Chocolate-Dipped Biscotti

1 cup sugar
1/2 cup (1 stick) unsalted butter,
  melted and cooled
2 tablespoons anise-flavored liqueur
1 1/2 tablespoons sour mash whiskey
2 tablespoons anise seed
3 large eggs
1 cup chopped almonds
2 3/4 cups all-purpose flour
1 1/2 teaspoons baking powder
1 12-ounce package semisweet
  chocolate chips
2 tablespoons solid vegetable
  shortening

In a large mixing bowl, stir together
the sugar and melted butter. Add the
liqueur, whiskey, and anise seed. Beat
in the eggs, then stir in the nuts. Sift
the dry ingredients together. Gently
stir in the dry ingredients until well

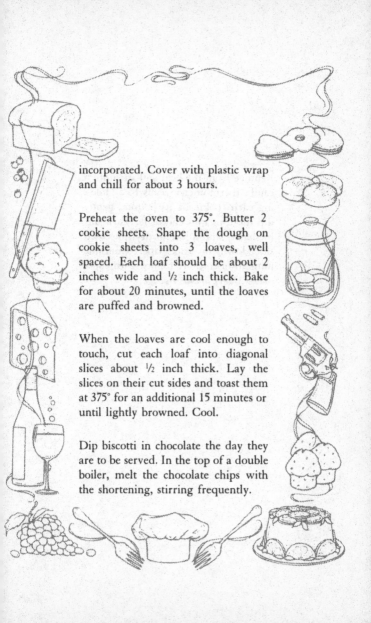

incorporated. Cover with plastic wrap and chill for about 3 hours.

Preheat the oven to 375°. Butter 2 cookie sheets. Shape the dough on cookie sheets into 3 loaves, well spaced. Each loaf should be about 2 inches wide and ½ inch thick. Bake for about 20 minutes, until the loaves are puffed and browned.

When the loaves are cool enough to touch, cut each loaf into diagonal slices about ½ inch thick. Lay the slices on their cut sides and toast them at 375° for an additional 15 minutes or until lightly browned. Cool.

Dip biscotti in chocolate the day they are to be served. In the top of a double boiler, melt the chocolate chips with the shortening, stirring frequently.

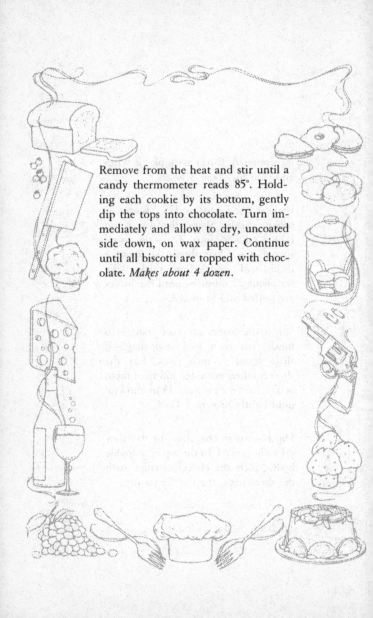

Remove from the heat and stir until a candy thermometer reads 85°. Holding each cookie by its bottom, gently dip the tops into chocolate. Turn immediately and allow to dry, uncoated side down, on wax paper. Continue until all biscotti are topped with chocolate. *Makes about 4 dozen*.

take the therapy route again. Arch had not, after all, thrown his own rock or strung up his own snake.

Being in a temper made me think I'd better keep busy. I cut butter into flour and swirled in buttermilk, caraway seeds, raisins, and eggs to make a thick speckled batter for Irish Soda Bread. This I poured into a round pan and set to bake while I nipped off to soak in a steaming bubble bath. Great-tasting bread and a great-smelling caterer. What else could Tom Schulz want?

Better not think about that, either.

When the bread was done, I began to wrap myself in a down coat, mittens, and earmuffs. After a two-day respite, thick, smoke-colored clouds had poured over the mountains. During the afternoon, the mercury had dropped fifteen degrees. The red sunrise was proving its warning. Flakes drifted down as I emerged from my front door. The icy wind made me hug the warm, fragrant round of Irish bread to my chest. I was thankful to see Julian chug up our street. Without telling him where I was going, I begged him for the four-wheel-drive Range Rover. I could just imagine myself facing a sudden blizzard and then saying to Schulz, "Oops, guess I'll have to spend the night."

Right.

Turning the Rover around sounded and felt like an advanced tank maneuver. But once I had managed it, I headed toward Main Street through the thickening snow and began to reflect on my relationship with the homicide investigator.

Being with Schulz was like . . . I smiled as I put the Rover into third and skittered through a channel of

Irish Soda Bread

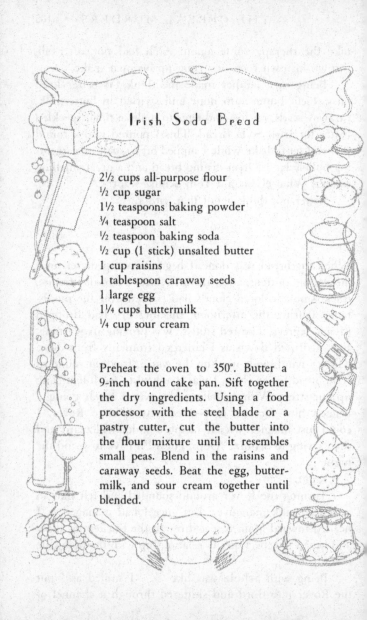

2½ cups all-purpose flour
½ cup sugar
1½ teaspoons baking powder
¾ teaspoon salt
½ teaspoon baking soda
½ cup (1 stick) unsalted butter
1 cup raisins
1 tablespoon caraway seeds
1 large egg
1¼ cups buttermilk
¼ cup sour cream

Preheat the oven to 350°. Butter a 9-inch round cake pan. Sift together the dry ingredients. Using a food processor with the steel blade or a pastry cutter, cut the butter into the flour mixture until it resembles small peas. Blend in the raisins and caraway seeds. Beat the egg, buttermilk, and sour cream together until blended.

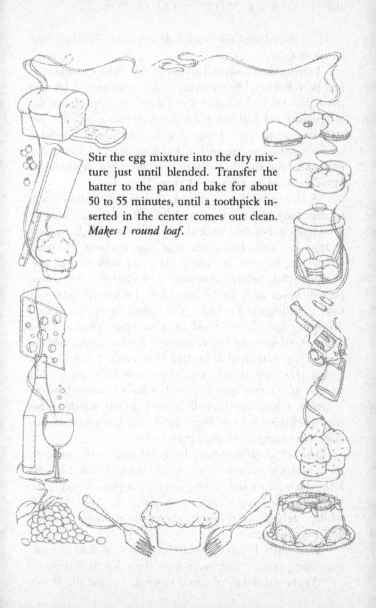

Stir the egg mixture into the dry mixture just until blended. Transfer the batter to the pan and bake for about 50 to 55 minutes, until a toothpick inserted in the center comes out clean. *Makes 1 round loaf.*

mud on the edge of the road. *Like what, Mr. Perkins? Like an enigma, sir.*

During the emotional stages of my divorce, numbness had been followed by hatred and then resentment. During that time I'd had neither the energy nor the desire for relationships. I had forsworn marriage, for ever and ever and ever. And since I was a good and faithful Sunday school teacher, swearing off marriage didn't leave many options in the fulfilling physical relationship department. Which was okay with me. I thought.

A strange thing happened, though, after the cocoon of animosity had worn off and John Richard had become merely an annoyance to deal with on a weekly basis. *Not so strange,* Marla had insisted at our frequent meetings where we, his two ex-wives, discussed addiction to unhealthy relationships. Anyway, I began to have unexpected waves of Sexual Something. I'd met Schulz, but kept my distance. I'd had a short-lived, nonphysical (but disastrous nonetheless) crush on a local psychologist. Then when Arch gave up his swimming lessons at the athletic club, I was surprised to realize how much I would miss his coach's easy smile. And there had been Arch's art teacher at the elementary school, whom I had helped on occasion. I had unexpectedly found myself watching his trim backside as he walked slowly from student to student, correcting their drawings.

Shame! Marla had teased me. Of course, she suffered from no such compunctions. Marla insisted that after the Jerk, she was not only giving up on marriage forever, she was going to have a great time doing so. And she had, while I felt guilty thinking about the swimming coach and the art teacher.

And then I met Schulz. Schulz, who had a commanding presence and green eyes the color of seawater.

As the fat flakes of snow swirled, I eased the Rover

into fourth and remembered a time during the summer when I had driven out of town alone to Tom Schulz's cabin. "Cabin" was much too diminutive a word for Schulz's stunning two-story home built of perfectly notched logs. He had bought it at an IRS auction after a locally famous sculptor had been caught for back taxes. Now, while the sculptor was carving license plates in a federal penitentiary, Schulz could leave the crises of the sheriff's office behind to retreat to his remote haven with its rocks and aspens and pines, its panoramic view of the Continental Divide.

On that night four months before, Schulz had fixed me an absolutely spectacular dinner that had helped get my mind off the crises of the moment, which included that ill-fated trademark-infringement lawsuit instigated by Three Bears Catering in Denver. Having the last name *Bear* had never been more trying. The same evening, our conversation had turned serious when Schulz had told me about his one and only fiancée. Twenty years earlier, she had served as a nurse in Vietnam. She'd been killed during an artillery shelling. Arch made an unexpected appearance after Schulz revealed this aspect of his past, and personal conversation had ended abruptly when our dinner for two became a cookout for three.

It was not long after this that the homicide investigator had asked me if I'd like to get rid of a whole bunch of problems by changing my last name to Schulz. He'd taken my negative answer with a heartbreaking look.

No matter how much I enjoyed Schulz, the memory of the emotional black hole within my marriage to John Richard still remained. Many of my single women friends complained of loneliness, now that they were divorced. But my worst experience of loneliness, of lovelessness, of complete abandonment, had come when I was married. For that I blamed the institution, and not the man. Intellectually, I knew this was wrong. Still, emotionally, I never wanted to get into another situation where it was even *possible* to feel that low.

I put the Range Rover back into third and chugged my way through deep slush on the dirt road. I thought back, involuntarily, to John Richard and his showers of blows, to the punch to my ear that had sent me reeling across the kitchen, to the way I screamed and beat my hands against the floor. I started to tremble.

Pulling the Rover to the side of the road, I rolled down the window. Take it easy, girl. The snow made a soft, whooshing sound as it fell. Listening to it, feeling the chilled air and the occasional icy flake on my face, chased away the ugly memories. I looked out at the whitened landscape, breathing deeply. And then my eye caught something on the road, half covered with snow.

It was a dead deer. I turned away immediately. It was an unbearable sight, and yet something you saw all the time here, deer and elk smashed by cars going too fast to swerve away. Sometimes the cracked and bloodied carcasses lay by the side of the road for days, their open, huge brown eyes causing pain to any who cared to be caught in that sightless gaze.

Oh, God, why had I been the one to find Keith Andrews? Had he, too, had that experience of thinking he was loved and admired? The black hole of hatred had come over him so suddenly, so prematurely, and now his parents were en route back from Europe to bury him. . . .

Involuntarily, I thought of my heart as I had imagined it after John Richard. It was an organ torn in half, a rent, ripped, and useless thing. My heart would never be healed, I had become convinced; it would just lie forever like an animal by the side of the road, smashed and dead.

Oh, get a grip! I revved the engine and recklessly gunned the Rover off the shoulder and onto the road. An evening with Schulz didn't need to cause such emotive eruption. *You're just going there for dinner, Goldy. You can handle it.*

7

When I pulled into his dirt driveway, Schulz was kneeling on the ground. Despite the weblike layer of new snow, he was spading soil energetically by the irregular flagstone walk that led to his front door.

"Hi there." I climbed carefully out of the Rover with the loaf of Irish bread. The image of the fallen deer still haunted me: I didn't trust myself to say anything else.

He turned and stood. Clods of wet soil clung to his jeans and jacket. "What's wrong?"

"I'm sorry, please finish what you're doing. I just—" My voice wobbled. Damn. The words were tumbling out; I was shaking my head, appalled at how shaken I was. "I just saw a dead animal by the side of the road and it reminded me . . . no, no, please," I said as he started to move toward me. "Please finish what you were doing."

He regarded me with one eye crinkled in appraisal. After a moment he crouched down again. "It never will leave you," he said without looking at me. "Seeing a real dead body is nothing like the movies." His large, capable fingers reached for a handful of bulbs and carefully pressed them at intervals into the newly spaded trough. Gently he refilled the area with potting soil from a bag. The gesture reminded me of putting a blanket around a sleeping child.

I breathed lungfuls of the sharp air. I hugged the fragrant bread. Although I wore a down coat, it felt as if my blood had stopped circulating.

"Cold?" Schulz asked. "Need to go in?" I shook my head. "I'm sorry you were the one who had to find him," he said gruffly. He finished patting down the soil, rose easily, and put an arm around my shoulders. "Come on, I made you some nachos. Then I need you to look at something."

We came through his sculpted-wood door and entered the large open space that was his living room. I stopped to admire the moss-rock fireplace that reached up two stories between rough-hewn mortared logs. A carefully set pile of aspen and pine logs lay in the grate. On one Shaker-style table was a pot Arch had made at the end of sixth grade. On a wall was an Arch-made woodcut print of a .45, the kind Schulz carried. A pickled-oak hutch held a display of Staffordshire plates and Bavarian glass. The sparse grouping of an antique sink and a cupboard between the sofa and chairs upholstered in nubby brown wool gave the place a homey feel. When I had complimented Schulz on his good taste during my last visit, he had replied without missing a beat: "Of course. Why d'you think I'm courting you?"

I moved away from that thought and arrived in the kitchen just as he was pulling an au gratin casserole out of the oven. The platter was heaped with sizzling corn chips,

Nachos Schulz

1 15-ounce can chili beans in chili
    gravy
9 tablespoons picante sauce
1 15-ounce bag corn tortilla chips
4 cups grated cheddar cheese
1 avocado
1 tablespoon fresh lemon juice
1½ cups sour cream
1 tablespoon grated onion
4 scallions, both white and green
    parts, chopped
1 cup pitted black olives, chopped
1 tomato, chopped

Preheat the oven to 400°. Mash the
beans with ½ cup of the picante sauce
until well mixed. Grease 2 9- by 13-
inch pans. Place half the chips in each
pan, then spoon the bean mixture over
them. Sprinkle the grated cheese on
top. Bake for about 10 minutes or un-

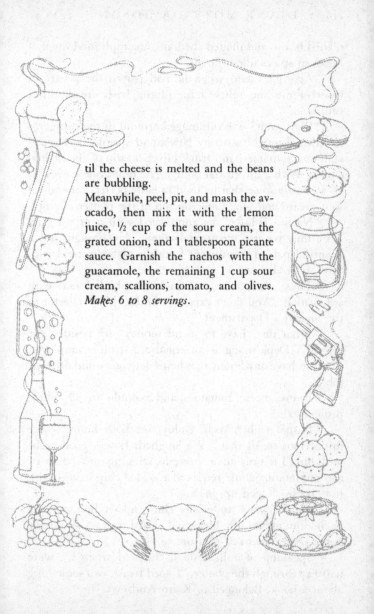

til the cheese is melted and the beans are bubbling.

Meanwhile, peel, pit, and mash the avocado, then mix it with the lemon juice, ½ cup of the sour cream, the grated onion, and 1 tablespoon picante sauce. Garnish the nachos with the guacamole, the remaining 1 cup sour cream, scallions, tomato, and olives. *Makes 6 to 8 servings.*

refried beans, and melted cheddar. A complicated smell of Mexican spices filled the air.

"Agony," I said when he had placed the platter in front of me and relieved me of the Irish bread. But I smiled.

"Wait, wait." He rummaged around in the refrigerator, then brought out tiny bowls and sprinkled chopped scallions, tomatoes, and black olives on top of the melted cheese. With a directorial flourish, he brandished—yes!— an *ice cream scoop* that he used to ladle perfect mounds of sour cream and guacamole on top of the platter of chips.

"Nachos Schulz," he announced with a proud grin. "For this, we use the special china." He brought out a beautiful pair of translucent Limoges plates painted with tiny, stylized roses.

"These must have set you back a bit," I said with admiration. "You don't expect to find a china collector in the Sheriff's Department."

"What do I have to spend money on? Besides, the Sheriff's Department is an equal-opportunity employer. You can have any hobby that helps get your mind off your job."

"Beans, cheese, tomatoes, and avocado are all aphrodisiac foods."

"Is that right? Well, Goldy, we both know you're impervious to all that." We laughed. It was good to be with him; I felt my anxiety recede. Digging into the Mexican mountain, Schulz retrieved a loaded chip stringy with hot cheese. "Open up, ma'am."

I held a plate under my chin and let him pop the nacho into my mouth. Heaven. I closed my eyes and made appropriate moans of pleasure.

"Speaking of aphrodisiacs," he said when we were halfway through the platter, "I need to ask you something about a book. Belonged to Keith Andrews."

"Oh, that reminds me . . ." I handed him the rock that had broken our upstairs window, then the Neiman-Marcus credit card. I had put the rock in a plastic bag; Schulz eyed it, turned it over in his big hands, then laid it carefully aside. Between bites he studied the credit card, ran his fingers over the letters and numbers, then pocketed it without indicating what he was thinking. He put a last chip into his mouth and slid off his barstool all in one motion. When I hesitated, he gestured for me to follow.

Like many of the more rustic homes in the mountains, Schulz's did not have a garage. I put on my coat and followed him outside to his car, where he opened the trunk and carefully emptied out a plastic bag onto some more plastic.

"Look but don't touch," he warned.

Not knowing what this was about or why I was doing it, I peered in and saw a jumble of papers, pens, and half-eaten pencils; Stanford, Columbia, and Princeton catalogues and pamphlets; a few books—a German-English dictionary, *Faust,* as well as the Cliff's Notes for same; *Professor Romeo* and *Aceing the ACT;* several old copies of the *Mountain Journal,* and some frayed articles held together with staples.

"What's all this?"

"Stuff from the trunk of Keith Andrews' car. You probably didn't notice his old Scirocco over in the corner of the parking lot at the school. I've got custody of this stuff until tomorrow. His locker had more textbooks and some papers, but given that he was a supposed computer whiz, it's odd we can't find any disks. The department's checking the locker contents out. No credit cards or bills, though, we know that."

"Why show me?"

He leaned against the trunk lid and looked up at the dark clouds. After a moment he shook his head. "I don't understand that school. I talk and talk to people and nothing comes up. The kid was smart, but not well liked. He worked hard on extracurricular activities, but nobody admired him for it. He brought back postcards from Paris for the whole French Club, and according to Arch, nobody thanked him. His windshield got broken, but by whom? Somebody hated him enough to kill him by bashing in his head. It doesn't sound like the supportive school community the headmaster is trying to convince me it is."

"His windshield got broken? When? What do you mean, according to *Arch*?"

"I talked to Arch this morning. He called me about some snake in his locker."

I shook my head. Unbelievable. Why not just label myself obsolete?

"Anyway," Schulz was saying, "Arch told me what I'd already heard from a parent, that Dawson fellow, that Julian and Keith Andrews had had some kind of argument a few weeks ago. I guess things got kind of out of hand. Keith's windshield ended up getting shattered, but not at the time of the argument."

"When, then?" Why didn't Julian ever tell me things like this?

"Before one of the bigwig college reps showed up at the school, is what I was told." He paused. "Do you think Julian's ashamed of being raised without money, his parents down in Utah, him having to work for and live with you his senior year, anything like that? Something Keith Andrews could have made fun of?"

"Not that I know of," I said firmly. Julian's financial situation caused him pain, but he had never mentioned students' ridiculing him for it. "I do think they had a girlfriend dispute," I said lamely. "Remember, Julian told us about it."

"This argument was different. This took place last

week in front of the *Mountain Journal* offices. Arch was in the Rover, didn't hear the whole thing, said that it had something to do with schools. Seems Julian was worried that Keith was going to write something negative about Elk Park Prep, when everyone was uptight enough already about the college application process. All they can say over at the paper was that Keith was doing some kind of exposé. They were going to read it before they decided whether or not to print it."

"Exposé about what?"

"About Elk Park Prep, I think." He gestured at the stuff in the trunk. "About test scores. About using Cliff's Notes. About a professor who thinks he's a Romeo. About taxes, for God's sake." Before I could ask him what he meant by that, he picked up a typed letter that had been done on perforated computer-printer paper. The letter looked like a draft. Words had been crossed out and new words hand-printed above. *Mr. Marensky,* it read, *I'd be more than happy to pay you your two hundred dollars if you'd call the director of admissions at Columbia for me. Or maybe you'd prefer I call the IRS?* IRS had a line through it, and *Internal Revenue Service* had been neatly written above it.

"I don't get it."

Schulz shrugged. "Stan Marensky had Keith do some yardwork for him. Marensky gave Keith a check for six hundred dollars for a four-hundred-dollar job with the agreement that Keith would refund him two hundred in cash. That way, Marensky could claim a six-hundred-dollar expense on his taxes. Petty thievery, not all that uncommon, and Marensky owned up to it pretty quick."

"So much for Saint Andrews. This is a pretty dark side. Maybe it explains why he wasn't universally liked. I mean, an exposé? Blackmailing a powerful parent?"

Schulz's hand grasped the trunk lid, making it creak. "Well, Marensky thought the blackmail was a joke, since he'd gone to Columbia so many years ago, and didn't have any influence there. He says. Claims he never got his two hundred dollars back. I asked the headmaster about Marensky, and he said he was like a, a, now, let's see, what did he say . . ."

I punched Schulz lightly on the shoulder. "Don't." Looking down at the jumble of papers in the trunk, I shivered. "I can't look at this stuff anymore. Let's go have some of your shrimp enchiladas."

"You peeked."

"Hey! This is a caterer you're talking to! Every meal someone else slaves over is a spy mission."

"Just tell me if you know whether Julian and Keith had any real animosity. Before I question Julian again myself. You think he'd break somebody's windshield?"

"He's got some hostility, but I doubt he'd do that."

"Do you know whether any of the teaching staff were Romeos?"

I felt my voice rising. "No! I don't! Gosh, what is the matter with that school? I wish I *could* find out what's going on."

"Well, you're doing those dinners for them. You hear stuff. I want to know about anything that sounds strange, out of place."

"Look, this murder happened at a dinner I was catering! It's my window that was broken and my son's locker that was vandalized! For crying out loud, Tom, the Andrews boy even *looked* like Arch. You think I want my kid in a school with a murderer on the loose? I have a stake in finding out what's going on out there. Believe me, I'll keep you informed."

He tilted his head and regarded me beneath the tent-like brows. "Just don't go off half cocked, Miss G."

"Oh, jeez, give me a break, will you? What do you think I am, some kind of petty criminal?"

Schulz took large steps ahead of me back to the house. "Who, you? The light of my life? The fearless breaker-and-enterer? You? Never!"

"You are so awful." I traipsed after him, unsure how I felt to be called the light of anyone's life.

Schulz settled me at his cherrywood dining room table, and then began to ferry out dishes. He had outdone himself. Plump, succulent shrimp nestled inside blue corn tortillas smothered with a green chile and cream cheese sauce. Next to these he served bacon-sprinkled refried black beans, a perfectly puffed Mexican corn pudding, and my fragrant Irish bread. A basket of raw vegetables and pot of picante made with fresh papaya graced the table between the candles. I savored it all. When was the last time I'd enjoyed an entire dinner that I had not exhausted myself preparing? I couldn't remember.

"Save room for chocolate," Schulz warned when the room had grown dark except for the candlelight flickering across his face.

"Not to worry."

Twenty minutes later, I was curled up on his couch. Schulz lit the enormous pile of logs. Soon the snap and roar of burning wood filled the air. Schulz retreated to the kitchen and returned with cups of espresso and a miniature chocolate cake.

I groaned. "It's a good thing I'm not prone to jealousy. I'd say you were a better cook than I am."

"Not much chance of that." He had turned on his outside light and was peering into the night. "Darn. It's stopped snowing."

So we had had the same thought. Once again I veered away from this emotional territory, the way you leap onto a makeshift sidewalk when the sign says HARD HATS ONLY!

Schulz wordlessly cut the cake and handed me a generous slice of what was actually two thin layers of fudge cake separated by a fat wedge of raspberry sherbet. Unlike my ex-husband, who had always had a vague notion that I liked licorice (I detest it), Schulz invariably served chocolate—my weakness.

Of course, the cake was exquisite. When it was reduced to crumbs, I licked my fingers, sighed, and asked, "Does Keith Andrews' family have money?"

He shrugged and leaned over to turn off the light. "Yes and no." He picked up my hand and ran his fingers over it lightly. The same gesture he had used with the credit card, I remembered. "Thought any more about my name-change offer?"

"Yes and no."

He let out an exasperated chuckle. "Wrong answer."

The firelight flickered over his sturdy body, over his hopeful, inviting face, and into eyes dark with a caring I wasn't quite willing to face.

"Goldy," he said. He smiled. "I care. Believe it?"

"Yeah. Sure. But . . . aren't you . . . don't you . . . think about all that's happened? You know, your nurse?"

"Excuse me, Miss G., but it's *you* who lives in the past." He took both of my hands in his, lifted them, and kissed them.

"I do *not* live in the past." My protest sounded weak. "And I have the psychotherapy bills to prove it."

He leaned in to kiss me. He caught about half of my mouth, which made us both laugh. The only sounds in the room were fire crackle and slow breaths. For a change, I was at a loss for words.

Without unlocking his eyes from mine, Schulz slipped one hand to the small of my back and inscribed gentle circles there. How I wanted to be loved again.

I said, "Oh, I don't know . . ."

"You do care about me, don't you?"

"Yes."

And I did, too. I loved having this beautiful meal, this hissing fire, this lovely man whose touch now made me shiver after all the years of self-righteous celibacy. The wax from the lit red candles on the dining table melted, dripped, and spiraled. I took Schulz's hands. They were rough, big hands, hands that every day, in ways I could only imagine, probed questions about life and death and feeling morally grounded in your actions. I smiled, lifted my hands to his face, and corrected the angle of his head so that when I brought his lips to mine, this time they would fit exactly.

We made love on his couch, our clothes mostly on, in a great shuddering hurry. Then, tenderly, he put his hands around my waist and said we should go upstairs. On the staircase, with my loosened clothes more or less falling around me, one of his hands caught me by the hip and pressed me into the wall. And this time he did not miss when his warm mouth found mine.

His log-paneled bedroom with its high-pitched ceiling had the inviting scent of aftershave and pinewood. Schulz handed me a thick, soft terry-cloth robe. He lit a kerosene lamp next to his hewn four-poster. The flame lit us and the bed, leaving the far reaches of the room deep in shadow. Beneath my bare feet the wood floor felt creamy-cold. I slipped between cool cotton sheets, keeping the robe on.

He bent toward me. "You all right?"

"I am very all right."

Schulz's body depressed the mattress next to me when he slid between the sheets and I involuntarily slid toward him. The sensation was odd after five years of sleeping alone. He pulled the down comforter around my shoulders and whispered, "I love you now and forever and ever."

I couldn't help it. Tears slid out of my eyes. My breath raked across the back of my throat. He hugged me tightly and I mumbled into his warm shoulder, "Thank you. Thank you," as his fingers tenderly worked their way under the robe.

This time the caresses were slow and lingering, so that the great heaving release took us by surprise. Just as I was drifting off to sleep, I saw Schulz, somewhere in my mind's eye, take my ripped carcass of a heart and gently, gently begin sewing.

I woke up with a start sometime in the middle of the night. I thought: *I have to get home, God, this is incredible.* Schulz and I had rolled apart. I turned to look at his face and the shape of his body in the moonlight streaming through the uncurtained window. His cheeks were slack, like a child's; his mouth was slightly open. I kissed his eyelids. They were like the velvety skin of new peaches. His eyes opened. He propped himself up on an elbow. "You okay? Need to go? Need some help?"

"Yes, I need to go, but no thanks, I don't need help." And I was fine. For a change.

I dressed quickly, gave Schulz a long, wordless hug, and hightailed it toward home in the Rover. It was just past midnight. The snow had stopped and the clouds had parted. The moon shone high and bright in the sky, a pure white crescent. The clean, cold air gushing through the car windows was incomparably sweet. I felt wonderful, light-headed, lighthearted, giddy. I steered the Rover with one hand and laughed. An enormous weight had lifted from me; I was floating.

Unfortunately, my hope of sneaking quietly to bed was not to be realized. When I pulled up curbside, it was my house, and mine alone on the snow-covered street, that shone like a beacon. Lights blazed from every window.

"*Where* have you been?" Julian accused when I came through the security system.

The house reeked of cigarette smoke. Julian had beer on his breath. He looked horrid. His face was gray, his eyes bloodshot. His unwashed mohawk haircut stood up in tiny tepees.

"Don't tell me you had more trouble with someone throwing—" I began, stunned out of my idyll. When he shook his head, I said, "Never mind where I've been. What is going on here? You don't smoke. You're a swimmer, for God's sake! And what's with the beer breath, Mr. Underage?"

"I have been so worried!" Julian hollered as he slammed into the kitchen ahead of me.

So much for my great mood. What in heaven's name was going on? How had Julian gotten himself into such a state? I came home late all the time, although now I recalled belatedly that Julian and Arch usually checked the calendar to see where my catering assignment was on any given evening. Maybe Julian just wasn't used to not knowing where I was. On the other hand, maybe he was worried about something else. Stay calm, I resolved.

I followed him into the kitchen. "Where is Arch?" I said in a low voice.

"In bed," Julian tossed over his shoulder, and opened my walk-in refrigerator. Next to the sink were three glass beer bottles, empty, ready to be recycled. Three beers! I could be put in jail for allowing him to drink in my home.

Chinese stars were scattered over the financial aid books stacked on the gingham tablecloth. Chinese stars are sharp-edged metal stars about the size of an adult's palm, which is where you can hide them, I had once been told. I had learned about the weapons unexpectedly, when a boy at Arch's elementary school had been caught with them. The principal had sent the students home with a mimeographed note about the weapons. Used in Tae Kwon Do, Chinese stars were banned at the school because when thrown, the letter explained, they could inflict great damage. The fellow who had brought them to Furman Elementary School had been summarily suspended. Looking straight at Julian, I scooped them all up and placed them in a pile on the counter.

"What is going on?"

Julian emerged from the refrigerator. He held a platter of cookies. In times of stress, eat sweets.

He said, "I'm going to kill the kid who threatened Arch." So saying, he popped two cookies into his mouth and chewed voraciously.

"Really. If you have cookies on top of beer, you'll throw up."

He slammed the platter down. "Don't you even care? Do you realize he's not safe at that school?"

"Well, excuse me, Mr. Mom. Yes, I realize it. Mr. Perkins seems to think it's a joke, however. A seventh-grade joke." I took a cookie. "Arch called Schulz, though, and told him all about the snake."

Julian slapped his compact body down on a chair; he ran a hand through the sparse crop of hair. "Do you think we could hire a bodyguard for Arch? How much would that cost?"

I swallowed. "Julian. You are very protective and sweet. However. You are overreacting. A bodyguard is not the answer to Arch's problems."

"You don't know these people! They're vicious! They steal and cheat! Look at what they did to Keith!"

"*What* people?"

He squeezed his eyes shut. "You just don't get it. You're just . . . indifferent. The Elk Park Prep people, that's what people. Perkins is always talking about trust and responsibility. Two coats, a cassette, and forty dollars were stolen out of my locker last year. Trust? It's a crock."

"Okay. Look. Julian, please. I'm not indifferent. I agree with you that there's a problem. I just don't know what to do. But I can tell you a bodyguard is out of the question."

His eyes opened; he scowled. "I went to the newspaper because I know there's a snake lady in Aspen Meadow. You know, she comes into the schools and does demonstrations with live snakes. Maybe we can find out who got the rattler by contacting her, I know she sells them—"

"Julian! For heaven's sake!"

"Don't you understand what's at stake here? He's not safe! *None* of us is safe!"

With a third cookie halfway to my mouth, I gaped at him. "Couldn't you please cool off? The way to react to this is not to smoke, drink, pull out your weapons, and put the screws on the snake lady, okay?" I put the cookie back on the platter and took a deep breath. "Won't you please go up and get some sleep? You're going to need your energy, with that midterm tomorrow and the college boards right around the corner. I need to go to bed too," I added as an afterthought.

"Do you promise me you'll follow through with Schulz?"

"I'm way ahead of you, Julian."

He thought about that for a minute, then shot an accusing look at me. "You never told me where you were."

"Not that I need to answer to you, but I actually had *dinner* with Schulz. Okay?"

He glanced at the ceramic clock that hangs over my sink. One o'clock. "Kinda late for dinner, wouldn't you say?"

"Julian, go to bed."

8

My phone rang at seven o'clock. I groped for it.

"Goldilocks' Catering, Where Everything—"

"Ah, Goldy the caterer?" said Father Olson.

"Oh, Lord!" I gargled into the mouthpiece. "Who told you?"

"Er—"

"I mean, how could you have found out? It was just last night!"

"What?"

I pressed my face into my pillow and knew better than to speak. An awkward silence ensued while I involuntarily recalled the Sunday school teaching on sexual activity between single adults—". . . either single and celibate or married and faithful."

Oh well. The silence lengthened. Father Olson cleared his throat.

I sat up gingerly, wondering if priests were frequently greeted with early morning guilt. Maybe they learned to ignore it. After a minute, Father Olson resumed a normal tone. "I'm sorry to call so early, Goldy. Ahh . . . but I have an all-day clergy meeting in Denver, and I wanted to give you the final count on Friday's luncheon board meeting. There'll be twelve of us."

I swallowed hard. "Twelve. How biblical."

"Can you tell me the menu? Because of our theological discussion."

"Fish," I said succinctly.

When I didn't elaborate, he mumbled something that was not a blessing, and disconnected. The phone immediately rang again. I flopped back down on the mattress. Why me?

"Come to Aspen Meadow," intoned Marla's husky voice, "the promiscuity capital of the western United States."

I rolled over and peered blearily at the early morning grayness. Clouds shrouded the distant mountains like a woolen blanket.

"I don't know why George Orwell bothered to write *1984*. He obviously never had to live in a small town, where Big Brother is a fact of life."

"So you're not going to deny it?" Marla demanded.

"I'm not saying anything. Tell me why you're calling so early."

"In case you're wondering how I suspected that something was up, so to speak, my dear, I called your fellow I like so much, that teen housemate-helper—"

"His name is Julian."

"Yes, well, I called you numerous times last night and got young Julian, who, as I say, is somewhat more forthright than his employer. He said your calendar didn't show any catering assignments." She stopped to take a noisy bite of something. "When he still knew nothing at eleven, but was obviously quite besieged with worry, I thought, This is our early-to-bed, early-to-work much-beloved town caterer?" She took time out to chew, then added, "Besides, if you'd been in an accident, I would have heard before now."

"How reassuring. Marla, I have a full day of cooking ahead, and so—"

"Tut-tut, not so fast, tell me what's going on in your love life. I don't want to hear about it from anyone else."

Well, you're not going to hear about it from me, either. I laughed lightly and replied, "Everything you suspect is true. And more."

"From the wounded warrior, Miss Cut and Chaste? I don't think so."

"Look. I had dinner with Schulz. Let me reflect a little bit before I have to analyze the relationship to death, okay?"

That seemed to satisfy her. "All right. Go cook. But when you take a break, I have some real news for you concerning the Elk Park preppies. Unless you want it now, of course."

This was so typical of her. "Make it fast and simple," I said. "I haven't had any caffeine yet."

"Don't complain to me that you're still in bed, when you could be trying to figure out what's going on out at Colorado's premier prep school. All right—that German pseudo-academic guy out there? The one who wrote the Faust dissertation?"

"Egon Schlichtmaier. What about him?"

"He helped you with that dinner, right?"

"He did. I don't know much about him."

"Well, I do, because he's *single* and has therefore been the subject of the usual background investigation from the women in step aerobics."

I shook my head. How women at the Aspen Meadow

Athletic Club could manage to step up, down, and side-ways at dizzying speeds while trading voluminous amounts of news and gossip was one of the wonders of modern physiology. Yet it was done, regularly and enthusiastically.

I ordered, "Go ahead."

"Egon Schlichtmaier is twenty-seven years old," Marla rattled on, "but he and his family immigrated to this country when there was still a Berlin Wall, in the seventies. Despite his problems learning English, Herr Schlichtmaier got a good education, including a Ph.D. in literature from dear old C.U. in Boulder. But poor Egon was unable to get a college teaching job."

"So what else is new? I heard the ratio of humanities doctorates to available jobs is about ten to one."

"Let me finish. Egon Schlichtmaier is also extremely good-looking. He works out with weights and has a body to die for."

I conjured up a mental picture of the history teacher. He was short, which meant I could look right into his olive-toned baby face with its big brown eyes. He had curly black hair and long black eyelashes, and whenever I had seen him he had been wearing khaki pants, an ox-ford-cloth shirt in some pastel shade, and a fashionable jacket. Ganymede meets Ralph Lauren.

"What else?" The lack of coffee was beginning to get to me. Besides, and I was astonished that I even had this thought, Schulz might be trying to reach me.

"All right, here's the scoop . . . he was a teaching assistant at C.U., and he was caught having affairs with no less than *three* female undergraduates. *At the same time.* Which is his business, I guess, except that the word got around at the Modern Language Association convention. The universities, when they got wind of it, wouldn't offer him a job scrubbing floors. Seems they thought the last thing they needed was a prof who would cause trouble among tuition-paying undergraduates."

Since I was no longer what we would call pristine in the lust department, I avoided judgment. But three at a time? Consecutively or simultaneously? I said, "Did all the academics from coast to coast know these details?"

"The way I heard it, only the hiring schools knew." She chewed some more of whatever it was. "The headmaster at Elk Park Prep owed the head of the C.U. comparative literature department a favor from some kid the department chairman helped to get into C.U., so Perkins hired Egon Schlichtmaier as a kind of interim thing to teach U.S. history. Mind you, this was after he had fired another American history teacher, a Miss Pamela Samuelson, over some unknown scandal last year. This year Egon was supposed to keep looking for a college teaching job."

"Miss Samuelson? Miss Pamela Samuelson? Why is that name familiar?"

"Pamela Samuelson was in your aerobics class before you quit the club, dummy."

"Oh, yes," I said, still unable to conjure up a face. "What about Egon Schlichtmaier's history with the female undergraduates? How could Perkins justify having that kind of guy around?"

Marla sighed gustily. "Come on, Goldy. First of all, as you and I both know, if nobody squeals about how awful a guy is, then his reputation remains intact."

"So the undergraduates weren't talking. And the news didn't outlive the MLA convention?"

"Apparently not. And if anybody else did find out, I think the spin Perkins was looking for was that this was youthful excess that people would soon forget if the issue were left alone. The word is, Perkins warned Egon not to get involved with the *preppie* females, or he'd be teaching

French to the longhorn steers down at the stock show. And there's no evidence Egon went after anyone who wasn't close to his own age. More on that later. Here's the problem. How willing do you think a college would be to hire Schlichtmaier if his background were exposed in a series of articles for the *Mountain Journal* by an ambitious student-reporter aiming to spice up his application to the Columbia School of Journalism?"

"No, no, not Keith Andrews . . ."

"The same. And *guess* who was trying to get Keith *not* to publish the articles? Your dear Julian!"

"Oh, God. Are you sure?"

"So I hear. And *guess* who was sleeping with Schlichtmaier until she supposedly heard the whole background thing from none other than her favorite student, Keith Andrews?"

"I can't imagine, but I know you're going to tell me."

"Mademoiselle Suzanne Ferrell. I don't know whether they have broken up irreparably, but I'm supposed to find out at the nine o'clock step class."

"Tell me about this unknown scandal with Miss . . . who was Schlichtmaier's predecessor?"

"Pamela Samuelson, I told you."

"Could you check on it? I'd like to get together with her."

"She's moved to another aerobics class, so it'll be tough."

"Okay, let me tell Schulz all this."

Marla giggled suggestively. "Really, I just told this story so you'd have an excuse to call him this morning."

She rang off with the promise that she would do all this snooping if I paid her in cookies. I promised her Chocolate-Dipped Biscotti, and she swooned.

• • •

I did my yoga, then reflected on the communications net-work in Aspen Meadow as I dressed. When the town developed from a mountain resort to a place where people lived year-round, the first social institution had been the fire department. In a climate so dry a fire could consume acres of forest in less than a blink, the need for mutual protection had drawn even rugged loners into social contact. With the weather and roads unpredictable in winter, now it was the telephone that people used to tell everything about everybody. That is, if you didn't have the benefit of step aerobics. But sometimes I would hear so much news about somebody that the next time I saw the person in question, he would look as if he'd aged. Egon Schlichtmaier could easily sprout gray hairs in the next week, and I would never notice.

By the time I got downstairs, the sky had turned the color of charcoal and was beginning to spit flakes of snow onto the pine trees around my house. But the enveloping grayness brought no dark mood. In fact, I realized suddenly, I felt fabulous. The weather was a quilt over a delicious inner coziness. I didn't want to admit—to Marla, Schulz, Arch, even to myself—what this new state was, but it felt a lot like falling in you-know-what.

Seeing Arch and Julian in the kitchen, however, gave me a jolt of alarm. Julian's skin was as ashen as the sky outside, and the pouches under his eyes were deep smudges. When we lived and worked at a client's house over the summer, he went to bed early, was up at six to swim his laps, shower, and dress carefully before setting off for Elk Park Prep. I couldn't remember when he'd taken the time to swim in the week since Keith's murder. This morning he looked as if he had had no sleep at all, and he was wearing the same rumpled clothes from the night before. I was beginning to wonder if living with us was the best thing for him. But I didn't want to get him upset by asking more questions, so I just gave Arch, who was dressed in three layers of green shirts complemented by dark green jeans, a cheery smile. Arch smiled back gleefully.

"Julian's heating his special chocolate croissants!" he announced. "He says we don't have time for anything else!" To my look of dismay, Arch added, "Come on, Mom. Have one with your espresso."

While a chocolate croissant would hardly be Headmaster Perkins' idea of a nutritious breakfast, I quickly surrendered. Julian was not just a good cook, he was an artist. He had the touch with food and the love of culinary creation that are truly rare, and he'd had early and excellent experience as an assisting pastry chef at his father's bakery in Bluff, Utah. Given his preference for healthful food, his experimentation with puff pastry was a delightful aberration. In helping with my business Julian had turned out to be worth his weight in Beluga caviar. Or radicchio, which he would prefer. But I knew he had a calculus midterm that afternoon, and I didn't want him to be bustling around making breakfast in addition to everything else.

"Julian, let me do this," I said gently.

"Just let me finish!" he said gruffly. He pulled a cookie sheet from the oven. The golden-brown pastry cylinders oozed melted chocolate.

I was saved from having to deal with Julian's hostility by the phone.

"Goldilocks' Catering—"

"Feeling good?"

"Yes, yes."

"How about this, then," Tom Schulz said. "Are you feeling *great*?" I could hear his grin. Unfortunately, I could also feel myself blush.

"Of course, what do you expect?" Something about

my tone caused both Arch and Julian to turn inquiring faces in my direction. I turned away from them, coloring furiously. "Where are you?"

"At work, drinking probably the worst coffee known to the human species. When can I see you again?"

I wanted that to be soon, and I needed to tell him Marla's news, but I wasn't going to say so in front of Julian. "Lunch? Can you come up here? Aspen Meadow Café?"

"If you call the entrées that they serve at that place *lunch,* then sure. Noon." And with that summary judgment of nouvelle cuisine, he rang off.

"Arch," I said when we were all munching the marvelous croissants, "you didn't tell me you called Tom Schulz about the snake."

Arch put down his croissant. "Mom," he said with his earnest voice and look. "What, do you really think I'm going to rely on Mr. Perkins to do anything for me? Come on."

"Boy, you got that right," Julian mumbled.

"Still," I insisted as gently as possible, "I want you to be careful today. Promise?"

He chirped, "Maybe I should just stay home from school."

"Come on, buster. Just keep everything in your bookbag. Don't even use your locker."

Julian lowered his eyebrows, and his mouth tightened stubbornly.

"Hey, *I* didn't put the snake in his locker," I said defensively. "I despise vipers, rodents, and spiders. *Detest* them. Ask Arch."

"She does," said Arch without being asked. "I can't have hamsters or gerbils. I can't even have an ant farm." He swallowed the last bite of his croissant, wiped his mouth, and got up from the table. "You should add insects to that list."

Arch clomped upstairs to finish getting ready for school. As soon as he was gone, Julian leaned toward me conspiratorially. His haggard face made my heart ache.

"I'm going to help him with his classes. You know, set up a study schedule, encourage him, like that. We're going to work in the dining room each night, if that's okay with you. There's more room there."

"Julian, you do not have time to—"

My phone rang again. It was going to be one of those days.

"Let me get it." Julian jumped up and grabbed the receiver, but instead of giving my business greeting, he said, "Yeah?"

I certainly hoped it was not an Aspen Meadow Country Club client. Julian mouthed, "Greer Dawson," and I shook my head.

Julian said, "What? You're kidding." Silence. "Oh, well, I'm busy anyway." Then he handed me the phone and said "Bitch" under his breath.

I said, "Yes, Greer, what can I do for you?"

Her voice was high, stiff, formal. "I've developed a new raspberry preserve I'd like you to try, Goldy. It's . . . exquisite. We want you to use it in a Linzertorte that you could make for the café."

"Oh, really? Who's we?"

She *tsk*ed.

"Let me think about it, Greer."

"Well, how long will that take? I need to know before the end of the school day so I can put it on my application that I have to get in the mail."

"Put *what* on your application?"

"That I developed a commercially successful recipe for raspberry preserve."

I detest ultimatums, especially those delivered before eight o'clock in the morning. "Tell your mother I'll stop into the café kitchen just before noon to try it out and talk to her about it." Without waiting for an answer, I hung up. My croissant was cold. I turned to Julian. "What are *you* mad at her about?"

"We were supposed to be partners in quizzing each other before the SATs. I didn't do as well as I wanted to last year, too nervous, I guess, so I really wanted to, you know, review. Miss Ferrell"—he pronounced the name with the profound disgust of the young—"says we shouldn't need this kind of cramming, but she encouraged us to go over a few things anyway. I quizzed Greer yesterday. But instead of quizzing me, Greer has to rush down to Denver for her last session of private SAT review." His shoulders slumped. "Oh, well. It'll give me more time to get started with Arch. We can use the school library."

"Why don't you go to the SAT review with Greer?" I asked innocently.

He pushed his chair back from the table. "Where am I supposed to get a thousand bucks?"

It was a rhetorical question, and we both knew it. But before I could say that I would be more than happy to quiz him myself, Julian slammed out of the kitchen.

9

After the boys left, I fixed a cup of espresso and took it out on the deck off the kitchen. Only a few pillows of white now floated across the sky. The heavy, dark clouds had passed after dropping less than an inch of snow. I brushed melting snow and ice off a redwood bench with one towel and sat on another. It was really too cold to be outside, but the air felt invigorating. In the deep blue of the sky, the sun shone. The snow heaped on each tree branch glittered like mounds of sugar.

It was the kind of moment where you wanted every clock and watch in the galaxy to stop. Yes, someone had horribly murdered Keith Andrews. And someone was threatening us; Arch was having trouble in school; loads of bookkeeping, cooking, and cleaning awaited me. I had people to call, food to order, schedules to set. But for the moment, that could all wait. I inhaled snow-chilled air. The espresso tasted marvelously strong and rich. One thing I had learned in the past few years was that when the great moments came, you should stop and enjoy them, because they weren't going to last.

And then the flowers began to arrive. First there were pots of freesias. Papery white, yellow, and purple blossoms filled my hall and kitchen with their delicate sweet scent. Then came daisies with heather and an enormous basket of gladiolus, astromeria, and snapdragons. Finally, the florist handed me a box of long-stemmed scarlet roses. He didn't know the occasion and looked to me for signals about whether to act sad or happy. I didn't give any clues, so the fellow remained stony-faced. They must teach you to be emotionally removed in florist school. I arranged the roses in a tall ceramic vase Arch had made in the same sixth-grade art class that had produced the woodcut at Schulz's. My kitchen smelled like a florist's refrigerator.

The phone rang. Apparently Schulz couldn't wait to see if the greenhouse had begun to arrive.

I trilled, "Goldilocks' Florist—"

"Huh? Goldy? You okay?"

Audrey Coopersmith.

"No," I said without missing a beat, "I need you to come help me. You see, after dealing with all these fruitcakes, I've gone nuts."

There was a pause. Tentatively, Audrey began, "Want me to call back in a little bit?"

Depressed people, especially those going through divorce, have a hard time with jokes. They need humor, but it's like a bank account that has been suddenly frozen. Still, I would be the last one to explain.

"Well, uh," Audrey continued, floundering, "we've got a bit of a problem. Headmaster Perkins just called. He was wondering if we could bring out some cookies around lunchtime. They're having an unofficial visit from the Stanford rep."

"Sorry to say," I replied happily, "I'm busy for lunch."

"But Goldy"—and there was a distinct whine in her voice—"I can help you. And I think it would be such a great experience for Heather to meet the Stanford representative. You see, Carl doesn't care at all about where she goes to school, so I'm the one left with the responsibility . . . can't you just help me with this? I'm really going through a bad time now . . . it's not that big a deal for you, probably, but . . ."

Heather? What did Heather have to do with the cookies? I had to *bake* in order to pave the way for Heather Coopersmith to interview for the college of her dreams—correction, her *mother's* dreams?

"Look, Audrey, I'm in a good mood and I'm trying to stay that way. Why didn't Perkins call me himself? I could give the school some ideas about snacks for the Stanford rep."

"He said he tried to call you earlier but your line was busy. I'm telling you, Goldy, he's willing to pay for at least six dozen, and I can help by taking them over to the school, with Heather, of course, and the rep—" She hesitated. "You just don't understand: Stanford *never* sends a rep to Elk Park Prep. They figure they don't need to—"

"So give the guy some frozen yogurt! Tell him to pretend he's in northern California!"

Audrey sighed bleakly and said nothing. I guess I wasn't acting like a caterer who wanted business, was I? I made a few rapid calculations. Okay, there was the Rocky Mountain Stanford Club, maybe they'd need a big catered luncheon sometime. And Stanford played the University of Colorado in football, so perhaps I could rustle up a tailgate affair in Boulder this fall or next. Impressing the rep might not be such a bad idea.

"All right," I said. "How about some granola?" Audrey's silence remained disapproving. "Just kidding. Look, I'll come up with something. But Perkins needs to make very clear to this guy the name of the caterer making the cookies. And you can also tell Perkins this is going to cost him. Six dozen cookies arranged on trays and delivered, thirty dollars."

"I'm sure he won't object. He even asked if you could make a red and white cookie. You know, Stanford colors. He was thinking"—and here she cleared her throat—"of something like, like . . . barber-pole cookies or . . . dough candy canes or—"

"One of these days, that guy is going to choke and they'll do CPR on his tongue."

Audrey said, "Is that a joke?"

"Also," I added firmly, "I can't bring the cookies out to the school because of this lunch engagement."

"But that's what I *told* you. Where are you going to be today? I can pick them up. The logistics are getting a bit complicated anyway—"

"What logistics?"

She took another deep breath and I prepared for a lengthy explanation. "Oh, well, the Marenskys heard from Perkins that the Stanford rep was coming, and they'd already been in to complain to him that Ferrell hadn't put Stanford on Brad Marensky's college list, not that he would *ever* have a chance of getting in there, he's fifth in the class, you know . . . let's see . . ." She trailed off.

"Logistics," I said gently, to get her back on track.

"Oh, yes, well. So Perkins told me he called the Marenskys—no doubt because they're such big donors to the school, although Perkins didn't mention *that*—and said Brad should be sure to see the Stanford rep today, and Rhoda Marensky *demanded* that they get a private audience with the guy—"

The pope from Palo Alto. I could just imagine this young fellow, entirely unaware of the intense power plays that his unannounced visit was engendering, or of the awesome authority currently being conferred on his head.

"—so the *Marenskys* are picking up the rep at the I-70 exit and driving him to the school, or at least they were until the Dawsons got wind of this private-interview bit, and they insisted that Greer get to meet with the fellow before the reception ever began—"

If in fact it ever did begin, I mentally amended.

"And then Miss Ferrell thought she'd better be present to arbitrate, so she gave her fourth period a study hall, which is when Heather has French, so of course I wanted *her* to meet the rep, since she did all that extra engineering work over the summer, and if they didn't have such a high percentage of minorities at that school, I think it's forty-seven percent, then she would be a top contender—"

"What is the bottom line here, Audrey?"

"What are you so upset about?" she asked, bewildered. "Where's your lunch get-together? I'll pick up the cookies, and bring Heather to meet the Stanford rep, and Miss Ferrell can be there at the same time—"

"I'll be at Aspen Meadow Café to taste jam at 11:45."

"To taste *jam*? Why not do that at home?"

"Well you may ask, my dear Audrey, but it's the Dawsons' idea. No doubt they'll also want you to taste some. I'm sure they will want Julia Child, Paul Bocuse, and the Stanford rep to taste it too."

She sniffed. "Well, that doesn't really make much sense, but I'll see. Oh, something else. The Tattered Cover folks think it might be a good idea for you to come down to the store early, maybe an hour before the signing Halloween night? I could show you where the third-floor kitchenette is, how they usually set up for a buffet, that kind of thing."

At last we were off the subject of the Stanford rep. Yes, I said, we should definitely case the third floor of the bookstore ahead of time. We decided Audrey would come over to my place after the penitential luncheon Friday so we could head down to Denver together. Then Audrey asked, "Why did you answer the phone like a florist? Are you thinking of expanding your business?"

"Sorry, I thought you were somebody else."

". . . Not meaning to be disrespectful, Goldy, but maybe you need a vacation."

That made two of us. I was still laughing when Tom Schulz called.

"Doesn't the caterer sound merry."

"She is, she is. First she had a great time with this cop last night." He *mm-hmm*ed. I went on. "This morning, though, she flunked out of surrogate-parenting. But to her rescue came this same cop, who quickly turned her house into the Denver Botanic Garden. Now for the rest of the day she has to make cookies, kowtow to some guy from California, taste jam, and have lunch with the cop."

"Uh-huh. Sounds normal to me. Glad you like the flowers."

"Love them. You are too generous. But listen, I need to tell you some stuff Marla's found out." I told him about Egon Schlichtmaier's allegedly shabby history and current alleged affair, along with the possibility that these items were going to get some journalistic exposure at the hands of the ambitious Keith Andrews.

"Okay, look," he said when I'd finished, "I may be a bit late for lunch. I'm going down to check on a murder in Lakewood. Ordinarily, it wouldn't involve me. But the victim's name was Andrews."

I was instantly sober. "Any relation to the late vale-dictorian?"

"Not that we can figure out. The victim's name was Kathy. They found her body in a field two weeks ago. Her head had been bashed in. Suspect is her ex-boyfriend, who owed her a couple thousand, but the investigators down there can't find him. Anyway, one of the things they're looking at is that Kathy Andrews' mail was stolen. And get this—she had an account at Neiman-Marcus. 'K Andrews' on her card, they said."

"I don't get it. Was it a robbery/murder?"

"That's the strange thing. Kathy Andrews was single, had a lot of money that she liked to spend. Looks like a *lot* of her mail might have been stolen, from the way she was complaining to the local post office. Maybe somebody was in the act of stealing letters and she caught them. That's what the Lakewood guys are trying to recon-struct."

"Why would someone steal her mail?"

"Same reason they take your purse, Miss G. For cash or checks, is what we usually see. Or vandalism. They're going through all Kathy Andrews' stuff, trying to check back with what she might have been expecting. But when something that was mailed—in this case a credit card—doesn't show up, you wonder. According to their records, Neiman-Marcus mailed it sometime in the last month."

I touched the phone wire, then quickly let go of it. I tried to wipe out the mental image of a woman I did not know. Kathy Andrews. "Did you talk to the Marenskys about their raccoon coat?"

"They claim it was stolen at some party."

"Well, I'm confused."

"You're not alone, Miss G. See you around noon."

· · ·

Something red and white. Not a barber pole, not a candy cane, not an embarrassed zebra. Something worthy of a visit from the school that had produced Nobel Prize winners, Pulitzer Prize winners, Jim Plunkett, and John Elway.

Since I thought a football-shaped cookie would be a bit too difficult to manage on such short notice, I decided on a rich white cookie with a red center. I beat butter with cream cheese and let my mind wander back to Julian. His abrupt departure that morning left me troubled. Julian, in his fourth year at Elk Park Prep, was bright and extremely competent. He had stunned me with the creativity of his project on DNA research. But his classmates were smart and productive too, and they had money to aid them in all their academic pursuits. I creamed in sugar and then swirled in dark, exotic-smelling Mexican vanilla, which I sniffed heartily. Julian cared about his school, not with a rah-rah cheerleader spirit, but with such a fierce loyalty that he was willing to risk a fight with Keith Andrews to keep a scandal out of the newspapers. I sifted flour in to make a stiff batter. Julian was passionate about people and cooking. The latter trait, I had long ago decided, was another way of being passionate about people. For all those therapy bills, I'd figured out a few things.

As my spatula scraped the golden batter off the sides of the bowl, I recalled the shy and happy look that had begun to creep over Julian's usually hostile face during the past summer, whenever Schulz or Arch or I had begged him to make his *tortellini della panna,* spinach pie in filo, or fudge with sun-dried cherries. Julian cared about me and about Schulz, and he was wild about Arch. The events of the past week had caused him great strain. Poor overwrought eighteen-year-old, I thought, what can I do to help you care less about us and more about your future?

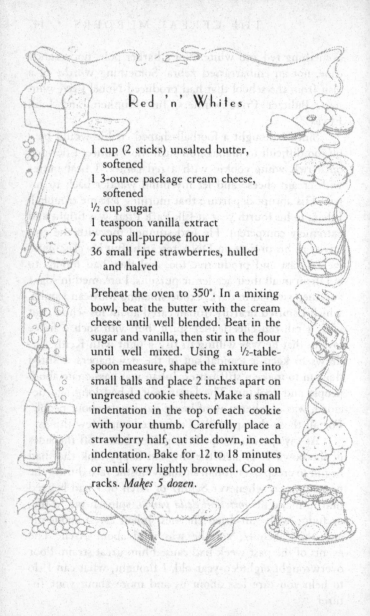

Red 'n' Whites

1 cup (2 sticks) unsalted butter,
  softened
1 3-ounce package cream cheese,
  softened
½ cup sugar
1 teaspoon vanilla extract
2 cups all-purpose flour
36 small ripe strawberries, hulled
  and halved

Preheat the oven to 350°. In a mixing
bowl, beat the butter with the cream
cheese until well blended. Beat in the
sugar and vanilla, then stir in the flour
until well mixed. Using a ½-table-
spoon measure, shape the mixture into
small balls and place 2 inches apart on
ungreased cookie sheets. Make a small
indentation in the top of each cookie
with your thumb. Carefully place a
strawberry half, cut side down, in each
indentation. Bake for 12 to 18 minutes
or until very lightly browned. Cool on
racks. *Makes 5 dozen.*

I stared at the creamy concoction. My supplier had recently delivered several quarts of fresh strawberries. I decided to cut them up and use them to top each cookie, for the red and white effect. The things a caterer is called upon to do. I rolled dainty half-tablespoonfuls of dough into spheres, thumb-printed the lot, and then put a half of a strawberry, seed-side up, in the little indentations. I slapped the cookie sheets into the oven, set the timer, then fixed another espresso.

Fifteen minutes later I was munching on the luscious results. They were like tiny cheesecakes, something you would have at an English tea. I decided to dub them something catchy. Red 'n' Whites, maybe. And speaking of something catchy, I decided then and there to beg Julian to let me help him with the SAT drill-questions, if he was still interested. How hard could it be? I already knew the opposite of *tranquil:* today's lunch.

Two hours later, toting three doily-covered trays and a wrapped package of six dozen Red 'n' Whites, I pulled into the parking lot of the Aspen Meadow Café. The Dawsons had tried hard to make their restaurant appear as continental as possible. There was no question that the café's sleek, glassed exterior was a far cry from the more casual health food and Western barbecue spots that peppered Aspen Meadow, places where tourists or construction workers or psychic massage practitioners could grab a noontime bite. No, the folks who frequented this café were, for the most part, not the kind who had to go out and work for a living, at least not full-time. Or they belonged to a growing group of professionals who could put on cowboy hats and wander out for a two-hour lunch.

I eased the van between a Mercedes (license plate:

LOIR; I guess ATURNIE was already taken) and Buick Riviera (URSIK; now, how was that to inspire confidence in an M.D.?). The café was sandwiched in the dark-paneled, turquoise-trimmed shopping center known as Aspen Meadow North. There was Aspen Meadow Florist, whose blossoms Schulz had recently decimated, and Aspen Meadow Interior Design, with its perennially southwest window display. Tasteful Halloween decorations adorned the windows of upscale boutiques. Next to the café was the undecorated window of Aspen Meadow Weight Control Center. Ah, irony!

I entered the café and passed the baskets of braided breads and puffed brioches, passed the cheese case with its Stiltons, Camemberts, and buffalo mozzarellas, and came up to the glass case of desserts. Luscious-looking apricot cream tortes, multilayered chocolate mousse cakes, and all manner of truffles called out for attention. I closed my eyes, trying to imagine the exclamations of delight that would greet my Happy Endings Plum Cake when it held a prominent place in front of the displayed concoctions.

Audrey had already arrived with Heather, whose pouty expression and slumped posture next to the Stiltons did not indicate happy-camper status. Audrey, utterly oblivious to her daughter's funk, sidled up to me and warned, "I made the mistake of asking the Dawsons if Greer had anything to impress the Stanford rep with. They went into a fit of preparation. Greer hightailed it into the bathroom and changed into a red and white outfit. Now they're all awaiting your presence in the kitchen for the big taste test. Oh." She lifted one eyebrow in her wide, humorless face. "The jam's *putrid*. Better say you'll make the Linzertorte they want at home."

Too much. I said, "Any sign of the Marenskys? Or Miss Ferrell?"

She pressed her lips together. "Ferrell's in the kitchen. I don't know about the Marenskys."

I said wishfully, "Is the jam just tart? Would it be better with some sugar mixed in?"

The smile she gave me oozed smugness. "Believe me, Goldy, you could take the sugar made by every beet farmer in eastern Colorado and put it in that jam, and it would still taste like solidified vinegar."

"Thanks, Audrey," I said dryly. "I trust you didn't let your opinion show."

"I had to spit it out. Either that or throw up."

"Great," I said as the Dawsons approached. They were like a human phalanx.

"Hey, Hank! Great game Sunday."

His face turned even more grim at my greeting. "They were lucky, you know that, Goldy. Washington's going to be tough. About as tough as this Stanford guy. We've just been talking about how to play him."

"I don't know why the Marenskys are even bothering to bring Brad," said Caroline primly. "Everyone knows Stanford is as demanding as the Ivy League schools. They *never* take anyone below the top ten percent."

I murmured, "But in a school as small as Elk Park Prep—"

"Never!" she interrupted me, her small dark eyes glowing. "Didn't you hear me?"

I was saved assuring her that my hearing was fine by the cheerful jingle of the bell hung over the café door. Stan Marensky came through, wearing a fur jacket, then Rhoda strutted regally past the bread baskets in a full-length fur coat, not the raccoon thing. She was followed by a diminutive fellow, presumably the Stanford rep. He wore blue jeans, a bow tie, and no coat. Bringing up the rear was Brad Marensky, a broad-shouldered boy who wore shorts and an Elk Park Prep varsity tennis T-shirt,

despite the fact that it was about thirty-eight degrees outside.

The diminutive fellow glanced around the café. He
did not look so very powerful to me. Yet beside me, Audrey Coopersmith was visibly trembling.

"Audrey," I said in as comforting a tone as I could
muster, "please relax. This is simply not as important as
you make it out to be."

Her look was chill. "You just don't get it, Goldy."

The Marenskys were chatting in loud, possessive
tones to the Stanford rep. They seemed extraordinarily
pleased with themselves, and acted as if some very important business had been resolved in the ten-minute car ride
from the I-70 exit. It occurred to me that while the
Marenskys, who were both as thin as models, ignored me,
the short, rotund Dawsons were always curious about my
every word or thought.

Hank Dawson leaned in close. "They sure seem
smug. I wonder what they could have told him about
Brad? That kid's only number five in the class, he'll never
make it. I need to get that guy away from them. Punt or
go for it?"

"Go for it," I said without hesitation.

"Welcome to our little restaurant." Caroline Dawson's lilting voice pronounced *restaurant* with a French
accent. I cringed. The Marenskys turned into two skinny
ice sculptures as they watched Caroline Dawson waddle
forward in one of her trademark crimson suits.

"We'd like to take you into the kitchen," Caroline
Dawson declared. She grasped the young man's arm
firmly. Once she had him in tow, she indicated with a
move of her head that she wanted me to follow her into
the kitchen. "Our daughter, Greer, who is third in her
class, is by the Hobart," she said with great sweetness.

"I'm so glad you came out on an early ski trip," she added as if she and the unfortunate rep were old chums.

"Should I kneel and kiss his ring?" I asked Audrey Coopersmith, who had timidly followed me in while tugging Heather's sleeve to bring her along. The Marenskys, trying to appear cool and unruffled, marched out into the kitchen to see what the Dawsons were up to with the rep.

While we were all assembling in the kitchen, Caroline engaged the Stanford rep in lively, empty conversation. Miss Ferrell, drinking coffee and leaning against a sink, had a pained look on her face. Well, that ought to teach the college counselor not to host unexpected reps. She *click-clack*ed her way over to me on her tiny heels.

"I have a teachers' meeting in Denver the next couple of days, Ms. Bear," she said under her breath. "But I would like to talk to you about Julian as soon as I get back. Can you free up some time? He came to see me this morning, and of course he's very upset about what happened to Arch . . . but he also has a number of questions about Keith. Oh, this all has become so dark—" She jerked back abruptly, suddenly aware that Audrey, Hank Dawson, and the Marenskys were all keen to hear what she had to say.

"What questions about Keith?" I asked.

"He was having some problems—" she began in a low voice. She looked around. The Marenskys began to whisper to each other. Hank reached for a cabinet door while Audrey pretended to be intensely perusing a menu she had found on the counter. "Some problems with this college thing," Miss Ferrell whispered.

"How about chatting Saturday morning before the tests?" I whispered back. I sneaked a sidelong glance at Audrey, but to read the menu she had put on her usual blank expression. It was hard to tell whether she was listening. "I'll be setting up that breakfast out at the school."

Miss Ferrell nodded and turned on her heels and *click-clack*ed back to the Stanford rep. Greer Dawson had made her appearance from the back end of the kitchen. As Audrey had predicted, the teenager was wearing a red and white striped shirt. The skirt matched. Her golden hair curled angelically around her diminutive heart-shaped face. I was reminded of the Breck girl. Daintily, Greer reached for a utensil and spooned a mouthful of the raspberry jam into the rep's reluctantly open mouth. Apparently, Greer didn't want me to preempt the rep in the tasting. With startling suddenness the rep's face took on the look of a two-week-old kiwi fruit.

He said in a high, uncertain voice over the expectant hush in the room, "What? No sweetener?"

Everyone immediately began bustling around, trying to make up for this faux pas. Everyone, that is, except Audrey, who leaned in to my ear and jeered, "Nanny-nanny-nana."

"Ah, well." Hank Dawson hustled forward. "This jam is still in development, I mean, this is a new batch, and Greer's just a rookie chef, after all, you can hardly judge—"

"We'll let Goldy decide," Caroline Dawson announced imperiously. "After all, she's the one Greer's been studying with."

Oh, blame it on the caterer! Well, excuse me, but the only thing Greer had studied while she was with me was whether you served pie with a spoon or a fork. Up until now, the girl had never shown even the slightest inkling of interest in food preparation. Of course, I knew what this setup was all about. If I pretended to love the jam, I'd get a Linzertorte job in addition to the plum cake assignment, and I'd show up Miss Ferrell and poor Audrey. Not to mention the Stanford guy. If I screwed up my face in disgust, I could forget about a Stanford tailgate picnic, and I could go elsewhere to peddle my plum cake. I also had the discomforting premonition that Schulz might walk in at any moment on this ridiculous scenario. The things a caterer has to do for business.

I stalled. "Fresh spoon?"

"In there." Audrey motioned to a wooden drawer.

I pulled the drawer open. It held one of those plastic four-part silverware trays. Each section bulged with utensils. I reached toward the spoon section, desperately attempting to *imagine* sweet jam.

"I'll get a big one," I said loudly.

But I wasn't going to taste jam that day. I should have looked more closely at the small object in the spoon section, the shiny black round form, the red hourglass on the bottom of its dark belly. But by the time I had the sense to draw back my hand, I had already been bitten by the black widow.

10

"Omigod!" I screeched.

The Dawsons, the Marenskys, Miss Ferrell, Audrey, all pressed forward with urgent queries: *What happened? Are you all right? A spider? Are you sure? Where?*

I backed up, my left hand clutching my right wrist. The stinging crept up my finger and into my palm. Furiously, I thought, Why did it have to be my *right* hand? I backed hard into Stan Marensky. When I whirled around, he appeared stunned. Involuntary tears filled my eyes.

Hank Dawson ran to the phone, Caroline Dawson began comforting a screaming Greer, the Marenskys demanded of one another and of a gaping Brad what the hell was going on, Miss Ferrell splashed cold water over a paper towel. Audrey was on her knees, looking for the spider, which she was convinced I had shaken out onto the floor. The poor Stanford guy was standing stock-still, his mouth gaping. You could see his mind working: *This place is weird.*

"Uh-uh," I said to the familiar person lumbering fast into the kitchen: Tom Schulz.

"What's going on?" he demanded. He reached out for my forearm and examined the spot I was pointing to on my right index finger. It was swelling up and reddening. And it burned. I mean, my hand was on *fire.*

From the floor, Audrey hollered up at him: "Do something, take her to the hospital, she's been bitten by a poisonous spider, do *something* . . ."

Tom Schulz gripped my shoulders. "Goldy," he said, demanding my gaze. "Was it small and brown?"

I said, "Uh . . . uh . . ."

"Would you know a brown recluse?"

"It wasn't . . . that wasn't . . ."

He seemed relieved, then raised his eyebrows. He said, "Black widow?" and I nodded. To each of his questions—"Are you allergic? Do you know?"—I shook my head and gave a helpless gesture. I hadn't the slightest idea if I was allergic. How often does one get bitten by a poisonous arachnid?

Hank Dawson trundled rapidly back into the kitchen. His voice cracked when he announced, "Oh, God, all the ambulances in the entire mountain area are tied up! Is she going to be all right? Should one of us take her to a hospital? Is she gonna die? What?"

Schulz hustled me out of there. Amid the siren, lights, squeal of tires, and Schulz's inability to get his cellular phone to work, we hightailed it out of Aspen Meadow North and got onto Interstate 70. As the dun-brown hills whizzed by, I held my hand by the wrist like a tourniquet. I tried to think of the spider venom as a toxic black ink that I was willing to stay in my palm and not travel through my veins into the bloodstream.

Once we were on I-70, Schulz's cellular phone kicked in and he announced to Dispatch where he was going. Then he called the poison center. Through the crackle of interference they directed us to Denver General Hospital. It had the closest source of antivenin, they told Schulz. My hand burned.

Cursing the welling tears and my shaking voice, I asked, "Isn't this supposed to go away or something? It's not really poisonous, is it?"

He kept his eyes on the road as we whipped past a truck. "Depends. Brown recluse would've been worse."

I cleared my throat. "I have to be able to take care of Arch. . . ." I was beginning to perspire heavily. Each time I took a breath, the bite throbbed. It was like being in labor.

Schulz said, "Feel nauseated?" I told him no. After a minute he said, "You're not going to die. I don't know why you go into that damn café, though. Last summer somebody pushed you into a glass case there. I'm telling you, Goldy, that place and you don't mix."

"No kidding." Perspiration trickled down my scalp. I stared at my swollen finger, now overcome with a dull, numbing pain. Strangely, I also felt a hardening pain developing between my shoulders. I took a breath. Agony. "I'm beginning to hurt all over. How'm I going to cook? Why did it have to be my right hand?"

He flicked me a look. "Why did it have to be you at all?"

Headache squeezed my temples mercilessly. I whispered, "Good thing you came along when you did."

"The posse," he said impassively.

In the emergency room a bleached-blond nurse asked in a clipped voice about allergies and insurance. A dark-complected doctor asked about how long ago this had happened and what I had been doing to make the spider bite me. Some people. While the doctor examined the bite, I closed my eyes and did Lamaze breathing. The childbirth experience, like the divorce experience, can give you a reservoir of behaviors to deal with crises for the rest of your life.

The doctor finally decreed that invenomation had not been severe. I did not, he said, need to be hospitalized. He checked my vital signs, then told me to take hot baths this afternoon and tonight, to relieve the muscular pain in my back. When I asked about working, he said I might be cooking again by tomorrow, that I should see how I felt. Before he breezed out he said tonight was for rest.

"Oh, gosh," I exclaimed, suddenly remembering, "the red and white cookies for the school! I don't know if Audrey remembered them!"

"Goldy, please," said Schulz, "why not let somebody else—"

"I can't, I worked all morning on those things," I said stubbornly, and scooted off the examination table. Dizziness rocked me as soon as my feet hit the ground. Shaking his head, Schulz held my arm as we walked down the hall to a pay phone. He punched in the number of the café and tried to cut through the barrage of frantic queries from Hank Dawson. Finally, sighing, Schulz handed me the phone.

Hank's inquiries about whether I was okay were immediately followed by a volley of questions designed to ascertain whether I was going to sue him. No, I wouldn't contemplate legal action, I promised, if he would retrieve the platters of cookies from my van and get them over to the prep school. Hank said Audrey had left in her "usual high-strung state" and had forgotten them, but that he would make sure they were delivered. Somewhat ruefully, he added that the Stanford rep had worried aloud about hygiene conditions at the café. To add insult to injury, Hank informed me, the rep hadn't even stayed for a free lunch. Greer's future at Stanford didn't look so hot.

After what seemed like an interminable wait—I couldn't decide if the doctor was waiting for me to die, get better, or just disappear—the blond nurse reappeared and announced that I could go. Schulz drove me home. I felt embarrassed to have taken so much of his time, and said so.

He chuckled. "Are you kidding? Most exciting lunch I've had all week."

Audrey Coopersmith's white pickup truck sat in front of my house. Audrey got out, and with her shoulders rolled inward, marched with her long duck-walk stride up to my front porch: the first official greeter. Bless her, she had brought a cellophane-wrapped bouquet of carnations. As Schulz and I came slowly up the walk, she stood, feet apart, hands clasping the flowers behind her back. Her face seemed frozen in anxiety. Schulz still held me gently by the right elbow, but he lifted his chin and squinted his eyes, appraising Audrey.

Under his breath he said, "Have you introduced me to this Mouseketeer?"

"Don't."

When we got to the front door, Audrey wordlessly thrust the flowers at me. Then, seeing my bandaged hand, she awkwardly drew the bouquet back and blushed deeply. I mumbled a thanks and reluctantly asked her to come in. It took me a minute to remember my security code. Put it down to spider toxin fuzzing the brain. After some fumbling we all stood in my kitchen.

Audrey's eyes widened at the vases and baskets of roses, daisies, freesias, astromeria. The kitchen smelled like a flower show.

"Gosh. Guess you didn't need carnations after all."

"Of course I did, now, meet my friend," I said, and

introduced her to Schulz, who was already ferreting through the freezer to dig out ice cubes for my finger. Schulz wiped his hands and courteously addressed her. I added that Audrey was a temporary helper for the catering business along with her work at the Tattered Cover. Schulz cocked his head and said he remembered that Audrey was one of the people who had helped me out the night of the Keith Andrews fatality.

She pressed her lips together. Her nostrils flared. "Well, Alfred Perkins has decided to move the location of the college advisory evenings."

"Yes," said Schulz with his Santa Claus grin, "going down to the bookstore, right? Terrific place. Will you be helping Goldy on Friday too?" Mr. Charm.

Audrey visibly relaxed and said yes to both questions. The edges of her mouth may have been starting to turn up in one of her rare grins. Then again, maybe it was my imagination. We were saved from more banter by the telephone. Schulz gestured toward it and raised his eyebrows at me, as in, Should I get it? I nodded.

It was my mother, calling from New Jersey because she had just heard that there had been a big snowstorm in Colorado. I try to tell my parents, This time of year, there is always *lots* of snow falling *somewhere* in the Rockies. Why this meteorological condition is so profoundly newsworthy for the national networks is beyond me. We take the precipitation in stride; the dire announcements just worry Coloradans' relatives who live elsewhere. I wedged the phone under my chin so I could keep the ice cubes on my right hand.

"Goldy! Is that the policeman you've been seeing? Why is he at your house in the middle of the day?" So much for the snow crisis. But if I told my mother what had just happened, there would be another flood of worried questions. I had never even told her Schulz was a homicide investigator. If she learned that, all hell would break loose.

"He's just helping me out," I told her. "I've, uh, had a bit of sickness."

My mother's high voice grew panicked. "Not *morning* sickness . . ."

"Mother. Please. It's past lunch here, thus well after morning. Not only that, but we've had only a tiny amount of snow, and Arch is due home any second—"

"Tell me again," she pressed, "is Tom Schulz somebody you knew from C.U.?" This query was designed to ascertain if Schulz was a college graduate. If she couldn't have a doctor for a son-in-law, Mom would at least go for well educated.

I said, "No, not from C.U." I wanted to say, *Last night I had my emotional life changed by this guy . . . today he drove me down to the hospital and back in a life-threatening situation, you're not going to believe this, Mother, I've finally found somebody who really cares about me. . . .* The phone slipped out of my left hand and bounced off the floor.

Her more distant voice persisted. "But he's not just . . . somebody you met, is he? This isn't going to be someone you just . . . picked up at a policeman's picnic or—?"

I picked up the phone. "Mother. No. This is someone"—I looked at Schulz and smiled—"very special, very smart. He is unique. He knows all about china and antiques and still was able to get a job with an equal-opportunity employer."

"Oh, God, he's *colored*—"

"Mother!" I promised to call over the weekend, and hastily said good-bye.

Schulz eyed me askance. "Didn't quite measure up, did I?"

"I heard her," Audrey said, and mimicked my mother's voice, " 'Someone you picked up?' Sorry, Goldy. Why do women of our mothers' generation worry so much about what kind of man we're seeing or married to? Why don't they worry about how *we're* doing? That's what I tell Heather, 'I'm worried about *you,* honey, not some boy you might be dating and what his background is.' " Audrey moved to the sink and poured herself a glass of water. She finished with, "You should have told her Schulz went to Harvard."

"Oh, Lord, don't remind me," groaned Schulz. He turned and gave me a half-grin. "I went out to Elk Park Prep to get a few things cleared up, and the headmaster asked me where I went to school." He shrugged. "I didn't know what he meant, so I said, 'Well, first there was North Peak Elementary—' and old Perkins waved his hand and said, 'Stop right there.' "

I was shocked. This hurt as much as the spider bite. How dare Perkins insult Schulz, who was in every way his superior? I felt the slight as keenly as if Perkins had criticized Arch. "That imbecile!" I blurted out.

Schulz turned his unruffled, seawater-green gaze at me. I felt my face redden and a flip-flop tighten my abdomen. "Not to worry, Miss G. I know the difference between a person who's educated enough to handle life's challenges and a person who just needs to brag all the time."

Audrey's mouth sagged open. She said, "Make that 'the difference between a *woman* who can handle life's challenges and a *man* who needs to brag all the time.' "

Schulz said, "Hmm."

I didn't know where this was going and I didn't care. But Schulz was interested. To Audrey, he said, "Er, tell me what you mean."

Audrey's tone was defiant. "That's what I'm trying to teach Heather. I say, 'Get ahead now, honey, while you're young, you don't want to get stuck taking care of some man's socks and ego.'" She took a shuddering breath. "You see, if you don't get ahead when you're young, if you just let things go along, if you trust people . . ."

A cloud of bitterness soured her features. "Oh, never mind. All I want is for Heather to have things I never had. She is phenomenally talented," she said, animated again. "She ran the virtual reality simulator this summer for exploring Mars." She glared at us fiercely. "Heather is going to be a *success*."

Schulz leaned back in his chair and gave Audrey and me a benevolent, questioning grin. "Success, huh?"

When we had no response, he got up out of his chair and cocked his head at us. "You feeling okay, Goldy?" When I said I thought so, he added, "I'm going to make some tea."

We were silent while Schulz rummaged for cups, saucers, and a pot, and then drew water. Finally Audrey said glumly, "Success is what I'm not." She ticked off on her fingers. "No meaningful work or career, no relationship, no money . . ."

Well, I was not going to interrupt my part-time assistant and say, catering is meaningful work for some of us, if not for you. Catering pays the bills. That's my definition of meaningful.

Schulz said, "I grew up in eastern Colorado and paid for my own college education until I was drafted. I didn't finish a degree until I got out of the army. Criminalistics, University of Colorado at Denver." He frowned. "I've killed people and thought it was wrong, killed them and thought it was right. Some criminals I catch and some I don't. I make a good salary and I'm unmarried, no kids."

He rubbed his chin, watching Audrey. "But I think of myself as a success. In fact"—here he gave me a wink—"I'm getting more successful all the time."

"Huh," said Audrey.

The teakettle whistled. Schulz moved efficiently around the kitchen, first ladling in China black tea leaves, then pouring a steaming stream of water into the pot. He ducked into the refrigerator and came out with a dish of leftover Red 'n' Whites. I glanced at my watch: 3:00. Arch and Julian would be home within the hour, and we had nothing for dinner. Maybe Julian would want to cook. This time he'd get no argument from me.

Audrey's hand trembled as she lifted her teacup and saucer. The cup made a chittering sound as Schulz slowly filled it. Audrey did not look at me when she went on. ". . . I didn't go to a school where I could make something out of myself. If only I had studied math, instead of . . ."

The pain in my hand was getting worse. I was having trouble focusing on Audrey's voice, *whine whine,* Caltech, *whine whine* Mount Holyoke, Heather's always been *so gifted.* Sudden exhaustion swept over me. I dreaded telling Arch and Julian about the spider bite. I longed to take my first doctor-prescribed hot bath. But now Audrey was complaining about how the best possible thing for Heather would be a big science-oriented school in California or the Northeast, since they had the best reputations and would assure her of landing a great job once she graduated. Maybe it was the bite, maybe it was my mood, maybe I had just had it with this kind of talk. Enough.

"Uncle! A big-name school is not going to *make* a person. You make it sound like it's sex or something!"

Schulz turned down the edges of his mouth in an effort not to laugh. He cleared his throat with a great rumbly sound and said, "Oh, yeah? Like sex? This ought to be interesting. Goldy? You haven't touched your tea."

I slouched back and obligingly sipped. "Let me tell you, my college counselor promised me the moon and I believed her."

Audrey said, "Really? Where did you go?" I told her; she was impressed. She said, "Gosh! A camel's-hair coat in every closet!"

"Spare me." I remembered undergraduate nights shivering in freezing rain mixed with snow. I didn't recall ever seeing a camel's-hair coat. I sighed. "Where do these reputations come from? People think, If you go to this or that college, you're in. Go to this or that school and you'll become beautiful and smart and get a great job and be a successful person. What a joke."

"She's getting cynical in her old age," Schulz told Audrey out of the side of his mouth. Then to me, brightly, "Would you pass the sugar?"

"I mean, just look at the catalogue." I slid Schulz the sugar bowl with my good hand. "Look at the close-up shots of Gothic spires . . . they do it that way so you won't see the smog. Look at the good-looking well-dressed preppy white Anglo-Saxon Protestant females striding together across the lush green campus. They and their friends vacated the campus over the weekend, while the less attractive girls stayed alone in the dorms, their minuscule numbers at meals an indictment of their own unpopularity."

I put down my teacup and held my hands open as if perusing an imaginary brochure. "Wow! Look at the picture of that energetic lecturer and those students eagerly taking notes—that must be a fascinating class!" I gave them a fascinated-class look. "The class is required for your major, but it took you three and a half years to get into it! Complain to your parents, as I did, and they say,

'For this we're paying thousands a year?' " I sipped tea and gave them a wide grin. "Man, I just *loved* going to a big-name school."

Schulz explained placidly to Audrey, "Goldy has an excitable temperament."

"Nah," I said, surprised by the passion in my little diatribe. "What the heck, I even give the school money."

The phone rang. Schulz raised his eyebrows at me again, and again I nodded. This time it was Julian. He had heard about the spider incident when Hank Dawson fulfilled his promise and delivered the cookies. Julian was frantic. Schulz tried to lighten it up by saying, "I've warned her not to try to cook with spiders," but Julian was having none of it. I could hear him yelling.

I signaled, "Just let me talk to him." When Schulz resignedly handed me the phone, I said, "Julian, I'm fine, I want you to quit worrying about me—"

"Who put that spider in the drawer?" he yelled. "Miss Ferrell? Trying to take attention away from her other problems?"

"Whoa, Julian. Of course Miss Ferrell didn't put it in the drawer. Come on. Everybody knows black widows live all over Colorado. I hardly think Miss Ferrell, or anybody else for that matter, would deliberately try something nasty like that."

"Want to bet? She just told me she doesn't know *anything* about food science! I'll bet she doesn't think it's worthy. She's not going to give me a good recommendation, I know it. She's a class A bitch from the word *go*."

"I'll talk to her," I volunteered.

"Lot of good that'll do," he replied bitterly. And then he sighed. It was a deep, pained, resigned sigh.

"What else is going on?" I asked, concerned. "You sound terrible."

"We're all staying until about six. There's a vocabu-
lary-review thing going on in Ferrell's room. Arch is in
the library, don't worry. We'll just be home late."

"How was the Stanford rep? Did you have some
cookies?"

"Oh, the room was packed. I didn't go." He paused.
"Sheila Morgenstern told me she mailed in her early decision application to Cornell. She's sixth in our class, but she
got 1550 combined on her SATs last year. I'm happy for
her, I guess, but it's bad for me. Cornell will never take
two kids from the same school. Especially if one of them
isn't going to get a good recommendation from the college
counselor."

"Oh, come on, sure they will, Julian. You're just making yourself miserable. Lighten up!"

There was a silence. "Goldy," Julian said evenly, "I
know you mean well. Really, I do. But honestly, you don't
know a thing."

"Oh," I mumbled, staring at my swollen finger.
Maybe he was right. My life did seem to be a mess at the
moment. "I didn't mean to—"

"Aah, forget about it. To make things worse, I
flunked a French quiz this morning. And I flunked a
history quiz too. Not my day, I guess."

"Flunked . . . ?"

"Oh, I was tired, and then Ferrell asked five questions about the subjunctive. Schlichtmaier asked about
Lafayette, and I guess I missed that part when he talked
about him." He mocked, "Vell, ve don't know for
shoor . . ."

"Don't," I said.

"Yeah, yeah, I know, don't be prejudiced. Forgot to
mention, half the class flunked too. Nobody's learning a
thing in there." There was a silence. "And hey, *I'm* not

the one making fun of Schlichtmaier. I stick up for him every chance I get."

"I'm sure you do."

But Julian's tone had again grown savage. "You want to know the truth, the guy who used to make fun of him is dead."

11

"Now, that's a happy note." I hung up the phone, somehow managing not to bang my injured finger. "Julian says I am totally ignorant. And worse, he's afraid Miss Ferrell isn't going to write him a good recommendation for Cornell."

"He's sunk," proclaimed Audrey. "He won't get in now if he invents a solar-powered car."

"Oh, give me a break."

"Come on," Schulz interjected. "That's just the kind of car we need down at the Sheriff's Department."

Audrey smiled shyly. On my index finger the bite area throbbed. I peeked under the bandage and saw that the redness had resolved itself into an enormous, ugly blister. I pondered it glumly. Schulz poured more tea. He wasn't going anywhere, and I didn't know whether this sudden lack of purpose stemmed from concern for me or curiosity about Audrey. I suspected the latter.

Audrey got to her feet. She left the bouquet of carnations on the table beside her empty teacup. "Well, I suppose I ought to be moving on. Think you're going to be okay to cook Friday? It's just a few days away."

I held out my hands helplessly, as in, Do I have a choice? I told her she could come by at six. "And thanks for the flowers. They're a great addition to the shop here."

"I'll walk you out," Schulz volunteered with unnecessary enthusiasm. I looked puzzled. He ignored me.

Outside, he stood talking with Audrey for a few minutes, then walked her to her pickup. After a few moments he came back, slowly sat in one of my kitchen chairs, then gently lifted my right hand and examined it. "I have to ask you the obvious, you know. Do you think that spider was intended for you? Or for somebody else?"

"I do not believe it was intended for me, or anyone else for that matter," I replied firmly. "There was a lot of confusion in the kitchen, a big crowd, a lot of chitchat about tasting jam." I saw my hand, as if in slow motion, go into the silverware drawer. "It just happened."

He mused about this for a while. For the first time I noticed the care he had used to dress for our lunch: pinstripe shirt, rep tie, knitted vest, corduroy pants. While I was looking him over, he winked and said, "Audrey didn't mention going to college herself."

"She went, all right, at least for a while. But it rained so much, she said her bike ran over fish on her way to classes. And I guess the classes themselves were awful. Dates were nonexistent. And everyone at her high school had told her it was going to be this *wonderful* experience. She got some therapy there at the school clinic. She hated that too. She finally concluded that what was making her unhappy was the school itself. So she left and got married. And now the marriage is breaking up."

Schulz gave me his impassive face. "How long's she had that pickup truck, do you know?"

The question was so unexpected that I laughed. "Gosh, Officer, I don't know. For as long as I've known her. Maybe it's part of her financial settlement. My theory is that she drives it because it's part of her image."

Schulz squinted at me. "Think she's capable of killing somebody?"

My skin went cold. I said, choosing my words carefully, "I don't know. What do you suspect?"

"Remember K. Andrews down in Lakewood?" When I nodded, he continued. "I went down, questioned all the neighbors, even though the Lakewood guys had already done it. Hardly anyone's around during the day, and nobody saw anything unusually suspicious. A blue Mercedes, a silver limousine, an old white pickup, maybe a new ice cream truck. No identifying features. One young mother glanced out her window and saw somebody stopped at Kathy Andrews' mailbox one day. She'd already reported it. 'Something unusual,' she says, 'something out of place. That's all I can remember.' "

"Something out of place?" I said, puzzled. "A moving van? A flying saucer? Is that all you could get out of her?"

"Hey! Don't think I didn't try. I say, 'Not a car from the neighborhood? Not Fed Ex or UPS?' She shakes her head. I go, 'Not the usual mail person?' 'No, no, no,' she says, 'it was something it was too late for, just one instant, there and then gone.' That's all that registered with her. I say, 'Too late for what? The mail?' And she says, 'I just don't know.' "

"So you checked with all the delivery people, limousine people, and nobody was late for anything."

"Correct. *Nada*. Same as the Lakewood guys found." He sipped his cold tea. "Then I see Ms. Audrey Coopersmith's pickup truck parked out front of your house, and I think, 'an old white pickup,' the way one of the other neighbors said. Kathy Andrews' old boyfriend drove a pickup, I found out. Would you say Audrey Cooper-smith's truck looks old?"

"Old? I guess it's not new and shiny . . . but why would Audrey steal some woman's credit card in Lake-wood and then beat her to death?"

"Don't know. The most frequent kind of credit-card fraud we have is a woman—excuse me, Miss G.—any-way, getting her friends' cards and signing their names to her purchases. Audrey works in Denver at the bookstore, and maybe she goes across the street to Neiman-Marcus on her break, sees some gal make a purchase, and the saleslady says, 'Thank you, Miss Andrews,' and Miss An-drews says, 'You can call me Kathy.' So maybe Audrey, who is having all these money problems, thinks of Keith Andrews, a convenient place to dump the card if things got hot. Then again, maybe all this investigating he was doing for the paper got him on her path."

"Pretty farfetched, I'd say. I mean, you can see for yourself that we're not exactly talking a designer ward-robe."

He smiled grimly. "But she was at that college advi-sory dinner, she has some unresolved feelings about her own past and present, and maybe all that got taken out on Kathy, and then Keith, Andrews." Again the raised eye-brows. "And she was at the café today when you were there with the Dawsons and Miss Ferrell. Maybe she put the spider in the drawer and it was intended for someone else, like the college counselor. Was she at the school the day Arch found the rattler in his locker?"

With a sickening feeling I remembered Audrey standing in the hall, telling me the headmaster wanted to see me. My finger ached dully. "Yes," I said, "she was."

Schulz asked to use my phone. When he had finished telling someone to check on Audrey Coopersmith's vehicle and background, he turned back toward me.

"Actually, I do know a cure for black widow spider bites."

"*Now* you tell me."

"You gotta stand up first."

"Tom—"

"You want to get better or not?"

I stood, and as soon as I had, he reached down and scooped me up in his arms.

"*What* are you doing?" I exclaimed when he was halfway down my front hall.

He started up the staircase. "Guess. I got the afternoon off, in case you haven't noticed."

In my bedroom he set me down on the bed, then kissed my finger all the way around the bite.

"Better yet?" His smile was mischievous.

"Why, I do believe I'm feeling some improvement, Officer."

He kissed my wrist, my forearm, my elbow. A tickle of desire began at the back of my throat. It was all I could do to keep from laughing as we undressed each other, especially when my bandaged right hand made me fumble. I reached for the fleshy expanse of Schulz's back. Only the night before, I had begun to discover hidden curves and niches there. Schulz's warm body snuggled in next to mine. His hands lingered on my skin. Tom Schulz was the opposite of John Richard's knobby edges and angry, thrusting force. And when it was over, I wanted him to stay in my bed and never leave.

"This is so great," I murmured into his shoulder.

"So you *are* feeling better."

"It's a miracle. No more spider bite pain. You see, Officer, *I* planted the black widow—"

We went off into a fit of giggles. Then we fell silent. Schulz tucked the sheets and blanket around my neck and shoulders until not a square centimeter of cold, foreign air could penetrate the warm pouch within. Knowing that the boys were due home late, I allowed myself to drift off to sleep. My mother was probably right to be suspicious. It was nice, in fact it was *delicious* to be so successfully up to something with this man in my house in the middle of the day.

The sun had already begun its blazing retreat behind the mountains when I woke to see Schulz standing beside my bed. My alarm clock said 5:30.

I said quietly, "The boys here yet?"

"No. You stay put. I'm fixing dinner."

I got up anyway and took the doctor-ordered bath. As I was putting on clean clothes, trying in vain not to use my right hand, my phone rang. I dove for it, in case it was my mother. The last thing she needed was to hear Schulz's voice again.

"Goldy, you *degenerate*."

"Now what?"

"Oh, tell me that policeman's car has been outside your house for three hours so he can teach you about security."

"Give me a break, Marla. I got bitten by a black widow."

"Old news. And I'm sorry. That's why I drove by, four times. I was worried about you. Of course, I didn't want to interrupt anything exciting. . . ."

"Okay, okay. Give me a little sympathy here. You wouldn't believe this bite I've got."

"Giving you sympathy is what I *hope* Tom Schulz has been doing, and a whole lot more, sweetie pie. *I* am going to give you help tomorrow with whatever kind of catering things you've got going."

"But you don't even cook!"

Marla snorted. "After tomorrow, you'll know why."

In the kitchen Schulz was playing country music on the radio and using a wok to steam vegetables. He had made a pasta dough that was resting, wrapped, on one of my counters, and he had grated two kinds of cheese and measured out cream and white wine.

"Fettuccine Schulz," he informed me as he jiggled the wok's steamer tray. "How hard is it to make pasta in this machine? That dough's ready."

I put a pasta plate on my large mixer and Schulz rolled the dough into walnut-sized pieces. Just as the machine began producing golden ribbons of fettuccine, we heard the boys trudging up the porch steps.

I felt a pang of sudden nervousness. "What's our story?"

"Story for what?" He laid out handfuls of pasta to dry. "You got bitten and I'm helping out. They're not going to say, Well, did you guys make love all afternoon? If they do, I'll say"—he put his big hands around my waist and swung me around—"yes, yes, yes, I'm trying to force this woman to marry me by making mad passionate love to her at least once a day."

The door opened and I squealed at him in panic. He put me down lightly, looking unrepentant. I glanced around hastily for something to do. Julian and Arch rushed into the room, then stopped, gazing in silent awe at the masses of flowers.

"Gosh," murmured Julian, "bad news sure travels fast in this town. All this for a spider bite?"

I didn't answer. Arch was giving me half a hug with one arm while keeping his other hand free to hold up my bandaged area and examine it. He pulled back and regarded me from behind his tortoiseshell-framed glasses. "Are you okay?"

"Of course."

He closed one eye in appraisal. "But something's going on. Sure it wasn't anything worse than a spider bite, Mom? I mean, all these flowers. Are you sick?"

"Arch! For heaven's sake, I'm fine. Go wash your hands and get ready for dinner."

Saved by the chore. To my surprise, they both sprinted out, calling back and forth about the work they were going to do together that night. Julian had volunteered to help Arch construct a model of the *Dawn Treader*. Then they were going to go over Arch's social studies homework. After the moon set, they were going to look for the Milky Way. Amazing.

When they came downstairs we all delved into the pasta. The velvety fettuccine was bathed in a rich cheese sauce studded with carrots, onions, broccoli, and luscious sun-dried tomatoes. It was not until we were eating the dessert, the final batch of leftover Red 'n' Whites, that Arch dropped his bombshell.

"Oh," he said without preliminaries. "I finally thought of something that someone warned me not to tattle about." We all stopped talking, and held cookies in mid-bite. Arch looked at each of us with a rueful smile. He was a great one for dramatic effect.

"Well, you know Mr. Schlichtmaier is kind of short and stocky? He works out. I mean with weights. I've seen him over at the rec center."

"Yes," I said, impatient. "So?"

"Well, one day I asked him if he used steroids to pump himself up."

"Arch!" I was shocked. "Why in the world would you do something like that?"

Schulz and Julian couldn't help it; they dropped their cookies and started laughing.

"Well, I was thinking about starting to work out myself!" Arch protested. "And you know they're always having those shows on TV about guys dying because they use those hormones. And now you have to be checked before races and games—"

"Arch," I said. It was not the first time I longed to throw a brick through the television. "What were you saying about tattling?"

"So Schlichtmaier goes, 'Steroids? Ach! Swear you won't tell?'" Arch's mouth twisted. "He laughed, though. I thought, weird, man. Anyway, that was a couple of days ago. Then the next day he says, 'You won't tattle on me?' I say, 'No problem, Mr. Schlichtmaier, you want to die of cancer, that's up to you.' He says, 'You promise?' Boring, man. I say, 'Yeah, yeah, yeah.' And then the snake thing happened and I forgot all about it."

Great. I looked at Schulz, who shrugged. Better to let go of it for now, especially after all we'd been through that day. Arch got up to clear the table. Julian offered to do the dishwashing. I walked out in the cool October night with Schulz.

"Sounds like a joke, Miss G.," he said, once again reading my mind. "Way to get a twelve-year-old kid to relax, have a relationship. Make a joke about artificial hormones."

"But you're willing to suspect Audrey Coopersmith of murder based on the age of her truck."

He said, "You know we're already checking on Schlichtmaier because of what you told us about the other gossip. If anything turns up, I'll let you know."

When we arrived at the doors of his squad car, we did not kiss or hug. We did not act as if we were anything other than police officer and solid citizen. You never knew who might be looking. I felt happiness and sadness; I felt the tug of a growing intimacy drawing me as ineluctably as the receding tide takes the unwary swimmer out to unexpected depths. I looked into his eyes and thanked him aloud for his help. He saluted me, then pulled slowly away from the curb.

I ran back inside and picked up the phone with the thumb and little finger of my right hand, then dialed with my left. In the dining room I could hear the cheerful voices of the boys as they constructed their ship.

"Aspen Meadow Recreation Center," came the answer on the other end after six rings.

"What time does the weight room open in the morning?" I whispered.

"Six. Why, you haven't been here before?"

"I've been there, just not to the weight room."

"Y'have to have an instructor the first time," said the voice, suddenly bored.

"Okay, okay, put me down for an instructor," I said quickly, then gave my name. A flash of inspiration struck. "Does, uh, Egon Schlichtmaier teach over there, by any chance? I know he's a language teacher somewhere—"

"The German guy? Nah, Egon doesn't teach. Sometimes he's here in the morning, brings a teenager. I asked if he knew Arnold Schwarzenegger, and he goes, 'He's from Austria,' like I was so dumb." There was a pause. I could hear papers rustling. "I'll put you down for Chuck Blaster. Twelve bucks. Wear sweats." A dial tone.

Oh, God. What had I done? Chuck *Blaster*? That couldn't possibly be his professional name, could it? But I replaced the receiver and crept up to bed.

He who wants to be a tattler . . .

I was not convinced it was a joke.

12

The throbbing in my finger woke me up Wednesday morning just as the sunrise began to brighten the horizon. I was lying there, feeling exceedingly sorry for myself when the radio alarm blasted me six inches off the mattress. Blasted, yes. Not unlike Blaster, now part of my ruse for a confrontation with Egon Schlichtmaier. But an early morning session lifting weights with one hand virtually out of commission was not my idea of fun. It seemed the mattress was begging for my return. I ignored its siren call and slipped carefully into a gray sweatsuit, stretched through the yoga salute to the sun and five more asanas, and tried not to think about lifting anything.

In the kitchen I wrote the boys a note. *Gone to rec center weight room.* This would engender surprised looks, no doubt. My double espresso spurted merrily into a new Elk Park Prep carry-along mug, a heavy plastic container that the seventh-grade parents had been requested (read "strong-armed") to purchase at the beginning of the school year as a fund-raiser for the kids' trip to a self-esteem workshop in Denver. Afterward Arch informed me he wasn't going to think positive unless he absolutely *had* to. And nobody can make me, he added. That's what I should have said when it was mug-buying time.

The grass underfoot was slick with frost, and my breath condensed into clouds of moisture in the cold October air. The van engine turned over with a purposeful roar. I ordered myself to think strong and muscular. Maybe *I* needed a positive-thinking workshop.

The van chugged obediently over streets whitened by a thin sheet of ice. Aspen Meadow Lake appeared around a bend—a brilliant, perfectly still mirror of early light. The evergreens ringing the shore reflected inverted pines that looked like downward-pointing arrows trapped in glass. Early snows had stripped the nearby aspens and cottonwoods of their leaves. Skeletons of branches revealed the previous summer's birds' nests, now abandoned. Without the trees' masking cloak of foliage, these deep, thick havens of twigs looked surprisingly vulnerable.

Like Keith Andrews.

And so did our household seem vulnerable now too, with accidents or pranks that were becoming increasingly serious. Julian appeared to be coming apart at the seams. And I had been nastily injured trying to deal with the Stanford rep's one and only visit to Elk Park Prep. As the caffeine fired up the far reaches of my brain, I tried to reconstruct: Why was someone targeting Arch? If indeed the spider in the drawer was intended for someone, was I that someone?

Without meaning to, I wrenched the wheel to the left and winced when pain shot up my finger. I'd have to watch the bite area with the weights. Either that or risk passing out. The *Mountain Journal*'s too cute headline would read: CATERER A DUMBBELL?

An image of the dreaded simile-speaking headmaster invaded my thoughts. Perkins certainly had not been overeager to find the snake-hanger who plagued Arch. But in the minds of most, which was what Perkins was after all concerned with, he might be considered successful. In his decade at the school, Alfred Perkins had raised hundreds of thousands of dollars for a much-publicized classroom expansion and renovation. He had masterminded a building program that included an outdoor pool and gymnasium. During parent orientation, some of the friendlier parents—of which I had to admit there were some—informed me that Perkins had superbly weathered the expected crises of administrative purges, teachers quitting or being fired, and students being expelled. Still, it seemed to me that Alfred Perkins hid behind his great wall of similes without letting too many folks know what was truly transpiring in his silvery-haired noggin. Perhaps that was how he and Elk Park Preparatory School had survived together unscarred, if not unruffled, for ten years.

Still, Perkins must view the past month as being unusually fraught with crises. First there was the splashy story in the *Denver Post* about the students' slumping SAT scores. Then, if you believed Marla's version of town gossip, there had been the threat of local newspaper coverage —by ambitious, clever Keith Andrews—of a sex scandal. Or some kind of scandal. After the coverage the *Post* had given the SAT scores, what they would do with a teacher-sleeps-with-students firebomb at the same school was barely imaginable. And then the most recent crisis, a whole order of magnitude more severe: the valedictorian had been killed—*murdered* on school property. Whether Headmaster Alfred Perkins could survive this lethal threat to his precious school's shaky stability and not-so-pristine reputation remained to be seen. How heavily he was involved in, or even worried about, these setbacks was a question mark too.

The word from Julian was that Perkins' tall, center-forward son, Macguire, despite his poor third-quarter standing in the senior class, had a good chance at a basketball school—North Carolina State, Indiana, UNLV. The acne-covered Perkins' dull voice and drooping eyelids had been eerily impassive even in the face of the chaos surrounding his classmate's brutal death. Macguire must be quite a disappointment to his status-seeking father, if not to himself. On the other hand, like many comics who acted the dunce, Macguire may have built up his own wall against caring.

I swerved too late to avoid a muddy puddle, then began the ascent to the rec center parking lot. Built in the seventies, the Aspen Meadow Recreation Center was a long, low redbrick building on the hill behind the town's public high school. "The rec," as it was affectionately known in town, predated the athletic club and catered to a different local clientele—working-class folks. Anyone who had to labor for a living didn't have a prayer of an early morning workout at the infinitely tonier Aspen Meadow Athletic Club, which didn't even open its doors until ten.

I pulled the van between the faded yellow lines of a space. To my astonishment, quite a few hardy souls were already parked in the rec center lot. Somehow, I had imagined I would be doing this body-building work in solitude. I devoutly hoped these fitness freaks were swimming laps. The thought that someone I knew might see me in sweats was more than I could bear.

My shoes gritted over gravel sprinkled with rock salt to melt the snow on the rec steps. Supported by an area-wide tax imposed by the residents themselves (since Aspen Meadow was fiercely proud of its unincorporated status), the rec was a no-nonsense sort of place with an indoor pool (shared with the public high school), a gym, a meeting room for senior citizens, and three racquetball courts. Here there were no steam rooms, no saunas, no massages, no tanning booths, no carpeted aerobics room, no outdoor pool. I didn't even know where the rec's weight room was until the woman at the desk, who at the age of forty had decided she needed braces, told me. She took my twelve dollars and then, through a mouth crisscrossed with vicious-looking metal, announced that they'd recently converted one of the racquetball courts.

"Folks just want to lift weights," she said with what I thought was too lingering a look at my lower-body bulges.

I felt my heart sink with each step up to where people actually lifted heavy things because they thought it was good for them. I mean, these people *wanted* to be big, they wanted to gain bulk, and they didn't want to do it by eating fettuccine Alfredo and sour cream cheesecake! They used powdered diet supplements! What were they, nuts? With some trepidation, I pushed open the door.

The place didn't just smell bad, it smelled horrific. It was as if the walls had been painted with perma-sweat, guaranteed to stay wet. Sort of an unwashed rain-forest-in-the-gym concept.

When I was about to pass out from the stench, a big guy—I mean a *really* big guy—with lots of knots and bulges and popping-out muscles on his arms and chest and massive legs, sauntered up to me. He growled, "You Goldy?"

I swallowed and said, "Aah—"

His eyes, tiny sapphires set in an expanse of facial

flesh, flicked over me contemptuously. "Don't work out much, do you?"

Not a good start. I looked around at the different instruments of torture, things you pushed up on, things you pushed down on, things you watched your shoulders dislocate on in the bank of—yes!—mirrors. Men of all ages, and one woman who I at first *thought* was a man, were grunting and groaning and pumping. It didn't look like fun.

"Really," I improvised desperately, "I'm just looking for somebody. . . ."

"You're looking for me," said Big Guy. "Come on over here. I'm Blaster."

Not one to argue with one so massive, I followed dutifully behind. I had a terrible blinding thought: What if I saw my ex-husband here? John Richard Korman would laugh himself silly. I cast a quick glance around. No Jerk. He preferred the more chi-chi athletic club. Thank God for tiny favors.

"First we stretch," announced Blaster.

Well now, stretching was something I knew about. I said hopefully, "I do yoga."

Blaster did a prune face of disdain and thrust a long metal rod at me. He said, "Do what I do," and then he threaded his huge arms around an identical metal rod. As he twisted his sculpted torso from side to side, I struggled to follow suit. But in the mirror I looked too much like a chunk of meat skewered on a shish kebab, so I stopped. Unfortunately I also let go. The rod Blaster had given me clattered to the floor with an unhappy *thunkety-thunk*.

"Hey!" he bellowed.

"Oh, don't be too hard on her," Hank Dawson said. "She had a really rough day yesterday. And she's a big Bronco fan." Unlike the young jocks in their scoopneck sleeveless shirts and tight black pants, Hank wore orange sweats emblazoned with the words DENVER BRONCOS—AFC CHAMPIONS! "Finger okay?" he inquired as he extricated himself from the thing he was pushing his elbows together in and walked slowly up to my mentor and me. One thing I had noticed about how the men moved in the weight room: They swaggered around bowlegged, as if at any minute they were going to face off against Gary Cooper. Tromp, tromp, tromp, *don't be too hard on her* tromp tromp *a rough day* tromp, *draw on three, pod'ner*.

"Actually," I said, turning pained eyes up to Blaster, "I did suffer from a terrible spider bite yesterday. . . ."

But Blaster had already clomped off to what looked like a stretcher lying on an angle. Hank Dawson gave me a grim apologetic look. "Are you sure you're well enough to do this, Goldy? Did you hear Elway pulled his shoulder in practice yesterday? I'm surprised you're here."

I said feebly, "So am I."

He grinned. "You know they *hate* food people here."

"I'm beginning to think this whole idea was a mistake." I meant it.

Blaster roared, "Hey, you, Goldy! Get on this thing head *down*!" Several men turned to see if I would do as commanded. I scurried over to Blaster.

"You don't seem to understand, I've changed my mind . . ."

He pointed at the stretcher. It was a long-fingered commanding point, not unlike when God brings a flaccid Adam to life on the Sistine ceiling. "Decline sit-ups," he boomed.

"You see," I ventured tremulously, "there was this black widow . . ."

The remorseless finger didn't waver. "Best thing for it. Get on."

A man of few words.

And so I started. First, sit-ups with my head lower

than my feet on the stretcher, which seemed unfair. Why not at least be level? Then incline leg raises and crunches (sit-ups on a level surface—why bother when I'd just defied gravity the other way?), then more torso twists with the skewer rod, then leg presses, leg extensions, leg curls, bench presses, and front lat pulls.

I'm dying, I thought. No, wait—I've died and I'm in hell. In the mirror, my face was an unhealthy shade of puce. My finger throbbed. Rivulets of sweat ran down my forehead and turned into a veritable torrent inside my sweatshirt. Blaster announced we were almost done, and that I would do better next time. Hey, Blaster! *There ain't gonna be a next time.*

Finally, *finally,* Egon Schlichtmaier walked in with none other than Macguire Perkins. Why I had not made an appointment just to see Schlichtmaier at the school was beyond me. I was going to need a heating pad for a week. No, not a heating pad—an electric sleeping bag and months of physical therapy.

"I need to talk to you," I panted when the two of them sauntered, John Wayne–like, over to where I was slumped on the floor, collapsed and terminally winded. Before they could greet me, however, Blaster loomed suddenly overhead. I was looking straight at his calves. Each resembled an oven-roasted turkey.

Blaster's beady blue eyes had a bone-chilling God-surveying-Sodom-and-Gomorrah look. "You're not done." His voice echoed off the dripping walls.

"Oh, yes, I am," I said as I scrambled to my feet, not without exquisite and hitherto undreamed of pain. "Stick me with a toothpick. I'm as done as I'll ever be."

But he was waving me over to the Stairmaster, unheeding.

Egon Schlichtmaier said, "It's not so easy the first time," only it came out, "Id's not zo easy ze furst time."

He gave me his big cow-eyed look. "Like sex, you know." The muscles in his back and arms flexed and rolled as he escorted me over to the aerobics area.

I hated him. I hated Egon Schlichtmaier for his muscles, I hated him for sleeping with those undergraduates, and I hated him for comparing what we were doing in this chamber of horrors to making love, which I had just begun to enjoy lately, thank you very much.

Blaster was punching numbers into the Stairmaster's digital readout with that meaty finger I had come to dread. He looked at me impassively. "Get on. Ten minutes. Then you're through." And joy of joys, he stomped away. I faced Egon Schlichtmaier and scowled.

"Better do what Blaster says," came the unnaturally low voice of Macguire Perkins. "Guy has eyes in the back of his head. We'll get on the treadmills and keep you company."

With such sympathetic exudings, the two of them mounted the treadmills and effortlessly began to walk. I wanted Macguire to go away, because what I was about to say concerned only Arch, Schlichtmaier, and me. Perhaps Macguire sensed my disapproval. He pulled out a headset while he was walking, tucked on earphones, and obligingly blissed out.

I stepped off the Stairmaster. Let Blaster come over and bawl me out. I dared him. I crossed my arms in front of Egon Schlichtmaier's treadmill as Macguire Perkins began to screech along with his tape: "Roxanne!"

To Egon Schlichtmaier I said, "I understand you've had some difficulty with my son."

Surprise flickered in his eyes. "I do not teach your son."

"Roxanne!" squealed Macguire.

"But was there something you didn't want him to tattle about?" I replied evenly. "He said you were teasing him about something he said. He said you teased him day after day, and it was about tattling on you for using steroids. I simply will not stand to have my son harassed, by you or anyone else." I narrowed my eyes at him.

And then I had a horrible thought: Maybe Arch wasn't the only one Egon Schlichtmaier didn't want to have tattle on him. A chill of fear scuttled down my back.

Damn. I should have left this whole thing to Schulz, as he was always telling me. Egon Schlichtmaier quietly turned off his treadmill and stepped off. He flexed his solid wall of muscles and I felt my heart freeze. Here I was among a bunch of bodybuilders, facing a possible multiple murderer.

"Roxanne!" screeched Macguire. His tall body rocked and heaved along the treadmill. His muscular chest shimmied to the beat. "Rox-anne!"

In his thick German accent Egon Schlichtmaier said, "Yes, I did tease your son. But that was all it was. Your son has had a hard time fitting in socially at the school, as you may or may not be aware." He crossed his arms: a standoff. "When he accused me of using steroids, which is no small accusation, as you know—"

Especially with all the other accusations you're facing, I thought but did not say.

"—I tried to joke him out of it. I mean, I work out, but I'm no Schwarzenegger, although we sound alike, no? I think your son has been watching too much TV."

I really hate it when people criticize Arch. Egon Schlichtmaier put his hands on his hips. He was muscled, this was true, and superbly proportioned. Just because I didn't like him didn't mean he couldn't have an athlete's body. But I had learned a few things about steroid use from one of the many parenting books I had read. Steroids cause mood swings. Egon Schlichtmaier may have been subject to these, who knew? His reputed sex life certainly pointed to an abundance of testosterone. But he had none of the acne, no sign of the female-type breasts that chronic steroid-users frequently develop.

Drug abuse. What was it that Hank Dawson had said to me at church the day after Keith's murder? *I understand that kid's had quite a history with substance abuse.* The kid was the headmaster's son. At the time, I had just ignored it; no one else had seemed to think the rumor was worth looking into. And if the police suspected marijuana or cocaine deals were going down at the school, Schulz would have at least mentioned it.

"Roxanne!" bellowed Macguire Perkins joyously as he jounced along the treadmill. My eyes were drawn to him. Not just his face, but his entire body, was covered with acne. And he looked as if he could use at least a Maidenform 36C.

13

"Why did you drive Macguire over here?" I demanded.

"His license has been suspended for a year. Drunk driving." Egon Schlichtmaier screwed his face into paternalistic incredulity. "I try to help these kids. I do not threaten them."

"Just trying to help, eh?" I didn't mention the dalliances at C.U. Sometimes teachers didn't know their own power. One thing I did know about steroids was that a large percentage of students who took them got them from coaches and teachers. "Does Macguire have problems with other drugs? I mean, that you know of."

"Sorry?" Egon said as if he had not understood me.

"Like steroids, for instance?"

His shoulder muscles rippled in a shrug. "Haven't the foggiest."

I peered hard at the darkly good-looking face of

Egon Schlichtmaier. He was an oily sort of fellow—evasive, glib, hard to know.

I said, "Because of Keith's death, I've been extremely concerned about things happening at the school. There was this snake, this . . . threat to Arch. Do you know anyone who would want to hurt my son?"

"No one." And then he added fiercely, "Including me."

"Okay." I stalled. Perhaps I was overreacting. "I guess I misunderstood the tattling banter the two of you had." Egon Schlichtmaier shrugged again. He closed his eyes and sighed asin, I'll let it go this time. I tried to adopt a cheerful tone. "Think you'll be staying at Elk Park Prep? I mean, past this year?"

He pondered the question. "What makes you think I would not?" I raised my eyebrows in ignorance. He seemed to accept that and shrugged again. "I have not decided."

At that moment a horrific shriek and reverberating metallic crash cut the air. On the other side of the room, a crowd gathered to see what had happened. A short, stocky fellow had dropped one of the largest barbells. I wondered how many pounds were involved, and if the barbell had landed on his toe. So much for clean and jerk.

Blaster started yelling at the poor guy who'd dropped the weight. Even Macguire pulled off his earphones. The Richter-scale vibration had come through the treadmill. With an air of exasperated defeat, Egon Schlichtmaier hunched toward the melee. But it seemed to me the teacher was only too glad to leave me standing there; we hadn't exactly been having a pleasant conversation. Macguire slouched off after Egon. I noticed with delight that the preoccupied Blaster had his back turned to me.

Time to boogie.

I showered quickly and drove home. By the time I eased the van in behind the Range Rover it was almost eight A.M. The Range Rover? Julian and Arch usually left for school around 7:30. Panic welled up. Were they all right? Had they overslept? I bounded inside and up the stairs to check, and immediately regretted the move. My thighs screamed with pain from the workout.

"Julian," I whispered after knocking on their door, "Arch!"

There were groans and the sounds of shuffling sheets. The air in the room was close, and it smelled of boy. As an only child, Arch took rooming with Julian as a great adventure. It had begun with a bunk bed. Of course, I hadn't been able to afford a new one, and we wouldn't be needing it after Julian went off to college. But a classified ad in the *Mountain Journal* had provided a secondhand two-tiered bed for fifty bucks. Unfortunately, it had cost another fifty for a carpenter to reinforce the upper bunk for Arch's weight.

"Guys!" I said more loudly. I glanced around the room. Their school clothes lay in piles on a chair. A gel-filled ice pack was on the floor next to Arch's slippers. "Is this a school holiday that I don't know about?"

Julian lifted his head and barely opened puffy eyes. His unshaven, exhausted face was a mottled gray. He made unintelligible sounds along the lines of, "Gh? Hnh?" and then, "Oh, it's you," and flopped back on his pillow.

"Hello?" I tried again. "Arch?"

But Arch only pulled himself under his covers, a typical maneuver. I bent down to pick up his slippers. They were wet.

"Julian," I said with frustration, "*could* you wake up enough to tell me what is going on?"

With great effort Julian propped himself up on one elbow. He announced thickly, "Arch and I saw your note. Arch went outside to get the paper and slipped on the top porch step. He landed on his ankle and really hurt himself." He yawned. "I took a look, and since it had already begun to swell, I put some ice packs on it and told him to go back to bed until you could decide what to do." Another, longer, yawn. "I didn't feel too good either. I'm really tired." He let out a deep, guttural groan, as if even putting this much thought into discourse were an effort.

"Uh, Doctor Teller?" I said. "After you diagnosed and treated the ankle, and sent the patient back to bed, what?"

He opened an eye. "Well," he said with just a shade of a grin cracking the expanse of youthful brown beard, "since I knew you wouldn't want Arch to be here alone, I mean after the rock and the snake and all, I decided to stay home with him. I can afford to miss a day." He flopped over. "You'll have to be the one who calls the school, though."

Oh, what was the use? "All right, okay," I said. Respecting kids' assessment of a situation is a finely tuned parenting skill. Not a skill I was sure I had yet, but never mind. "Arch? May I please take a look at your ankle?"

He grunted an assent and thrust the offending foot from underneath his covers. Julian's makeshift ice pack had already begun to unwrap, but there were still two frozen gel-filled packs inside a gently knotted terry-cloth towel. The ankle was swollen all right. The skin around the ankle was a pale blue.

"From the steps?" I was confused. "That's awful." Arch was not usually clumsy. In fact, his lack of athletic ability was in direct contrast to what I thought of as his physical grace, which of course you could see when he skied. Admittedly, as his mother I was somewhat prejudiced. "Can you stand on it?"

"I *can* stand on it and it is *not* broken," said Arch.

"One more thing," muttered Julian, his head on the pillow, his eyes closed. "I don't know if I'm getting paranoid or something. Did you spill water out front?" When I said that I had not, he said, "Well, it looked to me as if someone had poured water over the steps. So anyone going out the front *would* fall and break his ass."

Hmm. In any event, medical attention was not warranted, at least for now. I backed out of the room, but not before I heard Arch's muffled and indignant voice say: "I did *not* break my ass!"

I went down to the kitchen. When other people's lives get chaotic, they smoke, they drink, they exercise, they shop. I cook. At the moment it seemed we all needed the comfort of homemade bread. I made a yeast starter and phoned Marla. "You said you were coming over to help me today, remember? Please come now," I begged to her husky greeting.

"Goldy, it's the middle of the night, for crying out loud. Or the middle of winter. I had a late date last night and I'm hibernating. Call me when spring arrives."

"It's past eight," I countered unrelentingly, "and it won't be winter for another seven weeks. Come on over and I'll make something special. Julian and Arch are both home. Arch fell and Julian's . . . tired. Besides, I want you to tell me more about the lost teacher, Pamela Samuelson, and this Schlichtmaier fellow."

"The former has been hard to find, and the latter is too young for you. Is Arch okay?"

"Just bedridden."

She groaned. "Lucky him. I'm so glad I'm the one you call when the kids are incapacitated and you don't have anything better to do. But if you're making something special. . . ."

"Doughnuts," I promised. Marla was wild for them. She made a cooing noise and hung up.

Within moments I realized I didn't have enough oil to fill even a quarter of a deep fryer. Well, necessity was the mother of all new recipes. Not only that, but I needed to develop something sweet but nutritious for the SAT breakfast that would follow Headmaster Perkins' directive of including grains in everything possible. Why not oat bran in a doughnut? I'm sure kids would prefer that to an oat bran muffin any day, especially when those kind of muffins usually tasted as if they'd come right out of a cement mixer.

I moved the college financial aid books that Julian had left askew on the counter, then sanctimoniously sifted soy flour with the all-purpose stuff and, ever virtuous, poured judicious measures of oat bran and wheat germ on top. After the yeast starter was warm and bubbly, I swirled in sugar, eggs, vanilla, and the flour mixture. I massaged it into a rich, soft pillow of dough that snuggled easily into a buttered bowl. After I'd put the whole thing into my proofing oven to rise, I put in a call to Schulz's voice mail. I said I wanted to talk to him about Egon Schlichtmaier, who taught out at the school. And how was he doing on the pickup-truck situation, and Audrey's background? As I hung up, Julian shambled in. He wore a T-shirt with the faded logo of some ancient rock concert, frayed jeans, and loafers with the backs crumpled down.

"Sorry I was so tired," he mumbled. He looked

around the kitchen hopefully. "What're you putting together? You going to make some coffee?"

"Doughnuts in about an hour and a half," I countered as I measured out Medaglia d'Oro and filled a
pitcher with half-and-half. "Cappuccino in a couple of
moments."

He stood in front of my calendar of upcoming events
and read what was coming: "Clergy lunch . . . Tattered
Cover dessert . . . SAT breakfast . . . Bronco brunch.
How do you figure out what to charge for these meals?"

Even when he was out of sorts, Julian had great enthusiasm for catering. He wanted to know everything. It
provided a context for our relationship, for his goal was to
work as a hotel chef or have his own catering or restaurant business. Vegetarian, of course. While steaming the
hot half-and-half for his cappuccino, I told him that the
basic rule in catering was that you tripled the cost of your
raw ingredients to include cooking, serving, and overhead. If clients wanted wine or any liquor, that was com-
puted into the cost per person of the meal. I had sheets I
gave to clients with the details of menus that were six to
fifty dollars per person.

"What if clients giving a party disagree on what they
should get and how much things should cost?"

I laughed. "Don't get me started on weddings this
early in the morning."

"So tell me what you're planning," he asked as he
sipped the cappuccino. We reviewed the menus and costs
for the four upcoming events. He nodded and asked a
question here and there. Then I asked how he was feeling
about the college-application process.

"Okay." He stood to fix himself another, weaker cup
of cappuccino. "I guess." He obviously did not want to
chat about the applications, though, so I let it drop. He
reached for the sugar bowl, then plopped back down at

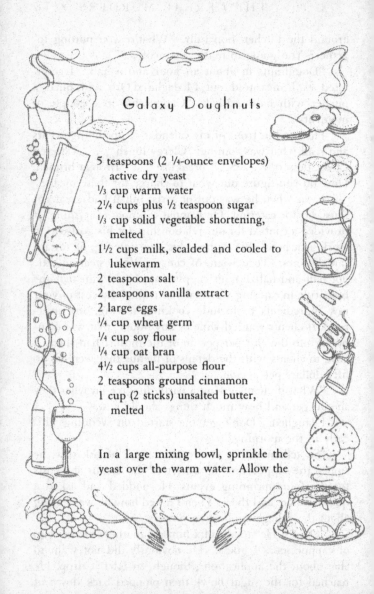

Galaxy Doughnuts

5 teaspoons (2 ¼-ounce envelopes)
   active dry yeast
⅓ cup warm water
2¼ cups plus ½ teaspoon sugar
⅓ cup solid vegetable shortening,
   melted
1½ cups milk, scalded and cooled to
   lukewarm
2 teaspoons salt
2 teaspoons vanilla extract
2 large eggs
¼ cup wheat germ
¼ cup soy flour
¼ cup oat bran
4½ cups all-purpose flour
2 teaspoons ground cinnamon
1 cup (2 sticks) unsalted butter,
   melted

In a large mixing bowl, sprinkle the
yeast over the warm water. Allow the

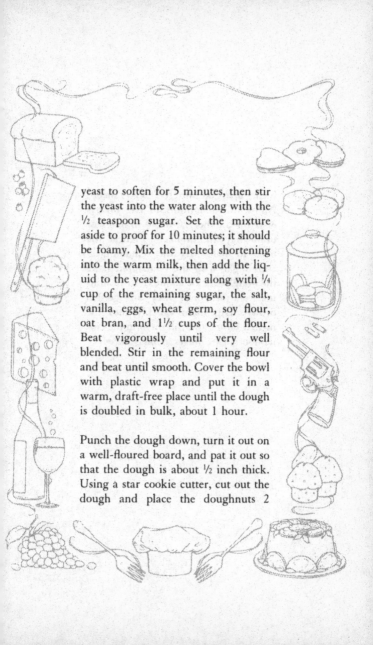

yeast to soften for 5 minutes, then stir the yeast into the water along with the ½ teaspoon sugar. Set the mixture aside to proof for 10 minutes; it should be foamy. Mix the melted shortening into the warm milk, then add the liquid to the yeast mixture along with ¼ cup of the remaining sugar, the salt, vanilla, eggs, wheat germ, soy flour, oat bran, and 1½ cups of the flour. Beat vigorously until very well blended. Stir in the remaining flour and beat until smooth. Cover the bowl with plastic wrap and put it in a warm, draft-free place until the dough is doubled in bulk, about 1 hour.

Punch the dough down, turn it out on a well-floured board, and pat it out so that the dough is about ½ inch thick. Using a star cookie cutter, cut out the dough and place the doughnuts 2

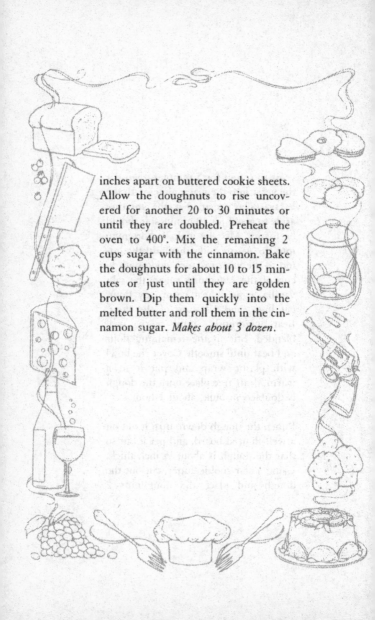

inches apart on buttered cookie sheets. Allow the doughnuts to rise uncovered for another 20 to 30 minutes or until they are doubled. Preheat the oven to 400°. Mix the remaining 2 cups sugar with the cinnamon. Bake the doughnuts for about 10 to 15 minutes or just until they are golden brown. Dip them quickly into the melted butter and roll them in the cinnamon sugar. *Makes about 3 dozen*.

the kitchen table. I managed not to wince when he ladled four teaspoons of sugar into the second cup. Ah, well, perhaps I should be glad that it wasn't drugs. Speaking of which.

"Tell me about the headmaster's son," I began conversationally.

"What's there to tell?" he asked between tiny slurps.

"Is he taking steroids?"

Julian choked on the coffee. Sputtering and coughing, he wiped his chin with a napkin I handed him and gave me a dark look. "Gee, Goldy, let's not mince any words."

"Well?"

Julian chewed the inside of his cheek. "You can't tell anybody," he began quietly.

"As if it weren't obvious."

Julian turned. "Macguire is under a lot of pressure."

"From whom?"

"Gosh, Goldy, *from whom* do you think? Do I have to spell it out for you, like, like, uh"—he cast his eyes heavenward in imitation of the headmaster—"like . . . ?"

"But Perkins, the son, I mean, isn't an academic type. He can hardly be expected to follow in his father's footsteps."

Julian got up and carefully covered his cappuccino with waxed paper before placing it in the microwave. When the timer beeped, he took it out. Then he shook his head. "You're not getting it."

"Okay, okay. Macguire excels in athletics. But that doesn't mean he needs to do a dangerous drug, does it? What happens if he gets caught?"

"He isn't going to get caught. Besides, he's not selling anything, so what's the penalty? Everybody feels sorry for him." He carefully sipped the heated cappuccino. Then he added darkly, "Almost everybody."

Wait a minute. "Was this what Keith Andrews was going to expose in the *Mountain Journal*?"

Julian, exasperated, snapped, "When are you going to believe that none of us *knew* what Keith was writing for the newspaper?" He ran the fingers of one hand through the blond mohawk. "That was the whole problem. I tried to get Keith to tell me what he was working on, and he said it would all come out. He made such a big deal about his secrecy, tapping away in the computer lab when no one was there. The CIA, man."

The front doorbell rang. I told Julian it was probably Marla, then cursed the fact that I'd forgotten to sand the front steps.

He said, "Oh, that reminds me, I forgot, you got a call—"

"Hold that thought."

Marla had safely navigated the steps and now stood in our doorway in her usual seasonal colors. This morning, three days before Halloween, the outfit consisted of an extra-large orange and black suede patchwork skirt and matching jacket. She held a brown grocery sack.

"You didn't have to bring anything," I said.

"Don't presume," she announced haughtily as her plump body breezed past me. "It's a hot melt glue gun, Styrofoam cone, and bag of baby Three Musketeers for Arch. Even sick people can do a craft project with candy. *Especially* sick people. And by the way, your front porch steps are covered with ice. Absolutely treacherous. Better put some salt on them." So saying, she dropped the bag at the bottom of the stairs, then yodeled a greeting to Julian, whom she passed on her way into the kitchen.

"You see, about this call—" Julian attempted.

"Just a sec." I turned back to slam the front door against the cold. Before I could close it, though, a small foreign car arrived on the street directly in front of my house. A young woman whom I vaguely recognized as being from the *Mountain Journal* delicately stepped out and peered up at me.

Julian came up beside me. "This is it, I'm sorry I forgot to tell you. This woman called from the newspaper around 6:45. She asked if it would be okay to come by and interview you this morning. I thought you'd want it for free publicity. For the business. It wasn't until I was about to hang up that she said it was about that night out at the headmaster's house." He added lamely, "I'm really sorry."

"Just take care of Marla, will you?" I said under my breath. "And check the doughnut dough." Then I shouted gaily to the intruder, "Come on in!" as if I were accustomed to having open house at nine o'clock every morning. "Just avoid the ice on the steps." After lifting weights, the last thing I needed was to lug a bag of road salt up from the basement to make my steps safe for the world of journalism.

The reporter tiptoed gingerly up the far side of my front steps. Frances Markasian was in her early twenties, wore no makeup, and had straggly black hair that fell limply to the shoulders of her denim jacket. An ominously large black bag dangled from her right arm and banged against the knees of her tight jeans.

"You don't have a camera in there, do you?" I asked once she was safely inside. I couldn't bear the thought of photographs.

"I won't use it if you don't want me to." Her voice was pure Chicago.

"Well, I'd really rather you wouldn't," I said sweetly, leading her out to the kitchen. Marla was already sipping cappuccino that Julian had made for her. Frances Markasian was introduced all around, and I asked her if it was okay if my friends stayed while she talked to me. She shrugged, which I took as consent. I offered her some coffee.

"No thanks." She dipped into her bag, brought out a diet Pepsi, popped the top, and then dropped two Vivarin through the opening.

Marla watched her, open-mouthed. When Frances Markasian took a long swig from the can, Marla said, "Mission control, we have ignition. Stand by."

Frances ignored her and pulled a pen and pad out of the voluminous bag. "I understand you were the caterer the night of the Andrews murder?"

"Well, er, yes." I had a sinking feeling she was not going to be asking about the menu.

Julian must have felt the reporter's eyes on him, because he got up, punched down the risen dough, and began to roll it out to cut doughnuts with a star cookie cutter.

"You want to tell me what happened?" she said.

"Well . . ." I began, then gave her the briefest possible account of the evening's events. Her pen made *scritch*-ing noises as she took notes.

"They've been having some other problems out at that school," she said when I had finished and was checking on the doughnuts, which had almost finished their brief rising.

"Really?" I inquired innocently. "Like what?" I wasn't going to give her anything. My previous experience with the *Mountain Journal* had been negative. They'd hired a food critic, who had viciously trashed me. The critic had been conducting a private vendetta in print. By the time I got the mess exposed, the unapologetic *Mountain Journal* had moved on to reports of elk herds moving through mountain neighborhoods.

"Problems like snakes in lockers," Frances said.

I waved my hand dismissively. "Seventh grade."

"Problems like a headmaster who might be having trouble raising money if bad news got out about the school," Frances continued matter-of-factly. "Take this dropping-SAT-score thing—"

"Oh, Ms. Markasian, sweetheart," Marla interrupted, "that news is so old, it has mold on it. Besides, if you were worried about your academic reputation, you wouldn't *kill* your top student, now, would you?" Marla rolled her eyes at me. "Those goodies ready?"

I turned to Julian, who wordlessly slid the risen doughnuts into the heated oven. "Fifteen minutes," he announced.

"Know anything about that headmaster?" Frances persisted. She tapped her pen on the pad.

"I know as much as you do," I told her. "Why don't you tell us about the story Keith Andrews was working on for your paper?"

"*We* didn't know what it was," she protested, "although he had been working on it for some time, and he'd promised something big." She tilted her Pepsi can back to drain the last few drops. "We were going to read it when he was done and then decide whether to run it or not. If it was a timely story. You know, truthful."

"You have such a good reputation for fact-checking," I said with a lying smile.

Without a shred of self-consciousness she tossed her can across the room into one of the two trash bags resting against my back door. Arch was supposed to take them out, but he was incapacitated.

"Three points," I said. "Except we recycle." I retrieved the can and dropped it into the aluminum bin in the pantry. I hoped she would take the hint and decide it was time to wrap things up. But no.

"How about the headmaster's son? Macguire Perkins? He drove his father's car through a guard rail on Highway 203 over the summer. Blood alcohol level 2.0."

I shrugged. "You know as much as I do."

Frances Markasian looked around my kitchen, her shallow black eyes impassive. The smell of the baking doughnuts was excruciating. I hadn't realized how hungry I was. "I understand some of the Elk Park Prep students and parents are pretty competitive. Would do anything to get into the right college."

I crossed my arms. "Yeah? Like what?"

She tapped her mouth with her pen but gave no answer. "Keith Andrews was the valedictorian. Who was next in line?"

Before I could answer, Arch came limping into the kitchen. I was thankful for the distraction. Julian asked Arch to join him out in the living room to make a sculpture out of the Three Musketeers.

"Wow," said Arch. "At nine-fifteen in the morning?"

"We're going to build a fire too. Is that all right? It is kind of cold." When I gave him the go-ahead, he said, "Can you handle getting the doughnuts out of the oven?"

"She's an old pro at removing cookie sheets," said Marla. "Besides, I think Ms. Markasian is almost done, isn't she?"

Frances Markasian closed her eyes and said, "Huh." She rounded her back and stretched her arms out in front of her. Journalistic meditation. The buzzer went off and I took the doughnuts out. Julian had prepared a pan of melted butter and a mountain of cinnamon sugar, so I quickly dipped and rolled, dipped and rolled. I brought the first plate of plump, warm doughnuts over to the table and placed them in the sunlight, so that cinnamon sugar sparkled on the veil of melted butter. Marla delicately lifted one onto a plate and then took a huge bite.

"Please have one," I said to the reporter.

She shook her head. Frances Markasian seemed to be unable to decide whether to share something with me. After a moment she put her pen and pad away in her enormous purse. "I'll tell you *like what* parents will do. Last week we got a call at the paper saying we should run a story on how Stan and Rhoda Marensky had sent a full-length mink coat to the director of admissions at Williams."

I couldn't help it. My mouth fell open.

"Listen," said Marla in her one-upsmanship voice. She reached for her second doughnut. "I wouldn't spend a winter in Massachusetts if I had a mink *house*."

At that moment, yells erupted from the living room. Julian banged through the kitchen door. A cloud of smoke billowed in behind him.

"Something's wrong!" he shouted. "The flue's open but the smoke won't go up! I'll help Arch out the front. You all need to get out!" His face was white with fear.

"Out the front, hurry!" I yelled at Marla and Frances. We bolted.

Julian and Arch were already halfway down the front walk by the time we three adults came hustling through the front door. Julian had Arch's arm draped around his shoulder and the two were half skipping toward the street. Frances Markasian reached the sidewalk first. With frighteningly effortless ease she spun around and scooped her camera out of her big black bag. Then she hoisted it and took a picture of Marla, midair, grasping a freshly baked oat bran doughnut, as she slipped on the iced steps and broke her leg.

14

With sirens blaring and lights flashing, the fluorescent chartreuse AMFD trucks arrived in a matter of moments, proving the local adage that the fastest thing about our town was the fire department. One of my neighbors had seen the smoke billowing out of the window Julian had hastily opened, and she'd put in the call. Over the incessant buzz of the smoke alarm, I screamed to Julian to stay out in the street with Arch. A wad of fur hit my calves and was gone—Scout the cat making a streaking escape. Flames were consuming my home. But I refused to leave Marla's side at the bottom of the front steps. Firemen clumped by us into the house. Marla clenched my hand and sobbed copiously. My schooling in Med Wives 101 adjudged it to be a broken right tibia. I shrieked for somebody to call an ambulance.

The firefighters rapidly assessed the situation and put a ladder up to the roof. Minutes later, clad in schoolbusyellow protective gear, the first fellow descended the ladder, holding a blackened piece of plywood and shaking his head. With a screaming siren, the ambulance arrived and carted Marla off to a Denver hospital. I hugged her carefully and promised to visit just as soon as the smoke cleared. She begged me to call her other friends so that everyone could know what had happened. Marla's idea of hell is enduring pain alone.

"What was that board?" I demanded of the one volunteer firefighter I recognized, a gray-haired real estate agent who had originally sold the house to John Richard and me.

"You had something on top of your chimney."

"Well, yes, but . . . how did it get there?"

"You have some gutter or roof work done? This your first use of the fireplace this season?"

"It is not my first use of the fireplace this season, and the only work I've had done on the house recently was a security system I had put in this summer." The blackened board lay propped against one of the tires of the AMFD truck. Two firemen stood in front of it, deep in conversation.

"Look, Goldy, it could have been a lot worse. We had this same thing happen to a summerhouse over by the lake. Smoke pouring everywhere. Usually it means you put too much paper on the logs, the chimney needs to be swept, or some birds have built a nest. Anyway, our guys went up. First one took off a nest, sure enough. Then he looked down the chimney and fainted. Second guy looked down the chimney and fainted. I had smoke, flames, and two guys out cold on the roof. Had to call an ambulance for the firefighters. Turns out this burglar had tried to enter the house through the chimney, got stuck, died of asphyxiation. In the spring some birds built a nest. Then the owners came back and built a fire. Once our guys pulled out that nest, they looked down at a perfectly pre-served skeleton."

I clenched my head with both hands. "Is this story supposed to reassure me?"

He shrugged one shoulder and moved off to help his men reload their equipment. The emergency, as far as they were concerned, was over. Several neighbors had gathered on the sidewalk to see what was going on. I asked if anyone had seen a person or persons on my roof recently. All negative. Then I crossed over to the house of a young mother, the only person on our street who had a good view of my place. Her forehead furrowed as she fixed the shoelace of one child and then gave antibiotic to another. She was raising four children under the age of six, and whenever anyone stupidly asked if she *worked,* she threw a dirty diaper at them. She told me she'd been preoccupied ferrying her kids to the pediatrician—three times in the last week—and no, she hadn't seen anyone.

Julian announced that he and Arch had decided they might as well go to school, was I going to be all right? I told them to go ahead. Frances Markasian stood on the sidewalk, snapping photos, as if the fire were the biggest news event to hit Aspen Meadow this century. The crash of the *Hindenburg* had less photo coverage. She took a picture of me as I walked up to her.

"I thought you promised not to do that." My life was beginning to feel out of control.

"Before, you weren't news," she said impassively. "Now you're news. Any idea how this could have happened?"

"Zero," I mumbled. "Did you see that plywood board they took off the chimney?" She nodded. "Maybe some workmen left it over the summer. I wish you wouldn't publish those pictures. People will think I burned something in my kitchen."

"If something more exciting happens before Monday, no problem." She shoved the camera into her bag and drew out a cigarette. No breakfast, diet cola with caffeine tabs, and now a smoke. I would give this woman ten years. She inhaled hungrily. "Listen, you were pretty discreet in there about the competition situation out at Elk Park Prep. So was I. But you're wrong."

"Oh?" I said innocently. "How's that?"

"Well." Fran blew a set of perfect smoke rings. "Parents seem to think we have an endless amount of newspaper space to run articles about their kids. First we did an article about Keith Andrews in September, at his request." She tapped the cigarette, scattering ashes on her denim jacket. "Maybe you saw it: 'First-place Andrews blends academics with activism.' I mean, Keith helped us a lot during the summer covering the Mountain Rendezvous and the arts festival, so we figured we owed him the article when he asked. Anyway. We ran the piece and Stan Marensky called us, shrieking his head off. Said Keith Andrews had never marched in front of his store the way he claimed. Said the kid didn't know a mink from an otter and couldn't care less about the anti-fur movement. So we went back and asked Keith about it, and he confessed that he had used a wee bit of exaggeration, but that the profile was really going to help his Stanford application." She exhaled another batch of white O's.

"If only you all would check facts before you print things," I murmured.

She flicked ashes. "Hey, what do you think we are, *The New York Times*? This was supposed to be a human interest thing. Then Hank Dawson shows up on our doorstep, waving a copy of the newspaper. He figures we should run a full-page profile on *his* daughter for our 'Who's Who' section. When we say his daughter isn't anybody special, Dawson yells he's going to withdraw all of his café advertising. We say, well, he can buy a page of advertising for his *daughter,* and he stomps out. Then he cancels both his advertising and his subscription."

The "Who's Who" page usually ran stories of veterinarians saving elk calves and national celebrities showing up at local Fourth of July celebrations. If we weren't talking the *Times,* we weren't exactly talking *People,* either.

"Perhaps you should have run the profile . . ." I murmured.

"Clearly, you don't read the *Mountain Journal*"—she crushed the cigarette savagely beneath her toe—"because we did. In 'Mountain Arts and Crafts' there was an article on little Greer Dawson and the Bronco jewelry she was making to peddle at her parents' café. Earrings dangling with miniature plastic orange footballs. Necklaces made of rows of teensy-weensy football helmets." Frances groped in the bulging bag and brought out a packet of candy corn. Dessert. She offered me some; I declined. "Now, how many women do you think actually buy jewelry like that? That article proved every stupid stereotype people have of rural journalism. We got the café's advertising back, but it was still a mistake because who comes in the next week? Audrey Coopersmith, whining that we should run an article on Heather and how her scientific know-how saved the ice cream social at the Mountain Rendezvous—"

"How do you save an ice cream social?"

She finished the candy corn and wiped her hands on her jeans. "Oh. You know, they have such a small power source in the homestead next to the park where the Rendezvous is held." I didn't, but I nodded anyway. "The freezer holding the Häagen-Dazs blew the fuses, and Heather Coopersmith saved the day by rewiring the whole thing . . . we are talking *way* boring. We didn't run an article for Audrey Coopersmith, and she cancelled her subscription. So what. I have to go. Sorry about your chimney." And with that she climbed into her car and discarded the candy corn bag out the window. She lit up another cigarette, revved the engine, and chugged away.

I picked up the bag from the street and went back into the house. The smoke alarm had stopped its ear-splitting buzz. I opened all the windows. After the commotion, the place felt absurdly quiet; it smelled like a camping site. I jumped when the phone rang—Tom Schulz. I told him what had happened, ending with poor Marla.

"How'd the board get over your chimney?" he wanted to know.

"That was my question. Think I should get the security people to come back out here?"

"I think you should move out of your house for a while. Go to Marla's, maybe?" His voice was slow and serious.

"No can do, sorry to say. Her cabinets would never pass the county health inspector. Anyway, whoever is doing this seems to know I have a security system, so I'm safe except for pranks."

He asked where the boys were, and I told him.

"Listen, Goldy, I don't care about your system. I don't want you in that place alone, especially at night."

I ignored this. "Thanks for the worry. Now, I've got a question for you. What was the story on the fuses at the headmaster's house? I mean, when the fuses blew that night, that was the moment that Keith Andrews' killer made his move, wasn't it?"

"There was a timer attached to one set of wires that had been stripped and coiled together. It was planned, sure, but you knew that, didn't you?"

I told him about the Rendezvous and Heather Coopersmith's expert knowledge of wiring.

"It's a long shot," he said, "but I'll go question her again. What's your take on that kid and her mother, anyway?"

"Oh, I don't know." My head ached, my finger throbbed, and I didn't want to go into the details of Audrey's bitterness, or how long it seemed to be lasting. "Audrey's unhappy, you saw that. Did the headmaster's place turn up anything else? I saw your guys out there sweeping the place after the snow melted."

"It did, as a matter of fact. Makes your discovery of the credit card in Rhoda Marensky's coat somewhat more interesting. Out by the sled there was a gold pen with the name Marensky Furs."

"Oh, my God."

"Problem is, Stan Marensky says the pen could have come from anywhere, and Rhoda Marensky swears she didn't leave her coat out at the headmaster's house."

"Liar, liar, raccoon on fire. Mr. Perkins specifically told me she'd be so happy to get it back."

"Headmaster Perkins said the coat just appeared in his closet the day of the dinner and he called Rhoda, who then forgot to take it with her after the lights went out. But she had been missing it for a couple of weeks. She says."

"If that is true, then whoever is doing all this is a phenomenally elaborate planner." I thought for a minute, and remembered only a glimpse of a fur-clad Stan Marensky whisking Rhoda out the headmaster's front door after the lights had come back on and order had been restored. "Look, I don't know what's going on with the Marenskys, their store, or pens from their store. What I don't understand is *why me*? Why a rock through *my* window, why ice on *my* steps, why a board over *my* chimney? I don't know anything. I never even met Keith Andrews."

"I swear, I wish you'd come to my place for a while,

Miss G. Or more than a while, if you're still of a mind . . ."

"Thank you, but I'm staying put."

"You're in danger. I'm going to talk to the team here about setting up some surveillance—"

I let out a deep breath.

He said, "I'll get back to you."

As usual, cooking cleared the head and calmed the nerves. I needed both. First I froze the doughnuts, which, miraculously, weren't smoke-damaged. Then I set about planning cooking times for the priests' luncheon on Friday, the Tattered Cover affair on Halloween night, and the SAT breakfast on Saturday morning. I called my supplier and ordered the freshest sole she could find, plus fresh fruit.

The rest of that day and the next passed placidly enough. I picked Marla up from the hospital Thursday morning and took her back to her house. She didn't want me to baby her. With all her money, Marla could pick anyone she wanted to take care of her; she had opted for a private nurse, arranged while she was still in the hospital. Arch's ankle healed nicely and gave him the much-desired excuse from gym class. He announced brightly that he was resting so he'd be completely better for skiing over the weekend. Julian sprinkled road salt on the iced front steps before the supplier arrived with her crates of boxes. I tried to believe that the board-over-the-chimney person had not also been responsible for the ice hazard. But that was sure to be wishful thinking.

Miss Ferrell called on Thursday afternoon and said she wanted to go over Julian's list for colleges with me after the SATs on Saturday, instead of our planned chat beforehand. She had too much organizing to do before the tests began, and she wanted to give me her full attention. I wasn't one of his parents, but she wanted to feel that some responsible adult was involved. "Julian can come too, if you like," she added. But I said I would feel better if she and I could just have a little time together alone. After all, I was new at this.

Friday morning brought gloomy clouds spitting snowflakes. Because his father was picking him up at three to go directly to Keystone, Arch busied himself packing up his ski gear before school. I washed crisp spinach leaves and poached sole fillets in white wine and broth. Then I chopped mountains of cranberries and pecans for the Sorry Cake. When I was putting the cake pans into the oven, Julian said he'd had an invitation to spend the night at a friend's house; they would go to the bookstore talk and the SAT testing together. But he was concerned—would I be all right alone? It was all I could do to keep from laughing. I told him if I could survive all those years with John Richard Korman, I could survive anything. Besides, with both boys gone, I knew just what guest to call.

I gave the boys pumpkin muffins for breakfast and helped Arch lug his skis, boots, and poles out to the Range Rover. Saying good-bye to him before he went off with his father was always difficult; before a holiday, even Halloween, it was excruciating.

At the last minute, Arch dashed upstairs to get his high-powered binoculars. "Almost forgot! I might be able to see the Andromeda galaxy once they turn out the night-skiing lights. You can see Andromeda in the winter, but never in the summer!" he hollered over his shoulder. When the boys were finally ready, I sent them off over their halfhearted protests with homemade popcorn balls and packets of candy corn to share with their friends.

They took off in a mood of high good cheer. Halloween was not a school holiday, but the snow, the buttery scent of popcorn, and Arch's cone sculpture of Three Musketeers bars made the two boys laugh giddily after a week that had been grueling for us all.

Despite his upbeat mood as he drove off, Julian's taut face and bitten nails told another story. During the past two weeks, he had spent hours at the kitchen table, studying financial aid forms and making lists of numbers. When he wasn't doing homework, he pored over tomes on test-taking and SAT review. Along with the rest of his class, Julian had taken the PSATs his sophomore year and the SATs his junior year. But this third time was *it,* he told me, the big one, make or break, do or die. These were the scores the colleges looked at to make their decisions.

I had tried to drill him a little bit Thursday night, using the SAT review, but it had not been a pleasant task. I mean, who made up these tests? For example, one analogy asked, *handsome* is to *corpulent* as *beautiful* is to . . . *obese, ugly, attractive,* or *dead?* Well, didn't that depend on whether or not you thought corpulence is an attractive trait? I happened to think that it was, and argued to that effect. And when, I demanded, were you going to use the word *epigrammatic* in day-to-day conversation? Now, I am all for reading and vocabulary-building, but as our generation used to say, let's get relevant. I told Julian he didn't need to know that one. He sighed. What did me in, though, was *"My friend is a philanthropist, therefore he . . . goes to church with his family, gives away his possessions, pays off his credit cards, or plays the glockenspiel."* Without hesitation I told Julian that he would pay off the credit cards, and maybe play the glockenspiel in the evening for the neighbors. Julian suggested I forget trying to test him, because the correct answer was "gives away his possessions." I argued that if you pay a high rate of interest on credit cards, you hurt your family, which should be your first area of philanthropy. Julian quietly closed the big book. I immediately apologized. The smile he gave me was pinched and ironic. But the review session was over. When Julian had retired to his room, I morosely poured myself a Cointreau and zapped the kernels for the popcorn balls. So much for philanthropy beginning at home.

On Halloween morning, with this spiritual thought still rocketing around in my head, I finished icing the Sorry Cake and took off for the church. A brief wash of snowflakes marked the end of the flurry. Wisps of cloud drifted upward from the near mountains. In the church parking lot sat only two cars: the secretary's pale blue Honda, and a gleaming new Jeep Wagoneer that I guessed belonged to the Marenskys—who else would have the license plate MINX? Nowhere in sight was Father Olson's Mercedes 300E, a four-wheel-drive vehicle that he claimed he needed to visit parishioners in remote locations. Well, our priest was probably off having one of his favorite things, a hilltop experience.

When I came through the church door with the first bowls of fruit, Brad Marensky almost mowed me down.

"Oh, I'm sorry," he yelped, and grabbed a teetering bowl of orange slices from my hands.

While he was getting control of the bowl, I took a good look at him. Of medium build, Brad was a younger, more handsome version of his father, Stan. There was the same curly hair, jet-black instead of salted with gray, the same high-cheekboned and olive-toned handsome face, smooth rather than deeply lined with anxiety. He also had his father's dark eyes. I imagined those eyes had elicited romantic interest from more than one girl at Elk Park Prep. In catching himself and the bowl, and then sidestepping me, Brad moved like an athlete. Even without the aid of the *Mountain Journal*'s sports section, Brad's all-round prowess, and his father's relentless drills, were well known. The mothers at the athletic club made a great joke of Stan Marensky's famous screech, "Come on, Brad! Come on, *Brad*!" Sometimes the coaches had to shut Stan up; they couldn't make themselves heard.

"Gosh, I'm sorry, I didn't mean to crash into you. Aren't you . . . doesn't Julian live at your . . ."

"Yes," I said simply. "Julian Teller lives with my son and me. And I know your parents."

He blushed. "Well, sorry about the"—he looked down at what he had rescued—"the fruit." He seemed tongue-tied. He held the bowl awkwardly, as if he were not quite sure what to do with it. Come to think of it, what was he doing in church on Halloween morning, anyway? Could the seniors just skip classes whenever they wanted?

"What about you? You okay?" I asked.

His face turned an even deeper shade of red. Avoiding my eyes, he pivoted on his heel and carefully placed the bowl on the tile floor next to the baptismal font. He turned back to me, pressed his lips together, and lifted his chin. Brad Marensky was not all right, that much was clear.

"I have to go," he said. "The person I wanted to see isn't here." His control slipped, and he added, "Uh, you don't know when Father Olson will be back, do you?"

"For lunch. I'm catering."

"Right, right, the caterer. A meeting, the secretary told me." He glanced around the cold, cavernous church. No altar candles were lit. The brass crucifix at the front of the church glowed with reflected light from the sacramental candle. In the pale light the teenager's face had the look of a jaundiced ghost.

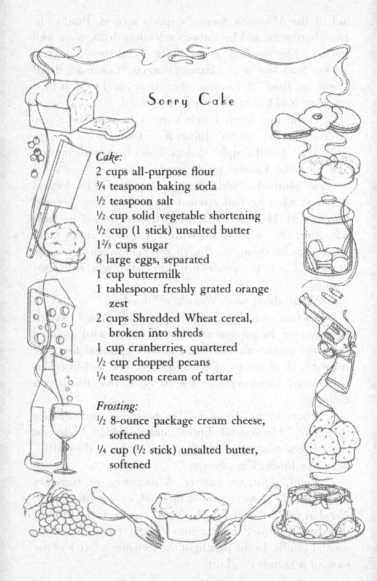

Sorry Cake

Cake:

2 cups all-purpose flour
¾ teaspoon baking soda
½ teaspoon salt
½ cup solid vegetable shortening
½ cup (1 stick) unsalted butter
1⅔ cups sugar
6 large eggs, separated
1 cup buttermilk
1 tablespoon freshly grated orange
 zest
2 cups Shredded Wheat cereal,
 broken into shreds
1 cup cranberries, quartered
½ cup chopped pecans
¼ teaspoon cream of tartar

Frosting:

½ 8-ounce package cream cheese,
 softened
¼ cup (½ stick) unsalted butter,
 softened

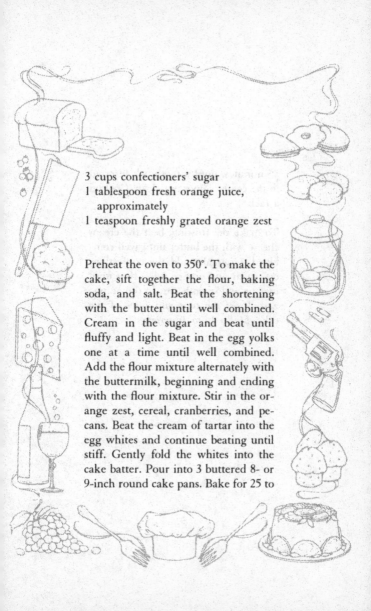

3 cups confectioners' sugar
1 tablespoon fresh orange juice,
 approximately
1 teaspoon freshly grated orange zest

Preheat the oven to 350°. To make the cake, sift together the flour, baking soda, and salt. Beat the shortening with the butter until well combined. Cream in the sugar and beat until fluffy and light. Beat in the egg yolks one at a time until well combined. Add the flour mixture alternately with the buttermilk, beginning and ending with the flour mixture. Stir in the orange zest, cereal, cranberries, and pecans. Beat the cream of tartar into the egg whites and continue beating until stiff. Gently fold the whites into the cake batter. Pour into 3 buttered 8- or 9-inch round cake pans. Bake for 25 to

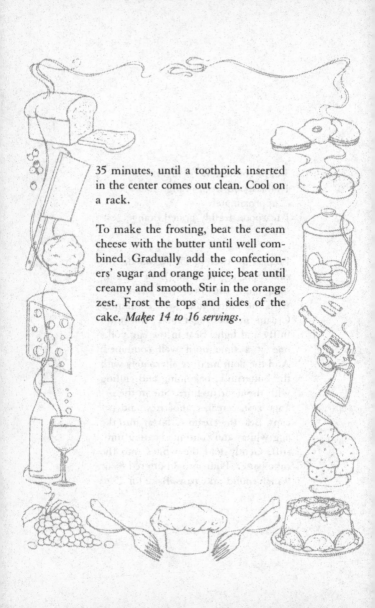

35 minutes, until a toothpick inserted in the center comes out clean. Cool on a rack.

To make the frosting, beat the cream cheese with the butter until well combined. Gradually add the confectioners' sugar and orange juice; beat until creamy and smooth. Stir in the orange zest. Frost the tops and sides of the cake. *Makes 14 to 16 servings*.

"Brad, are you sure you're all right? Do you want to sit down for a while?"

He lifted an eyebrow and considered. "I saw you at that college application meeting."

"Yes, well, I needed to see Miss Ferrell about my son, Arch. He's . . . having some problems at school." When he didn't respond, I rushed on with, "Maybe you'd like to help me in the kitchen until Father Olson gets here. When I'm waiting for something, it always helps me to take my mind off—"

"Julian says you're good to talk to."

"Oh. He does?"

He regarded me again with that same lost-Bambi expression, and then seemed to make a decision. "I'm here because of something in the bulletin."

"Something . . ."

His teeth gnawed his bottom lip. "Some discussion they're having."

"Oh, the committee! Yes, they're talking about penance and faith, I think. I'm . . . not sure the meeting is open to the public." I try to be delicate. Sometimes it works, sometimes it doesn't.

"Wait." His eyes widened. "You're the one who found Keith, aren't you?"

"Well, yes, but—"

"Oh, God," he said with a fierce dejection that twisted my heart. His shoulders slumped. "Things are such a mess. . . ."

"Look, Brad, come on out to the kitchen for just a while—"

"You don't understand why I'm here." Tears quivered in his protest. And then he said, "I need to confess."

15

"Let's go sit in a pew," I whispered. I had fleeting thoughts of calling Schulz, of telling this troubled boy to wait for Father Olson. But there was urgency behind Brad's distress and I wanted to help him. Whatever his problem was, I couldn't absolve him. Nor would I feel comfortable turning him in. He'd have to do that himself.

We slipped into the last hard wooden pew and sat down awkwardly. Think, I ordered myself. If Julian said I was good to talk to—a surprise—then maybe all I had to do was listen.

"I . . . I've been stealing," said Brad.

I said nothing. He looked at me and I nodded. His handsome face was racked with pain. He seemed to be expecting something. "Go on," I told him. He was silent. In a low voice I prompted him. "You wanted to talk about stealing."

"I've been doing it for a long time. Years." He

hunched his shoulders as if he were small and very lost. Then he straightened his back and let out a ragged breath. "I felt good at first. Taking stuff made me feel great. Strong." With sudden ferocity he said, "I loved it."

I *mm-hmm*ed.

"When Perkins used to say in assemblies, we don't need locks on the lockers at Elk Park Prep, I would laugh inside. I mean, I would just howl." Brad Marensky wasn't laughing now. He wasn't even smiling. His mouth was a grim, suffering slash as he silently contemplated the diamond-shaped window above the altar. I wondered if he was going to continue.

"It wasn't for the stuff," he said at last. "I had plenty of stuff. My parents have money. I could have had any coat in the store I wanted. My biggest thrill was ripping off a jean jacket from somebody's locker." A silent sob racked his lean body. He seemed to want to cry, but was holding it in. Perhaps he was afraid someone would walk through the doors. The muffled clatter of the ancient mimeo machine in the church office came across as a distant *crunch, pop; crunch, pop*. A cool, hushed quiet emanated from the stone floor and bare walls. Brad Marensky's confession was a murmur within that sanctified space.

"I was going to quit. That was what I swore to myself. I had even decided to give something back. . . . I don't even know why I'd taken this thing from a kid's locker."

He seemed poised to go off into another reverie. I thought of the table and food I had to prepare, of the twelve committee members who would be arriving within the hour. "Another kid's locker," I prodded gently.

"Yeah. Then one day a couple of weeks ago, I decided to put this thing back. After school. When I was slipping it back in and closing the locker, the stupid

French Club let out and all these kids filed into the hall. I just, like, froze. I figured Miss Ferrell, Keith Andrews, the other kids, even your son—sorry, I don't know his name—saw me and thought that instead of giving something back, I was taking it." He sighed. "It was the new Cure tape. I don't even like the Cure."

"Wait a minute. A tape? Not money, or a credit card?" I blurted out the question without thinking.

"Huh?" He said the word as if he'd been punched, and gave me a puzzled glance. "No. I took money, but not credit cards. You can really get in trouble for doing that." He looked uneasily at the front door. Before he finished, however, there was one thing I needed to know.

"If you thought Arch—my son—might have seen you, and was going to tell, did you try to stop him? With a rattlesnake in his locker? And a threatening note?"

"No, no, no. I wouldn't do that."

"Okay. Go ahead, I interrupted you."

But he couldn't. He started to cry. He cradled his head and sobbed, and impulsively I put my arms around his shoulders and murmured, "Don't . . . don't cry, please . . . it's going to be okay, really. Don't be so hard on yourself, everybody messes up. You tried to make things right. . . ."

"That was the weird part," he whispered into my shoulder. "As soon as I decided to quit, everything went wrong. First someone smashed Keith's windshield . . ."

"When was that, exactly?"

Brad sat up and swiped at his tears. "The day the Princeton rep came. I remember because Keith seemed not to be bothered by the car, he just went on as calm as ever. He was early for the rep and had a zillion questions about the eating clubs and whether they'd take his summer school credits from C.U., that kind of thing."

"A zillion . . ."

"Yeah. But later I heard he was writing this article for the newspaper, and I got scared. So I did steal something. Just one last thing, I told myself. Oh, God"—his words came out in a rush—"then he was killed." His brown eyes were sunken and fearful. "It wasn't me. I didn't kill him. I'd never do something like that. Then somebody put that snake in your son's locker." In disbelief, he shook his head. "It's like everything went haywire as soon as I decided to go straight."

"But after you stole that last thing, you did try to get rid of it. You put the credit card in your mother's coat pocket."

His boyish face wrinkled. "What is this with the credit card? I didn't take a credit card, and I don't know what the story is on my mother's coat, because I didn't steal that, either. After Keith saw me putting the Cure tape back, I was sure the article he was writing for the local paper was about stealing. About *me*. So I pried open the door to Keith's computer cubbyhole and took his disks. I thought I'd find the article for the newspaper and erase it." He reached under his sweatshirt and pulled out two disks. "There's an article in here, but it's not about stealing. Can you take these? I can't stand to have them anymore. I'm afraid if someone finds them, I'll get into big trouble. Maybe you could give them to the cops . . . I don't want a criminal record." He didn't say it, but the question in his eyes was *Are you going to turn me in?*

I held the disks but did not look at them. This was a boy in torment. I wasn't the law. But there was something else.

"Look at me, Brad."

He did.

"Did Keith know you were stealing?"

"I am almost positive now that he didn't," he said without hesitation. "Because if Keith had something on you, or if he didn't like you, he couldn't keep it to himself. Once he tried to blackmail my father over some tax stuff. When Schlichtmaier called on him, he would say, *Heil Hitler.*" He thrust his hands through his dark hair, then shuddered. "After the French Club got out that day, he never said anything to me. I figured I'd gotten off. But then somebody killed him. Do you believe me? I can't stand having this hanging over my head anymore."

Softly, I said, "Yes, I believe you." Brad had chosen me to help him. I was duty bound to do at least that. I met his eyes with a level, unsmiling gaze. "Have you decided to stop stealing?"

"Yes, yes," he said as his eyes watered up again. "Never again, I promise."

"Can you give back what you took?"

"The cash is gone. But . . . I can put the *stuff* in the lost and found. I will, I promise."

"All right." Tenderness again welled up in my heart. The world thought this vulnerable boy had everything. I put my hands on his shoulders and murmured, "Remember what I said a few minutes ago. It's going to be okay. Believe me?" Tears slid down his sallow cheeks. His nod was barely perceptible. "I'm going to leave you now, Brad. Say a prayer or something."

He didn't move or utter another word. After a moment I slid out of the pew. As I stood in the aisle, trying to remember what I'd done with the bowl of orange slices, Brad turned and caught my hand in a crushing grip.

"You won't tell anybody, will you? Please say you won't."

"No, I won't. But that doesn't mean people don't know. Like Miss Ferrell. Or whoever."

"Mostly I'm worried about my parents . . ."

"Brad. I'm not going to tell anybody. I promise. You

did the right thing to get it off your chest. The worst part is over."

"I don't know what my parents would do if they found out," he mumbled as he turned his head back toward the altar.

Neither did I.

I ferried the pans of Sole Florentine out to the church kitchen and heated the oven. Around twenty minutes before noon, members of the Board of Theological Examiners began to arrive. Father Olson whisked through the parish hall first. He was in something of a state, going on about the one laywoman on the committee having a stroke and what were they going to do now? Canonically, the committee had to have twelve members to conduct interviews of candidates for the priesthood in December; the same group would administer the oral ordination exams in April. Father Olson pulled on his beard, Moses in distress. If he didn't find a competent replacement soon, the feminists would pressure the bishop and he'd be in hot water. I wanted to ask him why, when men were looking for a woman to do anything, they assumed they'd have a problem with competence. Perhaps the real worry was that they'd find somebody who was more competent than they were.

"Oh, dear," Father Olson was wailing, "why did this have to happen just when I've been named head of the committee?" He slumped morosely into one of the chairs I had just set up. "I really don't know what to do. I just don't even know where to begin."

Although I thought a prayer for the stroke victim might be in order, I murmured only, "Start by resetting the table" to his unhearing ears. He traipsed unhappily off to the office while I removed the twelfth place setting. The two laymen on the committee came in and sat next to each other. Both had an air of quiet seriousness, as if they were awaiting instructions. The first group of priests plunged through the heavy doors like a gaggle of blackbirds, laughing and jostling and telling clerical Halloween jokes. *What do you get when you cross a bat with an evangelical?* Heads waggled. *You get a hymn that sticks to the roof of your mouth.* The two laymen exchanged looks. This was not their idea of a joke. I served a tray of triangles of sourdough toast spread with glistening pesto. Father Olson made his somber appearance.

"Olson!" one of the blackbirds shrieked. "You're doing trick-or-treat as a priest!"

Father Olson chuckled patronizingly, then intoned the blessing. I hustled around with the sole while the meeting began. The food elicited numerous compliments. While the news of the stroke victim was being relayed, the priest of the bat joke even ventured jocularly that I should be the replacement on the committee.

"Then you could bring food to every meeting!" he said in an astonished tone, as if he seldom had such great ideas.

It's a compliment, I reminded myself as I quick-stepped out to the kitchen for the Sorry Cake. When I returned, Father Olson stared at me and ruminated. Perhaps he was reviewing his standards of competence in the light of culinary prowess.

"You do have some experience as a Sunday school teacher," he murmured as if we were in the middle of an interview.

I nodded and doled out large pieces of cake.

"We *are* looking to see that the education of seminarians is complete before they begin to minister to others. What are your academic qualifications, Goldy?"

"I'll send you a résumé."

"Tell me," he continued, unperturbed, "how would you define faith?"

"What is this, a test?" Careful, careful, I warned myself. After all, Brad Marensky had had enough faith in me to make me his confessor. And if this group would ever pay, I could always use more bookings. "Well," I said with a bright smile while they all listened attentively, "I have faith that if I put chocolate cake in the oven, it's going to rise." There were a few ripples of laughter. Encouraged, I slapped down my tray and put my hand on my hip. "I have faith that if I cater to any group, even a *church* group, they're going to pay me." Guffaws erupted from the two laymen. "Faith is like . . ." and then I saw Schulz in my mind's eye. "Faith is like falling in love. After it happens, you change. You act differently with faith. You're confident, *con fidem,*" I concluded with what I hoped was an erudite lift of the eyebrows. In heaven, my Latin teacher put a jewel in my crown. I picked up the tray.

"Ah, Lonergan," said one of the priests.

Father Olson looked as if he were about to have an orgasm. He cried, "You've just paraphrased a prominent Jesuit theologian. Oh, Goldy, we'd *love* to have you on our committee! I had no idea you were so . . . learned."

I bathed them all in a benevolent smile. "You'd be surprised at what a caterer can figure out."

I hightailed it home as soon as the dishes were done, so I could get started on my next assignment of the day. Father Olson was in a state of high excitement, for all the priests had credited him with giving me such a good theological education. I made him promise that if I did cater to the ecclesiastical heavyweights, I would be paid standard food-service rates. Father Olson waved his hands, muttered about the diocesan office, and said something along the lines of money being forthcoming. Good, I said, so was my contract. Education was nice; practicality, essential.

Arch had left me a surprise note in the mailbox. *Mom,* it said, *Have a great Halloween. Be careful! I will be, too. Forgot to tell you, I got a B on a social studies test. Love, Arch*

When I got inside, the phone was ringing: Audrey Coopersmith. Would it be all right if Heather came down to the Tattered Cover with us? She was supposed to go with a friend, but that hadn't worked out. Of course, I said. Audrey said they'd be over in fifteen minutes.

The computer disks! In the rush with the committee, I had completely forgotten them. I pulled the stolen disks Brad had given me out of my apron pocket. Each label was hand-printed with the word *Andrews.* Call Schulz or see if I . . . oh, what the heck. I tried to boot first one, then the other, on my kitchen computer. No luck. I pulled out the platters of food for the bookstore reading and phoned Schulz. His machine picked up. I left a three-fold message: A confidential source had just given me Keith Andrews' computer disks; I would be catering to the prep school crowd tonight at the bookstore; and would he like a little trick-or-treat at my house afterward?

The doorbell rang: the Coopersmiths. As usual, Audrey clomped in first while her daughter hung back, skeptically assessing the surroundings. Two spots of color flamed on Audrey's cheeks. Knowing her ex-husband was on a cruise with the long-term mistress, I couldn't imagine what new crisis would bring such anger.

"You okay?" I asked unwisely.

"I have had it with that bitch Ferrell," Audrey spat out.

"Now what?" Out of the corner of my eye I saw Heather approach the platters of food on the counter next to the computer.

"Do you know what college she recommended for Heather? Bennington! *Bennington!* What does she think we are, hippies?"

"It's unstructured," murmured Heather over her shoulder.

"She's getting a kickback," Audrey fumed. "I just know it. Ferrell recommends some college to the school's best students, and the college gives her—"

"What is *this*?" exclaimed Heather.

Oh, damn. One Andrews disk was still in the computer, one was on the counter. I'd never make it as a Republican; I couldn't cover up a thing.

"How did you get this?" demanded Heather. Her pale eyes narrowed behind the pink-tinted glasses.

"I . . . don't know," I said, fumbling. "I can't say."

"You stole it," she accused me. "Nobody can put anything down at that school without it getting lifted."

Not anymore, I longed to say. "Please don't give me a hard time," I chided the girl gently. "Somebody gave Keith's disks to me because I found him that night and because Arch was threatened. They thought the disks might help. I can't make hide nor hair out of them and I'm just going to hand them over to the cops."

"Huh," grunted Heather. Disbelief was heavy in her voice.

"What is it?" Audrey was momentarily distracted from her harangue against Miss Ferrell. I took the disk out of the drive and slipped it into its sleeve. Audrey picked up the other one from the counter. "Oh, my God," she said with a sharp intake of breath, "where did you get this?"

"Never mind." I reached over and deftly unplugged the computer. The screen flashed and went blank. "The police will deal with it." I slipped the disks into my purse.

"They won't deal with it if they don't use WordPerfect," Heather announced smugly.

"You see how smart she is?" Audrey's voice gushed pride.

"We need to hit the road," I replied. And with that we began trucking platters of goodies out to the van. But if I thought Audrey was going to relinquish the subject of the superior and underappreciated intelligence of her daughter, I was sadly mistaken. As the van sped down I-70 toward Denver, Audrey ordered Heather to tell me about her summer internship at a Boulder engineering firm, Amalgamated Aerospace. It was a complicated thing dealing with a simulator. To me, virtual reality was something you dealt with when you did your finances. To Heather, it was something quite different.

"I was doing Mars," Heather began in a thin, superior tone.

"This is why she should be going to MIT, not Bennington," interjected Audrey. Did this imply MIT students were like Martians? Best not to ask.

"It was an astronaut-training exercise," Heather prattled on, "and I was working as an assistant to a programmer in the software department."

"Isn't this wonderful!" her mother exclaimed. "I told her to put this in the essay. They'll *have* to take her. Second in her class. You know . . . now." An awkward silence descended on us.

Heather said crisply, "Are you going to tell this story or am I, Mother? Because I wouldn't want to interrupt you."

"Go ahead, dear, I know Goldy *really* wants to hear it."

Goldy really *didn't* want to hear it, but never mind. There was a volcanic sigh from Heather. We were clearly testing her superior intelligence to the limit.

Heather rolled out the words quickly, as if she were a recording put on seventy-eight. "We used photographs taken by the Viking I and Viking II Mars Landers. We developed 800 gigabytes of video image data so that simulated real-time viewing of the Martian surface was possible when the virtual reality simulator display device was in place."

"Simulator display device?" I ventured.

"We used a modified F-16 helmet," she explained tartly. "Anyway, when you put on the helmet, you saw Mars. Look to the left, red rocks of the Martian landscape to the left. Look to the right, red rocks of the Martian landscape to the right." She sighed again.

"Wow!" I said, impressed. "Then what?"

"The programmer was laid off while he was viewing the surface of Mars. The President postponed the project until 2022, when I'll be forty-eight, the programmer will be sixty-eight, and the President will be dead." Sigh. "I think I *should* go to Bennington."

We all silently contemplated that brutal prospect. Then Audrey said miserably, "I can't afford Bennington."

Heather harrumphed. "You can't afford MIT."

Audrey swung around and glared at her daughter. "Do you have to contradict everything? I think I should have a say in where my daughter goes to school. I've earned that, haven't I?"

"Oh, *Mother*."

16

When we arrived at the intersection of First Avenue and Milwaukee, I cast a fleeting glance across the street at Neiman-Marcus.

"Did you two know the bookstore building used to house a department store?" Audrey asked brightly as I wound up the concrete ramp to the same entrance I'd used the night of the stir-fry.

Heather harrumphed. She hadn't said a word since the flap over tuition money.

"Yes," I mused, "I know about when this place was a store . . ." Did I ever. In fact, I'd often reflected that my acquaintance with different establishments of commerce depended on my financial status at any given stage of life. Neusteter's had been an upscale department store during my tenure as a doctor's wife. I had made frequent visits to the jewelry, cosmetics, shoe, dress, and suit departments. Not visits suffused with happiness, I might add, although,

I used to think, for example, that getting my hair done for an astronomical sum in the top-floor salon would make me feel better. But it never did. On my last visit there, I winced whenever the hairdresser touched the back of my scalp, because that was where John Richard had slammed me into a wall the night before. Now I much preferred a blunt cut from Mark the Barber in Aspen Meadow. Freedom cost eight bucks.

I firmly put these memories out of my mind as we unloaded the first trays of concentrically arranged Chocolate-Dipped Biscotti and strawberries. Audrey said the doors were already unlocked, and led the way to the tiny kitchen. The whole area was no more than five feet by five feet, but it would do. In fact, it was so small, we could start the coffee brewing without extension cords. Thank God.

"What do I do if the lights go out?" I demanded of Audrey when I'd filled the large pot with water and fresh coffee.

"The lights?" Her look was puzzled.

"The last time you and I catered this group— Just tell me if there's an auxiliary lighting system."

"Come with me." Audrey spoke with the resigned tone people use to deal with needlessly worried bosses. She guided me through a maze of shelves to an empty clerk's desk. The desktop was a jumble of books and papers. Set at an angle was one of those complicated phones with flashing buttons and finely printed instructions on paging and transferring calls. Audrey reached deftly under the desk, yanked, and brought out a flashlight. "There's one under every employee's desk in this entire store, in case a thunderstorm or power failure takes the lights out. Satisfied?"

"Yes," I said, feeling dumb. "Thanks." Before we could get back to the subject of food, the trade book buyer, a plump woman with papery white skin and curly black hair, came up and introduced herself: Miss Nell Kaplan. While Audrey replaced the flashlight, I invited Miss Kaplan into the kitchen to taste a biscotto. To be sociable, I had one too. Chocolate oozed around the crunch of almonds and cookie. Wonderful, Miss Kaplan and I both agreed.

"The chairs are all set up," Miss Kaplan informed us. "Now all we have to do is find the books the author is going to autograph. You wouldn't think this happens, but it does. Would you consider sharing that recipe for biscotti?"

"My pleasure."

"You should write a cookbook."

"One of these days."

Miss Ferrell *click-clack*ed into the tiny kitchen, wearing a black tent dress. A matching black scarf was wound around her bun of hair. I immediately worried how to keep her away from the wrath of Audrey, who was still Bennington-fixated, but was saved from that task by Miss Kaplan. They had found the books, she announced, and now she needed only a returning Audrey to help her open the chilled wine.

Her face bright with anticipation, Miss Ferrell said, "I'm so glad we're finally getting back on track with our college advisory nights." When I made a vague acknowledging gesture, she added in a lower tone, "Has Julian told you his news?"

"What news?"

She frowned and wrinkled her nose. "Perhaps Julian should be the one to tell you. We just found out this afternoon." She giggled. "What a trick-or-treat!"

Worry nagged behind my eyes. I thought of Julian's haggard face, the piles of review books. "You . . . wanted to meet with me tomorrow morning to talk about his college choices. If something has changed, I . . . think I'd like to hear about it now. If that's okay."

She put a finger mysteriously to her lips and guided me out to the open area where our meeting was to be held. Chairs were set in neat rows facing a table and podium. A bookstore employee was arranging bright, fragrant flowers at the table where the speaker, author of *Climbing the Ivy League,* was going to sign books. Apart from that we were alone.

Miss Ferrell leaned toward me. "He's been given a *full* scholarship."

I jerked back in astonishment. "Who? Julian? To what school?"

"Any school. He can go wherever he wants now. Wherever he gets in. Perkins just got the news this afternoon from the College Savings Bank in Princeton. Eighty thousand dollars wired to an account for Julian Teller." She rolled her eyes. "From an *anonymous* donor."

"Does Julian know who this donor is?" I said, confused. General Farquhar, who had given Julian the Range Rover, was in prison and unable to do anything with his money, which in any event had been largely spent on legal fees. I couldn't think of any other potential benefactor, unless it was a wealthy person at the school. But why a scholarship for Julian? I was utterly baffled. Unless someone wanted something from him . . . My mind rocketed around wildly. Was Julian being bribed to do something? To keep something quiet? I closed my eyes to stop the chattering in my head. In the face of recent events at the school, paranoia loomed.

"Is Julian here?" I asked wishfully.

Miss Ferrell's smile faded. Perhaps my response was not what she had anticipated. "I'm sure I don't know. What's the matter? Aren't you thrilled?"

"I am, I am," I said unconvincingly. In true paranoid

fashion, I didn't feel I could trust anyone. "It's just that . . . I need to talk to him. Now I must go tend to the food. Happy Halloween." I nipped back to the kitchenette, my mind reeling.

Heather sidled up while I was arranging the fruit. She straightened her thick pink glasses and whispered, "You didn't tell Miss Ferrell how mad my mom was, did you?"

"No, no, no . . ." Why did these teenagers, first Brad and now Heather, seem to think I was the resident tattler? Perhaps paranoia is contagious. "Miss Ferrell had something else to tell me," I told her.

"I heard about Julian's scholarship. It's supposed to be very hush-hush." Heather gave me a quizzical look. "One of the kids said maybe it was you, but then the headmaster's son said, Nah, you were poor."

Audrey rescued me from commenting on this untoward assessment of my financial state by announcing that we had a big problem where we were supposed to be setting up. I was saved from asking her what it was when I heard the all too familiar sound of parents' voices raised in heated dispute.

"Oh, come on, Hank. *Nobody's* heard of Occidental." Stan Marensky. "You must be joking!"

Audrey whispered to me, "I'll bet Hank Dawson just heard of Occidental himself. He probably thinks it's a Chinese restaurant. Or an insurance policy, maybe."

I rubbed my forehead, trying to think what to do. The Dawsons, the Marenskys, and Macguire Perkins stood together near the signing table. The mothers—short, crimson-suited Caroline and thinly elegant, fur-coated Rhoda—were eyeing each other like two wild animals in a life-and-death standoff. The fathers—lanky Stan and squat, beefy Hank—stood stiffly, bristling. All were glaring, and the air around them crackled with hostility. Macguire, as usual, had his eyes half closed and was observing the verbal brickbats fly back and forth as if the conversation were some kind of sporting event.

"You just don't know what you're talking about," Hank Dawson spat out. He clenched his fists at his sides; I was afraid he would raise them at any moment. "It's on *U.S. News & World Report*'s list of the top twenty-five liberal arts colleges. Greer is extraordinarily gifted, in the top ten percent of her class. That's more than you can say for Brad. What does he do, anyway? Besides play soccer, I mean."

To my horror, Hank turned and winked at me, as if I somehow shared this assessment. I recoiled and looked around for Brad Marensky, whom I had not seen since our encounter in church. But when I caught the teenager's eye, he turned away.

"You know, Stan," Hank went on, rocking back and forth on his heels and looking up into Stan's lean face with a smug grin, "you could always give the director of admissions at Stanford a mink coat, but I think it's too hot out there."

"I'm getting so *tired* of this from you! We used to be friends! And really, you don't know the first *thing* about colleges." Stan was white with anger. "*Jam* for the Stanford rep! What a laugh!"

"Oh, yeah?" shrilled Hank. His face flushed the color of a cherry tomato. "Greer's sixth-grade teacher said she tested out at the highest intelligence level they'd *ever* found."

"*Brad* has been in gifted and talented programs since he was eight. And he's an athlete, named all-state in soccer and basketball. Not just *girls'* volleyball," rasped Stan, his nostrils flaring. "You think you can improve Greer's chances with this stupid campaign of yours? Does the world know that Hank Dawson *flunked* out of the University of Michigan? You don't have a credential to your name."

"Oh, shit," muttered Macguire Perkins. "Oh, man," he said, looking around for Brad, who had sunk into a nearby chair rather than witness the intensifying conflict.

"Honey, stop," protested Caroline Dawson. But both men stood their ground. At any moment, someone was going to get punched in the nose. I tentatively offered my tray of biscotti to the little group. All ignored me.

Stan Marensky smiled largely. His tall body loomed over Hank Dawson's. "You're just jealous because you know Brad's gotten better grades than Greer—"

"Man, who cares?" interrupted Macguire Perkins.

"Shut *up!*" both fathers cried simultaneously to the headmaster's son.

Macguire raised his palms. "Whoa! I'm outta here." He slunk off. Brad Marensky slumped miserably and put his head in his hands.

Hank squinted up at Stan Marensky. He was breathing hard. Instead of addressing the jealousy question, he used Stan's own mocking tone to respond. "Six generations of Dawsons have attended the University of Michigan. That's more than you can say for the royal Russian Marenskys, I'm sure."

Stan Marensky grunted in disgust. His fists clenched.

I had resolved not to get involved in this, of course, but perhaps I could get us *out* of this.

"Please, men," I said amicably, wafting biscotti under their noses—I'm a great believer in the peace-making abilities of good food. "The kids will get the wrong idea of what college is all about if you don't quit arguing. You're both winners. I mean, remember the time when the Broncos—"

"Who asked you?" bellowed Hank Dawson as if I had unexpectedly betrayed him. He certainly was not in the mood for Bronco talk. Well, hey! I was just doing my referee imitation. I whisked off to set down the tray. Audrey and I had food to set out, conflict or no.

In catering weddings, I had discovered that there is absolutely no time to become overly involved in arguments between clients while you are trying to serve. To my great relief, and in the manner of wedding receptions, the Marenskys and the Dawsons now settled on opposite sides of the meeting area. More students and parents joined us. Audrey and I kept the trays filled and tended to the glasses. Miss Ferrell, who had watched the bitter exchange between the two sets of parents but sagely declined to interfere, pointed Julian out to me when he sauntered up the stairs to the third floor. I handed my tray to Audrey and rushed over to him.

"Congratulations," I gushed. "I heard. This is so—"

But the hard look in his eyes stopped me short. His face was cold with defiance.

"What is it?" I stammered. "I thought you'd be ecstatic."

He raised one eyebrow. "Even in the catering business, you know there's no free lunch."

"I'm happy for you anyway," I said lamely. The initial doubts I'd had about the scholarship loomed.

Julian nodded grimly and walked over to join the chatting students and parents. Several members of the crowd took their seats in response to Headmaster Perkins' agitated appearance at the table where the evening's speaker, a young fellow with wire-rimmed glasses and slicked-down blond hair, had just settled himself next to an enormous pile of books.

"I think we should have a moment's silence for our" —Headmaster Perkins gushed into the microphone— "our classmate and friend, Keith Andrews."

There was shuffling and rearranging of chairs. Along

with the noise from the customers on other floors, it was not exactly silence.

Miss Ferrell stood to introduce the author. Now, I would have thought that a Halloween speaker would at least have had a few lighthearted things to say about how scary the college-application process was, or something along those lines. But when the blond fellow regaled us with no jokes, and instead began with a fluttering hand gesture and the line, "When I was at Harvard . . ." I knew we were in trouble.

There would be no more serving until the man had finished his spiel and the question-and-answer period was over, so I slipped around to the back of the room and found Audrey.

"Any way I can get out of here without creating a fuss?"

"You can't go by the main staircase, they'd all see you. Where do you want to go?"

"Cookbooks?" Any port in a storm.

She led me around to the back of the third floor and then circled the room through another maze of bookshelves. Eventually we made our way to the other side of the main carpeted staircase from the speaker. Audrey stopped in front of a door taped with a photo of Anthony Hopkins as Hannibal Lecter.

I said, "Not a cookbook by *this* guy."

"We're in Crime, silly," Audrey said quietly so as not to disturb the stultifyingly boring speaker, who was declaiming, "College is an investment, like real estate. Location, location, location!"

Audrey whispered to me, "Go down two flights and you'll come out in cookbooks."

"What's on *that* window, a poster of Julia Child?"

"They just do it up as a refrigerator door." She

glanced over at the speaker. "I'll handle things. Better not be gone more than thirty minutes, though."

I thanked her for being such a great assistant and pushed through the *Silence of the Lambs* door. It closed behind me with a decisive thud. With the guilty enjoyment of escaping duty, I quickly descended the concrete stairway. Once I made it down to the cookbook section, I felt immediately at home. I searched out a recipe for piroshki, then flipped through a marvelously illustrated book on the cuisine of Italian hill towns. *Educating Your Palate* was the name of one of that cookbook's subsections. I sat in an armchair next to one of the windows.

My uniform-coated reflection looked back at me, cookbook in hand. *Educate your palate, huh?* I had never had a formal education in cooking; I had taught myself to cook from books. But I made my living at it. Naturally, the courses I'd had on Chaucer, Milton, and Shakespeare hadn't helped, although they'd been enjoyable, except for the Milton. And needless to say, the psychological savvy needed for the business had no referent in any of my papers on the early thinking of Freud.

But so what. I was educated, self-proclaimed. Period. With this delicious insight I walked over to the first-floor bank of registers to buy the Italian cookbook, then realized I'd left my purse upstairs. I reached into my apron pocket, where I always kept a twenty in case someone had to run out for ingredients, and had the satisfaction of paying for the book with cash earned from catering.

When I pushed past Hannibal Lecter again, Tom Schulz stood waiting near the door. The speaker said, "One last question," and moments later the parents were milling aggressively around and standing in line to have their books signed by the expert. Audrey and several other staff members began folding up the chairs.

"I'm glad to see you," I said to Schulz. I looked

around at the breakdown of the room. "I really should help them."

Schulz shook his head. "The food's gone, the people are leaving, and you have some disks to give me so I can deliver them to the Sheriff's Department tonight."

"Oh, my God," I said suddenly. Stupid. Stupid. Stupid. Why *hadn't* I taken them down to the first floor with me? I fled into the kitchen. No purse. I rushed back out to Audrey.

"Seen my purse?" I demanded.

"Yes, yes," she answered primly, and snapped a metal chair shut. "But don't ever leave it out like that again, Goldy. Kids at that school have a terrible reputation for stealing. The only time I bring a purse is when I need my wallet with all my cards. Otherwise, I *wear* my keys." She went to a closet and returned with my purse. I almost snatched it from her. The computer disks were inside.

I handed Schulz the disks. He hadn't mentioned coming over to my house later. Perhaps he didn't want to. I immediately felt embarrassed, as if I'd overstepped some invisible but important boundary.

Once again he was reading my mind. Leaning toward me, he whispered, "Can I meet you at your house in ninety minutes?"

"Of course. Will you be able to stay for a while?"

He gave me such a tender, incredulous look: *What do you think?* that I turned away. When I looked back he was saluting me as he sauntered out the third-floor exit. Julian had gone, presumably to his friend Neil's house; the Marenskys and Dawsons had disappeared. Chalk another one up for Greer not helping with catering cleanup. Maybe that wasn't required for Occidental.

Audrey and I cleared the trash and washed dishes. My heart ached for her as she recited all the latest cruel deeds foisted on her by Carl Coopersmith's insidious lawyer. Finally, but with some guilt, I told her I was expecting a guest at my home momentarily. With Heather's begrudging help, the three of us loaded our boxes into the van. In an extremely casual tone Audrey inquired, "What was that policeman doing at the store tonight?"

"I told you, I was giving him those disks."

"It's like he doesn't trust us," she said darkly.

"Well, can you blame him?" came Heather's sharp voice from the backseat.

"When I want your opinion, I'll ask for it," Audrey snapped.

"Oh, *Mom*."

And we drove in unhappy silence all the way back to their house in Aspen Meadow.

Plumes of exhaust drifted up from the tailpipe of Schulz's car when I pulled up by the curb in front of my home.

"Everyone will see you if you park here," I said when he had rolled down his window.

"Oh, yeah? I wasn't aware I was doing anything illegal." He hauled out a plastic bag. It said BRUNSWICK BOWLING BALLS.

"What did the disks say?"

"Talk about it inside."

I pushed the alarm buttons and opened the door. The bowling ball bag yielded a bottle of VSOP cognac. In a cabinet I found a couple of liqueur glasses that John Richard had not broken on one of his rampages. As we sat in my kitchen and sipped the cognac, Schulz said he wanted to hear about my evening first. I told him about the bookstore spats, and about Macguire Perkins getting in the middle of it. I also told him about my suspicion concerning Macguire's use of steroids.

"Was that what Keith's newspaper article was about?" I asked.

"No," he said pensively, "it wasn't."

I toyed with my glass. Relax, I ordered myself. But Arch's problems at school and Julian's troubling anxiety seemed to be in the air, even though neither of the boys was at home. And despite the afternoon interlude with Schulz the day of the spider bite, I was not used to being alone with him in my house. At night.

Schulz refilled my glass. "How about Julian? Did he get involved in the argument at the bookstore?"

"Oh, no." I brightened. "Good news on that front, in fact." I told him about Julian's scholarship.

"No kidding." Schulz seemed both pleased and intrigued. "That's interesting. Who gave him the money?"

"No one knows. I'm wondering if it's some kind of bribe."

He sipped his cognac. "A bribe. For what? Did you ask him?" I told him I had not. He pondered that for a minute, then said, "Now tell me how you got those disks."

"Can't, sorry, they were given to me in confidence. Do they contain evidence? I mean, is it something you'll be able to use?"

"I don't know how." But he reached inside the Brunswick bag and handed me some folded papers. "I got a printout of Keith's article. The rest was notes for a paper on Dostoyevski. The other disk had a list of expenses from his visits to ten colleges. The article sums up the trips." Seeing my puzzled expression, Schulz added, "That's what Keith was going to expose, Goldy. His personal views on college education as he'd already experienced it. I wanted you to take a look at it, but it just looks like his opinions."

If that was all it was, I told him I would read it in the

morning. I was too tired even to read the word *midterm* tonight. "If it's just Keith's opinions on what's going on in higher education in the world at large, what's the big deal?"

"I don't know. But nobody I can find seems to have had the slightest idea what he was researching for that article. Sometimes people are more afraid of what they *think* you're going to expose than they ever would be if they knew exactly what you were going to expose. You fear what you don't know."

"Oh, yeah?" I said as I drained the last of the cognac in my glass. Heady stuff.

"Like with this smoke stunt. Someone wants you to *think* you're going to be hurt."

"Marla broke her leg," I pointed out.

"She may have gotten off easy." He put his glass down. His face was very grim. "I know I've said this a few times already, Miss G., but I'd feel a lot better if you'd all move out, quietly, until we solve this murder."

I blinked at him. How many times had I run away in fear? Too many. The running part of my life was over, and I was not going to budge.

17

Schulz moved restlessly in his chair. I poured us some more cognac and had the uncomforting thought that if we got really drunk, we wouldn't even notice if someone smashed another window or stopped up every chimney in the neighborhood.

I sipped and looked at the clock. Ten o'clock. The odd feeling of being alone in my home with Schulz brought full wakefulness despite the fact that catering in the evening usually exhausted me. My mind traveled back to the Marenskys and the Dawsons, Brad Marensky morose and silent, Macguire Perkins embarrassed when ordered to shut up. When our tiny glasses were again empty, Schulz stood and walked out to the living room. I followed. The place still smelled faintly of smoke, and the pale yellow walls were the color of toasted marshmallow. In the near future I would have to hire someone to do a

THE CEREAL MURDERS · 251

cleanup. Schulz got down on one knee to peer up the chimney.

"Any ideas? Did you ever hear anything out on the roof?"

"No ideas, no weird sounds. My theory is that this is the same person who did the rock and the snake. I wish I knew who was so pissed off with me. Arbitration would be cheaper than making glass repairs and paying for professional cleaning."

"Somebody strong, somebody athletic," Schulz mused. "The only thing all these things have in common is a threat to Arch. Scare him while he's home alone, put something in the locker, fill the house with smoke while he's here with you and Julian . . . but that part wasn't planned, was it?"

"Being home? No, he fell on the icy front steps, prelude to Marla. Maybe that one was meant for me," I said wryly, remembering the spider-bite incident.

"Who's mad at you? Or Arch?" His eyes probed mine and he gently took my hand, then reeled me in like a slow-motion jitterbug dancer.

"I don't know," I murmured into his chest. He was warm; the clean smell of aftershave clung to his skin. I pulled back. Around his dark pupils was only a ring of green luminosity.

"All this talk about starting fires . . ." I said with a small smile.

And up we tiptoed to the silent second story. The cognac, the desire, the comfort of Schulz, seeped through me like one of those unexpected warm currents you encounter in the ocean. In the dark of my room he stood beside me while we looked out at the glowing jack-o'-lanterns in the neighborhood. He rubbed my back, then kissed my ear. I set my alarm for four and then slipped out of my clothes. We both laughed as we dove for the bed. It was a good thing Schulz always used protection. Ever since we had started making love, I had forgotten the meaning of the word *caution*.

When he pulled me next to him between the cool sheets, his large, rough hands brought calm to nerves inside and out. When he kissed me, something in my brain loosened. Before long I had abandoned not only caution but all the other petty worries that had crowded into my brain.

After our lovemaking Schulz went downstairs.

He came back up and said, "Twenty minutes," then got dressed.

"Until what?"

"Until the first shift of your surveillance shows up."

"Oh, for heaven's sake, why? I mean, why *now*?"

He counted off on his fingers as he enumerated. "Two murders, broken glass, anonymous phone calls, a poisonous snake followed by a poisonous spider, booby-trapped steps, and a vandalized chimney, which I didn't get to see *until* now. And a woman with two boys who won't move out, despite the best advice of her local cop."

"Arch will call his friends," I retorted mildly, "focus on the squad car with his high-powered binoculars, and pretend we're in the middle of a coup. Your cops will think we're nuts."

"You'd be surprised at how many loonies we get."

"Actually," I ventured, "why don't *you* just do the surveillance?"

"I wish."

I pulled on a bathrobe and stood by a bedroom window. Glowing pumpkin-candles illuminated the silky night air. Schulz went outside to his car. Five minutes later, an unmarked police car showed up. I watched Schulz leave, then I watched the jack-o'-lantern flames flicker and die. Eventually I slipped back into my empty bed that smelled of Tom Schulz. I slept deeply, dream-lessly, until the alarm surprised me.

Groaning, I slipped out of bed to start stretching in the dark. My yoga teacher had told me once that if you were just going through the motions, it wasn't yoga. So I emptied my mind and my breath and started over, salut-ing to the east, where there was as yet no sun, then breathing and allowing my body to flow through the rest of the routine until I was revitalized and ready to meet the day, even if we were only four and a half hours into it.

Too bad they didn't have a resident yogi at Elk Park Prep, I mused on my way downstairs. How could you have class rank with yoga? Its whole essence was noncom-petitive, the striving with one's own body rather than be-ing obsessed with the accomplishments of others. Which is what education should be, I decided as a jet-black stream of espresso spurted into one of my white porcelain cups. Stretching oneself. But no one was asking me. My eyes fell on the folded papers still on my kitchen table—the article printout from Keith's computer disk. Correc-tion: *Schulz* had asked me. I sat down with my coffee and started to read.

WHAT'S IN A NAME?
—Anatomy of a Hoax

As a senior at Elk Park Prep, this fall I have visited ten of the top colleges and universities in this coun-try. The qualification "top" is commonly given by the media and, of course, by the colleges themselves. I went to these schools because this higher-educa-tion journey is one I will be taking soon. It's a journey I've been looking forward to. Why? Because of what I thought I would find: 1) enthusiastic teachers, 2) a contagious love of learning, 3) academic peers with whom I would have mind-altering discussions, 4) the challenge of taking tests and writing papers that would give me 5) an introduction to new fields of learning so that I would have 6) the chance to develop my abilities.

I expected to find these things, but guess what? They weren't there. My parents could have shelled out eighty-plus thousand dollars for a hoax!

The first place I visited I went for two days of classes. I never saw a full professor the entire time, although several Nobel prizewinners had prominent photographs in the college catalogue. I went to five classes. I wish I could tell you what they were about, but they were all taught by graduate students with foreign accents so thick I couldn't tell what they were saying. . . .

I went to an all-boys school next. I never even saw humans teaching courses, only videotaped lectures. Over the weekend I wanted to have intellectual discussions. But all the guys had left to go to the campus of a girls' school nearby.

The next place had real people teaching. So I went to a section meeting of the introduction to art history. It turned out the class was concentrating on thirteenth-century Dutch Books of Hours. The instructor said at one point that something was a prelude to Rembrandt, and one of the kids said, Who's Rembrandt? After the class I asked why the instructor was teaching such an obscure topic, and one of the students said, Well, that was the subject of the instructor's dissertation, and he was trying to do his research while teaching the class. . . .

I knew somebody from Elk Park Prep at the next place I visited. She graduated from our school five years ago and was now a graduate student. She needed to talk to her advisor about her dissertation, but he was doing research in Tokyo, and hadn't been at the college for two years. . . .

Finally I visited a school with a fantastic teacher! I went to his class on modern European drama. It was jammed with students. They were having a lively discussion of Ibsen's *Hedda Gabler* and nobody was using Cliff's Notes. The professor was storming back and forth, asking why did Hedda Gabler just keel over at the end. After all the disappointment at the other schools, I came out feeling great! But when the class was over, the other students were glum. When I asked why, they said that this fabulous assistant professor, who had just won the Excellence in Teaching award, had been denied tenure! He hadn't *published* enough. . . .

Who is supporting this hoax in higher education? Certainly not yours truly. Do American students really want this false pedigree? Do we want good teaching, or an empty reputation? Do we want an educational process, or an impersonal stamp of approval? Students in the schools, unite. . . .

Well, well. He sounded like a valedictorian, all right. In a number of ways the article resembled Keith's speech the night he died. But this essay was not an exposé. There was really nothing in it anyone would kill to keep secret. Not that anyone else knew that, however.

Keith Andrews must have posed a threat to *someone*. Julian hadn't liked him, and neither had a number of the other students. And in the last two weeks, somebody or bodies had been trying to hurt Arch and me. Why? What was the connection between the murder and the attempts on us? Was the murder of Kathy Andrews in Lakewood part of the killer's scheme? How did the Neiman-Marcus credit card figure in what was going on? None of it added up.

Outside, the chilly Halloween night had given way to a snowy All Saints' morning. Because the first Saturday in November is notorious for heavy snowfall, the College Board opted to give the SATs locally in the mountain area rather than have all the Aspen Meadow students attempt the trek to Denver, forty miles away. In the spirit of noblesse oblige, Headmaster Perkins had ordered me to prepare quadruple the amount of morning snack, so we could serve—his words—"the masses." Time to get cracking.

I got out strawberries, cantaloupe, oranges, and bananas, and began to slice. Soon hills of jewellike fruit glistened on my cutting boards. Worry about Julian again surfaced. Had he been safe at his friend Neil's house? As far as I knew, he had slept less than twenty hours this entire week. Julian, the college-scholarship kid. Why had someone done that for him?

When I finished the fruit I started mixing the muffin batters. From the freezer I took the doughnuts I had been making during the smoke episode, along with extra homemade rolls from the clergy meeting. With these set out to thaw, I mixed peanut butter into flour and eggs for the final batch of muffins and set it into the other oven, and then began to put together something I had only been thinking about, something with whole grain but sweet, like granola. My food processor blended unsalted butter into brown and white sugars. I repressed a shudder. Given the school's reputation, I should call these Cereal Killer Cookies.

I scraped ice cream scoopfuls of the thick batter onto cookie sheets, took all the muffins out of the oven, then nipped outside with two hot ones wrapped in a cloth napkin. The policeman doing the surveillance accepted them gratefully. He wouldn't follow me to the school. His orders were to watch the house, not me. Back inside, the enticing scent of baking cookies filled the kitchen. When they were done, I packed up several gallons of chilled vanilla yogurt along with the rest of the goodies and set out for Elk Park Prep, waving to the officer in his squad car as I pulled away. He saluted me with a muffin and a grin.

The heavy clouds sprinkling thick snowflakes reminded me of detergent showering into a washing machine. Someone had the foresight to call the county highway people and get the road to Elk Park Prep plowed. At seven, after carefully rounding the newly plowed curves, I arrived at the school driveway, where a pickup with a CAT was smoothing a lane through the thick, rumpled white stuff.

I skirted the truck, put the van in first gear, and started slowly up the snow-packed asphalt, already much traveled by vehicles carrying test-taking students. In a spirit of Halloween festivity, the elementary grades had carved row upon row of pumpkins to line the long entrance to the school. But the sudden cold wave had softened and crumpled the orange ovoids so that their yawning, jagged-toothed mouths, their decaying, staring faces now leered upward under powdery white masks of snow. A jack-o'-lantern graveyard. Not what I'd want to see the day of a big test.

The parking lot was already three-fourths full. With relief I noticed the heavily stickered VW bug that belonged to Julian's friend, Neil Mansfield. When I came through the front doors that were still draped with wilted black crepe paper, Julian spotted me through the crowd of students and rushed over to help.

"No, no, that's okay," I protested as he took a box. "Please go back over to your friends."

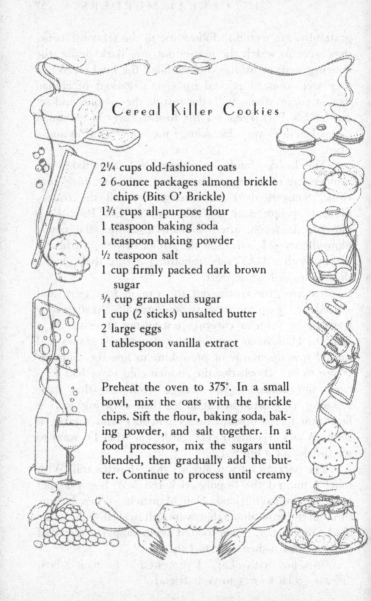

Cereal Killer Cookies

2¼ cups old-fashioned oats
2 6-ounce packages almond brickle
    chips (Bits O' Brickle)
1⅔ cups all-purpose flour
1 teaspoon baking soda
1 teaspoon baking powder
½ teaspoon salt
1 cup firmly packed dark brown
    sugar
¾ cup granulated sugar
1 cup (2 sticks) unsalted butter
2 large eggs
1 tablespoon vanilla extract

Preheat the oven to 375°. In a small
bowl, mix the oats with the brickle
chips. Sift the flour, baking soda, baking powder, and salt together. In a
food processor, mix the sugars until
blended, then gradually add the butter. Continue to process until creamy

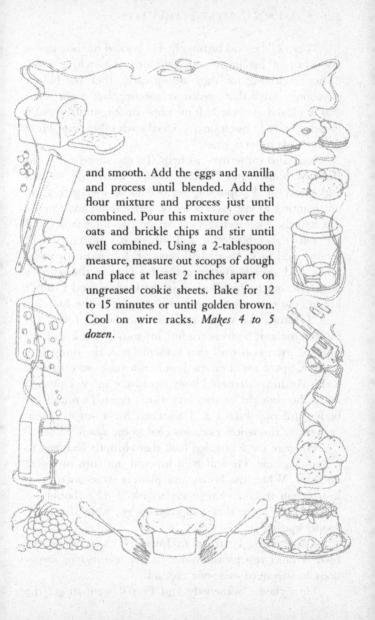

and smooth. Add the eggs and vanilla and process until blended. Add the flour mixture and process just until combined. Pour this mixture over the oats and brickle chips and stir until well combined. Using a 2-tablespoon measure, measure out scoops of dough and place at least 2 inches apart on ungreased cookie sheets. Bake for 12 to 15 minutes or until golden brown. Cool on wire racks. *Makes 4 to 5 dozen*.

"I can't," he said brusquely. He hoisted the box up on one knee of his jeans and shot me a beseeching look. "They're driving me nuts asking each other vocabulary questions. After that bookstore meeting last night, Neil and I played five-card draw until midnight. It was so great! The only question we asked each other was, How many cards do you want?"

Neil also came over to help. To my surprise, so did Brad Marensky and Heather Coopersmith. My sudden and unexpected popularity seemed to be owing to their not wanting to test each other on last-minute analogies. I directed the four teenagers to set up two long tables and lay out the tablecloths and disposable plates, bowls, spoons, and forks that I had brought. Julian, to my great relief, had already started coffee brewing in the school's large pot, but he had done it in the kitchen, and I didn't know how to move the immense pot out to the foyer.

"I wanted to start the coffee out here," Julian informed me as if he were reading my mind, "but I couldn't find the extension cord that's usually with the thing."

Oh, spare me. For the hundredth time since finding Keith Andrews' battered body out in the snow, I pushed away the thought of the dark cords twisted around his body. "Julian," I said as I searched for a sugar spoon, "never say the words *extension cord* to me again. Please?"

He gave me a puzzled look that abruptly changed to a knowing one. He and Neil brought out cups of coffee on trays. When the bowls and platters were uncovered, kids began to come up to me to ask if they should eat now, where were they supposed to go, were the classrooms marked?

Desperately, I turned to Julian. "I need to do the food. Would you please find a faculty member or somebody to shepherd everyone around?"

He sighed. "Somebody said Ferrell went to get the

pencils." Before we could worry about it further, thankfully, a pair of faculty proctors appeared. The kids could take another twenty minutes to have their breakfast, they announced. Then alphabetized assignments were made to classrooms. The students crowded around the serving tables, shouting encouragements and vocabulary words to one another as they juggled muffins, doughnuts, cookies, bowls of yogurt with fruit, and cups of coffee. I was so busy refilling platters that I didn't have a chance to talk to Julian again until just before he went into the P–Z classroom.

"How do you feel?"

"Okay." But his smile was halfhearted. He clamped his hands under the armpits of his gray sweatshirt. "You know, it's funny about that scholarship. Somebody— somebody besides you—cares about me. Maybe an alumnus, maybe one of the parents of the other kids. Not knowing who did it is kind of neat. I kept waiting for Ferrell or Perkins to say, Well, you have to do this, or you have to do that. But nothing happened. So now I think it doesn't matter so much how well I do on these tests. They're not the be-all and end-all. And that gives me a good feeling. I'm all right."

I said, "Great," and meant it.

Egon Schlichtmaier, his hair fashionably tousled and his hands in the pockets of a shearling coat, came up and shooed Julian along to the classroom. I went back to clean up. The foyer was empty except for one lone student. Macguire Perkins stared morosely at what was left of the Cereal Killer Cookies.

"Macguire! You need to go take your test. It's starting in five minutes."

"I'm hungry." He didn't look at me. "I'm usually not up this early. But I can't decide what to have."

"Here," I said, quickly grabbing up a handful of

cookies, "take these into your classroom. Follow Schlicht-maier down the hall."

Still not meeting my eye, Macguire stuffed them into the pouch of his baggy sweatshirt. "Thanks," he muttered. "Maybe they'll make me smart. I didn't have any last year, and I only got 820 combined."

"Oh, Macguire," I said earnestly, "don't worry . . ." His miserable pimpled face sagged. "Look, Macguire, everything's going to be okay. Come on." I scooted out from behind the long table. "Let me walk with you down to the classroom."

He shrank from my attempt to touch his arm, but slouched along next to me without protest toward the classroom where Egon Schlichtmaier had just closed the door. I glanced up at Macguire. The boy was shaking.

"Come on!" I exhorted him. "Think of it as being like basketball practice. Do it for a couple of hours and hope for the best."

He looked down at me, finally. His pupils were dilated with fear. Dully, he said, "I feel like shit." And without waiting for my response, he opened the door to the classroom and slipped inside.

I scolded myself all the way back to the foyer, where I scooped up dropped napkins and paper cups, cleared away paper bowls and plastic spoons, and covered the remaining muffins, bread, and fruit. There were crumbs everywhere. Basketball practice? Maybe that was the wrong thing to say.

The SAT was scheduled to take three hours. There would be only two five-minute breaks. The headmaster and Miss Ferrell had determined that it would be best not to try to serve the food more than once. And speaking of the college advisor, I had to find out where we were supposed to meet after the test. I poured myself a cup of coffee and walked down to Miss Ferrell's classroom. Unlike the other unused classrooms, it was unlocked but dark. I turned the lights on and waited. The desk was a mess of papers, indicating perhaps that she had been in to do some work but was coming back. Sipping my coffee, I waited for her over an hour, through the two five-minute breaks, but she was obviously involved with students.

Returning to the foyer, I decided to consolidate the food and wash my own empty dishes and bowls rather than haul them all home dirty. I found liquid soap, filled the porcelain basins of the old hotel kitchen with hot soapy water, and got to work, humming. Without a dishwasher the task took quite a bit longer than I anticipated. Oh, well, at least I wasn't in one of those classrooms, trying to figure out the meaning of words like *eleemosynary*.

Once the dishes were laid on the counters to dry, I came back out to the foyer. Crumbs and bits of fruit still littered the floor. I had only fifteen minutes before the kids would be done. On their way out, their shoes would grind every last morsel into the smooth gray rug.

The things a caterer has to do, I thought with great self-pity. I wiped the crumbs off the tables. No telling what my chances were of finding a vacuum among the plethora of closets in the kitchen.

Well, process of elimination, as Julian had told me of the multiple-choice SATs. The first closet held phone books and boxes. The next one I opened was the storage area for old Elk Park Prep yearbooks. I never did find out whether the third one held a vacuum cleaner. When I opened the door, I faced the dead body of Miss Suzanne Ferrell.

18

Her petite body swayed in the slight stir of air I had created by pulling open the door. I touched the bruised skin of her arm. No response. I stumbled backward. Incoherently, I called for help, for someone, anyone. I scanned the kitchen wildly: I needed something—a footstool, a ladder—to climb up and cut her down. Maybe I could help her. But she couldn't be alive. There was no way. I had just spent the last hour cleaning in this room and I would have heard her. If she had been alive, if there had been a chance . . .

Julian and a gray-haired, hunched-back teacher, a man I had seen earlier that morning, hurtled into the kitchen. Their voices tangled in shouts.

"What? What's wrong? What's the problem? The testing is still—"

"Quickly," I rasped, gesturing helplessly, "cut her—" I choked.

The older man limped forward and gaped at the contents of the open closet. "God help us," I heard him say.

Voices clamored at the kitchen door. *What's going on? Is everything all right?*

"No, no, don't come in," I yelled at two startled students who rushed into the room. Wide-eyed and openmouthed, they stood motionless, staring at the closet.

"Keep everybody out," I ordered Julian tersely.

He nodded and pivoted toward the kitchen entrance, where he motioned to the students to leave. Then he stationed himself at the door, where he spoke in low murmurs to the people there.

The voice of the older man broke as he asked me to get a knife. I groped for one in a drawer and handed it to him. At the door, Julian watched my every move. I think the sight of my face scared him.

Once the gray-haired man was at the top of a stepladder he'd pulled from the first closet, he said brusquely, "Have the boy go back to his classroom. I'll need your help."

Julian nodded and left. Together, the man and I grasped Miss Ferrell's tiny body and lowered her to the floor. I could not look at her grotesquely frozen grimace again.

The teacher told me to call the police. He choked slightly and coughed, then asked me to find a teacher who could pick up the answer sheets from his room. Yes, the one he and Julian had left when they heard my shouts. He would wait with the body. I did not need to see medals to know this was a war veteran. His impassive tone and the grief in his eyes said all too clearly that he had seen death before.

There was no phone in the kitchen. My head pounded. The kitchen door fanned me as it closed, and a sudden sweat chilled my skin. When I arrived in the hall, there was the beginning of distant scuffling from the classrooms. The clock in the hall said five to eleven; the SATs were almost over. Dizziness swept over me. Should I make some kind of announcement? Should I tell the students to stay? That the police would be here soon, and they would all be questioned? I walked quickly to the phone in the hallway.

I pressed 911. I identified myself and where I was, then said something along the lines of, "I've just found a body. I think it's Miss Suzanne Ferrell, a teacher here." There was a whirring in my ears, like being inside a wind tunnel.

"Are you there?" The operator's voice sounded impossibly distant.

"Yes, yes," I said.

"Don't let anybody leave that school. Nobody. I'll put in a call to get a team up there right away."

Groping for words within my mental fog, I hung up and stumbled to the P–Z classroom. I tersely told Julian to announce to his class and the others' that after their booklets were collected, they must wait.

"If they ask, you know, because they heard me screaming, don't . . . tell them anything else," I said hesitantly.

Julian turned back to his class, his face tight with worry. Sweat now covered my skin like a mold. The pounding in my head intensified agonizingly. I walked in slow motion back to the kitchen door.

"The police are on their way," I told the gray-haired man. Down on one knee, he had stationed himself next to the body. An unfolded white napkin shrouded Miss Ferrell's face. The teacher acknowledged my announcement with a grim nod, but said nothing.

The room felt oppressive. I could not stay there next to Suzanne Ferrell's corpse. In a daze, I went back out to the foyer. I found paper and pen in my supplies bag to make signs for the doors. Gripping the pencil was difficult. My shaking hand wrote, *Do not leave until the police say you can.* The room looked like the abandoned set of a surrealistic foreign film: What was all the debris, where did these bits of fruit come from, why were boxes of mine up on the tables? I grabbed a corner of one table to steady myself.

The recollection washed back, horrid, filthy. I saw my hand opening that door, saw a body swaying heavily in a bright orange and pink dress, saw a grotesque purple face that in no way resembled the perky French teacher. My fingers had blanched the darkening skin when they touched her. Her body had been strung up like the snake in Arch's locker. I squeezed my eyes shut.

The police arrived in a blur. I glanced at my watch: 11:45. The sky through the foyer's windows had begun to drop millions of snowflakes. An extremely tight-lipped Tom Schulz strode in. He was all business as the homicide team bustled around him, taking orders, falling into the grueling routine brought on by sudden death. They took the kids in the classrooms one by one. I knew the drill. Name. Address. When did you arrive, what did you see, and do you know anyone with a grudge against Miss Ferrell?

And of course the question that pressed in on my brain, caused throbbing at my temples, was the inevitable corollary: Who hated *both* Keith Andrews *and* Miss Suzanne Ferrell?

I sat on one of the benches and numbly answered Schulz's questions. When did I arrive? Who else was in the school at that time? Who had access to the kitchen this morning? Pain still knocked dully at the back of my brain, but I also felt relief. This horror was now in the hands of the police. In the kitchen, their team would be painstakingly processing the scene: taking photographs, making notes, sprinkling black graphite fingerprint powder everywhere. Julian came through a doorway, crossed the room, and slumped down next to me. "Ninety-eight percent of the people who were here can be eliminated," I heard Tom Schulz say to a member of his team. Julian and I were mute while the other seniors, finally dismissed, somberly filed past. I could feel the students' eyes on me. I didn't look up. All I could hear was my heartbeat.

When the lobby was again empty, Schulz sat down on the bench next to Julian and me. He said that Julian and his friend Neil had been the first to arrive that morning after the gray-haired faculty member, whose name was George Henley. Henley, it appeared, had found the outer doors unlocked upon his arrival shortly before 8:00. He had been given a set of keys by Headmaster Perkins, and had assumed Miss Ferrell, who was assigned to help him set up that morning, was "around somewhere," because the door to her classroom was open, although the light was off. No, the unlocked doors had not puzzled him because of the headmaster's much-touted belief in the "environment of trust."

"What we're looking for," Schulz said wearily, "is how this could relate to the Andrews murder. Know anyone who had problems with this woman? Someone who maybe disliked Keith too?"

I repeated what I had already told him about Egon Schlichtmaier and the supposed romantic link with Suzanne Ferrell. He asked if we had seen any exchange between them—we hadn't. Or between her and anyone else.

"This took place at the school. Because of what's already happened here, we need to look at the school first," Schulz insisted. "Is there anything else?"

A number of people, I told him numbly, might have

resented Miss Ferrell. Why? Schulz wanted to know. Because of their own highly emotional agenda concerning grades, recommendations, the college issue. She was the college advisor, after all. And there were things she might have known. From what I had learned about the school in the past couple of weeks, the place seemed a veritable repository for secrets.

"Jesus Christ," Schulz muttered under his breath. "When does anyone around here have time to learn? What about this headmaster? Any animosity there?"

"None that I know of," I said, and turned to Julian, who opened his hands and shook his head dumbly.

"We'll talk to him." Schulz looked at me. I could see the strain of this second murder in a week in his blood-shot eyes and haggard face. "She's been dead about six hours. Our surveillance guy can verify when you left your house, so you're not a suspect."

"For once," I said dryly. I felt no relief.

"Either one of you feel okay to drive?" Schulz asked.

Neil Mansfield of the bumper-stickered VW was long gone. Julian said, "Let me take Goldy home in her van." His face was bone-white. "Will you call us later?" he asked Schulz.

Schulz gently touched the side of Julian's head. "Tonight."

Snowflakes powdered the smooth lanes made by the CAT. Snow continued to swirl. The pumpkins edging the drive were now mounds of white, their leering faces long ago obscured. Julian edged the van around State Highway 203's winding curves. I wondered how I would tell Arch about Miss Ferrell's murder. After a long stretch of silence, I asked Julian how the tests went; he gave a non-committal shrug.

"Know what I feel like doing?" he said abruptly.

"What?"

"I need to swim. I haven't been near a pool in two weeks. Probably sounds crazy, I know." He fell silent, concentrating on the increasingly treacherous road. Then he said, "This stuff at the school is getting to me. I can't go back and sit in that house. Do you mind?" He gave me a quick sidelong glance. "You probably don't feel like cooking."

"You got that right. A swim sounds good."

We parked in front of the house. With the heavy snow, it was hard to tell if anyone sat in one of the cars lining our street. Schulz's surveillance cop had to be there, I told myself. Had to.

Once inside, I gratefully stripped off the caterer's uniform and quickly slipped into jeans and a turtleneck. We gathered swimsuits and towels. There was a message on the machine from Marla: Could we come by for an early dinner? She had finally located Pamela Samuelson. Pamela Samuelson? Marla's taped voice reminded me: "You know, that teacher out at Elk Park Prep who was involved in some kind of brouhaha with the headmaster. She really wants to see you." Marla added cryptically, "It's urgent."

I dialed Marla's number. The private nurse said her charge was taking a nap. Don't disturb her, I told the nurse. Just tell her when she wakes that we'll be there at five.

We switched to the Rover because of the roads. As we drove to the rec center, my heart felt like a knob of granite. Or maybe it wasn't my heart that felt that way, but some unexpressed emotion that had solidified inside my rib cage. Was it fear? Anger? Sadness? *All of the above.*

I wanted to cry but could not. Not yet. I wanted to know if Arch was all right, but I reassured myself that of course he was. After all, he was in Keystone with his father, miles away from these ugly events. *Just keep going,* some inner voice said. Of course, that was what I had always done. But the rock in my chest remained.

At the pool Julian dived in at once, landing with an explosive crack that sprayed water everywhere. He plowed down his lap lane like a man possessed. I eased myself with infinite care into the water, then moved like a person drugged to the lane to Julian's left. Closing my eyes, I allowed my arms to wheel into a slow crawl. Warm water washed over me. Twice I started to think about the events of the morning and accidentally inhaled water. I sputtered and changed to a backstroke, while in the next lane Julian repeatedly lapped me. After I had done a halting, uneven set of about twenty laps, I stopped Julian as he was about to do one of his rolling turns off the concrete wall. I was taking a shower, I told him. He said he was almost finished.

I shampooed my hair four times. The pine-scented shower gel would dry it out to straw, but I didn't care. The sharp, woodsy scent brought back memories of boarding school with its comforting routines: history class, field hockey, wearing pearls to dinner and gloves to church. Too bad Elk Park Prep was not nearly so safe a place.

Waiting for Julian in the lobby of the rec center, I stood at the window, watching the snow. It drifted down like bits of ash from a distant fire. I suddenly realized that I was famished. Julian came out shaking droplets from his hair, and we drove in silence to Marla's house in the country club area.

Marla greeted us with a shriek of happiness. Her leg

was in a thick plaster cast that already bore a number of colorful inscriptions.

"I thought you might be along," she said to Julian, "so I ordered you a grilled Gruyère sandwich along with our cheeseburgers. There'll be jalapeño-fried onions and red-cabbage coleslaw too," she added hopefully. Embarrassed to be so attended to, especially by someone in a cast, Julian flushed and mumbled thanks.

"Come on, then." Marla hobbled forward. "Goldy's been bugging me to find this person since last week." Over her shoulder she said to Julian, "You may know her already."

Pamela Samuelson, former teacher at Elk Park Prep, sat perched at the edge of a muted green and blue striped couch in Marla's living room. A generous fire blazed inside a fireplace edged with bright green and white Italian tiles.

"Oh, Miss Samuelson," Julian said in a surprised tone. "Eleventh-grade American history."

"Hello, Julian." Pamela's hair had the look and texture of a much-used Brillo pad, and the fire reflected in her thick glasses. She was about fifty years old and slightly doughy, despite Marla's introduction of her as "one of the regulars" at the athletic club. "Yes," she said with a touch of irony, "eleventh-grade American history."

"Pam's selling real estate now," Marla interjected with genuine sympathy. Realtors were not Marla's favorite people. "She got shafted out at that school."

I said, "Shafted?"

Pamela Samuelson threaded and unthreaded her plump fingers. She said, "One hates to hang out dirty laundry. But when I heard about Suzanne, and Marla phoned me—"

"You've heard already?" I exclaimed. Why was I surprised? My years in Aspen Meadow had certainly taught me the terrifying efficiency of the local grapevine.

"Oh, yes," Pamela said. She touched her wiry hairdo. "The fall SATs. First Saturday in November."

I glanced at Julian. He shrugged. I said, "Please, can you tell me more about the school? I hate to say it, but . . . dirty laundry may help us figure a few things out."

"Well. This was what I was telling Marla. I don't know if it's relevant." She fell silent and looked down at her hands.

"Please," I said again.

She remained silent. Julian got up and added a log to the fire. Marla studied her cast, which she had propped up on a green and white ottoman. I heard my stomach growl.

"Before I was dismissed," Pamela said at last, "I gave a final exam in American history. The essay question was, *Discuss American foreign policy from the Civil War to the present.*" Her eyes narrowed behind the thick lenses. "It was the question I myself had had on a preparatory school American history exam. But several Elk Park Prep students complained. Not to me, mind you," she said bitterly, "to Headmaster Perkins. Perkins gave me hell, said he hadn't had such a challenging question in a test until graduate school."

I said, "Uh-oh."

"I said, 'Where'd you go to graduate school, the University of the South Sandwich Islands?' And oh, that wasn't the worst of it," she continued sourly. "It was soccer season, don't you know. The weekend before exams, Brad Marensky performed brilliantly as goalie down in Colorado Springs. But he hadn't studied for his history exam, and on this essay question he unfortunately left out both World Wars."

Julian said, "Oops."

Pamela Samuelson turned a face contorted with sudden fury toward Julian. "Oops? Oops?" she cried. When Julian drew back in shock, she seemed to will herself to be calm. "Well. So I flunked him. Flat F."

No one said *oops*.

"When the honor roll came out at the end of the year," Pamela went on, "there was Brad Marensky. He could not have gotten there with an F, I can assure you." She spread her hands in a gesture of incomprehension. "Impossible. I demanded a meeting with Perkins. His *secretary* told me the Marenskys had protested Brad's grade. Before the meeting I checked the master transcript kept in a file in Perkins' office along with old grade books. The F history grade had been changed to a B. When I confronted Perkins, he wasn't even defensive. Smooth as silk, he says he gave Brad Marensky credit for the soccer game. I said, 'You have a pretty screwed up idea of academic integrity.' "

Not to mention American foreign policy.

"Perkins told me I was welcome to seek employment elsewhere, in fact, that he already had a superb replacement for me in mind. I know it was some young German man that a friend of his at C.U. was pressuring him to hire. I'd heard that from the secretary too." Pamela hissed in disgust. "The article in the *Post* about the lower SAT scores at Elk Park Prep made me feel better for a little while, but it didn't make me happy. I'm still trying to sell five-thousand-square-foot homes during the worst real estate recession in a decade."

I murmured sympathetically. Marla rolled her eyes at me.

"Suzanne Ferrell was my friend," Pamela said with a large, unhappy exhalation of air. "My first thought was, She wouldn't cave in to them."

"Them who?" demanded Marla.

"The ones who think education is just grades, class rank, where you go to college." Pamela Samuelson's voice was thin with anger. "It's so *destructive*!"

The high peal of the doorbell cut through her fury. Marla started to lift her cast from the ottoman, but Julian stopped her.

"I'll get it," he said. When he returned, Marla smilingly handed the goodies she had ordered all around. Pamela Samuelson announced hesitantly that she couldn't stay, and left, still radiating resentment. Clearly, the disgruntled teacher had said all she was going to on the subject of the headmaster, Egon Schlichtmaier, and the altered grades. Marla sweetly asked Julian to retrieve a miniature Sara Lee chocolate cake from one of her capacious freezers. I sliced and we each delved into large, cold pieces.

"Let me tell you what I think the problem is," Marla said matter-of-factly, delicately licking her fingers of chocolate crumbs. "It's like a family thing."

"How?" I asked.

She shifted her cast on the ottoman to make herself more comfortable and eyed the last piece of cake. "Who are the people you most resent? The people closest to you. My sister got an MG from my parents when she graduated from college. I thought, If I don't get a car of equal or better value, I'm going to hate my sister forever and my parents too. Did I resent all the other girls my age who might have been out in Oshkosh or Seattle or Miami getting new cars? No. I resented the people close to me. They had the power to give me the car or deny it, I figured, reasonably or unreasonably." She reached for the piece of cake and bit into it with a contented *mmm-mmm*.

I nodded and conjured up Elk Park Prep. "There could be seven thousand people out there applying for a thousand places in the freshman class at Yale. If you'd kill to get into Yale, do you stalk all seven thousand? No. The killer doesn't worry about all those people out there who might be better than he is. He thinks, I have to remove the people right here who are standing in my way. Then I'll be guaranteed of getting what I want. Fallacious reasoning, but psychologically sound."

"You just better be careful," Marla told me. "Somebody out there is vicious, Goldy. And I have the broken bone to prove it."

When Julian and I arrived back on our street, I was relieved to see a cop sitting in a regular squad car right outside my house. Schulz had called and left a message that the investigators were working all day Sunday, and that the school would have counselors on Monday to deal with the kids' reactions to the latest murder. I should not worry, he added. Not worry. Sure. Sleep came with difficulty, and Sunday morning brought weak sunshine and a return of the headache.

Overnight, we'd received ten inches of snow. Not even the brilliant white world outside raised my spirits.

I brought the newspaper in from my icy deck and scanned it for news of Suzanne Ferrell. There was a small article on the front page: PREP SCHOOL SCENE OF SECOND DEATH. I started to tremble as I read of Suzanne Joan Ferrell, 43, native of North Carolina, graduate of Middlebury College, teacher at Elk Park Prep for fifteen years, whose body was found while seniors took their Scholastic Aptitude Tests . . . parents in Chapel Hill notified . . . her father an architect, mother the chairman of the French Department at the University of North Carolina

. . . police have no explanation, no suspects . . . death by strangulation. . . .

I took out a sheet of notepaper and performed that most difficult of tasks, writing to Suzanne's parents. My note to Keith's parents had been short, since I had not really been acquainted with the boy. This was different. *I knew her,* I wrote to the unknown architect and professor, *she was a wonderful teacher. She cared deeply about her students* . . . and then the tears came, profusely, unapologetically, so many, many tears for this unexplained loss. I allowed myself to cry until I could not cry anymore. Finally, painfully, I penned a closing. I signed my name, and addressed the note to the Ferrells in care of the French Department at U.N.C. Perversely, I found the university's address inside one of Julian's college advisory books. I slammed the book closed and heaved it across the kitchen, where it hit a cabinet with a loud crack.

With shaking hands I measured out espresso. While it brewed, I stared out the kitchen window and watched Stellar's jays fight for supremacy at my bird feeder.

I turned away. One thing was clear. Suzanne Ferrell had not killed herself. My espresso machine hissed; a fragrant strand of coffee streamed into the small cup. Had Suzanne Ferrell preferred café au lait? Had she been enthusiastic about French food? Did she leave a lover? I would never know.

Let go of it. I wiped a few fresh tears from my face and sipped the espresso. Julian appeared and thankfully said nothing about my appearance or the college advisory book lying facedown on the floor. When he finished his coffee, he reminded me that we had another Bronco halftime meal to cater for the Dawsons. *An Italian feast,* I had specified on the appointments calendar. I groaned.

"Let me fix the food," he offered. When I was about

to object, he added, "It'll help me get my mind off of everything."

I knew how cooking could help with that particular emotional task, so I agreed. Julian rattled around, collecting ingredients. As I watched, he deftly grated Fontina and mozzarella, beat these with eggs, ricotta, Parmesan, and softened butter before blending in chopped fresh basil and pressed garlic. I felt a burst of pride in him as he sizzled onion and garlic in olive oil and added ingredients for a tomato sauce. The rich scents of Italian cooking filled the room. After he had cooked the manicotti noodles, he stuffed in the Fontina-ricotta mixture and ladled thick tomato sauce over it all.

"After it heats, I'm going to garnish it with more Parmesan and some chopped cilantro," he informed me. "I'll make it look good, don't worry."

Food was the least of my worries. I pulled myself up from my chair, tore fresh greens for the salad, and mixed a lemon vinaigrette. I had made some breadsticks and frozen them the week before. Julian said he would put together a mammoth antipasto platter. I would bake a fudge cake when I returned from church, and that would be that.

Julian did not accompany me to the Sunday service. I came in late, sat in the back, slipped into the bathroom when tears again overcame me during the passing of the peace. I left quietly as soon as communion was over. A couple of curious sidelong glances came my way, but I resolutely averted my eyes. I wasn't in the mood to discuss murder.

The glumness on Hank Dawson's ruddy face when he opened the door to let me in that afternoon seemed to emanate more from the prospect of the Broncos having to face the Redskins than from anything to do with Elk Park Prep. The Dawsons had even invited the Marenskys. Bizarrely, Hank and Stan seemed to be friendly, resigned together to weather another tragedy out at the school. Either that, or they were both awfully good actors.

Caroline Dawson was a completely different story, however. Instead of her usual menopause-red outfit, scrupulously made-up face, and stiff composure, Caroline was dressed in an unbecoming cream-colored suit that was made of a fuzzy wool that kept picking up stray watts of static electricity. She looked like a squat, electrically charged ivory post. There was an edginess, too, about her untidily pinned-up hair and too-fussy inspection of the food and the way we were setting the table for her guests.

"We pay a lot of money for Greer to go to that school," she said angrily during her fifth unexpected appearance in her kitchen. "She shouldn't have to put up with crime and harassment. It's not something I expect, if you know what I mean. They never should have started letting riffraff into that school. They wouldn't be having these problems if they'd just kept their standards up."

I said nothing. Everybody paid a lot to go to that school, and I didn't know how Caroline would define riffraff. Julian, maybe?

Rhoda Marensky, dressed in a knitted green and brown suit with matching Italian leather shoes, made one of her tall, elegant appearances. She conspired with Caroline in misery. "First there was that Andrews murder. One of our coats, mind you, was involved, and the police said they found a pen from our store out by the body . . . and now Ferrell. Poor Brad hasn't slept in two weeks, and I'm afraid he hasn't even been able to start his paper on *The Tempest*. This is *not* what we're all paying for," she

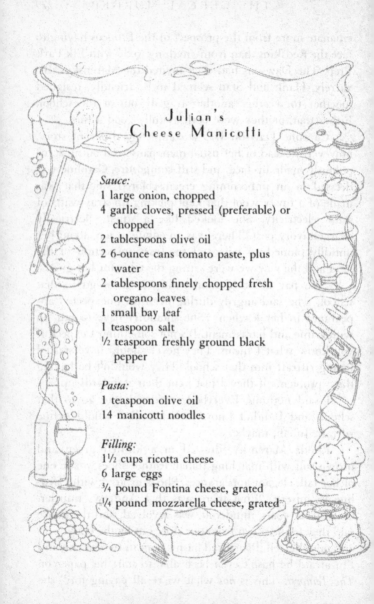

Julian's Cheese Manicotti

Sauce:
1 large onion, chopped
4 garlic cloves, pressed (preferable) or
 chopped
2 tablespoons olive oil
2 6-ounce cans tomato paste, plus
 water
2 tablespoons finely chopped fresh
 oregano leaves
1 small bay leaf
1 teaspoon salt
½ teaspoon freshly ground black
 pepper

Pasta:
1 teaspoon olive oil
14 manicotti noodles

Filling:
1½ cups ricotta cheese
6 large eggs
¾ pound Fontina cheese, grated
¼ pound mozzarella cheese, grated

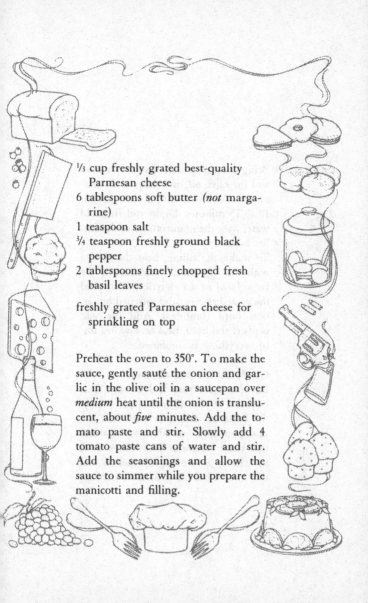

⅓ cup freshly grated best-quality
   Parmesan cheese
6 tablespoons soft butter (*not* marga-
   rine)
1 teaspoon salt
¾ teaspoon freshly ground black
   pepper
2 tablespoons finely chopped fresh
   basil leaves

freshly grated Parmesan cheese for
   sprinkling on top

Preheat the oven to 350°. To make the
sauce, gently sauté the onion and garlic in the olive oil in a saucepan over
medium heat until the onion is translucent, about *five* minutes. Add the tomato paste and stir. Slowly add 4
tomato paste cans of water and stir.
Add the seasonings and allow the
sauce to simmer while you prepare the
manicotti and filling.

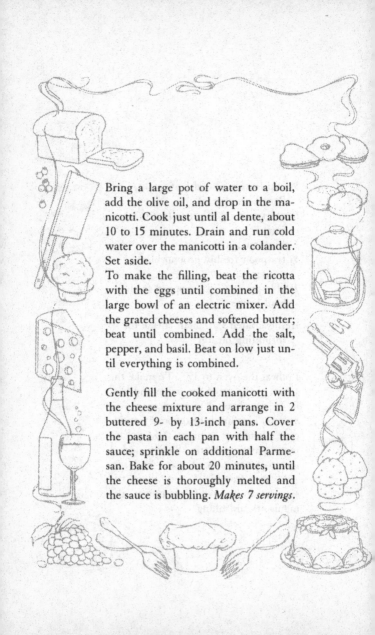

Bring a large pot of water to a boil, add the olive oil, and drop in the manicotti. Cook just until al dente, about 10 to 15 minutes. Drain and run cold water over the manicotti in a colander. Set aside.

To make the filling, beat the ricotta with the eggs until combined in the large bowl of an electric mixer. Add the grated cheeses and softened butter; beat until combined. Add the salt, pepper, and basil. Beat on low just until everything is combined.

Gently fill the cooked manicotti with the cheese mixture and arrange in 2 buttered 9- by 13-inch pans. Cover the pasta in each pan with half the sauce; sprinkle on additional Parmesan. Bake for about 20 minutes, until the cheese is thoroughly melted and the sauce is bubbling. *Makes 7 servings.*

exclaimed, eyes blazing. "It's like someone's *trying* to disrupt our *lives*!"

"Rhoda, honey," Stan called from the kitchen doorway, "what was the name of that lacrosse player from a couple of years back who graduated from Elk Park and went to Johns Hopkins? I can't remember and Hank just asked me if he was National Honor Society."

In a blur of green and brown, Rhoda brushed past Caroline Dawson, Julian, and me as if she had never even spoken to us. Strands from Caroline Dawson's hair and beige outfit now stood completely on end. Flaming spots of color stood out on her cheeks. Would we please hurry up? she said. Catering was *so* expensive, and with all the college expenses they would have next year, they couldn't afford to go for hours and hours without eating.

As soon as she'd banged out of the kitchen, Julian erupted. "Well, excuse the fuck me!"

"Welcome to catering," I said as I hoisted a tray. "You always think it's just going to be about cooking, but it never is."

We served the manicotti to a few grudgingly bestowed compliments. I felt terrible for Julian, especially since my own taste test had rated them mouth-watering. But what could you expect when the Redskins were smearing the Broncos? There was energetic kibbitzing about why this was happening: The coach had changed the lineup, Elway was worried about his shoulder, a linebacker was the subject of a paternity suit. When Washington won by three touchdowns, I feared we would receive no tip. But Hank Dawson reluctantly handed me twenty dollars as we trucked out the final boxes.

He lamented, "When Greer was in the state volleyball finals, we were going to take a gourmet box lunch. But Caroline said no, we had to have ham sandwiches the way we always did or we'd jinx it!"

"Oh, my," I said sympathetically. I didn't quite get the connection with the manicotti.

"Anyway," he continued morosely, "you should have done the same food you did last week. It would have been luckier."

It's always the caterer's fault.

19

"Lucky?" Julian groused on the way home. "Luckier *food*? What a dork."

"I keep telling you, people eat for different reasons. If they think eating sausage is going to win them the Super Bowl, then get out your bratwurst recipe and rev up the sausage stuffer. It pays in the long run, kiddo."

After we'd unloaded, he announced he was going to work on his college application forms. He called over his shoulder that anything was better than the thought of pig intestines. I laughed for the first time in two days.

John Richard left Arch off outside the house late that afternoon, the end of their Halloween skiing weekend. There he was, a strong, athletic father not lifting a finger to help his diminutive twelve-year-old son with skis, boots, poles, high-powered binoculars, and overnight bag. Should I scold him for forcing Arch to struggle halfway up the sidewalk with his loads of stuff? Never mind. This was, after all, the Jerk. If I uttered a word, then the whole neighborhood would rediscover why we were divorced in the first place.

I walked carefully down steps Julian had salted liberally that morning, relieved Arch of his skis and boots, and noticed with dismay that his face was sunburned to a brilliant pink except for the area around his eyes, where his goggles had left the skin eggshell-white. The resulting raccoon effect did not bode well for Monday morning. Then I noticed that what I had taken from him were new Rossignol skis boasting new Marker bindings.

"What is going on?" I asked.

Arch kept his eyes cast down as he hauled his overnight bag up the steps. "Dad forgot sunblock," he muttered.

"So he paid you off with new skis?" I said, incredulous.

"I guess."

His tone was as downcast as his voice. I realized with a pang that I hadn't even welcomed him home, much less told him about the tragic events of the weekend. Oh, spare me John Richard and his lavish attempts to bribe his way out of misconduct. The fact that I could not even come close to affording these luxurious trinkets didn't make dealing with them any easier. Not to mention what kind of message Arch was picking up from this kind of behavior.

"I'll be embarrassed to death if I have to go to school tomorrow looking like this," my son said with a crack in his voice. "I look like a red giant."

"A . . ."

"Oh, never mind, it's just a kind of star. Big and ugly and red."

"Oh, Arch—"

"Just don't say anything, please, Mom. Not a word."

"You can stay home tomorrow," I told him, giving him a hug. "The police are watching the house, so if I have to go out, you'll be protected."

"All *right*! Cool! Can I invite Todd over to watch the surveillance?"

Give them an inch . . .

"You can invite him over for dinner," I replied. At least this would give me some more time to lead up to the news of the Ferrell murder. It was my hope that Todd, a seventh-grader at the local junior high, would not be aware yet of the most recent crisis at Elk Park Prep.

Julian, who had fallen asleep working on his college applications, was in the kitchen drinking a Coke when Arch trundled in to greet him. To Julian's credit, although his eyebrows peaked in surprise upon seeing Arch's speckled facial condition, he made no comment. Over supper—fettuccine with hearty ladles of leftover tomato sauce—Arch regaled Todd, Julian, and me with stories of how he *caught about six feet of air going down a blue* and *cruised through a totally monstrous mogul field before biffing on top of this guy from Texas.* The Texan, one presumed, survived.

Before Arch went to bed I broke the news of Miss Ferrell's death. There would be counselors at the school the next day, I told him. So if he wasn't too worried about the sunburn . . . Arch said Miss Ferrell wasn't his teacher, but she was so nice. . . . Was it the same person who had bashed Keith, he asked. I told him I didn't know. After a few minutes Arch asked if we could pray for the two of them.

"Not out loud," he said as he turned away from me.

"Not out loud," I agreed, and after five minutes of silent offering, I turned out his light and went downstairs.

A windstorm kicked up overnight. Pine tree branches whooshed and knocked against the house and cold air slid through all of the uncaulked cracks. I got up to get another blanket. The police car at the end of our drive should have provided soporific assurance, but it did not. I prowled the house at midnight, two-thirty, and four A.M. Each time I checked on the boys, they were sleeping soundly, although Arch had stayed up late with his binoculars, watching for movements in the police car. Around five I finally drifted off into a deep sleep, but was sharply awakened an hour later when the phone rang.

"Goldy." Audrey Coopersmith sounded panicked. "I need to talk. I've been up for hours."

"Agh," I gargled.

"Carl's back," her voice rushed on, as if she were announcing a nuclear holocaust. "He came over and talked to Heather about his . . . girlfriend."

"He came over," I repeated, my nose deep in my pillow.

"He's thinking of getting married."

"Better to her than to you," I mumbled.

"The police were here when he came. He didn't even ask if I was all right. He didn't even ask what was going on."

Sadly, I said, "Audrey, Carl doesn't care anymore." I bit back the urge to talk about waking up and smelling the coffee. Mentioning caffeine would make me desire it too deeply.

"I just don't understand why he's acting this way, especially after all these years. . . ."

I pressed my face against my pillow and said nothing. Audrey was determined to recite the lengthy litany of Carl's wrongs. I said, "I'm sorry, but I need to go."

"Carl's upsetting Heather terribly. I don't know how she's going to survive this."

"Please, please, please, Audrey, let me go back to sleep. I promise I'll call you later."

She snapped, "You don't care. *Nobody* cares."

And with that she banged the phone down before I had a chance to protest. Grudgingly, I got out of bed and went down to smell, as well as make, the coffee. Julian was already up and showering. Audrey had not mentioned Suzanne Ferrell, but that was certainly why the police had visited her. I wondered if they would also be stationed out at the school.

Arch stumbled down to the kitchen at seven. His bright pink raccoon mask had faded somewhat, and I noticed with surprise that he had dressed in a ski sweater and jeans. He pulled a box of cereal out of the cupboard.

"Sure you feel okay about going today?"

He stopped sprinkling out Rice Krispies and gave me a solemn look. "Julian says that if you go to school with this kind of sunburn, kids don't make fun of you. They think you're cool because you skied all weekend. Besides, I want to listen to the counselors and find out if the French Club is going to do something for Miss Ferrell. You know, send flowers to her parents, write notes."

Within an hour both boys were out the door. Schulz called and said he was going down to Lakewood again to work on the Kathy Andrews case. He asked how we were, and I said truthfully that I was exhausted.

"I keep trying to figure out what's going on. Since Miss Ferrell wanted to talk to me about Julian, I need to at least make an attempt to chat with the headmaster about him."

"Keep at it," Schulz said. "You inspire great trust, Miss G."

"Yeah, sure."

He promised he would meet us at the Tattered Cover for the last college advisory affair this coming Friday night. Was it still going to happen, he wanted to know. I said I would call the school to find out if I was still the caterer of record.

"Look at it this way," Schulz soothed. "It's your last one of these college advisory things."

Small comfort. But I smiled anyway. "Getting to see you will be the best part."

"Ooo, ooo, should have gotten this on tape. The woman likes me."

I savored his wicked chuckle for the rest of the day.

The school secretary brusquely informed me that Headmaster Perkins was completely tied up with the police, parents, and teachers. He wouldn't have a free moment to see me for days. Then she put me on hold. In that time I managed to put together a Roquefort ramekin for our vegetarian supper, so I guess I was on hold for a long time. She returned to tell me that yes, they were going ahead Friday night; I should just fix the same menu. And Headmaster Perkins and I could discuss Julian Teller Friday morning at nine if I wanted. *If,* I thought with indignation.

The week passed in a flurry of meetings with clients who were already planning Thanksgiving and Christmas parties. I called Marla every day, but that was my closest link to the grapevine around the adults connected with Elk Park Prep. Unable to attend her exercise class with a broken leg, Marla had precious little access to information herself, although she did tell me that she'd heard Egon Schlichtmaier was dating somebody else from the athletic club.

"In addition to Suzanne Ferrell? Really?"

"She swears his relationship with Ferrell was just platonic. This other woman is disgustingly thin," Marla pronounced. "I just *know* she's had liposuction." She asked how Julian was doing, and I assured her he seemed fine. When I asked her why she cared about Julian, she said that she had a strong sympathy for vegetarians. News to me.

On Thursday, both Julian and Arch attended the memorial service for Miss Ferrell at the Catholic church. I had an unbreakable appointment with a client who had booked me for Thanksgiving itself. This client wanted a goose dinner for twenty that I would have to balance with my other commitments. Generally, I limited myself to ten Thanksgiving dinners. I would do most of the cooking Tuesday and Wednesday, deliver fixings for nine of them early Thursday morning, then actually cater one. John Richard habitually took Arch skiing that weekend, and I earned enough during the four-day period to support Arch and me for any sparsely booked spring month. Not only that, but I had learned that clients with relatives visiting over that weekend didn't want to see turkey Tetrazzini, turkey enchiladas, turkey rolls, or even poultry of any kind until the following week. So it was a great time to showcase any fish recipes I had been working on. Clients were famished for anything without gravy or cranberry jelly.

The windstorm raged all week. Temperatures dropped daily, and a skin of ice formed over the dark depths of Aspen Meadow Lake. Friday morning, after I had finished my yoga, I set out at nine o'clock and wished for about six more layers than my turtleneck and faded down coat. The fierce cold and snow had even encouraged the Main Street merchants to bring out their Christmas decorations early. The digital readout on the Bank of Aspen Meadow sign provided the grim reminder that it was November in the mountains: eleven degrees. Uneven ice coated the roads, the result of snow being churned up by the plows and then frozen solid. I drove carefully up Highway 203 toward Elk Park Prep and wondered if you could make a decent living doing catering in Hawaii.

The telltale side spotlights, huge mirrors, and low-to-the-ground chassis announced the fact that the only other vehicle in visitor parking at the school was an unmarked police car. More investigators for the Ferrell homicide? Catching up with me from the faculty parking lot, Egon Schlichtmaier, elegantly sartorial in a new fur-trimmed bomber jacket, held one of the massive doors to the school open wide and bowed low. Someone, I noticed, had finally removed the black crepe paper and Keith's picture.

"Tardy today?" I asked.

"I do not have a class until ten o'clock," he replied cheerfully. "I was working out, but did not see you."

I eyed him and said, "Nice jacket." He swaggered off.

The headmaster was deeply involved in a conference call, but could see me in a bit, the receptionist informed me. I went down the hall to check on Arch—undetected, this time. To my surprise, he was standing in front of his social studies class, giving a report. Before creeping off to find Julian, I scanned the facial expressions of Arch's classmates. All listened attentively. Pride lit a small glow in my chest.

A uniformed police officer stood guard outside one of the classrooms of the upper school area of the old hotel. I nodded to him and identified myself. He did not reply, but when I looked through the window into the classroom, he didn't ask me for ID either. Egon Schlichtmaier's American history class had just begun: Macguire Perkins was giving an oral report at the front of the room. On the board was written: THE MONROE DOCTRINE. Sad to say, Macguire and the justification for hemispheric intervention were not receiving as much attention as Arch. Greer Dawson was combing her hair; Heather Coopersmith was figuring on a calculator; Julian looked perilously close to slumber. For one brief moment my eyes locked with Macguire's, and he signaled hello to me with one hand. I shrank back from the door. The last thing I needed was for Egon Schlichtmaier to claim I'd been bothering his class. I slunk back toward the headmaster's office.

"He'll see you now," chirped the secretary without looking up from her computer monitor. I marched into the office, wondering vaguely how she'd known it was me. Did I smell like a caterer?

Headmaster Perkins was once again on the phone—although this must have been less important than the earlier conference call—as he covered the receiver with his hand and waved me over to a side table laden with a tray of baked goods and silver electrified urn.

"Help yourself," he said in a low voice, "I'll be right off."

There must have been an early morning meeting of the board of trustees, I thought vaguely, for all the *profiteroles*, miniature cheesecakes, chocolate chip bars, and frosted cupcakes on the tray. I poured myself a cup of coffee but decided against the sweets. How come Perkins hadn't called me to cater an early-morning meeting? Did he save me for the easy stuff like getting up at oh-dark-thirty to make healthful munchies for hordes of seniors? Or was he afraid I might hear how he presented the murder of Suzanne Ferrell to the big contributors?

"Yes," he was saying now into the phone. "Yes, quite tragic, but we must go on. Still seven P.M. Yes, on stress reduction in test-taking. Ah, no. I will be taking over the college counseling myself." He took a deep, resigned sniff. "Same caterer, indeed." But before he could say "ta-ta" again, the person on the other end hung up.

"Tattered Cover," he explained to me with a shake of his Andy Warhol hair. He looked around his desk, which was cluttered with papers and an enormous basket of fresh flowers. Someone obviously thought he needed sympathy when it was one of his teachers who had been murdered. Gray pouches of wrinkled skin hung under his eyes. He wore a navy sport coat instead of his usual *Brideshead Revisited* tweeds, and it suddenly occurred to me he hadn't used a single simile since I'd walked into the office.

"Are you all right, Headmaster Perkins?"

He looked straight at me with enormously sad eyes. "No, Ms. Bear, I am not all right."

He rolled his swivel chair around until he was looking at the painting of Big Ben. "George Albert Turner," he said thoughtfully. "Great-grandson of Joseph Mallord William Turner. Not exactly 'Burning of the Houses of Parliament,' though, is it?" Then he turned toward me again, and weak sunlight from outside illuminated the capillary veins scrawled across his face. His mournful voice intoned, "And so far am I also removed from the real thing."

"Ah, I'm not quite following you."

"Purity of pursuit, my God, Ms. Bear! Purity of artistry, purity of academic inquiry . . . all the same." Perkins rubbed his forehead with both hands. "Unlike"—he gestured to indicate the elegant room—"unlike all *this*."

"Mr. Perkins, I know you're upset. I can talk to you about Julian some other time. You've obviously had some meeting—"

"Meeting? What meeting?" A harsh laugh escaped his throat. "The only people I meet with these days are police."

"But"—I gestured to the urn and trays of baked goods—"I thought—"

Again the sad, ironic look, the voice of distress. "Midterm grades, Ms. Bear! The flowers are a gift! The owners of the flower shop want their son to go to Brown after he graduates next year. They want me to write the recommendation after I change the boy's French three grade from a C to an A. Miss Ferrell wouldn't do it, you see." I stared at the headmaster, incredulous. Was he losing it? He prattled on. "The baked goods are *also* a gift. One of my teachers has a new fur coat. He asked if it was all right for him to keep it, since it cost more than his entire wardrobe. He swears the donors haven't asked him to change a grade. I told him, 'Not yet, they haven't.' "

"But these people who wanted Miss Ferrell to . . . do this for them, could they . . ."

He shook his head. "They're in Martinique. With their son. You see, they go every year at the end of October, and the boy gets rather behind in his work." He raised his eyebrows at me. "They want me to give him credit for going to Martinique! They say he speaks some French there, so why not?"

"Purity of pursuit," I said softly. "Did you change the grade?"

He stiffened. "That's not the kind of question I answer. You wouldn't believe the pressure I'm under."

"I would believe it," I said truthfully. "Just look at what's happened around here the past two weeks. Speaking of gifts, could you tell me any more about this scholarship Julian received? I'm afraid there may be strings attached. Maybe not at this very moment, but as you yourself would say, not yet. Like your teacher with the coat. Maybe next week, or next month, Julian could get some anonymous message saying if he wants to keep his scholarship, he has to flunk a test, not apply to a certain school, something like that."

Perkins shrugged and looked back at the neo-Turner.

"I know as much as you do, Ms. Bear. We received a call from the bank, period. To the best of my knowledge, nobody at this school knows the donor. Or knew," he said, to my unanswered question about Miss Ferrell.

"Why do you think someone killed her?"

"We all have a constituency, Ms. Bear. You do, I do, Miss Ferrell did." He held up his hands in his mannered gesture of helplessness. His voice rose. "As a caterer, you must do what you know is bad for your constituency, because it is what they want. If the obese want fudge rather than oat bran, well, why not? When it comes back to haunt them, you'll be long gone. Displeased parents make my life a misery with phone calls and letters and all kinds of threats."

"Yes, but are you saying Miss Ferrell wouldn't play along? Sort of like Miss Samuelson?"

Anger blazed in his eyes. I felt myself recoil at the unexpected intensity of his obvious distress, his loathing at my bringing up this topic. Perkins had tried to disguise his dislike for me by trying for sympathy in—unprofessionally, I thought—sharing details of his emotional load. But it hadn't worked. Now he pressed his lips together and did not respond.

I said, "Did you tell the police that Miss Ferrell wouldn't play along, perhaps?"

His haggard face turned scarlet. "Of course I did," he snarled. "But they think somebody might have been searching her room that morning. They can't find her grade book; they don't know what was going on or who might have been having problems. And I doubt that any parent or student would dare put the pressure on me *now*." He leered. "But perhaps I don't know all she did."

"What about Egon Schlichtmaier? Have you talked to the police about him?"

He ran his hands impatiently over the cottony mass of

hair. "Why are you so interested? Why not just leave it to the authorities?"

"Look, the only person I'm worried about is Julian. I want to know who would give him this scholarship and why."

He tugged the lapels of his sport coat. "Julian Teller is a fine student." His lips closed firmly.

I mumbled something noncommittal, and Perkins said he'd see me that night for the last of the college meetings. The bell signaling class change rang, and I made noises about it being time for me to leave. But instead of the usual metaphorical sendoff, Headmaster Perkins merely swiveled back to the painting by Turner's great-grandson. As I left his office, my mind groped wildly.

Someone searching her room . . . they can't find her grade book . . .

In the hallway I saw several seniors I recognized. All avoided me by looking away or starting to talk animatedly to the person nearest to them. Discovering two dead bodies can get you ostracized, I guessed. Except by Macguire Perkins, who came lumbering down the hall and nodded when I said hello. I pulled his sleeve.

"Macguire," I said, "I need to talk to you."

"Oh well, okay." He led me out the school's front door.

I looked up. For that was where he was, this lanky, painfully acne-faced basketball star—way up. A blue plaid lumberjack shirt hung out over jeans that ended in weathered hiking boots. No preppie outfit for the headmaster's son.

"I want to talk to you about Miss Ferrell."

"I, uh, I'm real sorry about Miss Ferrell."

"So am I."

"You know, I know she was mad about my college visit, and . . . other stuff, but I think she liked me."

"What other stuff?"

"Just," he said, "stuff."

"Like having your driver's license suspended for drinking and driving? Or stuff like your use of steroids to muscle yourself up?"

His scarred face turned acutely red. "Yeah. Anyway, I stopped the steroids. Last week, I swear. Ferrell was talking to me about it, said I could be strong without them, like that."

"She was right." I hesitated. "There's something I need, Macguire. Something she might have feared would get stolen."

"What?"

"Miss Ferrell's classroom might have been searched last Saturday. It was a mess when the police got to it. I've just had a talk with your father and it made me think. . . . Listen, I need her grade book. You of all people know your way around this school. Is there any chance she could have hidden it somewhere?"

Macguire looked around the snowy parking lot before replying. Was paranoia a side effect of his brand of drug abuse?

"As a matter of fact," he said reluctantly, "I may know where it is. You know, being tall, I see things other folks don't see."

"Tell me."

"Remember when I read my essay about I.U. at the front of the class?" I nodded. "She has those big posters up there by the blackboard. Behind that framed one of that arch in Paris, I saw something. Like a brown notebook. I could go look . . ."

"Please do."

He trundled off, and within two minutes he was

back, grinning triumphantly. He shrugged his backpack off his shoulder and unzipped it. Another quick visual scan of the parking lot. "Luck," he said simply. He pulled out a brown fake-leather spiral grade book and handed it to me. I hadn't brought a purse, so I just held on to it.

"Give that to the cops," he said. "Maybe it'll tell them something."

My heart ached for this sad, loose-limbed boy. "Thank you, Macguire. I was so worried about you Saturday morning. You seemed so nervous about the test."

"What, me?" He backed away and held up his hands in protest. "Your cookies were great. I thought later, why should I have been so worried about the SATs? I'm not going to be somebody by going to Harvard. What the hell, I'm never going to be anybody."

20

I phoned Tom Schulz when I got home in the hope that he might have returned from Lakewood. No luck. I told his machine I had Suzanne Ferrell's roll book with the class grades, and where was he? The evening's event loomed and I knew I had food to prepare. Still, I was getting close to the answers to a lot of questions; I could feel it. Cooking could wait. I sat down at my kitchen table and opened Suzanne Ferrell's grade book.

It was larger than most grade books I had seen, about eight by eleven instead of four by six, and with many more pages. The notebook was divided into three parts: *French III, French IV,* and *CC*. When I flipped to it, *CC* proved to be college counseling. There I saw an inked list of the top-ranked seniors: 1. Keith Andrews, 2. Julian Teller, 3. Heather Coopersmith, 4. Greer Dawson, 5. Brad Marensky. . . . A quick check showed that Brad Marensky and Greer Dawson were in French III; Julian and

Heather Coopersmith were in French IV. Keith Andrews had also been in French IV. They were all, including Macguire Perkins, in college counseling.

In French III, Brad Marensky had a solid stream of C's and B's; his midterm grade was due to be a B minus. Greer Dawson's showed wide swings: two F's early on, the rest B's. Her grade: C. Julian had made A's at the beginning of the quarter, then a B and an F on a quiz last week. He had also received a B minus for the midterm. Heather Coopersmith had B's punctuated by two A's, and was due to receive a B plus. Keith Andrews had received all A's and one B. There was a line through his name.

Well, that didn't tell me much. Or if it did, I hadn't a clue how to interpret it. Would this finally all come down to mathematical calculations of grades? Is that what people would kill for?

With some trepidation I turned to the college counseling section. In addition to the class rank, the students were listed alphabetically. Reactions and conferences with the students, headmaster, and parents had been duly noted in careful handwriting.

KEITH ANDREWS—*Disillusioned by recent trips to universities. Parents in Europe. Wishes he could join them, visit Oxford, etc. Says someone should start a college made up of all the winners of Distinguished Teachers awards who didn't get tenure. H. says K. can't be trusted; writing something for paper. I said probably harmless.* RECOMMENDED: STANFORD, PRINCETON, COLUMBIA.

HEATHER COOPERSMITH—*Mother worried. Sat next to her at dinner. H. says mother obsessing on college thing because father dumped. Wants control of life. Jealous of K. Claims others have $$ they* *can spend to help their kids get into college. H. dreamy and distant. Wants less structure, less pressure in academic life. H. says mother a pain.* RECOMMENDED: BENNINGTON, ANTIOCH.

BRAD MARENSKY—*Parents brought in media rankings. Wanted to know Dawson list! They think B. "deserves" top-ranked school. Says stories about them offering fur coat to admissions director at Williams untrue. But do I think it would be a good idea? (Said no.) Unpleasantness from last year apparently resolved. B. indifferent to schools, but seemed to be watching me. Told me he wanted to be "far away from parents." Asked, "Did I know?" I said, about what? No response. H. doesn't have a clue.* RECOMMENDED: WASHINGTON AND LEE, COLBY.

GREER DAWSON—*Very difficult. Wants Ivy League or Stanford, but SATs not high enough; grades erratic. Parents offered me a year's free meals if I'd recommend her. Not amused. H. warned, "trouble if the school doesn't get Greer into Princeton."* RECOMMENDED: OCCIDENTAL, UNIVERSITY OF NORTH CAROLINA.

MACGUIRE PERKINS—*Asked about drinking record, drugs. Said he has talent for drama, but he thinks not; says he's depressed. Recommended psychotherapy. H. opposed, looks bad.* RECOMMENDED SCHOOLS FOR BASKETBALL: INDIANA, N.C. STATE, UNLV.

Uneasily, I turned to the dead woman's comments about Julian.

JULIAN TELLER—*Vulnerable. Wants to study food science. Not covered in Rugg's. Will phone around for help. J. knows Cornell has a program (Jane Brody alum); would fit with his academic bent. Meet with foster mother (caterer) morning of 11/1.* RECOMMENDED: CORNELL, MINNESOTA (?).

None of this made a whole lot of sense to me, except to confirm my suspicions about these people. Miss Ferrell was one smart cookie, except that she had not fathomed Brad Marensky's question: Did Miss Ferrell know about his stealing? Apparently she had not.

I also remembered vaguely about Rugg's—a reference book that rated colleges and universities by departments. If food science wasn't in there, perhaps I could check the cookbook section when I went to the Tattered Cover that evening to see where the most recent culinary writers had gone to school. It was something I could do to help, anyway. Even though Julian now had the funds to go anywhere he wanted, he might as well get the most his money could buy.

I tried to let go of academic worries while I put together more biscotti, some fruit and cheese trays, and started in on a recipe I was testing for Valentine's Day: Sweetheart Sandwiches. A Sweetheart Sandwich consisted of a pair of fudgelike cookies separated by a slide of buttercream filling. Serving these rich little cookies was inspired by the subject for the evening's lecture: "Stress Reduction in Test-taking." My prescription for stress was simple: *Take chocolate and call me when it's over.*

Audrey called, contrite over her early-morning explosion, and assured me she wanted to help tonight. Could she have a ride to the bookstore? Heather was doing some calculations for her classmates on their new class rank, and she had to deliver the results to her friends on their way down to Denver. Heather didn't want Audrey to embarrass her, Audrey told me sadly. Were we wearing white uniforms, aprons, what? I told her black skirt, white blouse, and her apron that said GOLDILOCKS' CATERING. She promised she'd come over at five-thirty.

Julian called. He said he would be eating over at Neil's; he would catch a ride with Neil and meet me at the bookstore. Unless I needed help? I assured him I had everything under control. Arch came home and announced he had to pack for an overnight with a friend. But first he would have some of the new cookies.

"If you'll pour me a glass of milk," he negotiated as he pushed his glasses up his nose and methodically placed three freshly baked cookies on his plate. With eyes closed, he tasted the first one.

"Well?"

He let me suffer a moment. Then he said very seriously, "Excellent, Mom. Any teacher would give you an A plus."

I grinned. "Are you feeling better in school?"

He swallowed, took a sip of milk, and wiped off the liquid white mustache. "Sort of."

"What does that mean?"

"Seventh grade is like . . ." Headmaster Perkins' mannerisms were contagious. Arch popped another cookie in his mouth and chewed pensively. "Seventh grade is like half happiness, half totalitarianism."

"Totalitarianism?"

"Oh, Mom." He adjusted his glasses. "Julian taught me that word for social studies." He paused. "Are they still working on finding out who killed Keith Andrews and Miss Ferrell?" When I nodded, he said, "You know, I just want to be in a safe place. It is scary in school, I have to admit."

"But nothing else has happened, right?"

"Mom, the police are there. How safe do you think it's going to be when they pull off their investigators and the surveillance?"

I didn't answer that question. "Don't worry," I said tensely, "we, or they, or somebody, is going to figure out what happened."

He didn't seem to want to talk anymore, so I went back to my cooking. By the time the friend's mother arrived at five o'clock, Arch had run through half a dozen cookies and declared he didn't want any dinner.

Neither did I, I decided after he left, but not because I was full of anything but dread. My stomach was churning in anticipation of yet another college advisory event. I wondered how many guidance counselors had ulcers. Perhaps when this final ordeal was over, Audrey could get a ride home with her daughter and Schulz and I could go out for a late supper.

Audrey arrived. We packed the trays into the van, hightailed it to Denver, and arrived at the Tattered Cover promptly at six. Driving up to the third-floor entrance, where I had parked before, I remembered my resolve to check the cookbooks for names of schools for Julian. I also suddenly remembered Miss Ferrell's grade book, which I had packed in one of my boxes in the hope that I could give it to Schulz after the program. With all the stealing going on among Elk Park preppies, I was going to make certain I personally handed this valuable volume to him for analysis. But I had learned my lesson with Keith's computer disks: I wasn't about to leave the grade book unprotected in the kitchen during the confusion of the catering. When Audrey was preoccupied with folding up box lids, I grabbed the grade book, wrapped it in a spare business apron, and headed briskly through the third-floor door and down two flights on the interior staircase. I wanted to put it in the secret closet Audrey had shown me

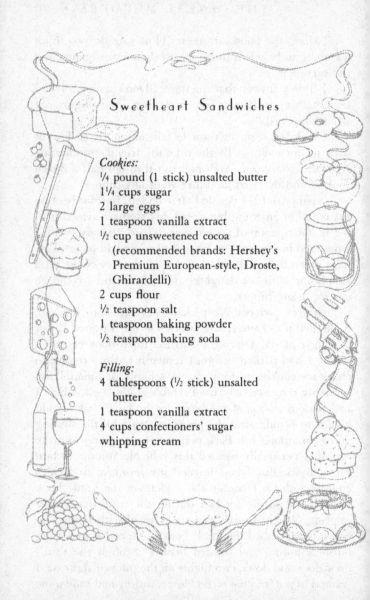

Sweetheart Sandwiches

Cookies:

¼ pound (1 stick) unsalted butter
1¼ cups sugar
2 large eggs
1 teaspoon vanilla extract
½ cup unsweetened cocoa
    (recommended brands: Hershey's
    Premium European-style, Droste,
    Ghirardelli)
2 cups flour
½ teaspoon salt
1 teaspoon baking powder
½ teaspoon baking soda

Filling:

4 tablespoons (½ stick) unsalted
    butter
1 teaspoon vanilla extract
4 cups confectioners' sugar
whipping cream

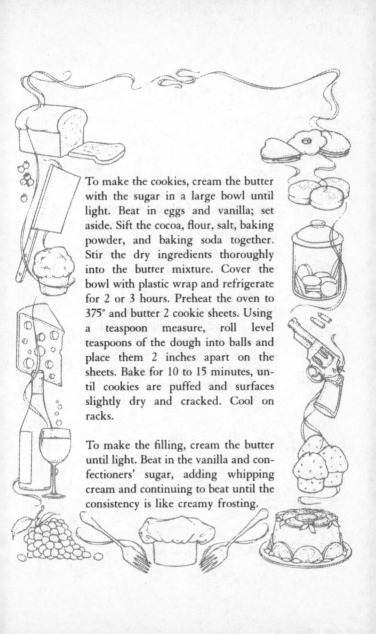

To make the cookies, cream the butter with the sugar in a large bowl until light. Beat in eggs and vanilla; set aside. Sift the cocoa, flour, salt, baking powder, and baking soda together. Stir the dry ingredients thoroughly into the butter mixture. Cover the bowl with plastic wrap and refrigerate for 2 or 3 hours. Preheat the oven to 375° and butter 2 cookie sheets. Using a teaspoon measure, roll level teaspoons of the dough into balls and place them 2 inches apart on the sheets. Bake for 10 to 15 minutes, until cookies are puffed and surfaces slightly dry and cracked. Cool on racks.

To make the filling, cream the butter until light. Beat in the vanilla and confectioners' sugar, adding whipping cream and continuing to beat until the consistency is like creamy frosting.

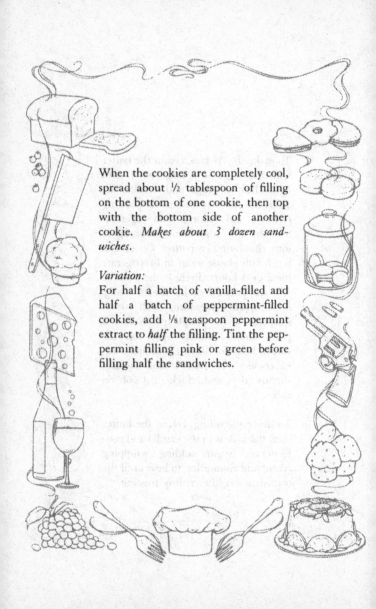

When the cookies are completely cool, spread about ½ tablespoon of filling on the bottom of one cookie, then top with the bottom side of another cookie. *Makes about 3 dozen sandwiches.*

Variation:
For half a batch of vanilla-filled and half a batch of peppermint-filled cookies, add ⅛ teaspoon peppermint extract to *half* the filling. Tint the peppermint filling pink or green before filling half the sandwiches.

in Business, but there was a cadre of people in front of the shelf, reading up on making millions in utilities stocks. I tried for a safer area.

The staffperson in Cookbooks recognized me from the previous week. She was delighted at my request to see the latest in culinary writing.

"Oh, but you have to go see our window display!" she exclaimed with a laugh. "It's a new display Audrey and I put together: 'What's new in food and cooking'! You must go admire what she did."

She directed me out the door to First Avenue, where I turned right and then faced a stage set behind plate glass that was designed to make people run—not walk—to the nearest restaurant. From every cranny of the big display window, photographs of food jumped out: splashy posters of Jarlsberg, Gorgonzola, and Gouda rounds vied with brilliant photos of jewel-red peppers, beets, and squashes, tangles of colored pasta, blackened fish and thick succulent steaks, loaves of shiny bread, creamy cheesecakes, gleaming raspberry tarts, dark chocolate soufflés. Stacked on tables placed in the visual display were at least a hundred cookbooks, thick and thin—Julia Child, Jane Brody, the Silver Palate people, the Cajun crowd, you-name-it. Hanging like flags here and there above the small stage were aprons, kitchen towels, and tablecloths. Hmm. I wondered if the woman could be persuaded to put a Goldilocks' Catering apron in there? The worst that could happen was that a negative response would be accompanied by the judgment that I was crassly, irredeemably commercial. Which I was. It was worth a try. None of us, I reflected as I trudged inside, is above bribery.

She would be happy to put the apron in, she told me cheerily. I accompanied her to the interior side of the window. There she slid expertly between the photographs, took down a red and white apron, and hung up my spare, the GOLDILOCKS' CATERING facing the street. Inspired, I sidled up to the front of the window and surreptitiously slipped the grade book underneath the latest Paul Prud'homme. It was, after all, *hot*.

"Watch your step," the woman warned as I accidentally backed into a pile of cookbooks.

"Not to worry," I assured her. I scooted off the platform in front of the window, where several street-side onlookers stood salivating over the photo display, thanked the cookbook person, and ran up the stairs to the third floor. The store staff was already setting up chairs, and Audrey had made the coffee and concocted the apple juice from concentrate. Her face was set in a studied frown.

"Carl bothering you again?" I ventured.

"No," she said after a moment. "It's Heather. She's having some problems with her classmates. Now she wants me to drive her home after this. And she said Carl called, just had to talk to me about some new crisis."

What else was new, I wanted to ask her. I refrained.

However, after spending a few silent minutes stacking plastic cups in the tiny kitchenette, Audrey faced me gloomily. "Heather's classmates told her they wanted her to figure the class rank because she's so marvelous with numbers. They were going to supply her with their midterm grades, which supposedly came out Tuesday. But she's tried for the past three days and she can't get some of the top people, like Brad Marensky or Greer Dawson, to give her their grades in French. Now, I know they both have team practices, but why not answer Heather's messages? I mean, they all said they *wanted* her to do this."

"I certainly don't know, Audrey. If you send Heather to Bennington, she won't have any grades."

Audrey *tsk*ed and shouldered a fruit and cheese tray. In the outer room, Miss Kaplan's microphone-enhanced voice introduced the evening's speaker, a Mr. Rathgore. I carried out the first tray of cups, returned to pick up the wine and apple juice, and scuttled back in time to see the troubled Heather deep in intense conversation with her mother, whose eyebrows were raised in perplexity.

Julian sat between Egon Schlichtmaier and Macguire Perkins. The three were chuckling over some private joke as Mr. Rathgore, a bald fellow in a shiny rayon suit, launched into his opening.

"We all hate to be tested," he said. A chorus of groans greeted this.

I stole a glance at the headmaster, who was nodding absentmindedly. Perkins appeared even more exhausted than he had that morning. The Marenskys and Dawsons had prudently decided to sit on opposite sides of the room. Brad Marensky wore a Johns Hopkins sweatshirt; Greer Dawson was again swathed in forest-green watered silk. A steely-eyed staring contest seemed to be taking place between the Dawsons and Audrey, who was seated in a couch to the side of the speaker. But after a moment Heather touched her mother's arm and Audrey looked away from the Dawsons.

"Worse, we can get caught up in the nerve-racking process of identifying with our children as they are tested," continued Mr. Rathgore. "Old patterns recapitulate. Parents take their children's poor performance much more seriously than the children themselves do. . . ."

No kidding. People began to shift uncomfortably in their seats, which I put down to the speech hitting a little too close to home. As I was setting out the paper cups one by one, I could see out of the corner of my eye that a few folks were standing up, stretching, milling about. Maybe they just couldn't take any more reminders of *their last chance at success.* I turned an attentive face to Mr. Rathgore, but instead met with the gray visage of Headmaster Perkins, who had crossed the room to me.

"Goldy," he stage-whispered, "I'm more exhausted than Perry when he finished traversing Antarctica." He favored me with a chilly half-grin. Apparently he'd forgiven me for bringing up the mess with Pamela Samuelson and her grading. "Please tell me this isn't decaf."

"It isn't," I assured him as I poured the dark liquid into the first cup. "Unadulterated caffeine, I promise. And have a Valentine's Day cookie, they're called Sweetheart Sandwiches."

His expressive brow furrowed. "Valentine's Day cookies? We haven't even endured Thanksgiving! Somewhat too early, wouldn't you say?"

Before I could answer, Tom Schulz appeared on the other side of the table and greeted me with a huge smile. "Got some of those for me?"

"Finally," I said with a smile I couldn't suppress. "You're back." And I handed him a steaming cup of fragrant black stuff and a plate of Sweetheart Sandwiches. The headmaster attempted a jovial greeting for Schulz, but it caught in his throat. He reddened.

"You have something else for me?" Schulz whispered in my direction, ignoring Perkins' discomfort. Mr. Rathgore paused in his talk to furrow his brow at the coffee-serving table. Several parents turned to see what was distracting the speaker's attention, and I drew back in embarrassment. Headmaster Perkins' too-bright smile froze on his face.

Alfred Perkins took a bite of his Valentine's Day cookie that was too early. There were too many snoopy folks around to give Schulz the grade book now, I decided.

"Have some cookies first, they're—"

But before I could hand him the platter, another parental squabble erupted in the audience. This time it was between Caroline Dawson and Audrey Coopersmith.

"What is the matter with you?" Caroline shrieked. She jumped to her feet and glowered down at Audrey Coopersmith. Audrey closed her eyes and raised her pointy chin in defiance. Caroline was as scarlet as her suit. "Do you think Heather is the only one with talent? Do you think she's the only one who can do math? Do you have any idea how *tired* we all get of your boasting?"

That shattered Audrey's calm. She blazed, "Oh, excuse me, but it was Hank and Stan who started this—"

Mr. Rathgore turned puzzled eyes to Miss Kaplan, who seemed at a loss for dealing with a civil disturbance during an author presentation.

"We did not!" Hank Dawson, irate, protested with his meaty hands. "Stan just said Heather wanted grades from Brad, but he's been busy all week, and Greer couldn't get her number in either, and all I said was that with the time it was taking, maybe the government should hire Heather to compute the deficit . . . really, let's just all calm down!"

"I will not calm down!" Audrey fumed. Now she rose to her feet and yanked at the strings of her apron. After she had flung it off, she wagged a finger at the Dawsons. "Hank, you don't know anything! How dare you make fun of Heather? To compute the deficit! Since when are you the economics expert? I'm so tired of you! You act like a know-it-all, and you know *nothing*! You— you think you buy a government bond to get out of jail!"

Not this routine again. Parents murmured and coughed; Schulz gave me one raised eyebrow. The Marenskys spoke to each other excitedly. They were probably bond investors.

"I'd like to know what business Hank Dawson has making snide remarks about computing the deficit," Audrey's shrill voice demanded of the stunned audience. "He thinks the Federal Reserve is where all the Indians live!"

Audrey did not wait for a response. True to form, she stomped out. Heather slithered out after her. So much for my post-catering cleaning help.

Miss Kaplan tried to restore order. "Why don't we all just . . . have some refreshments, and if you have questions for Mr. Rathgore . . ." Her voice trailed off amid the noise of people scooping up their coats and scrunching shopping bags. A couple of parents lined up to buy Mr. Rathgore's book: *The True Test.*

"Don't worry." Julian appeared at my side, holding a tray of biscotti. "I'll give you a hand. You know, Heather's mom is always stressed. Stressed *major.*"

Schulz helped himself to two biscotti. "As you were saying, Miss G., about my having cookies—"

But before I could try any thoughts out on him, there was a distant explosion of crashing glass.

Macguire, who'd been leaning against a bookcase, was so startled he almost fell down. Julian's tray dropped with a bang. Headmaster Perkins looked appalled.

"Don't move, anyone!" cried Tom Schulz. He loped out the nearby exit to the adjoining garage. Bewildered parents turned to one another; an anxious buzz filled the air. The unfortunate Mr. Rathgore turned to the trade buyer. He had forgotten he was wearing a microphone.

"What the hell is going on?" his voice boomed out.

Miss Kaplan steepled her hands and pressed them to her lips. First a parental argument, then a glass-breaking disruption. Unlikely Mr. Rathgore would agree to another signing anytime soon.

Schulz returned. "It's your van," he announced laconically.

"Whose?" the ill-fated Mr. Rathgore screeched into his microphone.

Julian cried, "Somebody's broken the windshield!

Just like . . ." But he didn't have to say just like which windshield.

Schulz quickly crossed the room to me, ignoring the confusion. "Goldy, I'm taking you to my car. I'll notify surveillance. I want you out of here and with me," he finished abruptly.

"I can't . . . I have to clean up."

"You have to go." Julian echoed Schulz. "It's what I keep telling you. You're not safe around these people. Go, go now. I'll clean up."

Schulz had taken me by the arm to lead me out. I stood firm.

"And how will you get home?" I demanded of Julian, refusing to budge.

"I'll get a ride or something. Now, go on, go."

I felt dazed. I took one long look at the assembled group of students, parents, school and bookstore staff. All stood immobile, as if suspended in a snapshot, watching the caterer make her unexpected exit under police guard. I wondered how many decided I was under arrest.

21

Tom Schulz's wheels shrieked as we rounded the parking lot's hairpin curves. Within moments he was gunning the car up First Avenue. "Where's Arch?" he demanded.

"Spending the night with a friend. I still don't understand why I should leave because of a broken windshield. I feel ridiculous."

"Come on, Goldy. You know you can't stay," was all he said.

When we arrived in Aspen Meadow forty-five minutes later, stillness enveloped my neighborhood. The only sounds were a dog barking in the distance and the murmurs between Schulz and the surveillance policeman.

Schulz shook his head as he walked back to me. "Nothing suspicious." He escorted me up the steps. At the door I hesitated.

"Had the surveillance fellow received any radio messages about who trashed my car?"

"Nope. Look, I've had another call, unrelated. But I'll come in and look around if you want."

"No need. The bookstore closed at nine. Julian'll be home by ten."

"I'll call you then."

I snapped on lights in each room, then checked the clock: 9:30. Every creak, every moan of breeze, every stray sound, made me jump. Finally, I made a mug of steaming hot chocolate, slipped on my down coat, and settled into a snowy lawn chair out front. Keeping the surveillance car in sight seemed like the best idea.

The hot chocolate was deliciously comforting. I leaned back to look at the expanse of stars glittering overhead. Because there was no moon, Arch was probably outside with his friend, wielding his high-powered binoculars and enthusiastically pointing out Sirius and Cassiopeia. I could find the Big Dipper and Orion, but that was about it.

At ten o'clock I went inside, checked my answering machine—no messages—and made more hot cocoa. Chocolate always tastes best with more chocolate, and I lamented that the windshield disruption had necessitated leaving the Sweetheart Sandwiches down at the bookstore. Actually, it was getting so that *any* Elk Park Prep catered event was likely to be disrupted.

Back on my lawn chair, I stared again at the sky. And then, it was as if a hole opened up in the sparkling firmament. Through it I could see Rhoda Marensky in the Dawsons' kitchen, exclaiming: *It's as if someone's trying to disrupt our lives.* I remembered Hank Dawson's different spin on that sentiment: *You should have done the same food you did last week. It would have been luckier.* Rhoda and Hank seemed to believe that if you ate the right things, got enough sleep, followed all the same routines, you'd do well.

But if someone disrupted your life, you wouldn't do well.

Someone had deliberately smashed Keith Andrews' windshield the day of the Princeton rep's visit. Not long after, that same person had probably killed him.

Someone had broken a window in our house, hung a snake in Arch's locker, and perhaps planted a deadly spider in a drawer. Our steps had been boobytrapped, our chimney stopped up, and one of our car windshields broken. The result had been police surveillance, worry, conflict, lack of sleep, quizzes failed, homework and college applications left undone.

The person who had suffered most had been a highly emotional person, someone who cared deeply about those around him, someone who was terribly vulnerable to criticism and cruelty.

Could it be that neither Arch nor I was at the heart of this campaign of harassment?

Excuse the fuck me. And then another time: *This stuff at the school is getting to me.*

I pictured Julian, who knew so many things that he was unwilling to discuss—the steroids, bitter conflicts between his classmates, perhaps even blackmail. He was also ranked number two in the Elk Park Prep senior class. Keith Andrews, the top student, was now dead.

I sat up straight, splashing cocoa down the front of my coat. I didn't have time to wipe it off or even curse it because I was running toward the house. The windshield incident was probably meant to lure *me* away. Dammit, *I* had never been in danger at the bookstore.

I fumbled with the front doorknob. My mind raced. Whoever had smashed my van knew who would be affected. Who stood in the way of a higher class rank? Who was vulnerable to a campaign of harassment of his employer and her son, whom he held so dear? *Who would volunteer to clean up in my absence?*

Julian had been the true target all along.

I called Julian's friend, Neil Mansfield. Had Julian asked him for a ride? No, Julian said someone else volunteered to drive him back to Aspen Meadow. Who? Neil didn't know. But, Neil added, he himself had been home for an hour, so Julian should be home by *now*. Great. Did Neil have any idea who *else* might know who offered this ride? No clue.

I tried to reach Schulz. No answer at his home. The Sheriff's Department dispatcher said he couldn't raise the homicide investigator on his cell phone. I glanced at the clock: 10:30.

I had no ideas, no plan, nothing but panic. I grabbed the keys to the Rover. If I called the police, I would not know what to tell them or where to send them. I willed the mental picture of Keith Andrews' bloody head out of my mind.

The bookstore. That was the last place I had seen Julian; that was where I would start. Maybe I could call Miss Kaplan, or some of the staff, maybe someone had seen him leave . . . but how would I get phone numbers for these people? Reluctantly, I dialed Audrey Cooper-smith, but got only a sleepy Heather.

"Mom's not here. She went out with Dad."

"What?"

"She said they were trying to work things out."

"Look, Heather, I have to talk to her. I . . . left something in the store . . . and I need to know how to reach somebody there *now*."

"Why? The bookstore's closed."

"You didn't see Julian, did you? At the end of the evening?"

"Ms. Bear, you're confusing me. Did you leave a thing or a person in the bookstore?"

Oh, God, the grade book. I *had* left something in the bookstore. If Julian was still alive, if somebody wanted the evidence of that grade book enough . . . maybe I could do a swap. But I didn't know who I was dealing with, what that person would want or when.

"Heather, look, I have a big problem. Julian's life may be in danger . . . and I do have something. I have Miss Ferrell's grade book."

A sharp intake of breath from Heather. "You? But we've been looking for it; I can't do the class rank without it."

"Listen up. I need you to call every senior's family. Be sure you talk to the senior *and* the parents—"

"But it's *late*—"

"Please! Tell *every single person* I have Miss Ferrell's grade book and that I'll swap it for Julian, at Elk Park Prep in"—I hastily consulted my watch—"two hours. No questions asked."

"Does that include my mother? Because I don't know where she is. And you still don't have a way of getting into the store."

"Find her. I'll figure out the store situation. Your mother and Carl must have a favorite restaurant or something. Find them. Please, Heather, find *everybody*."

"You're out of your fucking mind."

"Trust me." I hung up before she could continue to analyze my mental status.

I ran out to the Rover. I shifted into first gear and thought, Audrey out with Carl? Unbelievable. But that was the least of my concerns.

The Rover engine roared as I sped down Interstate 70

to Denver. At the First Avenue light I turned left on Milwaukee and pulled up to the parking garage entrance. The first thing I had to figure out was whether Julian had taken my van anywhere.

Glitch: the lot was closed. Worse, the horizontal bar was down.

What was a barricade to the rhino guard of a desert vehicle? I backed up, gunned the engine forward, and crashed through the horizontal bar.

The growl of the car engine echoed off the concrete walls and through the cavernous space of the deserted garage. Up, up, I went to the third-floor level. And there was my van, parked ominously, alone, next to the entrance. Glass sparkled at its tires.

My heartbeat banged in my ears. How *was* I going to get back into the store? Could Audrey, in stomping out of the bookstore in a rage, have forgotten her purse in my van? I desperately hoped she had left her security entrance card behind. Unless she had manufactured her tantrum . . .

Best not to speculate until I had the grade book in my hands. I hopped out of the Rover and slid open the van door. The sound reverberated eerily.

"Julian?" I whispered into the van's cold depths. Silence. And then I looked in shock at the mess of papers, boxes, and cups that the overhead light illuminated. The vehicle had been trashed.

I was so angry, I almost slammed the door. But then I saw Audrey Coopersmith's overturned purse on the floor. I searched desperately for the magnetic-striped security card. It was not there. Now what?

An explosion cracked the stillness. A gunshot. I fell forward.

The sound had come from inside the store.

I ran up to the back entrance security post. The light

was green: Whoever had ransacked my van had probably used Audrey's card to open the electronic lock. I wrenched open the first glass door and then the second. I cursed wildly to overcome fear as I stepped into the dark depths of the bookstore.

The air was black, tarlike. The silence was absolute. I stepped carefully out onto the soft carpet. The smell of the bookstore was rich: paper, carpet, bindings, books, chairs, wood, dust. The odor of humans still lingered. I was near the kitchenette but could see nothing. The desk was close by; Audrey had shown it to me. . . .

The flashlights. One under each desk. I walked through the darkness, not knowing whether I was going in a straight or crooked path, but heading in my mind's eye toward where that desk must be. My foot thumped the side of a chair. It squeaked forward on tiny, unseen wheels. Damn. I groped underneath the desk until I found the cold metal clips holding the flashlight. My fingers closed around it. When I turned it on, I heard another shot. Louder, this time. Closer.

"Julian!" I shouted into the darkness.

The phone. Call Schulz. I extricated myself from underneath the desk, stood, and directed the light to the phone. I dialed 911, begged them to come to the Tattered Cover right away, and hung up. The silence pressed down on me.

"Julian!" I shrieked again.

My flashlight beam washed across the carpet to the steps.

And then I saw something out of place that made my heart freeze. Near the steps there was a large, dark splotch on the carpet. I dashed toward it, then stopped and swayed backward. Blood in a bookstore. But wait.

What had I just said to myself?

Something out of place.

My mind reeled.

What had the woman in Lakewood said? *Something it was too late for, something that was out of place* . . . What had Arch said? *You can't see Andromeda in the summer* . . . and, of course, I couldn't buy a Good Humor bar from the ice cream man in the winter, now, could I? And I wouldn't see a spider in an immaculate kitchen, would I? Tom Schulz had always told me: *If you see anything that's out of place* . . .

And now I knew. The crimes, the perpetrator, even the methods . . . *I* knew. I sank against a bookshelf, sickened.

Move, I ordered myself.

Down the wide, carpeted stairs I went, flashing the light ahead of me, until I reached the second floor. The scents were different on this level—more people had been here, more sweat hung in the air. There had been no sound since the two shots.

"Julian?"

"Goldy!" came a bloodcurdling call from somewhere below me. "Gol-dy! Help!" Julian's voice.

"Where are you?" I yelled, but heard only shuffling, someone running, thudding footsteps. I nearly tripped running down the last flight of stairs.

Here, on the first floor, there was more light. It poured through the first-floor windows from the street lamps on First Avenue and Milwaukee Street.

"Agh!" came Julian's muffled voice again. And then there was a scuffling sound from . . . where? From over by Business books.

I ran through the shadows to where I thought he was, near the exit to Milwaukee Street. I swept the flashlight across the rug . . . nothing. When I was almost to the first-floor cash registers, something slammed against me. I fell forward with a great crash, sending the flashlight skittering across the carpet. I came to my knees and leapt for it just as the body hit me again. I grabbed the flashlight and whirled around. The light shone on the furious, leathery face of Hank Dawson.

"You son of a bitch!" I screamed, and swung wildly with my flashlight. "Where's Julian?"

He leapt for me, but I sidestepped him. With a curse, he drew back, then lunged for me again. Frantically, I grabbed for a wire display of oversize paperbacks and tipped it over in front of him. Hank tripped and fell hard. Desperately, I reached for books, any books, on nearby shelves and flung them on top of him.

To my amazement, his sprawled body remained motionless. I scuttled around the corner to Business books.

"Julian," I called into the shelves, "it's me! You have to come out quickly." Which one of these godforsaken shelves was the one that opened outward? I couldn't remember. But slowly, absurdly, as if I were in a horror movie, I saw a shelf begin to move. Books wobbled, then toppled out to the floor. A face peeked out of the vacant shelf.

"Is Mr. Dawson . . . dead?"

It was Julian. "Down but not out," I said when I had caught my breath. "Oh, God, Julian, is that blood on your face? I'm so glad you're alive. The police are on their way, but we've got to get out."

"I can't move," he whimpered. "He shot me . . ."

Hank Dawson groaned and moved under the pile of books.

"Go!" Julian whispered desperately. "Get out!"

"Scoot back in there," I ordered. He groaned, then inched back into the tiny space. I shoved the wall of books back in place just as Hank Dawson came around the corner of shelves.

"Hi, Goldy," he said absurdly. I might have been there, in a darkened bookstore, to cater a Bronco brunch.

"Hank—"

"I want what I came for," he told me with enormous, terrifying calm. "I want the kid."

"Hank—"

"Should I just start shooting into these shelves? I know he's in here somewhere."

"Wait!" I yelled. "There's something else you're going to need. Something you wanted before."

He shone his flashlight into my face. The light blinded me. "What?"

"Miss Ferrell's grade book. You were looking for it in her room, weren't you? And . . . in my van? I have it here in the store." I added fiercely, "You'll never be able to prove Greer's high class rank without it." I had to get him away from Julian. Julian was the key.

Hank was breathing hard. "The book," he said. "Where is it?"

"Here in the store. I hid it, I was going to . . . to give it to the police," I sputtered. I was afraid. I was also passionately, blindly angry.

Hank glanced at the unmoving bookshelves. Satisfied that Julian was immobilized, he growled, "All right, let's go get it." He shifted to one side of the shelves; I pushed past him. He stank of sweat.

My feet shuffled across the carpet. Hank clomped close behind. Where was my damn flashlight? I wanted to look at him. I wanted to look into the eyes of a man who had murdered a teenager, a teacher, and a woman in Lakewood all to get his daughter into a top school.

"Don't stall!" He swung his flashlight up and caught me under the chin. Pain flashed up through my skull. I staggered, and Hank shoved me into the cash register counter.

I reeled away from him. Damn you, damn you, damn you. I had to find a way to get him. But for now I had to think, to walk, to do what he wanted until I could figure out how to escape. "I'm not going to be able to find the grade book unless I get my light. Okay if I get it?" I said to the stinking form behind me.

"Walk ahead of me with it. You so much as move an inch out of line and I'll put a bullet through your back."

I did as directed, walking slowly and trying not to think of Julian. Or of Hank's gun.

I bent and slowly, very slowly, picked up my flashlight. "Why did you kill Keith Andrews?" I asked, straightening slowly.

"He was in the way," Hank muttered. "Pompous little creep."

"You sure planned it out. Break his windshield so he'll mess up with the Princeton rep. Psych him out. Just like in the NFL. But Keith didn't psych easily. So you looked up someone with the same initial and last name and stole her credit card so you could plant it in one of the Marenskys' coats and try to psych *them* out. But Kathy Andrews caught you stealing her mail, so you had to kill her."

"I didn't care about that Lakewood woman. You haven't had to listen to the Marenskys brag for eighteen years. Getting them arrested for Keith Andrews' murder would have killed two birds with one stone." He chuckled. "Too bad it didn't work out that way."

"Someone saw the van you used, Greer Dawson the Hammer's van, down in Lakewood, with the initials *GD HMR*," I ventured. "All the person who saw it could think of was, too early, something out of place in October. That person thought the initials stood for *Good Humor,* but I didn't figure that out until tonight. I saw"—I gritted my teeth—"something out of place, and I thought how out of place an ice cream truck was in the fall."

"Brilliant," he snapped. "Put you in the fucking Ivy League."

We were half a room away from the window display.

"And then you tried to intimidate Julian. Number two kid in the class, you figured if you scared Arch and me, you could get to Julian, right? Shake him up badly enough so that he'd blow his aptitude tests. And you almost succeeded, throwing a rock through our window, putting a snake in Arch's locker, stopping up our chimney, planting a spider in your own immaculate drawer, manufacturing a conflict with Audrey tonight to get rid of me—"

"Shut up!" Again he chuckled horribly. "You know what they always say, Goldy. You gotta make the other team sweat, make them think they're going to lose. It was going well until the cops started watching your house."

"Yes, they scared you off." I hesitated. "And then Miss Ferrell. She wouldn't give Greer an A in French, but you figured you could go to Perkins about that. After all, it had been done before at that school."

"Don't I know. Now, I told you to *shut up*."

I stopped by the magazines. "Why did you have to *kill* Miss Ferrell?" I persisted.

"I didn't pay over a hundred thousand dollars for Greer to go to that school so she could end up at some podunk place in the Midwest. Now, quit talking and move."

Some podunk place in the Midwest? You went to a school in the Midwest, didn't you? Only, as Stan Marensky had pointed out so cruelly, you flunked out of Michigan before you could ever end up anywhere, Hank. Macguire's words haunted me: *I'm nobody.* And who was nobody most of all in his own eyes? A flunk-out with a restaurant whose two pastimes in life were lifting weights and expressing his violent hostilities on Sunday afternoons in front of a televised playing field. But he was a nobody who would become somebody if his offspring went to Princeton. I should have known.

One last section of magazines loomed before we got to the window displays. I tried to think of how I would shove him into the door, try to knock him out the way I had before with the wire display.

He poked my shoulder hard. "Where is this damn grade book?"

"It's less than twenty feet away. If you don't let me get it, all your plans will fall through. . . ."

Apparently satisfied, Hank poked me again. "Go get it."

Actually, I wanted to tell him, you don't need it anymore. In that streetfront display, no one would find it for weeks. Even then, it probably would be discarded. To bookstore workers, who was Suzanne Ferrell? How could she have had anything to do with Goldy the caterer and her assistant, Julian Teller, found murdered in their bookstore?

Stop thinking like this.

"We have to squeeze into a display," I warned Hank.

"If you are lying, I'll kill you right now, I swear it."

"We're close. Good old Hank," I said grimly, "it's like your final goal line, isn't it? My one Bronco buddy, turned on me."

"Shut *up*."

I played my flashlight over the last shelf of magazines. I couldn't hear a thing from Julian. There were no sirens or flashing lights. Desperation gripped me. We arrived at the narrow entrance to the platform.

"Now what?" demanded Hank.

"It's in here. Underneath a pile of cookbooks."

"Is this a joke?" he demanded. "Get in there and get it for me. No, wait. I don't want you going out some door on the other side. Get in there, then you tell me where it is."

"All right, all right," I said. I put down my flashlight. "Flash your beam over on this pile." I motioned to the small table between the window and where I stood. "It's right under the first book."

In my mind's eye I saw Arch. Adrenaline surged through my body as I moved laboriously across the platform.

"Move over," Hank ordered impatiently. Obediently, I moved a few inches to my right and spread my feet to steady myself. There was about a foot of space between Hank and me, and then another eighteen inches between him and the window. He tucked his gun in his pants and reached greedily for the pile of cookbooks. One chance.

I bent over and shoved into Hank Dawson with all my might. I heard a startled *oomph!* as my head sank into his belly. He hurtled into the glass with an explosive crack. I felt the plate glass breaking. The window broke into monstrous falling shards. I pulled back. Hank Dawson screamed wildly as his body crashed through the shattered glass. The heavy blades fell like a guillotine.

"Agh! Agh!" he screamed. He writhed on the pavement, howling.

Shaking uncontrollably, I crept to the broken window. Beneath me, Hank Dawson lay sprawled on the snowy sidewalk. His face stared up at mine.

"Agh . . . argh . . ." He was reaching desperately for words.

I started to say, "I'm sorry—"

"Listen," he rasped. "Listen . . . she . . . she could read when . . . she was . . . only four. . . ."

Then he died.

22

"I swear, Goldy," said Tom Schulz an hour later, shaking his head, "you get into more damned trouble."

The ambulance carrying Julian pulled away from the curb. He had been shot in the calf, but would be all right. I had several bumps, none of which were life-threatening, according to the paramedics. "I swear also," Schulz went on grimly, "that's the last time I leave you or Julian in a potentially dangerous situation."

I looked around at the police cars and fire engines. Clouds had moved in again, and snow was falling in a gauzy, unhurried way from a sky tinted pink by urban streetlights. Audrey had shown me some of the Tattered Cover's charms. But it was great to be out of the bookstore and into the sweet, cold air, especially at one o'clock in the morning.

"You didn't know. And I did try to call you," I told him.

Tom Schulz grunted.

The Denver police officers who had answered my 911 call had questioned me repeatedly: the same story over and over. "For college?" they said, bewildered and disbelieving. "Because of class rank?"

Indeed. I wondered vaguely if Headmaster Perkins would face any charges. Altering grades was probably not illegal, even if you had the damning evidence of a teacher's grade book. The only crimes I knew of besides Hank's had been Macguire Perkins' drug use and Brad Marensky's thefts. I was hardly going to turn the boys in. Sadly, both teens had merely followed the example, both implicit and explicit, of their purported mentors—their parents.

"This was over who was first in the class?" a bewildered Denver sergeant had asked me at least six times.

Yep. With Keith Andrews gone, with an A in French and an uncooperative college counselor out of the way, with Julian incapacitated or dead, Greer Dawson would have passed Heather, been at the top of her class and on her way to the Ivy League, to all the things Hank coveted for his daughter—and for himself.

But this was not really over who headed the class. It was—heartbreakingly—about trying to make your child the kind of success you never were yourself. I felt a terrible pity for Greer Dawson. I knew she would never be able to measure up.

"How can you *buy* grades?" the cop kept asking.

"Same way you buy drugs," I answered.

"Huh," Schulz grunted under his breath. "Cynical, Miss G."

I asked the Denver police officer to phone Elk Park Prep, to alert the headmaster to some strange inquiries he might get from parents who might have been worried by

Heather Coopersmith's calls. How Alfred Perkins would react to this last event in the saga of collegial competition I could not imagine. Nor did I really care.

Now the picture takers were done. Hank Dawson's corpse was being removed. I did not look. The sergeant said I could go.

Schulz suggested that we exit through the brick walkway between the Tattered Cover and the Janus Building. His car, he told me, was on Second Avenue. He took my hand. His was warm and rough, entirely welcome.

"You were brave," he said. "Damn."

The memory of Hank Dawson, sprawled bloody and dead on the pavement, made my legs wobble. I stopped and tilted my head back to catch a few icy snowflakes in my mouth. The air was cool, fresh, sharp. Sweet. I drew it deep into my lungs.

"There's just one thing I never figured out," I said. We were standing on the pink-lit brick breezeway between the two buildings. Several late-night passersby had been halted by the police activity. I could hear their engines humming; music lilted from a car radio.

"One thing you haven't figured out," repeated Schulz. "Like how to get on with your life."

"Yes, that . . ." A breeze chilled my skin, and I shivered. Schulz pulled me into his warm chest.

"What else doesn't Miss G. understand?"

"I know it sounds petty after all that's happened, but . . . the scholarship for Julian. What was Hank hoping to gain from that?"

"Ah, nothing." Tom Schulz kissed my cheek, then hugged me very gently, as if I were breakable. The tune on the car radio changed: "Moon River." The bittersweet notes filtered through the snowy air.

I said, "You seem pretty sure of that."

Schulz sighed. "I'm just so happy to have you and Julian alive—"

"Yes, but . . . is the money gone now, or what? Julian will need to know."

He let go of me. Snowflakes drifted down onto my face and shoulders.

"The money is not gone," Schulz said. "It is not gone because I donated it, and I got your friend Marla to go in halvsies with me."

"What?"

He cupped my hand in his, then said, "Smart detective like Miss G., I should have thought you'd figure that out. I told you I didn't know what to do with my money. Good for Julian I'm a saver. Without kids of my own, this felt like a great thing to do. Marla likes Julian too, and God knows she has enough money. She said"—and here he drew his voice into an astonishingly accurate imitation of Marla's husky voice—"'Oh, oh, I'll never be able to keep a secret from Goldy!' And now look at who told."

"Aah, God . . ." I said, faltering. I was losing consciousness. My body was falling, falling, to the pavement, and I could feel Schulz's hands gently easing me down. It was all too much—Keith Andrews, Suzanne Ferrell, Hank Dawson . . . death everywhere.

"You're going to need counseling," Schulz warned. "You've been through a lot." He stroked my cheek.

The pavement was cold. Yes, counseling. I had witnessed too much. After all the death, my own mortality again loomed large. What really kept me going? What was I going to have faith in? I had Arch, Julian. I had . . . An ache filled me. What else?

Hank Dawson had wanted desperately to have a successful family. So had Audrey. The Marenskys. Headmaster Perkins with hapless Macguire. And so, too, had I. We had all reached out for success—or the image of success we had in our minds. I'd had a picture of John Richard, Arch, and me, a happy family, and that had certainly failed. *What had gone so wrong?*

This was what was wrong: my idea, Hank's idea, Caroline's, Brad's, Macguire's . . . that if you have *this* educational pedigree, *this* money, *this* fill-in-the-blank, you will be successful.

But really, I thought as I lay on the cold pavement and looked up into Schulz's concerned face, success was something else. Success was more a matter of finding the best people and then going through life with them . . . it was finding rewarding work and sticking with it, through thick and thin, as if life were a succession of cream sauces. . . .

Suddenly my head hurt, my stomach hurt, everything hurt. Schulz made patient murmuring noises, then helped me up.

I was shivering. "I'm so embarrassed," I said without looking at him.

"Aah, forget about it."

I tilted my head and again tasted a few blessed flakes of snow. Schulz motioned at the sky.

"Too bad Arch won't be able to look for galaxies tonight."

"Oh, well. You know how he's always complaining to me about the clouds obscuring the stars. The way all my troubles have obscured my appreciating you," I added.

"Listen to this woman. She's using metaphors like some headmaster I know. And it sounds as if she's gone soft—"

"Tom, there's something I have to tell you."

He took my hand and waited. Finally he said, "Go ahead."

"Yes."

"Yes, what?" said Tom Schulz.

"Yes," I said, firmly, with no hesitation. "Yes, I will marry you."

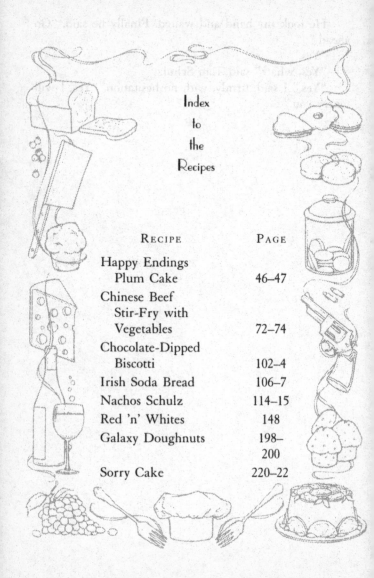

Index
to
the
Recipes

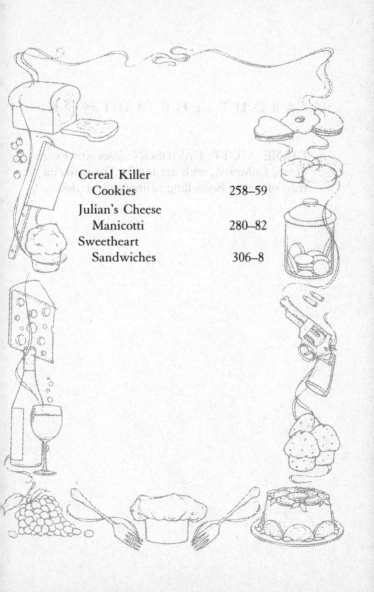

ABOUT THE AUTHOR

DIANE MOTT DAVIDSON lives in Ever-
green, Colorado, with her family. She is the author of eleven bestselling culinary mysteries.

If you enjoyed Diane Mott Davidson's *The Cereal Murders*, you won't want to miss any of the tantalizing mysteries in her nationally bestselling culinary mystery series!
Look for *CHOPPING SPREE*, the newest mystery, at your favorite bookseller's.

CHOPPING SPREE

by

Diane Mott Davidson

Turn the page for an exciting preview. . . .

Success can kill you.

So my best friend had been telling me, anyway. Too much success is like arsenic in chocolate cake. Eat a slice a *day*, Marla announced with a sweep of her plump, bejeweled fingers, and you'll get cancer. Gobble the whole *cake*? You'll keel over and die on the spot.

These observations, made over the course of a snowy March, had not cheered me. Besides, I'd have thought that Marla, with her inherited wealth and passion for shopping, would *applaud* the upward leap of my catering business. But she said she was worried about me.

Frankly, I was worried about me, too.

In mid-March I'd invited Marla over to taste cookies. Despite a sudden but typical Colorado blizzard, she'd roared over to our small house off Aspen Meadow's Main Street in her shiny new BMW four-wheel drive. Sitting in our commercial kitchen, she'd munched on ginger snaps and spice cookies, and harped on the fact that the newly frantic pace of my work had coincided with my fourteen-year-old son Arch's increasingly rotten behavior. I knew Marla doted on Arch.

But in this, too, she was right.

Arch's foray into athletics, begun that winter with

snowboarding and a stint on his school's fencing team, had ended with a trophy, a sprained ankle, and an unprecedented burst of physical self-confidence. He'd been eager to plunge into spring sports. When he'd decided on lacrosse, I'd been happy for him. That changed when I attended the first game. Watching my son forcefully shove an opponent aside and steal the ball, I'd felt queasy. With Arch's father—a rich doctor who'd had many violent episodes himself—now serving time for parole violation, all that slashing and hitting was more than I could take.

But even more worrisome than the sport itself, Marla and I agreed, were Arch's new teammates: an unrepentant gang of spoiled, acquisitive brats. Unfortunately, Arch thought the lacrosse guys were beyond cool. He spent hours with them, claiming that he "forgot" to tell us where he was going after practice. We could have sent him an *e-mail* telling him to call, Arch protested, if he only had what all his pals had, to wit, Internet-access watches. *Your own watch could have told you what time it was,* I'd told him, when I picked him up from the country-club estate where the senior who was supposed to drive him home had left him off.

Arch ignored me. These new friends, he'd announced glumly, also had Global Positioning System calculators, Model Bezillion Palm pilots, and electric-acoustic guitars that cost eight hundred dollars—and up. These litanies were always accompanied with not-so-tactful reminders that his fifteenth birthday was right around the corner. He wanted everything on his list, he announced as he tucked a scroll of paper into my purse. After all, with all the parties I'd booked, I could finally afford to get him some really good stuff.

And no telling what'll happen if I don't get what I want, he'd added darkly. (Marla informed me that he'd already given *her* a list.) I'd shrugged as Arch clopped into the house ahead of me. I'd started stuffing sautéed chicken breasts with wild rice and spinach. The next day, Tom had picked up Arch at another friend's house. When my son waltzed into the kitchen, I almost didn't recognize him.

His head was shaved.

"They Bic'd me," he declared, tossing a lime into the air and catching it in the net of his lacrosse stick.

"They *bicked* you?" I exclaimed incredulously.

"*Bic*, Mom. Like the razor." He rubbed his bare scalp, then flipped the lime again. "And I *would* have been home on time, if you'd bought me the Palm, to remind me to tell the guy shaving my head that I had to go."

I snagged the lime in midair. "Go start on your homework, buster. You got a C on the last anatomy test. And from now on, either Tom or I will pick you up right from practice."

On his way out of the kitchen, he whacked his lacrosse stick on the floor. I called after him please not to do that. I got no reply. The next day, much to Arch's sulking chagrin, Tom had picked him up directly from practice. *If being athletic is what success at that school looks like,* Tom told me, *then maybe Arch should take up painting.* I kept mum. The next day, I was ashamed to admit, I'd pulled out Arch's birthday list and bought him the Palm pilot.

Call it working mom's guilt, I'd thought, as I stuffed tiny cream puffs with shrimp salad. Still, I was not sorry I was making more money than ever before. I did not regret that *Goldilocks' Catering, Where Everything Is Just Right!* had gone from booked to overbooked. Finally, I was giving those caterers in Denver, forty miles to the east, a run for their shrimp rolls. This was what I'd always wanted, right?

Take my best upcoming week, I'd explained to Marla as she moved on to test my cheesecake bars and raspberry brownies. The second week of April, I would make close to ten thousand dollars—a record. I'd booked an upscale cocktail party at Westside Mall, a wedding reception, and two big luncheons. Once I survived all that, Friday, April the fifteenth, was Arch's birthday. By then, I'd finally have the cash to buy him something, as Arch himself had said, *really* good.

"Goldy, don't do all that," Marla warned as she downed one of my new Spice-of-Life Cookies. The buttery cookies featured large amounts of ginger, cinnamon, and freshly grated nutmeg, and were as comforting as anything from Grandma's kitchen. "You'll be too exhausted even to make a birthday cake. Listen to me, now. You need to decrease your bookings, hire some help, be stricter with Arch, and take care of yourself for a change. If you don't, you're going to *die*."

Marla was always one for the insightful observation.

I didn't listen. At least, not soon enough.

The time leading up to that lucrative week in April became even busier and more frenetic. Arch occasionally slipped away from practice before Tom, coming up from his investigative work at the sheriff's department, could snag him. I was unable to remember the last time I'd had a decent night's sleep. So I suppose it was inevitable that, at ten-twenty on the morning of April eleventh, I had what's known in the shrink business as a *crisis*. At least, that's what they'd called it years ago, during my pursuit of a singularly unhelpful degree in psychology.

I was inside our walk-in refrigerator when I blacked out. Just before hitting the walk-in's cold floor, I grabbed a metal shelf. Plastic bags of tomatoes, scallions, celery, shallots, and gingerroot spewed in every direction, and my bottom thumped the floor. I thought, *I don't have time for this.*

I struggled to get up, and belatedly realized this meltdown wasn't that hard to figure out. I'd been up since five A.M. With one of the luncheon preps done, I was focusing on the mall cocktail party that evening. Or at least I had been focusing on it, before my eyes, legs, and back gave out.

I groaned and quickly gathered the plastic bags. My back ached. My mind threw out the realization that I *still* did not know where Arch had been for three hours the previous afternoon, when lacrosse practice had been canceled. Neither Tom nor I had been aware of the calendar change. Tom had finally collected Arch from a seedy section of Denver's Colfax Avenue. So what had this about-to-turn-fifteen-year-old been up to this time? Arch had refused to say.

"Just do the catering," I announced to the empty refrigerator. I replaced the plastic bags and asked the Almighty for perspective. Arch would get the third degree when he came down for breakfast. Meanwhile, I had work to do.

Before falling on my behind, I'd been working on a concoction I'd dubbed Shoppers' Chocolate Truffles. These rich goodies featured a dense, smooth chocolate interior coated with more satiny chocolate. So what had I been looking for in the refrigerator? I had no idea. I stomped out and slammed the door.

I sagged against the counter and told myself the problem was fatigue. Or maybe my age—thirty-four—was kicking in. What would Marla say? She'd waggle a fork in my face and preach about the wages of success.

I brushed myself off and quick-stepped to the sink. As water gushed over my hands, I remembered I'd been searching for the scoops of ganache, that sinfully rich mélange of melted bittersweet chocolate, heavy cream, and liqueur that made up the heart of the truffles.

I dried my hands and resolved to concentrate on dark chocolate, not the darker side of success. After all, I had followed one of Marla's suggestions: I *had* hired help. But I had not cut back on parties. I'd forgotten what taking care of myself even felt like. And I seemed incapable of being stricter with Arch.

I hustled over to my new kitchen computer and booted it up, intent on checking that evening's assignment. Soon my new printer was spitting out lists of needed foodstuffs, floor plans, and scheduled setup. I may have lost my mind, but I'd picked it right up again.

"This is what happens when you give up caffeine!" I snarled at the ganache balls. Oops—that was twice I'd talked to myself in the last five minutes. Marla would not approve.

I tugged the plastic wrap off the globes of ganache and spooned up a sample to check the consistency. The smooth, intense dark chocolate sent a zing of pleasure up my back. I moved to the stovetop, stirred the luxurious pool of melting chocolate, and took a whiff of the intoxicatingly rich scent. I told myself—silently—that everything was going to be all right. The party-goers were going to *love* me.

The client for that night's cocktail party was Barry Dean, an old friend who was now manager of Westside Mall, an upscale shopping center abutting the foothills west of Denver. I'd previously put on successful catered parties at Westside. Each time, the store-owners had raved. But Barry Dean, who'd only been managing the mall for six months, had seemed worried about the party's dessert offering. I'd promised him his high-end spenders, for whom the party was geared, would *flip* over the truffles.

Maybe I'd even get a big tip, I thought as I scraped down the sides of the double boiler. I could spend it on a new mattress. On it, I might eventually get some sleep.

I stopped and took three deep breaths. My system craved coffee. Of course, I hadn't given up espresso *entirely*. I was just trying to cut back from nine shots a day to two. Too much caffeine was causing my sleeplessness, Marla had declared. Of course, since we'd both been married to the same doctor—consecutively, not concurrently—she and I were self-proclaimed experts on all physical ailments. (Med Wives 101, we called it.) So I'd actually heeded her advice. My plan had been to have one shot at eight in the morning (a distant memory), another at four in the afternoon (too far in the future). Now my resolve was melting faster than the dark chocolate.

I fired up the espresso machine and wondered how I'd gotten into such a mental and physical mess.

Innocently enough, my mind replied. Without warning, right after Valentine's Day, my catering business had taken off. An influx of ultrawealthy folks to Denver and the mountain area west of the Mile High City had translated into massive construction of trophy homes, purchases of multiple upscale cars, and doubling of prices for just about everything. Most important from my viewpoint, the demand for big-ticket catered events had skyrocketed. From mid-February to the beginning of April, a normally slow season, my assignments had exploded. I'd thought I'd entered a zone, as they say in Boulder, of *bliss*.

I pulled a double shot of espresso, then took a sip and felt infinitely better.

I rolled the first silky scoop of ganache into a ball, and set it aside. What had I been thinking about? Ah, yes. Success.

I downed more coffee and set aside the porcelain bought-on-clearance cup, a remnant of my financial dark days. Those days had lasted a long time, a fact that Arch had seemed to block out.

When I began divorce proceedings against the ultra-cute, ultravicious Doctor John Richard Korman, I'd been so determined that he would support our son well that I'd become an Official Nosy Person. Files, tax returns, credit card receipts, check stubs, bank deposits—I'd found and studied them all. My zealous curiosity had metamorphosed into a decent settlement. Wasn't it Benjamin Franklin who'd said, *God helps those who help themselves*? Old Ben had been right.

I bathed the first dark ganache globe in chocolate. OK, I'd replaced marital bitterness with bittersweet chocolate and bitter orange marmalade, right? And my life had turned around. Two years ago, I'd married Tom Schulz. As unreal as my newly minted financial success might seem, I did not doubt the miracle of my relationship with Tom, whose work as a police investigator had actually brought us together in the first place. Tom was bighearted and open-armed toward both Arch and me. So far, Tom and I had passed the tests that had been flung our way, and emerged still together. In this day and age, I thought, such commitment was commendable.

I rolled ganache balls, bathed them in chocolate, and set them aside to dry. Scoop, bathe, set aside. Marla could grouse all she wanted; I savored my new success. I was even considering purchasing a new set of springform pans, since I'd already bought a new computer, printer, and copier, not to mention new tableware, flatware, and knives—a shining set of silver Henckels. I *relished* no longer renting plates, silverware, and linens! I laughed aloud when I finished the twentieth truffle, and made myself another espresso. The dark drink tasted divine. No wonder they called financial solvency *liquidity*.

I rewarded myself with a forkful of ganache, which sparked more fireworks of chocolate ecstasy. I did a little two-step and thanked the Almighty for chocolate, coffee, and business growth.

Roll, bathe, set aside. I was appreciative that I had scads of new clients. In hiring me, they offered testimonies from friends (Marla in particular), or claimed they'd caught the reruns of my short-lived PBS cooking show. Some even said they just *had* to hire this caterer they'd read about, the one who helped her husband solve the occasional murder case. Well, why they hired me didn't matter. New clients were new clients, and glitzy parties paid the bills. It had been stupendous.

For a while.

Now I looked and felt like zabaglione, frothy after being beaten too hard. And I was unsure of what was going on with my son. I rolled, bathed, and set aside more truffles, all the while avoiding my reflection in the kitchen window. I knew what I'd see there: a haggard face with licorice-black bags under bloodshot eyes, not to mention a fretwork of worry-wrinkles. My freshly shampooed, too-busy-to-get-a-cut blond hair, which people had always likened to Shirley Temple's corkscrew curls, now gave me the look of a soaked poodle.

You're obsessing again, I scolded myself as I set the thirtieth truffle on the rack. *You'll just make things worse.*

I took a deep breath and ordered myself not to indulge in another taste until *all sixty* of the chocolates were made. Instead, I *had* to start planning Arch's birthday.

At the moment, Arch was still asleep, as the Elk Park Prep teachers were meeting for an in-service. School that day didn't start till noon, my son had announced the previous night, and could we spend the morning shopping? I'd said no, I had to *work*. And besides, where had he been the previous day? He'd sighed. Then he'd pushed his glasses up his nose so he could give me the full benefit of his pleading eyes, which seemed huge against the background of his shaved head. Had I started purchasing *any* items on his birthday list? he asked.

I swallowed. I'd only bought the Palm; I hadn't had time for anything else. Arch had hoisted his bookbag and stalked out of the kitchen. I yelled after him that no matter how much money you had, it was never enough. He'd called back something unintelligible.

I rolled another ball of ganache and longed to stuff it into my mouth. Instead, I dipped it into the dark chocolate. Marla's warnings haunted me. What, exactly, was *enough*? On our day of planning, Barry Dean had told me about the jewelry-event-cum-cocktail-party guests, members of Westside's Elite Shoppers Club. The "Elites," as Barry called them, spent a minimum of a thousand dollars a *week* at the mall. Membership in the group guaranteed special coupons, special sales, valet parking, and events like the jewelry-leasing extravaganza I was catering that night. One thing I had asked Barry: Where did the Elites *put* all the stuff they bought? He'd winked, done his endearing-bachelor shrug, and said usually they rented storage sheds.

My business line rang. I put down the truffle, swiped my fingers on my stained apron, and actually prayed that this was *not* another new client.

"Goldilocks' Catering—"

"You're working," Marla accused.

"No, really, I was sleeping in. Then my best friend called and woke me up."

"Yeah, sure." She swallowed something. I guessed it was her latest version of hot chocolate, which consisted of hot cream, cocoa, and low-cal sweetener. Even though Marla had had a heart attack almost two years before, she'd had little luck losing weight on a low-fat, high-carb, low-protein diet. So now she was trying a some-fat, some-carb, high-protein diet. She claimed she'd lost six pounds and felt much better. When I'd asked what her cardiologist thought of the new regimen, she'd hung up on me. You had to be careful with Marla.

Now I said, "OK, I *was* trying to roll truffles, until my best friend called and forced me to smear chocolate all over my new apron."

"Quit bellyaching." She started munching on something, I didn't want to imagine what. "Yesterday I gave Arch a package for you. It's in your freezer. I want you to open it."

I sighed, thinking of all the work I had to do. "While I'm *talking* to you, if you don't mind."

I knew my life would be much easier if I just tucked the phone against my shoulder, wrenched open the freezer door of the walk-in, and did as bidden. So I did. After a moment of groping, I pulled a very cold brown paper bag from a shelf. The bag contained—oh, joy—a pint of Häagen-Dazs coffee ice cream, hand-labeled "A," and a brown bottle of time-release vitamins, marked "B."

"OK, get a spoon and a glass of water," Marla commanded when she heard the paper rustling. "Take a spoonful of A, then a capsule of B. *Now.*"

I again followed orders. The ice cream improved my mood, no question. But when I tried to swallow the vitamin, I choked.

"I can't believe you're doing the event tonight," Marla cried, not heeding my wheezing gasps. "You'll wreck *my* shopping experience, and everyone else's. You think people want a caterer who looks half dead? Shoppers want to *escape* reality, Goldy. They want to feel *rich*. They want to feel *young*. They'll take one look at you and say, *Why should I shop? She's gonna die and so am I.*"

I finally swallowed the vitamin and croaked, "Are you done talking about me kicking the bucket? 'Cuz I've got truffles to coat."

Marla went on, her husky voice laced with anger: "I *was* going to lease the double strand of diamonds for the first month. They're *perfect* for the March of Dimes luncheon. But six thou a month? What'll I have left to give the March of Dimes?" She paused to devour more food. One of the whole-grain muffins I'd made her? Unlikely. "Then I heard that Page Stockham, also an Elite Shopper, wanted the same necklace. So now I'm trying to decide between a ruby chain and an emerald set in three rows of diamonds, in case Page gets it first. Oh, Page Stockham just makes me so *angry*. And to think I asked her to go with me to tonight's event."

"To *think*," I murmured sympathetically.

She ignored me. "Making matters even worse, Ellie

McNeely wants the double pearl strand with the aquamarine, which I've had my eye on forever to go with a dinner I'm giving in May, that I was hoping you'd cater, if you're not dead. Wait a minute, there's someone at the door."

Waiting for Marla to return to the phone, I kept on with the truffles. Six to go. Roll, bathe, set aside. What had I been thinking about? Oh, yes, money to burn. I wasn't resentful, though, because moneyed folks were my best clients. And anyway, who was I to judge anyone else's *shopping*?

My eyes traveled to the carved wooden cupboard hanging over our kitchen table. I truly did *not* want to look down on folks who engaged in retail therapy. The reason was that during my divorce from The Jerk, and despite near-dire financial straits, I'd been a shop-to-feel-better gal myself. On weekends when it was John Richard's turn to have Arch, I'd visited every shopping center I could find. I'd strolled through perfume-scented air, by gorgeously stacked goods, past gaggle after gaggle of smiling, prosperous people. I'd loitered in front of brightly lit displays of embroidered baby clothes, rainbow-hued designer sheets, sleek copper pots and pans, even sugared, sparkling cinnamon rolls. I'd allowed myself to feel rich, even if my bank account said otherwise.

Come to think of it, maybe that was what Arch had been doing the previous day: shopping. Still, there weren't any luxury shops on East Colfax.

I retucked the silent phone against my ear, rolled another truffle, but stopped again to ponder the cupboard shelves. On each of those long-ago shopping trips, I'd bought myself a little something from the "Drastically Reduced" tables. My white porcelain demitasse cup and saucer, a tiny crystal mouse, a miniature wooden car laden with painted wooden gifts—all these had made me uncommonly happy. At home, I'd placed my minuscule treasures on the old cupboard's shelves. Without the stores' strong overhead lights, the little crystal mouse had not looked quite so brilliant; the cheap china cup had lost its translucence. But I'd never cared. Each piece had been *mine*, something for *me*, a small token of an inner voice, too long silenced, saying, "I love you." So who was I to judge Marla or her friends, Page Stockham and Ellie McNeely? They all wanted someone, even if it was themselves, to say, *I really, really care about you! And to prove it, have this!*

Marla came back to the phone and said Ellie had arrived, and she had to go. Before the event, she, Ellie, and Page, who was driving down separately with husband Shane, would be getting the mud soak, the coconut-milk bath, and the vegetable-and-fruit wrap at Westside Spa.

"I'll watch for a moving luau."

"I'll catch you at the party," Marla retorted, undaunted, and signed off.

I rolled the fifty-eighth truffle. Then, lowering the scoop of ganache into the melted chocolate and setting it aside to dry, I made another espresso. To the far west, just visible out our back windows, a bright mist cloaked the mountains of the Aspen Meadow Wildlife Preserve. On the nearer hills, white-barked aspens nestled between dark expanses of fir, spruce, and pine. I peered at our thermometer. The red line was stubbornly stuck at twenty-nine degrees. *So this is Springtime in the Rockies?* newcomers always asked. *This is it,* I invariably replied. In June, you can take off your snow tires.

I slugged down what I vowed would be my last coffee. Once again, worry surfaced. Where *had* Arch been yesterday?

I disciplined myself to roll the next-to-last truffle. It broke into two pieces when I dunked it in the dark chocolate. Oh, darn! Guess I'll have to eat it, maybe with a fifth espresso! I pulled out the chocolate chunks swimming in the dark coating, placed them on the rack, then refilled the espresso doser. I rinsed the old porcelain demitasse cup and closed my eyes. Worry for Arch nagged at me. I balanced on one foot. I was *so* tired. . . . And then my much-loved cup slipped from my fingers. It shattered on the floor with a heartbreaking crash. Shards raced across the wood; bits of china smashed into the molding and sent reverberating tinkles throughout the kitchen.

My best shopping treasure was gone. Later, I tried not to think of it as an omen.